STEFAN

THE NEW GENERATION

The Porn Star Brothers Series

L.J. DIVA

★ ROYAL STAR PUBLISHING ★

Chances is an imprint of Royal Star Publishing
www.royalstarpublishing.com.au

First edition paperback published in 2019
All Rights Reserved, Copyright ©L.J. Diva 2019
Song lyrics reprinted with permission

Trade Paperback ISBN: 978-1-925683-58-5
Dust Jacket Hardcover ISBN: 978-1-922307-34-7
E-book ISBN: 978-1-925683-57-8
A catalogue record for this book is available from the National Library of
Australia.

Cover design: Royal Star Publishing/Odyssey Books
Cover photos: Casther/Shutterstock.com, SofiaZhuravetc/Shutterstock.com,
Glovatskiy/Shutterstock.com, kuzmafoto/Shutterstock.com,
FabrikaSimf/Shutterstock.com, sergeycauselove/Shutterstock.com
Typesetting in Minion Pro by Royal Star Publishing

Dedications

In 2014 a vague idea to write a book about a porn star came to me. In 2015 the idea brewed and grew and when my idol, Jackie Collins, passed away, the idea flourished with a vengeance.

Jackie Collins is the only inspiration in my life when it comes to writing. She had the passion, the brains, the ballsy rollicking attitude, and the kind of life that made me want to *be* her.

Without her, these books would not exist, for I would not have had the inspiration to follow in the same 'write whatever you want' league. Without her, I will continue trying to write the kind of books she wrote. Real, ballsy, and bonkbustingly good.

Jackie,

the Porn Star Brothers book series is dedicated to you as so many of my other books are. I thank you for the inspiration you have given me and hope you continue giving me, to go on and write more. I hope that you are well and having a good laugh wherever you are. I miss you and will continue doing so. Sometimes I think I feel you egging me on with my writing. Maybe that's true, and maybe it's just my rampant imagination; the same imagination that has given me the books I have written so far in my life. And sometimes, I really wished I could be you. You will forever be my idol and inspiration and I thank you.

RIP, Miss Jackie C.

And to the three Stefanovic brothers, Carlos, Pedro, and Tomas, without whom I would not have had names for my porn stars.

May 2007

Greek-Australian pop star, Alena, strutted across the concrete path, miming to her latest hit single, *Baby, Hit Me Up,* while keeping her eye on the camera. She stepped onto the sand in her black, sky-high, silver-studded stiletto platform heels and her feet buckled beneath her.

Down she went.

"Cut," yelled Carlos Stephanopoulos, world-famous movie writer, producer and director. But before he could say more, he was interrupted by his little brother.

"You okay, Bubba?" Pedro called out to his daughter.

Alena jumped up and quickly flicked sand from her hair. "I'm okay, Daddy. Just fell in these heels." She looked down at the sand-covered designer shoes. *Holy mother of God they were awesome shoes.*

"Well, that's what you get for wearing such ridiculous things, especially on sand," Vivian Villiers, world-famous supermodel, stylist, author, and wife of Carlos, said. "I may be the stylist, but *you* demanded those shoes." She watched the assistants brush Alena down, making sure all sand was off her jet-black, skin-tight Lycra bodysuit and studded black leather bomber jacket, while the hairstylist brushed out her hair.

"I *know,* Aunt Viv!" Alena exclaimed. "But I *love* them."

"You *may well* love them, but you *clearly can't walk* in them," Viv said. "Not on sand anyway." She stood by Carlos's side under the huge tent they had set up on their favourite Mykonos beach.

It was May, and already warm, with early summer tourists lined up to watch them record the 58th film clip of Alena's career. And it had been a long career, even though she was only twenty-eight.

Alena Jennifer Stephanopoulos was born to musical parents, her father being Pedro Stephanopoulos, world-famous DJ since he was eighteen, who'd taken his career into music writing and become a world-renowned producer for many artists. The family had its own studio, *Sync,* on Mykonos, and an even larger one at their headquarters, *Stefan Productions,* in Athens. Her mother was Angelina Stephanopoulos, Juilliard-trained pianist and violinist, coming together with her husband to write music not only for other artists, but for their own children. Alena, being the eldest of four, had always been musically gifted. Performing from an early age, she'd sung on music tracks her parents had written, and they'd been played in the family's nightclub, *SB3*, making her an overnight sensation at fifteen.

During her schooling, she had released four songs with film clips every year until she was twenty-one when she could take over her own career. She chose to continue the way it had been, but this time she released a full-length album every year and did small European tours as well. She had become mega-famous, not just in Greece, but the whole of Europe, the Middle East, India, China and Japan. By twenty-five, she had cracked the American market in 2003 with her and her family's eclectic mixes of Greek and pop, with a bit of techno, house, disco and every other kind thrown in, and did small promo tours there, but this summer she was set to do a huge stadium tour across all fifty states of America. It would take ten to twelve weeks.

She had hoped to take a few months recuperating at the family's penthouse in their NYC apartment building in fall and spend some time seeing New York, where she'd been born the day after her cousin, Diana Villiers. The family had moved back to Mykonos when they were three because their uncles, Tomas and Roger, were critically ill. But luckily there had been a miracle, and her uncles recovered, later setting up *In Shape*, a private gym for the rich and famous who came to the island, or the clients of *Stefan Productions*, either musically, or film-wise. Many actors and musicians had stayed in the private home they had for clients, so Alena had met many famous people over the years and now counted herself as one.

Shaking the sand out of her shoes, she went back to the original spot and waited for her uncle to call *action*. This time, she completed the walk without falling over, and the scene was done. And so was the shoot. "How was that, Daddy?" She bounded over to her father and flung her arms around his neck.

At fifty, Pedro was still incredibly gorgeous with slicked back jet-black hair, which he refused to admit he occasionally helped along with hair dye, fair skin that he religiously sunscreened when out in the sun, and bright blue eyes he inherited from his Australian mother, Jenny. Alena looked exactly like him.

"That was awesome as usual, Bubba." Pedro hugged his daughter proudly. "You're doing well. I'm so proud of you." He looked down. "*But not* proud of that outfit. A bit tight."

Viv laughed lightly. "Didn't Angelina wear an outfit like that back in the '70s and '80s? You definitely loved it then."

"That's where I got it from, Mama's closet." Alena stared down at her slick black outfit. "And then we restyled it for the current clothing line."

Haus of Stefan, the fashion company Alena and Diana owned, had started as an idea when they were teenagers, dressing up in their mothers' clothes. With Viv being a supermodel, Diana had a massive amount of fashion to delve into, so the girls had played dress-ups and talked about making their own clothes. When they reached twenty-one and could draw wages from the trust funds their grandmother had set up for them, they used the money for setting up the business. And with help from Grandma and Uncle Carlos as owner and co-CEOs of the Stephanopoulos Empire, the girls had their own fashion house by their twenty-fifth birthdays. And it had been a rocking success. With Diana, a world-famous model like her mother, and Alena being a mega superstar, the fashion label had dressed all the cool Gen X and Gen Y kids old enough to wear it. The label sold worldwide with stores in Milan, Paris, London, L.A., Tokyo, China and Australia. *Haus of Stefan* was everywhere, just like her music, just like Diana's modelling shots.

The girls were as famous as their parents. So were Diana's twin brothers, Cabot and Antonio, or as they called themselves, Steele and Phoenix Stefan, world-famous models in their own right, and so was Alena's sister Alexis who sang and designed for *HOS*. At ten years apart, the two sisters showed how *Haus of Stefan* could dress adults and teens.

"And you've done a good job of redesigning it for today," Viv told her. "It looks stunning with your hair."

Alena's black hair hung straight and long, but the bottom was cut in an edgy new style, making it look like the crenels and merlons of a castle's battlements. It sported long sections with short sections in between. Her bold, blunt bangs framed her electric blue eyes and pale complexion.

"Thanks, Aunt Viv. Anyone know where Diana is today?"

*****

Twenty-eight-year-old American-Greek-Australian beauty, Diana Villiers Stephanopoulos, was standing in front of the Acropolis in Athens. High on the hillside, she was wearing a white flowing dress with her abundance of golden-brown curls rolled into an updo with flowers woven through it. She was doing a photo shoot for *Flair* magazine, the go-to bible for fashion in the industry, and they had decided to capture her on one of Greece's most famous monuments.

"Hold your left hand out, so the dress blows back in the wind," photographer, Charles Kensington, called as he snapped away. "Perfect, perfect, now hold out your right arm. Head up and out."

Diana stood like a tree, arms out at awkward angles, her white Grecian style dress flapping in the wind, her neck forward, her head facing the sky. She was getting cramps from standing there and needed a break.

"Okay, I'm done," she told them. "I need a break, my arms hurt, my feet hurt, and I need a drink." She walked over to the tent that was set up for the shoot, where she got an ice-cold water with lemon from one of the assistants and sipped it slowly, so it didn't give her a freeze headache.

"We weren't finished." Charles strode over to her.

"I told you I need a break," Diana snapped. "I can't stand in the sun too long, or I burn. And I'm hot, so I need a drink, or I'll dehydrate and collapse. You got a problem with that?" Her electric blue eyes burned brightly. She was sick and tired of being told what to do by photographers who thought they had a dictatorship over her.

"You're just the hired model for the shoot," Charles barked at her, seething at the dressing down she was giving him. No model had ever spoken to him that way before, and he didn't like it. They were just the hired help, and it was his job to make them look good. Not that Diana Villiers needed help looking good, because she was incredibly beautiful, and it was all natural, but she infuriated him beyond belief by not doing things the way other models did. She did it to her own timetable and how *she* wanted, *not* how she was told. Her reputation preceded her, and it was a reputation she held onto fiercely. Punctual, friendly, observant, damn good at what she did, polite, but she did it her way, running the show to her health management, and *not* what anyone else wanted.

It amazed him *and* pissed him off. That this incredible, beautiful woman could tell him what to do and he did it. Just like that. Just like he had no say in the matter. Like he had no say when it came to her, and he seethed inside. Seethed because she had turned down his advances, and now, staring at her, his erection was threatening to burst from his pants. "So, *when* is Princess ready to work?" he asked icily.

Diana arched a perfectly groomed brow. She knew his attitude from previous shoots. He thought his own shit didn't stink, but she'd told him otherwise when he suggested getting a drink. Turning him down was not a problem. His attitude was a turn-off. His occasional chauvinism made her feel like slapping him, and the way he spoke to her during shoots made her want to do much more. His arrogance was mind-blowing. His body to die for, his lips so damn kissable… *wait, what the!* She snapped the hell out of it and drew her eyes from his full lips to his stunning blue eyes and short dark hair that hung in a boyish lock to the left side. He was taller than her at five ten and had an athletic build. A hint of chest hair sneaked out over the unbuttoned shirt he wore, the sleeves rolled up to his elbows revealed a dark tan and dark hair. His hands were strong and masculine.

"Is Princess ready?" he repeated, watching her eyes roam his body. It disgusted and electrified him. Disgusted because she was looking at him as if he was some kind of meat, electrified him because it turned him on. She was checking him out, and that was a good sign.

"Is *court jester* ready to do *his* job?" she asked in return, oblivious to all around them and the prying eyes that stared.

Flinching, he spat, "I'm no court jester."

"And I'm no princess," she returned. "Just because I set my own timetable and take a break when *I* know *I* need it, doesn't make me a princess. But yes, I *am* ready to finish this job, and then I won't have to see *you* any longer." She sneered and stormed over to the rock she had been standing on.

"Okay, everyone," he seethed. "Princess is ready to work again, places, hair, make-up." Making his way back to his spot, he wondered who the hell she thought she was.

Diana Villiers Stephanopoulos didn't take shit from anyone. At almost twenty-nine, she had been raised to be polite and nice by her mother Vivian, and to fight and stand up for herself by her father Carlos, and grandmother Jenny. And even though she looked like her mother, she took after her father and grandmother in every way. There was no way she'd tolerate some two-bit magazine photographer. She'd been in the business far too long to tolerate any kind of bull from anyone. Starting to model at fifteen, she'd always had her mother on hand to guide her. At nineteen, she was modelling on her own, at twenty-one she was setting up *Haus of Stefan* with her cousin, and now at twenty-eight, she was experiencing the most arrogant, the most despicable, the most narcissistic photographer, let alone person, she'd ever met. If only he wasn't so damn gorgeous as well.

"Ugh." She rolled her eyes and shook her head to clear away all thoughts. *Get out of my head, get out of my head, get out of my head.* Putting her face to the sun, she breathed and simply stood. She didn't move, she didn't speak, she just *was.* Letting the world slip away.

Charles stared at her through the viewfinder on his camera,

breathing in her ethereal beauty. A few tendrils had loosened and hung lightly around her face, framing it in golden light. The sun shone down upon her like the goddess she was and created a halo effect around her. He stared and hardened once more. Lowering the camera, he couldn't take his eyes from the breathtaking beauty standing in front of such an iconic monument.

At forty, he'd never met such an incredible woman, certainly not one that had captured his heart the way she had. Though she didn't know it. He wondered if she hated men. Maybe she'd had some bad experience in the past which was why she didn't respond to his obvious advances. Maybe she was uptight and frigid. Hell, maybe she was still a virgin and hadn't had a man before. With the way she was standing there looking so damn beautiful without even trying, maybe she wasn't into men. *Or maybe, she just isn't into me,* he thought. *In which case, I'd better change her mind. And if she's as virginal as she looks, all the better for it.* Lifting his camera, he finished off the roll.

*****

Steele Stefan slammed the young man face first into the toilet wall of *Nightmare*, a hot new club in New York City. His right hand had the man by the hair, his left had the man by the cock, and he was ramming his into the young blond, making him grunt.

"Oh, God, yes," the blond gasped, his own hands over Steele's on his cock. "Oh, God, yes, yes, oh, God." He didn't mind being taken from behind, or with such powerful force. The young man got off even more.

"Do you want it, huh?" Steele asked, thrusting his condom covered appendage into the man's anus. "Like it rough, do you?" He towered over the man before him; six foot to the man's five seven.

"Yes, oh, God," the man breathed. "Fuck me, Steele, fuck me hard. Oh, God."

With a final grunting thrust, Steele bashed the man's head into the wall before releasing him and withdrawing. Staggering backwards, he inhaled huge gasps of air to calm his racing heart.

The man pulled up his jeans and turned, seeing his idol with his dick still hanging out. "Do you mind if I take care of that?" He moved the few steps over to his one-time lover, kissing his neck and chest, and running his fingers through the light spattering of hair covering it.

Steele's shirt hung open as it was hot in the club, and the gay man took full advantage, kissing and groping his way down Steele's body to his crotch where he rolled the condom off. He proceeded to suck it into erection and ejaculation, swallowing it like the good little gay boy he was.

"Oh, God, that's good." Steele felt the warmth of the mouth and release of his seed.

The man's hands slid up Steele's body as he stood; his tongue sliding along the path his hands had taken.

"But now, it's enough." Steele shoved the man back and zipped up his jeans. "I'm done." Turning, he checked himself in the mirror, straightened the blue bandanna wrapped around his forehead, and washed his hands with the soap from the dispenser, noting the chipped black nail polish, and wide silver studded and skull rings he wore when in the mood for rebellion, along with the black leather and silver chain bracelets and necklaces. It was a look he'd stolen from his DJ cousin Dominic. He had added his own touches by piling on triple the amount.

Steele Stefan, international model, was formerly known as Cabot Conroy Stephanopoulos, son of Vivian and Carlos, and named after some fag photographer friend of his mother's. He'd hated the name all his life and couldn't wait to change it, choosing Steele Stefan as his new moniker when he and his brother started modelling.

Derek Zoolander's got nuthin' on my blue steel, he thought, eyeing himself in the mirror and seeing his bright blue eyes glare back, made even brighter by the thick black/blue eyeliner he wore when he went clubbing. He raised a brow and blew himself a kiss. *Fuck, I'm hot!*

"Well, I'm not, Steele. I want more." The man sidled up to him. "I love being taken from behind. Take me again, Steele." His hands went around Steele's waist to play with the penis belt buckle. "Take me again."

Steele pushed the hands away and turned from loving himself sick in the mirror. "I never fuck the same man twice, so I'm done. Find yourself another butt fucker." Sauntering into the club, he went in search of his brother.

Phoenix Stefan slammed the young woman against the back wall of the club, hidden by curtains and piles of boxes. He'd taken a fancy to her earlier in the night, and she'd shown him she was interested. A couple of beers later, and they were fucking against the club wall off a hallway. He had her pinned as his condom clad appendage entered from behind, making her groan in pleasure, or in pain. He wasn't sure which one, but her head was back, and her eyes were closed. Her mouth hung open, still in an o shape from sucking his cock moments earlier. He thrust hard, making sure his full eleven inches went all the way in. She was a hot little black number with a wild afro and no underwear. Her mouth knew how to pleasure a man, and so did her pussy.

Grunting to a stop, he withdrew, staggered back, and rolled the condom off. Dropping it where he stood, he breathed deeply to regulate his heartbeat.

"Are we done?" she purred. "I could do that again."

"We're done." Phoenix zipped up his pants and adjusted the bandanna wrapped around his forehead. "How do I look?"

"Gorgeous." The woman ground against him. "Perfect."

"Good," he said and shoved her away. "I need to go find my brother." Walking back into the club, he made his way through the crowd to come face to face with his other half. Standing, they observed each other. Six feet, both had golden-brown hair in a short boyish style, although Steele had an undercut on one side. Locks hung over their foreheads. They were broad and muscular thanks to the training from their uncles, and had eleven-inch cocks thanks to their father and his Greek lineage. They were identical in every way except for their eyes, and it was the only way to tell them apart unless one wore contact lenses.

Steele's eyes were blue, exactly like their father's. Phoenix's was green, just like their mother's.

Born Antonio DeLuca Stephanopoulos, Phoenix hadn't minded his name, unlike Steele. But when they turned fifteen and started modelling together, they came up with stage names. Liking Steele and Phoenix, they adopted their family's old moniker of Stefan and ran with it. They were the toast of the modelling world. Identical twins as gorgeous as they were was a rare thing indeed.

Sliding an arm around each other's waist, they moved in circles, scanning the crowd for wannabe mates. This was something they did. Had each other's back. It had been mentioned as strange, but to them, they shared a bond no one understood. Theirs wasn't a physically intimate relationship, more of a 'twin brother, I'm looking out for you bro' kind of thing. But made emotionally intimate after they'd found their father's stash of porn videos. And not just any porn videos, but movies with their father and uncles. They had watched all of them, surprised by their father's and uncles' lengths and prowess in *and* out of bed. The movies, they learned, held them in good stead for their own sexcapades, because seeing their father and uncles naked and fucking gave them ideas at eighteen, and started them on their own sexual exploration. Now, at twenty-four, they would be twenty-five in two months, they'd lost count of the lovers they'd had and the things they'd tried. Like when they'd had a foursome in the family's penthouse there in NYC. Whenever any family members were in town, they'd use the penthouse, and he and Steele had taken lovers there to share the bed.

He'd picked an African woman of twenty-five, and Steele had an African male of twenty-one that he was ramming home in. Phoenix sat back and watched, having pulled a chair over to the side of the bed so he could rest his legs on it. His right hand brought a beer to his lips as he watched his brother finish up with his one-night stand.

"Do you always do the fucking, or do you ever get fucked?" he asked his brother as his own date slid her hands down his body to his cock.

Steele rolled off and grabbed his own beer. "Always fuck. I like being in control. But just once in a blue moon, I'll be fucked. I don't like it that much."

"Men or women?" Phoenix went on.

"I've had both, as you know. Don't mind both. Do both. Depends

on the mood I'm in." Steele took another mouthful and watched his lover crawl over to his brother.

"And what do you like?" Phoenix asked the black man. Names were never asked or given.

"I like cock," the man said and wrapped his mouth around Phoenix.

Phoenix sighed in contentment. His eyes closed, and his hands gently stroked the man's face. "I like getting sucked." Staring down at the man working to pleasure him, he slid his hand over the man's head and back as he moved, watching Steele move across the bed to lie on his lover, his head resting in his hand, his elbow on his lover's back as he stared up at his twin. "I like cock too."

The black man raised his head. "Feeling left out?"

"Yes."

"Roll over then."

Steele rolled over, spread-eagled, the top of his torso hanging off the bed next to his brother's chair. He groaned in pleasure as his lover inhaled his cock, manipulating it to do what he wanted it to. "Oh, that's good." His fingers slid up Phoenix's leg and found his hand. Their fingers entwined, and he squeezed as he came. "Oh, God."

"Oh, God indeed," the black man said, making his way up Steele's body to find Phoenix's manhood willing and waiting.

Phoenix welcomed him and took his own lover's breast into his mouth as she lay across the chair. Hearing the man grunt, and getting a sharp suck, he glanced past the woman to find Steele back inside the man. Both of them working to please the man they were connected to, and with the woman forgotten, they moved as a threesome while Phoenix never tore his gaze from his brother's.

*****

Dominic Spiros Stephanopoulos leaned back in his chair with a sigh. He was in the family recording studio trying to put together some tracks, but it just wasn't gelling, and he didn't know why. He'd been at this for a week, coming in every day, working in the family's club every night as the resident DJ. At twenty-four, he'd made a name for himself just like his father, Pedro, had by the time he was the same age. He looked like his father too. Jet-black hair slicked back with a slight undercut and a lock overhanging bright blue eyes. He was the eldest son, but second in line behind Alena, the big sister who had ignored him for the first two years of his life and then bossed him around for the next nineteen years, stopping once he'd turned twenty-one. Although she still did it on occasion, he soon stopped her. At six foot one, he was an inch taller than their father, but five inches taller than her, and he always used his height as an intimidation tactic. And it worked. But Alena didn't bother much with the rest of the family anymore. She had her own music career and the fashion line with Diana, while he was into his music like their parents.

He'd grown up watching Pedro play night after night, falling in love with music and dancing in the process, and learning the craft from his father as well as piano from his mother. So, not only was he able to write it, he could play it and manipulate it all he liked in the studio, and he'd come up with some pretty sick beats. He'd worked in the family business for the last ten years, first as a watcher and coffee maker, then as an artist and musician, while learning from the master craftsmen of the era who came to record at their studio. The Stones, Eric Clapton, Madonna, U2, Elton John, David Bowie. They had come from far and wide to Mykonos to record with Pedro as a producer, and he'd taken full advantage of it, learning guitar and bass, music composition, lyric writing, and recording and producing. As with Alena, his music was played in the club and had become huge European hits. He went by the name Dom Stefan in the club and on his songs, but for some reason, his mojo just wasn't happening this week.

"What's the matter, bro?" Whitey asked from the couch. "I thought that was awesome."

"Yeah," Petey added, wiping his nose on his sleeve. "Cool, bro."

Dom spun around in his chair to look at the people in the studio with him. Whitey was Dan White, an average looking kid he'd gone to school with. They weren't best friends, but they still hung out on the odd occasion. Petey, Pete Marker, was a snivelling little toe rag friend of Whitey's. He sniffed so much that Dom thought he had a perpetual cold, or else he snorted drugs. Either way, he didn't know and didn't care as long as it didn't affect him.

Smallzy was Ben Small, a wannabe rapper who thought his ticket was Dom and his family's company; that they'd make him famous like the rest of the family. He wore his cap backwards and still emulated rappers from the '90s. With bleach blond tips and pants hanging off his butt, he believed he was the coolest. He wasn't.

Then there was Fryzy. Danny Fry was a friend of Ben's, and for some reason, they all had stupid nicknames. They were his posse, or as some of them joked, his pussy posse, as some scored with the women that hung around the stage in the club waiting for Dom to give them a wave. But he wasn't interested. Not that he wasn't interested in women; he was, just not that often. Sex wasn't a big deal to him, his music was, and he figured it would be mind-blowing with the right woman when she came along. But so far, she hadn't.

He wondered why he hung out with these boys. They weren't his friends. He had no best friend because he'd been working so damn hard and just figured he'd hang with whomever, but this lot were boring him, and he knew they were using him for their own gain.

"Look, I can't think with you lot here; why don't you go?" He spun back to the soundboard and tried thinking about his song while absentmindedly playing with the wide black leather cuffs around his wrists. *Why wasn't it working?*

"But Dom, we're your posse," Whitey said. "We'll help you through this. What's wrong? The song sounded good."

"Get out." Dom threw a scowl his way. "I can't work with you lot here."

"Maybe if I get on the board and helped you out?" Smallzy got up, eager to help.

"Are you all fucking deaf?" Dom yelled, his anger simmering below the surface. "I said get out. I don't want you here. Try listening to what I'm saying and have enough decency to respect it and leave. You're not welcome here anymore."

"Everything all right, Dom?" Mono, their big, black security guard asked from the doorway.

"No, Mono. Can you get this lot out of here? They're not welcome anymore. I'm sick and tired of them and don't want to see them again." Dom turned his back once more.

"Aw, why not?" Whitey asked. "We're your posse, Dom. You and I went to school together."

"We may have gone to school, Dan, but we were never friends. Just schoolmates, nothing else," Dom replied. "In fact, *none* of you are my friends. Just tragic wannabes and hangers-on. Get out and don't come back. Mono, make sure they're gone."

"Yes, boss." To Mono, every member of the Stephanopoulos family was boss, because the family paid his very healthy salary every week. He herded the boys out of the door while they threw scowls at Dom

Sighing, Dom replayed the track, spinning his wide music stave silver ring while trying to figure out what was wrong with the sound.

*****

Alexis Fallon Stephanopoulos, named after her mother's favourite characters from the US soap *Dynasty*, lay back on her sun lounge sipping her mocktail. She and her two best friends, twins Summer Rain and Melody Song Gatos, were spending the day on the beach under their umbrella, sipping drinks, and watching the cute boys go by.

All three girls had been born in 1988, hence the unusual names all three had, and with Summer and Melody's parents being Mike and Maggie Gatos, who were best friends of Alexis's parents, Pedro and Angelina, there was never any doubt the girls would be as well. At nineteen, they had been friends all their lives.

"So, does this mean we've started our summer holidays early?" Summer asked, eyeing the group of guys to her left. A petite fake blonde, she and her twin had been working until recently, having saved up enough to spend their summer months lounging around.

"I'm always on holiday," Alexis said from behind her dark sunglasses. With her mother's looks, brown eyes and jet-black hair, at five ten she was taller than her friends by two inches. She was also taller than Alena, the family tragic who believed she was a star and had made sure to tell anyone who'd stop and listen. Alexis had put up with it all of her life, and it irritated her beyond belief.

Alena the singing superstar, Alena the fashion house designer, Alena the model, Alena, Alena, Alena. That's all she'd heard her entire life.

Except from her grandmother who always made sure to spend time with each of her grandchildren, nurturing their loves and passions, and later, their careers. The Stephanopoulos clan was very career orientated indeed, but Alexis had no idea what it was she wanted to do. Her grandmother encouraged her to try music, and she could sing, but it wasn't overly interesting since Alena did it, and big brother Dom was into it too.

Then their grandmother had encouraged modelling the *Haus of Stefan* lines which she did to irritate Alena, and while she had fun doing the teen lines, she didn't think modelling was for her in the long term. Then her grandmother had suggested the creative side of things, such as designing fashion and accessories with the bag, shoes and jewellery lines. She had moderate success with the label, making some of her designs, but she didn't feel that was really for her either.

She was competitive with Alena, always had been, but there didn't seem to be much left to do that the family hadn't already done. And while she didn't want in on *Haus of Stefan,* she needed to be able to make her own mark somewhere away from her sister and cousins. The world-famous Diana, Steele and Phoenix. She snorted. What stupid names the boys had chosen. But then Cabot and Antonio were only remotely better.

She'd done some acting in Uncle Carlos's movies, as had the rest of them, but that didn't excite her, and she had no need to be a DJ.

"God," she groaned. "What am I going to do with my life?"

"Haven't you figured it out yet?" Melody asked. With dyed blonde hair like her twin, her green eyes sparkled with the summer fun to come.

"No." Alexis took another sip of her drink, but let the straw linger in her mouth while she took in the hot hunky man meat in front of her. At nineteen, she definitely wasn't a virgin, but had only been with one boy and now wanted a man. She watched him swim away before continuing, "You'd think with everything my family does, *something* would have interested me, but it hasn't. Once I try it, and I've done it, that's it. I want to do something else."

"You haven't found anything worthwhile to do then?" Summer asked. "What about volunteering for a charity or something?"

"Ugh, no, thanks. I've gotten that from Grandma." Alexis adjusted her bikini, much to the delight of the guys to their right, getting catcalls and whistles. "Ugh." She turned her nose up. "No thanks."

"You're not interested in men at all?" Summer asked.

"It's not that I'm *not* interested," Alexis replied, closing her eyes. "I just don't care to be whistled at."

"I think it's kinda sexy." Melody eyed off the guys, all hot and hunky and foreign.

"Well then, you take them," Alexis told her and felt her body go cold as something blocked the sun. Opening her eyes, she looked up at the most delicious-looking man she'd seen in ages. "You're blocking my sun."

"I came over to ask if you'd wanna grab a drink, maybe go for a swim out to some little island somewhere."

"What? So I can be raped by you?" Alexis spat. "Why would I go anywhere with a strange man? I don't know you."

The man had been eyeing off her large provocative breasts and well-packed body, but now he smirked. "Frigid bitch are you? You're just a whore and a tease. Lead men on then turn on them."

Alexis, not liking those comments one bit, daintily got to her feet and followed the man as he walked away. "Do you know who I am?"

The man turned. "What?"

"Do you know who I am?" she repeated, hands on hips, sly smile on lips.

"No. Should I?" tall, dark and gorgeously stupid asked.

"Well, considering the way you just treated me, you clearly have no idea, so let me just tell you." Her hand snaked out to grab his cock in his tight little speedos. He went down like a lead balloon. Still holding on while he was screaming in pain, she raised her voice and said, "My parents are world-famous musicians and record producers. My sister is world-famous singer Alena, my cousins are world-famous models Diana Villiers and Steele and Phoenix Stefan. My uncle is a world-famous movie writer, director, producer; my aunt is a world-famous model, stylist, cosmetics queen and author. My uncles and grandmother are world-famous gay and AIDS advocates and activists. We are the Stephanopoulos family, we own half the island, and you just called the wrong girl a frigid bitch, a whore and a tease." With a final wrench, she let go. "The next time you want to hit on me or call me names, just remember who my family is. We *are* the *Stefans.*" Dusting off her hands, she went back to her friends.

"He could have you for assault, you know," Melody told her. "Look, he can't even get off the ground."

They watched him crawl back to his friends who laughed and pointed.

"Ugh. What.Ev.Ah!" Alexis went back to sunbaking and sipping her mocktail. "So, what did you girls want to do this summer? Travel? See the sights? Go to Italy with my uncles?"

"When are they going?"

"After Princess Alena's birthday in June."

Summer snorted. "You two will never get along, will you?"

Alexis grinned wryly. "Probably not."

*****

Danté Pedro Stephanopoulos and his best friend, Nicholas Michael Gatos, son of his parents' best friends Mike and Maggie, were in the club preparing for that night's show. As the youngest child of Pedro, Danté Stefan was next in line behind his brother Dom, who already had a career DJing and making music. But at fourteen, Danté wanted to be a rapper. He wanted to write lyrics and make music, and what better training ground than his family's company, starting with *SB3*, their nightclub slash function room? And, as his initiation into DJing, he was allowed to spend one night a week behind his father's decks rocking out to music. He was already well-trained, having watched from a baby. He'd learned all he could, being a sponge when it came to educating himself on the art of music. And his best friend Nick was always there to support him. Their mothers were Juilliard-trained, had played in world-famous orchestras, taught music in schools, and did private tuition. Nick's dad had started as the head bartender at *SB3*, and moved up to assistant manager, and was then promoted to manager twelve years ago when his grandpa had retired at seventy.

Nick's parents had moved to Mykonos two years after Dante's had moved back in '81, and after a brief holiday and work experience in '82, had made the permanent move in '83. Nick was a year older than him, but the two of them had grown up together and were the best of friends.

"Any ideas what I should play tonight?" Dante asked, flipping through the record rack behind the deck set up on stage. It was a world-class system; all a DJ could want or ask for. They also had CDs, 45s, twelve inches, a computer system, and as much music as it could all hold.

"You have to do the latest stuff," Nick said from the CD rack. "Your father plays old school vintage, your brother plays a lot of '90s and pop, so you need to make your own stamp. It's 2007, play what's cool now, mixed with a few years ago that everyone will remember. Have you got anything that's new out? That no one here would have heard of?"

Dante sighed. "We have all sorts, but nothing really new that I know of." He pulled out an old Red Hot Chilli Peppers album. Every time he put it on he rapped along to it, giving the crowd something to cheer about. But he wanted to be different from his brother and wasn't sure how to be since they looked alike, except for the eye colour difference. Dom had blue eyes while he had brown. There was a height difference too; at fourteen he had a few inches to go until he was six foot one like his brother. "I could ask your dad if the new stuff has come in. We get stuff every two weeks from record companies around the world. We're one of their first stops for pop and club tracks. We play it here, and it hits all of Europe within the week and becomes a huge success."

"How great's that?" Nick said. "You play it, and it becomes a hit.

That's how big this club is, that's how big your family is."

"Yeah, I know. If only I knew how to make my mark in it."

"What do you mean?" Nick sat on the side table watching his friend. At fifteen, he'd lived his whole life on Mykonos, only occasionally seeing the rest of the world when his family went on holiday, so he always lived vicariously through his best friend who had the best family in the world. He had a huge crush on Alena, Alexis and Diana, thought Dom was pretty cool, but loved how Danté's grandmother ran the show. He rarely saw his own grandparents, maybe once a year for each, so he always took whatever he could get out of Mrs Stephanopoulos, whether it was sleepovers, food, holidays, or presents. Whatever Danté's grandmother offered, he took, and it wasn't too shabby that he got to meet world-famous musicians and actors just from hanging out with the family. You couldn't beat Arnie, Sylvester, or Van Damme to butt kick everything into gear. The summers were the best, and he couldn't wait to be out of school. "What are we doing for summer anyway? Are you gonna work on your music all the time, or are we gonna have fun?"

"What fun is there to have unless it's about music?" Danté asked, coming up with a playlist for that night.

"Ah…swimming, snorkelling, girl watching." Nick shook his head in disbelief. "I know you love your music, dude, but seriously, there is more to do than just that."

"If you didn't have a crush on my sisters and cousin, you would see there *is* more to the world than just girls," Danté teased.

Nick blushed. "Yeah, well," he mumbled. "They're hot."

"Ew, don't say that about my sisters." Danté screwed up his nose. "Gross, dude."

"Just because you're not interested in girls at fourteen, doesn't mean I'm not at fifteen," Nick retorted. "I've already sprouted two inches taller, *and* I'm getting a beard." He lifted his face for Danté to see.

Danté looked and kept looking. "You mean that bit of bum fluff as Grandma would say. That's no beard. You're so stupid, dude." He laughed.

"I am not," Nick argued. "I'm turning into a man."

Unable to control his laughter, Danté bent over and leant on his knees. "A man? You're turning into a man? Dude, *you're fifteen*, that's a long way from being a man."

"No, it's not." Nick crossed his arms. "I'll be a man at eighteen."

"Says who?" Danté slapped Nick on the arm. "The Wheaties box?"

*****

Tomas Stephanopoulos finished up his set at his gym, *In Shape*, and wiped the sweat from his brow with a fresh fluffy white towel. After all these years he still loved the feeling a workout gave him, and at fifty-two he was in great shape. A healthy diet, healthy lifestyle, work-life balance, and an amazing husband all made it possible.

He had it all and was eternally grateful to his mother for fighting hard to keep him alive. He had put back into the universe by being active in the fight for AIDS, and as a gay advocate, but he still preferred to be at home on Mykonos, staring out at the ocean and living a happy life with Roger, the love of his life. They had been together nearly thirty years, and he and his brothers would be celebrating their anniversaries that year in November. All of them had been married nearly thirty years and their parents for fifty-five. And *their* anniversary was in a couple of weeks. It was already a big year for birthdays and celebrations. His little brother had turned fifty, his sister-in-law had turned seventy, and the next couple of years would bring more.

Next year, Roger would be sixty, and he was already planning his birthday party, plus his mama would be eighty. The girls would be thirty, the year after Angie would finally hit fifty, and Alexis would be twenty-one, so the next few years were very busy with significant celebrations. Two years ago when he'd reached fifty, he had celebrated in style. For at the age of twenty-six, he'd never believed he'd reach twenty-seven, let alone see everyone turn thirty. But he had, thanks to Jenny fighting hard to save his life, and he had celebrated his thirtieth four years later with a big party, then his fortieth, then his fiftieth. And in a few months, he would be celebrating thirty years with the love of his life, Roger Dencott.

They'd had an amazing life together, meeting back in '77 when he was twenty-two, and Roger was twenty-nine. Roger was his second lover, with Tomas being very new to sex, and male sex on top of that. He'd only realised he might be gay a month before meeting Roger, who was a porn star. To spend time together, Tomas had joined him, becoming a porn star for all of about two months before leaving the industry.

His mother had sent the two of them on a worldwide travelling holiday, and they didn't work for years after. But 1981 was the worst time. For over a year he and his brothers lost friends to what was now known as the HIV/AIDS virus, and it had been rough. Pedro lost co-workers, Viv lost friends, and he and Roger lost both. The virus had absolutely devastated the gay community back in the '80s and '90s, and into the new century. It may have been 2007, but many were still dying from it, and in 1981, he had been told he had it; that he and Roger had contracted this disease that gay men were getting. It was so new at the time that no one knew what it actually was, how it was contracted, how to cure it, or how to deal with it. So men died, in the hundreds of thousands. And he and Roger were on their death beds, believing what the doctors told them; that they had the gay disease and would die of it. And he had.

In July 1981, after Jenny had packed them all up and taken the family back to Mykonos, Tomas had passed away. He was dead for five minutes while three doctors worked hard to bring him back, and they did.

It turned out, he didn't have the disease after all. He had a parasite that manifested symptoms incredibly similar to those of the gay disease. That's where the confusion lay. Because the diseases ate his blood and caused his T cells to drop, they thought he had the dreaded gay plague, the 4H disease, the gay disease, GRID, and however else it was known then. But he'd survived, though his body was so ravaged by all of the diseases he'd had as a result of the parasite. He'd taken nearly five years to get back to good physical, mental and emotional health. The only lasting effects were the permanent dusting of grey through his hair which he'd gotten as a result of the stress on his body, and the eye damage sustained by the CMV, which meant he'd needed glasses ever since.

He and Roger had stayed with his parents for all of that time, not wanting to leave the safety and comfort of his room and his mother's love and care. And he'd blossomed under it. But eventually, he and Roger moved into their own house beneath his parents' and knocked down the walls between the two front bedrooms to make a mega-master and art room, so they could take advantage of the magnificent views to continue painting the seascapes and landscapes he and Roger did.

After decorating everyone's homes, their artwork decorated the family's hotel, *The Windmill,* that they'd bought in 1983, where they'd all celebrated their weddings thirty years ago, the gym, the studios and *SB3.* Any other paintings left over were sold off, and the proceeds went for research and medications towards the fight for AIDS. Thus he and Roger could afford to work only once or twice a week in their gym, and to protest or educate the rest of their time while still enjoying holidays and long, languid days together.

He preferred the peace and quiet, so they had hired staff to take over when they weren't there, and trusted Julio, their manager, to take care of the place for them.

Grabbing a bottle of water from the bar fridge, he stood staring out at the magnificent view of the island. The gym was in a private section of Mykonos, known as the Stephanopoulos compound, so celebrities felt comfortable going there on any given day. There was always one there, especially in summer. Many came through winter to film movies or music and used it as their private gym. It was a part of the family business and a mega business at that.

Each son or in-law had a piece of the family company, *Stephanopoulos Inc.,* or *S.Inc* as it was affectionately known. Carlos had his movie productions, Pedro and Angie their music studio, Viv still had her cosmetics and style company that she'd started back in 1980 with the financial backing of Jenny, which was absorbed into the business, and he and Roger had the gym. Even the kids had gotten into it by following in their parents' footsteps, with modelling, music and fashion.

He thought about his nephew Cabot and his adventurous sex life. The rumours were that Cabot was into both, which was okay, and condom usage had been drummed into all the kids' heads along with safe sex and HIV/AIDS knowledge. After their scare in '81, there was no way his mother was going to let the kids grow up and have unprotected sex.

Taking a long drink of the icy lemon flavoured water; he felt a kiss on his shoulder and smiled. "Hey." He rested his head against Roger's. "You finished your workout?"

"Mmm, I have," Roger murmured. "Finished yours?" He nibbled his lover's ear.

"I have." Tomas felt himself falling. Even after all these years he still got weak at the knees when his husband touched or kissed him.

"You know…" Roger's hands slid around Tomas's waist. "No one's due in for a few hours…so the steam room is free."

"Roger!" Tomas exclaimed, looking up into his big brown eyes. "We can't do it here."

"Why not?" At six foot three, Australian born Roger was as fit and healthy as his husband, having not suffered to the degree Tomas had. With brown eyes and matching hair that was greying at the temples, he gazed into his husband's black eyes. "It's *our* gym, and we'll tell them not to disturb us. Come on, T. Let's take advantage and make memories." He led his lover toward the steam room, calling out to staff to not disturb them until they came out.

*****

Carlos Stephanopoulos wandered over to his wife, Vivian Villiers. Just two months earlier, Viv had turned seventy and didn't look a day over forty, the age she was when he met and married her. His bright blue eyes blazed up and down her firm slim body, and pert boobs and ass. The brown curls that once swayed gently against that pert ass now swayed against her shoulder blades, but were still as golden-brown as ever. She looked incredible and had taken care of herself in the thirty years they'd been together. It was nearly the 30th anniversary of their first meeting, and he was planning on recreating that moment, but that was next month. He slid his hands over that ass and around to her stomach, still as flat as a tack despite having twins nearly twenty-five years ago.

"Hey, you." She smiled at her gorgeous golden Greek god; the man that had captured her starving heart and fed it till it was full and flowing over with love and passion and desire. She'd loved Carlos from the moment she'd laid eyes on him; she just didn't know it until months later. It was definitely lust at first sight, having heard from good friend Harriet DeVille about the golden god pleasing her good friend Connie DeLuca. She'd jumped the ferry from Santorini to see for herself, and she had seen all ten glorious inches of him within thirty minutes. And those ten inches had never stopped pleasing her. "Ready to go?" She packed the final container into the make-up kit. "I'm done here."

"Ready to go." Carlos kissed her cheek. He had his brother Tomas to thank for helping Viv, himself and Pedro stay in shape all those years. They still had abs and biceps thanks to Tomas and Roger, and the healthy lifestyle they all shared saw to it that he still looked young at fifty-four, sixteen years Viv's junior. The age difference never mattered to him, but he knew it had mattered to Viv at first. He'd found out later that his mother had worried about it too, but they'd all gotten over it and moved on.

He was world-famous, something he'd been for a long time for so many reasons, with his own massive production company based in Athens, even though they lived in Mykonos. And he did a lot from the studio office he had on the island. It was all part of the business he ran with his mother. When they moved home in 1981, during the months Tomas and Roger were dying, Jenny had made a decision and consulted with him. She was going to move the family forward by giving her children what they wanted, and it was going to be on Mykonos as a base. She wanted him, as eldest, to be co-CEO with her, even though she owned it outright, and the company would pass to the boys once she and Spiros were gone. He'd marvelled at her faith in him and took on the challenge with gusto since he'd already delved into business and filmmaking with Viv's company, *Villiers Inc*, which she had set up in 1980. With film school and a business degree behind him, he'd set up the movie studio, *S'Reel,* in Mykonos as a starting base, and had *Stefan Productions* with Pedro in Athens two years later.

In the years since, he'd made documentaries on gays and AIDS in conjunction with his mother, Tomas and Roger. He'd made Alena's film clips, as well as many other singers' videos. He'd made big money-earner movies set in and around Greece, and had many celebrities coming from all over to work with him. Just like his mother, he was tough, but fair, and people always knew how far to push him before he pushed back. It was also fun working with his brother at *Stefan Productions*. Anything that got made would be under that name, regardless of what it was. And having Pedro around made it easier to get music for their movies, as he recorded it all in Athens, and it came under their publishing company, so they owned everything outright. It was a great set-up, and he loved working with his mother and hoped to continue working with the kids once he was too old to run the place.

"You get Mama and Papa's present yet? I have absolutely no idea what to get them. What do you get for a fifty-fifth? God, I can't believe they've been married for fifty-five years."

"We've been married for nearly thirty." Viv's laughter floated along on the sea breeze. "That's a long time too." Turning, she moved into her husband's arms and slid her own around his neck. "You'd better not forget to get me a present come November."

He gazed into her emerald cat-shaped eyes, still sparkling and vivacious. "Don't worry, babe, I've got your present right here." He pushed his crotch against her. "Right where it always is."

Viv snorted. "Oh, for God's sake. Are you kidding? One, you're still calling me babe, and two, you think I only want your penis for my anniversary?" She rolled her eyes. "You'd better think again, buster, because I can have that old thing any old time."

"Who you callin' old?" Carlos demanded. "I'm only fifty-four, but it's a young and youthful fifty-four. In fact…" He stopped her from butting in. "Carlos junior is still very much a healthy twenty-four, just like when you met it. Remember that? Our anniversary's next month. Thirty years since we met. And I think," he flashed back in his mind, "it only took maybe thirty minutes for you to get your hand on it."

Viv laughed at the memories. "Oh, I definitely remember. That Barbie girl was calling you out at the bar, so I called her out before giving you the eye. You were hot back then, darling, with your golden hair." She slid her hands through his short hair, still golden-brown, but secretly getting touched up every month to cover the greys creeping in at the temples. "I do miss tangling my hands in it from time to time."

"At least I still get to tangle mine in yours. I *miss* your long hair." His fingers played with a golden tendril.

"Oh, God, I don't." She shook her head to let the curls shimmer down her back. "I think now that I'm seventy I might go shorter still, like your mother. I like her hairstyle."

"Yeah, it suits her and is easy to maintain, she reckons." Carlos wrapped his hand in Viv's hair.

"Ugh, mine isn't anymore, so it's getting shorter," Viv said, then paused. "I was remembering before how we met. I had a call from Harriet, who'd gotten a call from Connie…" She paused, sadness washing over her even after all these years. "I still miss them."

Carlos pulled her closer. "Yeah, I miss all of them too."

Connie DeLuca was a friend of Viv's back in the mid to late '70s, and at the time, one of Carlos's women. Back in '77, Carlos was sex mad, making money left, right and centre, taking money from women who wanted his ten-inch cock to pleasure them. And he made big money, especially from Connie. After a frightening shootout at the hotel where he worked as a masseur at night, Connie and Viv got him out of Mykonos to L.A. where they had introduced him to Harry and Harriet DeVille, the porn king and queen of Hollywood. Harry gave him a job, and Carlos Stephanopoulos became Carlo Stefan, the Greek god of porn.

Sighing, he remembered back. He'd gone from starring in, to

writing and producing the movies, but after '78's *The Greek Gods* film, that was it. He was out of the business just like his brothers.

Once Tomas and Roger had become sick in '81 and *Stefan Productions* was set up, Carlos had phoned Harry and bargained with him to get his movies back. And it had come at a cost. Each of the movies he had starred in cost him five hundred thousand dollars each to get all rights moved over. *The Greek Gods* cost him one million, and the ones he wrote cost one hundred thousand each. But with the financial help from his mother, he'd bought them all back. He'd done the same with Marcus Seralift, buying Tomas and Roger's films, and Angie offered the Poulos fortune to help pay half the costs, paying off Greta Von Burro for all of Pedro's movies at a cost of eight million dollars.

Seralift was out of business by 1987 thanks to AIDS, and both Marcus and his co-owner ex-wife Violet were long dead, along with Harry and Harriet DeVille. Greta Von Burro shut down her company in 1997, but she was still alive at seventy-five and retired. He'd also found out how much the AIDS virus had cost Harry with the cast and crew he had to rebuild. He'd adopted Alfonso, the son of his maid, Suzy Q, as she'd died from the disease, and prepared him to take over when he passed.

Harry was also the one who had informed him back in 1981 of Connie's death. Her estranged husband, Spanish bullfighter Stephano DeLuca, had given her countless STDs and the gay virus, for her husband had been having wild affairs with men including a dead co-worker of Pedro, and a cop they had all known back in the '70s. Connie had been driven into depression and killed herself. A week later, their only child, Antonio, an ex-bartender friend of Carlos from the hotel he worked at, shot himself from the depression of what his parents had done. The news had been devastating because Carlos could have prevented it a year earlier when they'd found out that Stephano was having sex with men. His family had stopped him, and that was a decision he'd regret for the rest of his life.

That was why they'd named one of their boys Antonio DeLuca Stephanopoulos, after Connie and Antonio DeLuca, but he went by the name Phoenix for modelling. Carlos laughed at the strange way he'd gotten to that.

"What's so funny?" Viv asked. She always wondered what her husband was thinking about when he went quiet and emotionally drifted off.

"About Connie and Antonio, how we named one of the twins after them, and how he now goes by Phoenix which is stupid. That's why I laughed. Our sons and their stupid names."

Viv chuckled. "They are unusual, that's for sure. But you went by Carlo Stefan, so not much different. Like father like sons."

"At least it was a very basic version of my own name." Carlos grinned. "Not something as stupid as Steele and Phoenix. If anyone deserves to be called Phoenix, it's Tomas, as Mama always says. So I'm with her on that."

"Yes," Viv murmured. "Very true. He did rise like a phoenix from the flames and is now a big name in activism. He used his return for good."

A soft smile crossed Carlos's lips. "He's done so well, and I'm so proud of him."

"We all are." Viv smoothed his shirt lapel. "After what happened." She shook her head to clear the thoughts. "I don't know if I could be as strong as your mother."

"No." He marvelled at his mother's emotional strength. "I don't think any of us could be. I still remember that day as if it was yesterday, and my gut still ties in knots. You know, it's already twenty-six years ago in July. July 27, 1981, when we lost and regained our brother. Mama's strength got us all through. And just the mere fact she looked after him and Roger for another five years is unbelievable. We'd better be getting her something amazing for her birthday."

"Yes, we are." Viv collected her bag and slung it over her shoulder. "And Diana said she'd make it back. She's only in Athens. But I doubt the twins will be here."

"They've turned into selfish brats." Carlos scowled. "I guess that's our fault for telling them they could do whatever they wanted. But to not even come home for their grandmother's birthday, or their grandparents' anniversary, that's just plain rude." They started walking for the car park.

"They didn't care for my birthday, their cousin's birthdays, or their father's birthday either. I'm surprised they made it home for Christmas, but that was barely two days, and they were gone." Viv brushed a flyaway lock of hair out of her face.

"And no Thanksgiving, or their parents' and uncles' anniversaries before that either." Carlos's scowl deepened. "I can't believe we have such selfish brats for sons. We raised them how Mama raised us, and yet look how they turned out. *Nothing* like Pedro, Tomas and me."

"No," Viv said. "Exactly where did we go wrong to have such selfish, self-centred narcissistic children?"

*****

"How did Alena's video go?" Angelina asked Pedro as he walked into the music studio's office, just down the road and up the hill from their home.

"Good, good." Pedro kissed his wife of thirty years on the top of her head and wearily sank into the lounge chair in the corner of the room. He gazed out over the Mykonos landscape. "She fell over at one point, but sprang back up and got on with it."

"So I saw." Angie chuckled. "I can see the beach from here. I just happened to look up and down she went. It was those ridiculous black heels, wasn't it?" Sitting back in her seat, she looked at her husband. Every inch of his six feet was still gorgeous and studly. She admired his black hair with grey seeping through at the temples, bright blue eyes, fair skin, a great smile that showed off perfect white teeth, and his body that was still to die for at fifty. While hers was a little worse for wear after four children, she was in reasonable shape, but had gotten a little nip and tuck after her last child. Her eyes roamed her husband's long, lithe body and a sly smile came to her lips. Oh, how she loved fucking him, even now at forty-eight she still had a healthy sex drive and they regularly had sex. Remembering back to when they had met, she had named his penis all sorts of things. Disco stick, microphone, love muscle. But they were young then, eighteen and twenty, and it was very free and easy in '77. They'd very quickly learned that that freedom came at a cost when she became pregnant with Alena and they'd gotten married. Not wanting another child until she finished her four years at Juilliard, they'd had one every five years, and that was down to planning, condoms and birth control pills.

"What are you smiling at?" Pedro saw his wife's sly smile and marvelled at how beautiful she looked thirty years on. But then she was still young. Her long black hair hung in the latest fashionable cut. Her brown eyes sparkled with love, health and happiness. At five foot five, she still came only up to his chin, and he could still rest his head on hers.

Her smile grew. "Just thinking about all the names I gave your disco stick."

He remembered, and his smile matched hers. "You did come up with quite a few names for it. Every day you'd come home from school and bounce away getting your rocks off and call it something else. Then I'd go to work. How many names did you come up with?"

"Can't remember. But it didn't last long. Once all of that kidnapping stuff happened, I found out I was pregnant, and we got married, and all of a sudden it was real, and the jokes were over."

"Yeah." He blinked at the memories. "The jokes and fun were over." His life flashed before his eyes as it did on occasion. Meeting Angie in Santorini at her father's nightclub where he worked as the DJ. Having sex with her on the beach every night before Andros Poulos, her father, found out and threatened him. Angie hitting him and the bodyguard over the head before they fled to her house for her things, then his house for his things. They made their way to New York where he'd gotten the job as DJ at the hottest club of the '70s. *Studio 69.* The friends he'd made, Mike Gatos, and Leon Talley who died from AIDS in 1980, the regulars who loved him like Stan Kosnov who also died from AIDS. Even the owner of 69, Eddie Monteif, had died in 1983 from AIDS, after shutting down the club in '82, a year after Pedro had left to be with his brother on his deathbed.

He'd been there for nearly four years, and so much tragedy had happened. The kidnappings Angie had referred to were by Stefano Papadopoulos, his father's ex-uncle-in-law. Stefano had wanted all three brothers dead because they were due to inherit their great-grandfather's estate as it went to blood, not in-laws. Stefano's wife, Marishka Stephanopoulos Papadopoulos had died, and they'd never had children, so Stefano thought he'd still inherit. But Giorgio Stephanopoulos, their great-grandfather, had sold off his entire business, so there was none left to inherit. Stefano didn't know that, but it didn't stop him from having his henchmen kidnap each Stephanopoulos brother and drive them to Chicago's O'Hare airport for the plane back to Greece. With the cops involved, all the henchmen were dead, and once the FBI got involved, they had flown back to Mykonos and then to Athens to see Stefano to find out why it was happening. That's when Giorgio showed up in his wheelchair and shot Stefano dead. It was all over, but not for Tomas who was critically ill at the time.

His former lover had poisoned him, and he'd ended up in the hospital while Roger was in jail. Luiz Manning, the former lover, had killed four *Seralift* porn stars and framed Roger for it. He poisoned Tomas to get him away from Roger, then kidnapped him from the hospital. Stefano's man found him and shot him dead, then took Tomas to Chicago. It was that poisoning that led Tomas to have a weak immune system when all the diseases took hold, and he was told he had the gay plague. But fortunately he didn't, because the main thought was Luiz had given it to him. And in one big fat irony, not only was Luiz the illegitimate child of Andros Poulos, making him Angie's half-brother, but Andros was once Stefano Papadopoulos's stepson.

Oh, the family was a tangled web indeed.

After all of that, the mood changed. There were weddings, Christmas, New Year's, birthdays and babies. Barely adults, they were still babies themselves at nineteen and twenty-one when Alena came along.

He sighed. "We have so much yet have lost so much more. All the friends, the co-workers, the family. We are so lucky to still have Tomas and the family we do."

"Yeah." Angie smile sadly. "I know." She had lost her mother when she was ten and had learned at eighteen that Andros may not have even been her father, and that she had an illegitimate half-brother who'd tried to frame her brother-in-law Roger and kill her husband's brother Tomas. Then Pedro's sick psycho stalker killed her father, and another killed her brother. All of a sudden she was alone in the world and pregnant. If it weren't for Pedro and his family taking her in, she'd have no one and nothing, and with four years of Juilliard to get through, she didn't know how she didn't have a breakdown. But Jenny and Spiros had become substitute parents, and she called them Mama and Papa as their sons did. And if it weren't for them, she could not have dealt with getting married and having a baby. They were absolute lifesavers.

"At least we still have Mike and Maggie. Can you believe they're still together?"

Pedro laughed. "No. But then we are, so why not? Everybody else has died or moved on to someone else. Must be Mama's influence rubbing off on everyone. Hopefully, the kids will follow in our footsteps."

"Alena's still single at twenty-eight, nearly twenty-nine. God, how did we have a twenty-nine-year-old?"

"We didn't." Pedro's lips slid into a grin. "We had a baby, and *now* she's nearly twenty-nine. How the hell did we have three more children? Dom's twenty-five, and he's still single. Alexis has only had one boyfriend. Danté's still too young."

"Oh, please. Didn't you have girlfriends at fourteen?" Angie swung back and forth in her seat, watching her husband think about it.

"Well…" His grin got bigger. "Not girlfriends as such, but girls I was interested in."

"There you go then. Are you headed home, or you wanna help me with this paperwork while you reminisce about old girlfriends?"

Laughter escaped his mouth. "Like you don't reminisce about old boyfriends."

"I only had two before you. You definitely weren't my first, but you *were* my last."

"Aw, thanks, babe. So were you. For me that is. What's with the paperwork?"

"Requests for songs to be written, musicians to be produced, music for films and movies. They want us to make them some music."

He gazed lovingly at his wife and got an idea. Getting up, he locked the door, drew the shades, and pulled out the couch that turned into a bed. "I don't know about you, but I think *we* should make some music of our own."

Giggling, Angie got thrown into the air and over her husband's shoulder before being tossed onto the couch bed.

*****

Jenny Stephanopoulos was going over the company's books with her accountant, Ron Myles, an American who'd moved to Mykonos in the early '90s hoping for a quiet life, but instead ran the accounts for the family company. A gay man, he had come over knowing Mykonos was a gay destination and had eventually obtained a younger lover. He was forty-nine, in fairly good shape, and could keep up with that younger lover of twenty-nine, who had gotten a job in the family's nightclub as a bartender and dancer. Working two to three days a week for *Stephanopoulos Inc.* suited Ron just fine.

"How are we with *Stefan Productions?* Both legs of it?" Jenny asked.

"Earning quite a lot every year," Ron said, glancing at the spreadsheets. "Because you own the music rights you're constantly making money every time a song, album, or movie is sold or played thanks to copyright laws. The movies make enough every year to stay in production and then some."

"Good, good." Jenny scanned the nightclub's paperwork. "We're coming into summer, so the nightclub will be open every night. The hotel's fully booked out, and the meat shop's still raking it in. How's *Villiers Style, Styled by Vivian,* and *Haus of Stefan?*"

Ron shuffled through the portfolios until he came to Viv's company and the fashion label. "Villiers is slowing down cosmetics and make-up wise, but the perfumes still sell well, even after all these years. The videos and new DVDs sell to women over the forty to fifty age range and sell really well to women sixty plus. The fashion and how-to-wear the latest styles DVDs are a big hit."

"That's because they think they can look as good as Viv," Jenny said. "If she can look like that at seventy, they'll believe they can too."

"Which is why the DVDs still sell well, especially the ones in conjunction with the fashion label. Because the clothes can be incorporated into fashion for older women, and she shows them how, so some older ladies are also buying the clothes. Although that's primarily bought by teens through to thirties."

"And it's doing really well by these numbers," Jenny said, closing the portfolio.

"That's because you've picked the right people to run each leg of the business. You've got managers and accountants who know what they're doing and report back."

"Are there any discrepancies between the cash coming in and the products going out?" Jenny glanced up as Spiros, her husband, came through the door. They were at her dining table in her home, though they had offices in the nightclub and the studios, and there in the house, she preferred the space of the dining room for conducting business.

"Everything going out and coming in is accounted for," Ron told her.

"And every part is making a profit?" she asked, gazing over more paperwork.

"Absolutely. *Stephanopoulos Inc.* is making a motza."

"Good," Jenny said. "What about the publicity side of things? Viv and I have our books that we print and distribute through *Prologue Press*. Fortunately, they've been well-received and are always ordered."

"At this stage, there's not much more for you to do. You promote yourselves well, paying for ads in magazines, store windows, selling them in your own businesses. You have Greece behind you, gay America behind you, and the gay community in general behind you." After arriving in Mykonos all those years ago, he'd learned of Jenny Stephanopoulos, her gay son Tomas, and his husband, Roger Dencott. After doing some background searching, he'd been quite surprised at how active they were in the gay community. Having been a fairly closeted gay when he lived in Chicago, he'd never heard of them before that and became intrigued. He'd offered his services as an accountant, and after a few months had gone through very rigorous interviews before he finally got the job. So rigorous, they had their own private detective look into his life, and do background checks of their own. He'd passed. She had no problems with him being gay, and he'd liked the family a lot. The pay was great too, which had helped attract the men, with him finding Antoine five years ago when he'd been on holiday in Italy. Within a month, Antoine had made the move, was tested for HIV which was a standard test if you wanted to work for *S.Inc,* and scored a bartender job at the club. And on some nights, he danced on the stage or bar all night with four other dancers to help keep the crowd going.

"That's fine for my books on HIV and education, but I doubt the gay community are buying up Viv's style books." Jenny shut the portfolio on Viv's business.

"True." Ron chuckled. "But as you were able to get distribution deals set in place, she's in every bookstore across America and Europe. The books are massive best sellers because you got those deals."

"All part of running your own company." Jenny smiled and closed the last folder. "I think we're done for another week. I'll see you same time next week."

"Okay, Mrs S." Ron stood up. "I'm off to enjoy some beach time with Antoine. He's waiting for me." Heading for the door, he knew what an awesome job he had. Tuesdays and Wednesdays he went over all the accounts, and Thursdays he went over them with Jenny. A three-day workweek was perfect.

"Don't forget the sunscreen," Jenny called before he shut the door. Sighing, she turned to her husband as he stood in the kitchen, cold drink in hand. "Oooh, I need that." Sipping it, she let the cold liquid slide down her parched throat.

"Everything on track as usual?" Spiros pulled her into his arms. At nearly eighty-two, he was holding up well. He had no need for a walking implement, and could still get around without help, his mind was smart as a whip, and he could still make his wife happy in bed. He'd long retired from running the nightclub at seventy, and only recently gave up running the meat shop at eighty. He still liked to get his hand in them from time to time to keep his mind working, and he knew Jenny kept hers working by overseeing the entire company, though Carlos ran it and the boys were taking over. It would always be Jenny's company; the business she started after Tomas had died. It was the one thing she knew would keep her sons together as a family; all together in the one place, by her side. And he was forever grateful that she had. After Tomas's death times had been hard emotionally, with the boys' ill health taking a toll on them as well. But love and hard work had prevailed, and they had nursed the boys back to health, all while setting up a business to keep their minds focussed on good things. And the idea of their own gym had helped Tomas and Roger focus on the future and on getting better, so they could get back to life.

He was so thankful he had Jenny in his life. The beautiful Australian girl he'd met off the boat as in immigrant in 1950 on the dock in Sydney, who he'd lived next door to, learned English from, and fallen in love with. She'd accepted his proposal and they married. They'd had Carlos, Tomas and Pedro two years apart, all on Valentine's Day. And she'd given up everything; her family, her home, all to move to Mykonos to live upon the death of his father when he'd inherited the meat shop. She had sacrificed so much for him, and his selfishness in 1978 had almost cost them their marriage. She'd wanted to stay in New York with the kids, and he'd wanted to come back to Greece. After separating for nearly four months, he brought his lonely exile to an end when he realised how selfish he was being. But Tomas's health had brought them back, and they were still there. They travelled every year and spent summer and fall in New York for Jenny, Tomas and Roger to do their AIDS work. And he had no problem with that. He loved and supported them all. And now Jenny was about to turn seventy-nine two days before their anniversary. Kissing her softly, he told her he loved her.

Smiling up at him, she said, "I love you too. I always have and always will." Her hand stroked his cheek and slid over his moustache. He'd had it since '78, and she loved it and the way it tickled her during lovemaking, so she'd made him keep it all these years. And they were about to celebrate fifty-five years as a married couple, and fifty-six years together. Where had the time gone?

"You're smiling. Happy?" he asked.

"Very," she replied, setting her drink down on the kitchen bench and putting her arms around his neck. "Very." They kissed, deeply, passionately before she pulled back. "What are you up to for the rest of the day?"

"*Up* to?" he asked slyly. "Anything in particular?"

"Mmm…might be." Taking him by the hand, she led him to their bedroom.

*****

After the photo shoot, Diana hopped on a plane to Mykonos and rolled her cases into the house she shared with Alena. It was next to Tomas and Roger's and below her parents'. As the eldest, she and Alena had been allowed their own space, but it had to be shared, and since it was rare for them to both be home at the same time, it worked well as a base to come back to. "Hey cuz, you home?"

"Up here," floated down the stairs.

Diana carried her two cases up the stairs to her room and went back down for her bags. After dumping them on her bed, she made her way into Alena's half of the top floor and found her wrapping material around a dressmaker's mannequin. "Come up with something new?" She shielded her eyes against the bright evening sun coming through the huge floor-to-ceiling windows.

"Yep. Thought of it today after the shoot," she muttered through a pin-filled mouth. She pulled one out and stuck it through the bright purple fabric to keep it in place. "How was your day?"

"Horrible." Diana threw herself onto the bed. "I had a photo shoot for *Flair* magazine and their horrible photographer, Charles Kensington, was doing it. He's such an arrogant ass."

"But a *hot,* arrogant ass," Alena told her. "What is he? Forty-five?"

"Forty, I think. You think he's hot?" Diana glanced at her cousin. "He's old."

"If he's nearly forty he's only eleven years older than us." Alena pushed the last pin into the fabric and stood back. "He's got that older, sexy vibe goin' on. You know, the maturity thing. He looks like a man and not a boy."

Diana thought about it. Charles did have that older vibe going on, and he definitely wasn't like all the young guys that normally hit on her. But then, he thought he could hit on her and she'd fall for his charm. How wrong was he! He was arrogant, narcissistic and full of himself, expecting that she would just go out with him the first time he'd asked. He'd convinced himself she'd said yes, so he'd kept on talking. But when she repeated several times that she wasn't going out with him, he was dumbfounded and just couldn't believe she'd turned him down and demanded to know why.

'*You're arrogant, self-serving and up yourself,' she'd told him.*

'*Yeah, and,' he'd replied, still not comprehending that she wasn't interested.*

"Ugh," she moaned from her spot on the bed. "He's such an ass."

Alena threw herself down next to Diana. "It's a hot ass. Have you seen it? It's tight and toned and fits into those vintage stonewash jeans he wears."

Diana frowned. "When exactly did *you* see his ass?"

"Last month at that function thing we were at. You pointed him out, remember?"

Diana thought back to Monte Carlo where they attended a fashion night. Charles was there covering it for *Flair,* while they were there to showcase their latest fashion line, *A Glittering Summer,* a fabulous range of sparkling summer tops, dresses, kaftans and pants, all for holidaying in the sun. "Oh, right. Yeah, I remember."

"He certainly couldn't take his eyes off you," Alena went on, watching her cousin's face. "Whenever he thought you weren't looking at him, he'd look at you. And every time I saw him, he was taking photos of you."

"What!" Diana exclaimed. "He was what? That was unauthorized."

"Well, I don't think those photos will be making it out to the public eye," Alena teased. "I think he wanted them for himself, for his own… *private* collection."

"Oh, how horrible." Diana sat up. "How *dare he* take photos of me without me knowing? Ugh, just one more thing to hate him for. Like he already isn't a chauvinistic, arrogant, hateful son of a bitch."

"You like him, don't you?" Alena asked, a smile forming at the corners of her lips.

"What!" Diana's voice went high. "How could you say such things? He's…he's…horrible." She stormed out of Alena's room and into her own, slamming the door behind her and leaning on it, trying to catch her breath.

"Oh, yeah." Alena watched her cousin go. "You do."

*****

Charles Kensington sifted through the photos from the shoot in his hotel room and laid them out on the floor. He had to get some type of order to them ready for the magazine layout the following week. Edie, *Flair's* editor, wanted at least ten pictures for the story on Diana Villiers, Grecian goddess, model, fashion designer, daughter of world-famous parents, cousin of a world-famous singer, sister to world-famous twin models, and niece and granddaughter of world-famous gay activists and advocates.

"Quite a family you belong to, Princess," he muttered, picking up the one of her gazing up at the sun, eyes closed, arms by her side. The sun had created a halo effect around her, and he knew it would be the cover shot. It showed her exquisite beauty, making her look ethereal and hauntingly breathtaking.

"My God she's beautiful," he murmured, knowing full well she wasn't interested and hadn't been since they'd first met. Years later, he'd fancied her, hit on her, and she'd rejected him. *She* rejected *him*. *No* woman had rejected him. Not that in recent years he'd dated many women. Since meeting Diana, he hadn't dated for longer than one date.

That was it. He'd hit on a woman, get a date, but that was it. The thrill of the chase was over with that date, and he was no longer interested.

For five years he'd done that and had no idea why. But he'd realised back in Monte Carlo that he'd had a massive crush on her. No, it was more than a crush. It was pure unadulterated lust. He wanted her, desired her, and wanted to make her his. The thing stopping him was the fact she was so young. She'd been only nineteen when they'd first met; a baby by his standards. He'd been thirty and wasn't about to touch an underage virgin, despite the attraction. She had been a beauty then and had only gotten better with age. A mature beauty that made her what she was today.

They'd worked off and on over the decade doing photo shoots for different magazines, but the last couple of years things had changed. He saw her as a woman to be tasted, wanted, desired and devoured, and every night he dreamed about her, waking up with an erection so hard he could have broken it when he relieved himself. And he ached to relieve himself within her. Ached to devour her whole, to taste her and feel her as he crushed her beneath him. He was aching now, needing relief. Just from looking at a photo of her.

Sitting on the bed, he took a gulp of beer and relaxed. Never had a woman gotten him so worked up before. Not like Diana Villiers Stephanopoulos. He'd read all about her history; the one she gave the press, but he wanted to know the whole history. How many boyfriends she'd had, how many lovers, when did she lose her virginity…and if she hadn't, he would take it.

"Whoa, hold on there, buster," he said. "Where the hell did that come from?" Was he obsessed with her? Was he willing to do damage to the beautiful Diana? *Of course not, but Jesus fucking Christ, she brings out something in me I've never felt before. Some sort of animalistic Neanderthal feeling…but oh, God she gets to me. Why the fucking hell does she get to me?* It had only been the last two or three years when she'd started getting under his skin, biting back at him, snapping, making comments to rile him up. All the while she did it with those big beautiful blue eyes, and beautiful full lips that turned into a smile or a sneer. Oh, she knew how to work a man to advantage.

Making big cow eyes at him and fluttering those lashes, pouting those beautiful lips. But for him, she reserved hatred, contempt, condemnation, disrespect, and yet it still got to him. Still made him want to grab her by the arms and plant his lips on hers, to feel her firm pliable body underneath his as he made her his woman.

His woman?

Jesus Christ get a hold of yourself, Charles. Why has this woman gotten to you? What has she done to you to turn you into a wreck? Glancing down at the photos on the floor, he couldn't figure out why she irritated him so damn much.

*****

Steele and Phoenix stumbled out of the club into the morning sun that had barely touched the horizon. Shadows still hung in the air, but the sky was becoming lighter. Followers and hangers-on came out behind them, namely young girls and guys who wanted a piece of the twin action.

The Stefan action.

With arms around each other's neck, the boys waved to the people on the street as they passed, believing they were there for them.

"Hello, hello, thank you for coming." Steele waved. "But the party's over now. We've left, so no point going in anymore." Tripping over some uprooted concrete, he was caught by Phoenix and burst out laughing.

"Dude, I think you're drunk." Phoenix laughed with his brother.

"Of course I am." Steele preened, showing off his rock-hard abs to anyone he passed. "And now I want some more. Got anything on you?" He felt his brother's pockets as they walked along. "Got anything in here, bro, besides your big dick?"

Phoenix grinned. "I got a joint or two, that enough for you? I think you've already had some by the look of you."

"Yeah, man." Steele eyed a tall, blond beauty standing by the roadside. "I have. Now I want some more. Hey, gorgeous." He veered over to the hot blond. "You a fag?"

The blond scowled. "Don't you know better than to call us that?"

He stared Steele up and down and vaguely recognised him, but couldn't put his finger on it until he saw Phoenix come and stand behind him. "The Stefan brothers," he breathed. "Oh, my God."

"Yeah, dude, that's us," Steele told him. "You suck cock?"

The blond arched a brow. "You paying?"

"I don't pay to fuck or suck. I get all I want for free," Steele said. "You interested or not, otherwise, fuck off."

The blond took in Phoenix. "You come with the deal?"

"Hell no." Phoenix frowned. "I'm straight. Only *he* likes both." He nodded at his brother. "So it's only him you'll get."

The blond considered. He matched the boys in height and was a fairly decent weight next to them. "Okay. Where do you want me to go?"

"How 'bout the alley?" Steele grabbed his hand and dragged him to the closest alley.

"I'm better than an alley fuck. Take me home or to a motel room, or I'm not doing it," the blond told him.

Steele pushed him against the wall and shoved his hands down the man's pants, getting a groan in return. "Whenever I say fuck or suck, you fuck or suck. Now get down on your knees and start sucking." He ripped open his pants and let his bulging erection free, and the blond took it willingly. All eleven inches.

Steele leaned against the wall with one hand, while the other held the man's head to his cock. "God, suck it, suck it. Yeah, get it down your throat, cock sucker, get it down ya."

Phoenix leaned against the opposite wall, one leg bent, foot against the wall, arms crossed, thoughtfully considering what was happening. Steele was high on God knows what, smoking the joint he'd scored from his pocket, getting his cock sucked by a stranger which wasn't much different to what had happened inside the club. But what he noticed was Steele's anger. The swearing, the grabbing of the hair which he did to the blond, and he watched as Steele slammed the blond into the wall face first.

"Just wait till I roll a rubber on," Steele spoke around the joint. He searched his pockets, but couldn't find one. "Hey, Phe," he said as he turned to his brother, "got a rubber?"

Phoenix searched his pockets and found one. Moving over to his brother, he handed it to him. "You wanna do this, Steele?"

"Yeah, Phe." He flicked the joint to the ground. "You know I love to butt fuck." Rolling on the condom, he yanked down the blond's pants and rammed into him. The blond grunted. "Come on, Blondie, you know you want it. Like it rough, do ya?"

"Not really," Blondie said. "And I prefer to participate than just get rammed."

"Puh-lease, what are you complaining about? You're getting fucked by Steele Stefan," Steele bragged. "That's one for the record." A few more jerks and he was done. "You can pull your pants up now." Rolling off the condom, he dropped it where he stood. "You're not the best I've had, but you've got a great ass."

"Gee, thanks," the blond dryly said as he buckled up his pants. "The next time one of my friends talks about fucking Steele Stefan, I'll tell them not to bother because he has no idea what he's doing. He's just some random little dickshit who can't fuck for nothing." With a dirty look, he quickly walked down the alley.

"Don't call *me* a dickshit, you asshole, coz that's all you are, an asshole." Steele found himself being held back by his brother.

"Dude, stop it. Stop making a dick of yourself," Phoenix told his brother. "We gotta get home, we got a shoot later."

Steele stopped yelling down the alley and calmed down. "What?"

"We've got a shoot later; we gotta get home," Phoenix repeated.

"What time?" Steele stepped back and straightened his shirt.

Glancing at his watch, Phoenix swore. "Shit! We have to be there in four hours."

"Well." Steele wiped his nose on his shirt sleeve. "What's the point in going home then? We may as well keep on partying. Come on, dude, let's go." He flung an arm around his brother's shoulders and they made their way back to the street.

"We'll have to go home to shower and change," Phoenix said, leading his brother to a cab. "We can't rock up to work stinking and unshowered." Opening the back door of the cab that stopped, he shoved his brother into the back seat and climbed in behind him, giving the driver their address.

"Why not?" Steele sniffed his armpits. "This is Eau de Stefan. If they don't like it, they can go fuck themselves."

Phoenix sighed. As much as he loved his brother, he knew he was out of control. "And telling them that is not very professional, is it? If you want to keep modelling and making people like us, then you can't tell them to go fuck themselves. You have to continue being nice and polite so we get the jobs."

"Yeah, yeah." Steele leaned back and groaned. "What.Ev.Ah, bro."

Shaking his head, Phoenix just stared out the window.

*****

Dom burst into his grandparents' home. "Can't stay, Grandma, gotta get to the club." He saw his family gathered around, ready to sit down, and spying Diana, quickly kissed her cheek.. "Hey, cuz."

"Dominic," she warmly said and took her spot at the table.

"You don't work until midnight, Dom. Why do you need to be there?" Pedro asked his son while pulling out Angie's chair. "It's Danté's night."

Dom stopped short and glared at his younger brother, his enthusiasm tumbling to the pit of his stomach. "Oh…yeah…forgot."

Danté stared back, knowing full well that Dom knew it was his night to hit the decks at the club, which annoyed Dom to the hilt and always had. Ever since their father had allowed Danté to try out DJing, Dom had been put out. With his nose out of joint, he'd proceeded to ignore his little brother most times, and constantly criticised or chastised him, telling him he was doing it the wrong way, or that's not the way he did it. It annoyed Danté to the core, but with his parents and grandparents support, he tried not to let it worry him too much.

"Don't worry, Danté." Alena tweaked her brother's ear. "Dom's like Alexis, they're both jealous of our careers."

Alexis snorted, rolled her eyes, and took the seat next to Jenny before Alena could, scoring a scowl for it. "What.Ev.Ah, Princess Alena.

It's always in your head."

Dom sat next to Alexis. "Our sister seems to think she knows so much."

"Oh, don't you know, Dom," Alexis said. "Princess Alena knows everything."

Giggles came from Diana who was seated between her parents, but stopped when Alena gave her a blazingly cold glare.

"Thanks for your support, cuz," Alena said icily and whipped the napkin across her lap. "Maybe I should tell everyone about Charles."

Diana's eyes went wide. "You wouldn't? There's nothing *to* tell."

"You sure about that?" Alena took a plate of steaming food and gave her cousin a sly smile.

"Charles?" Viv asked, curious to find that there was a man in her daughter's life.

"No one." Diana blanched and accepted her plate. "Just a horrible photographer Alena wants to make up lies about."

"Alena," Jenny chastised. "You know we don't lie about each other in this family. We love and support." Sitting at her end of the table, she looked at her family. Carlos, Diana, Viv, Angie, Danté, and Pedro were squeezed in to her right, with Tomas, Roger, Alena, Dom and Alexis to her left.

"Sorry, Grandma," Alena said sweetly. "Just pulling her leg."

Diana flashed her a warning look.

Alena gave her an arched brow in return.

"Now, Dom, why do you need to be at the club so early?" Pedro repeated.

"Ah," Dom faltered. "Dunno. Forgot it was Squirt's night. But I still need to get my set list done and I need to know what he's playing."

"Then you can escort him to the club after dinner," Jenny said. "The club doesn't open until eight. You don't need to be there until seven-thirty." She paused. "Do you." It was more a hard-toned comment than a question.

Dom heard that tone and knew not to argue with his grandmother. They *all* knew that tone. It was the warning tone. The tone that told them not to keep going once they'd started. The tone that told them she knew what they were up to. He backed down. "No, Grandma."

Alexis smirked. "She told you."

"Shut up!" Dom elbowed her.

"Not at my table," Jenny snapped.

Everyone grew quiet.

Dom blinked, and a red blush crept up his cheeks. "Sorry, Grandma."

"And…" Jenny prompted.

"Sorry, Alexis," he muttered and buried his head in his food.

Alexis sneaked a glance at everyone quietly going back to their food. "Geez, you really know how to bring a party down, Grandma," she murmured.

Jenny gave her a look, but started laughing, unable to keep a straight face with her granddaughter, whom she adored. The mood lightened, and the conversation continued.

"How long are you here for, Diana?" Viv asked, enjoying the succulent lamb and citrus salad Tomas and Roger had prepared.

"Until tomorrow afternoon then I hop on a flight for Italy. We're doing a photo shoot in Milan, Venice and Rome. It will take about a week."

"You will be back in time for your grandmother's birthday, and your grandparents' anniversary, won't you?" Carlos asked her.

"Count on it." Diana smiled at her grandmother who smiled back. "I wouldn't miss those celebrations for anything."

"Unlike your brothers," Alena muttered. "Are *they* coming?"

Viv sighed and set down her cutlery. "I doubt it. Sorry Jenny, Spiros." She grabbed her wine glass and knocked back the contents.

"Not your fault, Viv. We all raised the kids the best we could. What they do as adults is up to them. It's just a pity they got so far out of line," Jenny said.

"Yeah," Carlos commented. "Who do we blame for that? We raised them the way you raised us, yet look how they turned out. Arrogant little brats."

"True," Jenny replied. "But then I see most of the kids aren't as close as you three were. You've got Alena and Alexis sniping at each other, and Dom gets constantly annoyed by Danté. Not much different to you with Pedro," she told Carlos. "But then you three grew out of it. This lot hasn't."

Pedro glanced at his boys. "I think it's because they haven't had an earth-shattering, life-changing problem to deal with. We did. Quite a few when we were their ages."

"You're not going to go over how you and Mama got married at eighteen and twenty, and had Alena at nineteen and twenty-one, are you?" Alexis complained. "Like we haven't heard *that* a billion times."

"There's more to the story than that, but none of you knows it," Pedro told her. "It was too much for us to deal with; you don't need to take it on."

Dom shrugged. "We know about Uncle Tomas and Roger getting sick, that's the story you drummed into our heads for the last couple of decades. Safe sex, HIV/AIDS, always wear a condom, don't do drugs."

"And there are parts of *that* story you have no idea about." Pedro sipped his wine. "And I doubt we'll ever tell you."

"Why's that, Daddy?" Alena asked. She had always been curious about her father and uncles' pasts, and the twins had hinted at something one day, but never elaborated.

"Well, Bubba, there's a lot of things your uncles and I dealt with when we were young that you all don't need to know about. But it made us stronger, *and* when uncles Tomas and Roger got sick, *that* made us stronger still. And that's the way families should be. Especially this one. *We're* all close, so we expect all of you to be." A soft smile touched his lips as he stared across the table at his older brother who smiled back. To Carlos and himself, losing Tomas had been the hardest thing they'd ever dealt with, and something they never wanted to deal with again. When he'd started recovering, they were still all there at home, doing their bit to nurse him back to health until the first anniversary, *SB3's* opening night, when Tomas had told them to move out of home and go on with their own lives. And though they'd moved next door, they still did their brotherly duties and helped out and always had dinner at their mama's house. Come hell or high water, they always made it for dinner and Sunday lunch.

"Why haven't you told us?" Alexis asked. "Aren't we old enough to know?"

"You're old enough, it's just nothing to do with you," Pedro replied. "It's *our* past, not yours, kiddo, so don't worry your pretty head about it."

Alexis shrugged and picked at the last of her salad. "Okay."

But Alena sat there, curiously eyeing her parents and uncle, and thought about calling the twins to see what info they had on their parents' pasts.

"What's everyone else doing for the next week?" Jenny asked.

"Rehearsing in Athens, Grandma. We're using the studio for practice and getting the concert ready to take on the road in the U.S.," Alena said. "We've got a month to go and start after our birthdays."

"Which both of you will be here for, I hope," Jenny replied.

"Of course, Grandma. We always celebrate our birthdays with you," Alena and Diana said.

After dinner, they went to the club to watch Danté do his thing, and Dom took over at midnight with his own brand and style. The two boys looked the same, but were so different when it came to music.

*****

"Turn left, turn right, cross your arms. No, you're not doing it right," the photographer snapped. "You do as I tell you." Jacques Theroux stomped his foot in frustration. They were in his studio, and he was trying to capture the twins for a line of alcohol they were promoting. As the faces of *Duo*, the latest tequila range, the twins were perfect. But Jacques was not.

Steele cast a cold eye at Phoenix who nodded.

"Mr Theroux," Phoenix said. "We don't do as we're told. That's not how we work. Didn't our manager tell you that?" Crossing his arms, he played it cool.

Jacques laughed. "I don't care how you work. When you photograph for me, you do as *I* say."

"Well, that's not the way *we* work, and if you don't like that, then you don't photograph us. Tilly." Phoenix snapped his fingers at their manager. "Tell him while we wait."

Matilda Day-Knight walked briskly over to Jacques and Mel Monro, the representative of *Duo* tequila. "Mr and Mr Stefan work when they are allowed to be themselves, not when they are dictated to. They each know how the other moves, and what the other's thinking, and give all of their clients exactly what they want without being yelled at by childish photographers who stomp their feet when they don't get their own way." She eyed Jacques and Mel. "Let the twins work their way, or get another photographer." With a spin on her heel, she marched over to the boys who sat waiting and getting their make-up done. At forty-four, she had been hired by their grandmother personally and was told by Jenny not to take shit from either of them. She worked for her, *not* the boys. Having been in management for over twenty years, she knew brats when she saw them. Steele was the biggest brat she'd seen in a while, and now Jacques was rivalling that.

Mel came over to them. "I've had a word with Jacques and told him we are doing it your way since you're the ones we're photographing. We've seen your work in many ads, and if you know how to work best, then please let's get on with it."

"All right then." Steele stood, adjusted his shirt, and flung his arm around his brother's neck. "Let's get to work, Phe." Getting back on set, they stood with their backs to everyone, breathing deeply and loosening up muscles.

"Wind maker," Tilly yelled. "Places, camera ready."

"Why do they have their backs to us?" Jacques complained.

"Just get your camera ready to capture the magic, Frenchie," Tilly snapped.

Jacques scowled and raised his camera, waiting for the boys to turn. And when they did, the magic occurred.

Steele and Phoenix Stefan showed everyone in that room exactly what had made them so famous. Their rock-hard abs, their enigmatic eyes, the way they moved together. Two souls in sync. They put arms around each other, smouldered into the camera, gave every man in the room a hard-on, and every woman an orgasm. When it was over, they stopped, shook it off, and walked over to their chairs.

The whole room burst into applause, even Jacques, who had never seen anything more magical.

"Thank you, thank you." Steele waved at them. "It was nothing, really."

Everyone started dispersing, casting winsome glances over shoulders, giggling behind hands, watching the boys change out of their clothes because they just didn't care who saw them naked.

"You boys get home on your own?" Tilly asked. "I gotta get some things organized for your next shoot."

"We're fine, Till," Phoenix said. "I'll deal with Steele."

"Okay, gorgeous. See you in a couple of days." They air kissed, and she left.

"Ready Steele?" he asked his brother, but found him wandering after Jacques. "Oh, God, no. Please don't let him be doing this."

Steele followed Jacques into his office and closed and locked the door behind him.

Jacques turned. "Mr Stefan. That was some performance you put on. I've never seen anything that magical." He eyed the young man before him.

Prime beef.

"Magical, huh? What about this?" Steele unzipped his pants and pulled out his cock. "This magical?"

Jacques stared, and his tongue slid out and licked his lips hungrily. "That's quite some magic."

"You a butt fucker, Jacques?"

Jacques blushed. "What?" He couldn't tear his eyes away as he crept towards the magical prize.

"Are you a butt fucker?" Steele repeated. "Take it up the ass. Fuck it and suck it."

Jacques finally tore his gaze from the appendage. "Are you propositioning me, Mr Stefan?"

Steele shrugged. "Either you are, or you aren't, you do, or you don't. If you want it, take it while I'm in the mood."

Jacques tilted his head, inching closer to the organ he sought. "You're offering your penis to me?"

"Got rubbers?"

Jacques hesitated only a moment before moving to his desk drawer and pulling out a box of condoms.

"Suck away," Steele said and watched Jacques greedily fall to his knees and take all eleven inches of Stefan cock into his mouth, groaning and moaning his pleasure.

"Do you like it rough, Jacques?" Steele grabbed his head and held it to him. "Do you like it rough up the ass?"

Jacques's hands moved up behind Steele and yanked down his pants.

Steele startled. "Oh, no, not me, Jacques. You. Suck it, Jacques. Suck it hard."

Jacques sucked hard and took all eleven glorious inches of Stefan cock. Once he swallowed, he came up for air, only to be lifted and thrown over his desk. "What are you doing?" he panicked.

"I did ask you if you were a butt fucker." Steele ripped open a condom and rolled it on.

"Oh, God yes." Jacques pulled down his pants and took Steele like a champion. "Oh, God." The pain was exquisite. "Oh, God yes, yes." He slammed a hand on the desk. "Fuck me, Steele, fuck me. Oh, God...yes..."

"Oh, God no," Phoenix groaned, standing at the closed door, hoping no one came along to find out where they had gone. *How could he? The photographer, oh, for fuck's sake. I can't believe he's doing this. I can't believe he's doing everyone he comes across. What if Grandma finds out?*

He paced back and forth. As much as he loved his family, he was deathly afraid of their grandmother when she got angry. When she got that look in her eye and that tone in her voice...

"Oh, God...God...oh...God..." Jacques slumped on the desk in blissful euphoria.

"Not God," Steele said, zipping up his pants. "Stefan. *Steele Stefan.*"

*****

While Alena hopped on a plane for Athens, Diana left for Italy, and Alexis hit the beach with Summer and Melody.

"Figured out what you want to do yet?" Summer asked. "We were here yesterday having the exact same discussion."

"And we didn't come up with anything then either," Melody added.

"I know, I know." Alexis groaned. "But at least Princess Alena has gone, so I don't have to put up with her for a while."

"Why don't the two of you get along?" Melody asked. "I think she's cool."

"She's a hog," Alexis said. "She hogs the bathroom, the mirror, our parents' attention, the spotlight, the stage, the business, everything. She hogs everything. I'm surprised she can share it all with Diana. But then being one day apart helped, as did growing up together, being the only girls until I came along ten years later. They were all they had, so they're like twins, and I get left out in the cold."

"Aw, poor Lexi." Summer smirked.

"Don't call me that," Alexis said. "I never did like it shortened."

"At least you had us." Melody ignored her sister. "We all grew up together."

"And thank God for that," Alexis said, changing positions on her daybed. "You two are all I had. All I *have*. Princess and I don't get along. Too many years between us. And she was always jealous of me after I was born. She wasn't the only girl in the family anymore. Just like Dom when Danté came along. Didn't like the fact he wasn't the only boy. Danté took his place."

"Wow, your family's a bunch of wackos," Summer said. "Regardless of the fact our parents are best friends."

"It's not our parents, it's us. And speaking of parents, aren't your grands in town?" Alexis asked.

"Both sets of grandparents are." Melody rolled her eyes. "That's why we didn't have dinner with you all last night. They flew in yesterday as a surprise. Totally stuffs up our summer. What are we going to do now?"

Summer shrugged at her sister. "Dunno. But I hope Mother doesn't make us stay. She said we could go away for two weeks."

"We'll probably have to wait until they've gone," Melody said. "She won't let us go while they're here."

"How long are they staying?" Alexis asked.

"Don't know," Summer said. "It could be two weeks, a month, the whole of summer."

"That would be a bummer," Melody added. "Imagine spending our whole summer with our grandparents."

Alexis frowned. "I spend most of the year with my grandparents. I only have one set, so I cherish them dearly."

"Yeah, but you're lucky," Summer said. "Your grandmother's so cool."

"Yeah, she runs a nightclub," Melody added. "That has under twenty-one nights."

"True." Alexis smiled. "That was my idea a few years back. Told Grandma they also had to cater for the younger crowds. So they have nights for the under eighteens, eighteen to twenty-one, and twenty-one and over. They're very popular in summer with the tourists."

"I bet." Melody sipped her mocktail. They were only allowed in on the eighteen to twenty-one nights, but Alexis got in whenever she wanted.

"I can't go anywhere unless I figure out what I'm doing with my life. I don't understand why I can't pick something to do. Why can't I find something to do?" Alexis complained. "Do you girls know what you want to do career-wise?"

Summer and Melody looked at each other across Alexis who was between them. "Marry your cousins."

"What?" Alexis lifted her huge dark sunglasses and looked at both of them. "You what?"

"Want to marry your cousins," they repeated.

Alexis struggled into a sitting position. "Let me get this right. The two of you want to marry my cousins. Cabot and Antonio?"

"Steele and Phoenix," the girls said dreamily.

"Ah, no. Cabot and Antonio," Alexis repeated. "That's their names, and you know Steele, uh, Cabot, is gay, right?"

Summer blinked in astonishment. "What?"

"*What do you mean, gay?*" Melody stared dumbfounded at her best friend.

Alexis moved her head back and forth between the twins. "Cabot is gay. He likes having sex with men. We've known for years though no one says anything. But we all found out."

"*No, he can't be*," Summer wailed, and tears sprang to her eyes. "How come you never told us?"

"Because it's no one's business, and you guys never told me you were interested in my cousins."

"Who the hell are we going to marry now?" Melody cried. "There's no one else I'm interested in."

"Well, there is Dom," Summer told her. "But there's only one of him."

Alexis arched a brow. *"My brother?"*

"Yes, your brother, silly. How many Doms do we know?" Summer said.

"Oh, my God." Alexis flopped on the lounge chair. "I've been taken to crazy town."

"Do you think Steele would ever come back to girls?" Melody asked.

"Oh, my God, oh, no," Alexis said. "Can we get off my cousins and focus on me?"

"What are *you* complaining about?" Summer retorted. "*You've* got a huge family business to go into. *We* don't."

"Your father is the manager of our club, and your mother helps Mama teach music and write and record stuff. They're a part of the business too. So are you two if you want jobs."

"Yeah, but I don't want to work. I want to have fun," Melody complained. "We've worked for the last nine months so we could take summer off, and now our grandparents are here, and we can't. It's not fair."

"What sort of jobs do you want?" Alexis asked, getting impatient at the conversation always going back to the girls.

"For summer, none. For the rest of the year, something fun. Like modelling for *Haus of Stefan*, maybe even work for the label. Getting to travel overseas, and model and design, and wear all of the awesome clothes like this kaftan top I'm wearing from the current line." Melody glanced down at the pretty blue and green swirl print top covered in sequins and Swarovski crystals.

"That one is *so* pretty." Summer admired the gorgeous colours.

"Oh, it is. I love it," Melody told her.

Alexis sighed, and not wanting to listen to the twins anymore, took off for the water. Swimming out, she dipped her hair to wet it and slowly floated around to look back at the beach.

"You're the frigid bitch from yesterday. I should teach you a lesson."

Alexis froze at the voice, but managed to turn her head to see the asshole from the day before. "You! Go away." Moving back toward the beach she tried to stay calm, but was yanked back by her hair.

"I didn't like the way you treated me yesterday," the male growled in her ear as he held her by the hair. "I should teach you a lesson right here where no one can save you." His other hand grabbed a breast.

"Help," Alexis screamed. "Help me, rape, rape."

Pedro, Angelina and Maggie were standing with Melody and Summer as they had decided to come down to the beach for a swim, and now heard the cries for help.

"Alexis," Pedro yelled, running for the water and slicing his way toward her.

The man, seeing him come, let go of her and tried to swim away, but Pedro got there first, getting him in a headlock while yanking his head back by his hair. "You ever touch my daughter again, I will hurt you. Do you understand me?"

"I wasn't," the man gulped. "I wasn't."

"Because if you do, it won't be me you'll have to worry about. I will hurt you, but her grandmother will kill you. Do you understand?" Pedro threatened.

"Yes, yes, please let me go. It was a misunderstanding." The male fought against the arm around his neck.

"I doubt it. My daughter doesn't cry rape for nothing." Pedro let him go and watched him swim off before returning to shore. "Alexis?" He ran up to her as she sheltered in her mother's arms. "You okay, Bubba?"

"Yes, Daddy," she sobbed. "He grabbed me and scared me. He said he was going to hurt me."

Pedro held on tight to Angie and Alexis. "Then I'm glad I came along when I did."

"So am I," Angie said. "Glad you suggested a swim." They had finished up at the studio and decided on an afternoon swim, finding the girls on the beach, and Alexis in danger.

"Who was that man, sweetie?" Pedro asked softly as he smoothed his daughter's hair.

"He was a horrible man from yesterday. He hit on me, and I ignored him, so he called me all sorts of horrible names. I showed him he was not to mess with me, but I guess he didn't listen." She sniffled. "I had only just gone for a swim when he came up behind me and grabbed me. That's when I screamed." She nestled in her parents' arms, enjoying the moment together.

"I'm glad we got here when we did. I warned him to stay away," Pedro told her and kissed her on the top of her head.

"Good," Alexis said. "I hope he does."

*****

Dom made it from the studio to the nightclub just after four. He had an hour or so before he had to be at his grandmother's for dinner, so had the time to get a set list together. Laying out the records, CDs, and tracks in order, he was alone, except for the odd barman who was also getting ready.

He loved the silence of the place before it opened. Most of the staff were yet to come in, and he had the stage to himself. The music, the decks, he thrived on it, loved it, lived it, breathed it. And he hated the fact that Danté was following in his footsteps.

Sure, *he* was following in his father's footsteps, and so was Danté, but he just wished that he could be the only one in the family to do it. Why did Danté and Alexis have to copy him and Alena with everything they did? Why couldn't they find their own interests, their own jobs? But with everyone being in the family business in some way, it wasn't likely that any of them would ever have a job outside of the family. No one wanted to work in the meat shop or hotel, so it was the nightclub and music studio, the movie business, style and fashion, or books and activism.

And none of the kids cared about writing books, or being an

advocate or activist. They all wanted to be in music, modelling, or fashion, and that's where it all became too much. Everyone was like everyone else. No one was different, and Dom wanted to be different.

Yes, he was DJing like his father who still got behind the decks once a week, but he wanted to show he was different to his father who made a name for himself in the '70s and '80s with disco and pop. At twenty-four, Dom wanted to stand out and not be like his father. They all wrote and made music, but Dom's was a mix of everything. Metal, thrash, techno, pop, disco. He jammed it all into his music to come up with something new, and every single he released always hit number one on any dance chart through Europe.

But with Danté getting to DJ one night a week, and thinking he was a rapper in the making, the spotlight was being taken away from him, and he didn't like it.

Just when he had found himself, found what he wanted to do in the family, Danté had come along and copied him. Tried to do better, tried to *be* better with his backward cap and baggy pants. He was a reject rapper from the '90s, and it was ridiculous. *Seriously, how can he think he's any good? He's only fourteen and lives in the '90s.*

Dom wanted to make his own path and not have some little kid brother try to be him. Try to do better than him. Hell, he wasn't even anywhere near their father, who played like he'd never seen a DJ play before. He danced, he sang, he spun. He did it all, and Dom had seen footage of him back in the *Studio 69* days, plus the '80s at *SB3*.

Everything had been recorded for prosperity, and he was glad it had. He got to see his father in his early years, and it was an awesome sight to behold. Even now when his father got on stage and did his thing, his thing still got the crowd going, especially the older women who came along who had known him back in the day. They were still around and came every summer. His dad still had the energy, and he watched every move he made, trying to learn from him. And he had. He had the same energy, the same dance moves. All while adding his own little Dom Stefan stamp on it. But Danté…

He sighed. He didn't *hate* his brother, just wished he didn't always want to be like him. Why couldn't he be himself? Danté irritated him.

Always had, but then it was probably the same for Alena and Alexis. Born ten years apart, they didn't have anything in common except for the family business, and it was a struggle to find a job that someone wasn't already doing. And that's why they all ended up doing the same thing. Their parents did it, so they did it. Music was in their blood, and it didn't matter how far they tried to run from it, they would always end up doing it.

He thought about Danté. The kid was only fourteen, had his own teen crowd that came to see him on the under eighteens night, and was talented, whether Dom liked it or not. *So if I don't hate him, and I think he's talented, why do I have such a problem?*

Danté stood watching Dom from the backstage area, hidden by the curtains so he couldn't be seen, watching every move his brother made. He desperately wanted his big brother to accept him, see him as his brother, not his enemy. But he didn't think Dom ever would. He had been ignored and rejected all of his life by his big brother, and it was only Alexis and Alena who had shown him any love. And his parents, of course. Grandma and Grandpa were the best at showering all of them with love and support their whole lives. But what he really wanted, was his older brother to love and accept him, play cricket and football with him, to go trick or treating with him, to hang out with. To Danté, Dom was the coolest.

The only other boys in the family were Cabot and Antonio and look where they were. Never with family, never at birthdays or celebrations. They were always off in their own world. So, the only one left was his brother. He'd seen all the old footage of their parents. The photos from all the years and each birthday, Thanksgiving, Christmas, New Year, whatever it was to celebrate, his father and his uncles were always there for each other. Hugging, holding, laughing. There were photos from every celebration of them in each other's arms, and every time he saw them, he wondered why he and Dom couldn't be like that. Why his sisters couldn't be like that. Why they couldn't love each other and be close and get along.

He felt the pang in his fourteen-year-old heart. He wanted to be accepted by his brother so desperately it hurt. And if it weren't for his best friend Nick, he wouldn't've had someone to be close to. He didn't know why Dom didn't like him, didn't know why he'd ignored him. He'd thought it was a great idea to emulate his father and brother and do what they did. Music was in their blood, it always had been.

They all had a healthy musical pedigree, with Alena first off the block with a singing career before he was even born. But there didn't seem to be a lot of love in this family among the kids. Alena and Diana were more like sisters than Alena and Alexis. Cabot and Antonio were twins and had been closer to Dom growing up, but now they didn't have much time for any of them. So, Danté and Alexis were all that was left. By the time they had come along, the first five kids had already set up a clique, the gorgeous, famous and talented, while they had struggled to find their own way. And at fourteen, he still had a long way to go.

Why, oh, why did Mama have us so far apart? he lamented. *If we'd been closer in age, we'd be closer as a family. Like Papa and Uncles Tomas and Carlos. Two years apart and still so close. Yet here we are all five years apart in age and friendships.*

His eyes stung with tears, his chest tightened, and his throat constricted. All he wanted was for his siblings and cousins to love him, to tell him, show him, instead of making him feel like an outsider in his own family. Making him feel unloved, unwanted, unneeded, unnecessary. It sucked. And he hated it. Hated feeling all of those things in his family. If it wasn't for Nick and his family, his own parents and grandparents, he didn't know how he would cope. They were his saviours along with music.

A lone tear slid down his left cheek, and he silently wept as he walked away.

*****

"Happy birthday and anniversary, Mama." Carlos kissed his mother's cheek. Since his parent's fifty-fifth wedding anniversary came two days after his mother's birthday, they always celebrated on the day in between.

"Thank you, my darling." Jenny accepted the brightly wrapped gifts from him and Viv.

"Happy birthday and anniversary, Jenny," Viv said, giving her mother-in-law a hug.

"Thank you, Viv. Is Diana on her way?"

"She said to give her half an hour to freshen up." Viv glanced around the room, seeing almost everyone but her sons.

"Antonio called earlier today." Jenny set the presents on the side buffet. "He sends his and Cabot's best wishes and says that a present is on its way."

"At least he did that." Carlos sighed. "Can't seem to be bothered turning up."

"No, but they want *SB3* for their own birthday," Jenny retorted. "They don't mind coming home for their own to see what they can get out of the family." She led the way to the dining table that was set up with munchies. "Help yourselves. We're not having a meal tonight, but there are plenty of yummy things for all. Tomas and Roger did everything."

"Including the drinks," Tomas called from the kitchen side of the room. Back in the '70s, there had been a wall separating the kitchen and dining rooms, but after the twins and Dom came along; Jenny had the wall torn down and remodelled the two rooms into one big one. A full floor-to-ceiling buffet cupboard full of family photos and knick-knacks was against the wall opposite the kitchen, floor-to-ceiling windows had been put in to bring in the ocean view, and they'd required two dining tables. The two rooms were separated by a huge island bench. A bar had been set up on the other dining table, with large glass drink dispensers holding deliciously healthy fruit mixes with mineral water, plus there was alcohol for those that wanted it. "Come and get it while you can."

"Cool spread, T," Carlos told him, using Roger's nickname for his brother that he and Pedro had adopted. "If you two keep things up, we'll have to get you to cater every celebration we have." He accepted a beer from his brother.

Tomas grinned. "All of this is just for Mama and Papa. The rest of you can cater your own." He refilled Pedro's glass with citrus water from the dispenser which had oranges, lemons and limes floating through it.

"And it's always Mama and Papa's birthdays and anniversaries. He *never* caters our birthdays and anniversaries," Pedro reminded Carlos.

"That's because *our* mother caters *our* birthdays since they're all on the same day." Tomas's grin grew bigger. "And our anniversaries are all in three days. She caters those too."

"He's got you there, bro," Carlos said to Pedro. "So, it looks like it's just Mama he caters to."

"After everything she did, she deserves it," Roger said from beside Tomas as he poured a drink for Danté. "The way she fought to keep us alive, we owe her the rest of our lives for that."

"Absolutely," Tomas agreed, sipping his own berry punch. "Every birthday, anniversary, mother's and father's day, I will cater it."

"With the food you make, it's no wonder we're all in good shape at the ages we are. We'll live forever at this rate," Carlos told him, watching his mother in his father's arms. They were still happy fifty-five years later.

"If only," Tomas murmured, following his brother's gaze. The love he had for his mother knew no bounds. The way she had so willingly accepted that he preferred men, and then gotten their father to understand and love him was still mind-blowing thirty years later. All she had done for him. Getting them both out of porn and to New York. Giving them a wedding ceremony in front of all their relatives, plus a reception. Looking after them that Christmas when they were sick, sending them around the world on a constant holiday, and then the one thing he would never be able to thank her enough for, saving his life. Bringing him home to Mykonos, getting all of the doctors to care for him, being with him, were the most precious moments he would never forget. When he was dying, all he could do was think about the good, because the bad would bring him to tears. And tears had fallen by the billion, from everyone. But she had hung on, and he had hung on for her until he couldn't anymore. And if it wasn't for Doctor Dan Ardent, he wouldn't be there now, and speaking of...

"Hey, Dan's here."

Dan Ardent and his partner of twenty-five years, Doctor Derek Blaine, waved hello to everyone as they came through the door with their luggage. "Hey, everyone. Happy birthday, Jenny, and happy anniversary, Jenny and Spiros."

"Dan, Derek, oh, you made it." Jenny moved over to them with open arms, hugging and kissing the doctors in whose company she'd spent the last twenty-five years fighting AIDS. "How are you? Did you just get in? Boys," she called to her sons. "Can you take their luggage into the spare room?"

"Oh, no, that's okay, Mrs S," Derek said. "We'll do it. We'd like to freshen up if you don't mind."

"Of course not. You know the way," Jenny said. "Beer or mineral water? We'll get it ready for you."

"Beer," Dan and Derek replied at the same time, carting their luggage into the spare room at the opposite end of the house. It was off the hallway off the lounge room, where the laundry slash extra kitchen was. They were back at the party in five minutes enjoying beers and munchies.

"How was your flight?" Jenny asked as Mike and Maggie came through the door with their kids and parents, Andrew and Marjory Boltworth, and Barry and Suzanne Gatos, in tow.

"Long. It may only be ten or eleven hours, but it's still a long haul," Derek said. At six foot, he was two inches taller than Dan. Both had dark brown hair, but Derek's eyes were blue to Dan's green. They had met in 1982 when Dan had finally flown home from Mykonos after spending another seven months with the family. Derek had been given Dan's old job at the hospital, and when they'd met, it had been love at first sight. After much discussion about AIDS, they had finally started dating and been together since. Both had gone on to be specialists in the field of HIV/AIDS, and worked with Jenny a lot, especially since she funded their clinic in New York.

"But we do get a lot done on those flights," Dan said, finishing off his beer. "Writing up reports, reading, research. We use it to our full advantage."

Summer and Melody hugged Alexis, and she spoke to their grandparents.

Nick brought his new computer game and wanted to play it with Danté.

Jenny excused herself and went over to speak with the Gatoses and Boltworths. "How nice of you to come." Since Mike and Maggie had moved to Mykonos, the in-laws had come over every year for a holiday, and she occasionally got to see and spend time with them.

"When Maggie said they'd been invited, we didn't want to intrude," Marjory said, looking around at everyone.

"No, no, that's fine. The more, the merrier. Mike and Maggie have been like family since we met them back in '77," Jenny placated them.

"I'm glad they know someone here. It seems so far away," Suzanne accepted a drink from Roger who brought a tray of drinks over.

"Yes, I suppose that's true," Jenny said. "But it seems the rest of the world wants to come to Mykonos across the summer months, so we all come together again. The world seems so tiny when everyone's here. How have you been since the last time we saw you?"

Summer and Melody pulled Alexis aside. "Our grandparents are staying until July. Can you believe it? That means we won't be going away until then."

"My family will probably be going to New York come August, Princess will finish her tour by September, and we'll spend a month or two there," Alexis said. "Why don't you come with us, and then I won't be so lonely."

The girls' eyes lit up. "Would your grandma mind?"

"Of course not." Alexis downed her drink. "She invites everyone. Just look at Dan and Derek. Two more honorary members of the family after you guys."

"They are hot," Summer murmured, eyeing off the two men talking to Tomas and Roger.

"Even if they are gay," Melody added. "God, look how gorgeous they all are."

Alexis turned to look. "Ah…ew!" she told them. "All gay, all taken. Two of them are my uncles. It was bad enough you told me the other day you wanted to marry my cousins."

Alena and Diana made it through the door. "Alena's here!" Alena exclaimed.

"Ugh, Princess always announces herself," Alexis scoffed and moved away from the table with the girls following.

"Hello, my darlings." Jenny got hugs and kisses from them both before they moved onto Spiros. "How was the photo shoot and concert rehearsal?"

"Good," they said at the same time and giggled.

"Italy is beautiful this time of year, and I spent three days in each city." Diana smiled. "Ah, Bellisima!"

"And the concert's great, Grandma," Alena added. "We've got the songs down, the dancing, the fireworks."

"Fireworks! I didn't authorise fireworks," Pedro called from the kitchen.

Alena turned to her father and saw the alertness on his face. He was standing next to her uncle whose blue-eyed expression matched his brother's. "They're only little ones, Daddy," she placated him. "Little whizzy things, not big boom, boom things."

"I hope you haven't burnt down my studio," Carlos told her. "'Cause you'll be paying for repairs."

Alena rolled her eyes. "Uncle Carlos, that's what *insurance* is for."

"Oh, is *that* what you think it's for?" Carlos raised a brow. "Free money so you can burn down my business and not pay for it." He watched her accept a wine from Tomas.

"Thank you, Prince Tomas." She kissed him on the cheek and got a sappy smile in return. It was something she had called him since she was little. She was Princess Alena, and he was Prince Tomas. And after the scary year of him being sick, they had grown closer though she was only three and four years of age.

"You're welcome, Princess A-ena," he replied, making her grin.

When she was little, she couldn't pronounce her ls, so it came out as A-ena. And Tomas adored her and Diana. The two little girls who had captured everyone's heart in '78 when they were born. Both curly-haired, Alena was dark and blue-eyed like her papa, and Diana golden-brown and blue-eyed like *her* papa. The girls had been the centre of the family, being loved and adored by all. And since he and Roger couldn't have kids or adopt any of their own, their nieces and nephews had been the light of their lives, looking after them whenever they could.

Pedro watched his brother's face, nudging Carlos to look.

Tomas noticed them and smiled as Pedro hooked an arm around his brother's neck. "You are *our* Prince Tomas." Pedro kissed him on the cheek, remembering back to their trip to Disneyland in 1980 when Alena had first called him Pince Tomas.

Tomas tried holding it together, but couldn't. Breaking down in tears, he turned and escaped out onto the balcony, trying to control himself. He would never be a father. Hell, he'd never thought he'd be married, but his mother had arranged a ceremony and reception for him and Roger, and that had sufficed though gay marriage still wasn't legal. But after the girls had come along, then the twins and the other kids, a part of him had still desperately wanted to have his own. He'd love to know that a little baby boy or girl had his blood, his genes, his DNA in him or her, and here he was at fifty-two, and it would never happen. He'd pushed the feelings down often enough. He flat out ignored them most of the time, but every now and then he would see or hear or remember, as with Alena at Disneyland. He removed his silver steel-rimmed glasses and sobbed into his sleeve.

Roger was first out the door to comfort his beloved, followed by Pedro and Carlos.

"T?" Roger stood by his husband's side. "Oh, baby. You okay?"

Pedro was on the other side, Carlos behind. "Remembering Disneyland, Prince Tomas?"

"And so much more," Tomas gasped through his tears.

"Like what?" Roger rubbed his back to soothe him.

Tomas finally looked up and wiped his face. "Like when we were sick, everything they said to me. Alena wanted to make me better and thought reading to me would do it."

"Yeah, I remember that," Carlos said. "She said it on the plane home."

"And the day at the beach, when she asked if she could sit on my legs and I told her I didn't have the strength, so she told me all about her day instead," Tomas said.

"And then I cried." Pedro nodded in remembrance.

"And I cried," Tomas added. "Then Mama cried, and we all cried." A ragged laugh came from him. "I'll never be a father. I'll never get to have my own son or daughter say those things to me, call me Papa." He fell into Roger's arms, crying. "We can't even adopt."

"I know, baby, I know." Roger held him tight. "We discussed this so many years ago."

"Didn't mean I was over it." Tomas sobbed against his chest.

"I guess not." Roger kissed his lover's head.

"If you wanna adopt the twins, you're welcome to them," Carlos said dryly.

That made Tomas stop crying and start laughing, and he raised his head. "No, thanks. I'll have Diana and Alena."

"Hey, what about Dom, Alexis and Danté? Don't they count?" Pedro pretended to be offended.

"Of course they do." Tomas wiped his face. "But Alexis and Danté are Mama and Daddy's little girl and boy; there's no way you're giving them up."

"True," Pedro agreed and told the others of the incident at the beach with Alexis.

"Jesus, what!" Carlos exclaimed. "Who was that little thug? He'd better not show his face anywhere near the rest of the family."

"I told the girls to get a photo of him if they ever saw him again, so we can ban him from the club if he comes," Pedro said.

"I should bloody well think so," Carlos replied. "Mama would kill him."

"That's what I told him." Pedro chuckled. "I told him I would hurt him, but her grandmother would kill him."

"Think he believed you?" Roger asked.

Pedro shook his head. "I don't know, but he'd better not try and find out."

Inside, Alena was chatting to Dan and Derek. "So, how's New York, Dan? I'll be there next month."

"New York is beautiful as always," Dan told her. "And your concert posters are everywhere. We *are* getting tickets, aren't we?"

"Of course," Alena replied. "Let me know when and where and I'll get you front row seats."

"How many shows are you doing in New York?" Derek asked.

"I'm starting there just after my birthday and then doing a second show at the end of the tour. The dates have just been added. Why not, right? It's where I was born, figured I'd start and finish there."

"It will have to be the last show then," Dan said. "We'll be here until August working with your grandmother and having a bit of a holiday."

Alena grinned. "The fam is planning on being in town in August for the last show and a bit of a holiday, so you'll be down front with them."

"Very cool." Dan grinned back. "Thanks, Alena."

"Thanks for saving my uncles, Dan." She bounced over to Spiros and hugged him. "Hello, Gampa."

Spiros laughed and remembered how she and Diana would call him that when they were little. "Hello, little A-ena."

"Is it time for presents yet?" Alexis asked everyone. "I want to see Grandma's face when she opens them."

"Oh, I guess we could since I have birthday and anniversary presents to open," Jenny said, and they all wandered into the lounge room. "Birthday presents first." At this late stage of the game, presents were always from families instead of individuals. It made it easier for everyone.

"Okay, from Carlos, Viv and the kids, two of which aren't here..." Jenny opened a beautiful box containing a crystal dressing table set with perfume decanter, tray, powder jar, and brush and comb. "Oh, it's beautiful."

"It's Italian, from the glass factories," Viv said. "We spotted it when we were there."

"Oh, I love it." Jenny kissed each of them. "It's beautiful."

"Come on, Grandma, open ours," Danté called, hovering next to his mother.

"Okay, I will." Jenny picked up the brightly coloured box and pulled out a crystal photo frame with a picture of Pedro's side of the family. Pedro and Angie, Alena, Dom, Alexis and Danté. "Aw, look at you all," Jenny cried. "Oh, I love it." Receiving a hug from all six of them, she came to Tomas and Roger's gift which made her pause.

Staring at it in the box, it was a crystal prayer book ornament with silver inlays. On the left page was the Corinthians passage she had read at their wedding, on the right a picture of them, Roger and Tomas, with her and Spiros taken on the previous Thanksgiving. "Oh…" she breathed as her voice caught in her throat. "It's just like the one you gave me in 1980, except that one was silver."

"And this one is crystal," Tomas said, gazing fondly at his mother. "With the same passage you read at our wedding thirty years ago, and without you and Papa, we wouldn't be here celebrating your birthday and anniversary. That's why there's a current photo of us to show thirty years on how much you still mean to us."

"Oh, Tomas." Jenny crumpled and went to her son. "I love you so much."

He held her tight, crying his tears with her. "I love you, Mama. And thank you, thank you for saving me."

She kissed his cheek, holding on to him. "I will always fight for my babies. Always." Pulling back, she looked him in the eye and held her hand to his face. "Always."

Tomas smiled through his tears. "Considering we ruined your party back in '81, we owe you big time."

Jenny remembered. "Yes, yes you did. But you were more important. Don't ever forget that. All of you." She turned to her children and grandchildren to see them crying and sniffling. "*All of you* are more important than a celebration. Birthday, anniversary, or otherwise. That's just all there is to it." Looking at Roger, she hugged and kissed him. "Thank you for looking after my baby all the times I couldn't or wasn't there to."

"You're welcome, Mrs S," he managed through his tears.

Wiping her eyes, Jenny said, "Okay, one more birthday present to go from my husband." Quickly getting the box from the cupboard, she opened it to find a beautiful crystal vase, "Did you all get a deal from a crystal factory?" She laughed and kissed him. "It's beautiful, my darling, thank you. I think I'll put everything on my dressing table, so I can look at them every day."

"And we'll fill that vase with fresh flowers every day too," Spiros said.

"Let's pop all of these things away and then I'll open the anniversary presents," Jenny said. With help from Angie and Viv, Jenny placed the crystal on her bed before clearing off her dressing table and setting it up with the new presents.

Back in the lounge room, she presented Spiros with his gift, which was a white gold signet ring with an inlaid emerald.

"Oh, Jenny." He slid it on his left ring finger. "This is beautiful."

"I've become as bad as you," she joked. "I have no idea what to get you anymore."

"It's definitely a handsome ring." Spiros held out his hand for all to see.

"And one I will be getting one day," Carlos murmured loud enough for all to hear, and cheekily grinned when they noticed.

"Carlos," Pedro chastised him as everyone groaned their dissatisfaction with his comment. "Not everything is going to you, you know. Tomas and I will get some too."

"Oh, for goodness sake." Jenny rolled her eyes. "Anniversary presents now. Whose do I open first?"

"Ours, Grandma," Diana said excitedly, knowing full well what it was.

"Okay, Carlos's family it is." Opening the gift box, she pulled out a velvet box. "Oooh, jewellery." Snapping it open, she gasped. "Oh, my God, they're gorgeous." Stunning white gold and emerald earrings sat on the velvet inlay card. "Oh, my, they're beautiful." Quickly, she slipped them on and looked in the mirror. "Oh, I love them. Thank you, so much." Taking all three of them into her arms, she smothered them in kisses while Spiros opened a box containing a white gold watch with emerald coloured face and leather band.

"Hey, leave some for the rest of us," Pedro called. "Tomas's present is next."

Reading the tag, Jenny opened another gift box with another velvet box inside. This one contained a white gold and emerald pendant in the same teardrop shape as the earrings. "Oh, I see a theme here."

Clasping it around her neck, she stared in the mirror. The teardrop hung just perfectly against her breastbone. "Thank you, my babies." She smothered Tomas and Roger in kisses and hugs while Spiros opened his present, white gold emerald cufflinks, with his initials, similar to the ones his boys had bought him for Christmas 1977.

"And now ours, Grandma," Alexis said, presenting her with it. This time it was a white gold and emerald bracelet, matching in teardrop shapes. "Oh, clearly you all got together and decided what to get me. It's beautiful." She slipped it on and admired the way it sparkled in the light before noticing Spiros had received an emerald and white gold tie clip.

"And these are from us, Jenny, Spiros," Dan said, presenting them with boxes.

One held a beautiful crystal and green leather writing set for her desk, and Spiros received a green leather travel wallet set.

"For all of those books you're yet to write," Derek told her. "The crystal for your birthday, the emerald for your anniversary."

"Oh, it's beautiful, boys." She admired the studded leather desk pad, which came with a crystal pen and pen holder. The pen was green with tiny green crystals around it. "I love it, thank you both."

"You're welcome, it's the least we can do considering all you've done for us," Dan said, proud that he and Derek had found such a gift for such an extraordinary woman who had changed their lives forever.

"You're part of the family, and always will be," Jenny said.

"How much bigger is this family going to get?" Pedro joked. "I think we've got enough members for our own cricket or rugby team."

"Oooh, team Stefan," Carlos perked up.

"Now you've got him started." Jenny laughed. "Leave it until tomorrow to worry about sports teams." She found the last present to be from Mike and Maggie and was surprised that there was none from Spiros. She glanced over and saw his sly smile. "Okay, let's see what Mike and Maggie got us." Opening the box, she found two delicate green crystal Tiffany lamps. "Oh, they're lovely. Are they tiny emeralds?" She peered at the small green stones spattered around the bases.

"Yes, they are. And the present is for both your birthday, which is why the crystal, and the emeralds for your anniversary," Maggie said.

After being invited into the family she and Mike had been eternally grateful to the whole family.

"Thank you, both of you." She kissed them, the girls, and Nick, whose hair she ruffled. If it weren't for the girls and Nick, Alexis and Danté would be alone, and she was grateful they weren't. "I'll just pop these in the bedroom, and by then I will expect a present from you, Mister," Jenny cheekily told her husband.

After placing the lamps on their side cupboards in the bedroom, and the desk set in her office, she quickly went back out. "Well!"

Spiros held out a small gift box which she took and opened to find another velvet box. "Let me guess, an oil painting." She grinned, flipped the lid, and gasped. "Oh, Spiros, it's beautiful."

"Happy fifty-fifth anniversary, my love. I know it's probably not as good as what I got you for our fiftieth, but—"

"No, it's beautiful." Jenny pulled the white gold and emerald teardrop ring from the box. "Put it on me."

He took it from her with shaky hands and, to oohs and aahs from the family, slid it onto her right ring finger.

"Oh, it's beautiful." She held out her hand as the family gathered around. "But then, I'm sure you've already seen it," she told them.

"Well…you know…" Carlos said. "We had to make sure we got you different things."

Touching the bracelet and staring down at the necklace, Jenny marvelled at the brilliance of the cut. "I'm sure you did. Just like with the crystal."

Spiros slid an arm around her waist. "Happy, my love?"

Glancing around, she saw two children missing and winced. "I am. Even though the twins aren't here. I am."

"We'll be seeing them soon," Spiros said. "And at least Antonio called."

"Yes," Jenny murmured, admiring her ring. "At least *he* called."

*****

"So, what did you send our adoring grandparents for their anniversary?" Cabot asked Antonio that night as they got ready to go out on the town.

"An emerald brooch for grandma," Antonio told him. "The rest of the fam said they were getting jewellery, so I said we'd send some too. Grandpa got a fountain pen set with emerald inlay."

"And who paid for that?" Cabot licked a bit of cocaine from his finger.

Antonio watched his brother snort another line. "Must you do that?"

"Do what?" Cabot asked. "It's only recreational. I'm not an addict."

"Bullshit!" Antonio exclaimed. "You're an addict all right. You're addicted to fame, to celebrity, to pot, to coke, to the lifestyle, to fucking men you don't know. Did you have to fuck that photographer, Jacques, last week after the shoot?"

Cabot shrugged. "Why not? I used a condom. That's what Grandma and our fag uncles Tomas and Roger drummed into our heads." He pulled a face to show how bored he was with the subject.

"Our uncles are not fags," Antonio snapped. "They're gay and so are you."

"I am not!" Cabot got indignant. "Just because I have sex with men does *not* make me a fag. I have sex with women too."

"So what!" Antonio scoffed. "You have sex with both. You're gay, and if Grandma heard you use the word fag, she'd slap you."

Cabot took a deep breath and blew kisses at himself in the mirror. He looked like a younger, taller version of his father. "Well, she's not here, so she's not hearing me. And there's *no way* she'd slap me. *I'm* her grandson."

Antonio snorted and stared at his brother. "Is that what you think? She'd lay a hand on you so fast your head would spin."

"There's no way I'm gonna let anyone lay a hand on Steele Stefan. Even my grandmother," Cabot told his brother. "She so much as touches me—"

"You'll what?" Antonio asked. "Hit her back? *Papa would kill you.*"

"*Our father* wouldn't touch me. I'm taller, broader, and more muscular."

Antonio shook his head. "You really are up yourself, aren't you? Living all by yourself on Planet Steele. You have no idea what Papa or Grandma would do, but I sure as hell don't want to find out. You're a smug son of a bitch, Cabot, and you need to pull your head out. It ain't all about you."

"*Don't call me Cabot, Antonio,*" Cabot warned. "That was another fag the family knew. Some fag photographer friend of our mother's back in the '70s. Ugh, what *is it* with our family? A bunch of fag lovers. Even Dan and his queer boy Derek are fags."

"*Stop using that word!*" Antonio balled his fists up. "Or do you want me to start calling *you* that? You're such a prat sometimes, Cabot." He walked into the bedroom of the penthouse and grabbed his jacket from the closet, not even sure he wanted to go out anymore. Sighing, he threw the jacket on the bed and moved over to the window, hands on hips, breathing heavily. His brother could be such an ass.

"Phe?" Cabot murmured as he followed his brother. "Don't leave me, Phe."

"*My name's Antonio,*" he snapped. "Phoenix is just a stage name, *like Steele.*"

Cabot sulked. "I know, Tone. It's just we've used the names for so long." He rested his chin on his brother's shoulder and looked up at him. "Don't hate me."

Antonio sighed. Sometimes he was just so sick of this shit. "I don't hate you, Cabot," he finally said. "I hate what you've become."

"Which is what?"

"A self-absorbed, self-centred, self-obsessed, selfish, arrogant, narcissistic jerk that doesn't care about anybody but himself. You didn't even want to go home for our grandparents' anniversary." He couldn't bring himself to look at his brother, who'd been acting like this for the last few years.

When they'd started modelling at fifteen, he was different. They were two normal boys who'd grown up with famous parents and a sister and had been gorgeous enough to be hired as twin models. And they'd made a career out of posing together. But since he'd turned twenty-one, Cabot had become big-headed, demanding, needy, and Antonio was bloody well sick of it.

"I didn't stop you from going. You could have gone," Cabot whined from behind his brother. "But you'd never leave me, Tone. That's why you stayed."

"I stayed because we have work," Antonio said. "We had that job the other day, and the day after tomorrow we have another. We couldn't just hop on a plane and go and come back like that. It would have been ridiculous." He stalked around the room. "I don't know if I wanna go out now."

"Come on, Tonee, we have to," Cabot wheedled. "It's the grand opening of *Slash*, and I've wanted to go to it since I first heard about it. Tilly got us tickets."

"I'm not into heavy metal, and neither are you. So, why are you so desperate to go to this club?" Antonio asked him.

"Well," Cabot murmured, going all shy. "The guitarist from the band on tonight is hot, and I'd like to meet him."

Antonio rolled his eyes. "Do you know if he's gay?"

Cabot shrugged. "What's that got to do with it?"

"Because *straight* men don't *fuck* men," Antonio said.

Cabot snorted. "Yeah, right! I haven't met a straight man yet who's turned down the Stefan rod of Steele. They all want it."

"I highly doubt it," Antonio scoffed. "I've seen you force yourself on a few of them—"

"They're all willing," Cabot interrupted.

"I doubt it." Sliding his jacket on, Antonio headed for the door. As much as he hated what Cabot did, the only person around to save Cabot from himself was him. But he had grown reluctant lately, didn't want to save Cabot anymore. He wanted to have a normal life. As much as he loved his twin, sometimes, he wanted time away from him, and that was becoming more and more forceful in his mind. He needed time away from the spotlight, from the celebrity, and his twin.

"Come on, Tone." Cabot trailed after him. "Let's go to *Slash* and check out *Slay My Way*. The guitarist is hot." He tugged his brother's sleeve. "*Come on*, Tone, live a little."

With a sigh, Antonio relented. "We have a shoot the day after tomorrow. We are *not* staying out all night, and *you* are *not* doing drugs."

"Me?" Cabot went wide-eyed. "Do drugs?"

"Don't shit me, Cabot," Antonio warned. "You're living up to the man whose name you carry. I did research on him, he loved it hard and fast in private, just like you."

"I'm nothing like that faggy little toerag," Cabot hissed as they went down in the lift, his temper seething. He wasn't a fag, no matter how anyone put it. Just because he liked both women and men, did *not* make him a fag.

*****

Alena sang into the microphone on stage at *Stefan Productions* in Athens. Her tour started in two weeks in the Big Apple, and she needed to be ready.

"Another day has come and gone,
And I am Still Without You,
Clouds are black, sun's disappeared,
And I am Still Without You.

The good is gone, replaced with pain,
And I am Still Without You,
I don't know how I'll love again,
And I am Still Without You.

Oooh, ooh, ooh, oooh,
Oooh, ooh, ooh, oooh,
Love, it hurts like hell and back,
Oooh, ooh, ooh, oooh,
Love has gone off the beaten track."

"We're having a problem with the microphone; can we get it sorted?" Rodney, the sound engineer, called out. "Everything else is good."

"Lighting's good, sound's good, instruments are good. I'd say we've got this down pat," Pat Richards, the tour manager told everyone. "Have you got the costume changes down, Alena?"

"Yes, Pat," Alena called. "Not quite to the second, but then anything can happen."

"We'll keep rehearsing that for the next week, and then we're off to New York to acclimatise and set up," Pat said.

"The tour doesn't start until the second week of June." Alena exchanged microphones. "Testing, testing, one, two."

"Sounds good," Rodney called.

"And you'll need to fly in several days before to rehearse," Pat said, watching Alena on stage. "It's a thirty date tour, three cities or so a week for nearly ten weeks."

"I thought it was fifty-one dates, one in each state with two in New York," Alena said.

"No. One stop every *second* state, but four states added extra dates," Pat told her. "You'll be done by mid-August, so you can have the rest of summer off."

"But you've got lots of publicity," Maria Baugh, her agent slash publicist slash manager said. At fifty-two, Maria had worked with Alena her whole career, and her family trusted her to do her job and protect Alena. Otherwise, Jenny Stephanopoulos would have her guts for garters.

Alena groaned. "How much publicity?"

"Magazines, papers, TV and radio shows from each state. I've tried to keep it to a minimum."

"That doesn't sound like a minimum, Maria," Alena said. "That sounds like a maximum. I don't want to be overworked. One of each, in each state. Make them the biggest because I won't be bothered with small stations and papers."

"Okay," Maria replied. "A lot of them you can phone in from the bus."

"Bus?" Alena inquired.

Maria grinned. "You're getting a tour bus."

Alena squealed. "I'm getting my own tour bus? Yay!" She danced around. "What colour is it?"

"Blue, black and white, your favourite colours."

"Yay." Clapping her hands excitedly, Alena asked, "Have you got any pictures?"

Maria dug a portfolio from her bag. "That's the company that did it."

Alena quickly flipped through the booklet. "Oooh, those look fabulous. Will the crew be with me?"

"Nope. Got their own," Maria said. "Yours is all for you and your family and friends."

"Oh, my God, I can't wait." Alena squealed again.

"And it will be fitted with your favourite flowers, food and drink. You'll have a big bed all to yourself. There are six bunks for guests, two bathrooms, kitchen, lounge and dining room."

"God, it sounds fabulous," Alena gushed. "I'm really looking forward to this tour now."

"So, how about you get back to rehearsing it," Rodney said. "We gotta check out that microphone."

"Yes, Rodney." Alena sighed and handed the portfolio back to Maria.

"And we'll do a full run through," Pat added.

"From start to finish?" Alena asked. "We just did one."

"And we'll do another one," Pat said. "Gotta make sure this all goes off without a hitch before we even get to New York."

"But we've already been rehearsing for weeks," Alena complained. "By the time we get to New York, I'm going to hate those songs and hate this show."

"That's why we're changing it up every night," Pat called out. "You've released fifty-eight singles in your career, two more will come out this year, and what, your tenth album will drop?"

"Ninth," Alena corrected.

"Well then, you've got plenty of material to work with," Pat said. "You won't get bored. And if you do, we'll get permission to sing other people's songs."

"Oooh, that would be cool. Maybe I can get my little brother on stage. He raps."

"Whatever you want, Alena," Pat told her. "In the meantime…"

"I know, back to rehearsal," she whined.

*****

Jenny received their presents from Antonio and Cabot in the post, and they opened them during dinner. The family sat around the two dining tables, eating another delicious meal that Tomas and Roger had made, and talking shop. "Oh, that's lovely." She picked up the brooch from the box. It was a beautiful teardrop emerald hanging from an emerald flower. "They obviously knew to get emeralds."

"That would have been Antonio," Viv said, thanking God her son had come through. "*He* still thinks about everyone besides himself."

"And the pen will come in handy for my memoirs." Spiros chuckled. "I would have thought the pen set would be for you," he told Jenny.

"You need a pen too," she said. "It's so hard to find new presents year after year. Unless you come back to giving the same things after a decade or two. And there's nothing wrong with writing your memoirs. You had quite a life before you met me. You immigrated to a new country, didn't speak English, got married, became a father, then went back home to take over your father's shop. Found out what the family business was, then ended up with three porn stars for children."

There was a clattering of cutlery and Jenny looked up at the stunned faces of her sons and their partners. "What? Oh..." She realised what she'd said and quickly looked at the four grandchildren along with their friends still eating and talking among themselves at the other table. "Ah, you kids didn't hear what I just said, right?"

"What?" The kids all looked at her. The girls had been discussing fashion, and the boys games or music.

"You say something, Grandma?" Diana asked.

"No, darling." Jenny smiled. "Just talking to your Gampa."

Diana laughed gaily. "Oh, I can't believe I used to say that. That's so funny."

Jenny shrugged at her children, and they all went back to eating.

"Yes, you did," Spiros told his eldest granddaughter. "You and Alena called us Gamma and Gampa."

"All because we couldn't pronounce Grandma and Grandpa. It must have sounded so silly," Diana went on.

"It was cute," Jenny said. "Like the two of you, with your curly hair and big blue eyes. You were so adorable I just wanted to moosh you."

"Grandma." Diana blushed.

"Grandma nothing," Jenny said. "You were both adorable little girls. And *then* the boys came along."

There was a collective groan around the two tables. The boys had been a handful from the moment they were born. Screaming, crying, demanding, running amok. They had worn everyone out.

"And then there was Dom who was a fairly quiet baby," Jenny said.

"Until you put music on." Pedro smiled at his eldest son and Dom smiled back. "And then he went to town, singing and dancing until he wore himself out."

"And then along came Alexis Fallon Stephanopoulos," Jenny said. "Adorable like crazy and fought with her sister for attention."

Alexis smiled at her grandmother from across the tables and Summer and Melody giggled. "But you loved me just the same."

"Of course I did," Jenny replied. "You're all my grandbabies. And then Danté, the baby of the family, unless Angie wants to pop out more." A wicked grin slid across Jenny's lips.

"Ah, no way, I'm long past done," Angie declared.

"And I'm not a baby, Grandma!" Danté exclaimed.

"You are until your sisters, brother, or cousins have children, then they'll be the babies of the family," Jenny told him.

"Grandma," Danté whined. "I'm fourteen. I'm not a baby, I'm nearly a man."

Nick dug his elbow into his best friend's ribs as if to say, 'that's what I said'.

Dominic snorted. "Is *that* what you think you are?"

"And *that* attitude isn't making *you* one right now, either," Jenny directed at Dom who blushed and lowered his eyes.

Pedro glanced from Dom to his mother with a 'what do we do with him' expression.

She sighed and shrugged again.

Pedro spoke to Danté. "You're a teenager, Danté, you're not going to be a man until you're old enough and can show you know how to be one."

Danté turned in his seat to look at his father. "When will that be, Dad?"

"Legally, you'll be an adult when you turn twenty-one. So, any time after that."

"Aw," Danté whined. "I have another seven years to go?"

"If that's what it takes," his father told him.

*****

Cabot and Antonio stood in *Slash*, New York's only thrash, heavy metal club, watching *Slay My Way* slam out their latest hit song. The guitarist, Adam Slayer, had a musical pedigree, and he'd started the band based on what he'd grown up listening to. Music was in his blood, and Cabot wanted to be in his body.

The band came to a screeching halt and told everyone they were taking a break.

Cabot watched, trying to see where Adam went, and found them at a table to the side of the stage. "Come on," he told his brother. "I've got to meet him."

"Cabot." Antonio held back. "I'm not interested in—"

"Don't be a party pooper," Cabot said and dragged him along. Finding the band, Cabot introduced them both. "I am such a huge fan."

The band nodded, eyeing the two six-foot pretty boys before them. "And how long have you been a fan?" Kinetix, the drummer asked, suspicious that such young good-looking guys could be into their music.

"Oh, at least two years," Cabot said. "Since the *Thrash Me* album. I found that and then tracked down the rest of your stuff."

"What's your favourite song?" Strings, the bassist inquired, leaning back in his chair with a beer.

"*Kill Me*, from the album, *Kill Me*," Cabot replied. "Easy to remember since every album has a theme running through it. *Kiss Me, Thrash Me, Fuck Me, Kill Me*. What will the next one be, *Resurrect Me?*"

Sharp, a.k.a. Frankie Vaughn, the singer, raised a brow. "How'd you know? You had people spying on us?" He stood up and puffed out his chest. "*No one* knows the name of the next album *but us*. You got spies, pretty boy?"

Antonio raised a brow and stepped back, but Cabot stood his ground. "It doesn't take much brain power to figure out the theme of the album titles. If the last was *Kill Me*, where were you going to go from there except for *Resurrect Me?* You don't need to be overly smart to figure it out."

Sharp sneered. "Yeah, well, lucky guess."

"Not a guess." Cabot smirked. "Simple deduction."

Sharp laughed. "Hey boys, did you hear that? Sherlock here used the word deduction. Like we don't know what the word means." He stuck his finger in Cabot's chest. "Pretty boy's assuming we don't know what it means?"

Cabot looked down at the finger then back up into the singer's eyes. "And you're assuming I give a fuck that you're stupid. I just came here to see Adam play."

"Oooh." Sharp turned to his bandmates. "Did you hear that? Pretty boy wanted to see Adam play. And why would you want to do that?" He stuck his forefinger in Cabot's chest again.

Cabot's blue eyes bored into Sharp's. "To see whether he's better live than his father was."

The band went silent.

"What?" Sharp asked, wondering what the kid was up to.

"To see whether he's better live than his father was," Cabot repeated and turned to Adam. "My uncle had all of your father's records from when he was in *Slay Me*. My uncle used to DJ at *Studio 69* in the late '70s early '80s and played *Slay Me's* songs a lot. He used to tell us stories about all of the celebrities who went there, and apparently, your dad met your mother there, Wednesday May, the star of the *Star Blade* movies. I wanted to see if you were better live than he was."

A grin slowly formed on Adam's lips. "Yeah. I remember my dad telling me about the '70s. The good old rock days. I think he's mentioned *Studio 69*. Not that he and Mom talk about it a lot anymore."

"Are they still together?" Cabot asked, noticing Sharp casting curious glances at his fellow bandmates.

"Nah. They broke up when I was in my teens. But they stayed

friends for me. How about we catch up after the show? You can tell me some more about your uncle, and I'll tell you about my dad."

"Sure." Cabot's grin was ear to ear. "Love to."

"Great. I'll see you then." With a flick of his long, sweat-soaked hair, he motioned the surprised band members back onto the stage.

An hour later, they thanked their fans for coming and waved as they left the stage and went out the back door.

"Wait, wait, Adam," Cabot yelled, trying to make his way through the crowd to the back of the club.

Adam saw them and pointed them out to a huge black dude that made his way toward them.

"Mr Slayer wants you to come with me." He led them backstage and into an alley.

"You boys know where I can get a beer and something to smoke?" Adam asked.

"Will a joint or two do?" Cabot asked.

"I'm up for it," Adam said, watching the rest of the band disperse. "None of them believe your uncle knows my dad."

"Come back to our place, and I'll tell you the stories he told us," Cabot said. "You need anything else. Like girls…"

Adam thought for a moment. "Could we get some?"

Cabot grinned. "I know some always up for a good time. We'll call them when we get back to our place. Come on." A cab ride and fifteen minutes later they were in the penthouse calling up girls they knew.

Cabot pulled liquor out of the built-in drinks cabinet. Gin, whiskey, vodka, and the pot was ready, as was the coke.

Adam was already knocking back a beer. "I just smoke man, I don't snort." He accepted a joint from Cabot who snorted a line.

"You sure?" Cabot came up for air and wiped his nose.

"Sure man." Adam knocked back the rest of his beer. "So, tell me the story."

Cabot went on to recount the tales from Pedro's days at 69.

Adam nodded at the stories he heard, tearing his attention away when the girls turned up. "Well, hello ladies."

"Hello Steele, Phoenix," the black girl, Gloria said. Marcy was with her. Both pros, both clean, both well versed in kinky sex. "Where do you want to start?"

"Let me introduce you to my friend, Adam Slayer." Cabot made the introductions.

"Well, hello Adam." Gloria straddled him on the couch.

"Well, hello there." Adam sucked on the joint then offered it to her. "Care for a blow?"

"All right." Gloria unbuckled his belt and got to work.

His head fell back. "I meant the joint," he groaned. "But this is just as good."

Cabot rolled another joint, this time adding a little coke to the mix. Lighting it, he handed it over to Adam. "Suck real deep."

"Me or her?" Adam asked, looking at the woman still on his dick.

"Both," Cabot said, wanting in on the action. But he knew he had to wait until Adam was well done. And that didn't take long.

"Oh, God." Adam groaned, helping Gloria bounce up and down on his cock. "I need a bed. You got somewhere we can stretch out?"

"Sure," Cabot replied. "Come this way." The four of them went up to the master, leaving Antonio to sigh in relief that he was on his own, but also in despair for what was coming.

Cabot flung back the bed covers and grinned. "Climb aboard."

Pulling his clothes off, Adam climbed backward onto the bed with Gloria on top, continuing the job she'd started downstairs.

As he watched, Cabot removed his clothes and got sucked by Marcy. It was a turn on, getting sucked, and watching a man get fucked. But he wanted to be the one who did it next.

"More whiskey, Adam?" He removed himself from Marcy's mouth and climbed onto the bed. Lying beside the guitarist, he poured the liquid into his mouth.

"Mmm, that's good shit man," Adam mumbled, licking his lips. "Got another joint?"

From his stash, Cabot rolled another, laced it with coke, and fed it to Adam as he came inside Gloria.

"Oh, that's good fucking shit," Adam said. "You got a shower I can use?"

"Sure, this way." Grabbing Adam's hand, he led him to the bathroom and ran the shower. "Planning on leaving so soon?"

"Nah, just feel a bit too sweaty." Adam swayed on his feet. "Got another drink?"

Cabot went into the bedroom for the whiskey and entered the shower. "Here, you drink, I'll clean." Grabbing a washcloth and soap, he washed Adam's long, lean body down, leaving the good bit until last. Kneeling, he took Adam into his mouth and sucked, eliciting a groan. Looking up, he saw Adam's eyes were closed, and he was leaning against the wall. Finishing up, he licked his way up Adam's body and helped him wash his hair.

"Good shit man, got any more?" He was quite drunk now and pretty much out of it.

"Plenty more where that came from." Cabot turned off the taps and dried Adam with a towel. He led him back into the bedroom, and they climbed onto the bed and drank, and snorted, and smoked. Drying Adam's luscious locks, Cabot watched Gloria and Marcy earn their night's wages.

Adam was in heaven. He was getting his cock sucked, and his hair dried. He had liquor and pot and was riding high, lying back against a pile of pillows in a penthouse on 5th Avenue.

Finishing with Adam's hair, Cabot lay beside him, trailing his fingers along his body, while he watched the girls. But he wanted in on the action. "Have you ever fucked a man, Adam?"

"What?" Adam's eyes were closed and his voice dreamy.

"Have you ever fucked a man." Cabot kissed Adam's neck. "Or been fucked by one?"

"What are you talking about?" Adam slurred, unable to open his eyes.

Cabot waved off the girls and slid onto Adam. "I want you. Tell me you want me." He kissed him, tangling his hands in Adam's hair. He held him, slid over him, lay on top of him. And Adam responded, hands groping, nails digging in.

"Oh, Adam, mmm." Cabot was all over him like a rash, naked flesh against naked flesh. He was between Adam's legs and entering. "Oh, Adam," he murmured against his lips.

"Mmm." Adam tried pushing him away. "What are you, mmm, doing?"

"Don't fight it, let it happen," Cabot told him, devouring his neck. "Let it happen. Oh, God." He hitched Adam's legs up around his waist and plunged in on final time. "Oh, Adam." He finished coming and collapsed on top of the guitarist.

"Ugh, what happened? What's going on," Adam jaggedly asked.

"You're having sex." Cabot kissed his chin. "Was it good for you?"

"Mmm." Adam struggled. "Something up my ass. What the fuck."

"That would be me." Cabot slid out and rolled off the condom. "Your turn, girls."

"You sure about that?" Gloria asked saucily and got to work seducing Adam who rolled her over and pinned her to the pile of pillows.

Cabot watched as he knocked back half a bottle of whiskey. Watched as Adam grew hard and entered Gloria. Watched as he rocked into her. Rolling on another condom, he slid his way up Adam's body, along his smooth muscular back, between his long, lean legs, and laid himself on top of them both. Getting into the rocking rhythm, he slid back into Adam.

"Oh, God, fuck man, what are you doing," Adam cried, trying to shift positions.

"Shh," Cabot soothed. "Let it happen. You in her, me in you. Let's ride this wave together." His face was beside Adam's and he grabbed the headboard. "Oh, God yes. Oh, God yes." He rammed into Adam which made Adam ram into Gloria who had hitched up her legs around them both. "Oh, God yes, oh, God. Come with me, Adam," he breathed in his ear. "Come with me, oh, God yes, fuck her, fuck her." He thrust, Adam thrust, all three groaned, and Cabot pummelled across the finish line. "Oh, God…yes." He collapsed on top of Adam, who collapsed on top of Gloria. "I'll have to show you how to do it to me," he told him. "Show you how to fuck me. I want you to fuck me, Adam."

Adam clutched his head. "Oh, God, get off me man, my head is pounding."

Cabot shifted. Adam backed out of Gloria and collapsed on the bed. Then Cabot collapsed onto him.

"I want to do that with you all night long, Adam." Cabot waved Gloria away, and she sat on the sofa with Marcy.

"What you doing, man?" Adam knocked back the gin Cabot gave him, vision blurry, head banging.

"Fucking you," Cabot told him and rolled a condom on Adam before sitting on him. "Oh, God yes, oh, fuck me, Adam, fuck me." He bounced up and down and came all over Adam before realising Adam was snoring his head off. "Oh, well, I'll just do what I want to you for the rest of the night."

In the cold hard light of day, Adam woke in a strange bed, with a strange woman on his left, and Steele Stefan on his right, with another woman beside him. All were naked, all were draped over each other. He moved, and the others stirred. He saw everything, alcohol bottles, condom wrappers, and an ashtray full of joints.

What the fuck? Looking around, he found his clothes and fled the room to dress in the hallway, and quietly made his way downstairs to find the twin brother. "What *the fuck,* man?" he panicked.

Antonio shrugged sympathetically. "Sorry, man. That's the way my brother is. If you don't say anything, he won't, and I *definitely* won't. None of my business. What happens in this place stays in this place."

"Did he…?" Adam gulped. "Does he…was he up my ass?" He was disgusted at the mere thought of sex with a man.

Antonio nodded slightly. "Yeah, man, sorry. But he always uses condoms…for what it's worth."

"It's worth fucking nothing if he raped me up the ass, and the fact he wore condoms is cold comfort," Adam spat. Panicked and freaked out, he ran from the suite, disgusted and alarmed at how much he had actually enjoyed it.

*****

"I can't believe we've been allowed in this place on an over twenty-one night," Summer said to Melody and Alexis. They were in the upstairs office at *SB3* enjoying her father's night at the club.

"Normally you wouldn't be since you're not over twenty-one,"

Alexis replied. "But since my family owns it, and your father's the manager, we're allowed up here. And *only* up here."

"Whoo," Melody yelled waving her arms in the air. "I *love* '70s disco. Who knew it was so great."

"My father." Alexis giggled. "He loves playing every Friday night and look at him." She watched him dance and sing, waving the crowd into a frenzy, just like in his *Studio 69* days. "Have you not seen all the old photos of our parents from back then? They're on the wall here in the office, and there are a couple of big ones of Daddy downstairs. Like a hall of fame thing."

"Oh, are they from then?" Summer asked. "I've never really noticed them. I see Dom and Danté have their photos on the wall too."

"Yep, it's a real family affair," Alexis went on, smiling at how happy her father was. "Even Princess has her picture on the wall as she started her singing career here."

"Do you ever call her by her name?" Melody rolled her eyes.

"Rarely" Alexis grinned. "She acts like a princess all the time, so that's what I call her. Besides, Grandma started it back when she and Diana were little. She called them Princesses Alena and Diana, so I can blame her for all of that. She started it."

"Are you ever going to get along?" Summer asked, sipping a juice.

"If we haven't gotten along in the nineteen years I've been alive, we won't now," Alexis replied, shaking her groove thang to the song. "We're too far apart in age, generation and attitudes."

"But that doesn't mean you can *never* get along," Summer continued.

"She's off living her life on her own," Alexis said. "She's only back for her birthday and celebrations. She'll be off on tour over summer, so none of us will see her until late August when we go to New York. We're too far apart, and she's too pompous." Scanning the crowd she saw the guy who'd attacked her. "Oh, my God, there he is. Quick, where's your father?"

Summer went and quickly found her father while Alexis kept an eye on the guy who'd attacked her in the water.

"Where is he?" Mike asked, peering over the crowd.

"Below us, near the bar, in the red t-shirt." Alexis pointed him out.

"Little Ted, can you pick up the tall brunet in the red t-shirt by the bar and throw him out?" Mike said into his walkie-talkie. "He's been banned from the club. And make sure the other bouncers know not to let him in again. We can't have the likes of him in this establishment."

"Yes, sir," came over the talkie.

They watched as Little Ted, their seven foot, three-hundred-pound bouncer strode over to the bar and stood behind him. Looking up, he pointed to the man's back. When he got the nod, he grabbed the man's arm and twisted it up behind his back. "I think you're in the wrong establishment, sir."

"What? Hey! Let me go," the tall, dark stud yelled, looking over his shoulder at the huge bouncer escorting him through the crowd. "Hey! Get off me." As he struggled, he happened to look up and saw the frigid bitch from the beach looking down at him, her two bimbo friends, and some old guy. Snarling, he was led out the door and shown to the bouncers.

"Boss man says this jerk is banned. Don't let him in again," Little Ted told them.

"Sure, Little Ted," Bubba said, and took a photo of his face.

Ted threw him into the crowd waiting to get in. "And don't come back."

"You won't get away with this. I'll complain to management," the guy yelled.

"It was management that threw you out," Ted said. "Get outta my sight."

The man stumbled backwards, trying to get his balance, and stalked off down the street. "I'll get you for this, you bastard. Tell that bitch I'll get her for this."

"Yeah, yeah." Ted waved a hand and went back inside.

"You girls okay?" Mike asked his daughters and Alexis.

"We're fine, Daddy," Summer said. "As long as he stays away."

"When you head home, do so together, and make sure Alexis gets home safe, just to be sure." Mike kissed his girls. "I'll see you later."

"Yes, Daddy," Melody said and went back to dancing when he walked away.

Alexis looked at her father on stage. He was looking up at her having seen the man being escorted out. She waved to show she was fine, and he nodded.

Staying on the balcony, the girls danced, trying not to worry about the guy from the beach. He was a nobody. Just some punk ass tourist who thought he could do what he wanted, and that was harass women and girls. But he'd messed with the wrong family.

At two in the morning, the girls wore out and decided to call it a night.

"I want to say goodbye to Daddy first, so let's go out the side door," Alexis said, and they all went downstairs to the backstage area.

"We'll wait outside," Summer said, dragging Melody to the door for fresh air.

"You guys go. I'll catch up," Alexis said, completely forgetting about Uncle Mike's words. She popped through the door to the stage.

"We should stay," Melody told her sister. "Remember what Daddy said?"

"But she'll only be a minute, and she knows the way home," Summer replied. "Besides, that guy's long gone. Let's get going."

"But Daddy said to stay together," Melody whined.

"Oh, for God's, sake, that jerk's gone," Summer said. "Let's go." Walking out the side door, they headed for home.

Pedro stepped over to the side of the stage. "Leaving, Bubba?"

"Yes, Daddy. Summer and Melody are waiting. I'll see you later today." She kissed his cheek.

"Stay safe, Bubba." He kissed her back.

"Yes, Daddy." Alexis ran outside to find the girls already far down the street. "Hey girls, wait for me." She took off as fast as she could in her espadrille wedges, but the girls had already turned the corner. "Girls! Wait for me." Hearing a noise behind her, she stopped and looked. But no one was there, so she quickly continued, getting halfway down the road before hearing footsteps. Looking over her shoulder, she saw no one, and determined to catch up with the girls, she moved faster, but tripped and fell to her knees.

"Damn it! These damn cobblestones." She barely made it to her feet before she was grabbed from behind.

A hand went over her mouth as she tried to scream. Her nails dug at it to get it off her face. An arm went around her waist and lifted her, carrying her to a small side alley filled with garbage cans and stacks of crates.

"Mmm," she screamed behind the hand, thrashing her legs, digging in her nails. She flung her hand back and scratched at the assailant's face, getting sworn at in return.

"You bitch, you fucking bitch." He slammed her face first into the wall, holding her there with the full weight of his body. "You fucking bitch. Just for that you really are going to get what you deserve." With his left hand still around her face, his right shoved her short skirt up and pulled down her panties.

She screamed and tried to lash out as he undid his pants and pulled his cock out.

"This is what you get for grabbing my dick, you bitch. You get it shoved inside you." In he went as she struggled and fought. His right hand pushed up her top to let her breasts free and groped and squeezed till they hurt. Then it found its way to her crotch and shoved its way down.

"Mmm." She grabbed his hair, his face. She scratched, she screamed, she cried, but pinned against the wall, there wasn't much she *could* do. He was raping her, and that's all there was to it.

When he was done, he withdrew, pulled her away from the wall, and sneered in her ear. "Frigid fucking bitches deserve what they get." Dragging his hand from her mouth, she managed to scream before he smashed her head into the wall.

"Ugh." She slumped to the ground, disorientated, and blurrily watched him zip himself up and back away from her.

"Alexis…"

Hearing the girls, he made a run for it.

"Alexis…"

"Hey, is that the guy from before?" Melody asked at the retreating figure.

"I can't tell," Summer said. "But maybe we should—"

"Alexis!" Melody exclaimed and looked at Summer. The two girls quickly ran down the small alley they'd seen him come from and found Alexis groaning on the ground. "Oh, my God, Alexis."

"Ugh," she moaned, seeing doubles of the girls as they came toward her. "Ugh."

"Can you walk?" Melody looked into her eyes while Summer helped redress her.

"Ugh." Alexis moved her hand up to her face and touched her forehead. Blood was on her fingers.

"Let's get you home." Melody gently lifted her into a sitting position. "You okay?"

"Ugh," Alexis breathed. "Dizzy."

"Okay, take a moment." They pulled down her top and covered her. "We'll get you home," Melody said. "Can you stand? We'll support you."

"Home?" Alexis murmured. "No home. No, go home." She was lifted by the girls until she was standing, and they were under each arm.

"Then where do you want to go?"

"Grandma's."

With a glance at each other, Summer and Melody helped Alexis all the way to her grandmother's house, arguing with one another how they should have waited and not gone off on their own.

"Do you have keys?" Melody whispered and dug around in Alexis's bag. "We don't want to wake your mother up next door." She found the keys, opened the door, and they quickly took Alexis inside.

"Who's there? Dan? Derek? Alexis! Oh, my baby, what's happened?" Jenny rushed to the girls' sides and grabbed her granddaughter who promptly burst into tears. "What happened?" she asked the girls who traded glances. "What happened?" she demanded, making the girls jump.

"We think she was attacked," Summer murmured, lowering her eyes, and pursing her lips. Her hands clutched one another in front of her. Jenny Stephanopoulos could scare her to pieces.

"What! Spiros! Come, Alexis, oh, my baby." She led her granddaughter into her father's old room, just as Spiros came from the master tying his robe.

"What is it? What's wrong?" He saw his wife with Alexis. "What happened?"

"Get Dan and Derek back here if they're not in their room. They were going to the club tonight." She helped Alexis into the bed and covered her. "Tell me who did this to you. Baby, do you know?" She smoothed Alexis's hair

She sobbed into the pillow. "He did. The jerk from the beach."

"The beach?" Jenny frowned and looked at the twins as they'd followed them into the bedroom. "What's she talking about?"

They traded glances. "The other day some jerk hit on her, and she showed him not to mess with her. Then he attacked her in the water, but her father got rid of him. He was at the club tonight. We pointed him out to Daddy, and he had him thrown out," Melody told her.

"Did he see you?" Jenny asked Alexis.

"Yes," came out of the pillow.

"And so he sought revenge. Do you girls have a photo of him?"

Summer pulled one from her bag. "Daddy made copies of the one the bouncer took so he could tell everyone at the club."

Jenny took it. "Girls, you stay with Alexis while I go and make a call. I'll be back in a minute," she told Alexis and slipped out the door.

*****

Dan and Derek were enjoying the show at *SB3*. They'd taken in as many nights as possible when they were in town, and Pedro was still the best DJ in Mykonos. On the dance floor, they waved their arms and strutted their stuff, having lived through the '70s in New York. They'd discovered they'd both been to 69 at different times, had both seen Pedro play, and agreed that he still had that magic thirty years later. Taking a break, they went over to the table they shared with friends against the side wall.

"Oh, God, I need a drink," Dan said, looking for his bag to get his wallet.

"I could do with a drink, but from my husband." Derek pulled Dan into his arms and kissed him, sliding his arms around Dan's waist, while Dan slid his arms around Derek's neck.

Like Tomas and Roger, they weren't legally married, but Jenny had thrown them a ceremony over two decades before.

"Mmm." Dan pulled back. "Is that enough?"

"Not what I was thinking of, but it will do for now." Derek smiled and then frowned as Dan's cell phone rang.

Sliding out of his husband's arms, Dan grabbed his phone out of his bag. "Hello?"

"Dan, Spiros, you need to get home now. It's an emergency, don't tell anyone."

"We're on our way." Snapping the phone shut, he grabbed their belongings. "We gotta go. Something's wrong."

"What?" Derek asked as they moved through the crowd to the door.

"Don't know," Dan replied. Fifteen minutes later they were in the lounge room talking to Spiros.

"Alexis has been attacked. Do you have your doctor bag?" Spiros asked.

"Yes, yes, of course. I'll get it." Dan quickly retrieved it from their room.

"Pedro's old room," Spiros told him, and he took off.

Spying him in the hallway, Jenny told the girls to go home. "You go home, go to bed and get some rest. We'll take it from here."

"You sure, Mrs S?" Melody asked, reluctant to leave her friend again.

"I'm okay," Alexis told her. "You two go, but don't say anything."

"Okay." Slowly the girls climbed off the bed and left the room.

"Alexis. Dan's here to check you over. We need to examine you."

"No," she cried and hid under the covers. "I don't want a man touching me."

"Sweetie, he's gay and a doctor; he's not going to hurt you. He doesn't have ulterior motives. We need to check that you're okay. Especially with that head wound."

Dan stopped snapping on his gloves. "Head wound? She may need x-rays and scans."

"She said he slammed her forehead into the wall, but she didn't lose consciousness, just got blurry vision." Pulling back the bed covers, she stayed by Alexis's side. "We need to examine you, okay."

"No, Grandma," she whimpered. "No."

"Then I'll do it," Jenny said. "Now, let me look at your arms and legs for scratches and scrapes." Rolling back the cover, she checked Alexis over for marks. "Some red marks around the thighs and buttocks, some on her breasts."

Alexis buried her head under a pillow.

"Broken nails. Did you scratch him, Alexis?" Jenny asked.

"Yes, Grandma. And I bit his fingers."

"Good." Jenny continued the examination. "Scrapes on her legs from the fall. Let Dan check your head, sweetie." She covered Alexis back over for the moment.

Dan flicked his light in her eyes, examined the cut on her forehead, and felt her neck and the back of her head. "Nothing feels broken, but you might have a concussion or fracture. You really should have an x-ray or scan to make sure." He cleaned and dressed the wound. "I need to do an internal."

"No," Alexis cried and buried herself back under the pillow. "No!"

"I need to check for cuts and scrapes. He might have done damage," Dan told Jenny, who was stroking Alexis's arm.

"Sweetie, I can't even begin to imagine what you've been through, but Dan has to examine you."

"No, Grandma, no," Alexis wailed. "I don't want a man touching me down there."

It was the second time Alexis had said that, and it made Jenny frown. "Alexis," she leant in close, "were you a virgin?"

The sobbing stopped, and the pillow was pulled back far enough to reveal her mouth. "No."

"How many?"

"One."

"The boy you dated last year?"

"Yes."

"How many times?"

"Four or five. He wasn't very good."

Jenny couldn't help but smile. "Okay. How about I help Dan out and we'll examine you together. You can keep your head buried in the pillow."

Sniffle. "Okay."

Jenny quickly pulled the blankets up from the bottom of the bed and lifted Alexis's legs. "Okay, sweetie, we'll be quick." She pulled Alexis's underwear down, and she and Dan got to work. Five minutes later she tucked the sheet and blankets back in. "It's over now, Alexis. We're all done."

"That was *so* embarrassing," Alexis murmured from under the pillow.

"I know, but we had to see that you were okay. Is she?" Jenny turned to Dan.

"Red, bruising, she'll be okay, but it was clearly rough." Dan filled a plastic bag with all the stuff they'd used. "Are you on the pill, Alexis?"

"Yes."

"Do you take it every day at the same time?"

"Yes."

"That might help her in not getting pregnant, but you never know," Dan said. "What do you plan on doing about it?"

"What any good grandmother *would* do," Jenny said as Spiros came to the door.

"Marco is here," he told her. "The team's outside."

"Marco's team? You called them in?" Dan asked, glancing from one to the other.

"Yes. I'm taking care of business," Jenny told him. "Alexis, I'll be back in a minute, sweetie, is there anything you want?"

"A drink…and some food." She peeked out from under the pillow.

"Okay. Grandpa will get that for you." Jenny ushered the others out the door and went to talk to Marco outside. She handed him the photo from Summer. "This is the creep that attacked my granddaughter. I want him found and taken to the cove. Pack his belongings and make it look like he just up and left to get out of paying his bill or something. *Do not be seen*, make sure he hasn't left yet, or doesn't leave the island if he tries. Knock him unconscious if you have to."

"Ma'am. We'll get right on it." Marco took the picture.

"And call me when you have him at the cove," Jenny said before going back inside to see Spiros taking a tray to Alexis. "Overall, how is she?" she asked Dan as he stood with Derek in the lounge.

"She'll heal," he said. "It was violent, but physically she's okay. Not too many marks and they will fade."

Jenny nodded. "And psychologically?"

"She'll need counselling," he said.

"Thank you for coming back. Why don't you two go to bed, and don't worry about getting up tomorrow."

They smiled. "Of course we'd come back. If there's a family emergency, we'll be there. What are you going to tell Pedro and Angie?" Derek asked.

Jenny sighed. "The truth. But I'll feed her and let her rest first. Pedro's still at work, Angie would be asleep. No point saying anything until later when we've all slept."

"Okay." Dan touched a hand to her arm. "We'll see you tomorrow. Night."

"Goodnight, you two," Jenny said and headed for Pedro's old room. She found Spiros on the bed with Alexis. She was munching on a sandwich and drinking citrus flavoured water. "There you are. Dan and Derek have gone to bed. Marco and his team are out searching for the bastard that did this, and everyone else is probably asleep." She sat next to her granddaughter. "You know we're going to have to tell your parents."

"No, Grandma, no." Alexis shook her head violently. "No, please, no."

"Sweetie." Jenny slid an arm around her. "I can't keep this from them. *You* can't keep this from them. They should know that their baby girl was attacked."

"No, Grandma, please," she whimpered. "It's so embarrassing."

"There's nothing to be embarrassed or ashamed about," Jenny told her. "It wasn't your fault, and it's being taken care of. So, you have nothing to fear."

"But Mama…and Daddy…he'll go berserk," Alexis sobbed. "I don't want Daddy getting into trouble if he does something."

"He won't," Jenny assured her. "I'll take care of your daddy, since he *is* my son, and I know your mama will be nothing but supportive. It will be okay, Alexis. We'll wait until later, when I'll let them know. In the meantime, you need some sleep and so do we. Have you finished eating for now?"

"Yes, Grandma." Alexis finished the last of her water and wiped her mouth. "Can you stay with me? I don't want to be alone."

"Of course, my baby." Jenny soothed back her hair. "Did you take some Panadol for your head?"

"Yes." Alexis snuggled down into her father's old bed.

"Can you make sure the house is locked before going back to bed?" Jenny asked Spiros.

"Of course." He kissed her and carried the tray from the room, and she closed the door behind him.

Slipping under the covers, she piled pillows behind her and watched as Alexis snuggled into her side, just as she had as a toddler. "You get some rest, Bubba. We'll sort all of this out tomorrow."

"Okay, Grandma..."

Jenny watched her sleep, boiling inside that some asshole could violate her granddaughter. She hoped that Marco and the team could find him because there was no way in hell she was going to let him leave after what he'd done. Oh, no, no way in hell would he ever leave the island.

*****

"What do you think of these designs?" Alena asked Diana in the *Stefan Productions* office Saturday morning. It was the only time the girls could get together to talk fashion, besides everything else. And they had an office in the production company lot as did Viv for her style and cosmetics company. The music and film studios took up the rest of the space. The whole company sat to the left of the city, halfway to the international airport, so it was close for their celebrity guests.

Diana took the A3 sized boards with designs on them and looked over the outfits. "These are awesome, but are they only going to suit you? They look edgy."

"Yeah, coz they're for the rock line. We *are* completely different, you know." Alena grinned at her cousin. "Those are for my line, but *these* are for you." She handed over more boards. "Those are more your style."

"Oh, they're so pretty," Diana exclaimed, taking in the gorgeous soft tones in rose, blue, green and pink. "So feminine."

"You know you dress like your mother back in the '70s and '80s."

"That's what she said." Diana laughed. "That I had raided her closet and was looking exactly like her."

"And you do. We've all seen her modelling shots," Alena said, looking over more designs. "That's the problem with both of us heading a fashion label, we're both so different and have different tastes."

"Isn't that the whole point, though?" Diana asked. "That's exactly the difference we use to sell products. You're the rock child every young girl and woman wants to be with your jet-black hair and skinny ass body. You can fit into all the edgy rock clothes. And then there's me, so they can be feminine and girly all day in pretty clothes, then change into yours for night-time." She spun around in her pretty peach dress, reminiscent of her mother's style from the '80s. It suited her complexion, big blue eyes, and long golden-brown hair. Except for the blue eyes which were from her father, she resembled her mother almost down to a T. "Complete opposite ends of the spectrum. That's why we do so well. We cater to both aspects."

"Yes, we do, and thanks to the twins being so popular, we have a men's line as well. Did you see the last shoot they did? *Smokin'* hot." Alena fanned herself with her hand.

"Yes, my brothers *are* gorgeous." Diana looked at the wall with all their photos on it. They had done men's lines to match the women's. One line for edgier rock wear, leather, denim, chains, and a classic line of suits, shirts and ties. The boys had worked well in both.

"And then we have the teen lines which Alexis and Danté do, with help from Summer, Melody and Nick." Staring at the photos, she saw another Alena, but younger. As much as Alexis didn't want to be like her big sister, she was very much the same. Black hair, fair complexion. The only difference was that Alexis had brown eyes, and Alena had blue. Alexis was taller, five ten to Alena's five eight. Both were naturally slim, and both were insanely gorgeous.

Danté, at fourteen, was already five eight and still growing. He was a shorter version of Dom, who wasn't interested in modelling their lines, and their father, Pedro. Danté got Angie's brown eyes like Alexis. The two teen lines had been a huge success, and every time she walked down a street in London, Milan or New York, she'd see teens and twenty-somethings wearing the clothes. *Haus of Stefan* was a huge hit.

"Why don't you get along with Alexis?" Diana sat down at the huge work table in the middle of the room. All of the next year's lines were spread out.

"She's jealous." Alena shrugged. "Ever since she could walk and talk she's been jealous. Always trying to do what I did. Always trying to take the stage. Always trying to be better."

"I never saw any of that," Diana said, going back to the winter line.

"Of course *you* wouldn't. But me being the eldest…it's like Dom and Danté. Danté's jealous of Dom. He and I did everything first, they didn't."

"Are you sure that's not your overactive imagination?" Diana asked. "All I see is Danté trying to emulate his brother and look up to him. Hell, I'd say he even *worships* his brother. And Alexis, she watches everything you do and wants to do it too. That's not being a copycat, that's wanting to be like your big sister or brother. That's wanting to emulate them, not copy, or be them." She just didn't understand the animosity between her cousins. She and her brothers got along. If they'd been girls, maybe it would have been different. Maybe if she'd had sisters, she'd be experiencing the same thing.

"Emulating!" Alena exclaimed. "I'm with Dom. Why can't they find their own thing to do? Why do they have to copy us?"

Diana shook her head at her cousin. "It's got nothing to do with copying. It's got to do with the family business. Mama was a model; and look at me. Mama's a stylist, look at us. My brothers do the same thing. Daddy's got a movie studio, so we've been extras in movies and films. Uncle Pedro's got a music studio and is a DJ. So all four of his children were going to be in music. Your mother's Juilliard-trained. The two boys want to be DJs, the two girls want to be singers and model their fashion lines. Grandma managed everything. Grandma is an author like Mama and goes around the world with Uncles Tomas and Roger who run the gym that we all work out at to stay in shape. There's the hotel, meat shop or nightclub left. We have a huge family business, Alena, it's no wonder we're all in it. And when our grandparents are gone, and our fathers and uncles run it, they will train us to run it for when they go. So, we'll all get to run it one day, and then our kids, and their kids. It's the family business; what else do you expect your brother and sister to do?"

Alena had been listening thoughtfully, but didn't believe for one minute that Alexis wanted to emulate her. Alexis was jealous, plain and simple. She wanted to do everything Alena had done, but she had never been better than Alena. She had always been a second-rate version of her big sister. Sure, she could sing. And sure, she looked good in the teen clothing line, but that was it. Alexis would never come close to being as good as she was.

"Don't believe it," she told Diana. "Maybe with Danté, Daddy's a DJ, so Dom and Danté would be too. Alexis could have been a pianist like Mama, but *no*, she wanted to sing and design like me. But she will *never* be better than me."

"Is that the only way you see her?" Diana asked, exasperated at the problems between her cousins.

Alena shrugged. "Yes."

"So, you don't see her as your little sister, who maybe *just wanted* to be like her big sister, and be loved by her and not treated like crap?"

Alena bit her lip. "No," she said uncertainly. "I never thought about it."

"Of course not." Diana sighed. "Because Alena is Alena and it's always about Alena. No one else is ever good enough to be your equal. You always have to be better."

"That's not true!" Alena exclaimed.

"Then what problem do you have with Alexis?" Diana asked. "I know she's ten years younger than you, but *so what?* I'd kill for a sister because hey, look at my brothers." She sat back in her seat, weary from family hassles.

"Aren't I your sister?" Alena whined. "We're sisters."

"We're *like* sisters," Diana said, "because we grew up together and did everything together. We are born one day apart. But *we're cousins, not sisters*, and we were the only thing either of us had that *resembled* a sister. Then came the twins. Ugh, boys, then Dom. We were nearly ten when Alexis was born. We were all we'd known as the only girls. But you got to have Alexis as a sister. I didn't get one. Mama was forty-five when she popped the twins out. She was hardly going to have another. You got lucky. I didn't."

Chewing on her lip, Alena thought about it. She didn't hate Alexis, just got annoyed that Alexis always wanted to copy her instead of being herself. And while it had been nice to see Mama pop out another girl, it was already too late. She was nearly ten and had grown up with Diana. They had done everything together. Gone to school, discovered boys, got their first training bras, their first make-up and ladies' cosmetics thanks to Aunt Viv. They had their first kiss from boys within a day of one another and had their first dates together. While their careers had taken them on different paths, they were still close and wanted to do a fashion label together, connecting whenever they could. And here they were, sitting in their own office, surrounded by previous and current lines, like the summer one, and they were preparing for fall, winter, spring and next summer. They had their own jobs, their own careers, and they forged them on their own. With no need to copy anyone.

"She's your only sister, Alena. What if something happened to her? What if we all went through what our fathers went through when Uncle Tomas was dying? And he *did* die. Dan worked for five minutes to bring him back. We were three and didn't realise or understand any of it. Just that he and Uncle Roger were very, very sick. What if that happened to us? What would we do then? Would you be able to live with yourself if something happened to Alexis and she wasn't here anymore? What about Danté? Could Dom live with *himself*? And as far as the boys, I know Cabot's a brat, but they're my brothers. I'd be *devastated* if something happened. Daddy and Uncle Pedro aren't the same. When it comes to Tomas and Roger, they fight like hell. Just like Grandma did. Do you *really* want to go through something like that? Watching your brother or sister die?"

"No, of course not," Alena jumped in. "I couldn't live with myself if I lost them. They're my blood…"

"But?" Diana prompted.

"But…" Alena desperately looked around trying to hit on the word she needed. "But…I don't know," she finally said. "I just *don't* know."

"Don't you know why you don't like her, or why you don't get along?"

"I don't *don't* like her. I definitely don't *hate* her," Alena said. "As for getting along, we get along. We just snipe at each other."

"So, you don't like her and don't get along. Do you know why?" Diana asked again.

After thinking, Alena shrugged. "I don't know. Maybe we're just two different people too far apart in time."

"Oh, for God's sake!" Diana exclaimed. "I get along perfectly fine with Alexis. We can talk about fashion, music, movies, work, life. There's nothing we can't talk about, and when *you're* not around *she's* perfectly fine to talk to. It's like she blossoms when you're not around."

Alena didn't like that one bit. "Well, how's that then? She won't have to worry because I'll be on tour soon. She can have the family all to herself for two and a half months."

"Oh, for God's sake, Alena. Can't you get along with her? For your parents' sake? Your *grandparents'* sake?"

"Hey, it's not me who can't get along." Alena put her hands up in protest. "She's the one calling me *Princess*, she's the one with the attitude, she's the one that doesn't want to get along. She walks away from me, doesn't sit near me at the table, doesn't talk to me."

"Would that *really matter* at the end of the day if something happened to her?" Diana all but screamed into Alena's stunned face. "*Is that really going to bloody matter?*"

*****

Knowing her son didn't wake until after four, Jenny took care of Alexis until then, talking to her about the assault, trying to come up with something for her to hang onto until she got a panicked call from Angie.

"Mama, is Alexis there? I sent Nick home and told him to send Alexis home, but she wasn't there, and the twins said they'd taken her to your place."

Jenny kept her voice calm. "Is Pedro awake yet? I was waiting to call so you could both come over."

"Yes, yes, he's awake. I woke him up when she wasn't with the twins."

"Can you both come over now? Without Dom and Danté."

"Okay, we'll be right over." They were there in two minutes, helpful since they lived next door.

"Mama, what's going on?" Pedro asked. "Dom and Danté have been at the club most of the day. It's Danté's shift until six, then Dom's on at eight."

"Okay, right, yes, that's good. It will keep them out of the way. What did the twins say?" Jenny stood in front of them in the lounge room.

"Just that they'd left around two and brought Alexis here. When we asked why, all they said was she asked them to," Angie said. "*Why* did they bring her here?"

Sighing, Jenny tried to come up with the right thing to say. "Pedro, stay here with your father, Angie, come with me." She led her to the hallway outside of the closed bedroom door. "Listen to me and listen carefully." She held Angie by the arms and stared into her eyes. "Something has happened to Alexis, and she is very freaked out. So keep your voice calm and low, and don't ask a lot of questions about it. Let her do the talking if she wants to. But stay calm and follow my lead."

"What happened, Mama?" Fear trickled its way through Angie's chest.

"Something...horrible. Just stay calm." Jenny nodded and led Angie into the room. "Alexis, sweetie, your mama's here to see you."

"Mama?" Alexis poked her head out from under the quilt.

"Sweetie? Oh, my baby, what's happened?" Angie crawled onto the bed behind her daughter and laid her head on Alexis's shoulder. "What's happened, sweetie?" Smoothing her hair, she kept her voice low. "Can you tell me? Can you tell Mama?"

Tears welled in her daughter's eyes, and she sobbed. "No." Hiding her head under the covers, she cried for the shame and embarrassment.

"Oh, sweetie, please don't cry, please don't cry." Angie shifted to lie beside her, putting her arms around her and putting her head next to hers. "It's okay, it's okay, sweetheart."

"Do you want me to tell her, Alexis?" Jenny asked, rubbing her granddaughter's arm.

"Yes, Grandma." The words came out muffled.

"Okay." Taking a deep breath, she looked at Angie. "Alexis was… assaulted…last night."

Angie blinked slowly while it tried to register. "What?"

"She was assaulted after leaving the club last night. She came here, and I had Dan look her over." She watched Angie's face, a frown now deep in place.

"How…assaulted?" The fear deepened in Angie's heart.

After another breath, Jenny went on. "By a man."

Angie's eyes flew open. "Sexually?" barely came out of her mouth.

Jenny nodded and laid her hand on Angie's arm. "Stay calm," she softly warned.

Alexis was sobbing into her pillow. "I'm so sorry. I'm so sorry, Mama."

Angie snapped out of it. "Oh, my baby, no, it's not your fault, no." Holding her daughter tightly, she saw Jenny indicate that she was going out to the others and nodded. "Come here, my baby, it's okay, it's not your fault."

Jenny walked into the lounge room, and Pedro and Spiros stood up from where they'd been sitting on the couch talking. "There's something I need to tell you, my baby boy."

"Mama." He hated it when she got that tone in her voice and that look on her face.

Taking his hands, she breathed in slowly and released it before continuing. "Last night, on the way home from the club, Alexis was assaulted."

"What!" he yelled and moved for his old room.

"No, no!" Jenny exclaimed. "Wait." She managed to stop him, seeing the panic on his face. "You need to stay calm for her sake. Stay calm. *Please,* Pedro, calm down." Waiting for him to be calm, she started again. "The girls got her here, and we had Dan examine her. She's going to be okay physically, but he suggested counselling. And I think that's a good idea because none of us has ever dealt with this before."

"Mama." The panic rose in his throat. "What kind of assault?"

Jenny glanced at Spiros, who nodded. "Sexual."

"What?" He crumpled. "No, no, not my baby." He stumbled backwards and Spiros caught him. "No, Mama. Was it that creep? The one from the beach?" Tears flooded down his face, and he quickly wiped them away.

"She said it was, and the twins gave me a photo. I gave it to Marco. The matter is being dealt with."

Pedro knew what Marco did. The whole family knew. "Marco found him? Does he have him? I want to hurt him. I told him I would." The fire fled through him, making him punchy and in the mood for revenge.

"The situation is being taken care of," Jenny told him. "Now, you need to be with your daughter. Keep your voice low and stay calm. It will help her stay calm. Okay?" She looked into his big blue eyes for confirmation. "Pedro." Her tone made him stop. "Stay calm for the sake of your daughter."

Breathing deeply, he nodded. "Okay, Mama." But inside he was going insane. He wanted to hurt and maim and kill the bastard who'd dared to touch his daughter.

"Come on." Going back to the bedroom, she saw Alexis sitting up a little. "Sweetie, your daddy's here."

"Alexis." Not waiting, he threw himself across the bed to be by his daughter's side. "Alexis, oh, my baby."

"Daddy." She burst into tears and snuggled into his chest as he wrapped his arms around her, pulling Angie into the embrace as well.

Seeing that everything was okay, Jenny shut the door and left them to it. "Oh, Jesus," she breathed and fled to the safety of her husband's arms. "Oh, dear God, what do we do?" Resting her head on his shoulder, she deflated.

"Why do I have a bad feeling about what you *are* going to do?" Spiros said.

"Because he deserves it," Jenny told him. "Any person that hurts my family like that deserves to be punished, and he will be."

"But Jenny…that's the kind of thing my grandfather used to do." He stepped back to look her in the eyes. "And I hated what he used to do."

"What do you expect us to do, Spiros?" She frowned. "Call the cops and let them take care of him? They'll give him a slap on the wrists."

"You know they won't because of who you are and who you were related to. You know full well your money talks on this island."

"I can't take that chance," Jenny said, shaking her head. "Not when it comes to rape. Not when it comes to my granddaughter. I will not take a chance on the God-forsaken Mykonos police department not doing their job. I will not put Alexis through having to go to court and recount her story over and over again. I will *not* put this family through that kind of public scrutiny. I won't, I just won't." Glancing at the clock on the wall, she saw it was already five. "Everyone will be coming for dinner soon. We'd better get dinner started."

Tomas and Roger came through the door with bags of food. "Hey, time to get dinner started." They continued into the kitchen and placed the bags on the island bench.

"Ah, Danté won't be here. Dom won't be coming," Jenny mumbled.

"Carlos, Viv, Diana?" Tomas unloaded the bags.

"Diana and Alena are in Athens working on the label. So, that's Carlos, Viv, us."

"Pedro, Angie, Alexis?" Roger asked, getting knives from the drawer.

Jenny rubbed her forehead, trying to think of a way around things. "I don't know. I'll have to find out. I need to freshen up." With a glance at Spiros, who nodded, Jenny went into her office to call Mike about Danté, and then headed for Pedro's bedroom. "Are you guys going to be up for dinner? Tomas and Roger are here preparing it."

"I don't want to see anyone," Alexis said from her father's arms. "But I am hungry. Can you bring a plate in for me?"

"Of course, my darling," Jenny said.

"I'm not sure we should leave her alone," Pedro added.

"Will *she* be here?" Alexis asked, sending a sly glance her grandmother's way.

A small smile came to Jenny's lips. "Alena and Diana are in Athens. Dom's staying at the club, so it will be just us and you. I just rang Mike and told him to send Danté home with Nick for the night. You know, Alexis, your aunt and uncles *will* find out."

"No, Grandma, please. I don't want anyone to know," Alexis cried out. "Please."

"Okay, okay," Jenny placated her. "But they *will* find out. And it's best coming from you. Now, are the two of you coming out? And will you be staying the night, or going home?" Jenny pointed at her son and daughter-in-law.

"I don't want to leave her," Angie quickly said. "We can take her home."

"No, Mama. I want to stay here," Alexis said. "I don't want to be around the boys, or Alena. I don't want them knowing. I want to stay here with Grandma."

Angie was offended. "But Alexis, I want you home with me, so I can take care of you. You're my baby, I'm your mama, I want to take care of you."

Alexis sniffled. "Mama, I'm so ashamed. I can't be around anyone else right now. And I'm safe here with Grandma, and I won't run into the boys, or Alena if she comes home. I need privacy, Mama. I need to deal with this away from my family."

"Oh, baby." Angie smoothed back her hair. "I want to look after you."

"You need to look after Danté, Mama. I want to stay with Grandma for a while. Just until I'm okay to venture out into the world."

"Okay, sweetie, but that won't stop me worrying," Angie told her.

"Oh, Mama. You can come over every day. I just need some space from the boys."

"Okay. Do you want me to bring over some of your things later?"

"Yes, please."

"Are you two having dinner?" Jenny repeated.

"You go," Alexis urged her parents. "Grandma brought in the TV for me, so I'll watch that while I eat. I can't face the family right now, so please, go out to eat."

"Okay, Bubba, if it's what you want." Pedro kissed her head.

"Yes, Daddy, please. Just act normal."

"Okay. I'll call you when it's ready." Jenny smiled and left the room.

"Mama?" Pedro followed her into the hallway. "Do you actually have him yet?"

Jenny sobered. "Yes."

"And when will you be teaching him a lesson?"

She sighed. "I don't want to get you involved with this. This is not something you should have on your conscience."

"I don't care, Mama." Pedro fired up. "He hurt my little girl, and I want to hurt him. Do you plan on doing it tonight?"

Another sigh. "Yes."

"Good." The steely-eyed determination raged within his eyes. "Because I want in."

Jenny shook her head wearily. "Pedro, no."

"Don't stop me, Mama," he warned. "I'm coming with you."

With another shake of her head, she left him to go back to the kitchen and found Carlos and Viv. "Pedro and Angie will be here."

"We'll have plenty to go around." Tomas fired up the grill, and everyone stood around chatting about their day, enjoying the sunset on the balcony before it disappeared beyond the horizon. "About fifteen minutes," he called a few minutes later.

Jenny saw Pedro and Angie come into the room.

"Five more minutes," Tomas called, and Roger prepared the salad onto plates.

"Make another," Jenny said when she saw the eight plates.

Startled, Roger said, "Who for?"

"Just make another plate please and say nothing," Jenny instructed quietly and got the tray down from the cupboard. Placing cutlery, a napkin, and bottle of drink on it, she waited for the first meal to be plated. "Say nothing," she reminded him, putting the plate on the tray and taking it to the room, but she knew everyone was watching. Knocking, she went in. "Here you go, sweetie, nice and hot from the grill."

Alexis was sitting up in bed watching TV. "Thanks, Grandma."

Out in the dining room, Pedro and Angie were getting strange looks from Carlos, Viv, Tomas and Roger.

"Who's in your room?" Carlos asked.

Gripping the back of his chair, Pedro ground his teeth.

"Pedro. Do you know who's—?" Carlos repeated, but was cut off.

"Alexis," Pedro blurted, breathing heavily.

"Why's she in your room?" Carlos went on, seeing his brother's reaction. He knew something was going on.

"Pedro," Spiros warned. "Say nothing."

"What do you mean, *say nothing*?" Carlos frowned and looked back and forth from his father to his brother for some sort of confirmation or comment. "We don't keep secrets in this family. Mama has told us enough times that we don't lie about each other, and we don't keep secrets."

"She was assaulted. She's staying here." Pedro's bone-white fingers dug deeper into the chair.

"What!" came from the four of them, and Viv's hand flew to her mouth in shock.

"Pedro," Spiros said. "Your mother—"

"Told you to say nothing," Jenny finished as she walked into the room.

"Mama?" Carlos mumbled in shock. "Is it true?"

Jenny remained calm. "It was not Pedro's place to tell you. It's Alexis's. She's not yet ready for the family to know. It was up to her when and *who* she told." Jenny eyed her youngest son.

"Mama," Pedro blurted. "My daughter was assaulted. I have a right to know. *This family* has a right to know, so we can come together and protect her."

"*Only* once she'd told," Jenny forcefully reminded him. "It's *her* story to tell, and she needs to feel ready to tell it. Not have you blurt it all over the damn countryside."

"It's not the countryside, it's *our family*. The adults that can deal with it," Pedro growled. "You raised us to look out for each other and to love, protect and defend. We taught the kids the same thing, but where the hell did we go wrong?"

"Keep your voice down," Jenny muttered. "She'll hear you and know you've blabbed to everyone when she didn't want anyone knowing and *told you* so." He calmed. "Now, it will be taken care of tonight. In the meantime, let's sit and eat." She nodded at Tomas and Roger who gave everyone a plate of steaming chicken and salad, before seating themselves.

In silence, they ate. The only sound was the occasional clatter of cutlery.

"God, look at this," Carlos finally said. "The last time there were so few of us at this table was before the girls came along."

Jenny smiled. "That was twenty-nine years ago, and it's been noisy ever since."

"Are you going to do something about it, Mama?" Carlos asked quietly.

"What?" she asked in return.

"The son of a bitch who assaulted my niece," Carlos replied, staring at the dead white fury on his little brother's face.

Everyone looked up from their plates to stare at her, waiting for a reply. Especially Pedro and Angie.

Jenny finally looked up, steely determination in her eyes. "It will be taken care of tonight."

*****

Danté finished his Saturday under-eighteen set and thanked everyone for coming. At fourteen, he always got the same age crowd. A few were as young as ten, some were older at sixteen and seventeen, but most were his age. He'd been on since midday and went until six. For six hours every Saturday, he got a chance to show his prowess on stage and rapped and sang to the delight of the crowd. And he had a lot of groupies who came every week. Kids from school, girls who had a crush on him, tourists. Any kid on the island that wanted somewhere to go on a Saturday. And every second Sunday he did the same and loved every minute of it.

Leaving the stage, he quickly wiped down and went out to greet the crowd, getting pats on the back from the boys, and hugs and kisses from the girls. He saw Mike coming towards him through the crowd.

"Okay, kids, time to go home. Danté, I'm to send you to my place with Nick. You're staying the night."

"How come, Uncle Mike?" Danté asked as Nick flung his arm around his neck.

"Your grandmother called, said you could spend the night. You guys grab your stuff. I'll get a cab."

"Okay, Uncle Mike." The boys went backstage to get their gear while bouncers cleared the kids out with a free drink.

"Okay, kids, off you go," Little Ted told them, herding them for the door and onto the minibuses Jenny had as part of the company. To keep the kids safe, they dropped them off home after every show. Bubba handed out drinks as they passed him outside the door.

Danté turned to the stage to see Dom sorting through records and CDs. He knew his brother had stuck around because he had a set to do that night, but also because it was his duty. His parents had made him do it. That's just all there was to it. He was underage and had to have a guardian in the club, and Dom was it. And for all intents and purposes, he hated it. Hated looking after the kid brother that got in his way of a life.

Saddened, after his high, he picked up his bag. "Bye Dom," he called, barely getting a glance in return.

"Come on." Nick saw the exchange and knew what Danté always talked about. "If he's going to ignore you, he's not your brother. I am. Come on, let's go home. We can grab some food on the way out, coz I doubt Mom's got any."

"Yeah…sure." Danté glanced back at Dom, whose back was to him. Feeling lonely and alone, he followed Nick out the door.

*****

After much discussion about who was going, Jenny and Pedro left the others and went silently down to the cove. It was part of the Stephanopoulos estate, a panoramic natural cove with a huge naturally built cave where they housed the yacht they'd bought over twenty years ago that the whole family used in summer. As a part of that cave, smaller rooms had been secretly hammered out, and now she and Pedro stood in one of them.

It was covered in plastic, and they were wearing suits that crime scene investigators wore. Marco and the team stood around waiting with the necessary equipment, and the guy that had assaulted Alexis was tied to a chair in the middle of the room. His legs were tied to the chair legs. His arms were tied behind the back of the chair. He was already sporting a black eye and a fat lip.

"You do that?" Jenny asked Marco as he handed her the man's wallet.

"He…struggled." Marco shrugged. "We had to restrain him."

Jenny looked at the driver's licence. "So, Mr Casey Farnsworth from Illinois, what made you think you could assault my granddaughter and get away with it?"

Casey looked up groggily. "What?"

"My granddaughter," Jenny repeated. "You verbally abused her on the beach, you physically assaulted her in the water, and you raped her in an alley. What made you think you could get away with it?"

Casey looked around at everyone, and his eyes landed on Pedro.

"Remember me?" Pedro cocked an angry brow. "When you attacked my daughter in the water the other day I told you that if you ever came near her, I'd hurt you, but that her grandmother would kill you." He pointed to his mother. "Her grandmother."

Casey's eyes went from Pedro to Jenny back to Pedro. "Yeah, right. She's going to kill me."

"Alexis said she told you who her family was Mr Farnsworth. Either you didn't listen, or you're an arrogant son of a bitch who thought he knew better. Now, in *our* family, my husband's grandfather used to be similar to a mob boss, in his own way," Jenny explained. "He had no problem getting rid of people he didn't like, or who caused his family grief. He died back in 1977 and my husband and I have run the family business ever since. But we've never had a reason to hurt or kill anyone until now. So, tell me, Mr Farnsworth, what made you think you could get away with raping and assaulting my granddaughter?"

Casey, knowing he probably wasn't going to live the night through, grew angry. "That fucked up frigid bitch thought she could lead me on and then back off. She fuckin' deserved what she got," he spat. "A good fucking from a real man."

Unable to hear any more, Pedro landed the hardest punch of his life on Casey's face, making Casey topple backwards in his chair, and fall with a thud onto the floor.

With his arms trapped under the chair back, there was a crack, and he screamed. "Fuck, my arm. You broke it. Fuck."

"Pedro stop." Jenny held him back.

"Don't stop me, Mama," he warned, swinging his arm back for another launch.

"I'm not; I just don't want you hurting your hand. Marco, give him something."

Marco handed him a baseball bat that he had handily lying on the bench behind him.

Weighing it up in his hands, Pedro took a moment before he swung. "Why did you rape my daughter?"

Lying on the floor, Casey balefully eyed him. "Because she's a whore who led me on and then turned me down." He saw the look in Pedro's eyes before the bat came down. He screamed as it connected with his leg. "You're just as fucking crazy." A hit to the other leg made him scream harder.

"Stick something in his mouth. I can bear the noise." Jenny said and watched one of her men roll up a towel and put it in Casey's mouth.

Pedro kept going, breaking his legs, his thighs, his ribs, his shoulders. He worked his way up the body until the only thing left was the head. He felt the anger, felt the sick feeling in his gut that his baby girl had been violated so brutally by this dog that was lying before him. He raised the bat above his head.

"No." Jenny put her hand on his chest. "I don't want that on your conscience."

Tears were slowly rolling down Pedro's cheeks. "I have to, Mama. I need revenge for Alexis," he said in a small voice.

"And *I* will get it, but I *do not* want you living with this for the rest of your life. Do you understand me? You've hurt him. Now *I* will kill him.

Go home. Clean up and go home to your family." She glanced at Marco who silently came over and removed the raised bat from Pedro's hands.

"Get cleaned up and go home," Jenny told her son. "Your job here is done."

Pedro slowly looked from the very bloody Casey to her, his body deflating with the exertion of his anger. He barely managed to nod.

Marco and another team member led him out, got the suit off him, and helped him clean up, then Marco watched the other man take him home and went back inside to see Jenny standing over the body.

"Mr Farnsworth, you're an animal, and as such, we're going to treat you like one. Untie him, we'll drain him and then dispose of the body and effects."

The men untied a very broken Casey Farnsworth from the chair and laid him out straight.

"Mr Farnsworth, you'll simply be a tourist who absconded from his hotel room without paying and disappeared from the island. There will be a manhunt, but eventually, people will stop looking for you, and your name will disappear from the newspapers and TV. You will disappear, and all because you couldn't keep your dick in your pants and leave my granddaughter alone. My son was right. He would *and did* hurt you. But *I* will kill you." Squatting down beside him, she looked into his very swollen eyes. "This is the punishment you get for hurting my granddaughter. Are you in pain, Mr Farnsworth?"

He tried to speak, but blood gurgled from his throat. *You bitch,* he thought dazedly. *You fucking bitch. All because of your cunt of a granddaughter, my life ends here. Fuck, fuck, fuck why did I have to go and get caught? Fuck. I'll never see my parents again, my friends, my girlfriend. Fuck, fuck, fuck.*

"Blood got your tongue, has it? Here. Let me help you clear your throat." In one swift motion, Jenny swiped a scalpel across Casey's throat.

His eyes widened at the end of his life, he gasped and gurgled, and blood poured from the wound.

"No point trying to save yourself, now." Jenny looked into his terrified eyes. "You raped my granddaughter. What on earth made you think you'd get away with it?" Standing back, she watched the blood pour down the drain in the middle of the room. "String him up and bleed him dry, then demolish the body. You know how. I want nothing left. No skin, no hair, no bones. Burn him in acid so there's nothing left, then grind him into dust. I want nothing left to be found. Do you understand me?" She looked from Casey to Marco. "Leave absolutely nothing."

"Ma'am." Marco nodded and got to work tying chain around Casey's feet and legs.

"Goodbye, Mr Farnsworth. Alexis will be so glad you'll never hurt her again. So glad you got what you deserved." She watched him being lifted, hung by his feet like a side of beef. All the years Spiros had worked in the meat shop, she had learned a lot. How to bleed an animal, how to cut it open, how to grind away what was left. And oh, how that information had come in so damn handy right now. Seeing the light leave Casey's eyes and hearing the last final outtake of breath, she left Marco to do the job.

Pedro stumbled into his parents' house where the adults were waiting. Glassily, and barely in control of his thoughts, he looked at his brothers and stopped at his father. "I can see why you didn't want anything to do with the business."

Spiros closed his eyes and sighed. "She should never…"

"She was seeking revenge for her granddaughter," Pedro told him. "So was I." Moving on, he fell into his brothers' arms, wrapping his own around their necks. "I can't believe I did that."

"Come outside." Carlos led him to the balcony off the kitchen, and the three of them held each other close.

"In all of my fifty years on this planet," Pedro murmured into Tomas's shoulder. "I never thought I would want to kill anyone. I never thought I'd go to the brink."

"Did you?" Tomas asked, rubbing his brother's back and wondering what the hell had happened.

"No." Pedro squeezed his eyes tight. "I beat him with a baseball bat. Broke every bone in his body, wanted to break his skull, kill him, but, Mama stopped me. I was ready to. But…"

"I didn't want you to have that on your conscience." Jenny stepped onto the balcony.

Sighing, Pedro turned his head. "Mama, did you?"

"I did," she said matter of factly. "He paid for what he did."

"Mama! How could you?" Shocked that his mother *could* go there, Carlos stared at her in disbelief.

"Quite easily when you let your anger get the better of you. And had I allowed Pedro to continue with that anger, he would have killed him, and I couldn't allow that to happen."

"I've never been so angry in my entire life," Pedro said, deflated and empty of all emotions. He sagged in his brothers' arms.

"But when it comes to your child you *could* kill." Jenny rubbed his back. "I know, believe me. This is not the first time I've felt this way. I felt it all the way back to Luiz."

The boys looked at her in shock.

"Mama," Tomas said, his head moving slowly from side to side. "It's been so long since his name…"

"I know, baby, I know," Jenny murmured. "But when I found out what he did to you, I wanted to kill him, and if Stefano's man hadn't already, I would have. You don't play nice when your children have been hurt, and I would do it for my babies in a heartbeat. And so I will do it for my grandbabies. Whether it was Diana or Alena, or even the boys. I would kill the bastards who hurt them."

"So, is this what the family business is getting back into?" Carlos asked, concerned by his mother's nonchalant attitude at killing.

"This is the only time it's happened," Jenny informed him. "It more than likely won't again."

"More than likely?" Carlos arched a brow in return.

"Where's Viv?" Jenny changed the subject.

"In with Alexis and Angie," Roger told her. He'd been standing quietly by on the balcony, watching the scene unfold between the brothers. He knew, like everyone else did, that sometimes the three of them just needed each other and no one else. And you didn't interrupt them when they did. It was a bond forged from birth that Jenny had created, and a bond that would last them until death.

Pedro looked up sharply and made a mad dash for the bedroom. Jenny wandered in after him, leaving the boys to murmur amongst themselves.

"Alexis, sweetie." He saw all three of them looking at fashion magazines on the bed.

"Daddy!" Alexis looked up at her shocked father's face. "Daddy's been a naughty daddy. He told everyone what happened to me when I said I didn't want anyone knowing."

"I'm sorry, baby." Tears poured down his cheeks, and his lips quivered. "I'm so sorry. I thought they should know." He watched Viv collect her shoes and get off the bed and crawled over and lay beside Alexis. "I'm sorry, baby." He laid his head on her stomach. "If the family knows we can help you, but I don't know how much we can since no one's been through what you've been through."

Viv stopped at the door. "Don't ever assume such things, brother-in-law." She closed the door behind her.

Blinking, he looked at the door. "What?"

"Silly Daddy." Alexis wrapped her arms around him and leant her chin on his head. "Aunt Viv and Mama were telling me how they had some horrible experiences too."

"Viv?" He blinked again. "Angie?" His head turned so he could look at his wife.

"Viv had a few hairy moments in her twenties, which clearly, none of us knew about," Angie said. "And then I had my moment when I was eighteen."

Pedro frowned while remembering. "That's going back. You mean...?"

"I didn't mention names," Angie quickly cut in. "No need to. But I explained to Alexis I had my own horrible experience back in 1977, and so it can happen to any woman that a man thinks he can control."

"You told her," Pedro said softly, gazing at his wife and recalling the horrible thing she had told him back then. He knew she'd never spoken of that night since. Not after the cops had arrested her father. And then Barbara Weston, an ex-schoolmate of Carlos's had become obsessed with Carlos and then him, and had killed Angie's father in the process of her obsession. Angie hadn't talked about it since.

"I know what you're thinking, and you're right. I haven't talked about it since it happened. And I didn't think I would. Ever. But, I have two girls, and I figured I might have to one day. That day is now. Not that it helps our daughter any." Angie gently swept Alexis's hair back.

"Of course it does, Mama. Knowing I'm not alone helps a lot," Alexis told her.

"Oh, baby. I wish I'd told you sooner to watch out for yourself and be aware of your surroundings." Angie's heart was in two, knowing her baby girl had been violated and she hadn't done anything to prevent it, let alone not being able to do anything to fix it.

"You did, Mama. So did Grandma. But I still got complacent and stopped worrying that something would ever happen. And then it did, so now I need to deal with it. And knowing you and Aunt Viv know what it's like, helps. I'm not alone. I just need to deal with it in my own time, in my own way."

"Okay, baby." Angie pushed her daughter's hair aside and planted a kiss on her temple.

"Did you and Grandma deal with him, Daddy?" Alexis hugged her father.

"Yes, Bubba. He won't be hurting anyone ever again." He couldn't look her in the eyes. Or Angie.

"Good!" Alexis exclaimed. "He got what he had coming."

In the lounge room, Viv put her shoes back on. "We had a nice chat, and I think she'll be fine. Knowing her mother and I went through the same thing helped."

"What! What?" Carlos perked up from his spot against the kitchen island. "You were assaulted? When?"

"In my twenties when I was modelling," Viv replied, smiling softly at her golden-haired husband. "It was common for men to think they could touch up young women and girls who didn't have chaperones. At least three tried it on with me, and one gave me more than I bargained for. That's why I prefer to work with gay photographers. They weren't interested in raping young innocent girls."

"Jesus, Viv." Carlos moved to her side and held her. "Did you ever tell Diana?"

"Not the details, but I definitely explained that she had to be tough and not take that kind of crap. A job is not worth being sexually assaulted for, and the family has money and jobs if she ever needed help. Hopefully, it all sank in, and she takes care of herself." She kissed him lightly on the cheek.

"That's why we had them learn self-defence growing up, but sometimes, even that's not enough to protect them," Jenny said. Seeing the tired looks on their faces, she added, "Why don't you all go home? It's late, and you need to spend time with each other. Come on, go home." She kissed them goodnight as she moved them through the front door and closed it behind them. Back in Pedro's room, she found all three of them asleep in each other's arms. A soft smiled touched her lips, and she grabbed a quilt from the cupboard, laying it over Pedro. She turned off the TV, turned out the light, and closed the door.

"Time for bed?" Spiros asked. "I've locked up for the night."

Sighing wearily, she nodded, and they walked into their room to change for bed. Washing her face in the ensuite, she thought back to what she'd done that night. Killed a man. Something she'd never done. But something she'd vowed to do again if one ever hurt any of her family. And it had been poor Alexis who copped it. No, there was no way she was going to allow any man to get away with assaulting any of her children or grandchildren.

Looking in the mirror, she saw a very old, very tired woman looking back. At seventy-nine, she had lived a good life and wanted that to continue. But right now, she felt very old and very tired. Needing her husband, she fled into the bedroom and climbed in beside him, settling into his arms. "I love you, Spiros."

"I love you too, my darling Jenny," he murmured against her forehead. "Always."

"Always," she repeated, nestling her head on his shoulder. "Always."

*****

In Carlos and Viv's home, they settled in for the rest of the night, in one another's arms. Carlos wanted to know more about her life before him. She told him that was for another time; she was writing her memoirs, and it would all be laid out in that.

*****

In Tomas and Roger's home, they were in the throes of passion, having been disturbed by all that had gone on, desperately needing to show each other how much they loved and wanted each other still, thirty years on.

*****

A few days later, with her parents at work, Alexis was at her wits' end. She'd holed herself up in her father's old room, and all she'd done was watch TV, listen to music, stare out the window, or go through her father's and uncles' closets. But most of their stuff had gone to their own homes, so there wasn't much left.

Sighing, she paced back and forth. The magazines had been read, and she was bored. She wanted to get out and about again. Summer and Melody had dropped by, but still, they didn't know what they wanted to do with their summer.

She threw herself down on the bed, flicked through the channels and came across a daytime TV show that had survivors of rape on as the guests. Sitting up, she watched. She listened. She cried when they cried, she got angry when they got angry. Holding a pillow to her chest, she heard word for word what each woman had gone through, how they had fought, how they had gotten away. How they were surviving, how they had tried to kill themselves. The anger, the guilt, the anguish, the shame and embarrassment. They blamed themselves even though they weren't to blame. And not one of them blamed the rapist. They all blamed themselves.

Crying until the show was over; Alexis buried her head in her pillow and wept, wept for all of her own shame and embarrassment, wept for all of her own pain and guilt. Wept for not knowing if she would ever be able to let a man touch her, kiss her, make love to her.

120

She was yet to find her one true love, the man she wanted to spend the rest of her life with, and now she doubted she ever would. She hated it. Hated never being loved, hated being alone, hated her sister and her life and how she looked. Hated everything and everyone, though she didn't really.

She ran into the bathroom and closed the door. Her tears blurred her image in the mirror, and she slid the cabinet door open and found an old pair of scissors. Taking a chunk of hair in hand, she cut it. And another, and another, sobbing the whole way.

"Alexis?" Jenny came through the door, seeing half of her granddaughter's hair gone and lying on the floor. "Oh, no, baby, no." She grabbed Alexis's hands and stopped her. "Oh, my baby, what are you doing?"

"I hate it," she wailed, falling into her grandmother's arms. "I hate it. He used it to grab me in the water, and he used it to slam me into the wall. I hate it. I hate it. I hate it," she screamed. "Get it off me. Get it off me."

"Alexis," Jenny said sternly. "It's okay. Calm down. I'll cut it." Soothing her granddaughter, she calmed her. "It's okay, my baby. We'll deal with it together. It's okay. You just wait a moment, and I'll get something to wrap around you." She ran to the other end of the house to the laundry for an old cloth and picked up a dining chair on the way back. Jenny sat Alexis down in the bathroom and wrapped the cloth around her neck. "Are you sure you want me to do this?"

"I've already started, Grandma, so you may as well finish it," Alexis said quietly.

Looking at the botched hack job Alexis had started, Jenny quickly cut off chunks of hair, laying it on the sink. She then trimmed it into shape, having cut Spiros's and then the boys' hair for years when they were young. She'd learned from her aunts who were hairdressers, so she could save money on haircuts.

She put her training into practice once more and trimmed Alexis's hair into a short, stylish do. Considering the hatchet job, Jenny could only give her a style similar to her own. Short back and sides, but still some length on top. Brushing Alexis's hair forward for a current trend, she wiped the hair from her neck and removed the cloth, shaking the hair into the shower alcove to be swept up and binned later. "There, stand up and see how you look."

Alexis stood, staring at herself in the mirror, seeing a completely different person looking back. The shock slid over her face, quickly followed by wonderment, surprise and happiness. "I look so different."

Jenny smiled. She was beside her looking into the mirror. "Sometimes a haircut does wonders for your looks, your personality, and your style. Haven't you read Viv's books or watched her videos?"

Alexis turned her head side to side trying to see the back, craning her neck to see. "It's…it's awesome, Grandma. I look so different."

"Yes, you do," Jenny agreed, seeing the happiness on her granddaughter's face. "You look like *you* now, and *not* your mother or sister."

Alexis stared at her and her grandmother's reflections. "Yes, yes." Her smile was bright and wide. "I look like myself. Finally. I look like *me*."

"Yes," Jenny replied. "And now you can finally find out who Alexis Fallon Stephanopoulos is."

Alexis's smile grew wider. She was finally coming into her own.

*****

"Oh, my God, Alexis, you cut off your hair," Angie said that night while they were waiting for dinner and Alexis had made her grand debut. She stared at her daughter who looked so different.

"Mama, it's only hair," Alexis replied. "It will grow back if I want it to. But I like it short." She watched as her mother stood in front of her, touching it. "I think it suits me and I finally get to be myself."

Angie gazed at her daughter, so stunning now that her face was on display and not covered in hair like hers and Alena's.

"I think you look stunningly beautiful." Pedro went to his daughter's side and kissed her temple. "My little girl is so beautiful."

"Thanks, Daddy." Alexis beamed happily as she always did in her father's love.

"My little girl isn't so little anymore," Angie said, hugging her daughter. "You look incredible."

"Thanks, Mama. But it's just hair."

"Did you get that done today?" Viv asked. "It's very stylish." They all stood around sipping pre-dinner drinks.

Alexis touched a hand to her hair. "Grandma did it."

"Jenny!" Viv exclaimed. "I didn't know you could cut hair."

"I used to do the boys when they were little. My aunts were hairdressers and showed me how." Jenny fussed around, setting the table.

"It's fantastic," Viv went on. "Maybe you should be doing hair for the photo shoots."

Jenny laughed. "I can cut, but I'm not that talented."

Dom and Danté came through the door. "Is dinner ready yet?" Dom asked then caught sight of the person with his parents. "Hey… who's this?"

"It's me, silly." Alexis giggled at the astonishment on her brothers' faces.

Dom's eyes widened. "Alexis? Whoa, you look so different."

"That's what *we're* all saying," Jenny called out.

Danté studied his sister. "So…you look more like *us* now?"

"I guess I do, Squirt," Alexis told him. "At least I no longer look like Alena."

"Wonder what she'll say about it," Jenny murmured as she laid out the cutlery.

"Probably jealous that she didn't think of it first." Alexis rolled her eyes.

"Wow, definitely different," Dom muttered. "You gonna wear it like that all the time?"

"Well, it is short, there's only so many ways I can style it," Alexis said, fluffing out the longer bangs that crossed over from right to left over her eyes.

"Nah, I meant brushed forward," Dom said. "Is that the only way you'll wear it?"

"Probably not. I can slick it back, do a side part, put it up, put it down. I can't wait." Alexis did a little dance. "It's kind of exciting having a new hairstyle. Just chopping it all off and going short like

Grandma did."

"I think you look amazing," Jenny said. "So, let's sit down and eat. Are Alena and Diana coming?"

"Not until their birthdays. Diana's busy with the fashion label, and Alena with rehearsals," Viv said. "So you won't see them for another week."

"Wait until they get a look at Alexis. They'll flip out," Jenny said.

June 2007

One week later, everyone was hovering around the dining room for Diana's birthday when Alexis came out of her room wearing skinny black ripped jeans, chunky soled boots, and a glittered, ripped, loose knit oversized sweater, all from the teen rock line at *Haus of Stefan*. She had long feather earrings in one ear, studs in the other, and wore black kohl eyeliner thickly around her eyes.

Diana's eyes widened. "Oh, my God, Alexis?" Her hands went to her mouth.

Alena turned to stare, shocked into disbelief that this was her sister standing at the other end of the table.

"Hey, cuz, happy birthday. I got you something." Alexis sat the box on the table.

"Oh, my God, Alexis." Diana quickly went to her cousin to see the new do. "Oh, my God, look at you. You have cheekbones and eyes and lips. Oh, my God, you're gorgeous, stunning." She hugged her. "You look amazing."

"Thanks, cuz." Alexis hugged her back. "Figured I'd take a leaf out of your mother's books and get a haircut."

Diana pulled back to examine the style. "Oh, you look brilliant. Look at you, and in our teen rock chick line. Oh, my God, you look fabulous. Just wait till the next line comes out and you'll model them. All the girls your age will want to look just like you."

Alexis smiled brightly, happy that she was getting some attention.

Diana had always been sweet and kind to her, unlike her sister. Her very own sister wanted nothing to do with her, but Diana did. "Thanks, cuz. Happy birthday."

"What'd you get me?" Diana asked.

"Open it and see," Alexis said, standing between her parents and grandparents.

Ripping the present open, Diana pulled out a beautiful multi blue swirl print dress in soft muted tones. "Oh, Alexis, it's beautiful. What label is it? It's not ours."

"Nope." Alexis beamed. "It's an *Alexis* original."

"What?" Diana's head flew around so she could see her cousin. "You made this?"

Alexis saw Alena scowl and smirked. "Yes, I did. Found the fabric, cut the pattern, and made it myself. All for you."

"Oh, Alexis, you beautiful, wonderful child. It's incredible, thank you." Diana hugged her once more and opened the rest of the presents.

Alena stood scowling, looking from the dress laid out over the box to her sister.

Alexis stared back, almost defying Alena to say something.

"Oh, the presents are all so wonderful." Diana hugged everyone. "Thank you so much. All of you, even you Danté." She pinched his cheeks. "I'll play the mixed CD all the time. You know they're my favourite songs."

He blushed. "But I changed them up a bit, so you won't get the usual ones."

"I think it's awesome that you want to be a rapper, and I've already bragged to all of my friends. Now I have something to play them."

Dom rolled his eyes and opened his mouth to say something, but he saw his grandmother, father and mother all stare at him. He closed his mouth and blushed.

A ringing popped up from somewhere. "Oh, that's my phone, give me a minute." Diana quickly got the phone from her bag. "Oh, it's my brother." Her eyes widened in surprise. "Antonio?"

"Hey, sis, happy birthday. You get your present I sent…*we* sent?"

She rolled her eyes. "Yes, Antonio. I got the present *you* sent. It's beautiful, thank you." She gently touched the pearl pendant around her neck. Pearl was her birthstone as a Gemini.

"You're welcome, sis. I sent them together to Grandma. Has Alena got hers?"

"Probably not." She didn't want to give too much away.

"All right. I don't know when we'll see you, probably when you all come to New York in a couple of months."

"I'll be there next month for Fourth of July, and I'll expect the penthouse, thank you very much."

"Ah…well…" Antonio muttered.

"Steam cleaned while you're at it." Diana raised her brows in amusement.

"Where will we sleep?"

"You'll have to go somewhere else, little brother." She chuckled. "I'm older than you, and what I say goes. I want the penthouse cleaned. Besides, you'll have to move out for August when the whole fam comes."

"Yeah, yeah." Antonio groaned. "Will you be home for our birthday? We're coming with a group of friends to *SB3*."

"I'll see what I can do, but considering you're not here for *my* birthday…"

"Yeah, yeah," he repeated. "I'll see you next month, sis."

"Okay, Tone, see you then." Hanging up, she relayed the message.

"Of course they'd be here for *their* birthday," Jenny said as she started setting the table.

"Boys *are* boys." Viv sighed. "We did our best, but clearly their horoscope got it wrong. Instead of being Geminis, they were Leos."

"Oh, Cabot definitely tries to prove he's the king of the pack," Diana said. "Have you heard the latest gossip from New York?"

"Ugh, can we not talk about your brothers?" Alena put her hands up in protest. "It's our birthday, and they're ruining it."

"Ah, hello," Diana stopped her. *"Whose* birthday? *Not yours."*

Exasperated, Alena rolled her eyes. "Duh! I know, but we've always celebrated for two days, and today you're twenty-nine, which means tomorrow *I'm* twenty-nine. So, I only have a few more hours before

I'm a year older and your age once again, and then we get to go and party."

Alexis scoffed. "God, you just can't *not* make it about you, can you?"

Alena turned on her. "At least it stops *you* making it about *you* and *your* new hairdo and look."

"Danté, come help with dinner," Tomas called to his nephew. "We're grilling on the balcony." He held his arm out for his nephew who went with him and Roger outside.

Pedro was grateful. Danté didn't need to hear what was about to happen and they all knew what that was.

"At least I don't look like *you* anymore," Alexis spat, hands on hips. "*My big sister.* The selfish, self-centred brat who only gives a damn about herself."

"Oh, and *you* don't," Alena cried. "Look at this." She waved her hand at Alexis's hair. "It's Diana's birthday, and *you* preview your new look."

"*Actually, I did this a week ago, so the family's already seen it,*" Alexis said. "Just because the two of you are flying off around the world doesn't mean the rest of us stand still and do bugger all."

Jenny raised her brows knowing full well Alexis had gotten that phrase from her.

"Well, you certainly haven't done anything except try and be like me your whole life. The hair, the singing, the fashion label. You *always* wanted to be me."

"*Because it's all about you,*" Alexis cried. "It's always about *you,* because *apparently,* nothing can happen to anyone *except you.* It has to be *all about Princess Alena* and *her* career, *her* dramas, *her* boyfriends. *It's always about you.* No one else can have anything to be proud of. No one else can go through shit because it's *all reserved for Alena. Princess fucking Alena,*" she screamed.

"Alexis; don't use that language at your sister," Pedro said, angrier at Alena than Alexis.

"*No, Daddy.* Don't tell me what to do. I'm sick of it. I'm sick of that selfish bitch and all the garbage she dumps on me." Turning, she fled for the bedroom. "I'm sick of being assaulted and abused all the time.

I'm sick of it." The door slammed, and they all stood stunned.

"A selfish bitch," Alena whispered, shocked that her sister could say such a thing. "Who the hell does she think she is?"

"Your sister," Jenny told her. "And yet look at you. *You're* the indignant one." Her heart was racing in her chest. She knew this was long overdue and had guessed that the residual effects of the assault would come out sooner or later. But she also knew she was to blame for Alena's attitude.

"Grandma, she called me a selfish bitch. *How dare she.*" Alena's attitude was ready for a fight.

Jenny slammed both hands on the table making everyone jump and go silent. Breathing hard, she knew it was time to clear the air, even if it meant ruining Diana's birthday. She saw Diana shelter in Viv and Carlos's arms, and Dom huddle beside his parents. "You *are* a selfish bitch, Alena," she said. Her voice was low in a tone they knew well and knew to say nothing to in return. "You are *so bloody selfish.* And that's *our* fault. *My* fault mainly. For the way you were raised made you the selfish, self-centred little girl you are today."

She stood and faced her shocked granddaughter. "*We* made you this way and *we* shouldn't have. I should have kicked that selfishness out of you years ago, but I didn't. It's our fault, *my* fault because when the two of you were born I called you princesses. You were the baby girls I never got to have, and I *doted* on you. I *spoilt* you, I called you princesses and gave you *everything,* all because I didn't have little girls of my own." Tears filled Jenny's eyes. "And for nine and a half years you and Diana *were* the only little girls we had until Alexis came along and we finally had another little girl to spoil. But it made you jealous because she was your sister, whereas Diana doted on her because she didn't have one." Staring into her granddaughter's eyes, she saw the pain of a telling off. "She's *your* sister and yet all you've done is ignore her and treat her badly. And all she wanted was her sister to love her and spend time with her, and show her how to put make-up on, and play dress ups with, and talk about boys and kisses and love with. And all you did was ignore her. You selfish, inconsiderate little girl. I blame myself. *I'm* at fault. *I* did this. *I* spoilt you and made the two of you believe you were everything. Diana grew up, you didn't, and even now, on your cousin's birthday, the day before yours, you make it all about you and attack your sister for her new look and makeover." Shaking her head sadly, she continued. "How selfish and self-centred can *you be*, Alena? To not think about *anyone* besides yourself. Did you even get her a birthday present this year?"

Alena gulped. No one in the family wanted to be reamed out by their grandmother. Not even her. "I sent a card," she said in a small quivering voice, trying hard not to let the tears fall. She loved her grandma and had never wanted to be at the end of a telling off.

"And that's supposed to be enough is it?" Jenny questioned. "The twins aren't here, but at least Antonio sends presents. What did *you* send? *A card!*"

A slamming on the table made them all turn around to see a huge brightly wrapped box. "There's your present for tomorrow. At least *I* bothered. But *I* never want to see you again, so *you* won't be seeing *me* tomorrow." Alexis's eyes burned with fury. "I *hate you*, Alena. I hate the way you've treated me my *entire life. I hate you, and I never want to see you again.* So, take your stinking present and shove it where the sun don't shine, because it's the last one you'll *ever* get from me." Walking around her parents, she headed for the door. "I'm going out. I'm sick of being cooped up. I'll be at *SB3*."

"Alexis, no!" Angie called. "Not on your own."

"Dom," Pedro said to his son. "You're working tonight, grab your gear and go after her. Don't let her be on her own, and don't let her out of your sight."

"Why?" Dom asked, getting his bag from the lounge.

"Just do it," Pedro demanded. "Look out for your sister. Go."

Weirded out by his parents' tone and wanting to get away from Alena and the entire situation, Dom left.

All was quiet with Angie and Pedro exchanging worried looks.

"What's going on?" Diana asked, pulling away from her parents' arms and studying everyone's expressions. "This is about more than Alena's selfishness. Alexis said before she was sick of being assaulted and abused. Who's assaulted and abused her?"

Jenny sighed and touched Diana's cheek. "I'm sorry your birthday turned out like this. None of us," she glanced at Alena who was silently crying, "wanted to get into any of this, I'm sure. But it was time it all came out."

Alena gasped through her sobs. "Alena's not selfish."

"Then stop speaking in the third person," Jenny said. "That's part of the problem, you talk about yourself constantly. Why not talk about your brothers or *sister* for once in your life, as though you actually *give a damn* about them and not only about yourself?"

"Grandma, who assaulted Alexis?" Diana pushed on.

With a backward glance at her son and daughter-in-law, she said, "A man. Nearly two weeks ago. I doubt she'd want you lot to know, and it's not my business to tell. But there it is. Alexis is going through something horrible and needs all the support she can get."

"A man assaulted her?" Fear snaked its way through Diana's chest. "Physical?" she paused, "or sexual?"

"The latter," Jenny told her.

"Oh, my God, no, not Alexis," Diana cried and punched Alena hard in the arm with both fists. "I said to you last week, what would you do if something happened to one of our siblings like it did to Uncle Tomas. What would you do? I told you you'd never forgive yourself. Oh, my God." She broke down and stumbled into her parents' arms. "Oh, my God, how could this happen? Oh, my God. Poor Alexis. Oh, my poor baby."

Alena tried to compute what was happening. "Someone hurt Alexis?"

"Yes." Jenny watched her face intently.

"A *man* assaulted Alexis?" Alena slowly went on.

"Yes." Jenny waited.

"Sexually…"

"Yes."

"She…" Alena stuttered. "She was…raped…"

"Yes."

Tears flowed out of her. "Oh…no…my baby sister…"

"Yes." Jenny knew what was coming.

"No." Alena's face crumpled, and she sobbed. "No, my baby sister. No."

Jenny took her into her arms and held her while she wept; knowing what Diana had told her was coming true.

No, Alena thought. *This can't be happening. Not my baby sister. No, why would, how could, why did Diana have to be right? Why did it have to take something bad happening for me to feel like shit and never forgiving myself? How can I ever talk to her about it? She'll never talk to me, she hates me. I never meant to make her hate me. I love her. Oh, God, I love her.* She pulled back. "I can't be here. I can't, oh God, I can't."

"Alena," Jenny warned.

"No, Grandma. I've been a horrible sister, and I deserve to lose her as my sister. I've been horrible." Grabbing the huge birthday present off the table, she ran for the door and down to the home she shared with Diana. Barging into her room, she stumbled, falling onto the bed, and crying. How could anyone do this to her sister? Her baby sister. And where had she been? Off rehearsing for her tour because that was her job, and rarely did she come home to her actual home and see her family because she didn't get along with her only sister.

"Argh!" she growled and got up, ripping off her leather jacket and flinging it on the bed. "Argh!" She stomped her feet and accidentally kicked the box across the room. It came to a stop at the balcony door, the lid half off, the fabric hanging out.

"Oh, no, her present. Oh, no, I've ruined it!" She ran over, fell to her knees, and peered at it, seeing black, white and silver fabric sliding out of the box. Pulling it out, she held it up. It was an off the right shoulder, asymmetrical dress with a batwing on the left arm that came down to the elbow. On the left leg, the hem ended mid-thigh, but it went down to below the knee on the right with a slit. The fabric was similar to that of Diana's dress.

"Oh, it's beautiful." She read the label. *Alexis* was all it said. "Oh, it's gorgeous. I love it, Alexis, oh, my baby sister, I love it. And I love you."

Upstairs in Jenny's home, everyone stopped crying long enough to serve dinner.

"Where'd everyone go?" Danté asked, knowing something was very wrong.

"Dom and Alexis are at *SB3*," Pedro said. "And I think Alena went home."

"Why?" Danté continued. "It's Diana's birthday."

"It's okay, Little D," Diana said, using her affectionate nickname for him. "We all have busy lives, and I don't mind having a birthday without Alena for once. I'll be able to get a word in now."

Quiet laughter went around the table as they celebrated the eldest Stephanopoulos grandchild's birthday.

"So, what will you be doing after today?" Jenny asked.

"I have a bunch of photo shoots this month, and then I'll be in New York for Fourth of July. And then more shoots, and the label, and more shoots. Oh, I forgot to bring the magazines up for you all."

"Magazines?" Viv inquired.

"The *Flair* story I did last month. It's out next week, and they sent me a box. I'll get them later. But what I'd like to do is this. If you all don't mind, when we've finished here I could go to *SB3* for the night with Alexis." Everyone looked up at her. "You don't mind, do you? I think she probably needs someone now, especially someone as annoyed with Alena as she is."

"The two of you are having problems?" Angie asked, surprised since the girls normally got along like sisters...much better than her own daughters did.

"More like, I'm exasperated and worn out." Diana sighed. "When we're working separately it's great, we're apart, but when we work together, it's...ugh!"

"Oh, we know," Pedro said. "We know very well."

"Well, who knows," Jenny added. "Maybe this will bring her to her senses."

Everyone looked at her.

"I hope so, Mama," Pedro replied.

A couple of hours later, Diana went downstairs to collect the magazines and change into the blue dress Alexis had made her. She put on the jewellery her family had given her, sprayed on the perfume they'd given her, and gathered her things. Not seeing or hearing her cousin, she went back up to her grandmother's house. "Here they are.

Wait until you see them." She set the box on the table.

"Oh, that dress really is beautiful." Viv admired the way it swirled around her daughter's shapely legs. "The workmanship is divine."

"Alexis has learned a lot from working at *Haus of Stefan*. She likes designing, cutting and sewing," Jenny said.

"It is lovely. I can't wait for Alexis to see me in it." Diana opened the box and pulled out the top magazines. "Get a load of this."

"Oh, Diana. That's stunning." Jenny moved closer and took the magazine she offered. "Look at you." It was the photo of Diana standing in front of the Acropolis, arms by her side, face up to the sun. She looked beautiful and ethereal, like a goddess.

"Oh, my darling, you're beautiful." Viv stared at the cover. "Look at our baby, Carlos." She held out a magazine for him to see.

"Aw, my little baby girl's all grown up." He grinned, and his heart overflowed with love for his daughter.

The family commented on the cover and inside shots.

"They're amazing, Diana, but then you do have the pedigree," Jenny said.

"It's surprising they turned out so well considering that jerk, Charles Kensington, took them. Ugh, he's worse than Alena to work with." A frown caused Diana's brows to furrow.

"You mean there's someone out there worse than Alena?" Danté asked.

Everyone laughed, and Diana ruffled his hair before sliding her arm around his shoulders. "Yes, Little D, there is."

"Wow." Danté's eyes widened in surprise before he rolled them. "Didn't think that was possible."

"Neither did I," Diana retorted. "But there it is. So, these are all for you guys, and I'm going to head off to *SB3*."

"Take a cab," Jenny said. "Don't take chances."

Diana paused, looking at her grandmother. "Okay, Grandma."

Five minutes later, she was in the cab heading for the family's club. Ten minutes after that, she was winding her way through the crowd looking for her cousin. Seeing Mike, she ran over. "Hey, Mike, do you know where Alexis is?"

"Upstairs in the office," he yelled above the blaring '90s music.

"Thanks." She went through the side door and up the stairs to the office to find Alexis sitting on the balcony overlooking everything. "Hey, cuz, I hear the DJ's good tonight."

Alexis looked at Diana, and her eyes lit up. "Hey, that looks really good."

"Good!" Diana exclaimed, picking at her sleeve. "It's insanely beautiful, Alexis. You're incredibly talented. I can't believe you made this all on your own from start to finish."

Alexis shrugged. "Yeah, well, I was taught by the women of Stefan, and they're pretty good." Watching her cousin, she sensed something. "Is everyone else here?"

Diana glanced up sharply. "Huh? Oh, no, just me. I told everyone I wanted to spend some time with my cousin."

Alexis studied her cousin's face. "Alena not good enough?"

"Alena took your present and stormed out of the house not long after you. I don't know where she is." Diana rolled her eyes at the drama and sighed.

Alexis raised a brow. "Got a talking to, did she?"

"Alexis." Diana took her hand. "Grandma…told us. Not in detail, just that you'd been assaulted by a man and we put the rest together."

Alexis pulled her hand away. "She shouldn't have."

"It was your comment about being assaulted and abused that got me thinking, and I pushed them to tell us."

"Great! So now the whole family knows."

"Not Danté, or Dom. Unless you told him on the way over?"

Alexis shook her head. "No. We just walked side by side, didn't speak."

Diana sat back in her seat on the couch and put an arm around Alexis. "You've got me to talk to if you want to, but since I haven't been here in a while, we could go down and dance."

Alexis cast a sideways look at her cousin. "*You* want to dance?"

"Why not?" Diana asked. "I know I'm not very good, but it's my birthday. Let's go and kick up our heels and fling our hair around." She glanced at Alexis's crop.

"Funny ha ha," Alexis retorted. "I have no hair to fling anymore."

Diana grinned. "No, but I do. I'll fling it for the both of us."

Laughing, Alexis allowed Diana to pull her down to the dance floor.

*****

It was Alena's birthday, and for the last twenty-four hours she'd thought, and cried, and screamed, and pummelled her pillow trying to get her feelings and thoughts straight. Her little baby sister had been raped, violated. Her *only* sister. The *only* sister she had. She'd always thought of Diana as her sister, but Diana was right. She was their cousin, and Alexis was her sister. And the thought that someone had hurt her baby sister made her sick to her stomach. Literally.

She had vomited in the bathroom at the mere thought of what Alexis must have gone through and sat crying at the rest of it.

Why hadn't she been a better sister to her? Why hadn't she taken on the big sister role and done her duties *as* a big sister? All the things her grandma said had hurt, but they were true. *She* was selfish. She had blamed Alexis for being selfish, and yet it was *her, Alena,* who was the selfish one; the one who ignored Alexis almost from the moment she was born because she saw how everyone doted on her as another girl. For nearly ten years it had been her and Diana, the only girls in a family of three boys, and then her mother had given birth to a daughter. She was beautiful. Brown-eyed and black-haired. She was gorgeous as a baby, and as a child, she wanted to be like her big sister, and Alena had hated it. Hated her for existing, for following her around and being annoying.

While she and Diana had experienced everything together, Alexis had experienced it on her own with just her mother, grandmother and Viv to turn to. She and Diana had it all, including each other. Alexis had no one. What sort of big sister was she? Selfish, self-absorbed, self-obsessed, just as Grandma had said. She *was* selfish, and she felt sick about it. Sick that she hadn't been there for the last nineteen years for her sister. Sick that she wasn't there now. Sick that she hadn't been there the night it happened. Not that she'd know what to do about it. What *could* she do? Except for starting over, it was too late. What could she do?

It's never too late, floated through her mind.

Nineteen years have passed, she thought. *Can I still be the big sister I should be? Can I still be the big sister I need to be?* Biting her lip, she came up with a plan she hoped would bring them back together.

Glancing at the clock, she saw it was nearly four. Two hours until the party for her. Was two hours enough time to sort through nineteen years of crap? She didn't know, but she was about to find out.

After packing up her outfit for the night, along with her accessories, she grabbed the latest designs from the upcoming rock chick line and went upstairs to her grandma's.

"You're early," Jenny said when she let her in. "Getting dressed here?"

"Um." Alena gulped. "Is Alexis here?"

"In your father's old room." Jenny studied her for a sign.

Nodding, Alena slowly walked toward the room to stand in front of it. Taking deep breaths, she knocked.

"Come in."

Opening the door, she saw Alexis sitting on the window seat looking out at the view. "Hey."

Alexis stared in surprise, watching with trepidation as her sister closed the door and laid down a bunch of stuff on the bed. "What do *you* want?"

"Um." Alena swallowed, having no idea where to start. "I…" She moved around the bed towards her sister, seeing her sitting there, so young and beautiful, but also battle-scarred by rape. Tears flooded her eyes. "Oh, my baby sister, I'm so sorry." She enveloped Alexis into her arms. "I'm so sorry you went through that. I'm so sorry I wasn't there for you. I'm so sorry you went through this. I'm sorry I've been a bitch to you all of your life. You didn't deserve that. I was selfish and jealous that another girl had come into the family, and it wasn't just about me anymore. Everyone doted on you and loved you and held you, and I got left out and I hated it. I was so jealous and I'm so sorry. It was just me and Diana, and I was a horrible selfish bitch, and a horrible jealous bitch, and I treated you badly, and so I wasn't there for you when you needed support, and I'm so sorry." She pulled back and wiped her sister's tears away. "Are you…still hurt? Did he…hurt you badly?"

Alexis couldn't stop her tears from falling. Not only for the rape, but for the words she had always longed to hear from her sister. Sobbing, she clung to what precious moments she had. "A little. He smashed my head into the wall to knock me unconscious, but I didn't pass out." She touched the faint mark on her forehead. "I had a concussion."

"Oh, my baby." Alena smoothed her sister's hair. "I'm so sorry. Do you want to talk about it?"

Looking at her sister, Alexis was wary. This was a side of Alena she had never seen, and she didn't know if it would last. She decided to take a chance. If it didn't work out, then stuff her! She moved her legs up so Alena could sit on the window seat, and she proceeded to tell her sister the story from start to finish.

Alena reached out and took her sister's hand while listening to the whole horrid tale, squeezing tight when she came to the part of the actual assault. "You shouldn't have gone through that," she murmured through her tears. "That must have been so horrible."

"It was," Alexis cried. "It was. But Grandma took care of it."

"What did she do?" Alena wiped her face with the back of her hand.

"I don't know. But she and Daddy went somewhere and didn't come back for ages. He said it had been taken care of, and the man wouldn't hurt me or anyone else ever again."

"That's good," Alena said. "You won't ever have to worry about him again."

"Yeah, I guess." Alexis looked out the window.

"What is it?" Alena asked, knowing there was something else.

"Dan…Grandma got Dan to examine me. He asked if I was on the pill and I said yes…" She looked down in shame.

"Alexis…" Alena became alarmed. "Are you on the pill or not? Are you…are you…?"

"Pregnant?" Alexis raised her head and looked at her sister under shame-filled eyelids.

Fear bolted through Alena. "Alexis…?"

Alexis shook her head. "No, I'm not. We've done a test, and Dan's put me on some medication just in case he had a disease."

Air whooshed out of Alena. "Oh, thank God. You shouldn't have to deal with a disease at your age, or a pregnancy."

"Mama did." Alexis eyed her sister. "She had you at nineteen."

Alena sighed. "Yeah…I know. But Mama and Daddy were married."

"Not when she got pregnant with you," Alexis reminded her.

A soft giggle came from Alena. "I know. I was made out of wedlock, but Daddy loved her and wanted to marry her, and they had me when they were nineteen and twenty-one. They had family to help. Grandma was there 24/7 helping to look after me and Diana. We've all heard the stories. But times have changed. This isn't the '70s, it's not thirty years ago anymore. No woman should have to have a child when she's just a teenager. God, I certainly couldn't imagine it." Another sigh. "But are you okay? Inside, I mean. No cuts or tears? He didn't cause damage?"

Alexis shook her head. "No, I'm okay."

"Oh, good. I couldn't stand it if he'd hurt you on the inside."

"No. I'm okay," Alexis repeated.

"I'm so sorry," Alena went on. "For everything. I was a selfish brat who only thought about myself. I should never have ignored you. You're my only sister. I should have loved you and doted on you like everyone else did. You were just a baby. I was nearly ten. I knew better. Can you…?" She bit her lip when tears welled in her eyes. "Can you ever forgive me for being a selfish bitch?" she sobbed.

Alexis wasn't sure. Was this a con that Alena was pulling, or was she actually feeling bad and wanted forgiveness? She decided to be honest. "I don't know, Alena. All the years you've treated me badly, and now I just don't know if it can be mended."

"I want to make it up to you," Alena gasped through her sobs. "I know I have a lot to be forgiven for, nineteen years. I want to start today, on my twenty-ninth birthday, so we can remember the date that I grew up and became the big sister to my little sister who needed me when I wasn't there. I want to make it up to you, Alexis, please let me, no matter how long it takes. I want to make it up to you."

Alexis thought about it. But could she be sure it was going to last? And what happened next time when Alena became all about Alena? Sighing, she finally spoke. "We'll give it a try, but it's going to take a long time for me to know you're serious, Alena. It won't happen overnight."

"I know, I know, but I *will* make it up to you, Alexis. I will be the big sister I should have been from the moment you were born. I'll make it up to you, I promise. We'll do everything together, and we can start tonight." Getting up from the seat, she rummaged through one of the bags. "These are from the next rock line. I want you to have them and wear them tonight."

"Aren't you worried I'll take the limelight off you?" Alexis cocked a brow. This was a new side to her sister, and it was scaring her a little.

Alena smiled and stared at her sister. "No. Because I love you and I'm proud of you, and you're my gorgeous baby sister. Now, I want to do your make-up."

By six, everyone had arrived at the house for Alena's birthday.

"Is Alena not here yet?" Angie asked, placing her daughter's present on the buffet. "I would have thought she'd be the first one here to be the centre of attention."

"She's been here since four," Jenny said, getting the table ready.

"What!" Pedro and Angie spun to stare at their mother.

Jenny glanced up from what she was doing. "Yep, she's been here for two hours in with Alexis."

"Have they killed each other yet?" Carlos joked.

"No." Jenny set down the cutlery. "No screaming, but I've heard crying, and lots of it."

"Well…maybe they've finally made up." Diana leant against the kitchen island sipping her wine.

"I hope so," Jenny told her. "After everything that's happened. After what I said to her last night, whatever it was you said to her, it all seems to have sunk in." She finished the table with the placement of the napkins. "I'll go and check on them." After knocking on the door, she opened it to see Alena doing Alexis's make-up on the window seat. The girls were dressed and just putting the finishing touches on. "Well, look at the two of you." Jenny smiled at the 180-degree change.

"Hey, Grandma. We're nearly ready. Just putting Alexis's lippy on." Alena slid the brush over her sister's lips. "There, all done."

"Wait till your family gets a look at you both, so beautiful." Jenny felt her heart overflow. "And getting along."

"Yes, Grandma. We're getting along, and I'm catching up on everything I should have been doing for the last nineteen years." Alena finished off her sister's hair. "We'll be out in a minute."

"Okay. Everyone's here and I'll let them know." Walking back into the living area, Jenny's tears fell.

"Mama, they *have* killed each other." Pedro stared at his mother's face, worried for his daughters.

Jenny shook her head and wiped away her tears. Taking a breath, she paused to collect herself. "I think Alena has finally grown up."

Brows rose at the announcement.

"You're kidding!" Diana exclaimed.

"Everyone," Alena called, and they turned to see her leading Alexis down the hall. "I want to introduce my insanely gorgeous sister, Alexis, in the upcoming rock chick collection that's out for Christmas." She twirled Alexis around. "We have the studded black leather skirt that makes her legs look a mile long. The silver and black sequin silk top tucked in which makes her waist look teeny tiny. And the new mega chunky platform shoes in black. Her jewellery is her own, and isn't she gorgeous?"

The family applauded, and Alexis blushed.

"And I am wearing the amazing dress by *Alexis.*" Alena spun around. "With black high-heel ankle boots, a wide black belt, and silver jewellery. And, if Diana will agree, I want to set up a new line of fashion at *Haus of Stefan*, and it will be called *Alexis*. Because," she added as she turned to her stunned sister, "these dresses that you made D and me are incredibly beautiful and amazing, and I want you to do them for the label. What do you say?"

Pedro and Angie traded surprised glances. Was the new Alena for real? And how long would it last?

"Uh, what?" Alexis was shocked. "I only did them for the two of you."

"Have you not made any for yourself?" Diana asked, excited that they were getting Alexis back into the business.

"Well, yeah. I make a lot of stuff for myself and the twins, but I never thought of doing them for *HOS* I've been there and done that."

"And now I want you to do it again." Alena squeezed her hand, amazed at how much her little sister had grown up. And she had selfishly missed it. "Buy as much of this fabric as you can. It's so beautiful, and you can do whatever designs you want to do. It's going to be based on the patterns and colours. What do you say?"

"Um." Alexis looked at her family, all giving her amazed, stunned, or encouraging smiles. "We'll see. I'm not sure I want to be rushed into that decision. Considering last time."

"Last time is gone," Alena said with a wave of her hand. "The time is now, and I want you to do it because you're incredibly gifted and I want the world to know it. Now, I need a drink and something to eat because I'm hungry."

"So, does this mean little Alena's finally grown up?" Jenny asked her granddaughter. Alena's arms were around Alexis, but Alexis was reluctant and just standing there awkwardly.

Alena grinned. "Yes, Gamma, Pincess A-ena has finally grown up."

"Aw, my babies." Jenny moved over and wrapped her arms around them. "So beautiful; look at you both. So beautiful and amazing and talented. You definitely don't get it from my side of the family."

"Mama!" Pedro exclaimed. "You're beautiful too. Look at you." He came up behind her and kissed her cheek. "Where do you think I got my genes from?"

"Your father," she said dryly. "Look at you. His height, his hair, his..." Her eyes went wide as she stopped herself from saying *his penis* and changed tack. "The girls have yours and Angie's hair and eyes."

"And where do you think Alena and Dom get *their* blue eyes from?" Pedro murmured in her ear.

"You." She grinned.

"Okay, everyone, food's ready," Tomas called as he and Roger started placing plates on the tables that had been joined together.

"Take your places."

With everyone beaming, Alena told the family she wanted Alexis to sit next to her and led her to the side of the table.

Pedro pulled out two chairs. "Princess Alena and Princess Alexis."

With a giggle, Alena helped Alexis take her seat and then sat beside her. "Thank you, Daddy," she said as he took the seat to her left. Angie took the seat to the right of Alexis, with Danté and Dom beside her.

Carlos, Viv and Diana seated themselves beside Dan and Derek, and Tomas and Roger finished serving the meal.

"Thank you, Prince Tomas," Alena said as he lay her plate before her, getting a sappy grin in return.

"Happy birthday, Princess A-ena," he whispered in her ear

Once everyone was settled, they talked about that night's plans.

"I would like to go to *SB3* tonight with Alexis," Alena said and turned to her sister who looked at her in surprise. "The rest of you can come if you want, but I want to go and spend time with my little sister."

"Um." Alexis gulped. "O-kay," she said slowly.

Alena sighed. "I get to spend so little time with family these days. I'm always busy, so I want to take you on tour with me as well," she told Alexis.

"What?" went around the table and all heads turned their way.

"Only if you want to," Alena went on quickly. "We don't spend time together and the only way for me to do that this summer is by taking you on the road with me. I have the room on the bus; we could make it a girls' trip. You and Mama can come, Diana and Aunt Viv and Grandma."

"Sorry, sweetie, I can't get away until August," Jenny told her.

"Neither can I," Viv added. "I've just released a new book and need to do a tour for it."

"And I've got modelling gigs," Diana said. "Sorry."

Disappointed, Alena turned to her mother. "Mama?"

"Well…" Angie paused. "I'm not doing anything for a while. A couple of weeks with my two daughters who are finally sort of getting along would be amazing."

"I don't know if I would want to do the whole tour," Alexis said slowly while she picked at her food. "That might be too much too soon. And besides, you'll be busy all day with interviews and stuff."

"Just come for a couple of weeks then," Alena implored. "We'll be starting in New York where Mama had me. We'll see the twins if they're in town, and you can be in the front row, or come backstage, and I'll wear this dress on stage and tell the world my little sister made it." She looked down at the dress with its swirly geometric pattern in black, white and silver before looking back up at Alexis. "Please. Let me try and make it up to you for all the years I was a mean and selfish bitch. Please." She batted her big blue eyes at her.

"Daddy does that," Alexis mused, glancing past her sister to her father.

"What do I do?" Pedro leaned back to look at his daughter.

"Bat your big baby blues to get what you want." Alexis smiled.

"I do not!" Pedro exclaimed.

"Oh, yes you do," came from almost everyone at the table.

"Ever since you were born," Jenny added, amused at the conversation.

"Mama." He batted his lashes. "I have no idea what you're talking about."

"Don't bother, it doesn't work on me anymore," Jenny told him.

"Liar." He grinned, and she laughed.

"Please, Alexis, will you and Mama come for a couple of weeks with me? It will be so lonely unless I have someone there."

Alexis sighed. "Let me think about it tonight. I'll let you know tomorrow."

"We leave the day after, so you'll need to pack tomorrow," Alena went on, munching on the summer salad her uncles had made.

"I don't have much. Just a whole bunch of *Alexis* originals and *HOS* stuff. That's all my wardrobe has consisted of for years." Alexis took a sip of mineral water, stringing her sister along.

"That will be easy to pack then. And if we need anything we'll buy it," Alena said, and finished off her meal before Tomas brought out the cake. She squealed and clapped her hands. "Cay."

The adults laughed, all remembering back to when she and Diana were little and could only say cay instead of cake.

"Oh, it's a concert stage," Alena cooed, taking in every detail of the gorgeous huge cake before her. "Who made this? Did you make it, Grandma?"

"Of course I did," Jenny said. "Don't I always?"

The cake was Alena's favourite, chocolate sponge, and the first piece went to Alexis. Once the cake was eaten, and the presents opened, it was time for Dom to go as it was his night at the club, and Alena mentioned partying again. "Can we continue this at *SB3*? I want to party with my sister." She squeezed Alexis's hand. "Everyone can come."

"I think a few hours back at the club sounds good," Jenny said. "We haven't been there for a while."

"Haven't seen Dom play for a while either," Spiros added. "If we're not intruding on the birthday girl's night." His eyes twinkled at his granddaughter.

Alena's eyes twinkled back. "Of course not, Grandpa. I want my family to be there. Can we go now?"

"Let's clean up and freshen up first, and then we can go," Jenny suggested. "Dan, Derek?"

"We're up for it," Dan said. "We haven't seen Dom play for a while either."

"It's settled. We're going dancing," Alena said and dragged Alexis off to the bathroom.

Thirty minutes later, they were walking in the back door of the club and hitting the dance floor.

Alena held onto Alexis's hand and danced with her, Diana and Angie. Viv and Carlos revived their '70s and '80s dance moves, Pedro tried break dancing with Danté, and Tomas and Roger, Dan and Derek kept to themselves, dancing with a group of mutual friends. Spiros and Jenny slow danced in one another's arms, still as madly in love as ever.

*****

In New York, Captain Webster was talking to his squad. "In five days, pop star Alena will be in town at Madison Square Gardens. We have been charged with public safety and patrolling the grounds. Almost twenty thousand people will be there, and it's our job to protect her and everyone else. It's only for one night, but she will be back for another concert in August, and we'll have to do it all over again. Any questions?" He glanced around the precinct. "No? Get back to work then."

"Have you heard her sing? She's awesome," Denny Nicolls said to his partner as they headed for the break room. "I've got all of her CDs, all of her film clips on tape, and some of her fashion label in my closet." At twenty-four, he was excited about seeing and hearing her in concert.

"Never heard of her," James said. "Where's she from?" At twenty-eight, James Gardo was one of New York's finest and hoped to make detective by thirty.

"She was born here in New York to a Greek mother and Greek Australian father, and *damn* she's fine," Denny gushed. "She's been singing since she was fifteen in the family's club in Mykonos, Greece. Hit it big here in the U.S. about '03. She and her cousin run a fashion label, and her cousins are models. Diana Villiers, and Steele and Phoenix Stefan."

"What sort of stupid names are those?" James asked, cracking open a bottle of water.

"Stage names," Denny replied. "The twins are Diana's brothers, Alena's cousins. Diana's pretty fine herself if you like the golden-haired blue-eyed type."

"And you said you were wearing ladies clothes." A sly smile slid over James's lips.

"*No, dude.*" Denny was exasperated. "Together they run *Haus of Stefan*. It has men's lines which are really cool and affordable for guys like me."

"You sound really involved with the family," James suggested, wondering if his partner was obsessed and he should watch out for him.

"Nah, man. Diana's mother was a world-famous model and stylist, her father is a movie writer, producer and director. Alena has two brothers and a sister, and her parents are world-famous music producers and writers. Her uncles are gay advocates and AIDS activists along with her grandmother. That's all over any interview she does."

James frowned. If she was so damn famous, how come he'd never heard of, or seen her and her family?

*****

"So, are you coming?" Alena asked Alexis at dinner the next night. They were sitting together at the table, much to the surprise of the family who were all trading glances, silently questioning how long it would last. "You'll have to pack your bags tonight if you and Mama are coming."

Alexis pushed her food around, making her sister wait. "Well…I still don't know."

"Alexis," Alena wailed. "How can you say no to New York?"

"Are you coming, Mama?" Alexis asked Angie, ignoring her sister and putting her off even longer.

"Only if you want me to, my darling," Angie replied, knowing what her daughter would say because she had been home all day packing her bags.

"Well," Alexis dragged it out, teasing her sister. "I suppose I could…"

"Yay." Alena hugged her sister tightly, catching her by surprise. "We're going to have so much fun. We'll be on the road, but we can watch TV together, and sing songs together, and you can get ideas for designs, and I'll get ideas for music. It will be so much fun being together, just you and me and Mama."

Everyone else looked at Alena and Alexis while they ate. Alena was hungrily devouring her food and oblivious to everything else, and Alexis looked at her sister in surprise, still caught off guard by the idea of them having fun together when they'd never had fun together in her whole life.

"So, who else is doing something over summer?" Jenny asked, moving things along.

"We're off to Italy in a couple of days," Tomas said. "You'll have to fend for yourself, Mama."

Jenny's laugh was light. "It's not as though I haven't cooked for us before."

"I know. I just want to take care of you the way you took care of me, us, when we were sick." Tomas sipped his mineral water. As much as he loved the occasional beer or alcoholic beverages, he preferred flavoured mineral water most days instead.

"That's sweet, my baby, but you don't have to," Jenny told him. "Italy sounds good; we might have to get back there one day. It's been a while."

"Italy sounds so nice right now," Dan said. "I'd love to go to Italy."

"We went there a couple of years ago. Don't you remember?" Derek's arm rested on the back of Dan's chair, and he tweaked his hair.

"Did we?" Dan remembered and shook his head in embarrassment. "That's right, we did too. It was so wonderful. But we're going to Santorini for two weeks, so we won't be here either. Hope you don't mind, Jenny."

"Why would I mind?" Jenny asked. "You're honorary members of the family; you can do what you want when you stay here."

"I know. I just feel like we just got here and already we're taking off for two weeks." Dan finished off his beer, grateful for the family environment Jenny had always offered since 1981 when he spent nearly a year helping Tomas and Roger with what they thought was the gay plague.

"Don't worry about it," Jenny said. "Have a holiday. We'll get work done when you get back."

"I can't wait to get back on the beach and do nothing," Dan went on. "It will be good to do nothing for a while."

"Mykonos beaches not good enough?" Tomas joked. "You seemed to think it was pretty spectacular twenty-five years ago when you came here."

"I did, and I do, but sometimes you just need somewhere different to get another perspective," Dan said. "I love it here; that's why we come every year. But I also want to see the other islands as well."

"Fair enough," Pedro said. "And sometimes we want to see the other side of the world. That's why every year we travel somewhere different. We've gone home to Australia, back to the U.S., and Europe. We make sure we take the kids somewhere different every school holidays."

"Definitely one way to get an education," Derek said. "You kids must've been world travellers from the time you were born?"

"D and I were born in New York as you know, so we try to get back once a year," Alena told him. "Are you all coming in August, Daddy?"

"Of course, Bubba," Pedro answered. "We'll all see your last New York show, spend some time in Central Park and Coney Island, and watch the leaves fall in October."

"How long will we be staying?" Carlos asked, surprised by Pedro's comment. "Weeks? Months?"

"Until October at least," Jenny said. "That's only a rough six weeks. I'd like to see autumn come in. What about Halloween?"

Groans went around the table.

"Can we be home by then?" Pedro asked. "We'll have our anniversaries in November, and then it's Thanksgiving, and Christmas tree time. I'd like to be back here for that."

"God, you're already thinking about Thanksgiving, Daddy?" Alena asked. "I'll be lucky to survive getting through the rest of summer. It's only June."

"And you won't be the only one working, Bubba," Pedro said. "Uncle Carlos has a movie to make, I have music to write for it, Viv has a book tour, Grandma has a mega-corporation to run, and Uncles Tomas and Roger are off on holiday."

"Hey, that's only for two weeks. We have some protests and marches to attend later in the year, so we'll be busy too. It's not like we have an easy life. We have a gym to run as well," Roger reminded him.

A grin lit up Pedro's face. "I know. But really, you two do less than the rest of us."

"That's because Mama put us on permanent holiday," Tomas teased. "You must be *so* jealous."

Rolling his eyes, Pedro added, "Yeah, not that I can complain. I love my music, so it's not work for me."

"It's not work for me either, Daddy. I love performing, but trying to figure out a tour is ridiculous. Everything has to be accounted for. I can't just get up on stage and sing because there's a million things to do before I can do it," Alena said. "And on top of that, there's songs to be written, and clothes to be designed, and the label to run."

"Which you have help with," Jenny reminded her. "We all have a business to run Alena, and one day you will be running it. For *your* children and *their* children."

"Oh, don't even think that, Grandma," Alena wailed. "I have too much living to do before I have kids. Mama was popping out Alexis at twenty-nine. I haven't even met someone to have kids *with*. Besides, I like my life that way it is. Lots of singing, lots of fashion, lots of doing what I want to do and not being told by a man." She finished off her drink, dessert long gone. "Now, I have to pack for tomorrow. Mama, you done?"

"I did it today," Angie replied.

"Alexis, you need help?" Alena asked her sister.

"Did it today." Alexis grinned.

"Good. You can come and help me, coz you know I'm horrible at packing." She grabbed her sister's and mother's hands and dragged them out the door.

"Good to see them getting along for once," Diana said. "Guess she really *has* grown up."

"Having something like that happen to your sibling makes you grow up pretty damn quick." Carlos gave Tomas a loving brotherly look.

"And makes you realise how damn special they are and that you can't live without them," Pedro added, from his seat opposite his brothers.

Tomas felt the love from both of them. "It makes you re-evaluate everything in your life, including family."

Jenny watched her sons and her heart beamed with pride. "So, let's hope that's what Alena has done."

*****

"Whoo, what a night," Steele yelled as the young Latino guy sucked his cock.

They were in the penthouse, and he was spread-eagled on the bed, half an hour after they'd stumbled out of a club on 54th and West.

The Latino boy looked up, a grin from ear to ear. "Am I doing it right, Steele?"

"Oh, you're doing it just fine, baby, keep sucking." It was just the two of them in the room. Phoenix wasn't there. He hadn't been interested, and Steele hadn't found another person that was interested enough to take home. So, the Latino boy was it.

Steele glanced down as he ran his hands over the boy's head and through his hair. He couldn't have been more than eighteen, if that, maybe a little too young, a little too inexperienced, but he could teach him.

The boy took what Steele gave him and wiped his mouth with the back of his hand. "Did you like that, Steele? Did I do it right?" He crawled up the bed to lie on top of his idol. His naked body was on top of Steele Stefan, international model and actor. He'd loved Steele for years and he knew he looked younger than his age. He was twenty-three and looked seventeen, or sometimes fifteen. He had Steele beneath him and planted kisses over his body.

"You did it just fine, my Latino lover. You took it like a good fag should. But I want more. Do you like it rough?"

"I like it any way you like it, Steele," the boy said.

Snapping on his condom, Steele kneeled on the bed. "Good. Get against the headboard."

The boy kneeled in front of the headboard and hung on as Steele probed and rammed. He squealed at the pain of such a large cock in his anus, but didn't want Steele to know it hurt. He hung on and grunted when Steele grunted.

"Like it up the ass, do you?" Steele rammed in, thrusting to his words.

"Any way you like it, Steele." The boy gritted his teeth and hung on for dear life to the headboard. He was definitely going to be sore after this.

"Like it rough, butt fucker," Steele said, hanging on to the boy's hair with his right hand, and the headboard with his left. "Tell me you're a butt fucker. You fuck it and suck it. Tell me."

"I'm a butt fucker." The Latino hunk squealed, feeling his luscious thick hair being yanked out by its roots. "I fuck it and suck it."

"Good, take this then." Steele grunted and thrust one last time. He held himself there until he knew he was drained and then slid out of the boy and onto the bed. "Oh, that was good. So good." He lay spread out, gasping while the boy ashamedly curled up.

It had hurt badly. Never had a cock so big done so much damage. He felt like crying, but he wanted to show Steele he could take it like a man. That he could *be* a man. Be the man that he could take home for the night. But this was rough, and he wasn't sure he wanted to stay. "Can I use your bathroom?"

"Mmm? Through there," Steele slurred and waved an arm in the general direction of the ensuite.

The boy got off the bed, grabbed his clothes, and went into the bathroom. Checking himself over, he ripped some toilet paper from the roll and dabbed his anus. Finding spots of blood, he flushed it down the toilet and got dressed. Fuck! Not the first time he'd had a bit of blood, but fuck that was rough. Moving quietly into the bedroom, he found Steele snoring his head off, and seeing his pants on the floor, rifled through the pockets for his wallet. He didn't find one, but found a wad of cash in a money clip instead. Counting it, he noted close to a thousand dollars and pocketed it. "That's for fucking me up rough," he whispered, and quietly and quickly got out of there.

Antonio heard the door open and close. He was in the spare room opposite the master, and figured it was the lover, one of Cabot's many, and wondered what the boy was thinking. They generally all thought the same thing. That getting to suck Steele Stefan was the best thing ever, but getting fucked by him was a nightmare. For some anyway. They couldn't take the roughness. But some could and took it well. Like they knew what to expect. He got up and went downstairs to find the boy going through the fridge and cupboards. "You need to leave now."

The kid, scared that Steele had come down, spun around to face him, but then realised it was someone different. He saw Antonio's outstretched hand pointing at the door and took off through it and downstairs, happy at least that he had over nine hundred bucks in his pocket.

Antonio closed the door and chucked out the food the boy had left on the counter. "No need to get germs from that."

*****

Denny was sitting in James's apartment. They had the day off, and he'd brought all things Alena over to show off. "Isn't she a babe? And look at her sister and cousin. Smokin' hot."

James studied the CD covers and fashion books Denny handed him. This was the first time he was seeing the woman they would be protecting. His captain hadn't even produced a photo. He looked at her big blue eyes framed by black hair, pale skin and petite features. She was definitely a stunner. Her younger sister was a replica, but with brown eyes, and the cousin, Diana, was beautiful. "This one's all right." He pointed to Diana.

"Yeah, she is, and check out her brothers." Denny flicked through to the men's section of the catalogue. "Steele and Phoenix Stefan. They are stunning."

James stared at the twins. One was a little darker, one a little blonder. One was blue-eyed, one green-eyed, but they were identical in every other way. With tight physiques, and pronounced abs, they had a visual look that was quite stunning, and something radiated in their eyes. "Wow, good-looking boys," he murmured without emotion.

"Yeah, but what about Alena? She's a little hottie. I'll put one of her CDs on." Getting up, he slid the disc into James's player. "It's a bit of Greek, a bit of pop, a bit of everything really. Her parents write the music and most of the lyrics. But she's been writing too. They record it all in their studio on Mykonos."

"Mykonos?" James tore his gaze away from the picture of Alena.

"Yeah, man. That's where the family lives. On Mykonos. I'd love to go there one summer. Lie on the beach, get a tan, get a hot girl. Alena preferably."

"Geez, you've got it bad, dude." James shook his head in boredom.

"Yeah, well, look at her. She's gorgeous in that dark exotic way. God, I'd love to plant one on those lips." His brain wandered off,

153

thinking about kissing Alena.

"Plan on stalking her at her show?" James set down the photos and books. "I don't think Cap would take kindly to that."

Denny shrugged. "I at least want to meet her, or get a photo with her. We can't *not* get something."

"I'd say you've got enough." James looked at everything Denny had brought over. "What else is there to get?"

"She'll have merchandise at the show. I wonder if I could get some," Denny said.

"What? T-shirts and jewellery? Yeah, that will really suit you." James snickered and got a beer from the fridge. Cracking it open, he took a gulp. "Better make sure you don't get arrested for stalking." He turned to stare out the window and saw his river view. His place was a small two-bedroom apartment on the west side of the island. He used the second bedroom for an office, and never shared the master. Not that he didn't have girls, just that he'd never asked anyone to move in. At twenty-eight, he was too focussed on making detective at thirty. He wanted to get in the hours and work his way up from the ground floor like his father, the man he looked up to. He wanted to be like him, emulate him, and carry on the Gardo name, so it wouldn't happen yet.

His parents wanted grandkids before they died, and with them in their late 70s and early 80s, it was a fair bet it wasn't going to happen. They held on to the idea of another child in the house, but he just wasn't interested yet. He told them he wanted to make detective, and he was sorry they had him so late in life, but grandchildren just may not happen. There were moments he'd even wondered if it would happen himself. He loved women, loved the way they felt and moved and looked, but he just hadn't found one he wanted to be with long term. Move in with, have a life with, have kids with, and so he kept apologising to his parents. Hell, his father had even asked him one day if he were gay. Not that it would matter, his father quickly added, but if he were, then at least tell them so they'd stop expecting the next generation.

James had been shocked at the conversation; not once had he ever suspected that he was gay. He had no interest in men that way, only women. And he enjoyed sex with women when he had it. Which wasn't often. As a cop, you didn't get a lot of time for recreational activities, so when you did, it had to be quick. At six feet with dark golden-brown hair, and a lean body with a smattering of chest hair, he could get any girl he wanted. Although it wasn't his body they said they cared about. They always said it was his aqua blue eyes that sucked them in.

*****

Alena, Alexis and Angie flew into New York and headed for their apartment building. Every summer it was free in case they came into town, and they could use it whenever they liked. Walking into apartment four, they finally dropped their bags and heaved a sigh of relief.

"God it's good to be back in New York!" Alena exclaimed, flopping down on the couch. "Even if it is just for one day."

"And back in our old apartment," Angie said. "This is where I had you." She sat beside her daughter. "You spent your first three years here."

"You tell us that every time we're here, Mama." Alena giggled. "Hey, I wonder if the twins are in." Calling upstairs, she found Antonio. "Hey cuz, we're in, come down."

Less than a minute later, he barged through the door. "Hey, cuz, whoa." He stopped and stared at Alexis. "Alexis?"

"Hey, cuz." She got up to give him a hug. "Where's Cabot?"

"Ah…" He stared at her hair. "Upstairs, asleep. You cut your hair. It's so cool. Who did it?" He twirled her around, taking in the new style Alexis.

"Grandma. After I hacked half it off," she said. "You like?"

"I *love*. You look hot." He noticed her mother and gave her and Alena hugs. "Hey, Aunt Angie. How come you three are here?" He waved a finger between them. "You two don't get along."

"We do now," Alena said and slid her arm around Alexis's waist.

"Why now?" he asked, perplexed by the fact his cousins had never gotten along, and now they were.

"Because something happened to make me wake up to myself," Alena said.

"What? And can you do the same for Cabot, coz he's a *total* dick lately." He rolled his eyes and crossed his arms over his chest.

Angie and Alena watched Alexis, and Antonio noticed. "What's wrong?"

"Um," Alexis started then slid a hand through her hair.

"What?" Antonio urged, getting a nagging feeling that it was bad. "Alexis?"

"Um…I was assaulted." She couldn't look him in the eye, and so she looked everywhere else but at him.

Antonio just stared, and his shoulders fell. "What?"

"I was assaulted…by a man…sexually," came softly out of Alexis.

"And it's made me realise what a selfish bitch I was, and I'm trying to make it up to my baby sister," Alena added. "Nothing's more important than family, as Grandma always says. I was just too selfish to care. But that's changed."

"Oh, Alexis. Cuz, I'm so sorry." Antonio pulled her into his arms and hugged her fiercely. "Does everyone know?"

Alexis nodded. "Except for Danté; he's too young. I told Dom before we flew out. It happened a couple of weeks ago now. I gave myself a makeover because he pulled my hair, so I cut it off. Grandma finished it. And I haven't told Cabot."

"Oh, cuz. I'm so sorry. Don't even bother telling him, he won't care." Antonio shook his head. "He's still in the same mode Alena was, only caring about himself. How long are you here for?"

"Just tonight," Alena told him. "I do a rehearsal this afternoon, and tomorrow, then take off on my tour bus after the show. Are you coming?"

"Got a spare ticket?" He grinned.

"And backstage passes." Alena mirrored the goofy Stephanopoulos grin. "Would Cabot be interested in coming?"

"I'm always interested in coming, cuz." Cabot managed to make it through the open door with just a robe on. "Hey, everyone. Whoa, Alexis?"

"Cabot!" Alexis greeted him warmly. "What are you on today?"

"Everything, darling." He hugged her and Alena. "Cuz, got tickets for us?"

"Yes, Cabot, as I was explaining to Antonio, you two can have backstage passes."

"Cool, thanks cuz. Aunt Angie." He walked between the girls to give her a hug.

"Cabot. I don't think your parents *or* grandmother would be too happy about this."

"About what, Aunt Angie? Me having fun?" Cabot flopped down on the couch, the robe barely hiding his eleven-inch cock.

"Oh, for God's sake, cover up, bro." Antonio slapped a cushion on his brother's crotch and sat on the couch arm beside him.

"Yeah, sorry, ladies present." Cabot softly blushed. "So, when's this concert, cuz?"

"Tomorrow night. You up for it?" Alena sat opposite him on the other couch.

"I'm always up for it." Cabot grinned.

"Apparently," Angie murmured. "You boys do know the family's coming here in August. Your grandparents will want the penthouse."

"We know, Aunt Angie," Antonio told her. "And Diana wants it for Fourth of July, so we'll get it steam cleaned for her and move into apartment 1."

"Good," Angie said. "And make sure you don't leave any drug paraphernalia lying around. Or condoms. Your grandmother won't tolerate it."

"Yeah, yeah," Cabot muttered. "I'm hungry. Got any food?"

"Go back upstairs." Antonio glanced at him. "There's plenty in the fridge."

"Okay." Cabot got to his feet and flung the cushion at his cousin. "Good seeing you again, cuzzes. We'll party tomorrow night." With a backward wave, he closed the door behind him.

"Jesus, Antonio. Your grandmother's going to kill both of you," Angie spat. "How could you let him get like that? She'll sack Tilly, that's what she'll do. Tilly was supposed to look after the two of you and keep you out of trouble."

"I know, Aunt Angie." Antonio collapsed onto the couch. "But even I can't handle him anymore. He's out of control, and I'm burning out. I don't know how much longer I can put up with his bullshit."

"Do you want out of the business?" Angie asked, noting the depressed expression on her nephew's face.

He shook his head. "No...not the business as such...just...I just need a break from my brother. I'm tired. I'm angry, I'm...I'm...I'm fed up with his garbage." A weary sigh escaped him, and a feeling of dread snaked up his insides.

"Maybe you should take a break then," Alena suggested. "Have fun for once and not worry so much about working. It's not all fun and games."

Yeah." He breathed slowly. "I know. Here it is summer, and we're booked up. When the hell do *we* get a break?"

"Whenever you want one," Angie told him. "Don't let yourself burn out. We've all told you that a million times. Don't overwork, don't burn out, take time out and reboot. Antonio..." Angie sat on the edge of her seat and leaned toward her nephew. "Don't let yourself burn out. If you feel you need time off, take it. Take a holiday away from Cabot. Catch your breath, take time off work. If the companies want you, they'll understand and wait while you have a break."

Another sigh left him, this one deflating him on the outtake. Exhaustion was looming with two jobs a week, flying everywhere; dealing with everyone, and bloody Cabot and his antics was driving a wedge between them. "Yeah, I get it, Aunt Angie. I need a holiday coz I feel I'm on the edge sometimes, and it's not through my own volition. Cabot's pushing me there, and I can't stand it anymore."

*****

While Alena was in New York, Diana was in Paris, having flown out the same day. She was there for a photo shoot with *Madame X* magazine, which was a little racier than *Flair*, so she knew to expect something a little off the books. Turning up at the studios for the shoot, she found everyone packing up. "What's going on?"

"We're taking the shoot on the road," a young woman rolling up cable said. "The photographer wants to get out of the city for something different."

"And how different is different?" Diana watched lights being packed up and carried outside. "The city is right here, we're in the studio."

"But there is no waterfall in the studio, Princess." Charles Kensington told her as he walked into the room. "Are you prepared to do *anything*, Princess?"

The sound of his voice spread chills down Diana's spine, and she turned. "What are *you* doing here? *No one* told me I was doing the shoot with you. You work for *Flair* magazine."

"I work for *the company*, Princess," he snapped. "One big multi corp owns both. They're sister magazines, and when one calls, I say how high." He made sure his cameras were in his bag and turned to Diana. "Ready to get wet, Princess?"

"What?" Diana was confused, but because Charles didn't stick around, she had to run after him. "What *are you* talking about?"

"We're sticking you under a waterfall," Charles told her, loading his bag into the van. "Get in."

"What? I'm not getting in a van with you." Diana defiantly crossed her arms. "Not until you tell me what's going on. I didn't sign up for this."

Charles rolled his eyes at the petulant, beautiful, gorgeous creature before him. No matter how much he tried to put her out of his mind, he couldn't. "You're doing a photo shoot for *Madame X* magazine. I thought we'd do something a little different and get out into the countryside. There's a waterfall about a half hour out, and it will be perfect. Now get in."

Diana, knowing full well what a tyrant Charles could be, considered backing out of the gig. But she didn't work that way and liked to keep business as business as much as possible. And it wasn't modelling, or the magazine, or the concept she didn't like. It was working with Charles Kensington. Arrogant son of a bitch who thought he was God's gift. Not that she had heard anything along those lines. He was ruthless at work and got results, but she'd never heard rumours or gossip of him bedding anyone. She stared at his blue eyes looking for some sort of ulterior motive, but found none. Sighing, she resigned herself to working with him once more and climbed into the van.

"That's a good princess," he sniped and climbed into the passenger seat.

"Stop calling me that you insufferable, arrogant, narcissistic, misogynist pig!" she snapped, surprising everyone within earshot.

He turned around to face her, displeasure on his face. "What do you want me to call you…little girl?"

"I'm *not* a little girl." Fury burned in her blue eyes. "I'm a twenty-nine-year-old woman who's sick of taking shit from the ass called Charles Kensington. This will be the last time we work together, *Mr* Kensington," she spat. "I'll have my manager make sure in future you're nowhere around the photo shoots I do."

"Fine by me, Princess." He slammed the door as the other crew got into the van. "I hate working with childish, immature, insecure, little brats anyway."

"Oh, you must have worked with my brother, Cabot, then," Diana jumped in. "Because I'm *nothing* like that."

"Oh, really," Charles yelled. "I've worked with your brothers, at least *they* know what they're doing."

"Ohhh," Diana growled through clenched teeth. *"How dare you!"* Crossing her arms, she stared out the window the whole way to the waterfall, giving Charles the silent treatment.

Not that he cared; he couldn't wait to see how she handled the choice of outfit he had planned for her, and since she'd be *in* the water, things were about to get real steaming hot, real damn quick.

After getting out in the car park, they walked ten minutes up the track to one of the most beautiful places Diana had seen. "Oh…it's beautiful."

"And perfect in this weather," Charles muttered. "Okay, everyone, get set up. We start shooting in half an hour." He got to work getting his cameras ready while the wardrobe assistant set up an area for Diana to change.

Not that it was much of a dressing room; just a portable, old-fashioned material screen on wheels that could cover her on four sides.

"Here," the assistant said, holding out an item of clothing. "Apparently he wants you to wear this."

Diana frowned. "A man's shirt?"

"That's what he said, and he picked it out himself."

"Is that all?" Diana asked, removing her top and pulling on the shirt.

Charles, being nearby, heard the conversation. "No, it isn't. I want you naked under it. Nothing on, just the shirt."

Diana froze. "You what?"

"I want you naked under it," he repeated, getting a thrill just from saying the words. He knew she'd done photo shoots before where she had a top or bottom off, so it wasn't new for her. In fact, he'd tracked down every photo shoot she'd done to make sure, and he'd found her naked body to be beautifully flawless and perfect. And one he wanted underneath him.

"I don't think so, *Mr* Kensington." She quickly put her top back on and barged out of the change room. "I'm not getting naked for you."

"You're not getting naked for me. You're wearing a shirt, so you won't be naked at all, and besides," he sneered, "it's for the magazine."

"I don't care who it's for, I'm not doing it," Diana declared. "Get yourself another model." Grabbing her bag, she was stopped short by his words as the crew looked on.

"You're being incredibly *unprofessional, Ms* Villiers. From all accounts, your mother was more professional than you."

Diana seethed inside. If it was one thing she wasn't, it was unprofessional. And she had done other half-naked shoots before. So, why did this one annoy her so much? Because of Charles Kensington, that was why. "I am *not* unprofessional," she spat icily and clenched her bag strap in a death grip. "I just don't want to be naked around you."

"You won't be," he countered. "You'll be wearing a shirt."

"With *nothing* underneath." She whirled around to face him. "Face it, you just want to see how far you can push me. How far you can dictate before I push back and tell you where to stuff it. Well, you know where you *can* stuff it, *Mr* Kensington. Right where that arrogant ego talks so much shit from."

"Pull the reins in," Charles snapped. "We're both professional people here to do a job, and when I suggested it, the magazine loved it."

"Oh, I'm sure they did," Diana yelled, her blood boiling. "*You* promised me wet and naked on a platter, and *I* wasn't even consulted."

"You don't need to be," he yelled back, noticing how her pupils dilated when she was angry, and a flush came to her cheeks. "You're just the model. *I'm* the photographer."

"Well, *if that's the way you feel, I'm just the model*, you can get yourself another one," Diana snapped and turned on her heel. Unfortunately, her heel caught between small rocks and tree roots poking out of the ground, and down she went in a flurry of arms and legs. "Argh!"

"Diana." Charles and the others rushed to her side. "Are you okay? Here, let me help you." If she injured herself on his shoot, he was a dead man.

"Oh, I hope I haven't scraped anything," she wailed softly as crew members helped her up into a sitting position. "It will take ages to heal."

Charles gently took her hands and cleaned them with a wet handkerchief while the assistant wiped her face over. Checking her legs, he gave her the all clear. "You're good to go," he said softly, looking into her teary eyes. "No scrapes, no cuts, your beauty is saved. Are you okay?" He was kneeling in front of her and waved the rest of the crew away.

Sucking in air, she calmed herself. "I haven't fallen like that since I was a kid. But I'll be okay, as long as I'm not scraped." She examined her arms and hands.

"No, you're not." Charles took her elbow and helped her stand. The closeness was driving him nuts, and he didn't even know the last time he'd touched her, or if he'd ever touched her.

"Oh, my clothes." She groaned, looking down at her soil stained top and skirt. "Oh, well, I guess it will come out. They're only clothes."

"You know, Nancy the wardrobe stylist here can clean them for you while we do the shoot. They should be dry by then," Charles suggested lightly, not wanting to put her offside again.

Diana's brow went up. "I don't like the fact you decided how *I* was going to dress for this shoot, *Mr* Kensington. So, I don't appreciate being told I need to be naked under a white shirt that will end up see-through if it gets wet, and then all *will* see that I'm naked underneath."

"It's for a *French* magazine." His brow matched hers by rising all the way up. "They like that sort of thing."

"Maybe so, but since I *am* a professional, unlike you pointed out, I will do it and hate it. And then I will *never* be photographed by you again. Because if you think I'm a piece of meat for you to ogle at, then you can think again. I am not here to do your bidding. I'm here to do my job," she said quietly. "And I would like as few people on set as possible." With a shake of her head, she walked over to the makeshift dressing room and changed into the shirt.

Charles went back to his cameras. "Okay, everyone, finish setting up, we're going to keep this professional. No unnecessary staring, no sly remarks, we're being professional here." Why the hell had he changed his tune? He'd never told a shoot crew to be professional. They'd always leer at the models, cracking jokes about their tits and ass and they didn't care if the models liked it or not. But Diana Villiers was different. She was classy and elegant, respectful and beautiful, and gorgeous, and a woman he wanted to kiss and kiss desperately.

Okay, Kensington, keep it in check, can't let her see how much you want to fuck her.

The models he *had* fucked had only gotten it once. They just didn't do it for him, but somehow, Diana did. "Okay, ready on set. Ms Villiers, we're ready for you."

Taking a deep breath to steady herself, Diana stepped out from behind the curtain wearing nothing but the shirt and her flip flops so she could walk over to wherever he wanted her. Her air hung in loose tendrils down her back, and she had barely any make-up on. "So… where do I start?"

Charles blinked. And stared. And blinked again. She was so naturally breathtakingly beautiful she took his breath away. "Ah…" He saw her staring at him. "We'll start in and around the pool, so you stay dry."

Directing her where to stand so she was in front of the waterfall, he took picture after picture as she posed in the sunlight streaming through the rich green canopy of trees. The whole waterfall was drenched in light, and it gave off a truly magical presence.

Diana moved naturally, standing carefully on the rocks, balancing, tiptoeing, flinging her hair back. Stretching her legs out, she moved over the rocks like a nymph, back and forth until Charles called time, and that it was the moment to move into the water.

He kept taking photos while she carefully stepped into the pool.

"Ooh, it's chilly," she said, watching for any creepy crawlies. "Anything in here I should worry about?"

"We've checked with the park rangers; nothing to worry about," a crew member said.

"Stand still and look over your shoulder," Charles called out and captured Diana looking ethereal. "Okay, keep moving."

She moved until she was waist deep.

"Look at me, great, great, beautiful," Charles said. "Keep moving."

She moved until the water just covered her breasts.

"Hold it there, face me, look at me, beautiful," Charles told everyone. "Okay, get wet, but not the face."

Carefully, Diana backed up to the water and let it wet her hair. "Oh, God, it's cold."

Good, Charles thought, *cold water equals erect nipples, and God how I want to suck on them.*

"What now?" Diana asked, trying to keep her face dry as she waded in front of the waterfall.

"Are you standing straight?" Charles asked. "We need you in front of the waterfall, but out of the water."

"How am I supposed to do that?" Diana frowned and kept an eye on the water for slippery things.

"Stand straight, walk forward, I'll tell you when to stop," Charles replied, readying his camera.

Standing, she found the water was still waist high and walked forward until it was thigh high.

"There, perfect, now pose." Charles snapped away as Diana posed.

Left, right, arms up, back arched, she did it all. Her beautiful pert breasts and golden thatch were on display through the wet shirt.

Oh, God how he wanted her right there in the water. How he could take her and give it to her how he wanted. But they were being professional, and he needed to lead by example. Shooting more pictures, he zoomed in on Diana's face, her breasts, her crotch and got every shot from every angle that he could. Once the sun shifted so there was no more ethereal light, he called time on the whole shoot. "We're done, start packing up."

Diana quickly moved to the edge and had help from Nancy, who gave her a towel to wrap around herself and her flip-flops to wear back to the change room.

"Half an hour people; be done by then," Charles called, packing his camera bag.

Diana changed into her clothes, which Nancy had cleaned and hung up to dry, and her shoes. She wrung out her hair with the towel, deftly braided it, and wrapped it into a bun at the back of her head. Making sure she had everything, she zipped up her bag and slipped out from behind the screen just as one of the crew folded it up to take back to the van. Except for the odd crew member, she and Nancy were the only ones left, and they hurried back to the van to find Charles barking into his phone from the passenger side.

"I've got them. You'll get them once I've developed them, not before…yes, I know they're for your magazine, but you don't need them until next week, so stop bitching and let me do my work." Snapping his phone shut he snapped at the crew. "Are we done yet?"

Yesses floated through the crowd, and van doors were shut.

"All right, let's get going then. We have to get Princess back to her life."

Diana's jaw clenched. He had been so placid during the shoot, bordering on respectful and well mannered, not calling her *Princess* once. And he had seemed to care when she'd fallen, looking over her to make sure she wasn't hurt. Now, he was back to his arrogant ass of a self, being rude and disrespectful. "Just when I thought you actually might be human and have some manners and respect, you turn back into the ass we all hate," she spat.

"Oh, please," Charles sneered. "Like I'd ever show Princess respect and manners. Too high and mighty for my liking."

"That's because it means I'm too good for you. I'm above you in manners, respect and decency. And you have none."

"Oh, and Princess has all of them, does she? Puh-leeze."

"Ooh," she growled. "I hate you."

"Get in line," he muttered.

Once again they journeyed in silence, and when they got back to the studio, Diana stormed out of the van and caught a cab back to her hotel room while Charles went upstairs to start developing the photos.

"Ooh, that insufferable, no good, two-bit, arrogant, hateful, jerk for brains." She ran out of gas, and having no one to talk to, rang her manager, Adrienne. "I hate him. I never want to work with Charles Kensington again. He's a jerk for brains, and I hate him. Whenever anyone wants me to do a shoot for them, tell them I'll only do it if it's not with him. I hate him. He made me fall over in the mud, and my clothes are stained."

"Are you okay?" Adrienne asked. "You're not hurt or scraped?"

"No, thank God." Diana exhaled. "That was probably the only moment he seemed to care about me as a human being. That I may have been hurt."

"Well, he would be at fault if you were," Adrienne told her. "He's the one who suggested that place, and if anyone got hurt, it would be on him."

"Ooohhh, if only it were," Diana growled. "I hate him. If I was hurt, I could sue him and teach him a lesson. Maybe I should fake an injury."

"You could try and get him to pay for the dry cleaning."

"But that's nothing." Diana paced back and forth. "He's, he's, insufferable and arrogant, and a jerk. Surely I can get emotional distress money, or something."

Adrienne laughed. "Are you kidding? What it sounds like is, the two of you have it bad for each other and all this *I can't stand him* is actually code for *I want to kiss him so bad.*"

"Oh, don't be absurd!" Diana exclaimed. "There's nothing about that man that I like. He's hateful and arrogant and narcissistic—"

"And deep down you're probably crazy about him and need to sort this rubbish out. You complain every time you work with him."

"Not every time," Diana defended. "Only the last couple of years. I worked with him when I was nineteen, and he was fine. *Better* than fine, and years after he was fine, but the last couple of years—"

"Maybe it's because he sees you as a beautiful woman now instead of a child," Adrienne butted in. "He could be interested in you, too."

"Oh, I doubt it. The only person Charles Kensington is interested in is Charles Kensington. Do you know what he said to me today? That he's worked with my brothers and Cabot acted better than me. Can you believe that? Cabot's as bad as *he* is. In fact, they're perfect for each other. Maybe I should set them up."

"Isn't your brother gay?"

"Bi. Even though he denies it." Diana frowned.

"But is Charles gay?"

"How the hell should I know!" Diana snapped. "What I *do* know is they would be perfect for each other. They're both so arrogant, narcissistic, self-absorbed, self-centred, egotistical—"

"Okay, I get the picture," Adrienne said. "Clearly, you don't want to work with him anymore, and that's fine. I'll inform all agencies in the future. But I'm going to suggest you get to the bottom of your ill feelings toward him and sort them out before it eats you away."

Diana flopped onto the couch. "I *do not* have feelings for him!"

"I said *ill* feelings," Adrienne repeated, amused at what was going on. *Ah,* she thought, *true love at work.*

Diana thought about it. "Well, I definitely have those. *Lots* of them."

"Then sort them out and get over him. I gotta go."

Diana got up and paced around her hotel room, not even noticing the lovely view of the Eiffel Tower. *Oh, I definitely have ill feelings. He's an arrogant jerk for brains who only thinks about himself.* The way he'd suddenly started sleazing over her two years ago after not working together for nearly five years was confusing. Had something happened to him? Had he gotten a bump on the head to change his attitude? *Well, I hope he gets over himself because he's a pain in the ass.*

*****

In the photography studio, Charles was processing the shots. At least, *he had been.*

He'd sat for the last ten minutes staring at a shot of Diana under the waterfall, arms above her head, back arched, eyes closed, hair hanging wet down to her pert ass. The white shirt clung to every beautiful curve of her body, showing off the dark nipples of her beautiful breasts, and the dark thatch between her legs. It was the perfect shot. *The* shot of the whole shoot.

The shot that showed what a woman she was. Showed what a womanly body she had. Showed him she was more than the princess he called her. When she'd fallen, he'd panicked and wanted to care for her. Wanted to wipe away all of the mud and leaves and twigs. When she was in the water, he'd wanted the world to disappear and it to be just them, and he'd imagined taking his clothes off and joining her in the pool, making love to her under the waterfall. It was beautiful, it was perfect. It was interrupted by the damn crew.

He sighed. *God, she's so beautiful. Like a young Vivian Villiers. Almost exactly the same except for the eye colour, and blue suits her perfectly. If we have a child, it would be blue-eyed too.*

Where the fuck did that come from?

He was so startled he nearly toppled the stool he was sitting on.

A child? What the fuck? What am I thinking about having a child with her for? We're not a couple. We certainly haven't fucked, but I'd like to. Oh, God, how I'd love to fuck her. He imagined her breasts in his hands, his mouth, the perfect areolas on the perfect breasts. Just the right size and darkness for her complexion. And her legs were long and shapely and would wrap around him, holding him in place while he let free his seed. Oh, how he wanted to release inside of her. Show her what a man he was and what he could do. She wouldn't want another, wouldn't *need* another. Just him. Just him to please and pleasure her as no other man ever had.

I wonder how many men she's had? One, two, a dozen? None! Oh, it would be even more perfect is she was a virgin. She certainly acted virginal all the time, but if she'd never had a man before he would be her first. Her last. Her only.

What the fuck, dude! Her only? What the fuck are you thinking?

*****

After rehearsal, and having dinner together at *Maxim's*, which was still going over twenty-five years later, Alena, Alexis and Angie took a carriage ride around Central Park and made it back to their apartment by midnight.

"Didn't you use to live across the park, Mama?" Alena asked as they stood out the front of their building, staring at the New York night.

"That's right, sweetie. We were only there a few months before everything changed."

"What changed, Mama?" Alexis asked, having always been curious about her parents' past. She always knew they left out the details when talking about it, as if they didn't want the kids to know certain things.

"Ah…" Angie knew she had to be careful. "Well, your daddy was at 69, I was in Juilliard, and then we ended up in Greece getting married and pregnant. Once that happened, your grandma got us this apartment building, and we moved in."

"There's more to it, isn't there, Mama?" Alena probed.

"I don't know what you mean, sweetie." Angie ushered the girls inside and into the lift. "We weren't there long before we got married. We'd only been here just three months, so they went quickly." They walked into their apartment. "It's late, and you have rehearsal tomorrow and then the concert, Alena, so we all need some sleep. Do you two mind sharing a room?"

"Of course not, Mama," Alena said. "We'll be okay."

"Okay. Do you need me to tuck you in?" Angie grinned at her lookalike daughters.

"Mama!" Alexis said.

But Alena cut her off. "Why not. You haven't done it for ages."

"Okay. I'll be in soon." Angie shooed them away and walked into the master to get ready for bed.

"You want her to tuck us in?" Alexis asked, grabbing the twin bed by the window.

"Why not?" Alena asked. "We never shared a room unless we were on holiday, and we're doing it now. I think it will be sweet of Mama to tuck us in."

"I wish she'd tell us the truth about their lives before we were born." Alexis slid into her nightie and picked up her make-up wipes from the chest of drawers between the beds. The bathroom was too small to keep their make-up *and* toiletries.

"What with?" Alena removed her earrings and popped them into her jewellery case.

"Haven't you ever noticed that whenever Mama and Daddy, or Uncles Carlos, Tomas and Roger, or Aunt Viv talk about their life before us, especially here in New York, they always leave bits out?"

"Like what?" Alena ran a brush through her hair and grabbed the make-up wipes.

"Like just before, when I asked about when they lived across the park. She skirted the issue. Have Diana or the twins ever mentioned something about back then? Do they know something?"

Alena thought as she used a second wipe. "Cabot did allude to something he'd seen, but he never elaborated. I've wondered if I should ask him more about it. See what he knows."

"Do you think he knows exactly what it is, though?" Alexis threw back the covers to her bed and fluffed up the ruffled pillow.

"Don't know. But we will know if we ask."

"Ask what?" Angie came in dressed in her nightie and dressing gown.

"Ah…" Alena glanced at Alexis, trying to come up with something in a hurry.

"If we can sleep with you tonight?" Alexis covered with a glance at her sister.

"What!" That caught Angie off guard. "It's been a long time since I've had one of my babies sleep with me."

"Yeah, but we're all here," Alena jumped in. "And we're your only daughters, *and* we're finally getting along, and you'll be *sooo* lonely without daddy."

Angie laughed. "Well, except for when I was in the hospital having you guys, we've never slept apart, so it will be strange for the next two weeks."

"Please, Mama?" Alena wheedled. "Please."

"Oh, okay," Angie said. "Have you finished up?"

"Just gotta go pee," Alena said and dashed into the small bathroom off the second bedroom.

Alexis followed Angie into the master and climbed in, snuggling under the covers as Angie got in.

Alena came bounding into the bedroom and got in beside her mother, hugging her. "Ooh, it's been so long. Is the bed even big enough?"

"Of course it is," Alexis said, and was enveloped into her mother's arms.

"It's big enough for all of us," Angie said. "Now, get some sleep, we have a big day and night tomorrow."

*****

"Tomas...Tomas..."

Visions of a man drifted through James's head while he slept.

"Tomas...Tomas..."

Jet-black hair and eyes; a tanned god stood before him.

"Tomas...Tomas..."

The face. The face he'd dreamed of all of his life.

"Tomas...Tomas..."

He was at a bikini bar on a beach. He was sitting there talking to the bartender.

"Tomas...Tomas..."

Why was he dreaming of that now...? That face...

They were on a dock somewhere, just coming off a ferry and there he was...

"Tomas...Tomas..."

He saw the man in a department store. He was in his father's arms and talking to a woman who was not his mother, and this beautiful man had come up to them...

"Tomas…Tomas…"

He'd said his name and reached out to him, but it frightened the man, and he ran. Ran from him, from the store. He was only little, seventeen months if that, but he knew the face, knew the man, and had dreamt of him ever since.

"Tomas…Tomas…"

He saw gym equipment. They were in a steam room; they were making love in the steam. He breathed in his lover and made him his.

"Tomas…Tomas…"

They were on an island making love…they were in an adult club… they were in a café…they were in a motel room…

He woke; panting, sweating, wondering what the fuck that was.

Throwing back the covers, he went into the kitchen and grabbed a bottle of water from the fridge, downing the whole thing in five seconds flat. *What the fuck was that dream?* He'd always had visions of a guy in a department store, seeing his face on a newspaper a few years later, but none of that other stuff had ever happened. He'd never dreamed about fucking another man before, and he wasn't interested in doing so now. He wasn't gay, but he'd just dreamt of having sex with a man. So, who the fuck *was* that man?

He remembered back to when he was little, in his father's arms at a big scary department store, and a strange woman greeting his father as if she knew him. And apparently his father had known her and liked her, and then *he* had walked up. This beautiful man whose voice he recognised, whose eyes and lips and face he knew. But *why* did he know? *How* did he know? What the hell was going on?

And then he remembered a year or two later, walking up to his father as he sat on the couch and seeing that man, Tomas, on the front of the paper he was reading, and pointing to him. Telling his father it was Tomas. His father had looked frightened, while *he'd* been angry. Angry that there was another man in the picture with Tomas. He didn't know who it was, just that he was angry that he had his hands on his Tomas.

He'd dreamt about it for the rest of his life. Seeing Tomas in the department store. Dreamt about him almost every night since. How happy it made him to see Tomas that day back in 1980. All these years, nearly three decades, and he still remembered hearing that name. Seeing that face. Seeing that beautiful Greek god he loved.

Leaning against the sink, James was more confused than ever. He'd always been told that Tomas was a figment of his imagination; a fairy godfather or something, but the dreams kept happening, and now, what the fuck were these new ones? Why was he dreaming of having sex with Tomas, whoever he was? He'd never found him; never bothered tracking him down. His father had told him one night he was a figment of his imagination after he'd woken, screaming his name. His father had come running in and soothed him, telling him it was just a dream, and that he was a guardian angel looking over him. But in all the years after, he'd never stopped dreaming. Never stopped wondering who the hell he was. And even after getting through the police academy and into the force, he'd never bothered finding out. In all these years, he'd never bothered finding out if he ever existed and who he truly was.

But the new dreams...he was older, he *felt* older in them. He was an adult and falling in love with this man, Tomas. They were watching each other at the beach bar, and on the dock. But where were they? What place was it? And the gym and steam room? That was their first time together, that much he felt. He knew, though it was a dream, it had to come from somewhere. The *images* had to come from somewhere, because he sure as hell had never actually had sex with this guy. But in the steam room, he'd sensed it was Tomas's first time, and he had been experienced. And then there was the beach. It was warm, tropical, beautiful, and desolate, and they were alone, making love all day and into the next. He was so beautiful. His body was gloriously tanned and lean and fine, and what a big cock he had.

"Oh, my God, I can't be thinking about a guy's cock," James groaned. "I'm *not gay* for fuck's sake. I'm not gay." But why was he dreaming about sex with the man he'd seen when he was little? Why did he know he was older in these other scenes? How could he know that, and why did it feel normal?

Why did it feel right? Why did having sex with a man that didn't exist, feel right?

"Argh," he growled and prowled around his small apartment. Why did he always dream about this man? Why did he always wake up with an erection after, and why was he now dreaming of other things, other places, other times? And why did he remember his name?

Tomas.

Tomas who? Was he real? Could he be tracked down if he was? Could he use his cop instincts and police resources to find him? Since he didn't have a surname, he had no idea what he could go on. *Maybe I should ask Dad?* But then he'd denied the guy existed. *Hang on; he was on the front of a newspaper. What year was that…I was…two, I think. Not long after I first saw him. Well, that was '81. Maybe I could track down papers from that time? That should be easy enough. I'd just have to go to the library. Why haven't I done that before?*

Pacing back and forth, he tried to get his mind off Tomas by thinking about Alena. *I have a pop princess to be on patrol at the Garden for. I wonder if her cousin will be there.* She was a hottie. He loved beautiful, classy looking women, and Diana was ethereal; whereas Alena had that dark exotic look with black hair, bright blue eyes, just like her cousin. *I wonder if she's a pop princess like so many others, coz if she is, this is not going to be fun.*

*****

Alena finished the rehearsal at the Garden and went for a late lunch with Alexis and Angie to *Buffalo,* a hot new steakhouse they'd heard of, before hitting their apartment for a quick nap and to pack their bags. At 6:30, they were back at the Garden and leaving their bags on Alena's tour bus.

"Oh, my God, was that Alexis?" Officer Denny Nicolls breathed, eyeing the dark-haired beauties as they walked inside. He and James were near the back entrance and had let the car through and watched as all three women piled out.

"Who?" James asked and stared in their direction.

"Whoa, she's cut her hair off and looks awesome. Wait." He looked at his partner. "What do you mean who? Alexis Stephanopoulos,

Alena's sister. That was their mother, Angelina Stephanopoulos. She's only five five, Alena's five eight, and Alexis is five ten. She takes after their father, Pedro, who's six foot. The eldest brother is tall too." He craned his neck to see more.

"Jesus, you really *are* a stalker, aren't you?" James sniggered. "Going to sneak onto the bus and paw through her underwear?"

"What! Dude, you suck." Denny punched him in the arm and kept watching. "These girls sure are beautiful. Hell, Alexis looks stunning with short hair."

"God, stop it. It's bad enough we have to be here, I don't need to hear you go on and on and on about her." James turned his back, rolling his eyes at his partner's carry on.

"Why? You got something better to do with your time, Officer Gardo? Got a hot date you missin' out on?" Denny teased, grinning from ear to ear as they walked back to the gate.

"Hardly," James muttered, seeing the crowd already down the driveway waiting for the pop star to leave. "Let's hope things don't get too rowdy."

"Nah, we should be fine." Denny glanced over the crowd. "We've got the gates, we've got the cops, the bus is in the underground car park. We should be fine."

"I hope so," James murmured, a bad feeling rising in his gut. "I hope so."

"Oh, my God, it's so awesome. Have a look." Alena led them inside the bus, and they all oohed and aahed at the opulence of it.

"At least you'll be comfortable for the next ten to twelve weeks," Angie said, leaving her bags on one of the guest bunks. "You seem to have everything you need. TV, kitchen, laundry. Wow, you even have a washer/dryer." She stared into the cabinet next to the bathroom.

"Everything we need, Mama," Alena said. "But now I gotta go get ready. Are you coming, or do you want to stay here a little longer?"

"We'll come now," Angie told her, and they followed Alena inside the underground labyrinth to her dressing room and helped her change into her first outfit.

"Mama? Help me with this zip." Alena spun around for Angie to zip up her dress. It was short black leather with cut-outs, and she wore silver knee-high boots and jewellery.

"Are you going to be able to get out of this in a hurry?" Angie asked, watching her daughter check herself in the mirror.

"Yes, Mama. I've got my costume changes down pat." Smoothing her hair, she critically eyed herself, and then her eyes lit upon Alexis's reflection. "Will you two stay backstage, or go down front?"

"Oh, I think we'll go down front," Angie said. "Be part of the crowd."

Alexis stopped watching the wardrobe assistant and turned to her sister. "You know you have the wrong boots with the wrong outfits?"

Alena smiled. "You sound like Aunt Viv. Yes, I know. But I always like to be a bit different."

"How long is the show going to be?" Angie asked, eyeing the short dresses and thigh high boots for the rest of the costumes.

"An hour and a half," Alena said before starting her vocal warm up.

"I wonder if the boys will make it?" Angie said to Alexis.

"Don't you mean, Steele and Phoenix Stefan?" Alena stopped her warm up long enough to say before going back to it.

Alexis giggled. "Yes, how can we forget. Steele and Phoenix Stefan."

"Someone mention our names?" The twins walked into the room.

"It was like Fort Knox, cuz. Every cop frisked us," Antonio said, giving everyone a hug.

"Which *I thoroughly* enjoyed." Cabot grinned and slumped on the couch. "When's this show start, cuz?"

Pat Richards, tour manager, came through the door. "Fifteen minutes. We'll get you to the back of stage now. Why don't the rest of you go out and enjoy the show." He held his arm out to encourage everyone to leave. "Alena, the band is warming up, go warm up with them."

"Yes, Pat," Alena sang and rolled her eyes, hugged her mother and sister. "Make sure I can see you from the stage."

"Okay, my baby, break a leg." Angie held on a little longer before letting go.

"Thanks, Mama."

"Hey, cuz, have a great show." Cabot gave her a quick peck on the cheek, but Antonio hugged her.

"Thanks." She followed Pat out of the room, singing all the way.

The rest of the group made their way to the front of the stage amid the frenzied screaming of the twenty thousand strong crowd.

"Jesus H Christ." Cabot covered his ears. "I hope they stop that. We won't be able to hear anything else."

Antonio cocked a brow at his brother. It had been a battle just to get him dressed and out the door on time, and he just knew in that outfit, low slung leather pants, unbuttoned shirt, and chains around his neck, that he was looking to get laid. "Jesus H Christ yourself Cabot. This is a concert, so there's going to be a lot of screaming."

"Yeah, but can they at least shut up?" Cabot whined. "It's giving me a headache."

"That's probably the coke you snorted," Antonio reminded him, and Cabot pulled a face in return.

The house lights dimmed, and the announcer came over the speaker. "Ladies and gentlemen…all the way from Mykonos, Greece, comes pop sensation…Alena…"

The crowd went wild as the curtain flew up to the strains of her latest hit, *Baby, Hit Me Up*. She danced, she pranced, she got twirled around by her dancers, and with five costume changes, she flew through fourteen years' worth of hits. One of the changes was the dress Alexis had made her, and she made sure to tell the crowd. "I wanna give a shout out to my stunningly beautiful sister, Alexis, who made this incredible dress I'm wearing." She smoothed it down and did a little twirl. "She's down front with our mother, world-famous music composer, Angelina Stephanopoulos, and my very good-looking cousins, Steele and Phoenix Stefan."

The crowd went wild, and Steele turned and threw his hands up in the air and waved to them. Antonio shook his head and traded amused glances with his aunt and cousin.

"I'm still trying to get her to do a new line at *Haus of Stefan*, so these awesome designs can be for everyone. Would you buy it?" Alena asked the crowd.

Twenty thousand people screamed in return.

"That's good, I hope you do. This next song will be the next single from my current album *Baby, Hit Me Up,* and it's *Love Will Shine Again.*"

At the end of the show, she did two encores and finally left the stage. The family made their way backstage to congratulate her and help her pack up and get ready to leave.

"That was awesome, my baby." Angie hugged her. "I'm so proud of you."

"Thanks, Mama, whoo, I'm hot and so thirsty." She grabbed a sports drink from the bar fridge and gulped it back. "Oh, I needed that. Are we able to go, Maria?" she asked her manager.

"You bet, kiddo. Unless you want to shower and change now…or you can go on the bus…and we'll leave soon after."

"I might just have a quick shower here," Alena said and looked around for her things. "Back soon." She dashed into the bathroom and was out in fifteen minutes with damp hair and dewy skin. "I'm done. Where are the boys?" She noticed they were gone.

"Cabot disappeared, and Antonio went to find him." Alexis rolled her eyes. "But then, what else is new."

"Ugh. I hope he's not getting into trouble," Alena said, and they made their way down the corridor.

*****

James eyed the crowd at the gate. It had gotten larger through the night, and larger still since the show had ended, and he knew a puny padlock was not going to stop a horde that big. He saw his fellow officers try and move people on, and they had called in reinforcements. But still, it wasn't enough. He heard a sound behind him and turned to see people come into the underground car park, climbing into cars and getting the bus ready. He didn't see anyone that looked like Alena, but she was probably on her way.

"They've broken through…" came over the two-way radio, and James glanced around to see a few thousand plus strong crowd racing down the driveway toward them.

"Inside," he yelled, and ran for the car park, hitting the button to bring the doors down to keep them out. But many of them dived under the doors and got in.

"Get back," he yelled, seeing the three dark-haired women step out of the back door and walk toward the bus. "Get back in." He didn't know how many were behind him, but he could hear the metallic banging on what he could only assume were the roller doors.

Tyres screeched, and cars drove into his line of vision, so he flew over the SUV's hoods. Everyone was frozen as more cars blocked the way of fans, frenzied and screaming.

Alena was frozen, as was her family, and she stared at James as he flew toward her. She had never experienced this type of frenzy in all of her years singing and didn't know what to do.

Loud pops went off and people screamed, grinding to a halt as they stopped and turned.

James dived at Alena, flying out of the way of the gunshots.

"Gun," someone yelled, and the crowd tried to run back the way they had come.

Denny, following James's lead, flew at Alexis, who stood stunned, and they fell to the ground.

Angie got flattened against the bus behind the open door.

Denny managed to get his hands behind Alexis's head, so it didn't smash into the ground. They landed and waited for the screaming to stop.

Alexis stared up into Denny's eyes, but instead of seeing him, all she saw was her attacker. "Get off me." She panicked. "Get off me, get off me, get off me." Her voice rose to panic level, and she crawled backward away from him.

"Alexis," Angie yelled and flew to her daughter's side. "Are you okay, my baby?" She saw the panic and fear. "Are you hurt? Where are you hurt?"

"Just get him off me. Get him off me."

"He's not on you, sweetie, it's okay. It's not him, it's not him," she soothed her. "It's just a police officer trying to save you, it's okay." She smoothed her daughter's hair.

"I'm sorry." Denny put a hand out. "Did I hurt you? I didn't mean to." He gazed at Alexis. Her beauty, made more alive and vibrant by the new short do, knee-length black leather skirt, black leather short sleeved top tucked in, chunky platform shoes, and a long dangly earring in one ear, drowned him. She was beautiful, and he was falling.

"No, no, it's not you," Angie told him. "She recently went through a traumatic experience, and it's still fresh. This obviously brought it back."

"Oh," Denny pulled his hand away. "I'm sorry."

"It's not your fault," Angie said and looked over at Alena to see an officer on top of her.

"Oh, oh." Alena gazed into eyes she'd never seen the likes of before. Aqua blue. Big beautiful eyes framed by brown lashes and brows, a light tan, and dark brown hair.

"Ah." James grunted. "Are you okay, miss?" He stared into beautiful blue eyes, pale skin, and black hair. "Oh, you're her."

"Um." Alena gulped. His crotch was pushing into hers, and she felt the enlargement. "Yes."

"Gardo, Nicolls." Captain Webster made his way through the dispersing crowd and around the SUVs blocking them. "The crowd is leaving, but we still haven't found a shooter or a gun. Is everyone all right?"

Denny stumbled back and stood, setting his hat on his head. "All good, sir."

"Good, Nicolls. Good." Webster waited for James, but he didn't move. Clearing his throat, he said, "Officer Gardo, is everything all right?"

Realising his captain was speaking to him, James quickly got to his feet and held out his hand to Alena, who lightly bounced to her feet.

"Gardo?"

James blinked. "Sir?" He looked from Alena to Webster. "Sir?"

"Your uniform." Webster raised a brow.

Glancing down, James quickly straightened his clothes and picked up his hat from where it had landed.

Pat and Maria came out. "What happened?"

"The crowd got through, and we heard what we thought was a gun. But we haven't found one, or a shooter," Webster told them. "We're getting rid of the crowd now."

They all glanced towards the driveway. The crowd was down to a hundred or two, and they were being moved on.

"Are you all right, Alena?" Maria touched her elbow.

Alena was still looking at tall, dark and gorgeous James. "I'm fine, Maria. This…*brave* officer saved me."

"Thank you, thank you so much." Maria shook his hand. "Fine officers you've got here Captain. Go beyond their duty to the public."

"Ah, yes, they do." Webster rocked back on his heels. "We are here to protect and serve."

"Good, good," Maria went on, seeing Angie and Alexis on the ground. "Mrs Stephanopoulos, are you and your daughter all right?"

"We're fine, Maria," Angie said, helping Alexis to her feet. "Just a bit shaken up." They brushed themselves down. "Looks like we have *two* fine officers to thank for saving us, Captain Webster."

"Ah, yes." Webster did the instructions. "Officer Denny Nicolls."

Denny tipped his hat at Angie and Alexis, not taking his eyes from Alexis's face. He was shorter than her by three inches, but realised that without her chunky shoes, she'd be shorter than him. *Perfect,* he thought.

"And Officer James Gardo." Webster turned to his star pupil.

"Gardo?" Angie stared at him and saw him turn, saw the most incredible aqua blue eyes she'd ever seen. They shone brightly in the underground car park. So incredible they were, they nagged at her memory. "Gardo? As in…Detective Giancarlo Gardo?"

James stared hard at the woman who seemed to know his father. "He's my father. Do you know him?"

Angie blinked and thought back. *Those eyes, where have I seen them before?* "Yes," slowly came out of her mouth. "A long time ago. Is he still alive?"

"Yes," James told her. "He and Mom are still alive and still living in their own home. They had it before I was born."

"Still alive," Angie muttered. "Well, I'll be. It's been a long, long time."

"Would he remember you, Mrs, ah, Stephanopoulos?" he asked, interested as to how a pop star's mother could know his father.

"Possibly," Angie said softly. "More than likely very probably, unless he's lost his memory."

"No, he hasn't," James said. "Still as strong as an ox and his mind is as sharp as ever."

"Mmm," Angie murmured. "That's interesting."

"Mama, I want to go now, that was scary." Alena moved to her mother's side, but kept her eye on James.

"We can't let you go until we've finished dealing with the area," Webster said, curious as to the conversation he'd just witnessed. "And if there *is* a gunman out there, it may not be safe to go yet."

"We'll hire a bodyguard," Maria said. "We'll get one to go on the bus with Alena. Will she be able to go then?" Watching Webster, she expected a yes.

"You can," he replied. "Do you *have* a bodyguard?"

"Well, no. Not one that can leave now," Maria said. "But I can get one."

"I have an idea," Alena piped up, still with her eyes on James. "Could Officer Gardo come with us?"

"Ah, no, that won't be possible," James protested.

"Nonsense," Webster told him. "That would be a splendid idea."

"What?" James's head swivelled from Alena to his captain. "Captain, I can't, I've got my patrols."

"Nonsense," Webster went on. "We can spare you, and it will be good PR for the NYPD. Officer saves international pop star from crazed gunman."

"Hardly crazed," James interjected.

"And hardly a gunman," Denny added. "If we haven't found one."

"Doesn't mean there wasn't one," Webster finished. "I think it's a fine idea. You can dash home and pack a bag. How long do you need? We'll be at least another hour here. Is that enough time?"

James looked from his captain's stern expression to Alena's bright smile and her mother's frown. That surprised him. He'd just saved her daughter's life, and she was frowning at him. "Captain, I really don't—"

"Enough said," Webster told him. "Get home and pack a bag. You'll be Miss Stephanopoulos's bodyguard for the rest of her tour. Do us proud, Gardo."

Resigned to his fate, James sighed. "I really don't—"

"It's a deal." Webster turned and walked off. "Do the NYPD proud."

Denny stared at James. "Dude, I hate you."

Casting a glance at all of them, James had a bad feeling about this family.

*****

Antonio had found Cabot, all right. He was getting his cock sucked by a gay crew member in some tiny out of the way space backstage. "For God's sake, Cabot!"

"It's *Steele, Phoenix,*" his brother reminded him. "And why are you forsaking God?" He could feel the urgency rising in his blood.

"I'm not, you moron," Antonio said through clenched teeth. "But you need to stop this. This is stupid."

"What is? And why do I need to stop?" Cabot came in the man's mouth.

"Because you're a shit," Antonio said. "Congratulations on being one, well done. You must be *so* proud, fucking different men every day, getting fucked and sucked."

"I never get fucked, I always do the fucking," Cabot said. "And there's nothing wrong with getting sucked when the need arises." He smiled at the crew member and zipped up.

The man smiled, wiped his mouth, and walked away.

"Seriously!" Antonio exclaimed, punching his brother hard on the arm and watching him rub it with a furious frown. "You had to score at your cousin's concert? It was bad enough you had to snort before you came here, but you had to get it sucked as well. You're disgusting, Cabot." He shook his head in dismay, saddened by his brother's behaviour that he seemed to have no intention of changing. "I'm leaving." Turning, he decided to head down the passage to the underground car park.

"Phe? Phe!" Cabot ran after him, not wanting to lose him. "Phe!"

"My name's Antonio!" he snapped, seeing a crowd of people around the door to the underground park. "What's going on?"

One of the crew hovering at the door heard him. "Apparently the crowd broke through, and a gun went off. Everyone hit the deck."

"Is anyone hurt?" Antonio pushed through to see his family on the bus. "Aunt Angie, Alena, Alexis." He ran up the stairs with Cabot behind him and stood staring at them. "Is everyone all right? Someone said a gun went off."

"We think so," Angie said. We have to wait for the crowd to disperse, and an officer to get back. He'll be coming with us as Alena's bodyguard."

"Cor blimey, cuz, you scored a copper as a bodyguard." Cabot put on his best English accent and casually slumped on the couch. "Good for you. Is he hot?"

Alena blushed. "Yes." She scored a dirty look from Angie, but she didn't see it.

"Aw, lucky girl," Cabot went on. "Do *we* get to meet him?"

"If you stick around till he gets back you will. He's gone home to pack." Alexis grinned. "You missed the whole thing." She was sitting next to Cabot, her legs crossed.

"So, what happened?" Antonio asked, and they told him from start to finish. "Will you tell the rest of the family? Your father and grandma in particular?"

"God, no!" Alena's eyes widened. "Daddy would worry and want to end the tour, and Grandma would want to come."

"She can't, she's busy until August," Angie reminded her. "But yes, your father would want you to end the tour."

"Then let's not tell Daddy," Alena implored her mother. "We'll only worry the family unnecessarily."

Angie's brows rose. "Unnecessarily? Your father would consider it *very* necessary to know."

"I know." Alena's voice came close to a whine. "But Mama, Daddy'll just make a big fat mountain out of an itty-bitty molehill and stress me out. Officer Gardo is coming. I'll be safe, and besides, they don't even know if there *was* a gunman, or a gun."

James came back with his bag and flashed his credentials at the bouncers standing around the cars. "The crowd has dispersed, and we're ready to go. We should get on the road." He stepped up into the bus only to be stopped by Cabot who had swooped out of his seat to see who the voice belonged to.

"Well, who *is this* hot looking stud?" He stared down at James in his light blue shirt, worn jeans, and cowboy boots. "You're gorgeous."

James blinked. He tried to recollect who the person in front of him was, but he couldn't. "And you are?"

"Steele, Steele Stefan, Alena's cousin." He held out his hand, but James didn't shake it, just looked at it with disdain. "Are you single?"

"That's none of your business." James took a step up, forcing Steele back.

"Gay?" Cabot's insides quivered in anticipation.

"No." James moved up another step.

"Do you want to be?" Cabot cocked a jaunty brow, hoping.

"Do you want me to rip your cock off and turn you into a woman?" James cocked his brow and forced his way up the last steps past a scowling Cabot to see the family. "Captain Webster said we can go now. The crowd is nearly gone, so there's no point keeping you here any longer." He watched the amused glances that Antonio, Alena and Alexis traded. "Is something wrong?"

"Not at all, officer." Antonio introduced himself, shaking James's hand. "You're the first man who's put my brother in his place."

James glanced over his shoulder at a still scowling Cabot. "I highly doubt that, but then there's a first time for everything. If you two aren't coming with us, you need to get off the bus." Turning back to Alena, he added, "And I need to stash these." He lifted his large blue case, matching overnight bag, and a backpack.

"Um, yeah, sure. There are some guest bunks back here." Alena showed him to the beds. "There's a space under them to store your case, and you can use the other bunks for stuff, and there's a small closet here." She showed him.

"And you'll be?" He eyed the bunks across from him.

"Ah, my mama and sister are bunking in with me in the master." She blushed. Of all times to get a cute guy on the bus and she had her mother and sister. *Bugger! Won't be able to make out.* The blush deepened.

"Are you okay? You look a little warm?" James noticed the flush to her pale skin.

"I'm…fine," she murmured, unable to look at him. Biting her bottom lip, she pointed to the bathroom. "Your bathroom's right here, next to the closet."

"Toilet, shower, great," James said unenthusiastically. "Let's get on the road."

They went back to the others, and Alena hugged her cousins goodbye. "Behave yourself, Cabot." She giggled. "But somehow I know you won't. Antonio, look after him."

"I don't know if I have the energy for that anymore." Antonio sighed, arms crossed, leaning against a counter. "I don't have the motivation *to* look out for him anymore."

"As long as you're both here, you have to look out for each other." Angie stood up to hug them. "I will see the two of you in July for your birthdays."

"Yes, Aunt Angie." Antonio kissed her. "Better get going." He pushed Cabot who longingly glanced at James as he got off the bus.

"Bye Officer Gorgeous," Cabot called and waved daintily at him.

James's brows rose in disgust.

"Bye everyone," Antonio called. "See you next month."

They watched as the door closed, and the engine started.

"Well," James said as they slowly rolled past. "*That* was interesting." He glanced at the three women. "Your cousins?"

"They're the golden-haired half of the family." Angie smiled, settling back into her seat in the lounge and watching her daughters kneel on the couch to wave goodbye to the boys.

"What's the bet Antonio caught Cabot having sex with some random crew member. Blech," Alena murmured in her sister's ear.

"Double blech." Alexis grinned.

"They're Uncle Carlos and Aunt Viv's kids. They have an older sister, Diana," Alena told James. "She's a famous model like their mother, as are the boys."

James vaguely remembered all of the pictures he'd looked at as they rolled out of the car park and along the driveway. He walked up beside the driver and stood in the stairwell as they drove through the remaining crowd who screamed and waved at Alena and Alexis. He watched out the window, making sure no one got in the way, or got in, or hung on to the bus in some way. Once they were clear, he went through the bus and looked out all of the windows and checked the monitors to see if anyone had climbed aboard. The bus had small cameras attached to the roof that monitored all four sides of the vehicle.

"All clear," he told them and took the seat behind the driver. "So, what's the itinerary?" Alena gave him a tour list, and he studied it. "Wow," his brows rose. "Twenty-five states, thirty dates. You must be famous?" He looked up into her blue eyes as she hovered close to him.

She smiled. "Yeah, kinda."

"That crowd was big tonight. We expecting more like that?" He stared at her, unable to look away.

"Every concert's a sell-out." Alena stared back. "The smallest will be about fifteen thousand seats, the largest about thirty thousand."

"Mmm, yeah, you are kinda famous," he murmured. "Is fifteen the smallest number of concert-goers we have to worry about?"

Her smile grew wider. "Yeah."

"Tell us about yourself, James," Angie interrupted, eyeing the man her daughter clearly had her eye on. "Detective Gardo's your father."

James blinked, swallowed, and turned his attention to Angelina. "Yes, he was a detective. A long time ago. He retired before I was born."

"And when was that?" Angie asked.

"Well, I was born in '79, so I think it was not long before." He studied her questioning gaze. "When did *you* know him?"

"In '77," Angie said. "Into '78. That was it for me, but my mother-in-law saw him in 1980 in a department store. She said he had you with him."

James moved his head side to side the shake out the cobwebs, and he frowned. "Your mother-in-law?" His eyes narrowed, his mind flashed back. "Average height, golden-brown hair, blue eyes."

Angie looked at him in surprise. "Yes. How do you remember? You were barely a toddler."

"Seventeen months," James replied. "We were buying something for my mother, and this woman popped up. She seemed to know Dad, and he her. Then…" How much should he say… Should he ask and not reveal too much while doing it? But if it was this woman's mother-in-law and the man was with her, then this was his chance to find out who the man was. The one he'd dreamt of all these years. But he had to stay cool and play it easy.

"Yes?" Angie urged, eager to hear what he had to say.

"From what I vaguely remember…" James licked his lips for effect. "There was a man who came up to us. Dark hair, dark eyes, they, my father and your mother-in-law, clearly knew him. I think his name was…" He pretended to think back, but the memory was as bright as day. "Dom…Dom…Tom…Thomas…Tomas, I think it was. He was taller than the woman."

"That would be my brother-in-law, Tomas Stephanopoulos. He was with his mother that day. I vaguely remember them mentioning seeing you and Detective Gardo when they were out. But it was oh, twenty-seven years ago now. July, I think it was. July 1980," Angie told him.

"Wow, that's a long time ago, Mama," Alexis said, listening with interest to the story and sensing there was more.

"Yes, sweetie, Alena and Diana would have been two, and it was before…" Her voice drifted off.

"Before Uncles Tomas and Roger got sick," Alena quietly finished, remembering back to the beach in Mykonos and the house and dancing for her uncles. They had celebrated their third birthdays while the boys had been in the hospital, sick and dying.

"Roger?" James questioned curiously.

"Yes, Roger Dencott, Tomas's husband," Angie said, eyes narrowing at the expression flitting across his face.

"He's gay?" James's brows rose in shock.

"Do you have a problem with that?" Angie inquired, puzzled by the comment.

"What…ah, no." James backed off. "What? I…ah…no, sorry. Until recently I'd never heard of your family, and now I'm finding out that it was your mother and brother-in-law in the department store that day, wow."

"Yeah," Alexis said slyly. "Small world."

"I had no idea anyone in your family was gay, sorry. But I take it your cousin is, the one that hit on me." James tried to keep himself in check.

"Cabot slash Steele? Yeah," Alena said. "Well…he's bi that we know of. But he seems to lean more towards men."

"Ah, so, he follows in his uncle's footsteps?" James was desperate to know more.

"*Do* gay people follow in other gay people's footsteps?" Angie asked, wanting to know what James's ulterior motives were.

"Ah, no, I guess not," James muttered, wishing the ground would open up and swallow him so he could get away from Angie's penetrating gaze. So, Tomas was gay and had a husband. "You said he got sick?" he asked Alena.

"Yes, in '81," Alena replied. "Now that we're older, we know that the doctors had told them they had AIDS and were dying. Grandma packed us all up and took us home to Mykonos for their last days."

"He's dead!?" James wasn't sure if that came out as a question or exclamation, and was worried he'd never find out what was going on.

"No." Alena smiled and drowned in his aqua eyes. "Grandma and Dan, his doctor, fought to save them, and it turns out, that while they had a lot of diseases gay men had, and this was before they called it HIV or AIDS, they actually had a parasite that showed the same symptoms. He was able to make them better. After Uncle Tomas had died for five minutes, Dan brought him back. It took years, but Uncle Tomas finally came good."

Alexis watched the range of emotions fly over James's face, curious about why he wanted to know. And she wondered if they'd ever find out about their parents' past themselves.

"So…he's alive. Where?" James asked.

"Why do you want to know?" Alexis asked, staring point blank at him.

Alena turned to look at her sister and opened her mouth to say something, but Angie discreetly shook her head no. Alena closed her mouth and turned back to James for his answer.

He blanched. "I've remembered that day for years and never knew who they were," he covered. "I'm just curious, as fate has now put me on this bus, and you happen to be related to the two people I saw."

"Yes…fate…" Alexis raised a brow.

"Yes…fate," James repeated, realising he'd have to be careful around her. "I've been told by my partner, Denny Nicolls, you're all a famous family, but I'd never heard of any of you until we were told we'd be on duty at the concert. Guess I run in different circles."

"How could you not have heard of us?" Alena was incredulous. She was famous worldwide, as were Diana and the twins. As were her daddy and mama, and uncles and aunt and grandmother.

James shrugged. "Sorry, don't listen to your music or buy your men's clothes. Don't read model magazines, or fashion ones for that matter."

"Has your girlfriend never left a fashion magazine around?" Alena asked coyly, hoping to get information out of him.

"Don't have girlfriends *to* leave magazines lying around," he said. "I've been busy working my way through the force. I want to become a detective by thirty."

"Like your father," Angie said.

"Yes." He smiled. "Like my father."

"Did you always want to be in the force?" Angie went on. "You didn't want to do what your mother did?"

He thought about it. "No. I loved the fact she worked part-time in the museum, and I could go in there and look at everything. But because I spent more time with Dad, I heard stories as I grew older and ended up wanting to be just like him and do what he did. I guess you could say it's in my blood."

"Like music is for us and our brothers." Alena glanced at her sister. "Daddy worked in a famous club as a DJ in the '70s, and Mama's a Juilliard graduate."

"The same for Diana and the twins," Alexis added. "They became models and actors after Uncle Carlos and Aunt Viv."

"And your Uncle Tomas?" James inquired.

"Doesn't have children," Angie said. "Gays aren't allowed to adopt."

"He could have tried a surrogate," James suggested.

Seeing they were crossing the border, Angie checked the clock. "No, they couldn't have," she stated. "Time for bed everyone. You girls need to get your beauty sleep." Getting up, she held an arm out to her daughters. "Goodnight, Officer Gardo, sleep well."

"Uh, thank you." He stood up as Alena reluctantly moved from his side.

"Night James," she said over her shoulder and followed her sister into the bedroom with her mother bringing up the rear.

Sighing, he slumped down on the couch and stared at the closed door. *Well, I'll be fucking blown away,* he thought. *All these years I've dreamt about a man named Tomas that I met in a department store when I was little, and now twenty-seven fucking years later I'm a fucking bodyguard to his niece. Fucking hell! Who would've thunk it? All these years I didn't look for him, didn't use my police influence to find him, all because I didn't have a last name, and now I find out it's fucking Stephanopoulos. Just like the pop princess I'm guarding. Fucking hell!*

He ran a hand through his hair. *All these years, all these dreams, and it's taken nearly twenty-seven fucking years to come back around. Well, now that I have a name I can look it up. Look into him. He's still alive, thank God, and maybe I can get it out of Princess. But her mother and sister, they're a different matter.* Her mother was definitely curious as to why he was asking all of the questions he was. And the sister was curious too, but he sensed for a different reason altogether. And now, *he* was curious about *that.* Oh, he had a lot to learn. If the mother went to Juilliard in the '70s, then maybe the rest of the family were there too, especially since it was the '80s that he'd seen them. He thought about the newspaper article with the picture of Tomas and Roger on the front.

Roger Dencott, the bastard who took my man.

Fucking hell. Where'd that come from?

The anger he'd felt twenty-seven years ago when he'd seen the photo came back. Anger, hatred, jealousy. All the things he'd always felt every time he'd had that dream. Every time he remembered that article.

At least now he had names to go on. Tomas Stephanopoulos and Roger Dencott. His husband. Husband? It wasn't legal for gays to marry, so how the hell were they husbands? And were they husbands back in the '70s, and when did Tomas meet Roger?

When he was broken up with me, that's fucking when. And how dare he fucking dump me because of fucking bloody Bertha. That fucking meddling bitch wrecked my poor Tomas and turned him against me.

Whoa, where the bloody hell'd that come from? And who the hell's Bertha? And when did Tomas and I break up? We've never been together. He must be what? In his fifties? So how the hell could I one, be having feelings for him, and two, be having memories of a time with him when I didn't exist? Fucking hell! How could this be happening?

Sighing, he slid back until he was full out on the sofa and comfortably settled.

In the master bathroom, Angie rang home while the girls got into bed.

Jenny hurried through the door and picked up the phone. "Hello, Stephanopoulos residence, Jenny speaking."

"Mama, Angie, you will *not* believe who we've met."

"Who?" Jenny gathered some papers from the dining table and watched as everyone wandered through the door ready for breakfast.

"Officer *James Gardo.*"

Jenny blinked. "Who? Gardo? James Gardo did you say? Giancarlo's son?" All eyes turned to her as she gaped open-mouthed.

"Yes. He was one of the officers patrolling the concert venue, and he's ended up coming along for the ride as a bodyguard. And *guess what*, he has *aqua blue eyes*. For the life of me, I *cannot remember* where I've seen eyes like that before."

"Yes." Jenny glanced at her family. "I noticed that when I saw him in the department store in 1980 with Giancarlo." She didn't mention that Tomas thought it was Luiz's eyes.

"Yes. He asked a lot of questions, and that got brought up. He said he vaguely remembered it even though he was seventeen months old back then. But something kept nagging at me."

"Like what?"

"Like…" Angie paused. "Like he was after information. He was digging for something, and then claimed he'd never heard of our family before, and to find out after twenty-seven years that it was the two of you in the store, and now here he was. It was all a bit sus to me, Mama."

"Mmm," Jenny mused. "It does seem strange that he would have remembered after all these years. How's his father? Is he still alive?"

"Strong as an ox, apparently. He was curious as to how I knew him. I vaguely mentioned it was back in the '70s, but I think he wants to know more, just as I do. So, what *do* I do?"

"Interesting." Jenny glanced at her children. Viv was off on her book tour, Tomas and Roger in Italy, Dan and Derek in Santorini, so it was just her and Spiros with Carlos, Pedro, Dom and Danté. Because whenever Viv or Angie were busy, the boys always came home for every meal. Just like old times. "I'd be curious to know more too, see what you can get out of him without giving too much away. Considering the kids don't know what went on back then, we don't want them digging around in that mess."

"Well, he knows everyone's name now," Angie said. "Alena spilled her guts. So, if he does go searching through old files and archives, he'll find a plethora of information."

Jenny sighed. "We can't have that. I wonder how much he's gotten from his father. If he was digging for info with *you*, I wonder if he's dug for info with Giancarlo. And I never did find out who his mother was."

"Worked in a museum." Angie wiped her face with a make-up wipe. "He said he loved going there as a kid, but he spent most of his time with his father who retired shortly before he was born."

"He was born on Valentine's Day 1979," Jenny told her. "I think Giancarlo was in his 50s then, so he'd be in his 80s now, like Spiros."

"Whatever's going on, I plan on finding out as much as I can about him as he seems set on finding out about us. I just hope Alena doesn't continue spilling her guts, because she seems taken with him. But I have a feeling she will."

"Well then, make sure she gets just as much out of him as he does out of her."

"Okay. Time to go, it's late, and we're on the bus."

"Okay, I'll say goodnight." Jenny saw Pedro come over, indicating that he wanted to talk to her. "Hang on, your husband wants to talk to you." She handed the phone over.

"Hey, babe."

"Hey, babe."

Jenny walked away, thinking about James Gardo. 1980, July, he was seventeen months old and he remembered? She remembered how he'd reacted to Tomas, reaching for him, saying his name, as if he knew him, as if he wanted him…

Twenty minutes later, they were sitting down to a hearty breakfast and digging in.

"So, what was that about?" Spiros asked. "Did I hear Detective Gardo's name mentioned?"

Finishing her mouthful of food, Jenny thought about it. "Yes. Apparently, his son James is an officer and was on duty at Alena's concert."

"The same son you and Tomas saw him with that day in the department store?" Pedro asked.

"Yes. He's all grown up and remembers that day." She buttered a piece of toast and took a bite.

"How long ago was that?" Carlos asked before finishing off his first cup of coffee.

Jenny swallowed and cleared her throat. "1980."

"And how old was he at the time?" Pedro asked.

"Seventeen months. His father was holding him in his arms, and he was a beautiful little boy." Jenny smiled at the memory. "Brown hair, blue eyes, he had a little t-shirt and shorts on like the ones I used to dress you boys in." Her smile turned to the boys. "He was adorable. I wonder what he looks like now."

"Probably like his father," Pedro said, noticing his sons eyeing them with curious stares. He gave them the eye back. "If you two are finished, you can go."

With nods, they dumped their plates in the sink and dashed out the door, disappointed they weren't going to find out more.

Pedro waited for them to be gone. "Did Angie tell you why he was on the bus as a bodyguard? She vaguely skirted the issue when I spoke to her."

"No." Jenny shook her head. "I suppose it had to do with the crowd. Maybe he's just along until she's out of New York. Who knows?"

"She told me Antonio and Cabot were there at the show, so at least they're supporting their family," Pedro told Carlos.

"At least they're thinking about someone besides themselves," Carlos replied. "But it's a safe bet it was Antonio who dragged Cabot along and made sure he got there."

"More than likely," Jenny said. "Antonio always showed more compassion and caring for others than Cabot."

"Yeah, but we raised them the same, so how come one's a selfish brat and one's not?" Carlos finished his food and refilled his coffee cup.

"They're twins; not every set is going to turn out the same. They're two different personalities. I think the problem is they've always been together, in birth, in life, in work. They stay together, live together, work together. They need to develop their own personalities instead of sticking to one between them."

"They're Jekyll and Hyde," Pedro said. "Antonio's the good one, and when Cabot realised that, he probably believed it allowed him to be bad. So, Antonio's the one who rings, the one who sends presents, Cabot's not."

"Cabot does what Cabot wants," Jenny said. "And to hell with whether it's right or wrong. Although if it's wrong, the more, the better, he can't say no."

Carlos shook his head. "Yeah. I know. So…where did we go wrong?"

"Who's to say we did?" Jenny asked. "Maybe he simply made the choice to be selfish and only think of himself. Was the original Cabot like that?"

They all looked at each other. Viv knew Cabot better than anyone. Carlos, Pedro, Tomas and Roger had met him only a couple of times.

"I don't know, Mama. Viv always said he was wonderful to work with and he was a good friend. But I think when it came to sex, like with all the others back then, it was to hell with everything and all about them. He did who he wanted, when he wanted, and to hell with his health and safety. And I'm thinking Cabot is doing the same." Carlos drank the last of his coffee and sat back.

"I'm afraid you might be right," Jenny said. "From all reports, he likes it with men and likes it a lot."

"Not that there's anything wrong with that," Spiros added wryly. After the telling off he'd gotten thirty years previously, he knew not to go against the grain.

"There is when it comes to the fact we've pummelled safe sex and condom usage into their heads for twenty years. If he's not doing it safely, he'll pay the consequences, and you know that," Jenny told him.

Spiros nodded soberly. "Yes, I agree with that, definitely. He needs to be doing it safely."

"I just wish he'd stop." Carlos sighed and ran his hands through his hair, letting them rest at the back of his head, interlocked. "I've got no problem if he's gay, but for God's sake don't screw so many. I worry. I worry about it coming back to bite him in the arse. What if it happens? Regardless of all the years. Look at what happened to Alexis. What if *he'd* had it? He would have passed it on to her."

Pedro's head swivelled from Carlos on his right to his mother on his left, fear rising at that possibility. "Mama?"

Jenny lightly shook her head. "I took samples for Dan to check. He was clean, so is Alexis."

The air whooshed out of Pedro. "Oh, thank God."

"And I have *that* to worry about," Carlos waved a hand at Pedro. "Why can't he find one partner and not screw everything that moves? God knows what germs he's got and could be passing on."

"That's not good," Pedro agreed. "Maybe a new talk would be wise. Do we know if he *is* using protection?" He looked in his brother's direction.

"Antonio claims he is, so does he, but he's not a rabid dog like his brother. He's choosy about where he plants it, and always wears a condom. But with Cabot, he can't be a hundred percent sure," Carlos told him.

"When was the last time we had a talk with the kids?" Spiros asked.

"I still discuss it with Danté and Nick sometimes," Pedro said. "He's into puberty and growing, and he'll start thinking about girls soon, though he says he's not interested. I know what his Uncle Carlos was like at fourteen, so I'm not taking any chances." He got a wry grin from his brother. "And Mike and Maggie have always been forthright about using protection with Nick and the girls. We lost Leon, Stan, Eddie, and a whole bunch of other people too. They get it, and make sure the kids do."

"But the problem is, we don't discuss *back then*, except when talking about nearly losing Tomas and Roger," Jenny said. "We tell them about the effect AIDS had on the country and the world, but I don't know if Cabot cares. We showed them those documentaries, the girls were moved by it, and so were Dom and Danté, but it just seemed to go over Cabot's head."

"Arrogance," Pedro said. "Just like his father at that age." He coolly glanced at his brother, a sly grin on his face.

Carlos frowned. "At least I only did it with women, and once I married Viv, I still used condoms until I was finished in the movies. In fact," his frown deepened, "I used condoms most of the time if not *all* of the time."

"Clearly, not with Viv." Pedro sniggered.

Carlos blushed. "No, but with all of the other women, either here or in the movies. I used condoms."

"With Connie?" Jenny asked softly.

Carlos glanced at her, a pang tweaking his heart. "Yes, with Connie. And I'm glad I did. Knowing she was still sleeping with her husband even though they were separated."

"Let's hope that we can knock it out of Cabot before something bad happens to him. I'd hate for him to end up like everyone you boys knew and worked with." Jenny placed her cutlery on her plate and dabbed her mouth with her napkin.

"Same here, Mama," Carlos said, the energy leaving him as Pedro clapped him on the shoulder and squeezed. "Same here."

*****

"I can't believe you screwed one of our cousin's crew members," Antonio told his brother as they walked up to *Nightmare*. The club was busy as always, but being megastars, they got in. The music was loud and drowned out Antonio's thoughts.

"Oh, come on, Phe," Cabot whined, throwing his arm around his brother's shoulder. "The night is young, life is short, get it sucked while you can."

"I don't want to get it sucked," Antonio spat. "And you shouldn't be either. You know the whole family taught us about safe sex and protection."

"And I *use* rubbers." Cabot put his hands up in protest. "You know I do. You've seen me, but life is too short for not getting laid."

"You don't wear condoms when you get sucked," Antonio told him. "You have no idea what sort of germs those men are passing on to you. What sort of germs they have in their mouth from sucking every cock that comes their way."

"Phe, stop worrying." Cabot pulled him into the crowd. "I got it covered at all times, don't worry about it, bro. Let's dance." Throwing his arms into the air, he whooped and hollered, dancing with any and all men that gravitated towards him. He loved it. Loved the attention. Loved the hands on him. Loved the lips and kisses and tongues, and the hands down pants. He was enjoying himself, being groped, and rubbed as the males clamoured around.

Antonio watched his brother. The shirt was nearly off, and he was being groped. *What sort of brother do I have? A slut, a manwhore? What the hell happened to the little old Cabot that I grew up with? Played football and games with? Started modelling with? Started living out of a suitcase with? What happened to* that *Cabot?* The one he loved, the one he treasured and cherished, where did he go? The

Cabot that the whole family loved. Instead, there was an arrogant, ignorant, selfish, self-obsessed, self-absorbed, self-centred asshole of a jerk who thought about nothing but himself. No *one* but himself, and it worried everyone. Him especially.

As his twin, he was scared he'd lose his brother to some stupid decision because Cabot always believed he knew best. And yet he never did. Antonio was scared that one day he'd wake up and Cabot would be dead from an overdose of his bloody cocaine, or find out he'd acquired AIDS, and when it came down to it, Antonio had absolutely no idea how he'd feel. Relieved or done.

Watching his brother, he knew he couldn't take it much longer. They were twenty-five soon, in just another month and a bit. Twenty-freakin' five. A quarter century. Could he tolerate it until then? Maybe it was time for them to take a holiday apart. Live alone. *Love* alone. But then he doubted Cabot could survive without him here. Cabot proved day after day that he couldn't survive without his brother. He could barely do the basic stuff for himself, not because he didn't know how, but because he was just too damn lazy to do it. Cabot left all the hard stuff up to Antonio so he could party and fuck his way through life. Well, he was sick of it. Sick of being the watchdog, the guardian, the fixer of everything. But how much longer could he take it? How much longer could he deal with Cabot and his reckless behaviour? He just knew he couldn't take care of things anymore. Couldn't be the gatekeeper. It had to stop and stop soon, before one of them wound up dead, and the other in a mental institution from exhaustion. He knew the time was coming, and knew it would more than likely be their birthday in July. But until then, he knew they had to do their jobs and get them done, and he had to watch Cabot in the meantime.

He decided to use the trick he always used when Cabot needed pulling into line. Making sure his brother saw him, he shook his head sadly and walked away.

"Phe?" Cabot strained to see where his brother had gone. "Phe?" He moved, looking for his brother. "Phe?" Seeing him heading for the door, he ran through the crowd. "Phe?" He couldn't lose Phe, couldn't lose his brother. He was all he had, and he couldn't be alone in the world, not without Phe. "Phe," he screamed, and followed him out the door, panicking that he was being left alone. And he didn't want to be left alone. Not in the world they lived in. Not without Phe. He ran out the door and saw his brother walking down the street and hailing a cab. "Phe?" Running up to him he grabbed him. "Don't leave me, Phe. I don't want to party without you." He threw his arms around him and rested his head on his shoulder.

"And I don't want to party. I'm tired; I'm going home. And my name's Antonio." He grabbed the cab that stopped and opened the door. "What you do is up to you, Cabot." Climbing in, he slid over to give his brother space if he wanted to get in. Giving the cabbie his address, he was pleased to see Cabot reluctantly climb in and shut the door.

It was a trick that always worked.

*****

Alexis had a restless sleep. Dreams of her attacker came back to haunt her, though they had calmed down in the last few weeks. The attack under the Garden had left her shaken, making the dreams pop up again. Waking, she rolled onto her side to stare at the wall on the left side of the bed.

Curling up, she relived the attack, the pain, the horror, the fear, and tried to remember what her grandma had told her. To treat it as a horrible sexual experience, but to not let it rule your life and emotions. She remembered the conversation. Her grandma said she had no words for her, no advice, no Jenny Stephanopoulos wisdom because she'd never been through it, and didn't know how to deal with it herself, so the only thing she could say was that. And it had helped greatly, to not see it as a rape, but as a horrible sexual experience. The counsellor she had spoken to didn't and had pooh-poohed her grandmother's advice and told her she needed to face up to the fact that it had happened and deal with it. But she hadn't told her how. So, Alexis turned back to her grandmother's advice and managed quite well. Pushing it to the back of her mind as a horrible experience helped, and so did finding out the jerk for brains that had done it got what he deserved.

And she was glad. They hadn't told her *what* happened, just that he wouldn't be hurting her or anyone ever again. She wondered if her grandmother had hurt him, killed him even. But since no one was talking, she couldn't find out.

The images of the concert flooded her head. The two officers, James and Denny, racing towards them, flying through the air, and Denny landing on her. His big eyes looking scared, his hands behind her head to stop it cracking on the ground. It was exhilarating, but so scary. Especially when she started reliving the assault. Freaking out because he was on top of her. *Oh, my God,* she inwardly groaned. *I can't believe I freaked out. The way he looked at me, all concerned, asking if I was okay. That was sweet and kind and caring, and I had to go and freak out all over the place. Oh, my God, what a moron.* She rolled her eyes. *What a bloody moron.*

She felt Alena move beside her, rolling over to curl up herself. The bed was massive and could easily fit three people, four if they wanted. So, they all had the space they needed. She wondered if Alena was dreaming of James.

The images flew through Alena's mind. The crowd screaming toward her, running down the ramp to her bus, it was almost like being in a zombie movie, where a horde had found its way through the barricades and were trying to get fresh meat. Her! It was horrible. She was frozen to the spot, unable to move, just watching them get closer and closer and closer, and then James came flying through the air, over the hood of the SUVs and toward her, flying *at* her, knocking her down to land on top of her. And oh, how he had felt so strong and masculine, and smelt so spicy and sexy and his eyes. Oh, my God, his eyes. So blue. So unusual, so sexy and sensual. He'd stared into hers for what seemed like forever, only for them to be interrupted by his captain. *And then what do you know, Mama knows his father, and his captain is telling him to come with us as a bodyguard. Oh, yes, I need a bodyguard,* she thought. A strong, good-looking, tall one. With dark brown hair and big blue eyes. Oh, yes, she definitely needed a bodyguard, and he could guard her body anytime. She inwardly groaned. It had been so long since she'd had sex, and now that she'd met James and found out he didn't have a girlfriend, she had her mother and sister in tow.

At least he'll be along for the whole tour. Mama and Alexis are only here for two weeks, so maybe we can get to know each other in that time. Mama can get more info out of him about his father, and I can get more info out of him about his life, and he can get all the info out of me that he wants, and who knows, maybe after the tour is over, we can get to know each other away from the spotlight and he can see me for who and how I am away from the stage. Yes, good plan, Alena, very good plan.

Angie racked her brain. Where had she seen blue eyes like James's before? The mere fact he was Gardo's son, and Jenny and Tomas had seen him twenty-seven years ago was more than unusual. It was highly improbable. But whatever the odds were, she couldn't for the life of her figure out where she'd seen eyes that colour. Or why Alena was interested. Sure, she was twenty-nine and a woman who might want to find a man to date, or marry, or have kids with. But James Gardo? Of all the men in all of the cities, she had to find the son of someone from their past. A past they all vowed to not tell their children about unless it was absolutely necessary. That time in their lives. Stefano Papadopoulos, and her father, Andros Poulos, were long dead, having died at the time, and what they did to the family the kids didn't have to know. Unless it was vitally important for them to know, and for the last twenty-nine years it hadn't been. But now a son of one of the police officers involved was hanging around and snooping and wanting to know who everyone was. What did he know? How *much* did he already know? He'd claimed he'd never heard of the family before, but could he be believed? Could she trust him? She didn't think so, and her gut was telling her to be careful and not say too much. To find out what *he* actually knew instead of telling *him* everything. If only Alena could keep quiet.

She knew her daughter. And knew she loved to brag about all of them, how they were all famous and talented and successful. But would she blab personal stuff? Not that she knew much, but what if

James found a way of getting that info out of her and she knew more than any of them realised? What if the older kids knew more than *any of them* realised. They were famous. Pedro was a well-known DJ, Carlos a movie producer, Viv a model, Tomas and Roger public faces of AIDS and gay campaigners. What if the kids had gone digging and found something out? What if they'd found Carlos's stack of porn movies and awards in the family vault where they'd been for twenty-five years? What if they'd found them and watched them? What if they knew?

James slowly woke to the hum of the bus motor and found he had fallen asleep on the lounge. The light was coming in around the edges of the windows, and the sun was rising fast. He thought about his new role as a bodyguard and what sort of woman Alena was. More of a girl. Young, pretty, a year older than him. She seemed so much younger. Was she sheltered? Naïve? He didn't know, but if she was, he planned on using that to find out more about her uncle.

Well, fancy that. Tomas Stephanopoulos. I know who you are. I know who I've been dreaming about for twenty-seven years. Who I dreamt about tonight. The beautiful Greek god who is the lover I've never forgotten. Not once, in the last thirty years that I've been gone, have I forgotten you, my love.

*****

After being on the road for two weeks, Angie and Alexis's time with Alena came to an end. They had spent six days in beautiful Miami where Alena did two concerts, and it was time for them to go so Alena could get to Alabama.

"I wish you could stay longer, Mama." Alena hugged Angie tight.

"So do I, my darling, but I have to get back to work with your father," Angie told her. "We'll see each other in another two months when we come to New York. The whole family will be there."

"I know. But that's two months without you." Alena let go to hug Alexis. "And we've just gotten back on track. I want you to stay for the whole tour."

"Baby steps, sis. Baby steps," Alexis said. "We need to take our time. Get to know each other in small doses. Find out what kind of people we are now."

"I know." Alena hugged tighter. "Doesn't mean I don't want you to stay."

"You sure? Coz it means you get James all to yourself," Alexis murmured in Alena's ear.

Alena giggled. "You naughty girl."

"No," Alexis replied. "*You* naughty girl."

"Well…he *is* gorgeous," Alena added, biting her lip to stop herself from laughing.

"He certainly is." Alexis pulled back.

Looking at her mother and sister, Alena went on. "I'm going to miss you both so much. Even if it is only for two months."

"And then we'll all be back together," Angie said. "You know you don't need to tour again if you don't want to. If family means that much to you."

"I know, Mama. And after what happened with Alexis, it makes me think I should spend some more time at home. And I will over the winter months."

"I'll look forward to it," Angie said. "In the meantime, we need to go." They were already at the airport in a hanger as they had the family jet to fly home in.

"Okay, Mama." Alena hugged her again.

"Bye, my baby." Angie patted her back and pulled away. "We have to go. Take care of her, James. It's expected of you."

"I will, Mrs Stephanopoulos." He raised a hand in farewell as he stepped over to Alena.

"Bye, Mama." Alena waved from beside James.

"Bye, baby, we'll see you in August." Angie waved from the door and five minutes later, they were flying off into the sky.

"Bye." Alena waved sadly, wiping her tears as her family left her. But she couldn't help herself; she burst into tears and leaned on James for support.

Startled, he cautiously patted her shoulder, not knowing what else to do.

"I'm going to miss them so much, especially Alexis." Wrapping her arms around him, she sobbed on his shoulder. His strong, broad shoulder. "I'm going to miss them so much." Actually, she was heartbroken, and it hurt like hell to not be going home with them. That was somewhere she'd really like to be right now.

"Come on, let's get you on the bus. We have to get to Alabama." James led her back to the peace and quiet of her tour bus, and they got on the road. It was late afternoon, early evening, and they sat quietly while Alena's sobs calmed down.

"I feel like going home with them."

"Then why do a tour?" James asked, curious to find out more now that the mother and sister were out of the way. The last two weeks he'd had to be careful with the questions he asked and the info he gave, for Angie and Alexis had been very curious indeed, and he couldn't give away too much. Now, he had free rein.

"Because I've never toured here." Alena wiped her nose. "I've done promo tours and small shows, but never a huge concert tour. We figured now was the time, but it came at a bad time."

"Why's that?"

"Because…my sister was assaulted in May while I was rehearsing, and that made me realise what a selfish bitch I'd been to her, her entire life, and I grew up. *Finally.* It wasn't all about me anymore. And so I want to spend more time with her, getting to know her. She had long hair until May, but after the assault she cut it off. I accused her of doing it for attention on our cousin's birthday. I didn't know she had been assaulted then." Wiping her face, she sniffed. "I have a lot to make up for."

"It sounds like a very complicated family. I'm glad I'm an only child." James shifted in his seat to get more comfortable.

Alena smiled softly. "You don't know the half of it."

"Do *you?*" His curiosity got the better of him. "From the bits you've told me the last two weeks, you've got quite a big family."

"Not really," Alena said. "My parents have four kids, my aunt and uncle three. My grandma and grandpa had three…well…four if you count the baby they lost. I was named after her."

"Really?" That intrigued him. "How sad." Knowing his parents had him when they were older; he'd often wondered if there were previous marriages and children.

"Yeah…" Her smile grew sadder. "Grandma had her nearly two years after Daddy. But she was stillborn. Grandma named her Alena. When Mama had me, Grandma suggested using the name; she believed I was her Alena come back for another go at life, but I was meant to be with Mama and Daddy, not her. I had to leave in order to come back nineteen years later. So, in honour of Daddy's sister, they named me Alena Jennifer Stephanopoulos."

"Jennifer?" James inquired.

"Grandma's name." Alena delicately dabbed a tissue to her eyes.

"That's sweet," James said, his heart aching for her. The last two weeks he'd grown accustomed to her ways and had gotten to know quite a lot about her and her family. He also got to gauge how she worked and could almost be in sync in certain moments, but she was also spontaneous and loved to drop everything and go and do something. And he'd lightened up. The three women were gorgeous, friendly, and well educated on music and activism, especially when it came to gay rights. And that led back to Tomas. "It must have been hard losing a child. Not that I know. I've never had any. So, your grandmother must have been ecstatic when Tomas didn't die."

"Yeah, she was. I was only three, but I remember everyone shouting and crying. It was scary, and Diana and I clung to each other as two men came running into the house and into his bedroom. We were kept back by our great-grandma, and we cried. It seemed like hours later they came out and told us Uncle Tomas and Roger were going to live and it would be a long fight."

"You remember that?" He brushed her hair away from her face. "You were three."

Alena blushed at his touch. "We were old enough to understand English, but not old enough to understand what dying and dead meant. I remember Mama hugging me tightly after that."

"And she hasn't let go since." James smiled. "You all seem incredibly close."

"Well, as I said, Alexis and I weren't for all of her nineteen years. I was horrible and hated her. Until she came along, I was the only girl in the family."

"But you had Diana," James pointed out.

"Yep. We were the only girls in the family until Alexis, and I became hateful, spiteful and jealous. But now, we're trying to put all of that behind us and start afresh. I think the last two weeks were an accomplishment."

"From what I saw, the two of you looked like you had been best friends for all of your lives."

His compliment brought a smile to her lips. "Yeah, it felt that way. But I have a lot to make up for. Nineteen years. So it's a small start."

"Will any more of your relatives be joining us in the next two months?" James secretly hoped he would meet Tomas. "Do I have to prepare myself?"

A girly giggle came out of Alena. "No. But I can't be sure. Grandma's busy until August; Aunt Viv is on a book tour. Daddy and Uncle Carlos have a movie to make. My brothers are busy being DJs in our club *SB3* on Mykonos—"

"*SB3?*"

"Stefan Brothers Three or some such thing," Alena said. "They opened it twenty-six year ago, one year after Uncle Tomas died and came back."

"He actually died?" James asked, hoping to get more information out of her now her family was gone. He'd been writing it all down in his notebook, so he had details to use when he went searching.

"Yes. His heart stopped, and Dan and the other doctors brought him back after five minutes. They plied him full of antibiotics, and he took ages to get better, spending nearly two months in the hospital. Grandma didn't give up, so he's vowed to spend the rest of his life looking after them."

"Are they sick?"

"No." Alena tucked a strand of hair behind her ear. "She did all she could for them when they were sick, and when he came back, she nursed him again. So, he and Uncle Roger vowed to take care of them until they died. They live in the house below, come up and make dinner every night. Sometimes lunch. He helps out around the house and runs the gym with Roger. They keep telling Grandma they'll look after them when they can't look after themselves anymore. Like they did for him when he was sick. He said he and Uncle Roger will do everything. But considering Uncle Roger isn't much younger than Grandma, I'm not sure what they'll do—"

"How much younger?"

"Twenty years."

"That's not *much* younger."

Another giggle. "I know, but Uncle Roger's sixty next year and Grandma's eighty. If my grandparents live another twenty years, Uncle Roger will be looking after her at one hundred, and he'll be eighty. Uncle Tomas is fifty-two now; he'll be seventy-three. I'm not sure how much a seventy-three and an eighty-year-old could do for a hundred-year-old."

"Your father or uncle won't be looking after them?" James mentally stored away the information.

She shrugged. "Uncle Carlos will run the family business with Uncle Tomas and Daddy, then they'll train us to take over and run it for our kids and their kids."

"And do any of you have kids yet?"

Shock flew over her face. "Diana and I are only twenty-nine, the boys are twenty-five next month, and the rest are too young. Danté's fourteen, Alexis nineteen, so kids are a long way off for us." She glanced out the window at the setting sun.

"Not really. You said you and your cousin are twenty-nine, so isn't it time to think about kids?"

"With what man?" Alena asked, daring to gaze into his aqua eyes. "We're both so busy we haven't dated in years."

"Then stop working. Allow yourself time off to meet people, travel, spend time with your family."

"That would be nice, and it will happen when the tour's over. We'll be in New York at the end of August and spend September there as well. You can meet the rest of the family."

"Will *Steele* be there?" He grinned wryly.

Alena snorted. "Probably, as they live in our apartment building. But you can meet Grandma and Grandpa, Uncle Carlos and Aunt Viv, Daddy, and my brothers. Maybe Diana if she's back."

"Back?"

"She's in Europe, modelling." Alena scratched her head and ran her hand through her hair. "But she usually has time off like we all do to meet up for late summer and early fall. Or autumn as my family calls it."

"Autumn?"

"Grandma's Australian. That's what they call it. She's lived in Greece since 1967, but she's still very Aussie in her accent and words, so we all picked it up and was taught it."

"Australia. Interesting. Your family is quite a mystery, Alena Stephanopoulos."

Her smile grew wider. "Why, thank you, James Gardo. And yet yours sounds too normal and boring."

He grinned. "Only child to older parents. Yeah, boring. No famous sibling, or cousins, or aunts and uncles. No world-famous anything in my family."

"That's not such a bad thing," Alena said, and her stomach growled. "Oops, time for dinner. What are you up for?"

James made spaghetti Bolognese, and over a glass of wine and garlic bread, they kept talking about her family.

*****

Arriving safely in Mykonos, Angie and Alexis were met in the Stephanopoulos hanger at the Mykonos airport by Pedro.

"Babe."

"Daddy."

The girls flew into his arms, and he hugged them fiercely. "Oh, my babies are here. But let's get you home, it's still night-time." He herded them and their luggage into the van and quickly took off. "We have to be quiet; most of the town is asleep."

"But not the club." Alexis spotted *SB3* in the distance as they turned a corner.

"No, not the club. But the family are, so we need to be quiet. Danté is with Nick at Mike and Maggie's. Dom's at the club; everyone else is asleep." He pulled up to the front of their house and unlocked the door, turned the light on, and piled the girls and their bags inside, locking the door behind them. "It's good to have you home." He took Angie into his arms and kissed her passionately.

"Ew, don't need to see it," Alexis complained. "I'm off to bed if you want to play kissy face like Alena and James. Night."

Angie giggled and pulled away from her husband, watching her daughter wheel her luggage to her room. "Night, sweetie."

"*Alena and James?* Are we on a first name basis now?" Pedro's brows rose. He was curious about all that had gone on the last two weeks. It was the longest he'd been without Angie by his side, or in his bed, and he'd missed her.

"Calling him Officer Gardo the whole time would have been silly." Angie picked up her bag. "Can we talk about this tomorrow when I can tell all of you together? I just want a hot shower and my own bed. Can you bring my case?"

"Can you hurry up and get naked? I want my wife." He dutifully grabbed her bag and followed.

She glanced over her shoulder and saw the determined look in his eye. "Down boy."

*****

The next day they gathered at Jenny's dining table for dinner. Dan and Derek were back from Santorini, Tomas and Roger back from Italy, and Tomas had prepared a delicious new pasta recipe he'd picked up during their travels.

"How's Alena's concert's going?" Jenny asked.

"Good." Angie dug into her meal. "Tens of thousands of screaming fans and travelling on her own tour bus. That bit was fun."

"And *now* you can tell us about James Gardo and *why* Alena's playing kissy face with him, and *why* he was hired as a bodyguard," Pedro said.

The kids snorted at their father saying *kissy face.*

Sighing, Angie looked at her food. "Can I at least finish my awesome meal cooked by your brother first? It's a long story." She changed the subject. "Dan, Derek, enjoy Santorini?"

The boys spoke of their holiday and passed on to Tomas and Roger who talked about Italy and the little towns they had never been to before.

"What date are you going to New York, Mama?" Tomas asked. "We won't be going with you."

"You're not coming to New York?" Jenny cried in alarm. "Why not?"

"No, we are," Tomas quickly said, seeing the expression on her face and resting his hand on hers to placate her. "We've just planned to go somewhere else for a couple of weeks."

"Where?" she asked, calming down. She hated it when plans were thrown into chaos.

Tomas looked at Roger. "Miami."

"What! Why?" Jenny asked, knowing he hadn't been back in decades and had never wanted to.

"Oh, we just left there," Angie said. "It's beautiful."

"Well..." Tomas breathed in. "On the first of August, it will be thirty years since Roger and I met." He grasped Roger's hand. "And, though I vowed to stay away from it, I think it's time to go back and say hello."

"Are you sure?" Jenny asked. "You stayed away for a reason."

"I know." Tomas nodded. "All of our friends and co-workers are dead. And after 1980 or '81 I refused to go back because it was too sad. Even on our tenth and twentieth, I refused. But we're older, and it hurts less. I made the choice to go, and it was *all my choice.* I booked the accommodations and hired a car. *I want* to go back," he said determinedly and dared his mother to say otherwise.

"When was the last time you were there?" Pedro asked.

Tomas sighed. "I didn't go back for Freddy's funeral, and that was '81."

"We got sick after that," Roger spoke up, watching his husband's face. "It must have been '80 for you."

"Twenty-seven years, same as James Gardo." Tomas mysteriously looked at his mother. "You believe in weird things and coincidences, Mama."

"Yes, I do, and unfortunately this is a big one." She looked at Angie. "Time for the full story, Missy."

Sighing, Angie finished her last mouthful and drank her wine. A half hour later, with excerpts from Alexis, she finished the story to oohs and aahs.

"Did they *actually* find a gun or gunman?" Pedro was astounded that his family had gone through that and not told him. "Angie, how could you not tell me?"

"Because Alena believed you'd want to shut down the tour and she didn't want you doing that."

"Damn right I would have shut it down," he snapped. "My daughter's life is at risk, a damn concert tour pales in comparison. Were the *two of you* okay?"

"Obviously." Angie raised a brow at her husband's tone and facial expression. "We're all fine. We're here, and Alena is being looked after by one of New York's finest."

"The coincidence," Jenny murmured, staring at the table's centrepiece. "It's weird, and now it's nagging at me."

"Lots of number making in this family," Tomas told his mother. "Are you matching up other numbers and sequences?" After what had happened to him, he'd become a big believer in nothing being a coincidence. Just like his mother.

"Numbers?" Dan asked, always ready to learn from his honorary family.

"All in alignment," Tomas told him. "*SB3* is turning twenty-five, same as the twins. Twenty-six years ago on the same day, I died and came back from the dead, at twenty-six. Alena is twenty-nine, same age as Angie when she had Alexis. Alexis is the same age as Angie when she had Alena. We saw James Gardo twenty-seven years ago, and I haven't been back to Miami in twenty-seven years. Dom is the same age as Carlos was when he left home in 1977, twenty-four, same as the twins until next month, July, when Pedro left Mykonos for New

York with Angie thirty years ago. In June, thirty years ago, Carlos left for Hollywood with Connie and Viv. On August first it will be thirty years since I left Mykonos for Miami and met Roger the same day."

"And I haven't seen, or heard, from or about, Giancarlo Gardo since that day in the department store," Jenny said thoughtfully. "Twenty-seven years ago. And now, twenty-seven years later, his son is on tour with my granddaughter and…" she paused for effect, "James Gardo was born on Valentine's Day 1979."

"But numbers are just numbers," Carlos argued. "They will always match up somewhere."

"True, but so many of them are far too coincidental," Jenny murmured. "In 1950 I met your father, he was twenty-five, same as the twins will be, same as *SB3*, I was twenty-two. In 1952 when we married, he was twenty-seven, I was twenty-four, same as you when you left Mykonos in '77 and then married Viv," she told Carlos. "Same as Dom and the boys now. When I had you, I was twenty-four, twenty-five that year. I turned twenty-nine the year I had Pedro. Twenty-seven when I had Tomas."

"But you weren't," Carlos continued arguing the matter. "Our birthdays are before yours, so you were twenty-four, twenty-six and twenty-eight."

"Ha! Twenty-six, same as the years I've been reborn," Tomas said. "And the number I was when I died."

"Oh, for God's sake this has gotten way out of control," Pedro jumped into the conversation. "What are we going to do about James Gardo and stopping him from playing kissy face with Alena?" That got more snorts and giggles from the kids.

"What *can* we do?" Jenny asked. "*She's* twenty-nine, *he's* twenty-eight, the same age I was when I had you," she reminded Pedro.

"Mama!" Carlos was exasperated, much to everyone's amusement.

"I haven't met the boy." Jenny ignored him and went on. "I can only hope he's like his father. What does he look like, Angie?"

"Tall, six feet or so—"

"So was Gardo," Jenny said.

"Dark brown hair, light tan, and those incredible aqua eyes." Angie drifted off.

Tomas glanced up at the eye reference and the memories it brought back for him, but he didn't say anything.

Jenny glanced his way before continuing. "Gardo is tall and has dark blond hair. He obviously looks like his father."

"I guess, but I can't even remember what Gardo looks like," Angie mumbled.

"Blue eyes, dark blond hair, moustache, tall, broad, built like a Mack Truck," Jenny said, looking at her daughter, and was surprised when everyone stared at her. "What?"

"And how do *you* remember what he looks like?" Spiros's eyes twinkled.

"Because *he* helped save *our* marriage," she reminded him.

July 2007

Diana flew into New York the weekend before the Independence Day celebrations. She had a lot to do; a photo shoot, interviews, going over *HOS* business and checking on the store. Plus, she'd be seeing her brothers if they were in town. They did most of their shoots in New York, using it as their base, but did travel overseas several times a year. Rolling her cases through the penthouse door, she called out to them. "Cabot, Antonio…you here?"

Silence.

"Boo!"

"Ah," Diana screamed and turned around, seeing her brother wetting himself laughing. "Antonio," she chided. "Don't scare me like that."

"Sorry, D." He swept her into his arms and spun around. "I waited until you got here and came in the door." Kissing her cheek, he set her down.

"Cabot with you?" She glanced around her brother.

"He's sulking down in A1. Didn't want to see you because you *demanded* the penthouse."

"Hardly demanded," she said, setting her bag on the coffee table in the sitting area. "I'm oldest, I get first dibs, that's the way it goes." Looking around, she added, "God, this place doesn't change. It looked the same when I was little."

"The décor *has* been updated." Antonio grinned as his eyes moved around, taking in the vibrant colours and upholstery. "It would have been in what, twenty-five, thirty years."

"True." Diana grinned back. "Of course, everything's been updated, but it's all still in the same layout. Did you get everything cleaned for me? I don't want to sleep in the same bed as the great sex stud Steele Stefan and his floozies."

A chuckle escaped Antonio. "The bed's covered in plastic, so the mattress is clean, but I had it steam cleaned anyway."

"Thank you, my baby brother. I really *did not* want to sleep on that after him. You know everyone back home knows about his sex life?" She sat on the couch, slipped off her heels, and stretched her ankles.

"Yeah." Antonio sat next to her. "I figured. With Tilly for a manager, I knew something would get back."

"Actually, I don't think Tilly does anything. Least of all tell Mama and Daddy, *or* Grandma. You might want to think about getting out of the business for a while and taking a break. Because if Steele doesn't change his ways, Grandma will come down on him like a tonne of bricks."

"Do you really think she will?" Antonio asked. "I worry, D. I really do. I'm so tired of being the one to look after him. I don't know how much longer I can do it for. I just…" He rubbed his eyes and forehead. "I'm tired of it all."

"You look it." Diana patted his hand sympathetically. "It must be a hard job, and no one would blame you if you stopped."

"I know…but…" He searched the room for answers. "We've always been a team. We've always worked together, lived together, done everything together."

"But?" She stared into his tired and discouraged emerald green eyes.

"But…" He sighed, and his eyelids lowered. "It's become a job in itself. Looking after him…he's become lazy and expects others to do it all, and then goes and does what he wants. Regardless of the cost. He's sucked all of my energy out of me, D, and we're not even twenty-five yet."

"Then maybe it's time for you to stop and take a break. Have a holiday, be by yourself for once."

"Yeah, yeah." He thought out loud. "I think our birthday's going to be the day it all changes."

"How?"

Antonio looked at her. "I think that's the day I stop being Phoenix Stefan."

****

Cabot woke, in the bed of apartment 1. Definitely not the penthouse, and it didn't have a view of the park. Well, it did, but not the best view.

Stretching, he lay spread-eagled on the bed. It wasn't as big as the one in the penthouse, but it would have to do. They would have it back at the end of the week if Princess Diana left on schedule. *How dare she kick us out? It's our penthouse, we can do what we want. But no, she's older and in charge. The hell she is! We are. We're the ones who live here nine months of the year. Why should we be kicked out over summer? And we'll be kicked out again in August and September. Who the bloody hell do the family think they are?*

Looking around, he heard nothing. "Phe?" he called out. "Phe? You there?" It had been a couple of weeks since Antonio had walked out of the club and he'd run after him. A couple of weeks during which he'd calmed down his routine. Well, just a bit. He'd still gone out and gotten sucked. Still fucked who he wanted, but he'd only done it a couple of times a week instead of every night. Plus, they'd been busy with photo shoots for winter campaigns. Since they modelled for *Haus of Stefan*, they didn't do shoots for other clothing companies, but they did do a bunch of other stuff. They were always asked to walk runways for parades and fashion weeks, but Tilly turned them down. He'd been angry about that the first time she'd done it. But Antonio pointed out how Cabot always snorted and screwed everyone, and that it wouldn't be appropriate to walk down a catwalk stoned or high on coke. They would be fired and blacklisted. So, they made sure they got invitations for the front rows instead, always wearing the latest *HOS* lines to the shows, always making sure they got their photo taken a hundred times more than the models on the catwalk. That was their way of staying in the spotlight and off the runway.

Scratching his nut sack, his hand moved over his cock and gave it a thorough going over. He hadn't had a lover the night before. Antonio had prohibited it, even though it was a Saturday night. Because Diana was coming in, he couldn't have a lover over. So, he'd fucked a few before coming home. He satisfied himself, lay in his mess and considered getting up.

"Phe?" he yelled. "You out there?" Still hearing silence, he figured he must be with Diana. Checking his travel clock on the bedside cupboard, he saw it was nearly lunchtime and decided to go up and see if anyone was making food. After rolling out of bed, he showered, wrapped a robe around himself, and went up to the penthouse.

*****

Diana's eyes widened. "What! What do you mean stop being Phoenix Stefan?"

"I'm tired, D. I want a break. I want to be myself again. Get away from prying eyes and gossip columns that know what I'm doing *before I even do it.* Besides, we've been doing this for nearly ten years. At fifteen we watched you and Alena have your careers, and had fun doing a couple of photo shoots, but then we got into it too, and here we are, tired and burnt out. Aren't you tired of it all?"

She thought about it. "I'm tired of sexist photographers. I'm tired of people who don't take me seriously because I model clothes. So, I must be dumb, right? I'm tired of flying everywhere, but love being in those places. I'm tired of not seeing my family much anymore… Yeah, I'm tired of it."

"You know how I feel then." Antonio ran a hand through his hair. "We've done it for ten years, you for fifteen. What else is there to do?"

"Well, Mama turned her modelling career into cosmetics and videos. I had a perfume named after me in 1980 I think it was, or '81. So did Alena."

"You still wear it, don't you," Antonio said, getting a hint of it in his nostrils.

"Yeah, and it still smells great. But I don't know how much longer I want to go on modelling. You can't really spend time with family or have your own. It's hard to find someone to date who'll take you seriously. And Alena and I have *HOS* to run and design for." She sighed. "Maybe I'll take a leaf out of Mama's book and move over to other things. Move more into *HOS* instead of modelling for other companies. I'll be more of the spokesperson for it and only model our stuff. I'm twenty-nine now. If I want a family, I've only got ten more years or so."

"Mama had you at forty-one, us at forty-five. You have a while," Antonio told her.

"Yeah, but I don't want to have children at that age. Mama's seventy now, and I'm only twenty-nine, you boys nearly twenty-five, and Daddy's fifty-four. That's a big difference. Don't you want children of your own, Antonio?"

He considered it and shrugged. "One day, I guess. Gotta find someone to have them with, and I'm young. I've got a few years yet before I have to worry about it."

"I don't," Diana moaned. "Ugh! I'm thirty next year. I'll get full control of my trust fund to do what I want with, and I know Grandma's put the stipulations of a prenup on it. No man I marry or live with is allowed to touch it. Same with Alena, same with all of us. I'll have the added pressure of finding a man that loves me for me and not for my fortune."

"Naw, poor Princess Diana." Cabot came through the open door. "The things you have to go through. There you are, Phe." He sat beside his twin, crossed his legs, and swung his left over his brother's.

Antonio raised a brow. "*What* do I keep telling you?"

Cabot blinked, a childlike quality coming over his face. "Tone."

"That's my name," Antonio said. "Use it. I'm not working, I'm off duty. I'm Antonio."

"Yes, Tone, sorry, Tone," Cabot said in a small voice before turning his attention to his stunned sister. "Thinking about getting married are we?"

Surprised at Cabot's toned-down persona, and getting a twinkling eye from Antonio, she replied, "God no. But I am twenty-nine, and I do want to have children before I get to forty like Mama was, so I'm going to have to seriously start thinking about it from next year."

"Next year?" Cabot played with his brother's hair.

"I'm thirty. I'll have been modelling for fifteen years, and I'll need to decide what to do with my life. So, I'll start thinking about having children."

"It's obvious I'll never have any, and I don't mind one bit," Cabot said. "Who wants a stinking dirty child to look after?"

"I don't, and yet I do." Antonio raised both brows at his brother.

Diana giggled. "*You* were those stinking dirty children once, you know. Mama and Daddy had to look after the two of you."

"Yeah, but that was us, and that was their job. They had us, so they had to look after us. We couldn't help pooing our pants, or eating worms," Cabot whined.

"And it was the eating of those worms that made you poo your pants," Antonio told him. "And you *still* poo your pants when you've done too much junk."

"I do not!" Cabot shrank back. "I have control over my bowels, thank you very much."

"Then why was I cleaning up *your* mess last week?" Antonio asked. He turned to Diana. *"See what I mean?"*

"Yes," she replied. "Looks like it's time for a lot of us to make changes."

"Who's changing? What changes?" Cabot perked up.

"I spoke to Alena a few days ago," Diana said. "She really wanted to go home with her mother and Alexis, so it's probably the last tour she'll do. And after what happened to Alexis, *she'll* probably want to change a few things too."

"What happened to Alexis?" Cabot asked, leaning his head on Antonio's shoulder.

Diana realised her cousin hadn't told him. Bugger! "Oh, she hasn't told you. She was assaulted back in May…by a man." It looked as if no one had told Cabot, and as far as she knew, even Danté still didn't know. But then, he was only fourteen and too young to understand.

"What?" Cabot lifted his head. "Why did no one tell me? She was raped? By who? How? When? What happened? Did Grandma kill the bastard?" So many thoughts raced through his head. His cousin had been raped, and no one had told him.

"For one thing, Alexis wanted to keep it quiet. She didn't even tell *us*," Diana told him. "Grandma did the night of my birthday. Alena verbally attacked her, and Alexis stormed off. Grandma attacked Alena and Alena stormed off. Grandma was the one who told the two of us. Not Alexis. Dom didn't know until just before she left for Alena's tour, and Danté still doesn't know."

"They told me when they were in town," Antonio said sending a scathing look in his brother's direction. "Just before you came into the room and made it all about you…as you do."

Cabot blinked in shock and thought about it. Someone had attacked his cousin, and he hadn't been told. That wasn't good. "What did Grandma and Uncle Pedro do?"

"All anyone has said is that it was taken care of. That *he* was taken care of," Diana said, surprised at the range of emotions flying over Cabot's face.

"Did they hurt him like he hurt Lexi?" Cabot's frown showed his displeasure.

"Alexis," Diana corrected. "You know she hates Lexi. As I said, they just kept saying it's been taken care of. *He's* been taken care of. If Grandma actually did him bodily harm, the bastard deserved it."

"Poor Alexis. What must she have gone through," Antonio murmured. "She must have been beside herself."

Diana shrugged lightly. "At my birthday she seemed okay; she'd cut her hair off, but other than that, she was holding it together."

"And she seemed fine at the concert when we were there," Cabot said, shaking his head in bewilderment. "Wow, our cuz was assaulted. That's shit, man!"

"It certainly is," Diana agreed, glad to see Cabot caring about someone other than himself for once.

*****

Alexis headed to Summer and Melody's house to catch up and flopped onto Summer's bed when she got there. "Your grandparents are finally gone then?"

"Thank God," Summer groaned, lying beside her. "Can you believe it's already July? One month of summer is over, and we haven't done anything."

"Well, not together." Melody lounged in a bean bag between the bed and the window. "But Alexis got to travel across America with her sister."

Alexis laughed. "It was hardly America. We only got to a few states."

"The whole eastern seaboard," Melody corrected. "New York, Miami."

"Five states," Alexis said. "She had concerts in five states, and we drove through a few more. But it's not like we stopped for shopping."

"Did you get to shop in Miami?" Summer asked. "Didn't she do two shows there?"

"She did, and we spent six days shopping."

"So, you did get to go shopping, you liar!" Melody exclaimed and threw a cushion at her best friend's head.

"And that was the only place," Alexis protested, clutching the cushion. "Everywhere else we were on the bus getting to the next stop. Miami was the one place we were in long enough to do anything worthwhile."

"How was it?" Summer asked. "Bring anything back for me?"

"What do you mean, you?" Melody chastised. "What about *me?*"

"I brought back stuff for both of you," Alexis told them and pulled stuff from the bag she'd brought with her. "Here. Snow globes for all." She produced two snow globes of Miami. The girls collected them and had many from all of the cities they'd visited.

"Awesome." Summer set hers next to the rest on the floor-to-ceiling shelves by the window. "Is that all?"

"Well, did you want t-shirts and caps and stuff?" Alexis asked.

"Not when we get to wear *Haus of Stefan* and *Alexis* originals. Are you going to design for the company?" Melody asked, shaking her snow globe and watching the glitter fall over the Miami beach scene.

"I don't know." Alexis shook her head. "I'm not sure what I want to do now."

"You didn't know in May either." Summer swung her legs off the edge of the bed. "We were all trying to figure out where we were going for summer, and now it's a third over."

"I'm not too worried about what I'm doing for the *rest* of summer," Alexis said. "I'm more worried about what sort of career I want. I love designing and sewing, but I'm not sure I could work full-time for Stefan."

"Then don't, do it in your spare time," Summer said. "Were you thinking of getting a job?"

Alexis shook her head. "No. I don't want to work full-time anywhere. Not even in one of the businesses, and you know we have many."

"What about one of the clothes shops, or that accessories store?" Melody put the ideas out there.

Alexis sighed and rolled over, staring at the coloured ceiling. "I don't know, I just...after the...what happened, I really don't know what I want to do. Oh, have you heard?" She rolled back to look at her two best friends.

"Heard what?" the twins asked in unison.

"What happened on the tour after the first New York show?"

"No, what! Tell us."

Alexis told them the whole sordid tale from start to finish. "I feel sorry for the officer who was saving me. He probably thought I was a halfwit or something because I was freaking out after he saved my life."

"Was he cute?" Summer asked, enthralled by the life of her best friend and wishing she had been there.

A blush crept across Alexis's cheeks. "Yeah."

"Do you like him?" Melody teased, seeing the red hue on her friend's face.

"I hardly know him, and I haven't seen him since. Besides, after the assault, I'm not sure I want to get involved with a man."

"Yeah." Summer sobered. "It must be hard still. How are you dealing?"

"Okay." Alexis shrugged. "I still have dreams, and they can make me queasy, but I'm okay." She picked at a loose thread coming out of the bedspread.

"Are you queasy from *other* things…?" Summer asked slowly.

"Oh, God, I'm not pregnant!" Alexis exclaimed. "Dan tested me."

"Oh, that's good." Melody let out a gasp of air in relief. "What would your Grandma do if you were?"

"Probably demand that I get rid of it," Alexis said. "I don't know. It was hard enough telling her I'd been sexually assaulted, I have no idea what she'd say if I ended up pregnant from it. God, can we change the subject? Have you two met any cute boys?"

Out in the hallway, Danté frowned. *Alexis has been sexually assaulted? When? Why wasn't I told?* He'd been visiting with Nick when he'd heard his sister come in and had stopped to listen on the way to the bathroom. The bathroom forgotten, he thought about what he'd heard. Alexis had been assaulted, and he needed to talk to someone about it. He went back to Nick's room and told him he needed to leave.

"But we haven't played Tube Racers yet," Nick complained.

"Next time, gotta go. See ya." Grabbing his bag, he quietly left and walked up the road to his grandparents' place, hoping his grandma was home. Letting himself in with his key, he called out. "Grandma?"

"We're out here, sweetie," Jenny called from the balcony.

He went out and saw Dan and Derek going over paperwork with her.

"Hey. You didn't want to stay at Nick's?" she asked as he leant down and kissed her on the cheek.

He was nervous about asking, but since Alexis had mentioned Dan, then maybe they could explain it to him. "No…I…ah…heard something and I thought…I'd come and ask you…coz you know everything."

Jenny laughed. "Well, not everything. What is it, sweetie?"

"Well—"

"Do you want us to stay?" Derek asked, seeing Danté's nervousness.

"No, um…you might be able to help, um..." Danté shoved his hands in his pockets.

"Has something happened?" Jenny asked, concerned by his reluctance to come out and ask. "Has something happened to you?"

"Um, no…" He glanced everywhere but at her. "Not me…"

"Nick?" she questioned.

"Um, no… I was with him, and Alexis came over to see the girls, and I heard them talking about the tour…"

"Yes," Jenny urged, putting her hand on his arm. "It's okay, sweetie, you can talk to us, you know that."

"Um…" He scuffed his foot. "You raised us to be safe, and you know…not force ourselves on women…"

Jenny's insides went cold, and she quickly glanced at Dan with a raised brow. "Go on, sweetie."

"Well, you told us it was rape and sexual assault and to never do it." Just saying the words made him sick to his stomach, and he wanted the balcony to collapse so he could die. The last thing he wanted to be doing was talking about sex and rape with his grandma.

"I…um…heard Alexis," he glanced out across the water, "say she was sexually assaulted. Why didn't anyone tell me?" rushed out. "She's my sister."

"Oh, sweetie." Jenny pushed her chair back and pulled him onto her lap. "We felt that you were too young to deal with that. Alexis was barely dealing with it herself. The family found out slowly, Dom was only told before she left on tour with Alena."

"So, why haven't I been told?" he asked, sliding his arm around her neck.

"Because you're too young. We didn't want to burden you with it," Jenny repeated.

"But she's my sister, you always said this family loves, protects and defends. So why wasn't I told so I could do that?" he asked.

"Because I took care of it," Jenny said. "I took care of the horrible person who did it to her, and neither she nor any other woman ever has to worry about him again."

"Did you hurt him?" Danté's blood was boiling, and he didn't know what to do with it.

"Yes, I did." Jenny nodded.

"So…" He bit his lip. "What did he do to her, and can we make it better?"

"Ah…" Jenny looked at Dan and Derek for answers. "Why don't you two explain that so he can understand? I have to pop inside for a minute. Take a seat, sweetie." She got up and sat him in her chair.

"Dan and Derek will explain it." Going inside, she called the girls and asked for Alexis to come over. Once she arrived, Jenny explained that Danté had overheard the conversation.

"Oh, no," Alexis groaned. "I didn't even know he was there."

"Well, he was, and he heard. He's out on the balcony with Dan and Derek who are explaining sexual assault and what he can do to help."

"Aw, cute Squirt. Guess I'd better spend some time with him and explain it all."

"You can use your father's old room if you want," Jenny said. "Or go for a walk."

"I might use Daddy's old room. I felt safe there when I came here that night."

"Okay." Jenny led the way to the balcony where Danté flew into his sister's arms.

"Did I hurt you?" he asked when she stepped back.

"No, you're okay, Squirt. Come on, we gotta talk. Let's go to Daddy's old room. Grandma will bring in some goodies for us to munch on."

"Oh, I will, will I?" Jenny raised an amused brow.

"Yes, Grandma, you will." Alexis smiled and slid her arm around Danté's shoulder. "Come on, Squirt, let's go have our own party." They walked off, and Jenny quietly got a rundown of what the boys had told him.

"Just the basics then." Jenny sighed. "Good. Not sure what Alexis will tell him, but I hope he can deal with it. *That's* why we hadn't told him."

"He'll be okay, Jenny. He's a smart kid, takes after his grandma." Dan grinned.

Laughing, she said, "Are you just trying to get some goodies to munch on?"

Dan and Derek sneaked a look at one another and replied at the same time. "Yes, please!"

*****

On Monday, Diana had a photo shoot and interview with *Sparkle* magazine, and since it was such a nice day, they went across the road to Central Park to talk and play.

"Tell me about your family," Fran, the red-haired interviewer said. "I know it's been a story told a million times, so tell me something no one else would know." They were walking along the path leading to the zoo.

"Well, my mother filmed her first exercise videos here in this very park," Diana said as the photographer snapped candid pics of them. "I remember being on the rooftop terrace of our building with Daddy and Grandpa when Grandma came up."

"Oh, my goodness, when was that?" Fran asked into her handheld recorder before pointing it back at Diana.

"It was 1980." Diana's laughter tinkled out of her. "A long time ago."

"And your mother is world-famous model turned cosmetics, perfume, make-up, book and style queen, Vivian Villiers. You're obviously following in her footsteps?"

"To a degree," Diana agreed. "Definitely with the modelling, and moving into fashion, but it's more the clothes design side than the styling side. We get her advice on colours and shapes and work with her on that, but as for the other things, I have no need to go into that too. She's done it all."

"Your mother even named a perfume after you, if I remember."

"Yes, she named one after all of us girls at the time. She had *Vivian* first and *Villiers* last, and in between came *Diana, Alena, Angie, Jennifer* and *Sarah.* They're still very popular, although there are many more now."

"Yes, and your father's a famous movie director, writer *and* producer; any thoughts about going into that side of the business?" Fran indicated to the photographer to take pics from a certain angle as they walked.

"We've been in some documentaries that Daddy's made, and did bit parts as extras on movies, so we've had the practice." Diana's smile shone brighter than the sun.

"Your brothers followed in the modelling footsteps and have quite a back catalogue themselves. Can you tell us something we wouldn't know about them?"

"Besides the fact they're actually named Antonio and Cabot after two dear friends of our parents who died before they were born?" They stopped by the side of the lake and she took her sandals off, dipping a toe in as the photographer snapped away.

"That's right," Fran remembered. "That's not a well-known fact, but it has been said. Which one's which?"

"Cabot is Steele, and Antonio is Phoenix." Diana moved her toes through the water, kicking high into the air and splashing water over everyone. She laughed.

"Wow, even Cabot's an unusual name," Fran went on, smiling at the great shots they were getting. "And your cousins and uncles are famous."

"The musical side of the family." Diana smiled, balancing on her tiptoes on the rocks. "My gorgeous cousins are very musically talented. Alena's on her tour right now."

"Touring a fantastic new album. I loved it," Fran told her. "Your uncles are activists, so what's it like growing up with that in the family?"

"We all know to practise safe sex," Diana said. "Had it drummed into our heads from an early age."

"And how often do you get to see the family?"

Diana slid her sandals back on, and they kept on walking. "Not often enough. We'll meet up after Alena's tour finishes in August, and spend some time here in New York. Then we'll go home for wedding anniversaries and Christmas."

"Wedding anniversaries?" Fran inquired, curious as to where the conversation was going.

"My parents and my uncles all got married across three days in November 1977. It's a three-day celebration for the family every year. This year's their thirtieth."

"That's fantastic. The whole family must have a lot to celebrate every year?"

"We do. Birthdays, anniversaries, Christmas, New Year, Father's day, Mother's day, Thanksgiving, Halloween, Fourth of July—"

"Even in Mykonos?" Fran was unbelieving.

"Oh, we celebrate everything in Mykonos. Any excuse for a party in our homes. We took a lot of traditions with us after we left."

"Left?" Fran asked.

"Yes. We lived in New York for four years from '77 through to '81. Well, the family did. I was born in 1978 with Alena, so we were three when we left. But we took a lot of traditions back and kept them going all these years. Which is good, considering there are seven of us kids to keep amused."

"It must be a non-stop party?" Fran laughed lightly.

"For the first half of the year, then we have a break from July until Halloween. Then it starts at the end of the year. Actually..." Diana stopped, hands in pockets, "Our year starts at Halloween and goes until July. It's very busy."

"Sounds like. So, what's next for Diana Villiers, supermodel and fashion designer?" Fran started walking again.

Diana followed and laughed at the phrasing. "I actually don't know and was talking to my brothers about this very thing yesterday. I'm thirty next year, so I'll decide then what else I'm going to do. I'll have been modelling for fifteen years, and maybe it's time to take my life and career in a new direction."

"Children?" Fran asked, desperately hoping for a scoop.

"With what man?" Diana asked in return. "I'm single, so there are no children coming in the next year."

"Since you're single, tell our readers what type of man you like, you want."

"Well," Diana thought for a moment. "Strong physically, emotionally, and definitely psychologically. He needs to be a man and act like one. Not be immature and insecure."

"Sure of himself," Fran cut in.

"But not *too* sure," Diana replied. "He needs to show emotions, needs to know how to defend and protect his family. Be loving, caring, happy within himself."

"He sounds perfect," Fran said. "But clearly he doesn't exist."

Diana stopped once more and smiled. "Oh, men like that *do* exist, Fran. My father is an incredible man, and so are his brothers, my uncles, even Roger, Uncle Tomas's husband. Four incredibly strong, loving, caring men who know how to be men and act like men, but can still have some fun. And they get that from Grandma and Grandpa. And hopefully, someday, three lucky girls will get my cousins Dom and Danté, and my brother Antonio."

"But not Steele, uh, Cabot?" *Now here's a scoop,* Fran thought.

Diana paused. "Steele, Cabot," she corrected herself, "is a free spirit. He loves who he wants, when he wants, and I really don't know if there's any *one* person in particular out there for him."

"The word is, he loves both." Fran shoved the recorder into Diana's face, not wanting to miss a single word.

"He does, and that's his business, Fran," Diana said calmly. "It's not mine to discuss."

Fran, realising the interview was coming to an end, started wrapping up. "So, what *is* next for Diana Villiers now she's twenty-nine?"

"Well, I'd like to spend the rest of the year doing my business, photo shoots, interviews, get it all out of the way, spend a few months with my family, and then make some resolutions and see where the new year takes me."

"Just before we go, the summer collection is currently out for *Haus of Stefan*, but what can we expect for the next year, fashion-wise?"

"I love our current summer range, *A Glittering Summer*, I think it's fabulous, and I'm wearing a top, pants and sandals from it, but what we have for fall is slightly darker colours, a little muted and dusty, but still colourful. For winter, we'll get into richer tones, sapphires, garnets, emeralds, violets, silks and satins, and leather, and we've got some fabulous faux fur goodies coming for fall/winter. Then we'll be back to spring with pastels and lights before hitting next summer with brights again."

"And all fabulously sparkling, I hope?" Fran asked.

"Of course." Diana laughed. "You *have* to have sparkle."

"Well, that's it for the interview. Diana, it's been a pleasure talking to you and walking through glorious Central Park. Have you got enough shots, Dave?" Fran asked the photographer.

"Sure have; they'll be great." He kept snapping.

"Great then, we'd better get going," Fran said and held out her hand. "Thank you so much, Diana, our editor will send you copies."

"Thank you." Diana shook Fran's hand. "That's one of the easiest interviews I've had." Taking her time back to the penthouse, Diana thought about the people in her life and what they meant to her. They meant everything. Her parents, grandparents, aunt and uncles, cousins, even her brothers meant so much, and with everything that had happened in the last few months alone, she realised that modelling may not be all that important anymore. Not at the rate she was doing it. Month after month, week after week, she had to deal with photographers like Charles Kensington.

Oh, God, where'd he pop up from?

But it was true, arrogant men who thought they knew how to shoot her, but who did nothing but annoy her. Stopping, she stared across the lake watching the ducks float by. Her family was the world, and if only she could find a man like her father or uncles, strong, supportive, loving and caring, not insecure when it came to her work, not insecure when it came to her earning more money. *And when my trust fund comes along…geez, that's going to attract some weirdos.*

Sighing, she thought some more. *Where am I going to find a man like Daddy and my uncles? A man that I can love, rely on, and trust.*

Turning, she came face to face with Charles Kensington.

*****

Steele and Phoenix were in the middle of their own photo shoot, downtown New York, on a pier overlooking the skyline, dressed in business suits with their shirts undone to show off their abs. They were actually modelling watches, but the photographer wanted abs. *And Steele.*

"Okay, Steele, look this way, hold up your arms, look at me, show off. The watch, I mean, turn, turn, turn. Phoenix, you're in the way, move."

"What do you mean, move!" Antonio stopped, bringing the photo shoot to a halt. "This *is not Steele's* shoot, it's *ours. We work as a team.* You don't tell me to move or get out of the way." With the mood he'd been in lately, he could easily pick a fight.

The photographer, Phan Lee, stared. Antonio's expression may have amused Steele, but it didn't amuse him. "If I want to take photos of Steele, then you will get out of the way."

"Then *we* don't do this shoot, and *the company* doesn't get Steele *and* Phoenix Stefan," Antonio told him, walking off the set. "You asked for both, you get both, you got that!" Swigging back the water Tilly handed him, he eyed her. "Why aren't you doing your job and telling them that?"

An amused grin was on her face. "You seem to be able to do that all on your own."

"And you're our manager, you made the booking, they either wanted both of us—"

"They did," Tilly interrupted. "But it seems Phan just wants Steele."

"Then he can have him," Antonio spat. "I don't get kicked off a shoot we were both hired to do. Tell *them* that!"

Tilly, being fluent in Japanese, spoke to the company's representative who was looking very flustered. She explained that the company had hired the twins, but with the photographer pushing him out of the way, Antonio didn't believe it was fair to the company, *or* him.

The representative bowed her head many times and spoke to Phan.

"If I want to take photos of Steele and not Phoenix, I will." The thirty-something Asian stomped his foot like a petulant child.

The representative spoke to him, and he calmed down.

"What are they saying?" Antonio asked Tilly.

"The company's exec threatened to fire him if he didn't take photos of both, oh…" Her eyes went back and forth between the company's representative and Phan. "Interesting."

"What is?" Antonio glanced over his shoulder to watch the exchange.

"Phan Lee owes them big money, and she's telling him he'll do as he's told or else."

"Or else what?" Antonio felt a rush of excitement course through him.

"Or else she'll see to it that he never walks again."

Steele strolled over to them. "So, I have a photographer who's only interested in me for my body. Should I take him up on his offer?"

"Oh, for fuck's sake, keep it in your pants for once," Antonio snapped, and saw the hurt expression flit over Cabot's face. They watched as Phan and the representative came over to them, red-faced with embarrassment, or shame.

"I will finish the photo shoot." Phan stared at Steele. "Of both of you."

"That is your job," Antonio told him. "Try doing it this time." He made his way back to the spot with Steele behind him. "And *you* keep it in your pants," he added to his brother. "Let's get this over and done with. I'm over it."

Surprised, and confused by his brother's reaction to it all, Steele prepped himself for the rest of the shoot.

Twenty minutes later, they handed back the watches and bowed to the representative who waved her hands and shook her head.

"She's giving them to you as a gift," Tilly translated. "They're yours."

"Oh, thank you." Antonio bowed his head. "Thank you, very much." He saw Steele follow his lead, and they watched the representative walk away. "Okay, let's strip off and go. I'm done." Fifteen minutes later, they were on their way home.

*****

"Charles!" Diana exclaimed. "How long have you been—"

"A while," he said, watching her blush. "Did I just see Fran and Dave leave a while ago?"

She frowned. "You've been here a while? Stalking me? Spying on me?" The anger burned inside.

"Don't kid yourself, Princess." He sneered. "I always come to the park when I'm in town. I saw you talking to them. Giving an interview?"

"Yes, not that's it any of *your* business." She pushed past him and moved on. Of all the insufferable people to come across…

"Talking about yourself again, were you?" He easily caught up to her, walking side by side as she stomped along.

"*Of course* I was." Diana rolled her eyes. "It *was* an interview." She needed to get away from him and get away now.

"Any chance to talk about yourself." Charles kept up, not sure why he'd ever bothered going up to her. He'd been minding his own business, sitting there eating, when he'd seen them all walk past. Curious, he'd followed and heard bits and pieces, especially the bits about what sort of man she was after. He'd also heard Fran mention babies, and Diana had said she was single. Well, at least there was no man to worry about. "Doing anything for Fourth of July?" he asked, keeping up.

"I wouldn't tell you if I was," Diana told him crossly. "Go away, Charles. I'm not working with you now."

"So, we can't talk and have a chat?"

She stopped and faced him, knowing her face was red. "Why would I talk to you? Why would I have a chat with you? I don't like you, *you're a pig.*" She walked away in a huff.

"In your words, but other models love me," he called, slyly watching her pert ass as she moved and raising his camera to take pictures.

"Bull they do," she yelled. "You're a repulsive, repugnant human being and you can get the hell away from me." She ran and kept running until she got to the penthouse where she locked the door. "Oh, my God why does he make me so angry?" she puffed. "Argh!"

*****

On Wednesday the third, Diana and the twins attended a pre-Independence Day party for *Flair* magazine. Accepting glasses of champagne, they separated, and Diana found herself talking to Edie, the editor.

"Hello, darling, did you get that box of magazines we sent you?" Edie eyed the stunning sequined dress Diana was wearing.

"Yes, we did. My family loved them and framed them up on the wall within twenty-four hours, they were so proud." Sipping her drink, she looked around the room, seeing Antonio chatting to a woman she didn't know. She couldn't even see Cabot…

"Good, good, we have to do another shoot soon, darling. You were our biggest seller for the year."

"Really?" Diana was surprised. "That's nice to know."

"That's why we want you to do another, and another, and another." Edie laughed. "You'll sell out every copy."

"But won't people get bored with me? There's only so much you can talk about, or ask me."

"People never get bored of you, darling. Look at you, you're gorgeous. We'll have to hook you up with Charles again. His photos were fantastic."

A scowl lit up Diana's gorgeous petite face. "I *never* want to work with that pompous ass again." She knocked back her champagne.

"Did you see the French shoot?" Edie asked, wondering what had happened between the two.

"No, not yet. I haven't received anything."

"You're beautiful," Edie said. "You're a stunning woman, Diana, and Charles makes you mind-blowingly, incredibly ethereal. You are a goddess when he photographs you."

"What? No, he doesn't," Diana replied. "I mean, what he does is good, I look awesome in them, but he does nothing special. He acts like a jerk all the time, that's what he does, and he never used to."

Edie moved closer, intrigued by the conversation. "When did you know him?"

"I first met him when I was nineteen. He was polite, friendly, a little…I don't know, quiet or something. I worked with him for a few more years and then didn't for a while. Then two years ago he was back, and we just got on each other's nerves. He was pompous and arrogant and a jerk."

"That's strange," Edie mused. "He's always been the same with me. I wonder what happened."

They drifted apart and spent the next hour mingling. Diana tracked down the twins and was talking when Charles came up to them.

"Oh, look, Princess and her twin lapdogs."

Diana rolled her eyes and looked away, embarrassed by the drunk behind her.

"Oh, look, the arrogant jerk that treats our sister like shit," Antonio snapped. "*Not cool*, dude, picking on a woman." He was two inches taller and proved it by leaning towards Charles.

That put Charles in his place. For about two seconds. "And the twins, Phoenix and gay boy." He coolly gazed at Cabot. "Still tapping anything that walks?"

"Only the men these days," Cabot replied, eyebrow raised. "But I seem to recall you turned me down, Mr Photographer. Don't like to suck?"

"Huh! I have no problem sucking pussies," Charles slurred. "The female kind. Not the arrogant cock kind. But I do recall you fucked one of my assistants."

"Well, after he told me you were no good, I felt sorry for him and decided to show him what a god was like." Cabot couldn't wait to hear Charles's line for that.

Diana cringed inwardly, wishing the ground would open up and swallow her. She frantically looked around for a way out.

"God!" Charles exclaimed. "You think you're a god? The poor bastard was left in a delusional state so deep he had to be admitted to a psych ward."

"All right, enough," Antonio spat, shoving his finger in Charles's chest. He pushed him back as he walked. "I have had *enough* of the way you treat my sister, you arrogant sod, and I don't care to hear you attack my brother. Whatever your problem is, Kensington, deal with it *away* from my family, you got that?" He stared coldly into Charles' terrified eyes. "Whatever reason you're hating on my sister for, you cut the crap out now, because it upsets her and pisses the rest of the family off. If you think you're a man being a rude cockhead to my sister, you'd better think again. It makes you an asshole, that's all it does. You're not cool, you're an ass for picking on a young woman. So you're going to stop it. Do I make myself clear, *Charles Kensington?*" He leaned in close, so they were eye to eye, completely unaware of everyone else in the room muttering and twittering amongst themselves.

Charles had been put in his place by almost no one. No one had come close to this, and it scared him. A little. The emerald eyes of Antonio DeLuca Stephanopoulos burned into his retinas, and they were almost the same height. The room became deathly quiet, all eyes on them, and they all knew who was going to win. Saying nothing, he straightened his jacket and walked away.

Cabot started clapping, and soon the whole room was too. "Good on you, bro, defending us against Mr Kensington."

Antonio came over to them. "You okay, D?"

"I'm fine." She kissed his cheek. "Thank you for defending me. I love you for it."

"You're welcome. Just doing what the fam taught us to do, defend one another." He pulled on his cuff and looked around the room, as whispers and amused glances were exchanged from person to person. "You sticking around?"

"No. I think I've had enough for the day. I need to go over *HOS* stuff for the next few days, so I'm going home." She trailed her hand across her forehead, feeling a headache coming on.

"Okay. We'll see you tomorrow." The twins each kissed a cheek and watched her walk away.

Making her way through the room, she didn't see Charles anywhere. *Good, let's hope he doesn't feel the need to assault me again. But then I'll never work with him ever again anyway.* She caught a taxi home, entered their building, and went up to the penthouse, where she showered and got ready for bed. Slipping into a white man's shirt made her remember back to the Paris photo shoot when she'd worn one, and it had felt so comfortable she'd grabbed a few from *HOS* headquarters. She wore them to bed and around the house. As she pulled a pair of panties from her bag, she heard a banging on the door. "Oh, damn it, the twins. What do they want?"

Her underwear forgotten, she ran downstairs and flung open the door. "Charles!" She stopped short in surprise.

"Princess," he slurred, drunker than he was at the party.

"How did you get in? We have a doorman." She was ready to call downstairs to have a go at their employee for letting him in.

"Wasn't at his post." Charles lounged against the doorjamb.

"Go home, Charles, before I call the police," she threatened, trying to show more bravado than she felt.

"Listen up, Princess, you don't get to decide." He slammed the door shut behind him. "How dare you tease me and torment me." He grabbed her face with both hands, saw her big blue eyes go wide, and planted a kiss on her lips.

"Mmm, mmm," she protested, pummelling him with her hands. But the feelings overwhelmed her, and all came rushing back. The reason she'd hated him in the first place, the reason she'd run every time he was around. Because when it all came down to it, she'd fallen in love with him when she was nineteen. But he'd clearly been unavailable at the time and wasn't interested, so she'd pushed down her feelings.

Charles probed with his tongue, allowing himself the release of all the feelings he had for her. And they boiled over. Seeing the photos of her in the waterfall had sent him over the edge. And finally, all of the emotions he'd ever had for her burst into a torrent, and then he'd drowned them in a torrent of alcohol. He couldn't believe that all of the years meant he was in love with her. It just wasn't possible. Not possible at all.

She gave in to the kiss, wanting to know what it was like to kiss him. Her fingers clawed at his shirt and his at hers. Somehow, they ended up against the wall, with him ripping open her shirt, her arms above her head, groaning as he devoured her neck. "Oh, God Charles." His hands were on her breasts.

"Oh, God such beautiful breasts." His mouth tore away and latched on the right one, replacing his hand. "Oh, God, you're so beautiful, so beautiful." His hands moved down to clench her ass, so perfect and ripe. Finding she had no underwear, he wrenched himself from his pants, clenched her, lifted her, and planted her where she belonged.

"Oh, God," she cried. "Oh, God." He was huge and filled her completely. "Oh, God, Charles." She gripped his hair as he thrust her against the wall. "Ah…ah…"

Charles plundered, moulded, kissed. He was inside the beautiful Diana Villiers, and he wanted it. "Where's the bedroom?"

"Oh," she breathed. "Upstairs."

He held her, and moved up to the bed, laying her down, moving in sync as her legs gripped his waist and his lips devoured her.

"Charles," she moaned. "Oh…uh…" She climaxed, enjoying the moment, the first moment with the man she actually loved. The consequence of her actions the furthest thing from her mind…

*****

After Diana had left the party, Cabot and Antonio stuck around and went on a fact-finding mission, going their separate ways. Although Antonio knew Cabot would more than likely be out for himself and what he could get, Antonio started questioning people about Charles and why he treated people like crap.

He found out from other models that he was rude to them, but found out from editors and publishers that he was hardworking and perfectly fine. So, it seemed to just be the models.

He thought back to their photo shoot a year earlier. He hadn't noticed anything in particular that was wrong. Charles hadn't called them names, been rude, or treated them badly, so maybe it was just the female models. Had Diana said something, done something, or retaliated in defence of something he had done or said? It must have started from somewhere for him to treat her so badly.

He left Edie till last, hoping she'd know more. "Edie, good to see you again. Haven't talked to you all night." He kissed her cheek.

She looked into his eyes to see which twin he was. "Phoenix, darling, how are you? I saw that little show of yours earlier."

"Everyone did," he cracked.

"Well, after what Diana told me, I have to wonder what Charles has done."

"That's what I'm trying to find out. He treats my sister like garbage and thinks it's okay. It's not. I've spoken to almost everyone here; the models say he's an ass, always hitting on them. Everyone else says they don't have a problem with him. Which is it, Edie? Is he Jekyll and Hyde, or does he just hate female models? Because he was fine with us a year ago."

"Diana told me he used to be fine with her too. She met him at nineteen apparently, and worked with him off and on for years, but it's been the last couple of years he's been a…what were the words she used…pompous, arrogant and a jerk."

"Do *you* remember what he was like back then?" Antonio asked, curious as to why someone could so radically change the way they treated someone.

"I vaguely remember something happening many years ago, but after taking time off, he was okay. I don't remember what it was. But he was really quiet and very polite. He stayed that way for years, but then he got a little harder. I think he'd actually gone overseas to work for some magazine. Went to photograph war-torn countries or something for a couple of years. When he came back, he was definitely harder, a little rough with his words, but not a whole lot different to how he'd been."

"He clearly treats female models very differently to how he treats everyone else," Antonio mused. "Maybe he came back thinking what a vacuous job modelling was compared to what he saw in war-torn countries?"

"Could be, but then why continue working with models?" Edie asked. "If he thinks that way, then why take the photos?"

"Money?" Antonio questioned. "Does he get paid well? Maybe it's how he makes his money. Maybe he donates his cheque to an orphanage or something. It's what he knows how to do, so he keeps doing it for the money."

"All very good explanations," Edie said. "He did come back a changed man."

"Yes, but changed enough to suddenly treat women like crap?" Antonio asked. "If he didn't treat her that way before, why would he simply because he would have seen what war did to people? You don't see that and then start treating people like crap."

"True," Edie replied. "Look, darling, I don't know what else to tell you. I really don't know a lot about his private life. He came onto the scene about sixteen or seventeen years ago, disappeared for a year, then came back, and your sister's shoot was the first he did. It landed him his next gig, and his popularity skyrocketed."

"Mmm," Antonio murmured. "Where did he go then?"

Edie shrugged. "Don't know, darling. Maybe you could do some digging?"

"Yeah, maybe. Okay, thanks, Edie." He kissed her other cheek.

"Darling, you and Steele have to do a photo shoot with us soon. You can't let your sister have all the *Flair* covers."

Antonio laughed. "Yes, Edie. Give Tilly a call." He went in search of his brother, unable to find him at the party. A cold feeling swept through him. If he wasn't in the room at the party, then he had sneaked off somewhere to do something...*or someone.* "For fuck's sake, Cabot," he muttered under his breath. "You'd better not be fucking someone."

*****

"Oh, God, oh, God," Steele groaned, getting sucked for the fourth time that night. He was in the service area, and had found a plethora of gay wait staff just ripe for the picking, and he was taking turns with them. They all sucked him, and he fucked all of them. "Oh, God, you're good. A good little fag boy who just wants some of the Stefan." He sighed as the mouth left him. "You like it up the butt, you little fucker?" He pulled the boy to him. "Do you?"

"I'll take it any way you want to give it to me, Steele," the boy said. At twenty-three, this was his first wait job, and wouldn't you know it, Steele Stefan, lover of men and women, but mostly men, had been at the party. Word on the street had everyone knowing his routine. You sucked him off then got fucked by him. You *never* fucked *him.* He wasn't interested in taking it up the ass, but he *gave it* up the ass, so you needed to decide what you wanted most. To suck him off, or get fucked by him. And most did both. They wanted the Stefan up their ass, wanted to know what it was like to be butt fucked by him, and most reports were good. Excellent in fact. But some cried of pain and violence. The most ignored the least, and many more still wanted to try him out. And he, Julio Varez, was trying him out; taking all eleven inches in his mouth, deep throating him the best he could. He'd never had an eleven-inch cock before, and it was choking. Ignoring the taste of it, he did his duty and pushed down his pants. "Take me, Steele, give it to me up the ass." He turned and bent over, leaning on a cupboard for support.

At the sight of the young Latino's naked ass, Steele hardened and removed a condom from his pocket. He'd brought ten out that night and had six left. Maybe he should go and buy more. Rolling it on, he grabbed the boy and pushed him against the cupboard, coming in from behind. He grasped the boy's hair with his right hand, pushing him against the cupboard. He towered a head above him. "Tell me you like it like this," he breathed in the boy's ear. "Tell me you like being butt fucked by Steele Stefan. Tell me, you little fag."

"I like it, Steele," Julio huffed, taking all eleven inches up his ass. It hurt, but the pain was exquisite and made his cock hard. "I *love* being butt fucked by you. Harder, Steele, harder."

Steele plunged in hard thrusts, grunting and groaning. He loved the power this gave him, to know he could make anyone do this. Suck him off then take it up the ass. He made them do it, just by being him. The sheer power of Steele Stefan made fags drop to their knees, or bend over, and it was exhilarating, liberating, life-changing.

"And what number's this?" Antonio asked from the doorway. He'd heard the whispers and seen the looks, the inquiring looks, to whether he was like his brother, and he'd found his way to the pantry, finding Steele up the ass of one of the wait staff.

"Hey, Phe!" Steele looked his brother's way, but didn't let go of the boy, or stop thrusting. "Number four, but who's counting?"

"*You* should be, Cabot," Antonio said. "And you should be ashamed of yourself. *I'm* ashamed of you." Pulling the door closed, he walked away.

Seeing his brother's sad expression, and hearing the words he'd spoken, Steele shrivelled up. Withdrawing, he whipped off the condom, shoved himself back into his pants, and went after his brother. "Phe? Phe?" His brother had said he was ashamed. Ashamed of him. *No, Phe, please don't be ashamed of me,* he thought, running down corridors and into the party.

He saw Antonio getting into the lift and ran for it, but the doors shut before he got there. "Phe?" Since there was only one lift, he raced for the stairs off the hall and bolted down ten flights to find Antonio getting into a cab. "Phe?" he huffed, seeing the door shut and the cab leave. "Phe," he screamed. "Phe, don't leave me. Phe, come back." He had to force himself to not fall apart. Not cry. Not break down. *Think, Steele, think. Where would he be going? Home. That's it, he's going home.* Hailing a cab, he gave his address and saw a cab leave their apartment building as he pulled up. Jumping out, he ran for the door, only to be stopped by the driver.

"Hey, you didn't pay." He was leaning out the window.

Cabot patted his pockets and realised why he generally didn't have any money on him. Because Phe always did. "Hang on," he told the cabbie and quickly spoke to their doorman as he raced through the lobby. "Pay him and come and get it tomorrow, thanks."

Mark Chapman paid, shaking his head because this wasn't the first time he'd had to pay for a cab for Cabot. He'd been the Stephanopoulos doorman for ten years, having known Martin Brewster, their previous employee, who'd recommended him for the job.

Upstairs, Cabot burst through the door to find Antonio in the kitchen getting a drink. "Phe!" he yelled, falling at his brother's feet and clinging to his legs. "Please don't leave me, Phe. I love you. I don't want you being ashamed of me. I love you, please don't leave me. I couldn't stand it if you left me. You're my brother."

Antonio gently ran his hand over Cabot's head. "It's okay, Cabot, it's okay."

*****

Up in the penthouse, Diana and Charles lay facing each other in bed. Not saying anything, not needing to. They traded small smiles and gazed into each other's eyes, silent in the wake of their passionate lovemaking.

Charles traced a finger along Diana's cheekbone and across her lips.

She opened them, and her tongue darted out to touch his finger.

He leaned in to kiss her and his own tongue replaced his finger. Her mouth opened willingly, her tongue mating with his. His arms moved around her, pulling her tight against his body. Her breasts squashed against his chest, and he felt the thatch between her legs tease him. He rose to meet the need burning deep inside, but she had other ideas.

Her breasts were on fire from his chest hair which ran all the way down his abdomen to his crotch, and she felt every millimetre of it against her. She also felt his manhood probing between her legs. Taking control, she rolled him onto his back, straddled him, and allowed him to enter. Her head fell back, and she let her shirt fall off her shoulders, leaving it where it lay.

"Oh," she breathed as his hands grasped her hips. Her hands slid through the nest of hair on his chest and clenched. "Oh."

He bucked up, watching her face. Watching her close her eyes against the delirium she was in. Oh, God how he wanted her. Wanted to be inside of her, against her, wrap his arms around her. She was a woman, and he was a man with needs he wanted only her to fulfil. He felt the overwhelming surge rise as she slowly slid up and down; tormenting him with her gasps and moans. Her muscles clenched around him, and he moved his hands to her beautiful breasts. Breasts he had longed to touch and hold and mould to him. They were beautiful, full, perfect, perky, well placed, and suited her perfectly.

She groaned as his thumbs flicked over her nipples and her head fell back. "Oh." Sitting up, her hands went through her hair and up into the air.

Oh, the perfection. She was flawless, but he already knew that from all of the pictures he'd seen. There was not a mark on her, and his hands explored all they wanted, even down to her thatch to flick her engorged clit.

"Ugh," she cried out, her arms falling for her hands to grip his arms.

"Ugh," kept coming out of her as he played with her, making her explode into a million pieces as she sat on him. Her eyes screwed shut tightly at the assault on her senses. But she had no control. No control when one hand went back to her breast. No control when he tormented both her nipple and her clitoris at the same time. No control when he sat slowly and took her nipple into his mouth. She was bending backward, no control over her body. No control over her senses. She was pounding inside. All of her pelvic mound was pounding and on fire. Wild and out of control.

His arm slid around her back to hold her, his mouth stayed on her nipple, his hand went back to her clitoris, and bringing up his knees, he moved her up and down until she was screaming, and he was coming inside of her.

*****

The fourth of July dawned bright and warm, and the boys lay in the master bed. After Cabot had finished crying the night before, Antonio had put him to bed. But Cabot didn't want to be alone, so Antonio got in the bed to hold his brother, and both had fallen asleep. The public holiday emerged, and it was going to be a day of barbecues and parties.

Glancing around the room, Antonio breathed in. Cabot was still wrapped in his arms, but he needed to move so he could take a leak and get some breakfast. Trying not to wake his brother, he slipped out of his arms and made his way to the small bathroom off the second bedroom, stripped off and stepped into the shower. The hot water felt good as he washed his hair and rinsed off, but just as he was grabbing for his washcloth, Cabot stepped in behind him. "What are you doing!?" He glared at his brother.

"Having a shower," Cabot said innocently. "We used to do it all the time when we were kids, and we *have* gotten naked for photo shoots."

"Yeah, but I always had my bits covered up," Antonio snapped. "We're not kids anymore, Cabot, we're grown ass adult men who need to have separate moments from one another. Like having showers."

"Oh, for God's sake." Cabot rolled his eyes and slid his arms around his brother's chest. "We're twins, Phe, ah, Tone. We were naked in Mama's womb, naked as babies, naked as kids when we ran around without nappies or jocks on. We're brothers, twins, two of a kind. We *have* seen each other's junk before. It's exactly the same too."

"Most of New York has seen *your* junk," Antonio said. "We're not little kids anymore, Cabot. Go and get in your own shower." Regardless of the fact Cabot was his brother, he didn't like the feel of his junk pressing up against his ass, knowing full well where it had been and what it had done. He didn't like it, and it made him uncomfortable. Sexually *and* physically. "Go and get in your own shower."

"Naw, Tone." Cabot pouted and reluctantly got out of the shower stall. "No fair." He grabbed the towel and wrapped it around himself.

"Hey, that's mine," Antonio yelled after him.

"Then come and get it," Cabot yelled back.

"Jesus fucking Christ," Antonio muttered through clenched teeth. "When is he going to grow the fuck up?" Finishing off, he used his hair towel to wipe the rest of him off and quickly got dressed. They were supposed to be attending a barbecue in the park and a couple of friends' places before another magazine party that night for the fireworks. But only God knew if he could get Cabot there, or make him behave. He sighed, knowing there was no one who could make him behave. Not him. Not their parents, probably not even their grandparents. He remembered their grandmother's disappointed look from when they were little. They were seven or eight and had done something. He couldn't remember what. But it had disappointed his grandma so much he remembered the look for the rest of his life. He never forgot it. The hurt it was hiding. He'd felt so bad he'd cried for hours over disappointing his grandma. Not even his parents could console him. Only Grandma could. And she had taken him into her arms and hugged and kissed him until it didn't hurt anymore. He didn't want to hurt his grandma, didn't want to disappoint her, but he had, and he felt so bad for it that it had taken years for him to be okay about it. And for Grandma to not be disappointed. He loved her dearly. She always seemed to understand what was going on with her kids and grandkids. It was as if she had a sixth sense about their problems and what they were and how they needed fixing. No one in the family understood how she did it. But she did. And everyone knew they could always turn to her for advice, or to fix things. Like Cabot.

He wondered if he should call her to get advice on how to deal with his wayward brother. But the problem was, what if she demanded or made them come home? Could he live with that? Not doing the work they did? He was in need of a break from it all. He had organized with Tilly to not book anything for August or September. They were going back to Mykonos for their birthday in a few weeks; maybe he could talk to her then. Get some good Stephanopoulos advice on how to deal with Cabot and have a break at the same time. Maybe he could reassess his life and what he wanted out of it as Diana meant to do. Maybe it was time they all did.

*****

Diana woke in Charles's arms, her head resting on his chest, hair tickling her nose. Inhaling, she stretched her legs and back and glanced up to see Charles watching her. "Hey." She smiled.

He smiled back. "Hey."

"Happy Fourth of July."

"Same to you." They kissed. It deepened, and they made love once more, not coming apart until the phone rang.

"Ugh, who is it?" she groaned into the receiver.

"It's Antonio. You coming to the party tonight or what?"

"Ugh, what time is it?"

"Six p.m."

"What!?" She looked out the window to see the setting sun. "But it's morning. I just woke up. It can't be evening already."

"Don't tell me you slept the day away?" Antonio laughed. "That's a first for you, sis. You never sleep all day."

"Guess I was tired." She casually glanced at the grinning face of Charles as the grin slid between her legs. "Oh, uh, gotta go."

"So, are you coming?"

"Oh, uh, oh, my God." She slammed the phone down.

He'd heard and was quite surprised that she had someone with her. "Guess she is."

"Who is?" Cabot asked, kneeling on the couch to watch his brother.

"Diana isn't coming to the party. She has a *guest.*"

"What sort of guest, and why are they more important than us?" Cabot demanded,

"A guest that is none of our business," Antonio told him. "Now, let's go and party."

*****

The Fourth of July fireworks weren't the only thing going off in New York that night. They were going off in the penthouse as well, as Charles brought Diana to orgasm over and over. They didn't pull apart, didn't leave the bed, didn't leave one another's arms, and stayed that way all night until the sun dawned on the fifth when Charles reluctantly got out of bed.

"Where are you going?" Diana yawned delicately and stretched like a cat under the white sheet.

"Grabbing a shower," he replied and went into the bathroom.

Deciding to follow, she got in behind him and soaped his back. "So, what are we doing today? More of the same?" She kissed his shoulder.

"Can't, gotta leave on my assignment." He shut off the taps and exited. Grabbing one of the towels, he wiped himself down and strode into the bedroom, leaving her standing naked and wet in the shower stall.

"Wait, what?" She grabbed another towel and wrapped it around herself, running into the bedroom. "You're leaving?"

"Yes, Princess, I have an assignment." He finished zipping up his pants and picked up his shirt. "The holiday's over. Time to get back to work, and I have a plane to catch in," he checked his watch, "three hours."

"Where are you going?" She was annoyed that he'd gone back to calling her Princess after what they'd done for the last God knows how many hours when they hadn't said much of anything.

"Overseas, Middle East, or Egypt, or Africa, or something. Not really sure, it's all in the paperwork." He grabbed his tux jacket and noticed her frown. "Don't worry, Princess, you're not the first to get the great Kensington charm and then be disappointed when it leaves."

That made her insides boil. "I seriously doubt you've slept with *that* many women. From the stories I've heard, most women turn you down."

"*You* didn't." He flipped his jacket over his shoulder and left the room.

"Well, *you* certainly didn't have a problem coming here in the middle of the night to take advantage of a young woman," she snapped, following him downstairs.

"And you certainly didn't have a problem with *coming*," he replied. "Quite experienced at what *you* do, Princess Diana." He opened the door and stood staring at her beauty. Even wearing a towel she radiated the love. "*Cleary* I'm not the only man you've been with."

Her brows rose in amusement. "Is that what you thought? That you were my first? The man who'd scored my virginity? Ha! So far from it. You're so far down the list you don't even matter."

"Must be a long list." He smarted at her comment. "A bit of a whore, are we?"

Her face darkened as her fury boiled. "*How dare you* call me a whore, you no good, arrogant, pompous pissant! I don't appreciate being used for social climbing. You're the one who came here, you're the one who kissed me and shoved his cock inside me. You're damn lucky I don't have you for rape, and break and enter."

He seethed inside at her words. "Rape? It was *hardly* rape. *You* wanted it, and *you* know it. And now because I have to leave for work, you become a pathetic immature, insecure little girl."

"I *am not* pathetic, *or* immature, and I sure as hell am *not* insecure, Mr Kensington. So get the hell out of my penthouse before I call the cops and have you arrested."

"On what charges?" he sneered. Storming out, he slammed the door behind him, and not waiting for the lift, ran down the stairs to hail a cab.

"Ooohhh," Diana growled, wondering why she'd just spent the last day and a half having sex with him.

*****

Friday the twenty-seventh was a beautiful sunny day in Mykonos, and Tomas and Roger were spending it at the beach. They only worked at the gym two to three days a week, took Fridays and most Mondays off, and always got to the beach as much as possible, especially from spring through to mid-autumn. They had swum the morning away, tanned in the sun, and now sat relaxing with drinks at the local beachside restaurant with Dan and Derek who'd joined them. Their table was on the sand near the water and under a huge umbrella.

"God, this is the life," Derek said, gazing over the water. "It's so beautiful here. Sometimes I wish I could stay forever."

"I thought that twenty-six years ago," Tomas said. "When we were brought back, and I was dying. I wished I could stay forever."

That sobered the moment, and Roger squeezed his husband's hand. "And here we are, twenty-six years later, still enjoying the view."

"Yep, all thanks to Dan the man." Tomas grinned at Dan who sat beside him. "If it weren't for you, I wouldn't be here now."

"*We* wouldn't be here now," Roger added since he'd been on his death bed too. It just happened that Tomas was closer to death than he was.

"That's true," Tomas replied. "I propose a toast to Dan Ardent, for saving our lives, making our family eternally grateful, and making him, and then Derek, honorary members of the family. To Dan."

"To Dan." Roger and Derek joined in.

"Thank you, thank you, it was nothing." Dan waved his hand. "Just doing my job."

"Bet you didn't think you'd be spending the rest of your life vacationing in the Greek Islands every year?" Roger asked.

"No, I didn't." Dan laughed. "That's definitely been a bonus, and we have a lot of anniversaries today. Twenty-six years since you survived, twenty-five years that we finally found out that it was named

AIDS, twenty-five years since *SB3* opened, twenty-five years for the twins to be born. Are they coming today?"

"I suppose." Tomas sipped his drink. "They booked *SB3* for a party, so they'd better be here." Running a hand through his hair, he noticed it was still damp. "Antonio will want to come. I'm not sure about Cabot."

"He still whoring himself out?" Derek asked, crossing his long, tanned legs.

"So we hear," Tomas said. "And no one in the family likes it. Least of all Mama."

"Carlos isn't too happy either," Roger added. "Although the bizarre thing is, Cabot's doing exactly what Carlos did when he was that age."

"Except Carlos charged for it, he didn't give it away for free unless the person was important, like Viv," Tomas reminded him.

"And then he ended up in the business doing the exact same thing," Roger said. "You can't really be too angry when his father put it out there too."

"That's part of the problem," Dan said. "You can't really demand your kid stop doing something you did yourself. It makes you a hypocrite."

"Yes, we know," Tomas said. "That's why we haven't really done anything to stop it. Because we can't. How can we?" He shrugged.

"You can't, so the only thing to do is keep an eye on him," Derek said. "Make sure he's told of the consequences, and try and keep him in line. Hopefully, he'll grow out of it."

"And what if it's a cry for attention?" Tomas asked. "It's not as though he wasn't loved or wanted, or didn't get enough attention from everyone. He got it in spades."

"Or it could be for another reason," Dan said. "Maybe he's just a free spirit like Diana said in her latest interview."

"Can you actually *be* a free spirit?" Roger finished his drink. "When does it stop being a free spirit and become a whore?"

"Good question," Tomas said. "Is there a line you cross from one to the other?"

"When you become an addict," Dan replied.

"And how do you know if you're a sex addict?" Roger asked.

"When you have a driving need for sex and don't care about the consequences." Dan called the waiter over and ordered another round.

"So, we have a sex addict on our hands?" Tomas asked after the waiter had gone. "Jesus, no one's going to like that."

"Your mother didn't when I suggested it. I gave her a book and some pamphlets on it. She's going to see what she can do about it." Dan sipped his icy cold beer.

"I suppose this weekend will be as good as any since they'll both be here." Derek stretched his legs before crossing them. "What *will* Jenny do?"

"I'm not sure, she didn't say." Dan sat thoughtfully. "But whatever it is, it won't be anything good."

"Roger! Tomas! Oh, my God, I hoped I'd find you both."

Roger looked towards the voice calling out. "David? David Marks? Oh, my God." He got up to hug it out with his old friend from Miami. He, Tomas, David Marks, Adam Zevon, and Zack Bryant had gotten out before AIDS had spread, and they lost all of their friends. He hadn't seen them since the opening of *SB3*. "Oh, my God, you're here."

"Yeah, man, yeah." David gave Tomas a man hug. "Thought I'd come for the anniversary of the club, and to see if I could find the two of you. Still alive, thank God."

"Yeah, yeah, we are. Hey, pull up a seat." Roger waved at the empty table beside theirs. "So, what's been happening with you and who's this?" He motioned at the man beside David.

"Oh, my bad," David said. "My boyfriend, Nevon Yeardly. We've been together nearly twenty years now." He looked at his five-ten dark Latin lover.

"Nineteen and a half," Nevon corrected. "And still loving it."

Roger introduced David to Dan and Derek.

"Roger and I knew each other back in Miami. I've told you about him before," David said to Nevon. "God what, '75 through '81, '82. The last time we saw each other was twenty-five years ago."

"In '82." Roger nodded. "A lot happened then. We were just talking about it. It was one year after we'd gotten sick from Freddy's funeral. Tomas's nephews were born, *SB3* was opened, and AIDS was announced."

"Yeah, quite a year, that was." David ordered drinks, and the waiter took everyone's order. "We're not intruding, are we? We didn't mean to."

"No, no." Roger looked at the others, and they shook their heads. "So, it's been twenty-five years, Jesus. What have you been doing?"

"Well, I kind of got into what you guys did, but in L.A. Activism, marches. I studied law so I could help out legally. It was four years of hard work, but I helped out with other things in the meantime. Then I met Nevon." He grasped his lover's hand and gazed fondly at him. "We've been together since, we are both HIV free, and practise safe sex most of the time."

"Good for you," Roger said enthusiastically.

Dan nodded. "I think I've heard of you. Are you that lawyer who sued that company on the grounds of discrimination when they fired their worker because they found out he had AIDS?"

David nodded. "Lyon, Rebel and Stand, yeah, that was me. And I won. How dare they bloody discriminate after the law was changed so no one could? Bastards lost and had to pay up big."

"Definitely good for you," Roger said. "What about Miami? Have you been back since Freddy's death?"

"Just once, about thirteen years ago to bury Zack." David frowned at the memory.

"Zack Bryant?" Roger asked, confused.

"Yep." David nodded slowly, gauging Roger's reaction.

"Oh, my God! It got him too?" Roger was shocked. "But how? When? What about Adam? You were all safe and free…"

David shrugged. "Zack took a while. We saw each other occasionally, and once he was sick, he lasted a few years. Tried the pills of the time, but they didn't work."

"AZT," Dan said. "They were replaced with HAART in 1995."

"Yeah, not long after he died," David said. "He wasn't sure where he got it from. He'd only had one partner after you saw us in '82, said he'd been safe, but he still got it and died from it. He was sent back to his family in Miami. I went to the funeral."

"Who else was there? Had anyone else survived?" Roger frowned, saddened by the news.

David's head shook left to right. "I looked up people, all gone. Every single one of them, including the Seralifts now."

"Yeah, yeah, we heard," Roger mumbled, trying to comprehend all of the news. "Everyone?"

"Everyone," David replied.

"And Adam?"

"Late '80s, about '87 or '88 I think. Then Zack about five years later."

"Both of AIDS," Roger muttered.

"Yes," David said. "I think we're the only ones left, Roger."

"Jesus, everyone has gone…" came out of Roger's mouth.

"This disease devastated the gay community all over the world," Dan said sombrely.

"That's what Mama once said. She predicted that we'd lose everyone we knew," Tomas replied. "She knew it before we all did."

Sighing, Roger shook his head. "I can't believe it. I just can't." A hand grasped his, and he looked down at it, following it up to Tomas's face. "Everyone's gone, T. Everyone but us." He felt like bursting into tears right there, but held himself back. "Jesus fucking Christ, everyone's gone." He got up and strode down to the water's edge and waded knee deep, walking back and forth, running his hands through his hair, trying to comprehend the pain and loss twenty-five years on.

"Everyone he knows is gone." Tomas gazed sadly at his beloved. "His parents died a few years ago. At least he got to see his mother back in '81, and he'd been in contact with her secretly. We even saw her a few times before they passed. His brother's gone, and his sister still doesn't care. Still won't accept that he's gay, so he's never seen most of his nieces or nephews, and now, Zack and Adam are gone too."

"It looks like it's hitting him hard," Dan said. "Maybe consider some counselling."

"Lots of crying in private." Tomas watched his lover wade about in the water. "We also heard the other day our good friend Bette Olander died at one hundred years of age. We're planning to go to Miami on the first of August. It will be thirty years since we met. Bette, Bertha and Willow took me there."

"Did we hear our names, darling?"

Tomas startled and turned around. "Oh, my God, Bertha, Willow!" He dived out of his chair and hugged both ladies, seeing Marie and Beatrice behind them. "What are you girls doing here?"

"Girls! Oh, would you listen to that," Bertha said, loving every ounce of attention at eighty-nine. She had been fifty-nine when she'd met Tomas way back in '77 and had been engaged to Luiz Manning at the time. Luiz had taken a fancy to Tomas and ruined everything, so they had dumped his sorry ass and left for Miami.

"You are *still* fabulously young." Tomas grinned. "Willow, we must dance together again while you're here. We were dancing at *The Joy Stick* when I met Roger."

"And speaking of tall, dark and handsome," Willow said as Roger walked over. "Hello, darling." Willow Bertran was eighty-one, and as full of zest as she had been thirty years previously.

"Hello, Willow." Roger kissed both cheeks and hugged the rest of the ladies. "What are you all doing back in Mykonos? We haven't seen you in what, ten years or so?"

"We're here to spread Bette's ashes, darling," Marie Von Burstenstore said. She'd been a close friend of Violet Seralift's, but knew all the ladies of Miami. At eighty-nine, she still followed the young crowd.

"Yeah, we heard. We're so sorry. It only happened a couple of weeks ago?" Roger asked.

"Yes, yes it did. The old bird made it to one hundred and dropped dead at one minute past midnight. She made sure to kick up her heels that day. Did everything she could," Bertha said.

"Including a lap dance from a hunky twenty-five-year-old." Willow giggled.

"Oh, my God, you're kidding!" Roger exclaimed. "Go, Bette!"

Bette Olander had been paramount in getting Tomas to Miami in 1977. If it weren't for her giving Tomas a place to stay and taking him to *The Joy Stick*, and later *Seralift Productions*, Roger would not have met him.

"You're spreading her ashes. When?" Tomas asked.

"Sunday," Beatrice said. At seventy-five, she was the youngest of the group. Most of their friends had passed, and there was only twenty or so left, and most of their ex-husbands had also passed, many from AIDS-related conditions.

"May we come?" Tomas asked. "I'd like to pay my respects."

"Of course, darling. That's why we came looking for you to invite you both." Bertha peered around him. "And if any of your hunky friends want to come along…" Soft laughter went around the table, and Tomas introduced the ladies to the boys.

"Oh, you're the doctor who saved our Tomas," Bertha said to Dan. "We read the obituaries. It made front-page news in Miami. When we came here five years later, we wanted to pay our respects and found out he was alive. A year later, we saw him and Roger doing their gay work."

Tomas smiled and asked if they wanted to join them. "Do you boys mind?" he asked the others.

"No, not at all," Dan said. "It will be interesting to hear first-hand. Bertha and I spoke on the phone in '81 when you two were sick."

"Oh, that was you? That's right," Bertha said as Dan, Derek, David and Nevon added another two tables to theirs and placed chairs around them. "Oh, we definitely have to talk." Seating themselves, they ordered lunch and sat chatting for the rest of the afternoon.

"So, you'll be spreading her ashes on Sunday. Anywhere in particular?" Tomas asked after several hours of the ladies regaling the boys with stories of Tomas and Roger in Miami.

"Somewhere private," Bertha said. "Across the water. She loved it here."

"I'm surprised she'd want them scattered here and not Miami, or her flower garden," Roger said. "She had a beautiful garden."

"Yes, she did, but no children to hand it down to," Marie said. "That's why she left the house to the two of you."

"What!" Tomas exclaimed, his jaw falling open. "She what? What do you mean, she left it to us two?"

"Just what I said," Marie replied. "That's why the lawyer rang to see if you could make it for the reading of the will. Apparently, you're coming in August?"

"Yes, I organised a holiday to celebrate our anniversary," Tomas said, dumbfounded. "The lawyer said to call his office on the third. He said nothing about the house."

"Well, Bette loved the two of you as if you were her sons," Beatrice said. "And left it to you both."

"Jesus," Roger murmured, in disbelief over the whole thing. "She left us that beautiful house."

"Yes, darling," Bertha said. "She left the two of you most of the estate. From what she told us, you get all the physical assets, her house, and what's in it, and all of the money went to shelters for gay people and women. I think she hoped you'd turn the house into some form of shelter too. But that's up to you."

"Oh, my God." Tomas shook his head. "This day just keeps piling it on."

"It certainly does," Roger said. "Too, too much."

*****

The sun was setting when Antonio and Cabot flew into Mykonos. They descended from the plane, already dressed up to hit *SB3* for their birthday.

"Look at that." Antonio gazed across the island where he had been born. "Gorgeous. It's good to be home!"

"What's the time, Tone? Is the club open?" Cabot watched his friends' eyes widen as each walked down the plane's stairs, taking in the beautiful tropical sunset.

"It's after six. Dom will be there, so it probably doesn't matter if we're early."

"Or we could take them to our place since we're all camping there tonight," Cabot said. "Let's dump our bags and chill for a bit. Where's the limo?"

"Over there." Antonio headed for the limo and handed his bag to the driver, stopping to take another look at the sunset.

"Wait up, Tone," Cabot yelled and ran over to his brother, grabbing him by the shoulders and jumping up. "We're twenty-five, woohoo!"

Antonio grinned. "Yeah. We made it to twenty-five. I'm definitely surprised *you* did."

"That's coz I'm fit, I'm young, I'm healthy," Cabot said, waving his friends to hurry up. They made it to their place fifteen minutes later, piled in through the door, and dumped their bags in the lounge room.

"Bathroom's down the hall on the right," Antonio told everyone. "There are four bedrooms upstairs, the front two are ours, don't hog the rest." Their house was next to Tomas and Roger's and under Pedro and Angelina's.

"The boys have come home," Tomas told everyone when he finally moved inside from his mother's balcony. "And they brought friends."

"How many?" Jenny asked with trepidation.

"About ten, from what I could tell," Tomas said.

"Not too many to wreck the place then," Jenny replied, getting the dishes ready.

"At least they made it." Viv sighed. "I wonder if they'll come up or just go on to the club."

Antonio had come quietly through the door and heard her. "I'm stopping by to see my family first. Cabot wasn't interested in coming up. He said he'd see everyone there." He hugged his mother. "Mama."

"Oh, my baby." She hugged him fiercely. "My baby's home."

"Mama," he complained. "Not a baby anymore." He let go of her to hug his father. "Papa."

"Antonio." Carlos was a good two inches shorter than his son, but he made up for it in width and strength. "It's good to have you home."

"It's good to be home. And you don't know how good," Antonio told him. "Sometimes, you just gotta come home."

"Yes, you do." Viv wrapped her arms around both her husband and son, glowing with motherly love. "Yes, you do."

"How about the rest of us, cuz?" Alexis said, standing by for her hug.

"Come here." Antonio picked her up and swung around. "It's good to see you."

"Same here," she said. "We didn't get enough time in New York."

"No, we didn't." He put her down and hugged his grandparents, uncles and aunt. "Dom at the club? And where's Danté and Uncle Pedro?"

"At the club," everyone said.

"It's Friday night; normally it's your uncle's night, but they decided since it's your birthday, they'd all do it as a present for you," Angie informed him.

"Aw, that's great. Well, we brought some friends with us, so Cabot's with them, and they'll probably meet us there," Antonio said.

"Probably?" Carlos asked. "You mean it's not a sure thing?"

"It is because he knows it's a free club, he doesn't have to pay to get in," Antonio said. "But if one of his friends suggests something else, you know he's susceptible to going off on a whim."

"That's Cabot," Jenny said. "Do you want dinner here, Antonio, or do you want to eat at the club?"

"What are we having?" he asked.

"Roast chicken."

"Cooked by you?" He loved his grandma's roast chicken.

"Of course."

"And Cabot?"

"Leave him."

"Good. I'll take his share, too."

*****

Cabot lounged with his friends, smoking pot, snorting coke. The club wasn't open until eight, and he wanted it to be going when he got there. Antonio had left to see the family, but he hadn't felt like going. He didn't want any lectures or disappointed stares. Besides, someone needed to stay with their friends. "What time is it now?"

"Half eight," someone said.

"We'll go soon. Maybe we should go now, come on, let's go now." Cabot was mentally all over the place and snorted another line of coke. "I wanna go now, come on."

*****

After dinner, they gave Antonio his presents. But with him being twenty-five, they weren't much. A new laptop, some CDs, a camcorder, and bits and pieces. With more hugs and kisses, they headed off to the club, running into Cabot and their friends when they got to the door.

"Hey, the fam's here," Cabot yelled, wild-eyed, and running around giving everyone hugs and kisses, hyper from the drugs. He turned to his friends. "Everyone, these are my parents, Carlos and Vivian. My grandparents, Spiros and Jenny, my aunt Angie and my cuz Alexis, my uncles Tomas and Roger. No Alena and Diana?" he asked the family.

"Alena's on tour, and Diana called before we left," Antonio reminded him. "Uncle Pedro, Dom and Danté are inside."

"Whoo," Cabot yelled, throwing his arms up in the air. "Let's go inside then." He ran inside with his friends following.

The rest of the family traded worried glances and followed.

"And here he is," Pedro said from the stage. Danté was pulling his shift, but Pedro had the mic. "Birthday boy, Cabot Conroy Stephanopoulos, also known as Steele Stefan." The crowd went wild as he ran around the room, whooping and hollering. "Oh, Jesus, he's fried," Pedro muttered to himself, then he saw the rest of the family enter. "And his twin brother, Antonio DeLuca Stephanopoulos, also known as Phoenix Stefan." He watched Cabot run up to Antonio and lift him up, spinning around. "The birthday boys are twenty-five today. The same age as *SB3* because the boys were born the night we opened way back in 1982." Another round of applause and screaming. "So, to celebrate the boys' birthday, and *SB3's* birthday, all the food and drinks are free all night." The screaming got louder. "We want you to enjoy yourselves, but drugs and smoking are not allowed, and you will be thrown out if we find you've brought it in. Enjoy your night." He turned off the microphone and left it behind the DJ deck. "You okay on your own, Danté?" he asked his son. Danté gave him the thumbs up and he left the stage to see his nephews. "Cabot, Antonio." He enveloped them in his arms. "Happy birthday."

"Uncle Pedro," Antonio said, while Cabot threw his arms around his neck.

"Uncle P," he shouted. "Whoo."

Pedro pulled his head back. "Cabot. Enjoy your night, you two. Behave yourselves." He left them to their friends and walked over to the rest of the family. "Cabot's already high, I see," he said to his brother. They stood around watching the boys as Cabot skipped around the room, shirt undone and flapping behind him, waving his arms around. Pedro spied his mother's expression. "Mama's up to something. That look on her face says it all. She's planning on doing something."

They all looked at her, seeing the steely determination in her eyes, the pressed lips, the frown. Oh, yes, Jenny Stephanopoulos was up to something. She was determined to save Cabot before he destroyed himself.

"It's my birthday," Cabot yelled, dancing in a group of friends and admirers. "It's my birthday, whoo, it's my birthday."

The family kept a close eye on him. Antonio was dancing with Alexis, Summer, and Melody, with Dom nearby, while their parents worked the crowd, the bar and the stage. All kept an eye out for drugs; all kept an eye out for bad behaviour.

Dan and Derek joined them, as did David and Nevon. The girls all turned up to celebrate Bette's passing and the club's birthday, and they spoke with Tomas and Roger all night. Tomas had his dance with Willow, and Roger took Bertha. Dan and Derek danced with Beatrice and Marie.

Jenny kept an eye on all of them from the upstairs office balcony. She kept an eye on Cabot mainly. She knew he had done something before he'd come, hard not to know. But she didn't know how to fix it without sending him off the rails, or making him run away. She'd thought of holding him against his will, detoxing him, but how could she rid him of his sex addiction? The need to screw anything that came near him; how could she stop him from doing that? The books and pamphlets Dan had given her explained why he did it, but they didn't really tell her how to stop it. And she knew if she didn't, something bad was going to happen. And after what Tomas had gone through all those years ago, she didn't want her grandson going through anything similar. Regardless of him using a condom, there was always a chance that one day he wouldn't, and that was going to be what potentially killed him.

Sighing, she kept vigil even as Spiros moved to her side.

"You cannot save all of them," he said, knowing full well what she was thinking.

"The hell I can't!" she replied. "If I can keep my boys alive, I can keep my grandboys alive too. Cabot has become his own worst enemy, and it's time one of us stepped in and said *enough*."

"He's an adult, Jenny. It's his life," Spiros told her. "I seem to remember you chiding me for wanting the boys to take over the meat shop. You told me it was *my* inheritance, not theirs, and if they wanted to do something else, to let them. They wanted to see the world. Cabot is no different."

"But our boys didn't do drugs and rampantly screw whatever they wanted. Well…" She winced. "With the exception of Carlos."

"Like father, like son." Spiros grinned wryly.

Jenny rolled her eyes. "Not quite. And certainly not in your case. None of them takes after you except for in looks."

"And I'm very proud of that." He smiled broadly. "I love the fact that at least one of my sons looks like me."

"Oh, you got the good one, and I got Carlos, is that is?" Jenny raised a brow. "So, Carlos takes after me?"

"Only in looks, my love. That seems to be all they take after us in." He put an arm around her, and they stood watching their grandson.

Pedro checked his watch and walked over to Dom. "You're on in ten minutes."

Dom glanced at his own watch and took off for backstage, ready to take on his shift for his cousins' birthday bash.

Danté saw him waiting backstage. There were two more records to play and then he was done for the night and could finally eat cake. And he knew his grandma had made one because he'd seen it in the club's fridge. After laying down the last track, he pulled off his headphones and picked up the mic. "I am Danté Stefan, Steele and Phoenix's cousin. We are here celebrating their twenty-fifth birthday."

That got *whoos* from Steele. "We are here celebrating *SB3*'s twenty-fifth birthday." That got *whoos* from the family and friends. "And I'm about to put on a special performance for my cousins." He started rapping to the song and got everyone cheering as he walked up and down the front of the stage.

Cabot whooped and hollered, climbing up on stage to jump up and down beside his cousin, and beckoned the family to join him.

Alexis grabbed Antonio's hand and dragged him up, and they all sang and danced.

Dom came on stage to get behind the decks. Once the song was over, he set the new track down and took the mic from his brother. "Hello *SB3*, I am Dom Stefan, Danté's brother, Steele and Phoenix's cousin, I'm with you for the next three and a half hours. We're getting into the '90s and noughties, so I hope you enjoy...*getting naughty.*"

"Whoo, let's get *naught-ay.*" Cabot threw his arms in the air and jumped off stage to dance with his friends.

Danté came running out from behind the stage and into Antonio's arms. "Tony."

"Dantie!" Antonio laughed and spun him around. He'd always been close to Dom and especially Danté. Cabot was too when he was younger, but he preferred being with Antonio only these days.

"Did you like my song?" Danté asked, waving a fist in the air to East 17's *It's Alright.*

"Loved it, Little D. You're becoming quite a rapper and muso in your own right. You're really good."

"Yeah? Cool! Just a pity Dom didn't think so." Danté's mood slumped down to his shoes.

Antonio put him down. "Dom's like Alena, selfish, and only thinks of himself. He was the only boy until you came along, and Alena was the only girl until Alexis. He's jealous that there's another son in the family and he hates the fact you're more talented than him." He ruffled his cousin's hair. "You're cool, kid, don't ever forget that."

A smile brighter than the sun spread across Danté's face. "Thanks, Tony."

Antonio had a soft spot in his heart for Danté because he was like a little brother that hadn't yet turned sour. "You're welcome, kid."

Pedro stepped on stage and picked up the mic, indicating for Dom to turn the music down. "Ladies and gentlemen, in honour of *SB3's* birthday, my mother had made a cake for you all to enjoy." He held an arm out to indicate its advent. They set it on a huge table to the side of the bar and Jenny had the knife ready.

"And to celebrate my nephew's birthday, they have their own cake just for them and the family," Pedro went on, watching Viv at the ready with her knife. "Ladies and gentlemen, my mother will do the honours of cutting *SB3's* cake, and my gorgeous sister-in-law Vivian Villiers, the boys' mother, will cut theirs. Please get ready for cake." He put the mic down and went to help, but saw the staff waiting with plates, forks and napkins, ready to hand out the pieces of chocolate vanilla sponge cake. He watched Jenny cut it and slice it up, then moved on to Viv to see Cabot and Antonio dig into their pieces.

"Mmm, great cake, Grandma," Cabot yelled with his mouth full and ran around the tables to kiss her on the cheek. He shoved more into his mouth and started dancing, moving out onto the floor while devouring his cake.

The family stood around chatting and eating the delicious cakes, keeping an eye on Cabot and his friends. Spiros took a piece to Dom, who inhaled it in seconds because being a DJ took a lot of energy.

Everyone was still dancing at half past two in the morning when Pedro took over. "Ladies and gentlemen. I am Pedro Stephanopoulos, resident DJ on a Friday night. I'm father to Dom and Danté whom you've already seen play. I'm uncle to Steele and Phoenix, welcome to *SB3*." That got everyone cheering with renewed vigour. "I was the DJ from 1977 to 1981 at *Studio 69* in New York. I was the biggest DJ in New York at the time. We opened *SB3* in 1982, and I've been DJing here ever since. Ten years ago my son Dom started DJing, showing what he was made of at the ripe old age of fourteen. And this year, my youngest, Danté, started playing, also at the ripe old age of fourteen. Must be in the blood." He grinned at the audience.

"You've heard Danté play the hits of today. You've heard Dom play the hits from the '90s and noughties. Now I'm bringing to you what I know and play best. The hits from the '70s and '80s; the hits I love to play and played often at 69. Those were the days, and to take you back, here's Slay Me's, *You Do It To Me.* I played this back in the day when the guitarist, Dan Slayer, would come to the club. He met his ex-wife, actress Wednesday May, there, back in '77. Enjoy." For the next two and a half hours he showed everyone what he was made of, which was why he was still the best in the world.

It took the family back to those days in New York, spending the boys' birthdays there, New Year's, and the way they partied. It also reminded them of those they lost. He saw some of the regulars still around and back for the anniversary. Bev Marie, Sara Holdare and Martine Krevnokov, who came every few years to celebrate. He remembered Leon, Stan and Eddie who had all passed from AIDS before anyone knew what AIDS was. He thought back to the days when he was a young man, fresh out of Mykonos, fresh out of his teens. Well, he was twenty when he and Angie had left, twenty when they got married, when he got the job at 69, and they had been some of the best years of his life. The freedom, the newness, the excitement, the money. Not that he needed that anymore. His family were well taken care of, they made plenty to live on; everyone was set and living comfortably.

At six in the morning, he retired from the stage and said goodnight to everyone as they were ushered out. Walking up to his family, he said, "God, I still love doing that."

"And I still love *watching* you do that." Angie kissed him. "You're still awesome. And it's like being back there at 69."

"Yeah." Pedro shook his head. "It's like I'm back there every Friday night when I'm on stage. I saw Bev, Sara and Martine before. I was remembering Dan Slayer and Wednesday May, and everyone else we knew and saw and met..." He sighed and looked down. "And everyone we lost."

"Yeah," Mike sadly agreed, standing with the family. "It's like being back there every Friday night. Every time I'm behind the bar, I look up and expect Leon to come rolling over for an order."

"That's because of the photos we have up on the wall," Pedro replied, glancing over at the black and white pictures of their 69 days behind the bar.

That sobered the moment for the family, but Cabot was still dancing in the middle of the floor, arms in the air, head back, dripping in sweat. His friends were lagging though, looking ready to go home.

"Guess that's my cue," Antonio said. "I'll leave you to your memories and get Cabot home. Don't expect us until dinnertime, Grandma." He kissed her cheek.

"Okay, sweetie. Just make sure he gets home safe." She watched him kiss his mother and father then head off to round up Cabot.

"Come on, bro, time to go home." He grabbed Cabot and turned him in the direction of the door.

"I don't want to go, Tone." He flung his arms around his brother's neck and rested his head on his arm. "I don't want to stop dancing."

"The club is closing, it's Saturday, it's not our birthday anymore, and we need some sleep, so come on. Come on, everyone." He called to their friends. "Time to go back to our place and sleep all day. Come on."

They followed him as if he were the Pied Piper, looking wet and ragged from a night of partying, and slowly, the family followed. It had been a very long time since they'd stayed all night at the club. The kids loved it, all the whooping and hollering, but the adults were a little the worse for wear in their later years.

*****

At six that night, Antonio managed to get his brother through the door of Jenny's house. It hadn't been easy. He'd woken Cabot an hour before and dragged him to the shower and had to help him dress, but still, they managed to make it on time. But he hadn't been able to stop Cabot snorting a line of coke.

"Steele Stefan is in the house." Cabot strode through the door. "And all the family's here. What's for dinner?" He kissed his mother and grandmother on the cheek.

"Roast beef and coleslaw," Viv told him. "Your Uncle Tomas is making it."

"Geez, Uncle T, do you make every meal? Time someone made it for you," Antonio said, walking into the kitchen to take a look.

"I don't mind." Tomas smiled at his nephew. "I enjoy torturing my family with new recipes."

"It smells good." Antonio clapped him on the shoulder and opened the fridge to see if there was anything. "Mind if I have a beer?" he yelled out.

"Ooh, I'll have one," Cabot called from next to Dom. "I'm so thirsty after last night." Taking his from Antonio, he sculled it back.

Jenny raised a brow. "You haven't eaten since the club?" She kept her tone neutral.

"No, Grandma. We slept all day," Antonio told her, seeing her eye his brother.

"Mmm, well don't have another of those until we eat," she said lightly. "You need food in your stomachs."

"Oh, come on, Grandma, don't be a party pooper." Cabot kissed her on the cheek as he passed her to go into the kitchen for another one.

"If you're thirsty, drink water." Carlos eyed his son. "It will hydrate you better."

"Ugh," Cabot moaned, throwing his head back. "Are you all party poopers today? It's our birthday."

"It was your birthday yesterday, Cabot, and you didn't see us until we all got to the club," Jenny said, becoming annoyed. "Today is Saturday, the twenty-eighth, it's not your birthday, you will not act like a brat, and if I tell you not to have another drink until you have eaten, you won't have another. Now, hand it over." She held out her hand and heard the family take a step back.

Cabot blinked. Whenever anyone took a step back, it was because Grandma was about to ream someone out. *By why would she ream me out?* "You can't be serious? It's a beer," he said.

She stepped closer. "And you can have it once you've eaten. The same for Antonio. One until you eat. Now, hand it over. If you're thirsty, there's juice and water. Tomas has made several varieties of flavoured water for you to drink; that will help hydrate you. Hand it over." She was standing in front of him staring into his blue eyes. The house was silent, except for the crackle of beef in the oven.

Cabot stared at her as if in a dream, unable to comprehend what was actually happening. "It's...*a beer*, Grandma, that's all."

"No, Cabot." Jenny kept her voice calm. "You know full well that's not all." She shook her head. "Did you do a line of coke before coming here? Did you do coke last night before getting to the club? How long have you been snorting, Cabot? How much longer will you keep screwing anything that wants you to screw them? How many more men and women do you need to have sex with? How many more times, Cabot? How much longer until you kill yourself and leave your parents devastated, leave *us* devastated? Why do you want to do that, Cabot?"

Cabot stared from her to his parents, to aunt, uncles and cousins. "It's just a beer, Grandma. I don't do those other things."

The disappointment rained down over Jenny. "Cabot," she said softly. "You know it's not. You know you do it; why do you want to ruin your life?"

Seeing the disappointment in her eyes, he gulped. He hated disappointing his grandmother, hated disappointing his mother. But the family were such freakin' hypocrites. "Grandma, why should I give up sex?"

Carlos inhaled sharply, and heads turned in his direction.

"I'm not asking you to give it up." Jenny ignored Carlos and kept looking at Cabot. "I want you to slow down and not do it so much. Take things slow and easy."

His eyes bored into hers. Blue versus blue, and she wasn't backing down. But then neither was he, and the anger raged inside. "Like my father did when he was my age?" he asked. "How many women did *manwhore Carlo Stefan* bed before he was my age? Huh?" He glanced at the surprised frown on his father's face and saw everyone else's expressions. Frowns on the adults, and confusion on the kids. "Well?" He went back to his father and grandmother. "*My* father, the great Carlo Stefan, *PORN STAR*," he spat. "How many women did you fuck before you married a woman sixteen years older than you? Huh? How many?"

"Don't you dare take that tone with me, Cabot Conroy Stephanopoulos," Carlos spat back. "You don't dare speak that way in this household."

"Bullshit! You're all a pack of fucking hypocrites." He spun and slammed the beer bottle onto the floor of the kitchen, surprising everyone. "You don't fuck hundreds of women and then want me to stop fucking. It makes you a hypocrite." He stalked past his parents, but stopped at the surprised expression on his brother's face. "Didn't think I'd ever tell, did you, Tone?" He turned and addressed his cousins. "*Our* fathers were porn stars back in the '70s. I found the stash in the vault years ago. All of the videos and master files, all of the porn awards in the shape of a ten-inch cock. Most with *my* father's name on them." He turned to his stunned parents. "Nice bit of information you kept from us, dear old Dad. All of those women, all of the movies, all of the shit you've never told us. Looks like I turned out *exactly* like *my old man*." His eyes flared brightly, matching those of his father.

"That's enough, Cabot," Vivian said quietly, wringing her hands together to keep from falling apart. "Our pasts are ours, not yours."

"You're kidding, Mother, aren't you? You named me after some fag photographer friend of yours who died from AIDS, I take it. Why the fuck did you think I wanted that horrible name dumped on me? *I hate it! I always have.* But you didn't care how *I* would feel as *I* got older. Oh, no, don't worry about Cabot, he won't mind being named after a *fag*."

"Don't use that language in this house," Carlos yelled, his face red with anger at his son. "You don't get to speak that way."

"Why not?" Cabot yelled back, fists clenched by his sides. "You've lied to us all of these years. Kept that from us, that you were all in porn movies for fuck's sake. Fucking women. Oh, wait," he spun around to face everyone else and waved his finger, "Uncle Pedro fucked two or three in every movie. And Tomas and Roger fucked men because they're fag fuckers!"

Jenny's hand flew hard and fast across Cabot's face.

Crack!

He spun around and stumbled, his hands flying to his face.

She waved her hand at the pain pulsating through it.

Hands flew to mouths in shock, and everyone took another step back.

Cabot stared at the floor in shock. His grandmother had just slapped him. He turned slowly and saw the blazing fire in her eyes.

"Don't you *ever* use that language in this house again!" Her voice was low and deadly. "Don't you *ever*, call *my* sons that ever again. Especially when *you* are one yourself, Cabot Conroy Stephanopoulos. *You* are the hypocrite. *You* can't even admit you're gay, yet you screw men. You call all of the men you screw that word, yet you are one yourself, and I will *never* tolerate the use of that word, or those words, in my house. That is the first, and only time those words will *ever* come out of your vile mouth in this household. Do you understand me?"

He swallowed and nodded, hands still on cheeks. They all knew better than to argue when she looked like that.

"Now, you have *one* choice. Apologise to my sons, Tomas and Roger, or get the hell out of my house. What will it be?"

Another swallow. He looked around at all of the disappointed expressions, sadness, frowns, confusion. His cousins clung to one another. Then he looked at his uncles and father and his blood boiled. "I won't apologise. Not after all the lies in this bloody family. To find out all of that, and to watch it." He saw his parent's shocked faces. "Yeah, dear old Dad, I got a lot of pointers from you. No wonder Mother couldn't say no."

"Cabot," Carlos barked. "Apologise. To everyone."

"No," Cabot shouted. "You're all a pack of fucking hypocrites, and I never want to see you ever again until you can tell the truth." He spun on his heel and stormed toward the door. "Don't you dare try and control my life when *you* did exactly the same thing." He slammed through the door and took off down the road.

"What the bloody hell?" Carlos moved after him, but Jenny stopped him with a hand on his chest.

"No! Leave him. He's right. You know that."

"But he doesn't get to talk that way in this family," Carlos argued, eyes flashing as he stared at his mother. He saw the sadness in the eyes that matched his own and deflated. "He doesn't get to act that way."

I know," she told him. "And I shouldn't have slapped him. He's your son, not mine."

"I don't care, I'm glad you did," Carlos said. "He *needed* slapping. And a damn good one at that."

Jenny turned to Tomas and Roger who were standing behind a shocked Antonio. "Are you two okay?"

"We'll live, Mrs S." Roger pulled a weary Tomas close. "Not the first time we've been called that."

"But the first time by my son, and I am *so* sorry," Carlos said. "We *did not* raise him that way, and he doesn't get away with talking to my brothers like that. I am disgusted and so sorry." He slowly walked over and hugged them.

"Antonio," Jenny said, holding out her hand to him.

"Grandma." He took her hand and went into her arms. "I'm so sorry. I'm so sorry I haven't done a better job of looking after him."

"It's not your job, Antonio. We clearly didn't do a very good job of raising him." She held him tightly. "But now you need to do me a favour because he'll talk to you."

"What is it?" He pulled back.

"Go after him and at least get him back to your place, or take the jet back to New York." She inhaled deeply and let it out slowly. "It's time for us to do our job. Will you do that for me?"

"Yes, Grandma." He kissed her cheek and ran out the door.

Turning, she noticed her three remaining grandchildren huddled together, standing in shock near their stunned, but frowning grandfather. "What Cabot said is true. But it's none of your business. It happened a long time before any of you came along and it has nothing to do with you now. Forget what you heard." She saw them nod unsurely and headed for the kitchen to clean up the mess Cabot had made. "Tomas, I think the beef's ready."

*****

"I need to get fucking drunk." Cabot stumbled down the road. "How fucking dare they be such fucking hypocrites," he spat. "How fucking dare they." He didn't know where he was going, just knew it couldn't be *SB3*. Otherwise, they'd find him. So, wherever he went, it couldn't be a place the family owned.

Heading for the beach, he ran to the water, gasping for air, trying to control his heartbeat. "The fucking hypocrites," he screamed into the night, getting looks from people walking along the beach. He was knee deep in the water and fell to his knees, bursting into tears, grasping at the moving sand beneath him, feeling it drain out of his fingers just as his life was draining away.

The pain inside of him was intense and immense, and he had felt it for years. Never really knowing what had caused it, never really knowing why it had never gone away. Never knowing why he couldn't resolve it and get rid of it, it plagued him constantly. That's why he tried to bury it beneath sex and pot and coke. But it was always there, always haunting him, always threatening to kill him on the inside by suffocating him, and it *would* kill him, he was sure.

Crying, he thought back to their shocked expressions. They'd never realised any of the kids would find out their secret. Yeah, sure, they'd locked the stuff away in the vault, but he'd found out, found the vault, found the combination, found the stash inside. All of the movies his father had made, all of the ones his uncles had made, including the one with all three of them together. What was it? *The Greek Gods*. What a load of fucking bullshit!

Slicking back his hair, he decided he needed a drink. He clambered to his feet, stumbled down the beach to the local beachside club, and rolled up to the bar.

"Steele, my man," the bartender said. "What will it be?"

"Vodka, and keep it coming." Cabot had no idea who the man was, but clearly, he knew him, even though he hadn't been to the club in years. If ever.

"Shot of vodka." The bartender placed the glass before Cabot.

"Leave the bottle," Cabot told him and grabbed it the moment he put it down. He drank half the bottle before coming up for air. "Whoo!"

He shook his head. "Let's party." He climbed on top of a nearby table, where he danced and drank the other half of the bottle. "Vodka all round," he yelled to the partygoers, "and get me another one while you're at it." He danced while the bartender brought him another bottle.

Watching Cabot dance on the table, the bartender knew they were in for a night. While Steele and Phoenix Stefan were rarely on the island, when they were, they were well-known. The whole Stefan/ Stephanopoulos family were well-known on the island. They kept a lot of people in business and gave a lot of people jobs. But this club was not theirs, and he knew Cabot would run up a tab.

"Partay!" Cabot yelled, and drank half of the second bottle then tipped the rest over his head. "Whoo," he screamed. "Another bottle." He jumped down and danced into the crowd, mostly men, a few women. The men seemed particularly interested, and he was up for it, having not had any in two days. He danced with a couple of men, and in particular with a Latin hunk in white pants and a tight white tank top. His hair was curling around his nape and was dark. Another man was dark, but he didn't quite look black. Some sort of exotic mix. Other men took his fancy, and as he drank his third bottle, they ground up a storm on the dance floor.

"Whoo," Cabot yelled. "Let's get fucked. Whoo!" He danced with more men, choosing a Caucasian male with black hair to stick his tongue down his throat. Hands went into pants and had a grope. But he knew the man was not up to standard. Moving on, he was intrigued by tall, dark and handsome, and excited by short, dark and gorgeous, but found himself coming back to the exotic mix. Dancing with him, he got a hand down his pants and found himself hard in an instant. "Wanna fuck and suck?" he asked.

"Where do you wanna go?" the man asked, brushing a finger across the top of the Stefan cock.

"I wanna go up your ass," Cabot said, and pushed the man backward until they were outside. Looking for a place, they found an alley just down from the club. "Get on your knees and suck it," he demanded, and the exotic mix did just that.

Falling to his knees, he pulled down Steele's pants and took him into his mouth, sucking it like a lollipop.

"Oh, my God, you're good." Steele groaned, his head falling back. "So good." He came quickly, and the exotic swallowed.

"What now, I get to fuck the gorgeous beast?" The man got to his feet.

"No. You get fucked by him. Drop your pants and turn around." Steele stopped drinking long enough to pull a condom out and roll it on. "Get ready, the Stefan is coming." He rammed it in and thrust in short, sharp motions.

The man stood there, taking it, clenching his jaw, his eyes narrowed as he gripped the wall in front of him. *At least the prick wore a condom,* he thought as Steele finished up.

Coming to a halt, Steele stumbled back. "Oh, fuck, that was good. You're good."

"Am I?" The man turned around, his own cock on display. "How much you gonna pay me? I ain't cheap."

"Pay you?" Steele laughed drunkenly. "The Stefan doesn't pay for sex. All give willingly." He pushed the condom off and tried shoving himself back into his pants.

"Well, *I don't* give willingly," the exotic blend spat. "I put out for money, so give it to me." He grabbed at Cabot's pockets.

"Hey, what'chya doin'? I haven't got any money. Hey, what'chya doin'?" Cabot grabbed the man's hand, trying to get him off. "Get out of it. I'm not paying you, I have no money, fuck off." He shoved the man back with both hands, and the man stumbled to the ground. "What the fuck do you think you're doing?" Cabot yelled. "You didn't say no. You didn't tell me you wanted to be paid for it. I wouldn't have picked you. What the fuck's wrong with you, you asshole?"

The exotic got to his feet and flicked a switchblade open.

"What the fuck, man?" Cabot was stunned that anyone could pull a knife on him. "Fuck! What are you doing?" He backed up a bit, but the man was quicker, flying up to him and sticking the knife to his throat.

"The great Steele Stefan will pay for what he's done." The man had Cabot by the shirt and flung him at the wall he'd just been bent over.

"Hey, man, what the fuck's wrong with you?" Cabot fell against the wall and tried to get to his feet. But the man was faster.

"Get to your feet." The exotic shoved the knife at Cabot and pushed him over the wall. "Now *I* will get *my* payment. Move, and I will cut your throat. Got that, you American ass?" Holding the knife to Cabot, he worked himself to get his cock hard and shoved it in Cabot's ass.

"Ow, what the fuck! Have you got a condom on?" Cabot panicked. He wanted to fight, but he couldn't keep anything straight in his head. He didn't have his wits, and he didn't want to be stabbed or cut. He pushed backward, but the man shoved the knife in. "Ow."

"I told you I would cut your throat," the man hissed.

Cabot swung his arm, his elbow connected with the man's temple and he ducked. Cabot swung his other arm, twisting his body around and trying to get him in the head. He succeeded.

The knife fell from the man's hand, and he bent over for it, giving Cabot the opportunity to grab him by the head and knee him. But he didn't have enough strength or balance to do a good enough job.

"You fag fucker. Who the fuck do you think you are fucking me up the ass?" He landed on top of the man who reached for the knife, but Cabot pushed it away and landed a punch on the man's face. He pummelled with both hands, but the man was stronger, and *not* drunk.

He managed to roll Cabot over and land a few punches of his own. "Who you calling fag fucker?"

"Hey, what's going on over there? Get out of that alley…" drifted across the wind, and it scared exotic blend enough to jump up and run off. But not before kicking at Cabot and saying, "Suck it, fag fucker, you've got the disease now."

Groaning, Cabot rolled to his side and managed to push himself up as a group of people came toward him.

"Oh, my God, are you all right?" A woman rushed over to him.

"He beat me, robbed me of my money. I tried to fight." Cabot was weak and spat blood out.

"Oh, my God, Brian, we need to help him," the woman said, and a couple of men helped him stand.

Cabot slowly pulled his pants up and checked himself for cuts.

"Are you okay, son?" Brian asked, seeing the blood on Cabot's face.

"He had a knife," Cabot dazedly said. "He said he'd cut my throat."

"Oh, my God, we need to get you to the hospital."

"No, no hospital, my friend...ah..." Cabot tried to think. "He's a doctor. I don't know his number though..."

"Cabot?" Antonio came running up to them. "Oh, my God, Cabot, what happened?"

"Hey, Tone." Cabot grinned drunkenly. "Got beat up."

"Oh, my God, we've gotta get you to the hospital, come on." Antonio put Cabot's arm around his shoulder then looked at the couples. "Thank you so much for helping my brother. I'm so glad you found him. I'd better get him to the hospital. Come on, Cabot. We'll grab a cab."

"Are you sure you'll be all right?" the woman asked, following them.

"I don't know," Antonio said. "But we need a cab."

"I'll wave one down." Brian ran ahead and flagged down a passing cab, opened the door, and watched while Antonio got his brother into it.

"Thank you so much, here..." Antonio pulled out his wallet and handed over two fifty-dollar notes. "Thank you, thank you so much." He climbed into the taxi. "Mykonos Private," he told the driver and shut the door.

The driver got them there, and Antonio pulled Cabot out of the back and into the wheelchair the nurses had brought out. "Help him, he's been beaten up." Flinging a fifty through the open window at the driver, he followed his brother into emergency. "Has he been stabbed?"

"Won't know till we look at him," the doctor said, seeing both boys. "You're Jenny Stephanopoulos's grandkids."

"Yeah, we are," Antonio said, watching his brother.

"Want us to call her?" the doctor asked.

"Ah, no, what?" Antonio finally looked up. "No. I'll make the call. First check him over, please." Watching as they took him into an exam room, he fumbled in his pocket for his phone and found Dan's number. Ringing, he found him. "Where are you?"

"At a nice little bar on the beach having a cocktail," Dan replied, sipping his margarita and glancing at Derek.

"Is anyone with you?" Antonio asked.

"Just my husband."

"Can you get to the hospital and not tell anyone?"

"What's happened?" Dan was immediately on alert.

"Please, just get here," Antonio pleaded, close to tears. "I'll pay."

"We're on our way." Dan snapped his phone shut and downed his drink. "Come on, one of the twins is in trouble."

"Gotta be Cabot," Derek said, and they rushed off. Ten minutes later, they stormed through the door and found Antonio sitting morosely in the waiting room.

Antonio lifted his arm and pointed to the room where they'd taken his brother. "He's being checked over by a doctor."

Dan rushed in and saw Cabot covered in blood. "What's going on," he demanded.

The young doctor saw him, his smile tight-lipped. "Ah, the Stephanopoulos private physician, Doctor Dan."

"Lorenzo," Dan replied. "Good to see you. What's going on?"

"He was beaten. We've taken x-rays, nothing broken or fractured, but he'll be bruised for many weeks. Lots of swelling, no stitches required."

"At least that's good news." Dan sighed. "Any sign of any other trauma?"

"We haven't looked. Should we?" Lorenzo asked.

Dan cocked a brow. "It may need checking. There was a rapist on the island in May, so who knows what sort is here now?"

Lorenzo eyed Dan. "Put on a pair of gloves and feel free."

Dan grabbed a pair of gloves and snapped them on, and after everyone but Lorenzo had left the room, checked Cabot's crotch and anus. "Redness, marks that could be from fingers," Dan murmured.

"Rough sex?" Lorenzo asked. "We all know he's gay."

"Yeah, but he usually does the talking," Dan said. "Doesn't get talked to. So why this, and why now?"

Cabot groaned. "Ugh, Tony."

"You can see him in a minute," Dan told him. "Cabot, I need you to tell me if you had sex tonight."

"Ugh, what?" Cabot squeezed his eyes shut against the bright lights.

"Did you have sex tonight, Cabot?"

"Ugh, the asshole," Cabot murmured. "He fuckin' attacked me."

"What did he do?" Dan pushed. "Tell me, Cabot. Did you have sex with him, or did he have sex with you?"

"Ugh." Cabot tried getting his thoughts together. "I fucked him, and then he pulled a knife, ugh."

"What then, Cabot. Tell me, it won't leave the room," Dan said, leaning in close.

"He pulled a knife and demanded money." His head felt as if it was cracked in two. His ribs hurt, and his face was killing him. "My face," he muttered, trying to touch it. "Bastard hit me in the face."

"What happened when he pulled the knife, Cabot?" Dan pushed harder.

"Ugh, he shoved it at me and told me he wanted payment."

"What sort of payment?" Dan urged.

"Sex."

"Did he force you?"

"He shoved the knife at me and forced me against the wall, said he'd cut my throat if I tried to fight him. Ugh," he whimpered. "He shoved it in me, but I swung my arms and hit him in the head, and he lost the knife."

"Then what?"

"I shoved him back and grabbed him. We fought, then those people came along, and he ran."

"Was the sex consensual?" Dan asked. "When he entered you. Did you want him to do that to you?"

"No, no." He shook his head slowly. "You know I don't do that, Dan. I only fuck men, I don't get fucked by them."

"Okay, you rest," Dan told him, seeing Lorenzo's brows rise. "We need to finish him up, and I need to talk to Antonio."

"I'll finish up." Lorenzo watched Dan leave the room. He knew the Stephanopoulos family, especially Jenny, having gotten a lot of help the last few years, and so he'd worked with Dan before. He liked the family, thought a lot of Jenny, and cared when her grandkids had been hurt, but not so much about Cabot. Knowing his reputation, he wasn't surprised by the turn of events. As he bandaged Cabot's head, he thought about the male members of the family. While he wasn't gay and loved women, he also didn't mind looking at the Stefan men and how they were still incredibly good looking, strong and virile in their fifties. And Dan wasn't bad either. But he was thirty, and they were all older than him. He'd dated Alena about five years ago, but like his, her career was important, and they went their separate ways.

Out in the waiting room, Dan approached Antonio and Derek.

"Dan, how is he?" Antonio bolted from his chair.

"He'll live," Dan said, taking him by the shoulders. "Have you told your grandmother?"

"No, oh God, no," Antonio muttered. "I can't tell her, or Mama and Papa."

"Why not? They're your family, they'd want to know," Derek said. "They'd be very upset if they weren't told. Very disappointed."

Antonio flagged, his energy gone. "I was supposed to find him and look after him."

"And you tried," Dan told him. "But he's not your responsibility." Watching Antonio fall apart, he sat him down. "I'll call."

"No, don't!" Antonio leapt up.

"Antonio, I need to." Dan was firm. "Now sit down. Derek, keep him there." He walked away to make the call.

"Hello, Stephanopoulos residence, Jenny speaking."

"I don't want you to say anything except yes or no, okay," Dan said.

Jenny glanced up at the wall in front of her, on alert. "Okay.

"Are Carlos and Viv there?"

"Yes."

"Are other people there?"

"Yes."

"Without making a fuss, can you leave with Carlos and Viv?"

"Yes."

"Come to the hospital."

"Why?"

"Jenny, just say nothing and come, please."

"Okay."

He hung up and went back to the others. "They're on their way."

"Ah, Carlos, why don't I walk you and Viv home? You should take some time to yourselves while the boys are out," Jenny said, trying to remain calm.

"We're all right, Mama," Carlos said from his comfy spot on the couch.

"No, seriously," Jenny urged. "After that performance today, you two need some time to yourselves. I'll walk you home."

"We just live next door, Jenny," Viv said. "No need for you to walk us." She stood up and stretched. "But I will be glad to get home after partying all night last night."

"Well then, I'll walk you." Jenny gathered her keys and opened the door. "Some fresh air will be good."

"Okay, night all." Puzzled, Carlos frowned at his brothers who had similar expressions, and got up, following his mother and wife out the door.

"What a lovely evening," Jenny said as they strolled the twenty-two steps to their house. "Okay." She stopped them. "No sounds, we need to go somewhere, come on." She headed for Carlos's car, pulling them along with her.

"What's going on?" Viv asked, flustered by the situation.

"I don't know. Dan was on the phone and said to get you both to the hospital."

"The hospital!" Viv exclaimed. "Oh, my God, the twins!" They jumped into the car and rushed up the hill, arriving to find Dan, Derek and Antonio.

"Now we know who's in trouble," Jenny said. "What's happened?"

"He was robbed and beaten," Dan told them.

"Oh, my God." Viv's hand flew to her mouth. "My baby."

"Some people helped him just as I came along," Antonio wailed. "I was too late."

"It's okay," Jenny soothed him. "It's not your fault. Can we see him?" she asked Dan.

"Sure. He's resting and will need to stay overnight." He led them to

Cabot's room to see Lorenzo checking on him.

"Ah, Mrs Stephanopoulos, Mr and Mrs Stephanopoulos," Lorenzo greeted them.

"I told them he had been robbed and beaten," Dan told him as Viv rushed to her son's side.

"Oh, my baby," she cried. "My poor, poor baby."

"Mama," Cabot groaned. "It hurts."

"I know, I know." She gently smoothed his hair back. "It will for a while." She turned to the doctors. "Has he been given painkillers?"

"Small doses, since he might have other things in his system," Lorenzo said.

"When can he come home?" Carlos asked, a mixture of fear for his son and disappointment in him, coursing through his body.

"If he's okay tomorrow, and the scans are clear, then tomorrow," Lorenzo told them.

Jenny stood at the end of the bed with Dan and Lorenzo watching Viv, Carlos and Antonio crowd around Cabot, speaking in low tones, holding his hands, smoothing back his hair and straightening the covers. It took her back to Tomas and Roger, but that wasn't the strange feeling she had in her stomach. That wasn't what was causing it. Motioning to Dan and Lorenzo, she left the room. They walked into the waiting room out of earshot. "What really happened?" She faced the two men.

They traded glances.

"You know I cannot speak of such things," Lorenzo said and walked away.

Jenny's eyes followed then turned back to Dan.

"Neither can I." He shrugged.

"Don't give me that crap. What happened?"

Sighing, he said, "I will only tell you what Antonio told me. He came upon him being assisted by a couple who helped him get a cab. Cabot had already been beaten up. It had just happened minutes before."

"How bad is the beating?"

"Not overly bad. I'd say they struggled. The punches are superficial, no fractures, no broken bones. He will heal."

"Anything else?"

"I technically and legally cannot say." He glanced away.

"Sex or rape?"

Dan breathed in sharply. How the hell did she do that? Know what was going on even if you didn't give her all the details?

"Both?" She eyed his discomfort, watching him squirm under his ethics. "So, we have another rapist on our hands then?" She crossed her arms and stood staring at him. "Do we?"

He guiltily looked away. "I can only surmise that being party season, there may be robbers and blackmailers, thieves and *rapists* in town."

"Great." She rubbed her forehead. "But unless he tells me, nothing can be done about it, and after I slapped him earlier, he will probably never want to speak to me again."

"Give him time. This may help him see the importance of family," Dan said.

Sighing, she glanced at him. "I doubt it."

*****

It was midday Sunday, and Tomas and Roger took Bertha, Willow, Beatrice and Marie out on the family yacht, looking for a place to spread Bette's ashes. They found it in a little cove with a view of the town and dropped anchor.

The ladies stood at the side, gazing over the scene before them. The town of Mykonos, the ocean, the sky, the sun. It was beautiful and perfect.

Bertha was holding Bette's urn to her chest and allowed her tears to fall. "Thirty years ago we were here. I had Luiz in tow, and we met Tomas." She glanced at his softly smiling face. "It was such a wonderful time, the '70s, free and easy. We did what we wanted, went where we wanted, had who we wanted, and now, all but a few of the people we knew are gone. Thirty years later, there's only a few of us left."

Wiping a wrinkled hand over her cheek, she smiled. "Bette Olander gave it her all for one hundred years. She lived, she loved, she got everything from her husbands that she thought she deserved, and she did well with it. She found young Tomas," she looked his way, "and decided to help him see the world, taking him in and helping him with his career. And when he found Roger, she encouraged the relationship."

Tomas and Roger traded loving smiles.

"She was so proud of you, Tomas. I think she told you that the last time we were here," Bertha went on. "She definitely considered the two of you as sons, and she was so proud of all you had achieved after your death. It killed her inside to see that newspaper article about your deaths. It killed all of us inside. But when we found you, our hearts sang. You were still with us and still alive, kicking on like the rest of us. And now you've been together for thirty years. Almost to the day when you met at *The Joy Stick*."

She wiped her tears. "We've lost so many. Marcus and Violet, our husbands, Webster, Bette. Bette was an incredible woman. She gave it all she had every day of her life, and she will be sadly missed." Opening the urn, she held it out. "Goodbye, Bette Olander, may you forever enjoy your life here on Mykonos." Tipping the urn upside down, she shook Bette's ashes to the wind.

The yacht's waiters handed out glasses of champagne, and they toasted.

"To Bette." Bertha raised her glass.

"To Bette." The others did the same and drank. After a few moments of remembrance, they sat on the lounges and reminisced.

"I can't believe she's gone," Tomas said, twirling his glass absentmindedly.

"Neither can I," Roger replied. "I thought she'd live on forever."

"So did we," Beatrice said. "With everyone we've lost, Bette was the one we thought would live forever."

"We gave her funeral home her kaftan from thirty years ago," Bertha told the boys. "The one she loved most. She'd often said '77 was her best year, and Mykonos was the best time. And then she joked about being buried in the kaftan she wore while we were here. That's why we're all wearing ours, to honour her." All of the ladies wore their best kaftans in memory.

"And you all look fabulous," Tomas said. "Just as you did back then."

"Tomas, darling." Bertha took a serious tone as the others tittered.

"Do you still think of him? It was thirty years ago."

Knowing something might be brought up, he'd assumed he was ready, but the pounding in his heart told him he wasn't.

"I don't mean to bring up bad memories, it's just that," she glanced at the other ladies, "it's thirty years ago for that too."

"Yeah, I know, and I try to get on with my life, and I have," Tomas replied. "Until someone brings him up."

"But does living here in Mykonos not make you remember every day?" Willow asked.

"No. Actually, it doesn't," he said. "When Mama brought us back, we believed we were dying, and I did." Playing with his glass, he sobered at the thought. "It was all about that, nothing more. Being with family as much as I could, making *as many memories* as I could. It took me years to get better, and by then, Mykonos had new meaning. Luiz wasn't a part of it."

Bertha nodded. "Yes, yes, I can see how things could make you forget him." She gazed over the sea. "It's so beautiful here."

The others agreed and celebrated Bette's life over succulent seafood and salad, plus more champagne, regaling each other with stories of Bette and her life. It was a long life to celebrate, and they stayed there reminiscing until well after sunset.

*****

"Oh, my God, they what!?" Alena said over Skype. She was in her hotel suite at the latest stop of Washington State for her concert in Seattle the next night.

"They were porn stars," Alexis repeated, looking at her sister on her Apple MacBook Pro computer. "Cabot threw a tantrum and blurted it out."

"That must have been what he hinted at," Diana said from her hotel room in Spain where she was doing a photo shoot.

"What do you mean, hinted at?" Dom asked. He was beside Alexis, huddled around their computers that they'd set up so that they could Skype Alena and Diana together.

"A few years back he hinted at some big secret," Diana told them. "But he never elaborated. Should Danté be in the room for this?" She leaned closer and kissed the camera on her computer. "Hey, Little D."

"Hey, Diana." Danté grinned. "I *am* fourteen, and considering everything else he said…" He glanced at his sister and brother.

"Unfortunately, he knows, and there's no way of taking it back," Alexis said.

"Have you googled it yet?" Alena pulled up another screen and typed in her father's name.

"It's just a bunch of stuff as a movie producer, and Daddy as a musician," Alexis said. "Uncle Tomas and Roger came up as activists."

"So, basically nothing from the '70s and '80s then?" Diana asked, twirling a tendril of hair around her finger.

"Not even when we put porn star after their names," Dom replied. "It's like their life back then never existed except for Dad's at 69."

"And Mama and Aunt Maggie came up under the Juilliard register of graduation," Danté added, and shrugged. "There's nothing."

"Bloody hell!" Alena said. "This family gets weirder and weirder."

"Well…" Diana started, then bit her lip.

"Go on, D," Alena urged.

"If *it is* true…" Diana went on. "Then it would explain Cabot's behaviour the last few years."

"Oh." Alena's mouth moved into an o shape. "So, you're saying that he would have seen those videos and then took on Uncle Carlos's persona?"

Diana shrugged a shoulder. "If he saw Daddy having sex with all of those women, plus Uncles Pedro and Tomas, then he probably figured, why the hell not."

"Mmm." Alena chewed on her bottom lip. "Could be. But Cabot's always been a bit different to the rest of us. He's not even like Antonio, personality-wise."

"I called him a free spirit in a recent interview, and I guess he is," Diana said. "He's always been the one to just go and do it."

"And to hell with the consequences," Dom replied.

"He didn't elaborate?" Alena asked. She was lying on her stomach on her bed while James had taken a walk. She was all alone with the door locked, but she had a view of it from the bed, so she could see who was coming.

"He said, all the women his father had, and that Daddy had two or three in each of his movies, and that Tomas and Roger had sex with men. And then he called them a bad name and Grandma slapped him," Alexis supplied.

"She what!" Diana exclaimed.

"What?" Alena added. "Grandma did what? *She wouldn't.*"

"*She did*, and he deserved it," Danté said. "It was bad. And then her voice got real low like it does when she's angry, and she told him off. Said he had one choice and he could apologise, or get out."

"What did he do?" Diana asked.

"He got angry, swore some more, and took off," Alexis said.

"Whoa, that's rough," Alena replied. "But, from the sound of it, he deserved it."

*****

"Do you want to come home to your old room, or stay at the house?" Viv asked Cabot as they helped him into a wheelchair at the hospital.

"I want to go to my home. *My* home with Antonio." He wasn't feeling much love for his family at that moment.

"Okay, well your grandmother had it cleaned up and sent your friends home," Viv said.

"She what! She had no right," he spat, feeling anger boil for the woman who'd taken her hand to his face.

"She had *every right*, Cabot," Antonio snapped back, making his brother look up. "Your friends are a part of your problem, and right now, you can't fly for a week, so that means you stay in the house."

"But what will I do, Tonee?" Cabot whined as Carlos wheeled him to the car.

"You'll rest and do as you're damn well told," Antonio told him and helped him out of the chair and into the car. "And you'll bloody well do it."

"Will you look after me, Tonee?" Cabot asked, gazing adoringly at his brother.

"You have parents for that." Antonio climbed in beside him.

Cabot cast a scowl at his parents. "I want you to do it, Tonee." He got the evil eye from his father in the rear-view mirror and could see his mother was upset. *Well, bloody well good,* he thought. *All the years they've lied to us about their pasts.*

"And what if I don't want to, Cabot?" Antonio asked. "What if I'm sick of looking after my bratty brother who acts like a child, who stomps his foot when he doesn't get his own way? What if I say no, Cabot?" He watched his brother's eyes widen as he thought about it.

"Tonee? You'd stop looking after me?" The thought was absolutely preposterous to Cabot, and he couldn't believe it.

Neither could Viv, who frowned at the tone of Antonio's voice.

"Yes, Cabot, I would," Antonio said as they pulled up to the house. "Let's get you inside." He alighted and helped Cabot out of the back of the car. "Let's get you in." They walked into the clean and tidy house and upstairs to the bedroom. "You need rest, Cabot. Take a painkiller and get some sleep." Antonio gave him his pill with a bottle of water from the drinks fridge beside the bed, and tucked his brother in. "I'll stay with you until you're asleep."

"It's not bedtime, Tone. I'm not tired. The sun is up. I want to party and get laid." Cabot stared at him.

"You did, two nights ago, which is why you're in the mess you're now in." Antonio stared back. "This is of your own doing, Cabot. You did this to yourself, and you need to fix it."

"I don't want to fix it, Tonee, I didn't do anything."

"You got yourself beaten up because you got drunk and fucked a guy who wasn't, and who decided he wanted payment for what he'd just done," Antonio told him. "That's *your* fault, Cabot. *You* got yourself beaten up. No one else. And now you need to grow up. Did he wear a condom?"

Cabot shrugged. "I don't know, the fucker didn't tell me."

"So, for all you know, you now have an STD up your ass?"

Cabot scowled. "Don't be absurd, Tonee. The Stefan doesn't get STDs, that's why I wear condoms." He slid down in his bed and yawned.

"But did he?"

Cabot's eyes closed. "Don't…know…"

Antonio patted his brother's hand and went downstairs to his parents. "He's out like a light. How long did Lorenzo say the pills will work for?"

"Four to five hours," Viv said, wringing her hanky. "Is this all our fault, Antonio? For what we did? For what your father did all those years ago?"

"Viv," Carlos chastised. "We're not to blame."

"Mama." Antonio held Viv by the arms. "This started in his teens. He'd ask questions, get curious, do things to find out if it worked, and he decided to have sex with women *and* men. Everything else was a gradual repercussion of his actions. I'm not even sure what's behind it all, but it started long before he found the movie stash, and somehow, I don't even think Cabot knows why he does it."

"He needs psychological help then?" Carlos asked his son.

Antonio sighed. "I'd say so, Papa."

"Ah," Carlos growled in defeat, his head falling back, the air leaving him. "*How* do we get him help?"

"Short of sticking him in a nutjob ward, I don't know," Antonio replied. "What I *do* know, is I'd like to take a break from him and get some air."

Viv looked at her watch. "The kids are all Skyping Alena and Diana in Alexis's room if you want to have a chat. They should still be going."

"Okay, I'll go and catch up." He kissed her on both cheeks and left.

"Where did we go wrong, Carlos?" she asked, turning to her husband, a deep frown on her face that was slowly becoming wrinkled with stress caused by her son. "What did we do wrong?"

He deflated. "I don't know, Viv. I really don't."

Antonio made his way up to Pedro's house where Angie let him in on her way out the door.

"We'll be next door; tell the kids."

"Okay, Aunt Angie." He kissed her cheek on the fly and walked into

Alexis's room to see them huddled around. "Hey all," he said wearily.

Danté spun around in his seat. "Tony!" He flew into his cousin's arms.

"Hey, Squirt." He hugged back, kissed Alexis, and slapped Dom on the shoulder. "Hey, Alena, how's the tour going?" Leaning in, he looked at his cousin on the monitor.

"Great, Tone. How are you?" she asked.

"Worn out. Hey, sis." He turned to his sister. "Lookin' good."

"And you're looking tired, Antonio. Or has you-know-who worn you out?" She worried about her brother and how old and worn out he was looking. "Where is he by the way? Out partying?"

"Asleep at home." Antonio sat on the bed, so he could see both computers, and his cousins pulled their chairs back to include him in the session.

"So, he *did* party hard." Diana snorted.

"No." Antonio grimaced. "He got beaten up and has just come home from the hospital."

"What!" rang out five times.

Antonio ran his hands through his hair and scratched his scalp. "The idiot ran out of here screaming Saturday night, did they tell you?"

"They told me," Diana said. "And about our fathers being porn stars. But back to Cabot, is he okay?"

"Got punched in the face, so he won't be working for a while, but nothing's broken or fractured, just bruised and sore."

"Jesus! Did he deserve it?" Dom asked.

Antonio looked at him and sighed. "Probably."

"What's going to happen now?" Diana asked, concerned for her brother. "After what he said, it sounds like he's gone off the rails."

"He's still angry at Mama and Papa and Grandma from the sound of it. I don't know what's going to happen. I don't know if we could put him in rehab, or get him into some facility to find out what his actual problem is." Antonio felt as if he'd lived a thousand lifetimes. "I don't know my brother anymore."

"Oh, Tone," Diana murmured. "I'm so sorry."

"So am I. Because now that we're twenty-five, I don't know if I even *want* to work with him anymore. Hell." He flopped back on the bed. "I don't know if I want to *work* anymore."

"You clearly need to take a break, and maybe you should. You said he was beaten, so he'll need to heal," Diana said. "Since he can't work, take time off and have a break."

"I wish I could," Antonio moaned. "But it's bigger than that. It's…I don't know…" He stared at Alexis's ceiling covered in colourful stars and rainbows that she'd painted herself. "Sometimes I wish I could just walk away from it all and go off into the land of rainbows." He pointed up to the ceiling. "It must be nice to live there. Just being free and not having anyone to look after."

"Won't you feel alone, Tony?" Danté asked, knowing what alone felt like. "Or lonely?"

"I don't know, Little D," Antonio said. "But sometimes, even when I'm with Cabot, I feel alone. I feel lonely. He's off in his own little world doing his own little things, and even though I'm standing there, I'm alone. On my own."

"So, you don't know if actually being on your own is going to help?" Diana sighed, wishing she could be there with them, and maybe she could talk some sense into her brother. Both of them.

"No, D, I don't," he replied, sitting up and looking at the computer. "I don't."

*****

"How is he?" Pedro asked after Jenny had explained Cabot's issue.

"He'll live," Dan said. He and Derek were getting ready to go out for a late lunch. "No breaks, just bruises."

"Jesus," Pedro muttered. "The kid gets worse and worse."

"And I don't know what to do about it," Jenny said, gripping the back of the dining chair. "I just don't. Short of locking him up and getting him a 24/7 shrink to get to the root of his problem."

"You can't do that—" Dan interjected.

"I damn well will if I have to," Jenny interrupted. "If it's the only thing that will help my grandson, I'll do it."

"Yes, I suppose you would," Dan replied. "Well, if you need recommendations, let me know. We're off to the beach."

"See you later." Jenny watched them leave and let go of the chair, wandering into the kitchen, not sure what she was even there for.

"We knew one day they might find out." Pedro came up behind her.

"But his reaction was ridiculous," Jenny replied, staring absentmindedly out the French doors across the ocean.

"He used it as an excuse to do it too. To be sexually rampant and screw whatever he wanted," Pedro added.

"Exactly what Carlos did," Jenny murmured.

"Yes, and now I'm paying for it," Carlos said from the doorway.

"How's Cabot?" Angie asked from her regular spot at the dining table. "Mama just told us."

Carlos slowly walked into the kitchen. "Sleeping. Antonio got him to take a sleeping pill. Lorenzo said to give him several a day, so he gets rest."

"Is that wise with all the other drugs he's been doing?" Spiros asked his son, reaching out and taking his hand and giving it a reassuring squeeze.

Carlos sighed and sat at the dining table next to his father, head slumped in hands. "I don't know, Papa. But he needs rest, and this is the best way to keep him calm, so he'll heal."

"Is Viv with him?" Jenny asked, walking over to her son and laying her hands on his shoulders.

"Yeah." Carlos finally looked up. "We both feel like shit. I feel guilty for loving sex at twenty-four, and Viv feels guilty because she doesn't think we did it right. She thinks we missed something when we raised him."

The kids walked through the door with the two laptops and placed them on the dining table.

Carlos saw Diana. "Hello, my baby, how's the modelling going?"

"Good, Daddy," she said. "Antonio told us about Cabot. That sucks. How is he?"

"He's…Cabot." Carlos sighed. "Angry, full of hatred, and I have no idea what we're going to do with him."

"How's Mama?" she went on.

"Feeling even more guilty than me."

"And um…" She bit her lip. "Is it true what they told us about your…*former* careers?"

Carlos glanced at his three grimacing brothers and frowning mother. "Yes, baby, it's true. But it has nothing to do with any of you kids, so don't worry about it."

"I can't believe Mama allowed Daddy to do such things," Alena said.

"I not only allowed it, I encouraged it, and it was before we were married," Angie said, leaning over to look at her daughter. "But as your uncle said, it's nothing to do with you."

"Mama, I'm shocked," Alena said, and her brothers and sister stood wide-eyed. "How could you!"

"Because we were young, it was the '70s, and people did things," Angie replied. "In fact, if it were the '70s now, Cabot would fit right in." She frowned at the thought.

A maniacal laugh burst out of Carlos. "Oh, my God, you're right. He would. Oh, my God, he's *exactly* like me." His head dropped back into his hands. "He's me back in 1977."

"But times have changed and we're 2007 now, and everything is different from 1977. Look," Jenny waved her hand at the computers, "We didn't have these back then; we used typewriters."

"Or the iPod, or iPhone. I got one of those when I was in New York a few weeks ago," Diana said. "Everything's technologically transportable." She screwed up her nose. "My God, that's a mouthful."

"Exactly. I use the computer for my books and running the business. We can call each other on our cell phones instead of worrying about when someone's going to call, or how we call them," Jenny said. "Times are different, but Cabot's attitude is a whole other thing, and it's more to do with something else other than the fact he watched his father having sex."

"Ew, Grandma," Diana said.

"That's what I think," Antonio told his grandmother. "There's something serious going on inside him, and even I don't know what it is. And I'm his twin."

Jenny let out a long breath. "Well, we need to do something, and clearly confrontation doesn't work."

"And he's still pretty angry at you for slapping him," Antonio said.

"I won't apologise if that's what he's waiting for. He'll get another one if this behaviour continues. And the only thing I can think of is locking him up. Either in the house or a mental clinic," Jenny said, one hand on her hip, one hand playing with her bottom lip.

"He needs help, whatever it is." Antonio sat next to his father. "Because I've had enough of dealing with it and need a break from it."

"Didn't you tell me that your twenty-fifth was when Phoenix Stefan stops existing or some such thing?" Diana asked him.

"What!" went around the room.

Antonio shrugged nonchalantly. "I'm done being Phoenix. I like modelling and all it's given me, but I'm bored with the lifestyle and just want to be me again. Just want to walk down the street and not have someone try and rip my clothes off. I miss my family, I miss spending time with you guys at birthdays and anniversaries and holidays."

"We miss you too, kid." Carlos grasped his hand.

"Maybe, then, it's time to come home," Jenny said.

*****

Alena was lying on the bed, staring up at the ceiling when James came back and knocked on her door. They were sharing the suite, so she had him nearby in case of emergencies.

"Hey, finished your family time?" He grabbed a drink from the fridge.

She continued staring up, lost in thought, and didn't answer him.

"Hello, anyone home?" He walked into the bedroom. "Alena?"

"Huh?" She turned her head to see him standing by the bed. "What? Oh, you're back." Twisting around, she rolled into a sitting position. "Hey, have a good walk?" Sliding back, she crossed her legs and indicated for him to sit.

"Did you have a good session with your family?" He tucked his right leg under him before he sat. "Clearly, since you didn't hear me come in, or talk to you."

She let out a deep breath and tucked her hair behind her ears. "My cousin was beaten up."

"What!" James's eyes went wide. "Which one?"

"Cabot. He and Antonio were home in Mykonos, but there was a huge fight, and he stormed off and got himself beaten up." She took a breath. "Antonio found him and got him to hospital. He's bruised, and his is face puffy from being hit, but he's okay and will get through it."

"Whoa. That must have sucked. They know who did it?" James asked, the cop instinct in him coming out.

She shook her head. "No, not that I know of. Antonio didn't say."

"Well…" James thought about it. "I'm sorry."

"Not your fault." She shrugged. "He's twenty-five and a brat. Probably time he learned a few lessons, and if getting beaten up is one of them, so be it."

"That's harsh."

"But true," she countered. "He's been off the rails for years, and could easily put his life in danger, but he doesn't care. He snorts, and smokes pot, but he doesn't care. He gets drunk and has sex with whoever, but he doesn't care."

"A bit of a troublemaker, then?" James asked. "Yeah, I saw that the night we met."

"Yep. Causes troubles for himself wherever he goes. No one in the family knows what his actual problem is, not even Antonio. And Cabot just doesn't care about the problems it causes for his brother, or the family. It's just all about him."

"So, a self-absorbed, egomaniacal narcissist, then."

Alena laughed. "Yeah, that's Cabot." She quietened and leaned back on the pile of pillows behind her.

"And there's something else?" James asked, curious as to what it was, or if it could tell him something more about the family. Googling hadn't been of any help except to give him info on Tomas's activism, and a whole bunch of photos. And he still didn't get why seeing his husband, Roger, made him angry.

"Huh?" She focussed on him.

"Is there something else?" He noted the faraway look on her face and in her eyes.

"Ah, yeah, but I can't really say."

"Why not?"

"It's ah, personal family business. Happened before we were born."

That got his juices flowing. "So personal you can't tell me?" Could this be it?

She blushed. "Ah, yeah…it kinda is. Has to do with my parents and uncles. We were told it had nothing to do with us, so…none of our business. Besides, we don't even have a lot of details. I couldn't tell you anything anyway."

"Can't even hint at it?" He gave a small smile, hoping to loosen her up.

She smiled back. "Sorry. Don't know anything, and it's none of my business, which means it's none of yours."

He blinked, surprised by her words. "Okay, fair enough. It's late. Why don't we hit the sack and go exploring tomorrow for some fun?"

Glancing at her travel clock, Alena saw it was after two in the morning. "Okay. I am tired. Night."

"Night." James left the room and closed the door behind him. Spreading out on his bed, he did some thinking. So there *was* something else before the kids. Something involving the parents. What could that be? Would have had to be from the '70s. Alena was born in '78 with her cousin, so what could be the big deal? He pictured Tomas naked, virile and twenty-two, laid out on the sand, underneath him. Oh, how glorious he was then, and still was now from the pictures he'd seen. Beautiful, tanned, muscular, just as he was back then… *Back when I loved him, and then he left me for Roger and got into those fucking movies. Is that what little Alena was going on about? The porn movies they were all in back in '77? Oh, how my darling looked so hot in them, but he should have been with me in them. ME! Not Roger fucking Dencott. He should have been my lover, my husband, my man because I loved him, not Roger fucking Dencott. I loved him and wanted to spend the rest of my life with him, but that bastard took my life, and took that choice, and took that chance away from me. He took my life with a bullet to the brain right when I was in the throes of passion with my man. The very last time I was with Tomas. But I'm back, and* I will *have another chance. You can count on it.*

*****

Cabot woke to find his mother beside his bed. He was worn out, even though he'd just slept for God knows how long, and needed a piss. He stared at his mother, still beautiful at seventy, sitting in the chair beside his bed, her head resting on her fist, eyes closed, her breathing soft. He hadn't meant to hurt her; hell he hadn't meant to blurt it all out that way, but when his grandmother had tried to stop him from drinking another beer, it had pissed him off. All because she had to bring up the coke and the pot and the sex. The sex had done it. Wanting him to cut back and slow down. What a preposterous idea that was. His father hadn't, so why would he? And they'd made such a big deal out of it. If they hadn't've done that, he probably would have kept his mouth shut. But they were such fucking hypocrites with their attitude.

I can't have sex, but my father could at the same age. Bullshit! They don't get to pull that crap on me. And what's the difference? There is none, except for what, Carlo Stefan got paid and did it on screen. Well, maybe I should get into the business, see how dear old Dad likes that then. Yeah, how about that. Steele Stefan, porn king. I'll outdo my old man any day. He wants to make this about sex, then I'll make it about sex. I'll get into the business and give him and Uncle Pedro a run for their money. I've got eleven inches, the only one who beats me is Tomas at twelve inches. But that's irrelevant. Maybe I should follow in their footsteps and get paid for it instead of giving it away for nothing.

Yes, he was going to stop giving away the Stefan to whoever wanted it, and start making a living doing it for money in movies. Yep, that was definitely a plan.

He quietly slid out of bed and padded into the bathroom for a piss. Not bothering to flush, he went downstairs and found his brother and father sitting on the lounge playing cards. "Tone, we got anything to eat?"

They looked up. "There's some roast chicken from Grandma in the fridge. It's from lunch today," Antonio replied.

"I don't want anything she's made," Cabot spat nastily, and that made Carlos and Antonio shoot up out of their seats and stare at him. He took a shocked step back, thinking they would hit him.

"Don't be a pig," Antonio snapped. "She's our grandmother. She slapped you because you deserved it, but at least she still cares."

Cabot blinked rapidly, trying to clear his thoughts. He was rarely chastised by his brother. *But considering the look on Tone's and Papa's faces, I'd better can it. And I am hungry.* Unnerved, he padded into the kitchen and removed the container from the fridge. Pulling off the lid, he saw juicy breast meat with skin, roast potatoes, carrots, peas and beans, with gravy poured over. *Good old Grandma, she does know how to cook a roast.* Hungry, he shoved a piece of chicken into his mouth and grabbed a bottle of water from the fridge before going into the lounge and curling up in an easy chair by the window. The ocean view was spectacular, and the breeze divine.

"Not going to heat it up?" Antonio flipped a card onto the coffee table.

"Too hungry to wait." Cabot shoved a potato in his mouth, followed by a carrot.

"Do you have your painkillers?" Antonio asked.

Cabot shrugged. "Where are they?"

"I have them here." Viv walked into the room and set them on the coffee table. "How are you feeling?"

He stared at her while finishing his mouthful. "Fine."

"Good." She sighed and wearily sat next to Carlos on the couch when Antonio vacated his seat to her and took the other easy chair. "It's time we had a talk, Cabot."

"Ugh," he groaned. "I don't need it."

"Shut up and listen, you snot-nosed little brat," Antonio snapped, his temper fraying at the edges. "Listen to your bloody parents for once. They may actually be able to help you."

Cabot stared wide-eyed at his brother, as did their parents. He gulped. "Tone?"

"*Listen to our parents, Cabot,*" Antonio repeated, giving his brother the death stare.

"Okay, Tone," Cabot said quietly, shoving more chicken into his mouth and moving his eyes away from his brother's glare.

"Cabot, my baby," Viv started. "We have no idea where we went wrong with you. We don't know what we didn't do, what we should have done, if anything. We have absolutely no idea what we have done to make you this way. And we're sorry." She wiped her tears and Carlos slid his arm around her, pulling her close. "Is it the fact you had a twin, so you had to share everything? Is it the fact Angie had Dom, so you weren't the only boys anymore? Did you not feel loved enough? Wanted? We don't know, Cabot. We just don't know where we went wrong." She cried on her husband's shoulder.

"We thought we loved you equally," Carlos took up the conversation. "We thought we *treated* you equally, taught you both the same things at the same time, and yet you've turned out completely different to your brother. Everyone's worried about your safety and health. Us, your grandparents, aunt, uncles, cousins, your siblings…oh, Cabot." Carlos sighed and saw Antonio wipe his eyes free of tears. "We have no idea where we went wrong. *What* we did wrong."

Cabot shovelled more food into his mouth to stop himself from crying. It wasn't them, they didn't do anything. It was something else. Something he couldn't put his finger on, and when he tried, it made him want to vomit. He swallowed it back with a few gulps of water. After a moment of quiet, he said, "You're hypocrites."

"Yes, we are," Carlos admitted, much to Cabot's surprise. "Your Aunt Angie said something today. The kids were Skyping each other and they brought their laptops into your grandma's house, so we could see them, and Alena was shocked that her mother allowed it. Angie admitted that she not only allowed it, she encouraged it, which shocked the kids. And then she said it was the '70s, we were young, and people did things like that. In fact, if it was the '70s now, Cabot would fit right in. I started laughing and realised that you are *exactly* like me back then. *Exactly!* We love sex, and I couldn't get enough of it. So, I started charging and made a motza. But regardless of that, I *never* did drugs, I *never* snorted or smoked. I kept my wits about me, and I made my way into a new life for myself. One that your mother suggested. But it was *my* choice," he told his stunned sons. "*My* choice to do porn. And it paid well. But after the birth of Diana, I was done starring in them. So I wrote and directed and produced. And I won a lot of awards for it. After Tomas died, I bought back all the rights from our movies and hid them all away. I thank God that was a long time before the internet. It's all hidden away to be remembered only on occasion."

Cabot blinked back tears. His family had never been this honest with him before. He chewed thoughtfully on a carrot. "How did you get into porn?"

Carlos exhaled and thought about what to say next. "Well, that's a long story in itself, and one that really has nothing to do with you guys, but, I have a feeling it will come out at some stage, although now is not the time. I had to leave Mykonos, and your mother and a friend of hers, Connie DeLuca, got me out and over to Hollywood. They knew someone who could help me out, and that was Harry DeVille. Porn king of L.A."

"You started working for him?" Cabot munched on a handful of peas and beans, scooping them up with his fingers.

"Yes. I loved sex and women and got paid well for it." Carlos felt the blood rise from his chest to his neck to his face. "It barely lasted a year, and I was done. We all were."

Teary, that his father was being honest, Cabot looked down at his food and chewed on another potato, thinking what it might mean for their relationship.

"We're not saying stop having sex, Cabot," Vivian said softly. "We just want you to slow down, take it seriously, and maybe pick a partner, maybe have an *actual* relationship." She shrugged. "To just be careful. We'd like you to stop doing drugs, stop snorting and smoking, but we know we can't make you. We'd like to see you and Antonio more often, but we know you're busy. We know that the two of you and Diana have busy lives and careers. But we hope you'd come home a little more often to see us. Or maybe we could meet up somewhere."

Cabot scooped up the last of the gravy with a piece of chicken. He didn't come home because he felt suffocated. All the family crowding around, getting in each other's business and lives, and he needed air; needed to be away from them. That was the only way he could keep his thoughts straight and breathe. Being in a city away from his family.

"We want you to be careful, Cabot," Viv went on. "With *everything* you do."

He finished off his food and licked his fingers, then swallowed the rest of his water. "She slapped me."

"You deserved it," Antonio said. "You acted like a bratty little child throwing a tantrum and expected to get away with it. You didn't. Grandma called you out on your bad behaviour."

"It hurt," Cabot whined.

"Good!" Antonio huffed. "It was supposed to. You'd just called her sons, *our* uncles, a pretty damn bad name. You deserved it."

"Tonee, you're supposed to be on my side," Cabot whined harder.

"Why? Because we're twins?" Antonio asked. "Doesn't cut it, Cabot. You were horrible yesterday and I'm not going to back up your horrible behaviour anymore. I'm done with it. We're twenty-five now, it's time to grow up and be an adult, and not the bratty little child you've been acting like. I don't want to look after you anymore. The only reason I happened along last night was because Grandma asked me to go look for you. Otherwise, you would've had to deal with that on your own. I want a brother, a friend, an adult I can talk to, not an immature little brat I have to look after and deal with." He sighed and rubbed his tear-reddened eyes. "I'm over your childish behaviour, Cabot. I want to work and live with a mature adult, not a child." He slumped wearily back in the chair. "Otherwise, I'm done."

"Done! Tonee!" Cabot was alarmed. "What do you mean; done? You can't leave me, Tonee." He stumbled past his parents to fall at his brother's feet. "Don't leave me, Tonee, I love you. Please don't say you're done."

Carlos and Vivian traded curious glances, and Carlos frowned at his son's behaviour. He'd never seen Cabot so dependent on Antonio, and now he realised why Antonio said he was over it.

"Cabot, it's time to grow up and be an adult." Antonio stared into his brother's scared eyes. "You need to do that now, Cabot. Grow up."

"But you won't leave me, will you, Tonee? Please say you won't," Cabot pleaded, tears sliding down his youthful cheeks. He laid his head on his brother's legs. "Please don't leave me, Tonee."

Antonio looked at his parents and raised a brow as if to say, 'see what I mean?' Instead of answering, he patted his brother's back.

Carlos and Viv walked into Jenny's house a half hour later, and re-capped what had just happened.

"Do you think he listened?" Pedro asked, cracking peanuts open on the dining table.

"God, I hope so," Carlos said, grabbing a handful of nuts and annoying Pedro. "But it seems there's only one person he actually listens to and sometimes obeys."

"Who's that?" Spiros asked, sipping an iced tea.

"Antonio," Carlos and Jenny said at the same time.

"Mama, how did you know?" Carlos stared in surprise at his mother.

"It's obvious," Jenny said, setting a jug of iced tea and glasses on the table. "It's mint, help yourselves."

Carlos followed her into the kitchen. "Have you noticed..." He kept his voice down. "How close they are? Mainly, Cabot to Antonio."

"What have you seen?" Jenny asked, getting the plates ready for dinner.

"That he's..." Carlos frowned and shook his head. "I don't know... he's *unnaturally* attached to Antonio."

Jenny paused and looked at him. "How do you mean, *exactly?*"

"Antonio had a go at him and told him he was done with his bullshit. It freaked Cabot out. His eyes went wide, he got scared, and pretty much threw himself at Antonio's feet, clinging to his legs, pleading for him to not leave him. *Don't leave me, Tonee, please don't leave me.* It was weird, to say the least." He leaned against the island bench. "And it makes me wonder what's really going on inside his head."

"Antonio did say earlier even *he* doesn't know what's going on in Cabot's head, and they're twins. So...if *he* can't figure it out, how the hell will we?"

Carlos sighed. "I don't know, Mama. I just don't know."

"Maybe a psychiatrist would help." Jenny handed the plates to her son.

"Maybe, but how the hell do we get him to one?" Carlos asked, holding the plates to his chest.

"That's something we're going to have to figure out," she replied.

*****

"Would you like to go upstairs for dinner?" Antonio asked Cabot as he lay on the couch beside him, curled up with his head on Antonio's legs.

"No."

"Because?"

"I'm clearly not welcome."

"You would be if you behaved yourself and didn't smart talk everyone."

"It would be too uncomfortable."

"That's your fault."

"Are you going to blame me for everything?"

"Yes."

"Even Grandma slapping me?"

"You're damn lucky it was Grandma and not Papa. He would've punched you."

Cabot thought about it. "Yeah, I guess."

"Don't really think about anyone but yourself, do you?"

"I think about you." Cabot turned his head to look up at his brother.

"Do you?" Antonio stroked his hair. "Does it matter to you how much your behaviour hurts me, shames me, disgusts me?"

Cabot rolled so he was on his back, his knees bent and leaning against the back of the couch. "Does sex disgust you, Tone?"

"No, but then I'm not a rabid dog like you."

"So, *me* having sex disgusts you?"

"Having me watch it, telling me about it, *that* disgusts me. Having to put up with it disgusts me. Put up with your cavalier behaviour, your coke addiction, your pot smoking. I'm over all of it, Cabot."

"What do you want me to do, Tonee?" Cabot was freaking out

inside. He could sense he was losing his brother and it was making his stomach clench.

"I want you to grow up, Cabot," Antonio told him. "You're twenty-five now; it's time to re-evaluate our lives, our careers, our choices. I'd like to do other things than model. Maybe do some more acting, or travel the world without worrying about doing a photo shoot."

"We could be actors together," Cabot suggested. "We could make movies of our own, become action stars. Do something like *Die Hard* or *Lethal Weapon*. That would be cool, Tone."

"And if I want to do it by myself?"

Cabot's smile faded. "You wouldn't want to do it with me, Tone?"

"What if I didn't?"

Cabot blinked as tears sprung to his eyes. "I…don't…know…"

"You'd be okay, Cabot," Antonio told him. "It's okay for twins to do things on their own every now and then. It's perfectly fine and healthy to have different lives and jobs, friends and careers."

"Yeah, but, we've done everything together. We were in Mama's womb, we were together in our crib and our room, and at school. We've lived together our whole lives. Worked together our whole lives. We haven't been apart, ever, Tone. Don't you love me anymore?" Fear gripped his heart.

"Of course I love you, but I hate your attitude and your behaviour. It's horrible what you called Uncle Tomas and Roger. No wonder Grandma slapped you. I hated it too. You're arrogant, self-absorbed, self-obsessed, self-centred, egotistical, egomaniacal, and narcissistic to name a few. You're selfish, Cabot, and it's time to stop and grow up."

"But you love me, Tonee." He panicked. "At least you still love me?"

"We *all* love you, Cabot. You're just driving us to hate you."

Cabot burst into tears and buried his head in his brother's lap. "I don't want you to hate me, Tonee. I love you. You're the only one who understands me and gets me. No one else does."

"That's because you don't spend enough time *with* anyone else *for* them to know who you are. And your behaviour sucks."

"I know. But I love being with you, and no one else gets me the way you do."

"Then maybe it's time for you to start letting *other people* get you. You have cousins, we have Diana, we have parents, grandparents and uncles who all love us. Let them in, Cabot. Let them see the person you are. Be the person you want to be, and not some stupid pseudonym named Steele Stefan."

"But I love the name Steele Stefan, and I hate Cabot Conroy freakin' Stephanopoulos." Cabot wiped his face and nose on his sleeve.

"I don't have a problem with Antonio, so why do you have a problem with Cabot?"

"Because he was some fag friend of Mother's. I was named after a fag, Tonee."

"You were named after a very close and personal *friend* of our mother who she cared for very deeply, and whose death affected her. Just like I was named after a friend of Papa's."

"Yeah, but your name is cool. Mine sucks," Cabot whined.

"Only because you want it to, Cabot. If you think everything sucks, then it will. Only *you* can change your behaviour, no one else. Only *you* can stop whining like a spoilt child and grow up and do something about it."

"I don't want to grow up, Tonee. I love my life."

"Do you? Really? Is that why you're trying very hard to run as fast as you can away from whatever's haunting you? What *is* haunting you, Cabot?"

Blinking rapidly to stop the forthcoming tears, Cabot screwed his face up, curled into a ball, and cried.

August 2007

On the first of August, Tomas stepped off the private plane of Bertha St John onto the tarmac at Miami airport. It was a beautiful bright day with not a cloud in the turquoise sky as the sun shone down, layering the world in a warm, soft glow. Tomas turned his face up toward that sun, feeling its warmth radiate on his face, and breathed the salty air drifting across on the gentle coast winds.

"Does it feel different?" Bertha asked

"To what?" Tomas looked at her in her bejewelled kaftan and kitten heels.

"To thirty years ago, darling," Bertha said, waving at all of their luggage that was being pulled from the plane, and indicating for the limo driver to put it in the trunk.

"It does," he finally said. "And it doesn't."

"Well, times *have* changed," Willow said from beside him. "But it must be bringing back memories?"

He smiled softly, looking at the ladies who had brought him there thirty years ago. "Good memories so far…when I arrived and stepped onto the tarmac…but life is different now. I have Roger by my side." He entwined his fingers with his husband's.

"Happy anniversary, T." Roger kissed him gently. It was thirty years ago to the day that they met.

"Happy anniversary, Roger." Tomas kissed him back. "Ladies," he turned toward them, "where are we going this time?"

Bertha smiled. "To the same place as last time. Let's go girls." They piled into the limo with Tomas taking the window seat.

Driving down the coast to Coral Gables, they rolled through still extravagantly wealthy neighbourhoods with magnificent mansions behind iron gates. They came to a stop in front of one of them.

Tomas's eyes widened as they stopped at the front door. "I can't believe it still looks the same after thirty years. It's still so beautiful." He gazed across Bette Olander's expansive home with its four round pillars, balcony with white railings, and lush green lawns spread across the plantation-style grounds.

"She did maintain it well," Willow told him.

"Come." Bertha motioned to Tomas. "I want you to see the inside." She led them through the front doors. "Thank you, Mikhale," she told the butler who'd opened the door and taken her things. She conducted everyone through the large entrance hall and opened a door on her right. The huge ballroom extended through the whole side of the house from the front to back, with French doors that folded back against the wall. "Mikhale, grab the door for me." Bertha opened them and slid one side back while the butler opened the other.

They all stood looking across the terrace onto the gardens with their waterfalls and pond and onto the emerald lawn beyond.

Tomas sighed. "I can't believe she kept it all up. Nothing's changed in thirty years." He breathed in as the soft scent of flowers wafted over them.

"It's not as if she couldn't afford it." Bertha gazed over the garden. "She left a trust fund for it, I think. But we all know your family's mega-rich, so you can afford it."

Roger raised a brow at the comment. He and Tomas weren't mega rich by any means, especially Bette Olander-rich. The gym did well as part of the business, and while they chose to live modestly so they could afford nice things, Jenny had bought and paid for everything; their home, the gym, the entire family empire. She controlled the money in the family, and they earned their keep.

"Even so, I still can't believe she kept the house. The upkeep must have been more than she could handle." Tomas noticed the butterflies floating from flower to flower.

"She had that garden company come in once a month and paid them to do it," Willow said. "We all use them, and they've become very popular."

"It's as beautiful as the first time I arrived, and I've loved seeing it, but we need to get to our hotel reservation," Tomas said.

"Oh, darling, you don't understand, this house is yours. The lawyer told us. You'll be staying here while you're in Miami," Bertha said. "The lawyer said it was fine."

"What! No, I—" Tomas shook his head.

"Yes, Tomas," Bertha shushed his protests. "You get to stay here. So, cancel your hotel and get your bags from the trunk. We'll leave you two lovebirds alone, but we'll be back to pick you up and take you out on the town like we did thirty years ago. Let us do this for you both. I know it's your anniversary, but this is our present to you, since we all had a hand in you meeting. We'll be back later." After kissing both their cheeks, she and the girls hastened out to the car, and Mikhale brought their bags in.

"Jesus, Roger, can you believe it? Bette left us her house." Tomas stepped back onto the terrace after the girls had gone and pulled a chair out from the table. Sitting, he admired the view as he had thirty years previously. "I haven't been back here since the day I left to move in with you. Do you remember that?"

"I certainly do." Roger thanked the butler as he placed tall glasses of lemonade on the table. "You moved into my apartment less than a month after we met." He sipped the sweet drink and leaned back in his chair. "I can't believe we're back here."

Tomas shook his head in disbelief. "Neither can I."

A half hour later, they were in the guest room, the same one Tomas had thirty years ago, overlooking the back garden, and wondering once more, how the hell he'd managed to get there. They unpacked their cases and carry-on bags, hanging their clothes in the closet. The bedroom was exactly the same, and Tomas remembered back to their first time in the bed.

"I see that smile." Roger grinned. "Thinking about our first time?"

Tomas blushed. "Yeah." Sitting on the edge of the bed, he looked out the French doors. "So much happened thirty years ago, so much is happening now, and look," he waved a hand, "it all looks the same."

"Like we've been transported back in time." Roger sat next to him. "Except this time we don't have to meet because we've been together for thirty years."

A smile came to Tomas's lips. "Thirty years ago today we met. Where the hell has the time gone?"

"Most of it has been spent on Mykonos running our first gym."

"Our *only* gym," Tomas added.

"The gym we talked about New Year's Eve at 69 in…" Roger thought back. "Was it '77?"

"I don't know, one of them," Tomas said and yawned. "Can you take care of our hotel? I need a nap." He spread out on the bed and relaxed.

"Sure." Roger kissed his cheek. "I'll join you in a few minutes."

*****

That evening, they cruised through the city and dined at *Cristal X*, an expensive restaurant where only the rich dined, feasting on lobster and caviar, and washing it down with Cristal champagne, for which the restaurant was named. It had been in business for twenty years and was on the site of *Sexe et Faveurs*, the restaurant the girls had taken Tomas to back in 1977. After dinner, they went to a new nightclub, *Pom Poms*, and walked into blaring music, flashing lights, and people of all races, colours and creeds.

"Oh, I love it. You can be so free here." Willow clapped her hands before wafting away in her gold lamé kaftan; the same one she had worn thirty years ago.

"I feel like I'm in a time warp," Tomas said above the noise, watching Willow twirl around in circles in the middle of the dance floor. The light reflected off the lamé, making her a human disco ball. The people around her cheered.

Someone grabbed Tomas's hand, and he saw it was Bertha, intent on leading him up a small flight of stairs to a seating area. "God, I really am in a time warp," he repeated when they sat.

Bertha, Marie, Beatrice, Tomas and Roger sat and watched all around them.

"This place is the old *Joy Stick*, darling," Bertha told them. "That's why we brought you here."

"What!" Tomas and Roger were shocked.

"*The Joy Stick* was here?" Roger asked. "I didn't even recognise the address." He had already been there dancing when the ladies had brought Tomas in, and he'd spied him dancing with Willow.

"A lot of rezoning, street name changes, the building was knocked down twice, and several clubs and restaurants have been here," Bertha said above the noise. "But look, thirty years on it's a club again. Happy anniversary. Let's dance."

They made their way onto the floor and joined Willow where Tomas got to dance with her once more. The crowd parted as they sashayed to the music. Tomas twirled Willow around and spied a hot looking guy over her shoulder. He looked away, but quickly glanced back. The man was standing at the edge of the crowd watching with everyone else. His dark hair was slicked back, his black shirt open to mid-chest, revealing a light covering of hair. He had a black suit, á la James Bond from any movie, and dark eyes that couldn't take themselves off Tomas.

Tomas swung Willow in another direction, so he didn't feel the connection from those eyes. He turned, straight into the path of the man in the James Bond suit. Their eyes met, the fire ignited, and a stunned Tomas turned again, this time heading for the bar. He wasn't a big drinker, but he needed a beer and knocked one back in five seconds flat then ordered a second.

"You're a good dancer. Do you take lessons?" the voice behind him said.

Tomas turned to see the James Bond lookalike.

James Bond grabbed a beer and leaned on the bar.

"What?" Tomas asked in a daze.

"Have you been taking lessons?" James lookalike repeated, his lips turning into a small smile.

Those lips turned Tomas on. "Yeah," he muttered, looking down at the bar. "No."

"Well, you're great. Hey, have you ever been on American Bandstand, or one of those shows as a dancer in the background? You'd be great."

"Um." Tomas shook his head. "No, never been on a show." *Be cool, just be cool,* he told himself. *Don't make a fool of yourself, just be cool. No expectations, nothing, just be cool.*

"How about videos? Have you ever been in a music video?" James went on.

"Ah, no, no music videos either."

"Mmm, well, if you need a job, I could get you onto the scene. A buddy of mine is a music producer and does video clips. He could always use extras."

"That's...oh..." Tomas knocked back another beer. "Sounds good."

"I'm Roger."

"What?" Tomas finally turned to look at the tall hunk of a man beside him.

"I'm Roger. Roger Dencott." The James Bond lookalike was holding out his hand.

Tomas stared from the hand to the deep dark eyes that he started drowning in. *Play it cool, Stephanopoulos, play it cool.* He started backstroking. "Tomas." Shaking hands, he felt the tingles go racing up his arm.

"Nice to meet you, Tomas," Roger said, hanging on a few moments more, feeling the tingle race up his arm and across his body. "Let me give you a card." He reluctantly let go to dig out a business card from his pocket. "This is my friend, get yourself to a recording and you'll be in a film clip."

Tomas took the card, never once taking his eyes off Roger.

"So, what do you do?" Roger asked, leaning an elbow on the bar and taking in the full length of the dark, brooding man before him, a dark, brooding man who'd taken his fancy and turned him on.

"Personal trainer." Tomas was feeling relaxed now, and he should after three beers. He casually glanced at the man beside him, and those tingles kept going and going and going down to his groin, stirring him.

Roger studied his face. "You're not from here, though."

"No, Mykonos. I've just come over. Landed today, actually."

"Ah, then you'll need a chaperone to get you around Miami." Roger took a swig of beer, wanting it to be Tomas sliding down his throat instead of the amber fluid.

"Ah," Tomas laughed lightly, "I have four of those. What about you? What do you do?" He finished off his beer and turned around to lean on the bar, so he faced the crowd.

"I'm a personal trainer too, but I used to be an actor. I used to help out with the setup and production of movies. Lights, cameras, etc."

"Cool." Tomas nodded. "Anything I would have seen you in?"

Roger grimaced. "Well, unless you've seen me in *Big Cock In Little China*, *Mount Cockmore* or *Big Cock Avalanche*, then probably not."

The titles bounced around in Tomas's brain. "Oh, my God." His eyes closed, and his head bowed. "Are they…gay…movies?"

"Porn, yes."

Tomas kept his eyes closed, scared to even open them. "You were a gay porn star?"

"Yes."

"Ah, Jesus." Tomas looked up into Roger's big, dark eyes and laughed. "How the hell do you remember the names of our movies?"

Roger grinned. "Because they were memorable. I did them with the man who became my husband." He sidled closer to Tomas. "Happy anniversary, my love."

Tomas matched his grin. "Happy anniversary, Roger." Kissing, they let the music take them away.

*****

Two days later, Bette's lawyer arrived at the house for the reading of the will, along with Bertha, Willow, Marie and Beatrice, and a few other people Tomas didn't know.

"Maxwell Montague," the lawyer introduced himself. "You must be Tomas and Roger."

"We are, please, come in." They led him out to the terrace. "Shall we get started?"

"Of course. Ladies." Maxwell nodded at the girls and laid his briefcase on the table. Clicking open the locks and flipping up the lid, he said, "As you all know, we're here for the reading of Bette Olander's last will and testament." After removing the papers, he closed the lid and spread them out. "Okay. To Bertha St John I leave the painting of Mykonos that I know she loves."

Bertha smiled brightly while the others congratulated her.

"To Willow, I leave my kaftan collection except for the one I'm buried in."

"Oh, I love Bette's kaftans!" Willow exclaimed.

"To Marie and Beatrice, I leave a jewelled brooch each, one they so admired." He went on to leave pieces to the rest of her friends. "Now, to my darling Tomas and Roger, I leave my home and grounds and anything else inside that can be useful. I would love it if you turned it into some sort of shelter for women or gay men with HIV/AIDS as a retreat when they're sick and dying. But I will leave it up to you. I also leave a ten-million-dollar trust fund for the upkeep of the house and grounds, and for setting up the shelter, for hiring staff, nurses, etc, and buying all of the medical equipment and supplies that you will need. I do hope you do this as we have lost so many to the disease."

Tomas wiped away his tears, but couldn't stop himself from crying.

Roger took him into his arms and held him. "Oh, T, that's fabulous."

"We told you she'd done it." Bertha went to their side. "And you get money to set it all up, so that's a big help."

Tomas pulled back and wiped his face. "That is so fantastic. I can't even believe it, that she'd do it."

"She did. And she also asked us to help you organise it all. How long are you in Miami for?" Bertha asked.

"We're only here for two to three weeks to celebrate our anniversary, and to see how the old place stacks up these days," Roger said.

"That's more than enough time to renovate, decorate and get everything done," Marie said. "We all have cleaners who will help."

"Or we could hire that new company," Beatrice added.

"We can get new beds and medical equipment," Willow joined in.

"We wouldn't even know where to start with that," Tomas said.

"Dan would," Roger told him. "Call him for a list of suppliers and see if he knows anyone else who can help out."

"Fabulous idea!" Bertha exclaimed. "I know Dan would love to help."

"He and Derek flew out for New York the same time as us, so they should be home. I'll give them a call." Tomas wandered back inside and called Dan on his cell. It rang ten times before he answered.

"Tomas. What's wrong?"

"Nothing's wrong, but you will not believe what's happened." Tomas went on to tell the whole story, ending in asking for suppliers of beds and medication.

"I think you need to apply to be a respite centre before you can store medicines on site, but I can email you a bunch of different suppliers I know from down that way. They should be able to help you. And I'll give you the name of a friend you can ask for help. He'll help you lay it all out and figure out how many of everything you'll need."

"Great. That's great, Dan. I can't wait for your email."

"I'll send it tonight. We just got back from a conference."

"Okay, bye." Tomas hung up and went to tell the others the news.

"And in the meantime, we can get everything out of the house and get it cleaned up," Bertha said. "A fresh coat of paint, new curtains, new bedwear, it will all be fabulous."

They spent the rest of the afternoon signing paperwork, hiring cleaning crews, and going through the house sorting out what would go and what would stay. The kitchen would need updating as well as the bathrooms. The carpet upstairs would need removing, and doorways made bigger. In all, there were five bedrooms in each wing of the house, giving them ten sizable rooms for turning into multi-patient wards. There were the two master suites running the width of the house which could be turned into wards for the sickest patients, and the other rooms would house two each. Bette had an elevator installed in her later years, so that would need maintaining, but overall, the house was still in good condition.

That night, Tomas got the email from Dan and printed out the list of suppliers and doctors who could help. Since they were spending the weekend seeing Miami, they were going to start work first thing Monday morning.

*****

Miami was bright and beautiful on Saturday, and they drove up and down the coast looking at old hangouts and haunts. Except none of them existed anymore. *Wood, The Bat and Balls* and others were all gone. Freddy's old place, *Love Stick*, had long disappeared. So had *Seralift Productions*. The studio they used to film their movies had made way for a housing development.

"Jesus, T!" Roger exclaimed as they pulled to a stop outside and looked over the houses. "We used to work here, now…"

"Time moves on, Roger," Tomas said quietly, feeling Roger's pain. The town he'd lived in for a few short months was gone; in its place was a brand spanking new one.

"I came to work here." Roger stared out the window, pain in his gut. "For years…I…" He shook his head at the memories. "Marcus and Violet…*Seralift Productions*…this is where we met again. Where we got to know each other."

"And we've been together for thirty years, Roger. It stopped being home when we moved on." Tomas gently touched Roger's arm. "Time moves on."

"It's only thirty years, T." Roger glanced his way. "And way too much has changed." With a last longing look, he drove on, taking them to the spot their old apartment was. Pulling over, Roger gazed up. Their old four-storey apartment building had been replaced with a twenty-storey apartment block. "Fucking hell! It's gone."

"Thank God!"

Roger turned. "Don't say that, T. I loved that apartment. It was the only one I had here, and I brought you home to it."

"Maybe," Tomas replied. "But it's also where Luiz broke in and poisoned my milk, took photos of us, stalked us, left a dead body in the underground car park to frame you, and where you were arrested for it. Not that many good memories for me."

Roger sighed at those memories. "Yeah. I guess you're right. Things did go south after a while. As much as I loved Miami." His mind wandered back to their days in '77.

"It's all changed," Tomas said, rubbing Roger's arm softly. "Everything's changed.

"Yeah, and I saw the start of it in the late '70s early '80s when AIDS was ravaging the gay community. They're all gone. We're still here, and now we're back, and it's changed way too much."

"That's the way the world works. We move on and move with the times."

"Yeah, I know. Doesn't make it suck any less."

"I know. And I'm sorry. This was your home before it was mine. You lived here longer, knew people longer, went to these places longer."

"And now they're all gone as though none of them mattered." Roger's brows slid into a frown.

"They matter to you, and that's what's important," Tomas said.

Another sigh left Roger's gut, and he turned away. "Yeah, but what does that matter now they're all gone, and no one's around to remember them?" He glanced back at Tomas. "Not even us."

*****

On Monday morning, everyone rolled into Bette's place. Bertha and the girls brought their friends, cleaners, helpers, and AIDS volunteers. Even the doctor Dan had emailed, William Fender, who was an AIDS specialist that helped set up hospices and care centres, turned up. He directed all that needed removing, such as carpets, curtains and walls. Paintings came down, furniture went out, and by the end of the day, they had the bare bones of the house.

During the rest of the week the floor was sanded, sealed, and hospital grade flooring put down. The bathrooms were gutted and made bigger, as was the kitchen and dining rooms. New cupboards were made to be installed, and the lift was upgraded.

In the second week, the bathrooms and kitchen were finished off and installed with everything required, the walls were painted, new curtains went up, new furniture went in, including the hospital beds that were appropriate for sick patients. New bedding was added to stop it looking so sterile, and the ballroom was decorated and furnished into five different areas for visitors and patients to sit and talk. The roof was checked over, the outside cleaned, and at the end of the two weeks, William had the paperwork in his hand for legalizing the place as a hospice/care centre.

"I can't believe all of this has happened so quickly." Tomas sat down on the back terrace as the kitchen staff served drinks and food. The girls had hired a medical food company to be kitchen staff as they were properly trained in meals for AIDS patients, and they would stay until a permanent chef and staff could be hired. The gardening company Bette had been using would continue doing the gardens once a month. A three-piece maintenance crew had been hired to keep the place on its foundation, and nurses and volunteers had been hired to care for future patients, of which there was already a long waiting list.

And after having Tomas speaking with his family every night for the last two weeks about Bette's amazing gift, Jenny had the centre placed under the *Stephanopoulos Inc.* umbrella of business, and she had already hired a manager to run the place. She reminded her sons the family would be there on the weekend for the grand opening before flying to New York.

"That's what happens when you have friends, darling. Between all of us," Bertha waved a hand at the twenty plus women sitting on the terrace, "and the people we know and companies we use, it was bound to get done quickly."

"And I cannot thank you all enough," Tomas said, grateful that they had been there. "We start bringing patients in tomorrow, and my family is coming for the opening before heading for New York. It has been a hectic two weeks. I cannot thank you enough. Especially Dr William Fender for getting the legal stuff happening so fast, and helping out with medical supplies, thank you all."

*****

On Saturday, patients started arriving at the home and were directed up to their brand-new rooms. The carers and nurses settled them in and stored what clothes and bits and pieces they had on the shelves and in the closets. Others were walking around looking the place over or sitting on the terrace drinking lemonade.

In all, there were twenty-four patients in the home, and all had AIDS in its advanced stages. The two master bedrooms held four each, the eight smaller rooms accommodated two each, and the waiting list to get in was still long.

Tomas saw the limo arrive and ran out to meet it, yanking open the back door and leaning down to look inside. "Mama?"

"My baby!" Jenny alighted in her summer pants and top, slid her huge black sunglasses on, and hugged him tightly. "Oh, it's so good to see you, and I can't believe what you've done. It's all happened so fast."

"I had help." He laughed and hugged the rest of the family. "Twins not here?"

"In New York, have been for weeks," Carlos said.

"And Diana's still on modelling assignments, but she'll join us in New York," Viv added, putting on her sunglasses and wide-brimmed hat.

"You do know it's Alena's last date for the tour tonight?" Jenny reminded Tomas and Roger as she settled her huge summer hat on her head and slid her handbag into the crook of her arm. "You'll have to fly up to see it and fly back tomorrow if you still have things to do."

Tomas groaned. "Damn! I forgot about Alena's concert."

"As I said, we can fly up, and you can fly back tomorrow," Jenny repeated. "When are you bringing patients in?"

"We did it already. They came this morning," Tomas told her. "So everyone's already settled in."

"Then why don't you show us around." Jenny grasped his hand and tucked it into the crook of her other elbow. "I saw the before pictures you sent."

Tomas led the family through the house, introduced them to the staff, the ladies, and anyone who was still around. They tried not to disturb the patients and ended up on the back terrace sipping cold drinks.

"It's a beautiful old plantation home," Viv said, gazing out over the back gardens. "She maintained it well."

"She did," Tomas said and checked his watch. "That's why the place will be named after her. How long does it take to get to New York?"

"Two to three hours," Roger replied, sipping his lemonade.

"We'd better get this place opened then," Tomas said and quickly disappeared.

"We in time for the opening?" Dan and Derek came through the open French doors. "Thought we'd jump a flight down and hitch a ride back."

"You're more than welcome," Jenny told them. "Tomas will be back in a minute."

"Okay everyone, for those of you who can, can you please gather at the front door, out on the terrace," Tomas called. "We're officially opening the place." Everyone who could, made their way to the front terrace and stood waiting while Tomas tied up the ribbon. He held a pair of scissors and addressed the crowd. "Thirty years ago, I met an incredible woman named Bette Olander, who brought me to this house to start a new life here in Miami. It's where I met my husband Roger, and we have just celebrated our first date anniversary of thirty years and taken possession of this house that Bette incredibly left to us. She wanted us to turn it into a care centre for women and men with AIDS who have nowhere left to go at their end. And since Roger and I lost so many friends to AIDS in the '80s and '90s, as well as my brothers and family losing their friends and loved ones, I am proud to announce that today, we are opening the *Bette Olander Aids Care Centre* in her honour. To Bette." He cut the ribbon.

"To Bette." Her friends all wiped tears from their eyes.

"Please look around, have some refreshments, say hello to people here, or goodbye as you leave, and thank you for coming," Tomas told everyone and watched Dan and William catch up, and people wander through the garden. He saw his mother introduce herself to the manager she'd hired and give him her death grip, and he was sure she was telling him not to take advantage.

Smiling, he watched his niece and nephews and their friends help serve food and drinks, and his brothers, sisters-in-law and Mike and Maggie help out patients. It was a pretty damn special day indeed; the changing of his feelings for Miami and all they had lost then. Now, he had a reason to come back, and come back often.

*****

Diana flew into New York, got to her parents' apartment, number 3 in the family's residence of 5th Avenue, and promptly threw up in the toilet in the second bathroom. She'd been sick for the last few days, with it starting in Tokyo. She'd been there for two weeks for magazine and TV photo shoots, had given a bunch of interviews, and had thrown up after eating sushi a few days earlier.

"Can't keep barfing up," she mumbled, climbing to her feet and washing her mouth out in the sink. "Agh, I didn't think food poisoning lasted this long. Oh, God, I want it to stop; ooh, my stomach." Groaning, she moved into the bedroom and lay down. It had two single beds, but she doubted her brothers would be staying. They probably had apartment 1 which was for guests or any extras the family had along.

Remembering to grab her alarm clock from her bag, she set it for two hours before the show. She didn't want to be late, but she was so damn tired...

*****

"Tone?" Cabot croaked through his dry throat. "Tonee?"

"What?" Antonio walked into the master bedroom of apartment 1. He knew the family were coming, and knew Mike and Maggie were joining them, which meant they needed to get out of there in the next hour or so, so he'd been packing his things and straightening the place up.

"I feel sick," Cabot whined. "My throat…" He reached out weakly to his brother who handed him two paracetamol and a bottle of water.

"Would you like something to eat? We don't have much, but we could order in. We'll have to vacate the apartment soon."

"Why?" Cabot whimpered.

"Because Mike and Maggie are coming with the kids and they'll be needing this place."

"Where will we go?" Cabot rolled over and buried himself in the quilt. They had been back in New York for two weeks, having stayed the extra week in Mykonos after Cabot's beating, and had hunkered down in the apartment while he continued his recovery.

Tilly had delayed shoots, citing that the boys were ill and needed time, and Antonio had gotten to spend time in the park. Cabot had confined himself to a life of misery by not going out, getting laid, or doing drugs, and was bored witless by it. And now the family were coming to town. "Why are they here?"

"Because Alena's giving her last concert of the tour tonight," Antonio said. "The whole family's in town. You know that, we holiday here every year."

"So, our parents will be here?"

"Yes."

"So, we can't stay in that apartment?"

"We could if we wanted to. I have no problem with it. Unless you want to stay in the penthouse with Grandma and Grandpa."

"Blech! No, thanks. She didn't apologise for slapping me."

"And I hope she doesn't. You deserved it."

"Tonee," Cabot whined, peering out from the covers. "You're still on her side?"

"Yes, I am. Now, I'm going to pack your things, and you're not going to complain about it. You just need to decide where you want to stay. I'm sure Uncle Tomas and Roger wouldn't have a problem if we stayed in their spare room."

"Ah," Cabot growled. "Tonee."

*****

Alena was busy soaking up the sun on the rooftop terrace of the family's home. She had slept there the night before, after getting back to New York yesterday afternoon, and was relaxing before her show. She thought about James and the trip they'd just had. And how hot he was. She blushed. *Silly, he's not interested in you. He hasn't even tried to kiss you. He is single, or so he says; doesn't mean he's interested.*

She wrestled with her brain about the hot cop who'd been with her for ten weeks and wondered why he hadn't tried anything. He hadn't tried to kiss her, or hold her hand, and except in doing his duty, he'd barely touched her. But he had flirted when he wanted information, and Alena was smart enough to know when a guy was flirting for info.

She'd had many of them want Diana's number, and a few ask for Cabot's, so she knew James was up to something. But what could it be? He always brought the conversation around to the family, namely Tomas and Roger, but why would he be interested in them? Maybe he was gay, despite what he told Cabot on the bus that night. Maybe he was interested in older men and liked the look and sound of Tomas or Roger. Otherwise, why would he keep asking about them?

Glancing at the clock beside her, she saw it was time to leave. After gathering her things, she went downstairs to apartment 4, not seeing any family on the way, and changed. Upon leaving, Mark told her Diana had arrived.

Well, at least my cousin's in town, and I know the boys are hiding in 1. Let's hope the rest of the family make it.

*****

After saying goodbye to everyone in Miami, the family hopped on the plane and headed for New York. If they were lucky, they'd make the concert before Alena started. Arriving and going to their home, they offloaded their luggage and Viv and Carlos found Antonio and Diana, who was looking quite pale, waiting for them in their apartment.

"Sweetie, are you okay?" Viv checked her daughter over.

"Food poisoning, I think," Diana murmured. "I got it in Tokyo."

"Will you be well enough to come tonight?" Carlos asked as they stood in their lounge room. Everyone had gone to their own apartments to freshen up and change. Cabot had taken his bags and sought refuge in a hotel down the street, telling Antonio he'd make it to the show.

"I'm going to give it a red hot go," Diana said. "I'm careful with what I eat and have been taking anti-nausea pills. Are we ready?"

After a quick change, the family met downstairs and piled into the two limos waiting for them to make it backstage just before Alena went on. They made their way to the front just as the announcer came over the mic.

"Ladies and gentlemen, to end her first American tour in the city she was born, welcome, Alena…"

Thunderous applause spread through the Garden, and she burst onto the stage. She spied her family down front, waved, and kept on performing. An hour later, she called for the guards to help her brothers on stage, as well as Alexis and their parents. "I want to show you what a musical family I come from, and since it's my last night here on tour, in the city I was born, I want my mama and daddy to come on stage with my brothers Dom and Danté, and my sister Alexis. Come on."

"No, no, no." Pedro waved his hands back and forth in front of him.

"Oh, go on," Angie urged. "Let's show 'em what we're made of." She pushed him ahead of her, as Dom and Danté had already bounced up on stage, and Pedro helped Angie and Alexis up. Three DJ decks and the piano were rolled out, and they all conferred on which songs to do.

Turning back to the crowd, Alena and Alexis took to the front while Dom and Danté picked a deck either side of their father. Angie was on the side behind the piano.

"We're going to do some songs from the '70s. I was born in 1978 when my father was the DJ at the infamous *Studio 69* here in New York. My brothers Dom and Danté," she pointed them out, "have followed in Daddy's footsteps, and Alexis and I sing. And Mama's still playing the piano because she was trained at Juilliard here in The Big Apple. So here we go. When you're ready, Pedro Stefan."

He looked up, grinned, and set the needle on it. Music burst out and on they went, doing funked up versions of the '70s and '80s classics *Venus, Lady Marmalade, Fame* and *Celebration.* Danté got to show off his rapping skills to thunderous applause, and Dom showed his love for music. Alexis got to belt out the high notes, Angie played her piano solos, and Alena got to see her family happy and united, if just for a few songs. When they were finished, the family waved and moved off stage.

"If you're ever on Mykonos you'll get to see my family DJ every night in our club *SB3*. Daddy plays the '70s and '80s on Friday nights, Dom plays the '90s and noughties weeknights, and Danté gets the under 18 gig on Saturdays and every other Sunday. Come and see the family play, everyone. This next song will be the next single released from my album, and it's dedicated to my family who are all down front. My grandparents, parents, aunt and uncles, cousins, even the great Steele Stefan made it. Nice to see ya, cuz."

The family turned to see Cabot hugging himself and hovering near Antonio. He gave a little wave and smile to Alena, but ignored the crowd. It was good to see him there, even if he was sick.

Diana was holding on, trying not to vomit. The anti-nausea pills were helping, but wearing off, and she knew she needed a bathroom. Hurrying backstage, she found the ladies and dropped her guts. "Argh," she moaned, washing it down the sink. There was no way she was going to stick her head in the toilet.

"Diana, sweetie." Viv came in behind her. "This food poisoning really has got you. Are you okay?"

Diana patted her face dry. "I am now. Ugh, that's horrible."

"Have you seen a doctor?" Viv asked, feeling Diana's forehead. "Maybe you've come down with something. You're quite warm."

"It is summer, Mama, and quite warm out there." Diana breathed in slowly. "I'll be okay. Let's get back out to the show."

"Are you sure?" Viv looked into her daughter's eyes.

"I'll be okay." Diana gently removed her mother's hands. "Let's get back to the show." They retraced their steps and found their way back to the front of the stage.

"You look as bad as I feel," Cabot croaked in her ear when he stopped her.

"You sound horrible," Diana told him. "What have you been up to?"

He smirked. "Nothing like that. I haven't since we came home."

"Busy healing and having a holiday?" She gently touched his face. "The bruises are gone."

"Yeah, some fancy anti-inflammatories or something. Helped get rid of it. You?"

"Food poisoning."

"Blech!" He pulled a face and went back to watching the show.

*****

James lurked backstage. Once he saw the family turn up, he'd disappeared out of everyone's sight. Not that people noticed, he'd been on the whole tour lurking in the background. People hadn't noticed him after a while, and he could do whatever he wanted. He'd been stalking the halls for hours, looking for the best escape route to execute his plan. Knowing full well the whole family would be there, he needed to separate them, so he could strike. And he planned on doing it tonight. In fact, he'd planned it for weeks. If he could just get Roger alone...

*****

Alena finished with her final encore and bowed. "Thank you so much, New York. I have enjoyed this tour so much, starting and finishing in my place of birth. My mama went to Juilliard, my daddy played at *Studio 69*, and we had a wonderful three and a half years here before moving back to Mykonos. We make sure to come back every year or two for late summer, early fall. It's a beautiful place to be, and I love it. I love you, thank you so much, have a safe journey home. Good night." With a wave, she left the stage, and the family made their way backstage to her dressing room.

"I'm going to have a quick shower, Maria," Alena told her manager and dashed into the dressing room.

Maria stood guard until the family turned up. "She's in the shower, I need to wrap things up."

"You go," Jenny said, and they piled into the plush room. The kids dived at the fridge for drinks and passed them around.

Cabot hovered in the hall, and Roger went off in need of the gents which was down the hall and around the corner.

Alena came out of the bathroom in her dressing gown with her hair wrapped in a towel. "Whew! What a show." She hugged the family and downed the ice-cold sports drink Alexis handed to her.

"Certainly was, Bubba, and I cannot believe you hauled us up on stage," Pedro said to her. "I was not expecting that."

"Of course not, Daddy, but I planned it anyway." Alena hugged him. "I wanted my family on stage for my final show. What did you all think?"

"The best thing since sliced bread." Jenny wrapped her arms around her granddaughter.

"Grandma, you think everything's the best thing since sliced bread," Alena complained, but grinned anyway.

"That's because it is." Jenny laughed. "You were fabulous, my darling."

Antonio stepped outside to give Cabot a drink and watched him crack it open and down it in seconds.

Cabot let the coldness numb his parched throat. "Ah, I need that. My throat's killing me."

"Take your pills?"

"Yes, doctor."

"Are you coming in?"

"Nah, I'll hang back here." Cabot watched Antonio walk back into the room and casually glanced down the hall, catching a figure all in black, sneaking across the hall and down the corridor to where the gents were. "What the hell?" Curiosity got the better of him, and he strode down the hall to have a look.

Roger pulled the door of the gents open and stepped through the doorway only to have something flung over his head and around his neck. He gasped, desperately pulling at the rope. It was cutting off his airway, and he couldn't breathe.

"Stay away from my Tomas," the figure in black rasped in his ear. "He's mine, not yours, and you will not take him away from me again."

He yanked the rope tighter, bringing Roger to his knees.

Roger flagged and was losing consciousness.

Cabot came around the corner and saw the figure with Roger. "Hey," he shouted through his raspy throat, but it came out less powerfully than he'd hoped. "Hey, let him go." He raced down the hall to the figure who spun to face him, letting Roger collapse on the floor. "What do you think you're doing?"

The figure darted past, but Cabot caught his sleeve. The figure swung Cabot around, and Cabot managed to land a punch on his chin. The figure went sprawling, but quickly scrambled to his feet and took off the way he'd come.

Cabot took off after the figure, sliding into the connecting hallway to turn the corner. "Come back here," he yelled. It came out in a rasp as he took off after the man.

Tomas, Pedro, Carlos and Antonio all came to a stop at the crossway watching after Cabot. They had heard him yelling, and went to see what was going on, and where Roger had gotten to.

Tomas looked to his left. "Roger." He ran to find his husband on the ground, pulling a rope from his neck. "What the hell happened?" He knelt down as his brothers arrived.

"Some nut job jumped me," Roger gasped. "Tried to strangle me."

"God; why would someone do that?" Tomas asked as they helped him stand.

"Dunno," Roger breathed. "I heard someone yell and come running. Who was that? Was it Cabot?"

"Yeah, it was," Carlos murmured, watching his brother-in-law dust himself off.

Cabot walked up to them, huffing and puffing from being unwell, a black ski mask in his hand. "Couldn't catch him, but I got this. No need though, I know who it was."

"You chased after him?" Roger asked, astounded by Cabot's good deed. "Pretty cool, kid." He offered his hand.

After shrugging, Cabot shook it, embarrassed. "It's not fun being assaulted."

"No," Roger agreed. "It's not."

"Thank you for helping." Carlos laid a hand on his son's arm. "You stepped up."

Cabot nodded, unsure of what to say to compliments from his father and uncle.

"How do you know who it was? Did you see his face?" Tomas asked.

"Nah, he had this on." Cabot held up the mask. "But I saw his eyes, and I remember those eyes as James Gardo's."

"How would you remember that?" Antonio asked as their father and uncles traded puzzled glances.

Cabot smirked. "Because he has those hot aqua blue eyes, and I ain't ever seen anyone with that colour. Ever."

Tomas's jaw dropped open, and Roger looked down at him. Gently shutting Tomas's mouth, Roger said, "At least we know who it was. But why would a cop's kid try and strangle me?"

"Don't know," Carlos said. "But let's get you back to the family." They helped Roger down the corridor to be checked out by Dan while the boys lingered behind.

"Pretty cool of you, bro." Antonio flung his arm around Cabot's neck. "Pretty adult of you to help out your uncle."

Cabot was pleased with the praise. "It was nothing, Tone." He flung his arms around his brother, knowing he was happy with him. After weeks of anger and grief, things were looking up. "You really think so, Tone?"

"Looks like everything everyone said has sunk in," Antonio told him, "but it's early days, so we'll see."

Cabot smiled, happy he was back in his brother's good books.

They made their way to Alena's dressing room to hear her say, "James? Why would he do such a thing? Is Cabot sure?"

"I saw his eyes," Cabot said from the doorway. "Aqua blue. And I should remember, he's gorgeous and I looked straight into them on the bus the last time we were here, remember."

"When you asked him if he wanted to be gay, and he asked you if you wanted him to rip your cock off and turn you into a woman?" Alena smirked.

"Alena, not in front of your brother." Angie covered Danté's ears.

"Bit late for that, Mama," Danté said dryly, looking at her.

Cabot blushed, embarrassed by that. "Yeah, well, that night."

"It looks as though James Gardo has a streak in him no one knows about," Jenny said. "And clearly it's time I met him."

*****

James ran full pelt through the car park, down the drive, over the fence, and down the road. He had his badge in his pocket in case he needed a quick getaway.

Damn it! He hadn't expected fag boy to get in the way. *Just when I was getting my revenge on Roger, that dumb fuck had to come along.*

He made it to his car, gunned the engine, stepped on the accelerator and headed for home. If that dumb fuck had seen him, he'd be in deep shit. Not just with the Stephanopoulos family, but his own.

His father would come down on him like a tonne of bricks, and they would get involved again. *Or maybe that's a good thing,* he thought. *Yes, bring our families back together. Jenny and Giancarlo.* From his memory, he remembered that his father was pleased to see Jenny, and she him, that day in the department store. *And I wonder if they know who my mother is? Would they know who Sheila Manning is?* During the tour, he'd googled what he could, but found nothing was on the web. It was too long ago, and he'd need to get into the police vault at his father's old precinct which just happened to be his as well.

*****

"Are you sure it was James?" Alena asked again, stunned that the good-looking officer assigned to protect her could try and kill her uncle.

"I saw his eyes, Alena," Cabot repeated. "If you know someone else with eyes that colour, tell me. But I never have."

Tomas traded a glance with his mother and Roger. They knew of one other person, but he was dead.

Roger frowned and thought about it. What the attacker had said. *'Stay away from my Tomas, he's mine, not yours, you will not take him away from me again'.* Why would James Gardo, a man he'd never met, a man who'd only ever met Tomas when he was a little kid, say such things to him? What the hell was James Gardo after?

"I think we should go home," Jenny told everyone. "It's been a long day for all of us. Dan, we'll drop you and Derek off first."

"Sure, Jenny," Dan said, and everyone made their way out to the limos in the underground car park.

"It's funny," Alexis murmured to Alena. "The last time we were here, James Gardo was the big superhero flying over an SUV to save you, now, he's trying to kill Uncle Roger."

"Mmm," Alena mumbled. "I have a weird feeling. It doesn't make sense."

After dropping off Dan and Derek, then Cabot at his hotel, the rest of the family split up back home.

"Mrs S, will you be awake a while? I want to talk," Roger managed to whisper to her.

She frowned. "I'll wait up."

After many decisions, the girls decided to have a slumber party up in the penthouse lounge room, which meant Danté could bunk in with Nick, and Dom with Antonio.

Jenny waited for Roger, listening to the girls giggle as Alena recounted stories of her tour, and a half hour later, Roger made his way up. Jenny took him to the rooftop terrace to talk freely. "What is it?"

He told her of his experience and what James had said. "Why would he say that? It makes no sense."

"Mmm." Jenny frowned. "I don't know, but I have a very sick suspicion." Remembering something from long ago, she told Roger to follow her downstairs. In the kitchen, she uncovered the built-in safe, and opening it, found what she'd left there twenty-six years earlier, having completely forgotten to get it out. She walked over to the girls, handed over the photo, and asked if it was James Gardo.

"Oh, yes, that's definitely him, Grandma. Same hair, same build. How come you have a photo of him?" Alena held out the picture. "Isn't he gorgeous?" The girls clamoured around to ooh and ahh before Jenny took the photo back.

"I know his father, remember," was all she said and walked back to Roger who'd heard the whole thing.

"How do you have a photo of James Gardo?"

"I don't." Jenny handed the photo over.

Roger recognised it from years ago. His eyes grew to the size of saucers. "You *are* kidding?"

"Nope. They said that's James Gardo, but that is Luiz Manning from 1977 on Mykonos." She glanced at the photo Tomas had given her after a trip back to Miami for a funeral in 1980 before he'd taken sick. It was taken by Bertha St John on Mykonos when they had holidayed there in 1977 and he'd met Tomas. She had given several photos to Tomas when he'd asked for them, and he'd showed the family. Jenny had kept them in the safe all those years. She stared at the aqua blue eyes of Luiz Manning and wondered what the hell was going on.

*****

James made his way to the precinct and slipped unseen down into the document room. Thanks to a fire and flood, there weren't that many records left, and not all had been put on computer yet, so he thought he'd give it a shot before hitting the computer upstairs since he hadn't had a chance to in the last ten weeks. He went silently through the room and started looking. S for Stephanopoulos. That was the family's last name, and he hoped to find something, at least. Trailing through the aisles, he came to RST and began searching. Luckily, not a lot had been lost in the second half of the alphabet, and he managed to find a file.

"Here we go," he muttered, pulling it out of the box. He started reading. Pedro Stephanopoulos accused of battery by Andros Poulos, unfounded. Andros Poulos, the father of Angelina Poulos, accused Pedro of battery but was arrested himself when his daughter filed charges. Charges were not laid against Stephanopoulos.

"Mmm, interesting." Looking through the rest of the papers, he came across the paperwork for Barbara Weston and the murder of Andros Poulos. "She had been stalking Pedro Stephanopoulos when she jumped in his car and drove at Poulos, pinning him against his limo, killing him instantly…mmm…" He noticed his father's name on the paperwork. The date, October 1977. Officers Burns and Devron were on the others.

"What's this?" He peered at the paper for a kidnapping. Pedro Stephanopoulos kidnapped by Stavros Christopoulos, an employee of Stefano Papadopoulos in Athens. Papadopoulos was taken care of by the FBI. "Kidnapped? Why would he be kidnapped?" He flicked through the rest of the file and found papers on Tomas Stephanopoulos's kidnapping by Luiz Manning, then twenty-five, and there was information on Luiz and his mother, Sheila Manning.

"Mom?" James frowned. "Mom had a son? I had a brother?" He kept reading and found Luiz had been murdered and Tomas kidnapped by another man. Luiz had poisoned Tomas and then kidnapped him from Miami General after killing four porn stars from *Seralift Productions* where Roger Dencott and Tomas worked, and tried to frame Roger for the murders.

"Jesus, fucking Christ," he murmured, shining his flashlight at the file. He searched through the rest of it then looked for more files under other names; Luiz Manning, Andros Poulos, Barbara Weston. He found none. Going back to the file, he went through it and found other witnesses and names. Mark Monroe and Sara-Michelle Dubois, Eddie Monteif, Greta Von Burro, Nedro Scarvo, and his father's name was all over the paperwork.

Rolling the papers up, he stuck them down the back of his pants and pulled his jumper over them. He didn't want anyone seeing what he had. Just as stealthily as he'd come, he left, and found his way to his station where he jumped on the computer and started tapping in names. He didn't find much. Anything before 1990 wasn't online except for reference numbers for files in the basement.

"Looks like I've got all I'm gonna get," he muttered and glanced around the room. The night shift was out, and there was no one around, so he left quietly and unobserved. At home, he laid out the paperwork on the floor and put it all in order. The file on the kidnapping, the shooting, the assault, the file on Tomas.

"Luiz Manning. Shit. Why didn't my parents tell me I had a brother?" He read the file carefully. Luiz was twenty-five and shot dead in October 1977, and, as it turned out, was the illegitimate son of Andros Poulos.

"What!" he exclaimed. "My mother had a kid that was Angelina Stephanopoulos's half-brother? And he kidnapped her brother-in-law? Fuck! He was shot not even one day after kidnapping Tomas from the hospital." He searched through the papers for photos, but found none; only photos of Angelina's bruises and her father's bruises from where she'd defended herself and beaten him back. There was also the car wreck, and a dead Barbara Weston, and Andros Poulos. He read every single line on each paper and stapled each file together.

"Why in fucking hell is there no more info on Luiz?" he muttered. The FBI were the ones to do all the legwork, his dad was just put in as an extra file. He'd mentioned in his report the meeting in Chicago where all three cities had come together when the Stefans were kidnapped, and he'd made a note of the timeline of all of them.

"Well." He sat back. "That's quite a story. If only I had a picture of Luiz Manning, half Manning, half Poulos."

I wonder if our mother has pictures of me…but then she kicked me out when I was seventeen, so why would she.

She wouldn't, he blinked. *Is that what those memories are about? I was remembering Luiz?*

No, stupid! I am *Luiz. Don't you get that?*

He rubbed his eyes. The headaches were worse, especially now the tour was over. So far, they'd been bearable, having started that first night he'd been dumped in it by his captain to be Alena's bodyguard. That's when they'd been constant. Before that, they'd come just now and then when he'd had the dreams. But *they* were constant now too. Sighing, he grabbed a beer from the fridge and slumped on the floor in front of the paperwork. It wouldn't help the headache, but it would make him forget.

*****

Early Sunday morning, Diana was the worse for wear. "Oh," she groaned. "I feel horrible." Getting up from the couch in the penthouse, she managed to make it to the bathroom before throwing up. Needing a proper bed, and trying not to wake the other girls, she crept down to her parents' apartment, glad they weren't up yet, and that Antonio or Dom wasn't there. She crawled into bed. Snuggling down, she fell back to sleep.

*****

Cabot woke in his hotel room, hot, sore and alone. He didn't want to stay with the family, and there was no room anyway. But he missed knowing they were around. And he really missed Antonio. "Tonee," he moaned, almost in tears. "Tonee." His bottom lip quivered. "Tonee," he cried, letting the tears flow. He missed his brother horribly, having never spent a night apart, like ever, not since they were born, and now when he needed him, he wasn't there.

There was a knock on the door.

"Tonee?" he called plaintively and weakly ran for the door. "Tonee!" He leapt into his brother's arms and Antonio carried him in. "I was so lonely without you, Tonee."

"How are you feeling?' Antonio asked, waiting for Cabot to get down. When he didn't, he gently pushed him off. "How are you?"

"Miserable," Cabot croaked. "My throat's sore, my body aches, I'm hot and thirsty."

"Maybe you should come home and let Mama and Grandma check you out. Diana's sick too."

"I don't want to go there. There's no room for me." Cabot pouted. "No place for me." Curling up on the couch, he stuck his bottom lip out farther.

"As I said, Diana's sick too, so maybe we could call in Dan to see to both of you." Antonio sat beside him on the couch. "Didn't go far from home, I see. You may as well have stayed."

"I'm not welcome there," Cabot complained.

"You don't know that," Antonio retorted. "You're just assuming it because you got told off and you think everyone's out to get you. They're not. They're out to help you, you just can't see it…or don't care. Either way, it's up to you." He stood up. "I just stopped by to see how you were. Still sick, I see. You really should see Dan. I bet he's in the clinic today. Want me to give him a call?"

"No. Can you look after me, Tonee?"

"No." Antonio's response was simple and to the point, and he headed for the door. "Be an adult, Cabot. If you're sick, see a doctor. If you want to be part of the family, come back home."

"But I'm sick, Tonee. What's the point in me being there?" Cabot whined

Antonio lingered at the door. "Because we're your family. I'll see you there." Closing the door on his brother, he left.

"Tonee." Cabot plaintively reached out. "Tonee."

Antonio arrived home and found everyone but Diana in the penthouse.

"How is he?" Viv rushed over, worried for her baby boy.

"Sick," Antonio replied. "Whiny."

"Has he seen Dan since Mykonos?" Jenny asked as she walked past with a plate of cookies for the kids who were in the sitting room.

"Not yet. I was trying to get him to go. What about Diana? She should see him." Antonio snatched a cookie and followed his grandmother back to the kitchen for a drink.

"Yes, she should," Viv said. "I've never known food poisoning to go on this long."

"Why don't I ring Dan and see if he can come over?" Jenny said and walked back to the phone. A moment later, she got him. "Dan? Can you come over to check on Diana? Cabot needs a check-up too, but he's in a hotel."

"Can't stop by, sorry, too busy. But they can come in, and I can do some tests."

"Okay. We'll get them in today, thanks, Dan." She dropped the phone into the cradle. "Looks like the kids will have to go in for tests. Dan can't leave."

"I'll do it." Antonio finished his drink. "I'll get D and take her, then grab Cabot if he still hasn't got there himself. I was trying to get him to see Dan or come home."

"What's wrong with him?" Jenny asked.

"Probably the flu or something," Antonio said. "It will give D and me time to spend as siblings. See you all later." He left and went downstairs to Diana's room. "D? You awake?"

"Ugh, what?" she groaned from the bed.

"The family wants you to see Dan, but he can't get away from the lab, so I said I'd take you. Come on, can you have a shower?"

"Ugh, okay. But why can't he come here?"

"He's busy. Besides, tests will get done quicker at the clinic, and he can give you something there, so come on. A shower will do you good. Maybe we can pick up Cabot on the way."

"Ugh, okay." She crawled out of bed and into the shower, brushing her teeth and spraying on perfume, so she didn't smell like vomit. On the way to the clinic, they stopped at the hotel, and Antonio went to grab Cabot, but he wasn't in.

"That's strange," Antonio told Diana. "Maybe he's already there."

At the clinic, Derek led them to the back room, and Diana sat on the examination bed.

"Is Cabot here?" Antonio asked. "He's sick too."

"No, he's not," Derek replied, taking Diana's blood and setting up a glucose drip. "Okay, we need to ask a bunch of questions." Ten minutes later, he left them alone to get the blood test done. There was a small lab on the premises and two staff in it. Half an hour later, he checked on her. "You doing okay?" He monitored her hydration.

"Better." She smiled. "Feel good actually. Better than I have in weeks."

"The tests should be done in half hour or so, and then Dan will talk to you about the results."

"Okay, thanks, Derek."

"What do you think it is?" Antonio asked, swinging his legs from his position on the other exam bed. The room was large, had two beds, and an array of machinery.

"With all this vomiting it has to be food poisoning, right?" she said. "I had sushi in Tokyo, and the next thing I knew, I was throwing it up. Clearly fish doesn't treat me kindly anymore."

"You're not allergic to it, are you?"

"Unless it was poisonous." She thought back.

"You mean puffer fish?" Antonio asked. "You'd be dead if that wasn't sliced and diced properly."

"Yeah, I suppose," she murmured. "I've never been this sick before. Even in Japan that time five, no, ten years ago now. I think that was because they made me eat something horrible."

Half an hour later, the test results were in and on Dan's table. "Okay then." He collected bottles of vitamins and got a B12 shot ready. "Derek," he called through the open office door. "Can you get Diana, please?"

"Sure." Derek went into the exam room and unhooked the glucose line then led them into Dan's office.

"Ah." Dan saw Antonio. "Can you wait outside?"

"It's okay, he's my brother," Diana said, pulling out a chair.

"You may want to take this on your own," Dan told her.

"It's okay, I'll go," Antonio said and went to wait in the outside room.

"It wouldn't have mattered," Diana said, sitting opposite Dan as Derek closed the door behind him.

"It might," Dan said. "You're pregnant."

Diana blinked and blinked again as her head twitched slightly. "What!"

"You're pregnant."

Another blink. She registered it. "No." A shake of the head. "I can't be."

"Can't you?" Dan asked. "When was the last time you had sex?"

"No, I…" She thought back. "July fourth."

He calculated. "That's about right for six to eight weeks. When did you have sex before that?"

She blushed. "A couple of years. I've been busy."

"You know who the father is then?"

The blush deepened. Oh, yes, she knew who the father was. A man she hadn't seen since; the only man she'd been with in years.

"I've got a bunch of vitamins and pills for you." He set them all out on the desk in front of her. "Some for you, some for the baby. I'll give you a B12 shot while you're here." He got up, rolled his tray over, cleaned a spot on her arm and jabbed the needle in.

The pain didn't hurt as much as the pain in her heart. She was twenty-nine years old and pregnant to a man who wasn't even in the country.

"You know I also did the usual blood test for HIV." Dan sat back down. "Negative as usual. He didn't have it either."

"That we know of," Diana murmured.

"After six to eight weeks it would already be in your system. So far, you're fine."

"Physically," she continued. "Don't tell anyone, especially Mama and Grandma. I'm not ready for that."

"You're not in a relationship with the father?"

She shook her head. "He's not even in the country."

Dan raised a brow. "Well...I can't say anything anyway, so it's entirely up to you, but your grandma will want to know your HIV test."

"That's fine." Diana picked up a bottle of pills. "Do I take these all together?"

"One every morning," Dan said and stood up. "I'll walk you out. Unless you have any questions?"

"No." Her head shook mechanically from side to side, and after slowly standing, she left the office.

"Hey, D." Antonio stood up as she approached. "You okay?"

"Mmm?" She glanced up. "Fine. Just needed some vitamins. Can we go? I'd like to get some air."

He followed her out the door, frowning at the obscurity of her information, but then, that was between her and Dan. "Anywhere you want to go for that air?"

"The beach. The ocean," she murmured, and they caught a cab through Brooklyn, all the way down to Coney Island Beach and sat watching the waves roll in.

"You okay, D?" Antonio asked after a while. As much as he enjoyed sitting peacefully with his sister, he knew something was wrong.

"Just wanted some air before facing the family," she said. "They'll want to know what's wrong."

"And what is wrong?"

She was silent, debating whether to tell him. If he didn't know, he couldn't tell. "Undernourished is all. Must be all the vomiting. I haven't eaten enough." She chose to lie. It wasn't a total lie, she was undernourished, but it wasn't from food poisoning.

"So, you're not going to tell me, huh?" Antonio grinned. "That's cool, it's your business anyway. Not mine."

"Do you think Cabot will go and see Dan?"

"I hope so. He's been sick for a few days."

*****

On Monday, in the privacy of her office, Jenny made a phone call. "Yes, hello, I'd like to speak to Officer James Gardo's superior please…what's his name…Webster…and what's his…okay, thank you." She waited while her call was transferred.

"Captain Webster."

"Yes, hello Captain Webster. I'm Jenny Stephanopoulos, and I'd like to talk to you about Officer Gardo. He was recently assigned bodyguard duty on my granddaughter Alena's tour, and we'd like to get in contact with him."

"Wasn't he at the final show, what was that, Saturday?"

"No, he wasn't. And no one seems to know where he's gone."

"Mmm," Webster grumbled. "Let me put you on hold a moment." He checked to see if James had logged in for the day and found he hadn't. "Martha," he yelled to his assistant. "Get Officer Nicolls in here if he's available." He went back to the phone. "I'm sorry, Mrs Stephanopoulos, he isn't in today, but I'll find him for you and let him know you'd like to speak with him. Anything in particular?"

"I'd just like to thank him for the job he did; that was all. And to finally meet the officer who's looked after my granddaughter. You don't happen to know how I can get in contact with his father, do you? It's been twenty-five or twenty-six years since I've seen him, and I would like to say hello."

"We do have his number on file, but I can't just hand it out, you understand."

"Of course. I wouldn't expect you to. Please let me know if you find James. We'd like to invite him to dinner, so he can meet the whole family."

"Of course, Mrs Stephanopoulos. I'll let you know." He wrote down her number and hung up.

"Sir, you wanted to see me, sir?" Denny Nicolls stood in his captain's doorway.

"Nicolls, have you seen Gardo?"

"Not since he went on Alena's tour, sir."

"No phone calls, emails?" The captain was surprised.

"Nothing," Denny said. "And I'm bummed about it. I wanted him to get me some tour merchandise, and I've heard nothing."

"Well, let me know if you see him. Alena's grandmother would like to meet him."

Denny's eyes widened. "The family's in town? Cool. I wonder if I could meet them too."

Webster raised a brow. "You?"

Denny grinned. "I'm a huge fan of the whole family."

Jenny thoughtfully put the phone down, wondering how she was going to find James and Giancarlo. Trying the phone book, she came across only a few Gardos and no J. There was a G&C, a G&M and a G&S. "I don't know Giancarlo's wife's name, but I could just try all of them." She tried the first number but was interrupted by Antonio.

"Has Cabot come over?"

She hung up the phone; the call not connected. "Was he supposed to?"

"I suggested he should yesterday, but he grumbled a lot, and I left him to it. I did tell him to go and see Dan, and he hasn't been in his hotel suite since yesterday morning."

"It's Cabot. I'm sure he's somewhere." She left her seat and walked out to the sitting room with him. "You and Diana took your time coming home yesterday."

"Diana wanted to go to the beach, so we sat and watched the waves roll in," he said with a smile. "It was nice. Just breathing and being with my sister. Taking time out from busy schedules. It was really nice."

"She seems better, so I guess Dan did the job." When they had come home, Diana had been better, but mostly silent, and it had Jenny wondering what was wrong with her granddaughter. She'd made a quick call to Dan, and he'd told her she just needed vitamins and more food because she had become malnourished with the vomiting. They joined Spiros and her sons while the kids were across in the park.

"He had her on some drip to get her fluids up and gave her some vitamins, I think. I wasn't there for the results. I just wish I'd gotten Cabot in there."

"Did you find James, or his father?" Spiros asked.

"No. James hasn't been to work, and I didn't get Giancarlo's number, although there are three Gs in the book, I haven't called yet." She sat next to him on the sofa and felt the cool summer breeze on the nape of her neck as it flowed through the open floor-to-ceiling windows. "Viv and Angie out?"

"Shopping," Carlos said. He was slumped in his seat with his feet on the coffee table. "Why would James Gardo, a person we've never met, do what he did to Roger?"

Roger looked up sharply, watching Jenny for her reaction.

"Who knows." Her brows went up. "Maybe there's something wrong in his head? Or maybe he's somehow fixated on Tomas all these years, and so, also on Roger. Angie did say he remembers our meeting in the department store. Maybe he's fixated on that and…I don't know…I'm just guessing."

"I'm gonna go join the others," Antonio said. "Any idea where they went?"

"Around the zoo somewhere," Jenny replied. "Or check the closest pond."

"Okay, see you all later." He left and ran downstairs.

Jenny had decided not to mention that James looked like Luiz because she was still trying to figure that one out herself. There was no way that Luiz would come back to Gardo. What did *he* have to do with anything? So, it was quite a surprise, and not a very nice one.

"Mama, is James Gardo someone we have to look out for?" Tomas asked from his seat beside Roger.

She cleared her thoughts. "I don't know, sweetie. But until I talk to him, and see what he has to say, only then will I get in contact with his father."

"Shouldn't you do that now and warn him his son's a nutjob?" Carlos said.

Jenny sighed. "I don't know. This can of worms is far bigger than any of us imagined. And I'm not even sure I want to crack it all the way open."

*****

The family spent a relaxing week seeing the sights of the city. Diana was feeling better, but reserved. The girls all raided the clothing stores and vintage shops, they stopped by *Haus of Stefan* to see how it was going, and they bought out the shoe stores. The family as a whole, with Mike, Maggie, Nick and the girls, along with Cabot who dragged himself away from the hotel with cajoling from Antonio, spent the day at Coney Island, although Cabot hung back and was quiet. And they took the ferry to the Statue of Liberty and climbed all the way to the crown.

At night, the adults went to bars, the kids to clubs, and those who couldn't get in stayed with the adults, or found under twenty-one entertainment.

At the end of the week, Pedro and Mike stood on the pavement of 254 West and 54th Street and leaned against their car, staring at the spot where they used to work.

Pedro crossed his arms and frowned. "This is what they've done with 69?"

"Yep." Mike mirrored Pedro with crossed arms. "It's funny; all the years we've come back to New York, and we've never stopped here."

"Jesus, what have they done to the place?" Pedro's frown deepened as the memories came flooding back, and he looked at the club it was now. "It's all gone. All of it. All of them."

Mike saddened. "Yeah, but it lives on in *SB3* every Friday night when you get onstage. It's like we're back there."

"But never the same," Pedro murmured. "No gold shorts or boots, no Eddie, no Leon, no Stan, no none of them. None of it."

"We still have a few old regulars over summer," Mike reminded him. "I'm surprised they still come. Didn't Bev Marie vomit on you one night way back when?"

A grin crossed Pedro's lips. "After I came back from getting married. It was my first night and thank God I had spare clothes in my locker."

Mike grinned. "Yeah, they were great times."

"They were." Pedro sobered. "But we've lost too many, and I wish the times could have gone on."

"But you couldn't, and *they* couldn't because of your brother."

"Yeah." Pedro nodded. "All the deaths, then Tomas and Roger. I'm surprised I finished off four years. I wanted to ditch it, but Mama said no, finish the month off. God knows how I managed by that time. Leon was gone, Stan, Jamal Devron, Thomas Derbon."

"Have you seen Greta since?"

"She, Stephanie and Carson turned up at *SB3* years ago, but I never see her when I'm here. I don't go looking either. God, Mike, it's thirty years. Thirty years since Angie and I ran away to come here. Thirty years since I started here and 69 opened. Thirty freakin' years. Where the hell did the time go?"

"I have no idea." Mike shook his head. "Hey, isn't this the spot Angie's dad was standing when that freak drove at him?"

Pedro jumped up from the car. "Uh, no, I think that was opposite the alley which is now a car park." He pointed to his right. "Two car lengths that way."

"Ah, the alley, where so much good stuff happened," Mike joked.

A scowl flew across Pedro's face. "Not funny! You mean the shooting, the crazy stalker killing my future father-in-law, or me getting kidnapped?"

"All of the above." Mike's grin got bigger.

"Ha, ha," Pedro joked dryly, but he quickly sobered. "A hell of a lot of stuff happened here in just a few short years. Too short, way too short."

"Yeah." Mike felt the pang. "Way too short. But look on the bright side. Because of you and Angie coming here, I got to meet Maggie, and we've been together ever since."

"Yeah, you have." Pedro nodded. "Angie and I are still together. We have our own club, our kids are best friends, you were at our wedding, we were at yours."

"And now we get to live the good life thanks to your mother. We owe her a lot."

"We all do," Pedro agreed. "We all do." Staring at the building they once called their night job, he sighed. "To 69." He raised an imaginary glass. "Thank you for the memories, the friends, the good times. I shared you with my family, I made my family, and we've continued the good times. Thank you. To *Studio 69.*"

"*Studio 69,*" Mike cheered.

*****

Cabot was on his deathbed by the weekend. Or so he thought. He'd gallantly gone to Coney Island with the family and tried to enjoy it, though he felt like the Titanic with icebergs surrounding him with their cold iciness. And he was sinking quickly. For the most part, his grandparents, father, aunt and uncles ignored him, whereas his mother made sure he had food and water, other than that, they were cordial and nothing more. He felt like shit, and hadn't been able to go out to the clubs. He really wanted to show his older cousins what Steele Stefan was made of and how popular he was. But he just didn't have it in him, and he was dying, having been sick all week. It was worse now, and Antonio had left him alone which he'd never done before. And he felt all alone in the world without love and care, but now he needed to be the adult.

He rang Dan.

"Doctor Dan Ardent."

"Dan," he said hoarsely. "Cabot. I'm sick; can you come and see me?"

It being a Saturday, Dan had spent the day catching up at the clinic to recoup his time off. "Can't leave. I'm busy. But you can make it in. Weren't you supposed to be here a week ago?"

"Too sick," he rasped. "I guess I could make it."

"Okay. Come in now and I can do some tests."

"Okay, bye, Dan." He hung up and searched his latest new craze iPhone for Dan's address. The clinic wasn't too far, and he could grab a cab. He hadn't gone to see Dan in the last week because he couldn't be bothered. When Antonio had left him, he'd gone for a walk through the park and sat thinking about things. It wasn't the first time he'd taken time off, but it was the first time he'd been ill since he was a kid. After the walk, he'd stayed in bed watching TV and having the occasional visit from Antonio who'd pulled him out of bed to go to Coney Island. But once he'd gotten back home, it was back to bed. He couldn't deny it any longer. He was on his deathbed and failing fast.

After managing to have a shower without scratching his anus off, he dressed and hailed a cab to the clinic where Derek took him into the exam room.

"You're going to need to change into this gown." Derek handed a clean one over. "And then Dan will examine you."

Cabot screwed up his face and grabbed it with two fingers. "Is this clean?"

"Steamed cleaned, just for you." Derek raised a brow. "He'll be in in a few minutes. Leave your clothes on the chair."

"Okay, thanks," Cabot croaked and got changed. He kept his underwear on and was walking around when Dan entered.

"Okay, let me hear you." Dan pulled a pair of gloves from the box on the wall.

"What do you want me to say?" Cabot asked.

"Oooh, that's bad. Okay, I'll give you an all-over physical. Derek will take notes." He grabbed Cabot by the head and dug his fingers into his neck. "Swollen throat glands," he told Derek who noted it. Dan stuck a stick in Cabot's mouth and shone his light. "Swelling, red." He probed Cabot's armpits. "Swollen glands under the arms." He examined his body. "No marks, no redness. Let me check your crotch."

"My what?" Cabot asked in alarm.

Dan smiled at him as if he was a child. "I need to check your penis and testicles."

"Dan!" Cabot joked lightly. "We haven't even been on our first date."

That made Dan laugh and even got a grin from Derek. "I already saw it in Mykonos. Now let me check you again."

Reluctantly, Cabot dropped his underwear and pulled his gown up to cover his face.

Dan handled him expertly. "Some swelling and red spots on the penis."

"What! I have what?" Cabot pulled the gown under his chin and peered at his aroused manhood.

"Still works," Dan said wryly. "But we'll need a swab to find out what it is, and hopefully a cream or an antibiotic will help it. Anything else before we take samples?"

"Well." Cabot lowered the gown to cover his manhood and blushed. "I…ah…"

"Yes," Dan urged.

"Um." Cabot looked away. "Have a really bad itch. It hurts so much."

Dan frowned. "Where? I didn't see anything."

"Um." Cabot reddened. "Um, up my…butt."

"Oh…" Dan glanced at Derek. "Okay. We're going to have to have a look."

"Oh, my God," Cabot groaned. "It's so embarrassing."

"Bend over the table, and I'll have a look."

"Oh, my God, Dan," Cabot squealed. "This is embarrassing." He knew he was beet red all over.

"I know," Dan soothed. "But if I can fix it for you, you'll feel so much better. Right?"

Cabot sighed. "I suppose." He flung himself face first over the exam bed and covered his face with both hands.

Moving the light over to have a better look, Dan spread Cabot's buttocks apart. Glancing at Derek, he said, "We have an STD present. We'll need to take swabs and apply a topical cream. You said it's itchy?"

"I keep scratching myself, and it's painful when I crap," Cabot muttered.

Dan looked at the red lumps on Cabot's anus. "When did you first notice this problem?"

"I don't know," he said as Dan let go of his butt. "It's been a couple of weeks, but I had the odd sore spot before that."

Removing his gloves, Dan said, "It looks like genital herpes, but we'll take a blood test and do swabs. Pop your underwear back on for now," he said and glanced at Derek who made notes. "I need swabs sticks, needles, and a topical antibacterial cream." Turning back to Cabot, he added, "Hop up on the bed, and I'll take your blood." He watched Cabot get up on the bed and squirm around. "How long have you had symptoms?"

Cabot shrugged. "I've had a sore throat for over a week. Felt like crap last week, felt a bit better, now I feel like death."

Dan plunged the syringe into Cabot's arm and withdrew three vials of blood. He had double gloved without anyone noticing, and was careful with the needle. "Okay, mark them down," he told Derek. "And I will start taking swabs." He grasped a long cotton stick and shoved it into Cabot's mouth. "Saliva." He handed it to Derek and took another one. "I need to swab your crotch. You can stand again and drop your underwear."

Cabot stood and dropped his pants.

Dan swabbed over the testicles and penis, especially the red spots. "Do you clean yourself after going to the toilet? Crotch swab." He handed the swab to Derek and picked up another stick.

"Of course, why?"

"Turn around and bend over the table. I'll take a sample of your butt." He swiped the stick over the red lumps and handed it to Derek who screwed up his face. "I'll need another stick and the cream." Within a minute he had covered the spots in antibacterial cream and Cabot was putting his clothes on. "Feel better?"

Cabot paused and thought about it. "It's stopped itching."

"Good. We'll need a pee sample too." He handed over a container and waited for him to come back. "We'll give you a tube of cream.

You'll need to apply it yourself every morning and night after a wash."

"But how do I…?" Cabot was mortified at the suggestion.

"Smear some on clean toilet paper, bend over, and dab it on. Then flush the paper when you're done and thoroughly clean your hands with soap or disinfectant wash." Dan removed his gloves. "Test results will be done in twenty-four to forty-eight hours. We'll give you some antibiotics for your throat, and some for your STDs which should disappear in about ten days. Make sure you take the pills every day as prescribed," Dan told him. "It's important. Now, I want to ask you some questions. When was the last time you had sex?"

Cabot blanched, not wanting to remember.

But Dan guessed anyway. "Mykonos?"

Cabot nodded, embarrassed. "I do it *to* men, they just get a suck, and then I fuck them."

"Wear a condom?"

"Always. You and the family have drilled it into our heads."

"Has anyone been up your ass?"

Cabot reddened further. "Rarely…"

"Mykonos?"

Another nod.

"When we examined you then, you didn't have an STD, so I'd say you got it from him if you haven't had sex since."

"I haven't touched anyone, scout's honour." Cabot held up three fingers. "That was the last time. Not that I haven't wanted to, but with my face and now being sick, I haven't wanted to go out."

"So, then you picked it up from him, which meant he didn't wear a condom. Did he say anything to you?"

"About what?"

Dan shrugged. "If he had anything, or if you noticed his penis or testicles looked normal."

Cabot mirrored Dan's shrug. "Didn't see them." He thought back. "We were fighting, calling each other fag fucker, those people came along, and then before he ran away he said something, but I didn't take much notice, I was drunk."

"What did he say?" Dan asked as Derek stood silently by, knowing something was coming.

"Um," Cabot thought hard. "Suck it fag fucker…you've now got… a disease…the disease, I think he said."

Dan looked up sharply from his clipboard. "Is that what he said precisely?"

Another nonchalant shrug from Cabot. "I dunno. I was drunk, Dan. Look, can I go?"

"Are you sure you haven't been with anyone since?" Dan pushed.

"Scout's honour, Dan," Cabot said. "Can I get something to numb my throat?"

"Ah, yeah, sure." Dan cast a glance at Derek who rifled through the cabinet for throat lozenges with a numbing agent. He found a pack and handed them over. "Suck on those, they'll numb your throat, and Derek will get you the cream and antibiotics on the way out."

"Great, thanks Dan, Derek," Cabot said around a lozenge. "Hey, these are working already."

"Yeah," Dan said, absentmindedly. "They do that." He waved goodbye and watched Derek follow Cabot out. *Fuck! Could he have?* He grabbed the tray of swabs and samples and walked into the lab to his technicians. "Priority case boys, STDs and potential HIV. Suit up, and I need all results pronto."

They nodded and got to work as Dan walked into his office. "Fuck! What do I tell Jenny? Oh, fuck, fuck, fuck."

"Oooh, can we?" Derek asked, closing the door behind him. He quickly sat down when Dan cast a dark glare his way. "Do you think he has it?"

"I bloody hope not," Dan replied.

*****

The next day, Dan got the test results and sat behind his desk staring at the folder. Twenty-six years ago he'd been almost reluctant to tell Jenny her son and son-in-law had the gay plague and were dying. But that was then, and they had no idea what HIV was, and AIDS hadn't been discovered. They just knew there was the gay plague, the gay disease, the gay cancer. And he'd had to tell her. Now was different. For all of the education, how Cabot had lasted this long was anyone's guess, but he had. And now it was possible that he had it. Two sexual assaults in the one family, and it would have to be the gay one who got it. Not that Alexis deserved it either.

Taking a deep breath, he opened the file. The throat swabs showed nothing. The crotch and anus swabs showed genital herpes as suspected, normal swabs for gay men, and could easily be fixed with the cream and antibiotics he'd given him. He moved on to the blood test and his eyes closed. "Oh, sweet Jesus."

*****

James was hiding out in his apartment, drunk off his face, and fading in and out of consciousness as his head pounded. Ten weeks of being on the road with Alena, learning all about the family; Tomas and Roger, in particular, had taken its toll. So had trying to kill Roger. That wasn't him, he didn't know what he was thinking, or if he was thinking at all. All he remembered was looking down at Roger and wondering why he was strangling him. It was as if he was standing there watching while someone else did the strangling.

He rubbed his eyes and yawned. He couldn't be bothered going in to work. Why should he when his captain had volunteered his services back in June? He deserved time off and wanted to be left alone, especially after what he had done. He didn't think the twin had recognised him; he hadn't seen his face, even when he caught hold of the ski mask and pulled it off. So far, so good. There were no cops on his doorstep, except for Denny who came by every day, banging away. But he ignored him.

There were plenty of phone calls every day from Captain Webster's secretary, but he'd left a letter explaining he needed time off on her desk. God knows why she hadn't gotten it. Either way, he wanted to be left alone. It had been a week, and he didn't care. The phone rang. He let the machine take it.

"James, it's your father. Are you there? Webster told us you were back, but had disappeared, and hadn't come back into work. He asked if we'd seen or heard from you, but I told him we hadn't. Are you there? Are you okay? Do you need help? Call us, we'll come for you, you know that. Call us, James, we're worried." Beep. The line went dead.

James slumped on his couch, paperwork around him. During the week he'd sneaked out to the state library into the newspaper archives to find more information, and had found quite a lot from 1977. It was all over the news. The legal problems at 69, the death of Andros Poulos and kidnapping of Pedro Stefan, porn king of New York. There were even stories about his brothers' being kidnapped, and he'd tracked down the story of the death of Tomas and Roger, then, five years later, the story of them being at the Act Up rally in New York and how they'd survived death and were now campaigners for HIV/AIDS.

He'd also searched for anything on Luiz Manning and had found minor reports from Miami about a suspect in the murder of four men, and the poisoning and kidnapping of Tomas Stephanopoulos. But again, no pictures.

"Damn it! Why were there no pictures?" He wanted pictures. He threw his beer bottle across the room and it smashed against the wall. He didn't care. His head pounded. He didn't care. All he cared about was getting Tomas back.

*****

Dan didn't call Cabot until Monday. He couldn't. He needed time to gather his thoughts, and he arranged to come over to the hotel after work to give him his test results.

He and Derek stood at Cabot's door with Dan trying to work up the courage to knock.

"Oh, for God's sake, he has to know," Derek whispered and knocked.

"I know, but Jenny—"

The door flung open and Cabot invited them in. "Hey, come on in."

Derek pushed Dan in, and they walked to the centre of the lounge room.

Cabot closed the door and followed. "So, what can you do for the flu? It is the flu, right? God knows how I got it in August, must have picked up some germ from somewhere." He stood expectantly waiting to hear the news, feeling much better since the visit to the clinic.

"Well." Dan swallowed and tried to find a way around telling him. "The STD is definitely genital herpes, so continue taking the pills for it and applying the cream. They will get rid of it over the next few weeks."

"Oh good." Cabot nodded. "How do I get rid of this flu?"

"Ah…" Dan glanced at Derek. "You…don't…have the flu."

Cabot frowned. "Wait, you're telling me I don't have the flu? Well…then, what do I have?"

"Ah…you have the symptoms of a virus that you've contracted. Influenza-like symptoms are common in the initial stages of infection." Dan couldn't look him in the eye.

"Okay, so you give me the meds for it and fix it." Cabot breathed in, his arms crossed. While he was better, he wanted to get the bug out of his body.

Dan looked down in remorse. "There are no meds to fix it."

Cabot's frown was back. "What do you mean? It's just a virus, get rid of it."

"You…" Dan shook his head and walked over to the window, his gut wrenching.

"Dan?" Cabot's frown deepened. "You can get rid of my virus, can't you?"

Derek looked from Cabot to Dan and back. "No, he can't. You can't get rid of Human Immunodeficiency Virus, Cabot. Once you have it, you have it for life. There is no cure."

"Human…Immune…Virus…" Cabot trailed off as it registered in his foggy brain. "H…I…V…"

"Yes, Cabot," Derek said softly, his heart breaking for the young man before him. "You've contracted HIV."

Cabot was stunned, looking back and forth from Derek to Dan who had turned around to stare forlornly at him. "No…I…no…" He shook his head. "No. I couldn't have… I don't take it up the ass… I give it, and I'm safe," he rambled, unable to breathe, or think, or see. Feeling faint, he sat on the couch. "I can't how...there's no way...no, Dan..." He desperately looked at his doctor who was sitting on the coffee table in front of him. "There's no way."

"The assault on Mykonos," Dan reminded him gently. "You said he told you, you now have the disease. Well...looks like he was talking about HIV, and he's given it to you."

"No," Cabot whined, shaking his head in disbelief. "No. I've always been safe. I've never not used a condom. I've never taken it up the ass. This can't be happening, Dan. No. No," he said forcefully, standing, stalking around the room. "No. I can't believe it, it can't be true. Do the tests again. I get it that I have an STD, fine." He waved a hand. "But not HIV, no Dan, not HIV. There's no way, no how, uh-uh, not possible. I...I..." He flagged. "I can't, I..." Slumping to the floor, he cried. "I can't...I can't..."

Dan and Derek went to his side. "It's not a death sentence anymore, Cabot. We can get you started on the medications, and you'll be able to live a relatively normal life. Of course, it means reassessing your life and doing things a little differently, but you can deal with this."

"Deal with it!" Cabot screamed, looking into Dan's eyes with fire in his own. "How the fuck am I supposed to deal with having HIV, Dan? Tell me, because I don't fucking know. It's a death sentence. I can't get rid of it. How the fuck am I supposed to live with it?"

Dan baulked. It wasn't the first time he'd told someone they had HIV, and it definitely wasn't the first time he'd been screamed at. "Cabot."

"No, Dan. There's nothing you can say they will make this go away," Cabot said. "I *do not* have HIV. I *just don't*, Dan." He ran to the bedroom and threw himself on the bed. After a few minutes of crying, he chose the best mode for him to be in.

Denial.

"Cabot?" Dan asked from the doorway.

Calmly, Cabot got up and started pulling clothes from the closet. "Yes, Dan?"

"Are you okay?"

"Fine, Dan," he said. "I'm going out tonight. What will you be doing?"

Dan frowned. "You're going out?"

"Yes." Cabot looked up from the black leather pants he held in his hand. "I'm going out. I haven't been clubbing in weeks."

Dan traded a confused glance with Derek. "Cabot, we just told you—"

"And I don't believe you, Dan," Cabot said calmly. "I choose to not believe it." He pulled out a shirt and leather vest to go with the pants.

"That's a very dangerous thing to do, Cabot," Dan warned. "We need to get you started on the medications. We need to get you—"

"I don't care, Dan." Cabot stared him in the eye. "I'm going clubbing."

"And if you don't take this seriously, I'm telling your grandmother," Dan threated.

Derek took a step back just as the family did when a fight was brewing.

Cabot didn't bat an eye. "Going to lie to her too? Go ahead, Dan. None of you can stop me doing what I want. It's my life."

"So we've figured out," Dan said, surprised that Cabot didn't care. "You know your grandmother will want to do something about it."

Cabot pulled off his t-shirt and slid into the shirt and vest. "I'm sure she'll try, but she'll have to find me." He slid into his leather pants. "I'll make sure none of you finds me."

"Cabot," Dan pleaded. "Please come to the clinic so we can get you started on the meds. Please. For the sake of your own life. Please."

"I don't believe I have it, so why do I need meds? You're just trying to control me, Dan, and *no one* controls me." He sprayed cologne on his torso, slid into his leather boots, and piled black leather bracelets on both wrists and chains around his neck. With a flick of his hair, he grabbed his wallet and keys and strode toward the door. "Find your own way out."

Dan and Derek watched him go.

"What the fuck was that?" Derek asked. "Did you *see* that denial?"

"Came on pretty fast, didn't it," Dan replied. "What am I gonna do? Do I tell Jenny, or try and keep getting through to him?" He pulled the door shut behind them as they left. "What do I do?"

"Well," Derek said thoughtfully. "There is patient-doctor confidentiality, but, on the other hand, HIV tests are a mandatory standard for all family and company employees. Jenny wants to know so meds and health care can be maintained, and people treated with kindness. It's all because of Tomas and Roger."

"Yeah," Dan murmured, and they stepped out onto the street. "You weren't there those few months. The way he wasted away, the tests I did, the things I did. I stayed with them in Mykonos for nearly a year." He shook his head at the memories, still so clear after twenty-six years. Taking a deep breath, he let it out slowly, trying to figure out what to do.

"And now you're going through it all over again." Derek hailed a cab. "You know they're just down the road."

"No, I—" Dan panicked. "No. I need to get my head around it. I'd like to get Cabot on side first, try and get his medications going, and some sort of good health regime."

"But he clearly wants nothing to do with it," Derek reminded him. "He went into denial pretty damn fast, and now we have to get him out of it."

Dan sighed. "Yeah, but how do we do that?"

*****

Steele Stefan stalked the streets of New York looking for a good time. It had been nearly a month since he'd been out partying, since his birthday on Mykonos. Between a puffy face and the flu, he'd been knocked on his back. But he was feeling better and was out to party, and he was starting with *Nightmare* where he could get lost in the music and atmosphere. It opened at eight, and he rolled up to the door and was ushered in as if he owned the place.

"Steele Stefan is in the house," he yelled and spread his arms out, so he looked like Jesus on the cross.

"Whoo, Steele, we love you." A group of girls came running over and crowded around.

"And I love you too, ladies." Flinging his arms around them, he walked them onto the dance floor. "Let's dance." He cut loose, losing control and letting go after weeks of hiding. Flinging his arms up, he danced with abandon as the gay men danced around, touching, feeling, wanting a piece of the Stefan.

He ordered bottles of alcohol and downed them, dancing like a wild man living his last tomorrow, and he had no problem ramming himself into an admirer's anus as he held the man's head against the wall. "Want a piece of the Stefan, do you?"

"Give it to me, Steele," the man grunted.

Steele plundered, but Cabot wafted through his head.

Are you wearing a condom?

Yes, I'm wearing a condom.

Why?

Because I don't want to catch an STD.

Like the one you already have?

Steele slowed as the acronym HIV/AIDS floated through his head. Looking down between their two bodies, he saw he'd rolled a condom on. At least he'd done it. He hadn't even remembered putting any in his pocket. Not feeling like sex anymore, he withdrew, frowning as he rolled the condom off and left it where it fell.

"Steele?" The man turned. "Want me to finish?"

Looking up, Steele's frown darkened. "No. No, I don't want to." Shoving himself into his pants, he washed his hands and strode back into the club, out the door, and onto the street. Hailing a cab, he went to *Slash*, the heavy metal club he and Antonio had gone to, to see Slay My Way and Adam Slayer. He was able to get in and found the thrash metal of the band somewhat soothing.

Trying to get a look at the stage, he was surprised to find Slay My Way on stage and caught a glimpse of Adam on guitar. He still looked good two months later, and he remembered their night together, or what he could of it.

Adam was beautiful, long, lean, and in great shape. Steele could still feel Adam's hair slide over his body as they moved. Adam Slayer had been a conquest, and he was glad he had achieved it. Spending the rest of the night watching, he didn't go near the stage to say hello. Adam didn't need to know he was here. Didn't need to be reminded of that night. As much as he'd love another night with him, he knew Adam wasn't into men. But he hadn't cared. He'd just wanted what he'd wanted and to hell with anyone else.

Watching until their last song, and seeing them walk off stage, he went in search of a refuge, walking in and out of five more clubs looking for some *thing*, some *one* that was going to take him away from his life right now. He needed to get lost, and no club was doing it for him.

Stumbling drunk from the club, he hailed a cab and went to his family's residence. His hotel was just down the road, so he let the cab go. "Hey…dude," he couldn't remember their doorman's name, even after all these years. "Is Antonio in?"

Mark Chapman cocked a brow. He was used to Cabot's lack of memory and even bigger lack of manners and respect. But he was paid well for his job and treated with respect by the rest of the family, so he ignored it. "Yes, sir, I think he might be."

"Can you ring him please, get him to come down?"

"Of course." Mark tried apartment 3, but found him in the penthouse. He told Antonio his brother was downstairs and wanted to talk to him. A few moments later, he hung up. "Master Antonio is on his way down."

"Thanks, I'll be waiting outside," Cabot told him and stepped out onto the pavement. Breathing deeply, he waited for his brother, sobering at the thoughts in his head.

Antonio came through the door. "Cabot."

"Tonee!" Cabot spun around in tears. "Tonee." He flew into his brother's arms and sobbed. "I've missed you, Tonee."

"Hey." Antonio patted him gently on the back. "What's going on, Cabot?"

"I've missed you. I went partying tonight, but it wasn't the same without you."

"You went out? I thought you were still sick?" Antonio was surprised.

"I saw Dan, and he gave me stuff. I feel better, so I went out coz I was sick of being cooped up for weeks on end." He finally pulled back and kissed his brother's cheek. "I've missed you so much, Tonee. I love you. And never want to live without you ever again. Will you come and stay with me tonight?"

Antonio looked into his brother's eyes and saw something he didn't recognise. "Are you okay, Cabot?"

Cabot shook his head, and his lip quivered. "I miss you. This last week I realised how much you mean to me, and I've missed you really bad, Tonee. Can you come and stay with me, please?"

"Why don't you come upstairs? Diana's staying in the penthouse, so we can have Mama and Papa's spare room."

Cabot baulked. "Uh, I don't want to see the family right now, Tone. Just you."

"It's after midnight, Cabot; most of us were ready for bed." He glanced at his watch. "It's nearly one. Why don't you come up?"

Cabot backed away. "I'd prefer not to. I don't want to see the family right now. Just you. Can you come, Tonee, please?"

Antonio saw what a mess Cabot was and knew something was wrong. Stepping in to the lobby, he asked Mark to ring upstairs to let them know he'd be staying with his brother for the night and went back to Cabot. "Come on, bro." He flung an arm around his shoulders. "Let's get you home."

They took off down the street and made it to Cabot's hotel. Upstairs, Cabot showered, applied the cream, and pulled on boxers and a singlet. "You want something to sleep in, Tone?"

Antonio had stripped down to his shorts and left his t-shirt on. "I'm fine. Time for bed." He watched Cabot scamper under the covers and eagerly wait for him to get in.

"Yay, Tone!" Cabot cuddled up and laid his head on his brother's chest. "Ooh, this feels good. I've missed you so much." He smiled happily, feeling good in his brother's arms.

Antonio knew, he could sense it; something was wrong. Something Cabot wasn't telling him. *I wonder if he's seen Dan and what's actually wrong with him. He seems okay. Better than last week, but still…there's something going on. Normally he's not into telling me he loves me. Even though he's dependent a lot, he normally doesn't say it. Maybe the illness has made him remember what really matters and not just himself?* He wondered if it was too good to be true as he lay there in the hotel room with his brother clinging to him like a life vest.

*****

The next morning, as Antonio got out of bed and dressed, he watched Cabot sleep. He was peaceful and looked like a child all curled up. *Probably the best sleep he's had in a while,* Antonio thought as he zipped up his fly. After quickly scribbling a note, he left it on the bedside cupboard and left, but was stopped by the mailboy on his way out.

"Package, Mr Stefan," the boy said.

"Ugh, thanks." Antonio quietly shut the door and looked over the bulky envelope. *Ah, from Dan. Wonder what it is.* After sneaking a look into the bedroom to see if Cabot was still asleep, Antonio opened the envelope and slid out the folder. "What to do when you have HIV/AIDS," he murmured, a frown sliding between his eyes. *Why would Dan...oh...* Casting a glance at Cabot, he opened the folder and found the note inside.

Cabot,

I know right now you're in denial, but the assault last month in Mykonos has resulted in you contracting HIV. For your own health and well-being, we must get your medication regime going. You can live a full life with this, Cabot. We just need to get you educated on it.

Dan.

Antonio's head mechanically moved between looking at the folder in his hands, and Cabot in his bed. His brother...no...he couldn't... *Is that why he wanted to see me...oh, God, what do I tell Mama and Papa? And Grandma? Oh, my God.*

Unable to think, he stared at the letter, re-reading it a dozen times. *Dan. I have to get to Dan.* He quickly sealed the envelope, laid it on the coffee table, and left, managing to find his way to the clinic where he stumbled into Dan's office.

Dan had to look into Antonio's eyes to tell him apart from Cabot. "Antonio, what's wrong?"

"Dan, Cabot…is he…?" He stared into Dan's green eyes, unable to comprehend.

"What? Is he okay? He took off last night." Dan came around his desk, "Antonio?"

"Is he…?" Antonio desperately tried forming the words. "Is he…?"

"Antonio." Dan grasped him by the arms and shook him. "What's wrong?"

"I was…at his hotel…and an envelope was delivered this morning… from you…" Antonio looked him straight in the eye. "I opened it."

Dan's face fell. "That wasn't for you, Antonio."

"Does he…? He can't have? Dan," Antonio wailed and collapsed into the chair Derek had placed behind him. "Dan," he wailed. "Dan."

Dan nodded for Derek to shut the door and grabbed the other chair. Sitting opposite him, he spoke firmly and calmly. "You read the letter I sent with the package." He got a nod. "So you know that the assault on your brother is when the infection occurred." Another nod. "And you know that there is no cure, so now it's a matter of medications to stop it progressing to AIDS." A third nod. "Since you weren't meant to see that package, does Cabot know you've seen it?" A head shake. "Good. Keep it that way."

"When did…" Antonio gulped. "You find…"

"He came in on Saturday for me to look at because he was still sick. I did swabs and took samples. He has an STD which he's being treated for, and the blood test revealed the virus."

"It was because of the assault?" Antonio wiped his face.

Dan nodded. "The man who Cabot had sex with told him before he ran away, that he now had *a* or *the* disease. I suspected, and we tested for it. I got the results on Sunday and told Cabot yesterday afternoon."

"What happens now? Do you tell Grandma?"

Dan exhaled. "I'm supposed to. But I know she will blow, and I'm not ready for that."

"You said in the letter you know Cabot's in denial."

"He refused to believe it after I told him. He went into full-on denial mode."

"So, then, what now?" Antonio slumped in his chair.

"It's not a death sentence, as you know. It can be controlled well with medication. It's just a matter of getting him out of denial and onto the meds. But as long as he refuses to believe it, there's not much I can do. I'd like to not tell your grandmother. She'd kill me either way. But I want to try and get Cabot onto the medicine before telling her."

"I can try and convince him," Antonio said, racking his brain.

"And what do you think will happen when he finds out you know?"

Antonio blinked back tears and looked at Dan. "I don't know."

"What if he goes off the rails?"

Antonio smiled sadly. "Then I'll have to be there with him and try and get him back on track."

A half hour later, after a quick information recap from Dan, Antonio was utterly sick, wandering from the clinic, all the way back to the park. He couldn't go inside. Couldn't see his family. Not then anyway. So, he sat in the park and thought. How did he get Cabot out of denial and onto the meds? He didn't know off the top of his head, but the one thing he could do was be there for his brother.

Sighing, he finally stood and went up to his parents' apartment where he packed his things. Luckily, they were out, but he found his aunt and uncle on the way out with the kids.

"Hey, Antonio, you okay? You leaving?" Pedro stopped.

"I'm going to stay with Cabot for a while." Antonio left it at that.

"Can't live without him?" Pedro smiled, watching his nephew and his strange behaviour.

All of a sudden it hit Antonio; what his father and Pedro had talked about all those years. The bond that brothers have. You'd do anything for them. His throat clenched, and his breathing hastened. "No, I can't," was all he managed, and he took off down the street with two suitcases and two bags.

"Antonio," Pedro called. "Antonio." He watched his nephew rush down the road to Cabot's hotel and waited until he couldn't see him anymore.

"Daddy, *come on*, we've got to go, we'll be late," Alena called from the limo. They were heading out to a musical, and it started soon.

"Pedro? What's wrong?" Angie asked as he got into the back and the driver shut the door.

"Huh? Ah, nothing." He shook his head. At least he hoped it was nothing.

*****

Antonio knocked on Cabot's door and wiped his face free from tears.

Stretching, Cabot jumped out of bed, where he had been languishing, and opened it. "Tone?" he said in surprise when he saw the bags. "I didn't even know you'd gone." Holding the door back, he watched his brother roll his bags in.

"Yeah, um, I was awake early and left you sleeping. I walked home and had a bit of a sit in the park and realised that…I miss you too."

"Does this mean we're going to be together again?" Cabot got excited and clapped his hands, running over to hug his brother.

"Yeah." Antonio hugged back. "Yeah, it does."

"Yay, Tone. We can share the bed, coz there's only one. You don't mind, do you?" He grabbed a case and rolled it into the bedroom.

"Ah, no." Antonio followed with the second, and they took a few minutes to unpack the essentials.

"So, how much longer are the fam in town? I want to get back to the penthouse."

"We could be in there now if you wanted to share," Antonio said.

"No." The scowl was deep on Cabot's face. "I don't want to be in the same room as Grandma."

"Why not?" Antonio asked. "She loves you, *regardless* of what you do."

"I doubt it." Cabot wandered into the lounge and saw the huge envelope on the coffee table. "She favours the girls and Danté because he's still young and controllable. Hey, what's this?"

"Ah, that arrived this morning. I left it there." Antonio saw Cabot open the envelope and withdraw the file. "Modelling stuff or something?"

Cabot read the title on the folder and panicked. Jamming it back

361

into the envelope, he resealed it. "Um, nah, just a bunch of brochures from companies. Must've thought they could bombard me while I'm here."

"Oh, for you, or both of us?" Antonio casually asked.

"Ah." Cabot glanced at the name on the envelope. "Just me, Tone, sorry." He rammed it into a drawer and slammed it shut. "Have you had breakfast?" He checked the clock and saw the time. "Or brunch or lunch?"

"No, not yet. But I am hungry." Antonio eyed his brother, knowing full well when Cabot was panicking.

"Cool. Let's order waffles and syrup and pancakes and really sickly stuff we normally don't eat." Cabot picked up the phone and ordered a big lunch. When he was done, he had a shower and was out by the time it arrived. "Yum, Tone. Dig in." They sat and ate like naughty children eating all the wrong things; the foods they weren't allowed to have because they were too sugary, or considered junk food, and when they were done, they were full and sick. Groaning, they lay back on the couch, put their feet on the coffee table, and watched TV for the rest of the day and into the night, just being together, just being brothers.

*****

Diana checked her schedule for the next four weeks and saw she didn't have jobs until mid-September in London.

London. The other side of the world. *Oh, wait,* she blushed, *no it's not.* Giggling at her mistake, she knew it was only a six or seven-hour flight from there, but from there she had Paris, Barcelona, Germany, Switzerland and Italy again. And she needed to get all of them in by the beginning of November for her parents' anniversary. *Must be baby brain,* she thought and then stopped. Stunned.

Baby…

I'm having a baby…

Oh, my God!

She threw herself down on the bed in her parents' apartment and burst into tears, thankful they were out. They couldn't know yet, not when she hadn't sorted out how she felt. And how *did* she feel? She'd been in denial all week, since Dan had told her, and she just couldn't get around that she, Diana Villiers Stephanopoulos, was pregnant at twenty-nine. Not that it mattered in the grand scheme of things. It was 2007, and she was twenty-nine. Her mother had been forty-one when she'd had her, her father twenty-five. And they'd been pregnant before getting married, and that was back in 1977, so it wasn't as if there was much of a difference.

Jesus, I'm pregnant. What am I going to do with a baby? What am I going to do with my career? What am I going to do with my life? And Charles? What about him?

What about him?

Do I tell him?

Do you even know where he is?

That shouldn't make a difference, he is the father, he has every right to know he's going to be a father. I wonder if he's ever had children, or been married for that matter? As far as I remember, he's never mentioned a wife or girlfriend, but the rumours have been of a lot of lovers. Or they could all be lies. And what if he wants to be a father? What then? Do we get married, live together, or none of the above? We barely get along, and that time we were together was a mistake.

Is the baby a mistake?

Oh, God no. Her hand flew to her stomach. *No, this baby is not a mistake. Because like him or hate him, I love him. I love Charles. But does he love me?*

Sitting up, she realised she hadn't heard anything about him since he'd left that day in July, and it was nearly September. *I wonder if he's still overseas? Maybe there's someone I could call to find out? Or maybe I just shouldn't bother. He doesn't care about me, so why should I care about him? I was just a fling, a conquest to him. Diana Villiers, conquest. Stupid, young, naïve, ignorant of the world and the men in it. Ignorant about Charles Kensington and his stupid games.*

She didn't know what he was up to, but she wanted no part of it. She didn't want anything to do with it then, and she didn't want anything to do with it now. She had been used for his own sexual enjoyment, a plaything, a prize to score, and score he had. Big time.

Oh, how could I be so foolish as to fall for him, she moaned. Him and his manly hands that know how to treat a woman, and those lips, and that tongue, and that body that she rode for hours. *Oh, how could I be so foolish?*

She smacked her forehead with the palm of her hand. *You stupid girl, and now look, you're pregnant, and your life has changed and will continue to change next year as you get bigger and give birth.* She calculated on her fingers how long she had. Until April. *The same as Uncle Roger, Aunt Angie, Dom and Alexis. Oh, God, how could I be so stupid?*

Flopping back on the bed, she realised it was two months before her birthday. *I'll be a mother at twenty-nine. I won't even be thirty yet. Oh, my God.* Rolling over, she buried her head in her pillow. *I'll be a single mother at thirty.*

Not that there's anything wrong with that. It is 2007.

I know, but Jesus. I thought I might be in a committed relationship by this stage, like Mama and Daddy were. Not single and without the father here.

Then call him.

But I don't know where he is.

Then find someone who does.

Well, he worked for Edie at Flair. Maybe she's got a contact number. Grabbing her phone, she dialled *Flair's* number. "Edie, please, it's Diana Villiers." After a few moments, she was put through.

"Diana, darling, how are you?"

"Fine thanks, Edie. You?"

"Can't complain, darling. What's up?"

"I need a number for Charles Kensington. He promised me some photos, and he hasn't come through. I want them for my portfolio."

"Oh darling, I'll have to look it up, but I think he's still overseas." She scrolled through her address book.

Still? Diana frowned. "I last saw him in July."

"Yes, he left then for some overseas assignment; no one knows what. We wanted him to do a shoot, but we were told he wasn't available."

"Oh." Diana tried to sound uninterested. "Didn't bother coming back then. Off on holiday or extended leave?"

"Don't know, darling. But I doubt you'll get him. Apparently, no one can." She read out his number and Diana wrote it down.

"I'll give it a shot, anyway," Diana said. "I'd really like those photos. Thanks, Edie."

"Will you and the boys do a photo shoot for us?"

"What about the whole family? My cousins are in town, my parents, grandparents, aunt and uncles. You could interview all of us. Imagine what an issue that would be."

"Oh, a bumper issue. Do you think your family would be in on it?"

"I'll have a chat and get back to you, thanks, Edie."

"Thank you, darling. I'll await your call."

Turning off her phone, Diana stared at Charles's number, too scared to call it. Too scared of what to say. Too scared of what he would say.

That night, she consulted with her family about the article and called Antonio to see if the twins would be interested. All agreed, *if* they had final say over the article. She rang Edie back, and it was arranged for Friday.

*****

On Thursday, Pedro and Angie, Carlos and Viv, Tomas and Roger, and Mike and Maggie did a tour of the city. Not a normal tour, but a tour of the cemeteries where their beloved friends were buried.

"Oh, look, Leon's mother and grandmother are buried here too." Angie stood in front of all three gravestones.

A frown creased Pedro's forehead as he read the dates. "At least they're together. His grandmother went five years later, his mother ten." He set flowers on Leon's grave and rested his hand on the gravestone. "Hello, old friend, it's been so long." Tears flowed, and Mike crouched down beside him while the others stood back with tears of their own. "Way too long. It was thirty years ago that we all met at 69. You loved it. Those short shorts and the roller skates, you loved it so much. Whereas I hated it. But you would walk into work in your fur coats and matching hats, get into those shorts and do your thing, and you did it well. You knew how to work the crowd."

"He sure did," Mike said. "Remember that time we all went to the theatre to see your brother's movie?" He glanced over his shoulder at Carlos, whose eyes widened. "Leon loved *every single inch* of it."

Angie burst out laughing, Maggie blushed, and Viv tried to hide her giggles behind her hands.

Mike turned back to Pedro. "And then he tried convincing *you* to get into movies. Was hoping you'd say yes to him, but he understood that you weren't into it."

"Yeah." Pedro grinned. "And that's when you met Maggie."

Mike stood up, grasped her hand and slid an arm around her. "Yes, it was."

"Oh, Leon." Pedro sobered and rubbed a hand over the gravestone. "I miss your disco ball style. And we always knew you were watching down on us every night when that disco ball turned. That was you turning it for us. And we celebrated your life. Just like the way we do now every Friday night at *SB3*. In honour of all our fallen friends. We named a drink after you. It's the *Roller-Skating Disco Ball*, and it's a mix of rum, vodka and tequila. Just for you, Leon. Just for you. I'm so sorry you're not here to see how life's changed. We know what you had, and there's medicine for it now. If only you hadn't gone so fast, maybe you'd still be with us."

Angie laid flowers on his mother's and grandmother's graves and made the cross symbol with her fingers.

"Goodbye, old friend." Pedro got to his feet. "We miss you."

"Leon," Mike muttered and touched the gravestone. The others followed suit, and they filed back to the limo.

"Ah," Pedro let out an anguished growl. "Who's next?"

"Eddie's next," Viv murmured, and half an hour later, they were leaving flowers on Eddie Monteif's grave.

"God, Eddie, you were only fifty-two!" Pedro exclaimed. "The same age Tomas is now." They all looked at the grave.

Eddie had passed in '83, they'd known in '82 at the opening of *SB3* that he was ill. He'd turned up to see Pedro play, to find out what had taken him from 69. But the headlines in '81 and '82 had said it all. His brother was dead, and Eddie would soon be too. He didn't fault Pedro for that and thanked him for his four years at 69. He was grateful and thankful that Pedro had made it the place to be and had said how sorry he was that he hadn't listened to him the year before. He had it. The gay plague, or AIDS as it was now known. And he didn't know how long he had left. That was the last time they had seen him.

"God, Eddie." Pedro breathed as Angie laid flowers on the grave.

"He made 69 what it was," Mike said. "And at the time, it was the biggest thing since sliced bread, to quote your mother." That brought smiles to everyone's faces.

"Yeah, he did," Pedro agreed. "He certainly did." Touching the gravestone, he added, "Goodbye, Eddie. You gave us all one hell of a time."

"Eddie." Mike touched the stone, and they filed solemnly out of the cemetery.

"Stan and Thomas are next," Viv said softly. "Then Cabot."

A sharp intake from Carlos was heard through the limo.

"I didn't mean ours," Viv quickly added.

"I know. But I got a chill when you said that," he told her. "And I don't like getting chills."

They laid flowers at the gravestones of Stan Kosnov and Thomas Derbon. They were buried in the same cemetery, but at opposite ends. Stan was a 69 regular who had a fling with Leon and Jamal Devron, plus Stephano DeLuca. All were dead from AIDS. Thomas was Greta Von Burro's publicist. She never replaced him, but did find another person to do the job, but no, it wasn't a replacement. Thomas had died peacefully after seeing Pedro at the penthouse on Valentine's Day 1980. It was hard, seeing all the names of people they knew, people they worked with, people they considered friends, etched into stone with their birth and death dates.

After leaving flowers, they left and went to pay their respect at

Cabot's grave.

Viv sighed. "He was so loved." She knelt down and placed the bunch of white roses she had specifically bought for him, leaning them on the stone. "It's been too long, my friend," she murmured. "And your namesake is turning out just like you. What do I do about that?" She brushed away the dirt and leaves and stared at his stone. "What do I do with you, Cabot?" She shivered and gasped, and quickly standing, backed away.

"Viv?" Carlos put his arms around her. "Are you okay?"

"I got a chill, just as you did," she said. "I…" Staring hard at the grave, she went on a few moments later. "I confused them. I said, what do I do with you, Cabot, but Cabot is dead, so I can't do anything with him, but for a split second I thought it was Cabot's grave and I was talking to him." She looked at Carlos. "Tell me I'm crazy."

Carlos examined Viv's face. "Is it your motherly instincts?"

She rubbed her arms as everyone stared. "I don't know. What would you think if we visited Antonio's grave?"

Carlos thought about it. "Probably the same thing."

"There you go then," she said. "I don't know. I can't put my finger on it."

"Maybe we should go," Tomas suggested. "All of this is freaking me out. Imagine if we went to all the graves of *our* friends." He looked at Roger. "We'd be all day."

"At least most of them are buried in the same cemetery," Roger replied. "Except for Zack and Adam, I think. Most of the others are in the same place."

"This is depressing." Tomas glanced around. "Let's go, please."

They solemnly left and ended up at a bar, cheering to their beloved departed.

*****

On Friday, the whole family, including Cabot who was still in denial, turned up at the *Flair* magazine studio for a photo shoot and interview. The family had their hair done, and fabulous clothes from

Haus of Stefan on hand. They were interviewed while getting ready, and once everyone was done, walked into the studio.

"Darlings." Edie came wafting over to gaze upon the gorgeousness of the beings before her. "Oh, I can't believe I have the whole family for a shoot. The magazine's going to be a sell-out, and I have the cover blurb ready to go. *Stephanopoulos Inc: The Making of a Family Dynasty.*" She threw her arms wide. "It's going to be huge."

Diana introduced everyone, and Edie called to the photographer. "Aneeka, darling."

"Aneeka!" Carlos exclaimed, looking in the direction of the table. "Aneeka?"

She turned and saw the family, her red-lipped smile beaming across the room. "Carlos, it has been so long. How are you?" They met halfway in a hug, and Pedro and Tomas moved over to say hello, trading hugs and how are yous.

Aneeka remembered Jenny, Spiros, Viv, Angie and Roger. "It has been so long, but I have followed your careers and am very proud of all of you." In her late 60s, African American Aneeka Ne Masta knew the family from 1977 when she had worked with Carlos. She'd been involved in Carlos's kidnapping, having been kidnapped herself for photographing the two men in the yard of her next-door neighbour, who just happened to be Carlos's then-girlfriend. She also photographed the 1987 Act Up rally that Tomas, Roger and Jenny had attended. To cut a long story short, she was alive and living a wonderful life. "Did you hear about Harry and Harriet?"

"Yes, they passed what…ten years ago, and Alfonso took over."

"Yes, legitimately, thankfully." Aneeka grinned.

"Wasn't Harry legitimate?" Carlos grinned back.

"So, you all know each other?" Edie asked, looking perplexed.

They glanced around at the curious onlookers. "Way back in '77 Aneeka did a couple of photo shoots of me. We got to know each other well, and you have held up well. Look at you," Carlos told her. "You still look as youthful as you did thirty years ago."

"It's all the Villiers cosmetics I use, keeps you looking young," Aneeka joked. "Now, let's get started." Directing everyone to their places, she had Jenny and Spiros sit on a purple velvet couch in the design of a throne. "You are the king and queen of the Stefan empire; we will take your shots first." She clicked a couple of dozen shots as she spoke to Jenny and Spiros, capturing natural expressions. "Now, the three boys stand behind them."

Carlos, Tomas and Pedro stood behind the couch.

"Give me natural," she called and clicked off more photos. "Now the partners."

Viv, Angie and Roger joined them, and more photos were taken.

"Now the kids." She directed them where to stand as she looked in the viewfinder and reeled off more pictures. "Okay, Jenny and Spiros, you are done. I will do the adults. If you can sit on the couch, just the three boys." Carlos, Tomas and Pedro sat in order on the couch, and laughed as Aneeka regaled them with stories of Carlos and Harry.

"And now the partners can come in." She photographed them with the boys, and as separate couples on the couch. "And now we have the kids. I want the girls on the couch and the boys behind them."

They arranged themselves, and Aneeka kept shooting. "Now just the golden-haired trio on the couch." Diana sat between Cabot and Antonio, trying not to barf. The anti-nausea pills helped, but she was in need of a bathroom.

"And now the parents, Carlos and Viv. Kids, stand up the back." More shots were snapped. "And now the Greek side of the family. Girls on the couch, boys either side." Alena and Alexis sat down, and Dom and Danté stood either end. "Pedro and Angie, can you join them?"

She also took photos of Tomas and Roger on their own. They didn't have kids, but were still a family.

"And we will break. If you need the bathroom, use it. I need to take more shots with you all standing," Aneeka called as Diana bolted out the door. Alexis and Alena followed, in need of a pee.

Standing around sipping cool drinks, Aneeka spoke with the family. "Quite an empire you've built, Mr Stefan." She grinned at Carlos.

"Mama had a big hand in it," Carlos told her. "But we all do what we can."

"And Mama still owns and runs the whole shebang," Tomas reminded his brother.

"I'm so glad to see the two of you still alive and healthy. I was glad to read that the two of you had survived back then, but it was a shock," Aneeka said to Tomas and Roger. "We had all gathered at Harry's to commiserate. It made the newspaper in L.A."

"Apparently it did everywhere," Tomas said. "And we're glad we're still here too. Especially me."

"Do you mind talking about that, darling?" Edie asked from behind him. "We want to interview you all separately to get *your* story. I want to do at least four to six pages on each family to let the readers know who *you really are.*"

Tomas shrugged lightly. "No. I don't have a problem."

"Fabulous, darling. I've got a bunch of questions for everyone and plenty of staff to do the interviews. We'll be recording them, so we can get every word."

At the refreshment table, Cabot shifted, scratched his neck, and sighed.

"Calm down, bro," Antonio said. "You're used to photo shoots."

"Yeah, but normally it's just us, and we get it over with." He was antsy and wanted to leave to go back to the peace and quiet of their hotel room. "I still feel awkward being around them."

"Who, our parents?"

"Have you seen the way Mama's been staring at me all day, like," he glanced at her to see her staring, with a worried frown, "like she knows something."

"And what would she know, Cabot?" Antonio asked, wanting his brother to come clean and get his diagnosis out in the open.

"Ugh," Cabot mumbled and turned away. "Nothing."

The girls came back into the room, and Aneeka called time. "This time, we'll do it all, but standing. Can I have the king and queen on their throne, please." After a few minutes, they were getting their photo taken.

Pedro had his arm around Angie's neck, admiring her new haircut. "So, what inspired this look, Mrs Stephanopoulos?"

Angie giggled. "If my daughter can cut her hair off, so can I. It was time for a change."

Pedro checked out the sleek new bob, cut to just above the hairline at the nape of her neck, but slanted down to frame her jaw and chin. She had a side part, and a choppy fringe was blown across her face from right to left. "It certainly is, yours has never been this short in the whole thirty years we've been together."

"My hair hasn't been this short since I was a kid," Angie said. "It was time for a change."

"I like it, Mama," Alexis told her as she stood next to them.

"My girls are changing," Pedro softly wailed. "First my daughter, then my wife."

"I've had a haircut too, Daddy," Alena had to get in. Her battlement edges had been cut into a zigzag, and her fringe was choppy, not smooth and straight.

"It's only hair, Pedro, it will grow out if they want it to," Jenny said, looking over her right shoulder at her children. "I think you look lovely," she told Angie.

"Thanks, Mama." Angie beamed. After losing her own mother at the age of ten, Jenny had been the substitute for thirty years and filled the hole spectacularly.

"I feel I should get a new haircut now." Viv joined the conversation from the other side. "I only cut a few inches off, but maybe I should go short since everyone else is."

"Don't you dare!" Carlos exclaimed. "I love your hair, it's your trademark."

"It's only hair, Carlos," Jenny reminded him.

"And we're done," Aneeka called. "Thank you so much for this, it's been fun. So much fun catching up after so long."

"Same here, Aneeka." Carlos walked over and hugged her. "You didn't get to tweak my nipples though," he said in her ear.

She laughed gaily and playfully slapped his arm, remembering back to the photo shoot at Harry's when she had made that comment. Picking up her bag, she left the room with a wave.

"What did you say to her?" Pedro asked.

Carlos grinned. "Just reminded her of something she said to me a long time ago."

"Can we get the interviews out of the way, please?" Edie called. "It shouldn't take too long."

Going to separate rooms, they were done in an hour, having talked about the business, what they did, how they did it, and how they all still got along.

Edie promised a hundred copies of the magazine and negatives of all the photos.

The family went back to the penthouse, Cabot and Antonio to their hotel, leaving Jenny and Vivian suspicious and worried.

*****

"Do you want to go out tonight, Tone? Go see some bands, eat, drink, be merry?" Cabot plonked down on the couch in his hotel room.

"Haven't you had enough for one day? I actually found that exhausting." Antonio sat beside him.

"Since when do you find photo shoots exhausting?" Cabot asked.

"Since the whole family was in it," Antonio groaned. "God, that went on, and to then do an interview that took another hour...I really don't need to talk about myself that much."

"Let your *body* of work speak for itself, huh, Tone?" Cabot grinned.

Antonio rolled his eyes at his brother's corny joke. "Ha, ha. Aren't you tired?"

"Nah, not really. Now that my face is pretty much back to normal, I want to get out and about again. Go back to the partying we were doing before we went home." He put his feet up on the coffee table and slouched back.

"Where you got drunk and had rough sex with whoever wanted it?" Antonio said. "Not my kind of fun, watching my brother fuck someone."

"You didn't say anything, Tone." Cabot frowned.

"I did. Plenty of times," Antonio replied. "Plenty of times."

Cabot shifted uncomfortably. "Well, I'm feeling good after having the flu, and I want to go out. Come with me, Tone. Let's go and dance the night away like we used to."

Antonio sighed. "Do you plan on having sex?"

Cabot shrugged a shoulder. "If I feel like it."

"You'll take condoms out with you?"

"Of course. That's what we had drummed into us all our lives." Cabot wondered where Antonio was going with the questions.

"Cabot." Antonio picked at a piece of material coming out of the couch. "I want you to stop having sex."

"Ugh, Tone. Not you too." Cabot let his head fall back. "I get that from Grandma and our mother. I'm free to do whatever I want."

"Except you're not, and I hate it, Cabot." Antonio blinked back tears. "I hate seeing you always up a guy's ass. It's horrible, and I don't want to see it anymore. I don't want to see, or know you screw anything that moves. I find it horrible and disgusting and wish you'd stop. I don't want to see it anymore, Cabot. I'm ashamed of it, and it worries me." Antonio wanted to broach the subject of HIV, but knew he had to take it easy.

"You're ashamed of me, Tone?" Cabot's lip quivered.

"I'm ashamed of your behaviour, Cabot. The need and want to screw everything needs to stop. It's disgusting, and God knows what germs they're giving you and passing on. And what about what *you're* passing on? It's gross and I want you to stop." He looked at his brother. "You never used to be that way. Yeah, you'd have sex with women, then men, but once you saw those videos of our father, you changed. You became rampant. Like you couldn't get enough. What *is* it? Can *you* explain it to me, because I don't understand it. What is this need you have that makes you fuck every man you come across?"

Cabot blinked, having never felt such concern come from his brother before. How was he going to explain it to Antonio if he couldn't explain it to himself? "I don't know, Tone. I just..." Another shrug. "Do it. I can't explain it to you when I don't know myself."

Antonio let out a deep sigh. "I want you to be safe, Cabot. I want you to re-evaluate what you're doing and cut it out. Figure out whether it's men or women you want, and then maybe search for a partner, have a relationship instead of one-night stands. That'll be so much more fulfilling. Don't you want something that's fulfilling, Cabot? Don't you want to come home to the one person every night knowing they're there for you, and will listen to your day and how good or bad things were?"

"Do you want that, Tone? You sound like you'd like a relationship," Cabot said, worried his brother was planning on leaving him.

Antonio thought about it. "Yeah. Yeah, I would. Sometime in the next few years, I'd like to meet a girl and fall in love, maybe live together. Think about marriage and babies. But we're nowhere near that right now. We're booked up the wazoo until next summer. We've *HOS* to model for."

"But you want to fall in love, Tone?" Cabot asked softly, watching his brother's facial expressions sweeten.

"Yeah." Antonio smiled softly. "I do."

"That's sweet, Tone. Where do you plan on meeting her?"

"I don't know."

"And where do you plan on living?"

"Don't know that either."

"So, at the moment it's just a dream?"

Sadness washed over Antonio. "I guess."

"Aw, Tone." Cabot wrapped his arms around him. "I hope you get to meet a nice girl one day and fall in love. I really do. But until then, you won't meet anyone by staying home on a Saturday night. Let's go out and meet people together, Tone." He jumped up and ran into the bedroom to change.

Antonio sat there, trying to come up with a way of bringing the subject to the fore. It needed to be discussed, but maybe getting him drunk was the way to do it. Cabot was free when he was drunk, unable to lie, or keep a story straight, so that was probably going to be the best chance he had. And because they had stayed in during the week spending time together, it hadn't come up then either. So maybe, this was it. The night it all came out. Reluctantly, he got up and walked into the bedroom, watching Cabot change into his party gear of open shirt, low slung pants, and black leather boots.

"Come on, Tone, get dressed," Cabot urged.

"Isn't it a little early? The clubs won't even be open yet."

"We can go and eat somewhere." Cabot threw some black leather necklaces around his neck. "We only got snacks at the photo shoot, how boring was that, didn't get decent food. Let's go eat and then we can par-tay."

*****

James sat drunk on his lounge room floor, looking out the floor-to-ceiling windows at the river across the street. He'd been drunk most of the week to quieten the voice in his head; the voice that claimed to be Luiz Manning. He had no idea why he would be thinking the thoughts he was thinking, or why the headaches were so bad, but they eased when he drank, so he drank all day, and he drank all night. The only time he didn't drink was when he needed to go out for more alcohol. He ordered his food in, but he didn't eat much anyway. He watched TV, slept, or tried to read, but the lines kept blurring.

Everything he had read in the files kept going around the inside of his head, and he wanted it to stop. That's why he drank. He forgot when he drank. It didn't hurt when he drank, it felt good, and he felt free, but he also knew he couldn't keep it up forever. Something had to happen, and he didn't know what needed to happen to make it all stop.

"Ugh," he groaned. "It needs to stop, but what the hell do I do about it?" He'd racked his brain in his fog-induced state, but couldn't come up with anything short of shooting himself in the head just to stop the ache and the thoughts and the garbage going around his brain. He had, however, wondered what would happen if he stopped drinking...

*****

Cabot and Antonio ate dinner at a local restaurant before heading out to party. There was a new club, *Angels & Demons*, opening up and they had received an invitation. The crowd snaked down the street, and bouncers stood at the door. But the invitation got them in.

"Oh, my God, it's Steele and Phoenix Stefan," girls screamed from the line.

"Hello, girls." Steele blew kisses at them. "Thank you for being fans." They breezed inside to more of the same adulation. Girls and guys crowded round as they made their way to the reserved section and took their place, inviting their adoring fans to sit with them. Champagne was served, and they partied like they hadn't since their birthday. Dancing with the crowd, they cut loose, especially Steele. Phoenix was more reserved. He knew the score. When they were home, they were Cabot and Antonio. When they were out, or working, they were Steele and Phoenix, and unfortunately, Steele had a reputation to uphold, one of his own making.

Phoenix saw Steele's tongue down the throat of a guy. Their bodies were together, and his brother's arms were around the man. *Jesus, he doesn't learn. Can't help himself, and clearly nothing I said today sank in. He really is in denial, but how the hell am I going to get him out of it?* Keeping an eye on his brother, he saw him go from partner to partner, playing tonsil hockey with most of the men, and some of the women in the club. At one stage, he lost sight of his brother and went searching, finding him fucking a guy in the back room. "I hope you have a condom on."

Steele's head swung around, but he kept on hammering. "Of course, Phe."

"That's good. Because you wouldn't want to give the poor bastard that STD you've got." Antonio turned and walked back the way he'd come, hearing the guy screech something about fucking STDs and how could Steele give it to him.

"I've got a condom on, don't worry," Steele said. "Look." He pointed at his dick still wrapped in the prophylactic.

The man looked down. "I don't care how many of them you wear, I don't want to catch anything. How could you?" He slapped Steele across the face and ran off.

Steele, angry that Phoenix had ruined his fun, rolled off the condom and shoved his privates back in his pants. Going in search of Phe, he found him trying to pay for their tab.

"It's on the house," the manager said. "Thanks for coming."

"Thank you for inviting us." Phoenix shook his hand. "It's a great club, and we'll let all our friends know to come here."

Steele waited for the man to walk away before pouncing. "What did you have to tell the guy that for?" He punched his brother's arm. "I was having fun, Phe."

"What? That you have an STD?" Phoenix stayed calm.

"And what would you know about that?" Steele crossed his arms.

"The cream in the bathroom," Phoenix said. "I've had enough, I'm going home."

"But it's still early, Phe." Steele ran after him.

"It's after one, and I'm going home. It's been a long day," Phoenix shouted over his shoulder. "It's up to you if you come or not."

"Well, it's not like I got the chance to." Steele pouted. Not wanting to be left alone by his brother again, he silently followed. He had enjoyed himself, dancing under the strobe lights, but the sex just hadn't cut it as it used to. *Maybe I'm bored with the whole club scene?* he thought, walking out onto the pavement after Phoenix. *Maybe I need somewhere new to go?*

They caught a cab back to their hotel where Cabot showered and applied his cream. Walking into the bedroom, he saw Antonio standing stoic, scowling, arms crossed. "Tone?"

"When were you going to tell me?"

"Tell you what?"

"You had an STD. You shouldn't even be having sex. Did Dan discover it?"

"What makes you think Dan—"

"His name's on the tube."

"Oh." Cabot's eyes fell, unable to look his brother in the eye. "I wasn't going to tell anyone, Tone. It's embarrassing."

"That you have an STD?" Antonio raised a brow. "We'd be more surprised if this is your first."

"Tonee!" Cabot's scowl matched his brother's. "That's not funny. *Of course* it's the first one I've ever gotten. That's why it's embarrassing."

"And is there anything else you want to tell me?" He realised for all the alcohol Cabot had drunk, it hadn't quite gotten him to where he needed him to open up.

"Why would there be, Tone?" Cabot crawled into bed, worried that secrets were coming out.

"Was it from the guy on Mykonos?" Antonio urged. "The one who assaulted you?" He got in beside Cabot.

Cabot couldn't look at his brother. Instead, he slid down into the bed. "It doesn't matter, Tone. Let's get some sleep. We can do it all again tomorrow night."

"You expect me to go clubbing tomorrow night?"

"Why not? It's still summer, it's still hot, we'll be back to work before we know it. So let's party."

September 2007

Saturday morning, James woke as a shaft of sun flashed across his face. "Ugh, what the hell!?" His hand flew to cover his eyes, and he slithered out of the way. "Ugh." He blinked a few times to clear his vision and glanced around the room. He was still sitting on the floor in his lounge, having fallen asleep drunk. But he'd made a decision, and knew it needed to start today.

Crawling to the bathroom, he stumbled to his feet and fell into the shower cubicle. A ten-minute ice-cold shower and a shave followed. He dressed, made himself a healthy breakfast and forced it down. Then he made a batch of health shakes he could drink all day. It was his normal routine, and he needed to get back to it. He had decided the night before he was going cold turkey. Instead of drinking to forget, he was going to let it happen, just to see what *did* happen, and he hoped it wasn't as bad as he feared. He was going to spend the day meditating on the roof for fresh air, drink his shakes to get his body back on track, and do some light exercise.

There had been fewer phone calls. Obviously, Captain Webster had found his letter asking for time off. So, the only people calling were Denny and his parents. And he wasn't ready to deal with them yet.

Why had he never known about his brother? Why had his mother never said anything? *But then, why would she when he died in 1977, and I was born in 1979? He died at twenty-five, and I'm now twenty-eight. At least I've lived three years longer.*

After grabbing his keys and sunglasses, he went up to the roof where there was a small seating area and table and chairs. One of the tenants had left their barbeque up there and the place smelled of burnt meat. Finding a quiet spot in the shade that faced the river, he sat comfortably and breathed. He hadn't meditated properly in a while, probably since before the tour, although, he'd grabbed a few minutes here and there during the ten weeks.

Watching the river water flow by, he calmed his breathing and allowed himself to drift. He drifted along on a cloud, floating above the river, floating above the water, floating above the island. An island with two people entwined on a beach. Two men. He saw it was himself and Tomas making love on the beach, lost in each other's arms and their surroundings. He watched for a while and then floated on. Floated into an apartment where he found Tomas and another man making love. It was Roger that was with him, and he was not.

Angry, he floated away and found himself in a strange man's bedroom, fucking a man he barely knew. His name was Aiden Head, and he watched himself pour drugs down Aiden's nose until he was unconscious. Watched as he hauled Aiden's body out to his car and drove him to Roger's apartment where he poured the lethal dose down Aiden's throat. The dose that killed him.

He watched himself leave and found himself in a room. He had bleached hair and was wearing an orderly's uniform. He was packing his belongings and talking to himself.

Floating along, he saw himself go into the hospital, find a wheelchair, and go into a room. Tomas was in the bed, and he got him out of it and into the chair. Whistling, he wheeled Tomas into the lift as his ex-fiance noticed from the other end of the hall. Panicking, he watched himself hurry Tomas out to the car, place him in the back seat, and drive off.

He followed, floating along on his cloud until it was night-time, and he was watching himself carry Tomas into a seedy hotel room and place him on the bed. Unable to contain himself, he pulled off Tomas's clothes and had his way. He watched from the corner of the room as a strange man sneaked in and stood watching as he climaxed inside his lover.

"Oh, God, oh, God, oh, God," Luiz cried out.

"Oh, God indeed," the man said, and fired a bullet right into a stunned Luiz's brain.

He watched, floating on his cloud from the corner of the room, as the man dressed Tomas, threw him over his shoulder, and left as quietly as he'd come. Floating over to the bed, he stared down at himself. Naked, eyes open, arms flung wide. A red fleshy spot in the middle of his forehead. He knew he was dead. Knew it would never be for him and Tomas again. Not in that lifetime anyway. *But I've been reborn. I've been reborn as James Giancarlo Gardo on Valentine's Day 1979. I came back, and I plan on taking my revenge.*

*****

Saturday night, Cabot dragged Antonio out of the hotel room and out for dinner.

Cabot wanted fun.

Antonio wanted answers, and he was determined to get them. Making sure Cabot drank more than the night before, he had him home and drunk by midnight. "Here we go." He sat Cabot down on the couch.

"Where are we, Tone?" Cabot yawned.

"Home, the hotel."

"Why aren't we still out partying?" Cabot blinked to stay awake.

"Because we need to talk, Cabot."

"I don't want to talk, Tone. I want to dance and have sex."

"Even though you have HIV, Cabot." Antonio sat on the coffee table, so he could face him. "When were you going to tell me, Cabot? I'm your twin brother. Don't I get to know?"

Cabot stared glassy-eyed at him. "HIV, Tone? I don't have HIV."

Antonio pulled the folder from the envelope he'd gotten from the drawer. "I had a look before I left the other morning. I was curious as to what Dan was sending you. His name is on it. I read the letter, Cabot."

Cabot gazed at the folder. "I have no idea what that is, Tone. I haven't seen it before."

"Sure you have." Antonio opened it and read the letter aloud. "You didn't read the letter the other day. I saw you glance at the folder and jam it into the drawer. I've been waiting for you to tell me, *your twin brother.* Why haven't you told me, Cabot? Why haven't you told me you have HIV from the assault in Mykonos? I'm your brother."

"Because I don't have it, Tone," Cabot murmured and stumbled to his feet. "I don't have it." He swayed. "I don't."

"You do, Cabot. And now you need to get help for it." Antonio stood behind his brother. "I'll help you. We *all* will."

"We all will?" Cabot's eyes blazed. "Who are you kidding, Tone? Grandma will be one big fat 'I told you so', and Mama will fall apart. Our father will shake his head, and the whole family will want nothing to do with me. I'm not telling anyone, Tone, because *I don't* have HIV. *I don't* have AIDS." He stumbled around the room. "*I don't* have it..." He wheezed. "I don't."

"Cabot." Antonio went to his side. "The tests say you do, and we need to get you to admit that you do, so we can start you on the necessary medications."

"I don't have it, Tonee. I don't need any medication," Cabot screamed. "I don't have AIDS."

"No, you have HIV, Cabot," Antonio said. "It's not AIDS yet, not if you start the treatment. You can prevent it from progressing."

"I did prevent it," Cabot yelled. "I wore condoms, and did my due diligence, and followed Dan's advice and Grandma's advice, and Mother and Father's advice, and I did it all and still do it all."

"It wasn't you that got it from something you did wrong, you got it from an assault. *Someone did wrong to you,* that's *not your fault.* But you have to admit it and get yourself help," Antonio told him.

"Help for what, Tone? I don't have anything. There's nothing wrong with me." Cabot's face crumpled, and he saw Antonio pick up the folder and listened to him read the letter. "Stop it, stop it." He covered his ears.

Antonio kept reading the letter, over and over as Cabot screamed at him. "You have HIV, Cabot, you need help. It's nothing to be ashamed of."

"I don't have it, I don't have it." Cabot fell to his knees and sobbed. "I don't have it."

"You do, Cabot, and you need to let me help you." Antonio knelt beside him. "Let me help you, Cabot."

"Help me with what, Tone? I don't need help." Cabot wiped his face and got to his feet. "I'm fine."

"No, you're not. You're in denial. You have HIV, you need to admit it."

A million things went through Cabot's mind. HIV/AIDS, the guy from Mykonos, Dan telling him he had HIV. "No." His head jerkily moved from side to side. "I don't." his face crumpled. "I don't."

"You do, Cabot." Antonio reached out to his brother. "You do."

"No." Cabot fell apart. "No."

"Oh, Cabot." Antonio pulled him into his arms. "You do. Oh, my brother."

"No." Cabot bent forward in his brother's arms. "No."

"Oh, Cabot," Antonio soothed. "Let's get you to Dan for your medication."

"Dan?" Cabot gasped for air. "Dan?"

"Yes, Dan. Let's get you to Dan, so you can get your meds."

"Meds?" Cabot murmured, straightening. "No...I...no...no," his voice rose. "No, no, no, no, no." He raced out the door and downstairs, with Antonio hot on his tail.

"Cabot," Antonio yelled, running after him. "Come back."

"No, Tony, no. I don't have it." Cabot raced across the road and into the blackness of Central Park.

Antonio followed Cabot across the road, but stopped just inside the park and breathed in, having no idea which way Cabot had gone. He'd expected that to go better than it did, and kicked himself for not keeping him there.

Cabot smashed through the park, across roads, and kept running until he got to the other side. He found himself somewhere near Central Park West, and stopped to catch his breath. Bending, he put his hands on his knees and gasped. *Tony knew, Tony knew, Tony knows, oh, God, how could he know.*

Sobbing, he went to his knees and thanked God no one was around. He stayed that way for a while. Time was no longer relevant, but then it never had been. Not for him. Antonio and Tilly always took care of the time and appointments. He just went where they sent him, and he got to where he needed to be on time, usually because he went everywhere with Antonio. Now, he had no one. No family, no Tilly, no Tony.

Wiping his nose on his sleeve, he looked around and cleared his eyes. Seeing a convenience store down the road, he patted his pockets, finding a wad of bills and condoms. Getting to his feet, he started off for the store and made his way inside to find a nice selection of whiskey, gin and vodka. Grabbing one of each, he also grabbed potato crisps and red licorice sticks.

"I need to see some ID." The clerk looked at him expectantly.

"What? Are you kidding? I'm twenty-five." Cabot rolled his eyes. "Don't you know who I am. I'm Steele Stefan, world-famous model." He pointed to the man's computer. "Google me, you'll see."

"I still need to see ID," the clerk repeated.

"Ugh," Cabot growled and pulled out the wad of money. Tucked in the middle was his driver's licence. He flashed it. "Happy, now?"

"That says you're Cabot Stephanopoulos." The clerk frowned.

"Steele Stefan is my stage name. I have a twin brother Antonio who goes by Phoenix Stefan. Our parents are famous, our sister is a model, our aunts and uncles and cousins are famous. Look us up." He flipped a fifty-dollar bill at the man and grabbed the bag. "Buh-bye." Walking out, he headed back to the park.

After Cabot had left, the clerk quickly googled Steele Stefan and found he was famous, did have a twin, and was twenty-five years old. And that he lived just across the park.

Cabot knew it wasn't totally safe to be walking the park at night, but he needed to be away from his family, and he knew of a secret hidey-hole where he could sit, not far from the family's home on 5th. Not that he would be going there, but he wanted to see people just in case. Munching on the licorice, he found the spot. It was a huge, naturally carved out hollow in the tree trunk. While it faced slightly away, he could still peer out of it and see their home.

Sitting back, he sighed. "What the fuck is going on? Seriously, what the fuck is going on." He cracked open the bottle of whiskey and took several gulps. It burned his throat, so he followed it with crisps which made him thirsty, so he opened the vodka and tried that. It didn't burn, but didn't yet dull the terrifying fear that was eating away at his heart.

Why had Tony said he had HIV? Why had Tony read the letter over and over? Why had Tony looked in the envelope? *Why did he intrude on my privacy? God, Tony, why did you have to intrude?*

He swallowed half a bottle and prayed there were no spiders or snakes in the hollow. Ten minutes later, the vodka was gone, and he was mellow. *Tonee,* he silently wailed. *Tonee, where are you when I need you, Tonee? Why aren't you here with me now? I need you, Tonee, you're the only one who loves me, and I need you, please, Tonee, don't talk about that anymore. I don't have it, I don't want it, I can't have it, no, Tonee.*

He cried hot silent tears, rocked back and forth, his knees to his chest, his arms wrapped around his legs. The tears burned. Burned his eyes, his flesh, his heart, his soul. His life was over. Over as he knew it. No longer could he be the person *he* wanted to be, *his family* wanted him to be, *his brother* wanted him to be. His life was over, and that's all there was to it.

The crisps were finished, the licorice eaten, the gin and whiskey drunk, so he sat nursing the empty vodka bottle and cried himself to sleep.

*****

Sunday morning, James awoke. In his bed, in his apartment, and not on the floor. And not drunk. His brain had been formulating a plan for the last twenty-four hours and had it all ready to go. He just needed an invitation. He rang Alena on her phone, having stolen her number while they were on tour.

"Oh, uh, hello? It's so early." She yawned from her bed and saw Alexis stick her head up for a second and then bury it again.

"Alena? James Gardo."

"James!" Alena exclaimed, quickly sitting up.

Alexis popped her head up to listen.

"Hi. I don't want to be too forward, but are you doing anything for lunch or brunch?"

"Um, just with my family, I think. It's Sunday after all."

"Oh, what about dinner?"

"What about you come over?" Alena asked boldly and saw Alexis sit up with interest.

"Oh, today? For lunch or dinner?"

"Ah, lunch. We'll probably converge on the penthouse about eleven and eat about twelve or so."

"That's a great time. Will your family mind?"

"Probably not. Grandma mentioned wanting to meet you."

"She did? Well, I certainly can't wait to meet your family. Will everyone be there?"

"Probably not Cabot or Antonio, but you never know."

"Okay, I'll see you at eleven. Thank you for the invite." Hanging up, he silently hissed in delight. It had gone just the way he wanted.

Alena clicked off her phone.

"You didn't say you had James Gardo's number," Alexis said.

"I don't." Alena put the phone on the cupboard between the two beds. "He must have gotten mine because I certainly don't have his."

"You'd better tell Grandma before he turns up. You know she sets out a certain number of places every Sunday meal time."

"Yeah." Alena looked at her clock. "Ugh, barely nine. Why did he call so early?"

"The early bird does catch the worm." Alexis grinned. "And looks like he caught you real easy."

Alena threw a pillow at her. "Silly, he's not interested in me."

Alexis threw the pillow back. "How do you know?"

"Because he never tried to kiss me or hold my hand or anything."

"Doesn't mean he's not interested. Maybe he was getting to know you, and now he wants a chance to ask the family for your hand in marriage."

"Ah," Alena shrieked, laughing her head off.

"Keep it down, it's still early," Pedro said from the half-open doorway. He held two steaming cups of coffee. "Your mother's still in bed. What's all the laughing about?"

"James Gardo called Alena to ask her out, but she ended up inviting him to lunch instead," Alexis said.

Pedro frowned. "You better tell your grandmother well before then. She'll want to know."

"Yes, Daddy." Alena fell back onto her bed. "I'll tell her."

"All right, we'll see you later." He went into the master and told Angie what had just happened.

"After trying to get in touch with him, he gets in touch with her." She sipped the strong brew. They were nestled in a pile of pillows, catching up on Sunday morning TV. "Seems strange to me."

"And me," Pedro replied, opening the Sunday paper their doorman had dropped off.

*****

It being a Sunday, and having the family around, Jenny was up early preparing her chickens for roasting. There was a ten-kilo bag of potatoes ready for peeling, bunches of carrots, and kilos of peas and beans. Everyone would be there at eleven, but lunch started around twelve, so it was already in the oven.

Tomas and Roger came through the door. "Mama, I need to grab some things from the store, do you need anything?"

"Ah." She looked around. "No, I've got everything, sweetie."

"Okay, it's ten now, I should be back within the hour."

"Take your time, you know we don't eat until later."

"Okay, bye Roger."

"Bye, T. Get me some chocolate," Roger called as Tomas raced down the stairs. He turned to Jenny. "Have you found him yet?"

"Who?"

"James Gardo. The L.M. lookalike."

Jenny frowned, kept her voice low and looked around the penthouse. "No."

Spiros was reading the paper in the sitting area, and some of the kids were watching TV in the lounge.

"What do we do about it?" he asked as Carlos and Viv came through the door.

"Smells good, Mama," Carlos called and joined Spiros on the couch. "Got the sports and entertainment sections?"

Pedro and Angie walked in with Mike, Maggie and their kids. "Hey, I want the music section."

"No," Jenny said to Roger. "I'll deal with it tomorrow." Joining the family, they read the papers and caught up on the news while the kids gathered around the TV.

"Oh, hey, Mama, is Alena up yet?" Pedro yawned, still half asleep, and not even noticing whether his daughters were in the room.

"Not yet, why?"

"She got a phone call this morning."

"From who?"

"James Gardo."

All adult eyes landed on him.

"What?"

"Apparently, he called and invited her out," Pedro replied, noticing everyone's stares.

"After all this time," Jenny murmured, thinking about what it meant.

"But, she invited him to lunch instead. I told her to make sure to tell you, but if she's still not here yet…"

"No, I haven't seen her." Jenny glanced at Roger. What the hell were they going to do when he turned up?

"Thought you should know. The twins coming?"

*****

"Oh, my God. Look at all the trouble you're going to," Alexis teased her sister, watching as she re-did her hair for the tenth time in their small bathroom.

"I want to look good. You saw him." Alena brushed her hair in the opposite direction from what it just was.

"But you said he wasn't interested." Alexis leaned on the doorjamb, smiling.

"Maybe he's changed his mind."

Alexis snorted. "Yeah, and hell froze over."

"Hey," Alena cried. "Guys are interested in me." She tied her hair up then pulled it out.

"So, why don't you date any of them?"

Alena shrugged and brushed it out once more. "I'm not interested in them."

"And you're interested in James Gardo?"

"Maybe."

*****

James had it all planned out, and that plan started now.

He left his home and took a cab to 5th Avenue and stopped down the road from the Stephanopoulos building. He was going to walk there, wanting time to get himself together. The whole family would be there. To see him as he was now; twenty-eight, strong, healthy, and not dead. He wanted Tomas to see him as he was now. The lover he once had. The lover he would have again.

Taking a deep breath, he started down the avenue, uneasy at first, but with every step, his confidence grew and kept growing. He felt like Tony Manero from *Saturday Night Fever*. He'd seen the ad for it before he died. 1977; what a year! He'd gotten engaged to Bertha and fallen in love with Tomas, the love of his life, and he'd known that from their first time in the steam room. The first time he'd touched him, the first time he'd kissed him. Tomas was so young and untroubled by relationships. He wasn't battle-scarred, but naïve and innocent, and willing. And he had taken and given, and he knew after that time, Tomas was the one for him. But thanks to Bertha St Bloody John, it was ruined. Tomas was his no more, and not long after, he was with Roger. And was *still* with Roger.

I just need to get him away from Tomas, so we can have some alone time. We need to talk, at length, about our future. In the distance, he saw a figure, tall, dark hair, sunglasses, carrying a bag of groceries. *Is that...?* His steps quickened, and he got closer. Tomas! Removing his glasses so he could see better, he was close to the Victorian the family called home. "Tomas," he called softly, seeing him stop outside of the building.

Tomas stared and removed his glasses. He stared, and his jaw dropped. "Luiz," he whispered, disbelieving. The man before him, just metres away, was Luiz. "No."

"Tomas," Luiz called. "My love." Reaching out, he saw the panic in his lover's eyes.

"No," Tomas yelled, and ran into the lobby straight into the lift, hitting the button non-stop, hoping it would make the doors shut faster so he could get away from his nightmare.

"Tomas," Luiz yelled and ran inside, only to be stopped by Mark.

"I'm James Gardo, I'm expected. I'm also a cop." He dashed past and up the stairs, knowing Tomas would go to the penthouse.

Bursting out of the lift, and flinging open the penthouse door, Tomas stumbled in and dropped the bag of groceries. "Mama, no, it can't be. No."

"Tomas!" Jenny flew to his side, scared that he was ill again, and they were about to relive that day in 1981.

Roger quickly picked up the bag and gathered the items, curious as to what had scared his husband.

"He can't be alive," Tomas babbled in his mother's arms, clinging to her like a lifeboat. "He's here, he can't be alive, he just can't be, he can't be."

The rest of the family stood, watching, concerned for their brother's welfare.

"Who are you talking about?" Carlos asked, seeing his brother's tormented face.

"Tomas!" Luiz burst through the door straight for Tomas.

Jenny reacted instantly. Letting go of Tomas, she smashed her open hands into his chest. "No, you don't. You were not invited here."

She stared into the aqua blue eyes of James Gardo, but she knew, she could see, that it was not him behind them.

Luiz stopped, staring down into her furious blue eyes. "Oh, you must be Mrs Stephanopoulos. I finally get to meet you. I didn't back then, Tomas dumped me before I could meet the family. Nice to meet you."

Roger was hanging on to Tomas, not believing what he was seeing. "No, it can't be. You can't be him."

Luiz hardened. "You," he spat. "You took my Tomas away from me, and now it's time for me to get him back."

"No." Tomas shuddered with his gasps, desperately trying to hold on to any moral and sober thought he could. "Get away from me. You're dead."

"Yes," Luiz said. "*Technically* I am, at least, my old body is. Killed by that man who sneaked into our hotel room. We were in the throes of passion when he planted a bullet right smack bang here." He planted his forefinger in the middle of his forehead. "So, my old body's dead, but then wouldn't you know it, I was reborn into *this* body, and I look *exactly the same*. What are the odds? Tomas, I still love you so much." He reached out, but Jenny stood strong between them.

Her heart was pounding, and she was sure the rest of the family could hear it. She knew Carlos, Pedro and Mike were nearby. The girls would have backed away with the kids. But Alena and Alexis weren't there yet, and she needed to keep the situation calm. "Are you saying you've been reincarnated and have become Luiz again?"

"Luiz," murmured through the family as the family looked at each other in shock.

"Exactly, Mrs S. Oh, may I call you that? You don't mind, do you?"

She gave a slight shake of her head.

"How was *I* to know that when I was shot dead in that seedy hotel room by God knows who, and my Tomas was going to be kidnapped from me, that I would be reincarnated back into a body that was going to look *exactly the same as the old one*? What are the chances, huh?" His grin looked like the Joker's from Batman. Maniacal. His hands moved in wild gestures, his eyes wide and dangerous. "Can you believe it? I certainly can't. Some poor dumb schmuck that got called James Gardo got my body."

That caused frowns all round.

"Well, little did *I* know that when he saw you and Tomas in the department store way back when, 1980, was it? That I was going to pop up when I heard that voice." He smiled longingly at Tomas. "I remembered you, Tomas. The sound of your voice, the way you looked. I *knew* you. I *remembered* you, my love. My lover. The only man I ever wanted with all of my heart, body and soul, and you turned away and gave it to him." He pointed accusingly at Roger. "You got my Tomas." His face screwed up into something unearthly. "*You* got what *I* wanted, and what *I* should have had. *You* got the man I love, and I will kill *you* for it, Roger Dencott. Just like I killed all of your ex-lovers at *Seralift.* Jeff Fastwater, Brock Hardwood, Brent Woodcock and finally, Aiden Head. *I will kill you.*"

"No, you won't." Jenny stood firm. "You and I need a little chat, Luiz. We never got to have one thirty years ago."

He calmed down and looked at her. "Okay Mrs S, what do you want to talk about?"

Tomas took that moment to spin around Roger and take off out the penthouse and down the stairs.

"Tomas," Luiz called and moved to follow.

But Jenny held on tight. "No, you don't, let him go."

Roger grabbed him by his t-shirt. "You leave him the fuck alone, or *I* will kill *you.*" He hovered over Luiz by three inches, and shoving him back, took off after his husband. "Tomas," he called.

"Luiz." Jenny turned him around to look at her. "Why are you back, Luiz?"

The others were still trading glances in confusion. What this *the* Luiz? Luiz Manning, who had killed four porn stars to frame Roger *and* poisoned their brother to then kidnap him from the hospital? Pedro and Carlos exchanged a glance, glad Mike was with them. Meanwhile, Maggie was with Angie and Viv, keeping the kids in the lounge room away from it all.

Alena and Alexis came through the door, looking from over their shoulders to everyone in the penthouse. "Hey, what's going on? Uncle Tomas flew down the stairs. Hey, James, you're here. Have you met the family?" Alena asked, curious as to why her grandmother had a hold of James.

Jenny shot out her left hand to stop Alena, while her right hand held on to James's white t-shirt. The girls stopped short at their grandmother's serious expression.

Luiz turned his head. "You're the little girl James has fallen for. But he never had the chance since I was always in his head."

Alena looked at him in confusion, and her father grabbed both her and Alexis and moved them out of harm's way.

"James? What?" Alena went on.

"Be quiet," Pedro murmured in her ear.

She looked at the terrified expressions on everyone's faces.

"Don't worry, I'm not about to hurt her, it's only Roger I'll kill," Luiz told everyone.

"Why? Because Tomas fell in love with him?" Jenny asked, wanting to find out more. She believed in reincarnation and was dying to see if it was actually Luiz.

Luiz scowled. "He loved *me*, Mrs S. I saw it. I felt it. But we didn't have enough time together. Bertha got in the way. She convinced Tomas to dump me and go home to Miami with her. To *leave me*, can you believe that? I loved him then, and I still love him now."

"Yes, I see that," Jenny soothed. "But you did so much to hurt him that he can never forgive you for it. Never take you back. You hurt him, Luiz, and you tried to frame Roger for murder."

"I know, Mrs S," he groaned. "But I wanted to break them up, so Roger would never be around him again and I would have him back."

"Why did you poison him then?" Jenny asked calmly; while boiling inside.

"Because I wanted to get him away from Roger. I planned the kidnapping from the hospital. I dyed my hair and got an orderly's outfit. I fitted right in."

"You kidnapped Tomas from the hospital?"

"I *removed* him from the hospital," Luiz told her. "I put him in the back seat of my car and drove off. I didn't know where I was going, but I knew I had to get away from Miami, so we stayed in a motel somewhere in Alabama. I carried him in and put him on the bed. I got him out of the gown and got all excited about seeing him again, so we made love. While I was going for the big O, someone spoke behind me. I turned my head and a man pointed his gun at me and shot me. The man took off with Tomas and that was it. I didn't get to see him again until the department store. I kept having dreams about him, but James's old man said it was just his imagination. Then I saw the newspaper article about him and Roger being dead. I felt so sad, it was horrible. And then James had to go and get himself on bodyguard duty, but I managed to find out Tomas was alive. That's when I came out."

"He's gay?" Alena's shocked expression said it all.

"No," Luiz snapped, glancing at her. "James isn't. *I meant I came out of his brain.*"

"And what will make you go away again?" Jenny asked, her hand cramping from hanging on.

He shrugged. "Probably nothing. I'm Luiz now, that's all there is to it."

"And what will it take for you to leave my son alone?"

Luiz looked her square in the eye. "Nothing. Because I won't."

*****

Giancarlo Gardo unlocked his son's front door and entered. James had been home for two weeks from Alena's tour and hadn't been to see them or call them. James's captain had called looking for James and said a Jenny Stephanopoulos was asking after him. Ah, Jenny. Jenny with the blue eyes Stephanopoulos. Once the girl of his dreams. But that was a hell of a long time ago. He looked around the apartment and found paperwork filed neatly on his desk.

"Ah, Jesus." He picked up one pile and saw it was his old file from 1977. *How the hell did he get these?* He found printouts of newspaper articles on the Stephanopoulos family and all that had happened for the last thirty years. "What in the blazes…?" He stood staring at the papers, his detective brain ticking over. Flicking through them, he saw Luiz Manning's name circled in red, along with his mother's. "Shit!" Had James realised Sheila had a son before him? A son they had never mentioned?

Collecting all the papers, he saw a small white piece flutter to the floor. Picking it up, he saw *Alena, 11 a.m. Brunch at penthouse.* "Bloody shit!" Giancarlo knew exactly what was going on. When James had quickly called from the night of the first concert, he'd told them it was Alena, and they knew full well who she was. Pedro and Angelina's daughter. Then, he knew trouble was brewing. Now, he knew it was about to blow. He just didn't know what was going to happen.

Taking the paperwork, he left, and went down to his car. Hitting the gas, he put the siren on the roof. It wasn't police issue, and at eighty-three he was too old to be playing detective, but he could still cut a mean figure when he needed to.

*****

Down in apartment 2, Roger found Tomas in the bedroom, clinging to the bedcovers as he sat on the floor sobbing his heart out. "Oh, Jesus, T." He slumped down in front of him, leaning on the bed.

"Roger," Tomas gasped. "It can't be, it just can't be."

"It isn't," Roger told him. "That is James Gardo. Detective Gardo's son."

Tomas frowned, but the tears kept flowing. "What? But he—"

"Looks exactly like Luiz?" Roger said. "Yeah, I know."

Tomas gazed around, unfocused, dazed, trying to collect his thoughts. "But how?"

"Who knows?" Roger said. "But this reaction has to stop, T. Look at you. Even after thirty years you're freaking out."

"What do you expect?" Tomas cried. "After what he did to us, *to me?*"

"Yeah, I know. I get it. And once we came back from the dead, he was no more. But Jesus, T, he's like fricken Voldemort, he who can't be named, because Jesus, look at the reaction he gets."

"He *poisoned me*, Roger. He *killed four people* we knew and tried to frame you for their murders. He *kidnapped me* from the hospital. *We thought* he had given me AIDS."

"And *he* has been dead for nearly thirty fucking years, Tomas," Roger shouted. "I know we haven't spoken of him since 1981, but fucking seriously. You see a guy who just happens to look exactly like him, and you freak the fuck out. *Why* does he still have this effect on you thirty years later?

Tears rolled down Tomas's cheeks. "I don't know, Roger. He poisoned me, the first man, the first *person* I gave myself to so incredibly intimately and personally, poisoned me. Kidnapped me, killed four men and tried to frame my new lover. You tell me how I'm supposed to keep reacting?"

"After thirty years," Roger said. "Not like this."

*****

Officer Denny Nicolls jumped out of his car and raced after the perp who'd just held up a convenience store. He was at the north end of the park, off Central Park North, and didn't plan on running through the whole park, but it was his job, and he knew that Alena's family were somewhere on 5th. But that was miles away.

"Suspect on foot and running through Central Park off Central Park North. Following," he gasped over the radio while trying to keep the perp in sight.

"We'll get officers at the other end and on all sides, stay with him."

"Roger that." He kept going.

*****

"Luiz," Jenny cajoled. "I'm so sorry you were hurt back then. We raised our boys to have morals and principles and standards. When Tomas found out you were the one engaged to Bertha, it nearly killed him. He felt so guilty."

"I know, Mrs S. But he could've hooked up with me in Miami. Or in Mykonos when Bertha dumped me. He didn't have to feel guilty after that. There was no need to." Luiz's heart ached for Tomas.

"But he did, and it hurt him so much. You were his first, Luiz, and it hurt him that you hadn't told him you were engaged to a woman."

"I know." He became crestfallen. "And I'm sorry for not telling him. The moment I first saw him I fell in love. He's so beautiful, Mrs S, you made one incredible man in Tomas, and I fell so hard. He's a beautiful Greek god, and I love him so much." His hands were enclosed over his heart. "I *still* love him, Mrs S, all these years later. I still love him and want another chance with him."

*****

Giancarlo sped through the city from the Meat Packing District to 5th Avenue, lights blazing. He didn't know what had happened to his son, but he planned on finding out. Seeing a traffic jam ahead, he veered off and took another route.

*****

"What am I supposed to do?" Tomas wailed. "What am I supposed to do?"

"Let him go. That man downstairs is *not* Luiz Manning. *Let Luiz Manning go.*"

"And how do I do that? How do I let the memories of my first lover, and everything he did, go?"

"What aren't you telling me?" Roger changed tack.

"What?" Tomas's head shook slightly in confusion.

"What aren't you telling me about Luiz?" Roger repeated.

"I don't know what you mean." A frown lit upon Tomas's face.

"There is something inside you that makes you cling to him. What is it?"

Tomas's voice hardened. "I don't know, Roger. But why don't you tell me what he meant when he said he killed off your ex-lovers at *Seraliff?*"

*****

Denny puffed. He had to keep going, but he wasn't that fit and was running out of steam. "Perp's on 86th Street Transverse, I'm after him." He bolted down the Central Park West side of the park, trying to keep the thief in sight. He wore baggy white pants and a red hoodie, so it wasn't too hard, but at eleven-thirty on a Sunday, there were a lot of people in the park, and they were getting in the way.

"We've got him, we're coming in from Central Park West."

Denny kept running.

*****

Giancarlo got to 5th Avenue and screeched to a halt outside the Stephanopoulos building, seeing a few cop cars, and cops running. He wondered what was going on, but didn't have the time to deal with business that was not his.

*****

"My what?" Roger frowned in surprise and fear and desperation at keeping his long-held secret intact. "That is not Luiz, Tomas. He has no idea what he's talking about. I told you thirty years ago, we only did movies together, nothing else. Why would you listen to what some whack job, who's not even who you think he is, says?"

But Tomas was still hardened. "Then who *is* he, Roger? And how does he know so damn much, that no one else does?"

*****

"But you can't have another chance, Luiz, because *you're not* Luiz. You are James Gardo," Jenny soothingly told him.

"No, I'm not," he spat crossly. "I'm Luiz Manning, and I still love Tomas even though I haven't seen him in thirty years." Tears rolled down his face. "I still love him, Mrs S, even though I've been gone all these years. But I'm back, and I want another chance with him."

"And what about my son?"

Luiz turned to see Giancarlo standing in the open doorway. "How did you…?"

Jenny was stunned. She hadn't seen Giancarlo since the department store in 1980. "Giancarlo?" There were murmurings among the adult members of the family.

"Jenny." He nodded, but he kept his eyes on his son. "I went to my son's apartment," he said to Luiz. "And found all of the paperwork. Paperwork he took from the precinct basement. My old police reports from 1977. Plus he had more, plus he left himself a note about brunch. I want my son." He took a step closer.

"You can't have him," Luiz snapped. "This may be the body of the boy you and that woman created twenty-nine years ago, but *I* am the one who controls it. You don't get it back."

Giancarlo took another step, slowly, slowly. "You are *not* Luiz Manning. Luiz Manning died in 1977."

"I know," Luiz spat. "I was shot in the head."

Giancarlo frowned and noticed Jenny's hand clawing at his son's t-shirt. "Luiz was shot in the head. *You* were not. *You* are my son, James Giancarlo Gardo. *You* are twenty-eight years old and an only child."

"Only child!" Luiz yelled. "Bullshit. *I* am Luiz Manning, bastard son of Andros Poulos and Sheila Manning. And you know who *that* is, and now you lay claim to this body as your son's? You didn't tell me I had a bro—"

"I want my son," Giancarlo yelled. "Get out of my son's head."

Pain seared through Luiz's head. "Ah…" He gripped it. "Dad?"

"James."

"Argh." Another burst. "He's not, I am Luiz."

"James." Giancarlo finally made it to his son and grabbed him by both arms. "James."

"I am not." The pain doubled Luiz over. "My head."

"James, let me get you to the hospital."

Luiz threw himself up and back in pain, and they could see a blood vessel had burst in his left eye.

"James." Giancarlo saw it and knew it wasn't good.

"I'm not James, I'm Luiz," he screamed and took off out the door and down the stairs.

Jenny stared at Giancarlo.

Giancarlo stared at Jenny.

"Stay here," she directed to her very confused family and took off with Giancarlo into the lift. "What the bloody hell!"

"It's good to see you, Jenny." He noticed her eyes were as blue as ever. "You still look incredible."

Jenny glanced at him in confusion, and when the doors opened on the ground floor, they saw James bolt out the door.

*****

"Perp is heading across the park to 5th Avenue," Denny gasped into his radio as he ran past people out for a relaxing Sunday.

"Hey, what the hell?" Cabot woke with a start to see police officers running past and toward the family's home. "What the bloody hell is going on?" Crawling from the tree trunk, he watched that gorgeous officer from Alena's tour come bursting from the building's lobby and across the road.

"James," Giancarlo yelled from the pavement, seeing his son bolt across the road and into the park.

James saw a pack of cops running for him and saw Denny in the lead. Then he saw the perp with the gun, and his brain kicked into cop mode. "Stop, Police," he yelled.

The perp, a twenty-four-year-old African Mexican mix and common street thief called Réjon José Sanchez, saw the man in front of him hold out his hand and yell. And instead of veering away, he chose to shoot at the man, not even realising he was a cop.

James went down, flat on his back, a bullet in his left frontal lobe.

"James," Giancarlo yelled, and he and Jenny dashed across the road to find his son lying, bleeding, and potentially dead.

"Shots fired, officer down, officer down," Denny huffed into his radio, coming to a halt at the body and collapsing on his knees in exhaustion. "Officer has taken a bullet, we need paramedics to 5th Avenue next to the zoo. Officer down."

"Holy fucking shit balls!" Cabot breathed, watching the scene. People were screaming, running for their lives, running from the park in all directions. He cowered in the tree, peeking around the edge. He saw his grandmother with a man he didn't know leaning over officer gorgeous. He also saw Antonio come out of the door, with his father, Uncle Pedro and Mike. "Fuck, I'd better get out of here." Looking around, but keeping an eye on his family, he took off for his hotel, keeping out of sight. Since his brother wasn't there, it was a good time to get home for a shower and change of clothes.

"James, stay with me," Giancarlo yelled, holding a cloth to his son's head. "Stay with me." The paramedics arrived, and within two minutes had him swathed and in the ambulance. "I'm his father. I'm coming with him." Giancarlo got in beside his son and the doors closed.

The van screeched away, sirens wailing, and Jenny finally realised what was going on. She saw Officer Denny Nicolls standing near her, along with other officers. But he was staring, smiling to her right. Her head turned slowly, and she saw her family standing on the pavement outside the door. Turning back, she saw Denny still grinning. Who's he? Her ears were blocked as if she were underwater, and she couldn't register what was happening. A man came up to her and spoke, her head turned toward him, but she still didn't hear.

"Mrs Stephanopoulos, can you tell me what Officer Gardo was doing here?"

Jenny blinked, her head slowly cleared, and she heard him on his third repeat. "Visiting," she said and turned to her family. Crossing the road, among police, paramedics and onlookers, she moved into her husband's arms.

"There's that officer that was with James," Alexis told Summer and Melody. "The cute one smiling like a lovesick puppy dog."

"Ooh, he's cute," Summer said. "Maybe you should go out."

Alexis's eyes widened in alarm. "I don't think so."

"Why not?" Melody asked. "He looks okay, and he's a cop too."

"So is James, and look what just happened. Cuckoo." Alexis twirled her finger in circles at her temple.

"Mama, what just happened? Why was James saying his name was Luiz Manning?" Alena asked her parents, troubled by all she had seen.

"We don't know, sweetie. It looks as though his father doesn't even know," Angie replied. "The best thing for him now is help. If he survives." She glanced at Jenny who stood stone-like in Spiros's arms. "Maybe we should get back upstairs. Show's over." She gathered her children, collected Maggie and her kids, and moved them into the lobby. Viv motioned for Diana and Antonio to follow, and Carlos came after them. Pedro and Mike joined them, but Tomas and Roger stood frozen.

Jenny watched her family move inside and turned her head to see Tomas frowning. "He's not Luiz, Tomas."

Tomas slowly looked at her. "Isn't he, Mama? He looks exactly the same."

"Luiz is dead. Thirty years ago." Jenny left Spiros's arms to take her son by his. "Luiz is long dead. But I can understand your reaction."

"Then can you explain it to Roger, because he doesn't." Tomas fled upstairs, leaving his husband with his parents.

"I don't get it." Roger shrugged. "Why does a dead man affect him so much thirty years later?"

"Because he was Tomas's first lover, period. He had an effect on him you may not be able to understand. But who knows? Maybe this will help him resolve any leftover feelings about him." She went inside, and Roger followed.

"But thirty years, Mrs S? Hell, he even called you Mrs S as if he knew you."

"*You* were shocked when I showed the girls Luiz's photo, so why are you surprised by *his* reaction to James now?"

"I don't know." Roger shook his head. "I guess it's freaked me out too, but Jesus!"

"Tomas needs to sort it out," Jenny said.

"After thirty years you'd think he would have," Roger said.

"Yes," Jenny murmured. "You'd think he would have."

*****

Giancarlo phoned Sheila when he arrived at the hospital. He told her James had been shot and she needed to come. She calmly said she'd be there soon, replaced the phone in its cradle, and promptly burst into tears.

Not another one. Not my boy, not again. Oh, dear God.

After sobbing for what seemed like forever, she got herself together and called a cab. The trip was twenty minutes of excruciating hell, but she made it to the hospital, finding Giancarlo in emergency.

"They took him up to surgery," he said. "They think they can remove the bullet."

She almost couldn't ask. "Where from?"

Giancarlo stared at her for a long time before answering, but she already knew. "His head." She collapsed into his arms, and he led her to the fifth-floor waiting area where he told her what he knew.

Her eyes grew wide at the mere mention of the Stephanopouloses and she knew what it meant. That unless she could avoid it, she'd be coming face to face with Jenny after thirty years. "I can't lose my son, Giancarlo. Not another one," she whispered.

"Then we'd better pray," he told her. "Because he actually thinks he *is* Luiz."

After the life she had lived with her first son, and the heart-wrenching decision she made to kick him out at seventeen because of him having sex with underage boys in the neighbourhood, she had never seen him again. But since she received the money from Jenny, she had tracked down his grave, had the body exhumed, and had him cremated. She kept him in a small urn on her bedside table, but the only pictures or mementoes she had of him were from before he left home, and they were hidden away in a box in the attic. They had remained unseen for nearly forty years.

*****

After a hot shower and a quick meal, Cabot rested on the couch.

Having spent the night curled up in a tree trunk, he was a bit itchy and a bit cramped. But, he was also restless, and flicked between all of the channels three times before throwing the remote down on the couch beside him. He saw the envelope from Dan, the folder sitting on the coffee table, and the letter on top.

Do I? Do I read it? Do I open the file? No, no need to. I'm perfectly healthy and don't have HIV.

But Tony said you did, and so did Dan.

Well, what would Dan know?

He's the doctor that did the tests.

Okay, well, what would Tony know!

He's your brother, and he read the letter.

No…I don't have it…I don't… He eyed the folder. *I don't…have it…* His hand snaked out and grabbed the folder and letter and placed it on his lap and he sat perfectly still. The letter was there, clear for all to see.

Cabot,

I know right now you're in denial, but the assault last month in Mykonos has resulted in you contracting HIV. For your own health and well-being, we must get your medication regime going. You can live a full life with this, Cabot. We just need to get you educated on it.

Dan.

Nope! Don't believe it.

His eyes re-read it.

Nope, still don't believe it.

He opened the folder and looked through all of the booklets and brochures.

Nope! Still don't believe it.

Everything registered in his head. Dan, his parents, his grandparents had all drummed it into their heads for decades. He knew it all by heart, so the package contained nothing new.

Nope! Don't have it.

A booklet talked about the medication he would have to take, explaining what it did and how it worked.

Nope! Still don't have it.

He crammed the booklet back in and closed the folder. *What to Do When You Have HIV.*

Nope! Still didn't have it.

He read the letter ten times.

Nope! Still don't have it.

He replayed Dan and Derek's visit when they had told him.

Nope…still don't…

He replayed the scene from the night before with his brother.

Nope…still…

He replayed the fear in Tony's eyes, the tremble in his voice, the panic in his body language.

Nope…

He replayed Dan and Derek. Dan's facial expressions, his sorrow, his sadness, his pain. He replayed it over and over. He replayed Tony's words from the night before.

No…

It replayed itself a million times, it all replayed a million times, and left him gasping for air. He clutched his throat, panicking at not getting that air. He saw the folder fall to the floor and scrambled to pick it up. Shoving the booklets back in, he shut the folder and saw *What to Do When You Have HIV* again and again and again. He saw Dan's letter, and the words swam before his eyes.

'Cabot, I know right now you're in denial.'

Nope not in denial, just don't have it. I can't have it. I just can't. Steele Stefan does not get HIV!

'But the assault last month in Mykonos has resulted in you contracting HIV.'

Nope! Fag fucker didn't do it, he just didn't. The Stefan doesn't get AIDS.

'For your own health and well-being, we must get your medication regime going.'

Medication? I don't need medication. Just have a little STD is all, and you said it would go away with the meds you gave me.

'You can live a full life with this, Cabot. We just need to get you educated on it.'

I already do live a full life, Dan. I always have, and I'm not about to stop because you claim I have HIV. I don't have it, nope, no way, no how, nope. Don't have it. I just don't.

He remembered Dan's face when he told him. He remembered Antonio's face when he told him. Why was it, that he could remember their faces from two very specific times, and yet he could not remember any of the faces belonging to the men and women he'd fucked? Except for the gorgeous Adam Slayer. Did they mean that little? Nothing? Just bodies to plant his cock in? He'd rebelled upon learning of his father's former career, but the one thing his father didn't do was get a disease. He didn't get AIDS. Neither did Tomas and Roger, and it was all but expected of them considering they had believed they had it back in '81. If anyone in the family was going to get it, it was them.

But no, how come it had to be me? How come with all of the education, all of the lessons, all of the talking to, it was me? Alexis was assaulted, did she get it? No! I was assaulted, did I get…? Did I get it…? Did I…? I…? I…got it… Of all the people in this family, I got HIV.

The thought didn't sit well, and denial came back full bore.

Grabbing his money and keys, he left to hit the clubs.

Cabot made his way to as many clubs as possible. *Nightmare, Slash, Vixen, Party Boy, Go Stop, Dude, Angels & Demons* and more. Each was barely a half hour as he walked in, drank, danced, fucked some random guy and left for another. By 2 a.m. he was wasted, and was surprised it had taken him that long, having started way before the clubs were open.

He found himself walking aimlessly, bottle of whiskey in hand. He had nowhere to go. The clubs were boring, the men more boring. It was the same old, same old. The same clubs, the same people, the same songs he danced to. There was nothing new, nothing exciting, nothing to excite *him.*

Sex had been mechanical and all with men. He rarely fucked a woman these days, preferring his conquests to face the wall, so he didn't have to see their faces as he did his thing, and even now, he was still wearing a condom.

God knows why I'm bothering, but it's probably something to do with safe sex.

He burst out laughing, surprising the passers-by who saw the bottle in his hand.

Safe sex! What a fucking joke! For all the condoms he used, he still got HIV. For all the times he did it safely, he *still* got HIV.

H.I. Fucking. V!

He staggered to a stop and looked around. His head was splitting, confusion rained down, the noise became unbearably loud. The lights blinded him and dimmed his vision. The city became too much for him. Looking around, he found a corner store and stumbled in for some painkillers. Squinting at the boxes, he grabbed as many packets as he could, another bottle of alcohol, and some licorice sticks, raspberry, as that was the only flavour he could tolerate. Showing his ID, he paid and stumbled out of the store.

Gazing left and right, he had no idea where he was, so kept walking on his right. A block later, he came to Centre Street that led to the Brooklyn Bridge. The bright lights dazzled him, and guided him, like a beacon to their flame. He followed, dazzled, chewing distractedly on the licorice; he wandered, following the pretty lights all the way to the bridge until he was standing in the very middle. Plonking himself down, he opened the bottle of vodka and drank a quarter, not even noticing the cars speeding by.

He had HIV.

What did it matter if he drank himself to death?

What would it matter if he died from an overdose of alcohol?

Alcohol poisoning. Can you die from eating licorice as you drink? his brain wondered. *What does it matter now? I don't have to watch what I eat or drink or do. I have HIV, my life is over. I'm fucked. Fucked royally. Fucked up the ass, royally, and that fag fucker gave me the disease. The one disease Grandma and Dan warned us about getting. H.I. Fucking. V. And if I don't get onto those meds, it will turn into AIDS. A.I. Fucking D.S. AIDS. Why should I care?* He wallowed, knocking back another quarter bottle and finishing off the licorice.

My life is over. I have it. I will never model again, work again, fuck men again. My life is fucking over. What a fucking con. The day after my 25th birthday, you give me fucking HIV you fucking asshole of a God. Who the fuck do you think you are giving me fucking HIV? What the fuck have I ever done to you except use what you gave me to work with? My looks. I'm so fucking gorgeous you made me a model. You made me and Antonio Steele and Phoenix Stefan. You made us gorgeous. You gave us to two gorgeous people. You made my mother and sister models. You made my father an actor with a big dick. You gave me an even bigger dick, so what was the point if not to use it? What was the point in giving me a huge cock if I wasn't supposed to use it?

He dug around in the bag for the paracetamol as the store didn't have anything stronger, and after cracking all twenty-four from the pack, he swallowed them back with the vodka.

"Goodbye God, you fucker. You fucking shit, fucking shit fucker," he rambled, holding up the bottle. "Goodbye, you cock sucking piece of shit asshole. You filthy, lying, no good piece of pussy who never got laid. Fuck you! If this is what my life's meant to be like, then fuck you." He opened another pack of pills and swallowed them with the rest of the vodka.

Pulling out his phone, he drunkenly dialled Antonio.

"Cabot? Where are you? You didn't come to brunch."

"Toneeeee," Cabot whined. "I luv yooouuu."

"I love you too, Cabot. Are you drunk?" Antonio had been searching the streets and clubs for hours, looking for his brother, worried after realising Cabot had gone back to the hotel while he'd been with the family, and noticing the HIV folder from Dan had been disturbed. He knew Cabot had read it, and he'd gone looking for him. "Where are you?"

"I'm on a ridge." Cabot giggled.

"And you're drunk."

"An' I'm runk." More giggles as he fell sideways.

"Where are you? I'll come and get you."

"Hang on, Tonee." Cabot hauled himself to his feet and looked over the railing. "I'm on a ridge, Tonee."

"Which one?"

Cabot looked around, the sights and sounds dulled by the alcohol. "I dunno."

"What are the buildings you see?"

"Ah…" Cabot blinked to clear his vision. "Lots of really tall ones all lit up like sparklers."

"What else?"

"Ah, another ridge."

"What else, Cabot?" Antonio ticked off bridges in his head.

Cabot squinted his eyes to clear his vision and noticed a huge red sign. "Lots of cars are speeding by and ah…a huge building with a red dick," he giggled, "I mean tick."

Cars? Antonio frowned. Hadn't he taken the pedestrian path? "Is it the Brooklyn Bridge? Cabot, are you there?"

"Toneeeee, I luv you, Toneeeee." Cabot slid to the ground, leaning his head against the concrete barrier. "I luv you sho mush, Tonee, it hurts."

"Just hang on, Cabot, I'm coming for you." Antonio wasn't that far away and he bolted down the road for the bridge. "What part are you, Cabot?" he huffed. "Near the end or in the middle."

"Middle." More giggles. "Rhymes with piddle." Laughter burst out of him, but he ended up in tears. "I'm dying, Tonee. I'm dying."

"No, you're not, Cabot. Listen to me. Get up and start walking back to the Manhattan side of the bridge and I'll meet you there. I'm nearly there." He turned onto the street that led to the bridge. "Tell me where you are, Cabot."

"Toneeeee," he cried. "I'm dying. I have HIV. I have no life anymore." He folded into himself and lay in a ball.

"Yes, you do, Cabot." Antonio headed for the bridge and ran. Thank God for all the years Tomas and Roger had trained them and kept them on a healthy diet. "You have plenty to live for. Me, for one."

"But I have AIDS, Toneeeee," Cabot whimpered. "I hate it. I hate it, Tonee. I hate having AIDS, so I'm ending it all. I have nothing to live for, Tonee."

"Don't say that, Cabot." Antonio was a quarter way across and desperately looking for his brother.

"I have nothing to live for anymore, Tonee." Cabot picked himself up. "Goodbye, Tonee, I luv you. You will be better off without me." Dropping the phone, he climbed up to hang over the railing.

"Cabot," Antonio screamed into his phone. "Cabot." Checking the phone, he saw the disconnected signal and ran pell-mell, seeing his brother standing at the railing. "Cabot," he screamed. "Cabot, don't."

Cabot, hearing his brother's voice, swung his head around. "Toneeeee," he wailed, "Don't come near me, Tonee. I'm poison. I'm diseased. I'll kill you."

Antonio came to a halt a few feet away from his brother. "Cabot, what are you doing?"

"I'm killing myself, Toneeeee." He swayed and clung to the railing. "I have nothing to live for anymore. I'm death."

"Don't be silly." Antonio put his hand out. "Come to me, Cabot. Let's do this together. We'll go and see Dan together and get you started on your meds. Come with me, Cabot. Give me your hand, come on."

"No, Tonee, stay back." Cabot swung an arm wildly. "Stay away from me, I'll give you AIDS. It's over, Tonee, it's over. *I'm* over, *my life* is over. No one will want to have Steele Stefan now. No one will want me, Tonee. No one." He burst into tears. "No one will want me, Tonee."

"Oh, Cabot." Antonio stepped closer. "I want you. You're my brother. I love you, our parents love you, Diana loves you, our whole family loves you. You just need to love yourself, Cabot. Let me take you home."

"No." Cabot stumbled away, but fell to the ground, knocking over his food bag, making the contents scatter across the path.

"Cabot, have you taken painkillers with alcohol?" Antonio frowned at the empty boxes. "Have you tried to OD, Cabot?" Fear rose in his chest and spread to his throat. Dialling 911, he called for an ambulance. "I need help on Brooklyn Bridge. My brother has overdosed on paracetamol and alcohol." He heard glass smash. "Cabot, no," he yelled, seeing his brother rake the broken bottle across his wrist. Blood spurted. "Cabot, oh, my God. I need help now." He launched himself at Cabot, but didn't manage to stop him from slashing his other wrist. They landed on the ground. "What are you doing?" he screamed, ripping up Cabot's shirt to tie around his wrists.

"Let me die, Toneeeee," Cabot wailed, flattened by his brother. "I have AIDS, let me die." His eyes were overflowing with tears, his head overflowing with fears. His stomach was full of alcohol and paracetamol, and his wrists full of glass shards. "Let me die." Sobs racked him as Antonio wrapped his wrists a second time.

"Why would you do this, Cabot?" Antonio didn't care if he got HIV, he just wanted to help his brother, and lying on top of him, he soothed the child below. "It's okay, Cabot." He stroked his brother's face as he cried. "It's okay. I'll take care of you."

Sirens wailed in the distance, but it was no match for the animalistic howls from Cabot.

"I'm dying, Toneeeee. I'm dying. My life is over."

"No, you're not. You're not dying. It's okay. Shhh. Your life isn't over, Cabot, it's okay, your life isn't over."

"Let me die, Tonee." Cabot felt no pain, hadn't when he slashed that broken bottle across his left wrist. Hadn't when he slashed the bottle over his right. But his heart was a different matter. It was dying along with him. His life was over, his partnership with his brother was over. His work, his career, his personal life, his sex life, his family life. It was all over. All over because of one fag fucker who thought it was funny to give HIV to men.

"Tonee." His voice was quiet over the blaring siren as it pulled up alongside them. "I luv you, Tonee." His eyes glazed over as he stared up into the warm September night.

"Cabot, stay with me, Cabot." Antonio shook his brother. "Cabot, stay with me, you bastard, stay with me."

"Sir; let us help." The paramedics pulled him away.

"He has HIV," came out of Antonio's mouth, but sounded dull and low in his ears. "He just recently found out. Got it from an assault…" He let himself be pulled back and stood watching as the two men took his brother's vitals. More lights, more people. Looking up, Antonio saw police running around and waving traffic on. His eyes went back to Cabot who was being put on a stretcher. "I'm coming." The words flew out of his mouth, distorted and mechanical sounding.

They nodded and rolled Cabot into the back of the ambulance.

Antonio followed in slow motion. That's what it was. Everything was in slow motion. Getting into the back of the van, he told the officers to get him to Mount Sinai where Dan and Derek worked part-time. The officer put in a call to the hospital to contact the doctors to meet them there. The doors slammed shut and off they went.

Clearing the bridge into the city, they veered off and made their way to the hospital, arriving at the emergency department fifteen minutes later to Dan and Derek who quickly took in Cabot's condition.

"I need charcoal and a bucket, plus I'll need to examine his wrists. Blood pressure, and x-rays just in case," Dan directed and helped roll him into an exam room. "When did he do this?"

"About half hour ago," Antonio mumbled from beside the door.

"But I take it he's been drinking all night?" Dan said.

"More than likely," Antonio told him, arms crossed, leaning against the wall and staring at the forlorn figure of his brother.

"Was he trying to kill himself?" Derek asked, getting the tube ready for insertion.

"Probably."

Dan and Derek glanced at Antonio. "Well then, let's stop him."

Dan shoved the tube down his throat and administered the charcoal, rolling him onto his side. They checked for vitals and hooked him up to the machines. The charcoal worked quickly, but there wasn't much vomit except alcohol. The paracetamol had already been dissolved into his system, so Dan gave him an injection to counteract it. Once he was done vomiting, they closely looked over his wrists.

"Artificial, not deep, nothing major cut." Dan peered through the microscope headwear he had on. "We'll get a specialist to check just in case, but he's got some glass that will need to be removed." He turned to the nurse. "Can you page Dr Varden for me, please."

"Yes, doctor." She left to call the specialist.

"In the meantime, we'll wash the wounds ourselves and get them ready for inspection." Fifteen minutes later, the wounds were washed when Dr Varden walked in. After a close inspection, he declared no need for surgery and Dan patched Cabot up. Derek wrapped each wrist afterwards, and they settled Cabot into his own section in ICU.

Antonio stood back. Watching. Breathing. Never taking his eyes off his brother. He felt the pain. Not just in his heart, but deep in his gut. It was partly his fault. He should have tried harder to stop Cabot from doing what he did. Fucking anything that moved. If he had, Cabot wouldn't have been at the club getting drunk. Wouldn't have been at that club dancing with that guy. Wouldn't have been at that club fucking in the alley. So…he wouldn't have been in that alley getting assaulted at knifepoint and now, here they both were in the hospital; Cabot unconscious from an attempted suicide bid, and he, Antonio, standing at the end of his bed watching over him. Other than that, he had no idea what to do.

"I don't see any point in calling your grandmother now." Dan stood in front of Antonio. "It's the middle of the night. He'll be here until he wakes up and is deemed fit and almost healthy. I'm ordering HAART for him. We can get him started on it when he wakes up and is alcohol and paracetamol free." He glanced from Antonio to Cabot. "And we'll have a good talk to him with an AIDS counsellor."

Antonio finally moved his head to look at Dan and heaved a sigh. "This will kill him. Kill my family."

Dan smiled softly. "Your grandmother doesn't die. She's been through this before and didn't let it stop her. Your mother, on the other hand, may end up on one big guilt trip."

Antonio rubbed his weary eyes. "Can we not tell anyone yet? Too many people may freak him out."

"I'll call your grandmother in the morning." Dan gripped Antonio by the shoulder. "She'll take charge and make everything okay. Don't you worry."

"Does this mean I go home and pack our bags?" Derek asked from the doorway.

Dan gave him an apologetic smile. "Do you mind? I'm not sure how long we'll be gone, unless you want to stay."

"Considering Jenny pays our wages, we go where we're needed. I'm going home; are you staying?" Derek asked his husband.

Dan glanced at Antonio and Cabot. "Yeah, I'll stay."

Derek nodded and kissed his cheek. "Figured you would. I'll see you later."

Dan watched him go and grabbed a chair for Antonio to sit on. "Here, take a seat. It will be a long night." After Antonio sat, he checked Cabot's notes and went into the hallway to keep a close eye, but to also have a break. What the fuck was he going to tell Jenny when he called?

Antonio sighed, deeply. Cabot was not just his brother, but his *twin* brother. He gazed at his peaceful face. His own face. A mirror image of each other. They were twins. The only difference was their eye colour, and whatever colour Cabot's hair was that month. Most people couldn't tell them apart, but family knew. Knew by their eyes. He remembered one time they had different coloured eye contacts in and had switched to fool everyone. And they had. Except for Grandma who knew her grandbabies better than their parents did. She knew which one was which. No, you couldn't fool Grandma.

He reached out and laid his hand over Cabot's. Everything else about them was the same. Their height, shoe size, cock size, hand size. Everything was the same. He squeezed gently and his face crumpled. As tears rolled down his cheeks, he relived every moment of their lives, from growing in their mother's womb for nine months, to sharing a crib, a pram, a party every year, a room, a classroom, modelling assignments, apartments, school projects, and girlfriends, when Cabot had been interested in girls. But that hadn't happened in a long time. No, they hadn't shared women in a very long time. He didn't have a problem with his brother preferring men, but he did have a problem with how rampant he'd become. It could all be blamed on watching their father's videos. But there had to be something else. Something else making him the way he was. What was he after? What he searching for? Why did he seem so desperately needy for sex? Not that all of that mattered anymore. Cabot's HIV status would need to come first. His medical and health regime would now take top priority. Nothing else would. Nothing else would matter. Ever. Cabot would need to take care of himself and change his priorities, and that's all there was to it.

Exhausted from searching all over New York for his brother, he sat back to find Dan handing him a bottle of chilled water, a cup of tea, and a couple of containers of sandwiches. "Oh, God, I need these, thank you." He set the tea on the roller table and sculled back the water. "Ah, thirsty. So good." He opened the first sandwich and shovelled half into his mouth.

"I thought you could do with it," Dan said softly. "When was the last time you ate?"

"Lunch at Grandma's. Hey, did you hear the news?" When Dan shook his head, Antonio went on to tell him all he knew about James Gardo getting shot in the head, and then the news afterwards as the family talked about it. "But us kids were kept out of it. Apparently, this Luiz Manning guy was Uncle Tomas's first lover and did some pretty weirdo shit. But we couldn't hear much, they were whispering madly in the kitchen while we were all in the lounge room. Do you know who this guy is?"

"Luiz Manning, or James Gardo?" Dan asked.

"Both."

Dan sighed. "Luiz Manning, I never met, but he *was* your uncle's first lover back in 1977. We thought he was the one who gave Tomas AIDS until we realised your uncle didn't have AIDS. As for James Gardo, wasn't he the officer you met on Alena's tour?"

"Yeah, yeah, he was." Antonio thought back. "But he was calling himself Luiz Manning, so we're all confused."

"Well, Luiz was before your time. What does your grandmother think?"

"Grandma thinks he was reincarnated just as he does."

"Mmm," Dan murmured. "Jenny does believe in that stuff. How did she handle it?"

"Alena and Diana said she took charge of everything when they were all panicking. Grandma kept him calm until his father turned up."

"His father?"

"Giancarlo Gardo, ex-cop detective or something. He had papers that were his old files. He found them in James's apartment. He'd stolen them from the precinct, I think Diana said."

"Wow." Dan raised a brow. "So…he tries to kill Roger at Alena's last concert, runs away, takes time off work while everyone's trying to find him, including Jenny, then suddenly turns up on Jenny's doorstep freaking Tomas out. And he's managed to steal police paperwork. Some cop." While sickened at the murder attempt, Dan was impressed.

"Yeah," Antonio said, and picked up the cup of tea. Sipping it, he thought about everything it meant. "James is in hospital fighting for his life with a bullet in his brain, and here is Cabot fighting for his life after trying to kill himself. We're quite a family, aren't we?"

Five doors away, James Gardo was on a ventilator. His surgery had taken sixteen hours of delicate manoeuvring to remove the bullet without doing permanent damage to his brain. But what stunned doctors was, when they removed the bullet, they found the remnants of an aneurysm. Shocked, they examined his brain, sucked out the leftovers, and put him back together. The ventilation was to help him breathe while in the induced coma the doctors put him under. With major swelling, he needed complete rest while he healed.

Giancarlo and Sheila sat by their son's side, praying, not that either one had been overly religious. But since James was Giancarlo's only son, and Sheila's second, they felt it necessary to call on all gods to help their son. Both of them were so fixated on praying for James to return to them, that neither knew Cabot and Antonio were down the hall in another room.

*****

On Monday morning, the family gathered in the penthouse, still talking about James, but also talking about Cabot and Antonio.

"Cabot's probably drunk somewhere," Pedro said. "You know what he's like. Gets drunk, sleeps all day. His hotel is down the road if you want to go see him, Viv."

Viv paced back and forth. "I know something is wrong. I can't explain it, but I feel it in here." Her closed fist went to just under her ribcage. "I don't know what it is, but I feel it."

Jenny was standing at the windows staring thoughtfully over the park.

The police tape was still intact, there was a huge bloodstain, and she saw a cop car pull up. Two officers got out and walked around the scene.

"Grandma." Alena stood by her grandmother's side looking down at the path across the street. "Why did James call himself Luiz? And who is Luiz?"

Jenny sighed. The secrets they had held back from the kids for thirty years were all coming out, and it wasn't pretty. "Luiz Manning was your Uncle Tomas's first lover. He was shot dead back in 1977. As for James calling himself Luiz, I have no idea why he would do that. Maybe he's sick, sweetie. Bipolar, schizophrenia, split personality, who knows? From what I could gather, he'd stolen his father's paperwork from thirty years ago, so maybe he was sick and thought he was Luiz. I don't know. I can't explain it."

"But you can always explain everything." Alena rested her head on Jenny's shoulder, making her grandmother smile.

Putting her arms around her, Jenny hugged her granddaughter. "And right now, I can't."

"What do *you* think, Tomas?" Carlos asked his brother, noticing the cold body language between him and Roger. They hadn't spoken since they'd arrived, and Carlos could only guess that their fight had continued into the night.

"Of what, Carlos?" Tomas looked questioningly at his older brother, seeing his eyes flit back and forth from him to Roger.

"James Gardo." Carlos eyed him carefully.

"I think he is a very unfortunate man to have been made to look like another human being so closely. A murderer no less. He stole his father's paperwork, so he'd know what Luiz did. But to then claim to *be* Luiz and scare the bejesus out of all of us was sick, to say the least."

"Particularly you," Pedro cut in, worried for his brother and his relationship.

Tomas sighed and stared down at his entwined fingers. "Particularly me. It was absolutely terrifying. I have no idea what's going on in his head, but that *was not* funny. What he did was scary and brought back very bad memories."

"Yeah," Pedro murmured. "Carlos and I can't even begin to

imagine what you went through. We were all kidnapped, but you were poisoned, stalked by him, Roger was framed for the murder of four co-workers, but then he kidnapped you from the hospital on top of that. And then four years later, you believed he had given you the gay plague." He shook his head. "I can't even begin to understand how you feel or what you're going through."

"Well, neither can Roger." Tomas sharply looked away, hearing an intake of breath beside him from Roger, seeing the kids watching them curiously from the lounge room. They were all there except for Cabot and Antonio.

"What do you think's going on?" Nick whispered to Danté. They sat on the couch peering over at everyone.

"No idea. But I'd love to find out." Danté was trying to read their lips.

"Maybe we *should* find out," Alexis said softly from between Summer and Melody on their own couch.

"How do we do that?" Diana asked, curious about James Gardo and his story.

"The library," Dom said quietly from beside her. "They have newspaper archives. We might be able to find something."

Alena came over and heard her brother's idea. "That sounds good. Let's go now and then I can ring the hospital and find out how he is. Come on." She turned. "We're going out. After yesterday, we need some fresh air, and we want to be a bit nosey across the road." She grinned. "If we see Cabot or Antonio, we'll tell them to call. And yes, we'll get our phones, so we can call." With a wave, all eight of them left.

Jenny watched the door close behind them. "They're up to something."

"Do you always have to be so suspicious, Mama?" Carlos asked.

"Do you always have to be so blind to what's going on with the children?" Jenny shot back, getting a frown in return. Seeing his annoyed expression, she sighed and turned back to the window. "I didn't mean anything by it."

"No, Mama." Carlos sat up in his seat. "You did, so spit it out." He wasn't the only one waiting for her to speak. They all watched as she stood staring out of the window.

"We knew they would find out," she murmured. "We thought we

had hidden it so well. The videos, the paperwork, it's not on the internet, so we didn't have to worry. But here it is, all coming out thirty years on." Another sigh. "We thought we were being so careful in keeping your pasts from the children."

Carlos stared down at his feet. "Yeah, we did." Running both hands through his hair, he rested his elbows on his knees.

"The children are up to something. They rarely go out in a group. In fact, I don't know the last time they went out in a group on their own." She watched as they crossed the road and stood at the police tape, looking at the bloodstain. "They seem very fixated on James Gardo. They're looking at the crime scene now." She watched as they circled the tape, looking from different angles. "They've become very curious about your pasts. They're asking questions. Who is Luiz? What did he do? What is he to James? Who was the man who kidnapped Uncle Tomas and killed Luiz? That all comes back to Stefano Papadopoulos. Are you ready to tell the kids the whole story of that?"

Carlos glanced at Pedro and Tomas who traded looks. "Not really."

Jenny saw Alena glance up at the penthouse and quickly usher the others on.

Where are they going? Jenny watched until she couldn't see them anymore, and turned and paced instead, thinking as she went. Thirty years ago Stefano had kidnapped her sons with the intent to kill them for the family fortune, but his ex-father-in-law, Spiros's grandfather, had shot him dead. Meanwhile, Carlos had to deal with a girlfriend being raped and killed, and his friend Aneeka being kidnapped for taking photos of the murderers. Pedro had to deal with Barbara Weston, Andros Poulos and Nedro Scarvo. And Tomas had to deal with Luiz on top of everything else that was going on, like four dead porn star co-workers and a poisoning. "Are *you* ready to tell them? They could be on their way to find out. James did. I vaguely heard the word library, so for all we know, they're heading off to find out for themselves."

"Personally, I don't want to tell them," Angie said. "It's none of their business."

"And I thought that way until James Gardo came into this home,"

Jenny said. "Did you not recognise him when you met him, Angie?"

"No." She was curled up next to Pedro on the couch. "I kept thinking I'd seen eyes like that before, but for the life of me, I couldn't remember where. But I don't know what Luiz looked like."

"Yes, you do. I brought home photos of Luiz in 1980. I got them from Bertha, and you all saw them. He was your brother; you wanted to see him," Tomas reminded her.

A frown crossed Angie's forehead as she thought. "That was so long ago, I don't remember it. And I certainly don't remember him."

Jenny wandered over to the safe in the kitchen and withdrew the photos of Luiz with Bertha, both with Bette and Willow, and Luiz on his own. She walked slowly back to the others and held the one of Luiz up. "Remember now?"

Everyone looked, and murmurs flew around the group.

"Jesus, that's Luiz?" Angie sat forward. "I think I remember now. I said he had Daddy's hair, but the eyes weren't ours."

"Sheila has blue eyes." Jenny glanced at the photo. "He would have gotten them from her."

"So, where did James get them from?" Tomas asked, unable to look at the photo.

"Giancarlo, he has blue eyes." Jenny studied the picture. "He looks exactly the same. It's not only uncanny, it's downright freaky."

"Add poisoning, murder, stalking and kidnapping, and now you know how I feel," Tomas said, staring out the window.

Jenny rested a hand on his shoulder. "Yes, you did go through more than the rest of us. Definitely went through more than your brothers." She sat on the arm next to him. "How in God's name does he look so damn identical?"

*****

The kids headed down 5th Avenue to the Public Library in the Stephen A. Schwarzman Building, and found their way to the manuscripts and archive division where they spoke to an archivist and were lucky enough to use the computers and troll through the card catalogue.

"Got something," Alena yelled, then quickly looked around, guilty for yelling out. They crowded around. "It's Daddy and Mama, and a car wreck. *Studio 69 resident DJ, Pedro Stefan, resident porn star, survived an attempted murder tonight by a young woman, who sources have told us, was stalking Mr Stefan's girlfriend, Angelina Poulos. New York post dug up assault charges on Mr Poulos, laid by his daughter only weeks beforehand, they came before Mr Stefan's first car crash in the city. Mr Stefan was taken at gunpoint from the second crash scene. Word is, his brothers Carlo Stefan and Tomas Stefan were also kidnapped from Hollywood and Miami respectively, and all are the subject of an ongoing case.*"

"Whoa." They all stood back.

"Daddy was kidnapped?" Diana was in shock.

"So was daddy and Uncle Tomas," Alena said.

"And Mama was assaulted by her father, *our* grandfather," Alexis said. "Bloody shit balls!"

Danté tapped a few keys and printed out the story. "Keep looking."

They went back to searching and found mentions of Tomas and Carlos, a few short stories about 69, plus the passing of Tomas and Roger.

"Can we get papers from anywhere else?" Diana asked Danté since he was the resident computer expert along with Nick.

"I can check for a nationwide archive," he said, and he and Nick got to work digging up newspaper articles on Carlos and the murder of Rosalee Brentworth and the kidnapping of Aneeka Ne Masta. "Whoa! Hey, isn't that the photographer we had the other day at that photo shoot?"

Once again they gathered round.

"That's her," Alexis said. "*Aneeka Ne Masta was kidnapped in conjunction with a next door rape and murder involving porn star Carlo Stefan.*"

"Oh, my God, Daddy didn't do those things," Diana wailed softly.

"It doesn't say that. The woman was his girlfriend, and Ms Ne Masta took photographs of the intruders, leading to her being kidnapped," Danté told her, reading the article. "*The kidnappers took her and Mr*

Stefan, but Ms Ne Masta got away outside of Las Vegas while Mr Stefan got away in Chicago where the second of the kidnappers were shot dead. No word on why Mr Stefan was kidnapped."

"Bloody *great big* shit balls!" Alexis exclaimed, grabbing the papers from the printer and adding them to the pile.

"Hey, here's Uncle Tomas," Danté called, reading the article. "It's pretty much the same except for whoa, *'his ex-lover Luiz Manning was found shot dead in the hotel room he'd absconded to with Mr Stefan. Manning, who once worked for Seralift Productions, a gay porn film studio, killed off four Seralift employees to frame current employee and Stefan's new lover, Roger Dencott. He also poisoned Mr Stefan after stalking him and breaking into his and Dencott's apartment. Dencott was released on no charges. Stefan was kidnapped from the hotel by another man and taken to Chicago, where he was found by Detective Jeremiah Barden. Barden told the Miami Star the FBI had taken over the case in Chicago. It seems there's an international flavour to this case, and it involves kidnapping, murder, and money. The Star has no more reports on the case to date, but will continue searching'."*

"Whoa! Poison, murder, kidnapping. Luiz Manning got up to a lot," Dom said. He peered at the computer screen over his brother's shoulder. "No wonder James Gardo freaked the crap out of him. He must look exactly the same."

Danté went searching for photos of Luiz. "Can't find any pictures of him. Obviously, no one had any."

"Check out James," Alena urged, and watched as photo after photo of James came up with news articles on commendations, drug busts, and capturing crims, and it was all down to James. "That's him, so, he looks *exactly* like Luiz?" She shook her head. "Is that even possible?"

"Here's a picture of him with his parents, Giancarlo and Sheila Gardo." Danté stared at it as it printed. "He doesn't really look like either of them."

"Has his father's height," Summer said. "And build. What did his father look like in his younger days?"

"Grandma would know," Alena said. "Mama said they knew him

back in the late '70s early '80s. Are there any more pictures of him?"

Danté scoured for Giancarlo and came across a few. One was for the kidnapping and murder in '77, one was for a commendation for a drug bust in '76, and the other had him at a crime scene in '75.

"Well, I guess James could have his looks. He has the build and height as Summer said," Alexis told everyone and gathered the printouts. "Any more?"

Another half hour search revealed nothing except for a few articles about Andros Poulos, the Seralifts, the DeVilles, and Greta Von Burro. All three porn studios were left reeling with AIDS deaths, but *DeVille* was still going. Greta had retired ten years earlier, and the Seralifts shut down in the '80s and died a few years back, along with the DeVilles.

"So, *they* were our fathers' bosses," Dom murmured, reading an article on Greta Von Burro.

"Do you think we could find their movies if we went looking?" Alena suggested. "Are there any porn shops around that sell old porn movies?"

"We could check out the phone book," Danté suggested. "I saw some upstairs."

After gathering their things, they went upstairs and raided the directories for porn stores and video shops. Armed with a list, they left and grabbed a couple of cabs, leaving the meters running while they ran inside each one. After ten, they finally hit the jackpot.

"Do you have any movies that feature a Carlo Stefan, a Pedro Stefan, a Tomas Stefan, or a Roger Dencott?" Alena said sweetly, smiling at the clerk. "We don't know the titles, I'm afraid." She stood with Diana and Dom since the others weren't old enough to be inside.

The clerk checked the computer. "You're in luck. We have one."

"Only one?" Diana was crestfallen.

"Yes, ma'am. It says here the movies went out of production in the early '80s and there are no more copies. So, whatever there is, it's as rare as hen's teeth. It's a display only copy and is on the back wall with the poster."

"May we look at it?" Alena asked.

"Of course." The clerk blushed. "It's through the door there to your right and on the back wall."

"Thank you so much." Alena smiled, and they moved through the door and over to the back wall. "What are we looking for?"

"That." Dom pointed, and the girls followed his finger to see a huge movie poster on the wall above them, showing Carlos reclining on a couch, Pedro playing with a harp, and Tomas flexing his pecs.

"*The Greek Gods,*" Alena murmured. "*The ancient times never looked so good.* That's the line they went with from the movie?"

"Looks like." Dom stared at the poster. "Anyone got a camera?"

"No," Alena said. "Didn't think to bring one."

"I have one on my iPhone, but I don't know if we can print it off," Diana said.

"Go see if Danté's got one," Alena suggested. "He's usually got something."

Dom left the store. "You got a camera? We need it," he said to his brother.

"A please or thank you would be nice." Nick scowled as Danté slid his backpack off his shoulder and set it on the ground, and got a raised brow in return from Dom.

Danté dug around and pulled out his brand-new camera. "Be careful, I only just got it for my birthday."

"Yeah, yeah, whatever." Dom snatched it and went back in the store.

Alexis sighed. They were all waiting outside since they weren't allowed in. "He's such a pig to you, Danté. Just like Alena used to be with me."

Danté shrugged a shoulder, trying not to let it hurt him, but he also knew Alexis could see right through it.

Dom walked into the room and started snapping pics of the poster and old VHS videotape box.

"I can't believe that's them," Diana said, staring at the poster. She was still coming to terms with her father being in porn movies.

"Ah, I've printed out a list of movies for you," the clerk said as they passed by. "We don't have any of them, but it's a list of the movies the Stefan brothers were in, plus there's a list of Roger Dencott's movies.

Plus all of the movies Carlo Stefan wrote, directed, or produced."

"Goodness." Alena took the papers and stared at the thick pile. Thanking him, she followed Dom out the door with Diana behind her.

"Here." Dom threw the camera at Danté who wasn't even watching, and it smashed onto the ground at Danté's feet, pieces scattering in all directions.

It left everyone speechless, especially Danté.

But Alena soon found her voice. "What the fuck did you just do that for, Dominic Spiros Stephanopoulos? That's an expensive camera that the family gave him for his birthday." The blood boiled in her veins as she watched the others help Danté pick up the pieces of the five-hundred-dollar camera.

Dom, surprised at the tirade, shrugged. "I didn't do it on purpose."

"Bullshit!" Alexis spat from the ground. "You didn't care that you were throwing it."

Dom burned inside. "He should have been looking."

"Don't you *dare* blame Danté, he's just fourteen." Alena slapped Dom clear across the face, surprising everyone, especially Dom. "You're just like I used to be, selfish, self-centred and arrogant. But I grew up because my sister was more important to me than some bullshit jealousy. Whatever you've got going on, you need to grow up. Just you wait until Mama and Daddy hear about this. And Grandma won't be too happy either." She turned from a shocked Dom to a tearful Danté.

He was trying to keep it in, but he loved that camera so much and had taken some awesome shots with it. Now it lay in pieces in a small bag he carried.

"Come on, Danté. We'll go and see if it can be repaired. If not, I'll get you a new one and make *Dom* pay for it." She glanced over her shoulder at her brother. *"And he will pay for it."*

"While you do that, I'm going home," Diana said. "My feet are killing me, and I really don't feel good."

"Still recovering from food poisoning?" Alena turned her attention briefly to her cousin.

"Guess it took more out of me than I realised. Plus, I have some things to do, so I'll see you all later." Diana flagged down a cab and left.

Dom, unsure of what to do, scowled and stormed off down the road.

"I *cannot* believe he did that!" Alena exclaimed. "I was right behind him, and he just didn't care whatsoever."

Danté wiped his face. "It's Dom. He never liked me."

"Well, I didn't like Alexis for nineteen years until something bad happened and it made me grow up. Now look, we get on like a house on fire. All Dom needs to do is grow up. Meanwhile, let's find a camera store."

They found one a few blocks away, but after an examination, were told the camera was deceased and needed a burial. Danté giggled, but managed to score another one for half price, so Alena suggested getting a whole bunch of extras that he didn't have. While he was doing that, she looked around the store and saw a sign for instant digital photos.

"Excuse me." She pointed to the sign. "Do you do photos from those thingy cards in cameras?"

"SD cards," Danté informed her.

"Yeah, those." Alena's face was still blank.

"Yes, ma'am," the assistant said, flirting with Alena. "It will just take a few minutes. Do you have your card with you?" He flashed his pearly whites.

"I do." Danté dug it out from his smashed camera. "What photos are you after?" he asked Alena.

"The photo of the poster in the store," Alena said and watched the clerk slide the card into a machine and little thumbnails of all the pictures on the card popped up on the screen. "They should be the last photos taken."

"And there we are," the clerk said, wondering why they had taken a picture of a poster.

Alena peered closely. "Can we have that one, please."

"Of course." The clerk clicked a button, and two minutes later, they had the photo in their hand.

"Whoa." Alexis looked over her sister's shoulder. "Is that one of their movies?"

"Yep, all of them with Roger," Alena said. "But the clerk gave us a really long list of movies they were in, so we can track them down."

"Aren't they in Uncle Carlos's vault?" Danté said. "Didn't Cabot say that?"

"Yeah, he did." Alena handed over her credit card to pay for their purchases, and they left. "I'd like to go and see James, but it's so long after lunch I'm starving. Anyone else hungry? My treat."

They lunched at a local bar and grill before leaving for home, and after dropping their things off, they headed upstairs to the penthouse.

"Dom back yet? He owes me five hundred and twelve dollars," Alena said as they came through the door.

"What does he owe you that for?" Pedro asked from where he was lazing on the couch.

"A replacement of Danté's camera that he smashed," Alena told them. "I booked it up on credit."

"He what!" everyone exclaimed.

"How the hell did he do that?" Pedro sat up, alert to trouble amongst his children.

"He borrowed Danté's camera, and instead of *handing* it back to him he *threw* it, and Danté wasn't even watching, so it smashed. I slapped him when he said it wasn't his fault. He tried to blame Danté for not looking."

Pedro saw his youngest tear up and knew what a jerk Dom could be. He went to his son and hugged him, feeling his body jerk with silent sobs. "Let's go downstairs and have a chat about your brother, hey." He looked into his son's brown eyes, an identical match to Angie's, and led him down to their apartment and sat him on the couch. "Dominic, you here?" Getting no reply, he quickly searched the second bedroom, but didn't find him. Sitting beside Danté, he gently put his hand on his cheek. "I'm so sorry your brother's a selfish asshole like Alena used to be."

Danté's brows rose. He'd never heard his parents use that name to describe their kids.

"Yeah, I know." Pedro grinned. "I shouldn't call him that, but when it comes to you, he is. And I don't know what to do about it. He's like Cabot. Off the rails, but not so bad, and I know what it's like to be the youngest in the family. I got ignored by Carlos too."

"But you had Uncle Tomas."

"Yeah, I did." Pedro nodded. "And I'm glad I did, because at least I had a brother who loved me and thought about me and not just himself. But your Uncle Carlos came good by the time we were older, and we became close again."

"Dom and I won't be close," Danté said. "He doesn't care."

"No, no, I think Dom only cares about himself, and that's not good." Pedro pulled his son close. "But we're going to fix that."

Upstairs, Jenny was talking to her granddaughters. "So, what did you kids get up to today? I think I heard the word library mentioned."

Alena and Alexis exchanged guilt-ridden looks, and Summer and Melody left them to it by side-stepping over to the lounge to watch TV.

"Well, we went for a walk, Grandma," Alena said. "And took some pictures; that's how Dom smashed Danté's camera. Then we went shopping for a new camera, had a late lunch, and came home. Have you seen Diana? She left early, said her feet hurt and she didn't feel well."

"Still!" Viv said. "I would have thought the food poisoning was long over."

"That's what I said, Aunt Viv." Alena sat on the couch arm. "Maybe her body's still getting its energy back."

"Maybe," Viv murmured. "But she didn't come here, so maybe she's in her room."

"What did you do at the library?" Jenny pushed.

"Looked at some books, Grandma." Alena glanced at her sister.

"And went through the archives for newspaper articles like James Gardo did?"

The girls looked up in shock. "Grandma…how'd you—"

"I know my grandchildren. Because they're *exactly* like their parents," Jenny said, casting a glance at Carlos. "Where are they?"

"Where are what?" Alena feigned ignorance.

"The printouts?" Jenny demanded.

Looking down, Alena gave in. "In Danté's backpack."

"And what did you find?"

"Um," Alena traded glances with Alexis. "A bunch of articles on Daddy at 69, his stalker, his kidnapping and um," she looked at her mother, "an article on Mama being assaulted by *her* daddy and him getting killed by some woman who stalked *our* daddy."

"Jesus." Angie frowned. "I hadn't thought about that in years."

Jenny grabbed the phone and dialled apartment 1.

"Mama?"

"Danté has a bunch of printouts in his bag, get them all and bring them up."

"Okay." Pedro looked at Danté. "What did you print out today?"

Danté reddened and glanced away. "Nothing."

"Grandma knows. She wants them," Pedro told him. "They're in your bag."

Signing, Danté grabbed his backpack from beside his feet and pulled out the papers.

"Jesus Christ, where did you find that?" Pedro saw the photo of the Greek Gods poster, and it immediately took him back thirty years.

Danté shrugged. "Some porn shop. I wasn't allowed in."

"Come on, Squirt, let's go upstairs." Pedro took him back up and handed over the papers.

"Oh, look at this." Jenny handed the poster photo to Carlos. "One of your posters."

"Wow, I haven't seen this since I packed it in the vault." Carlos stared at the picture, remembering back to making it. "God, that was a great movie."

Tomas snorted. "For you, maybe. You wrote it, directed it, produced it—"

"And made us a motza," Carlos reminded him.

"And here's a list of movie titles. I can only assume all of them are yours," Jenny said. "Oh, my God, am I seeing right? *The Vagina Diviner?* Oh, good grief, Carlos." She handed the list to him. "Seriously? Is that what you called yourself?"

Blushing at the raucous laughter going around the adults, Carlos flicked through the papers. "Yep, those are mine. And yes, Mama, that was a movie name. Took it from the water diviners back home in Aus. Figured if it rhymed…why not."

"What's a water diviner?" Alena whispered to Alexis, Danté and

Nick, and got shrugs in return.

"What's a vagina?" Danté whispered back.

Redness crept over Alexis's face, and Alena stifled a giggle. "Part of a girl's anatomy," Alena whispered. "One you'll know about when you start having sex."

A look of horror swept over Danté and Nick, and their faces screwed up at the mere mention of a girl's privates.

"Newspaper articles on Pedro and 69." Jenny handed them to Pedro. "His stalker, Andros Poulos," she gave those to Angie, "the DeVilles, Seralifts, and Von Burro, Tomas and Roger..." She smiled sadly at the front page obit from 1981 before giving it to her son.

Tomas looked at it sadly. "We made the paper."

"Yeah, T, we did," Roger replied softly, laying his hand on his husband's arm. He got a cold shoulder instead as Tomas shifted away.

"We have articles on the kidnappings, Luiz and the poisoning, stalking, kidnapping, and so much more." She handed those to Tomas. "No wonder he thought he was Luiz. What, no photos?" She looked at the girls.

They had been watching curiously, with Danté and Nick, wondering why their parents weren't concerned with everything they had found. The girls shrugged. "We couldn't find any."

Jenny went back to the pile. "And we have Leon's death, Eddie's death, the end of 69," she handed them to Mike, "and ooh, we have Giancarlo from '75. He *was* handsome."

"Hey," Spiros protested, a twinkle in his eye.

"Hey, yourself." Jenny went back to the articles as she walked around the sitting area handing out the paperwork. "And we have Giancarlo, Giancarlo and James and his commendations, following in the footsteps of his father, and we have James and his parents at his graduation." She read the caption under the photo. "*'Retired NYPD Detective Giancarlo Gardo and his wife Sheila celebrate their son's graduation.'*" She stopped and stared at the photo and the wheel turned. The cog clicked into place. Memories came flooding back. *"Sheila?"* The person stared back. The wheel turned. The cog clicked into place. Memories came flooding back. *"Sheila?* It can't be," she murmured. "It c*an't* be."

Thirty years came back, and thirty years' worth of memories hit her, clicking into each slot on the cog like a jigsaw puzzle.

"Can't be who, Grandma?" Alena asked, always wondering what went through her grandmother's razor-sharp mind.

The department store flooded back. Giancarlo mentioned no name, but she noticed James's eyes. She remembered Tomas flinching, and she remembered their conversation on the way home. If Luiz had been reincarnated why would he come back to Gardo? What did he have to do with Gardo? Fast forward twenty-seven years and that same boy was standing in her living room declaring to be Luiz Manning. Mentioning he was the bastard son of Andros Poulos and Sheila Manning. *'And you know who that is…' he'd said. 'You didn't tell me I had a bro…'*

"Oh, my God." She stared at the photo. "*Oh, my bloody God.* All these years, all this time, I questioned why he would come back to Gardo and now I know why." Her hands screwed into fists, screwing the papers with them. "Oooh," she growled, and spinning around, threw the ball of paper across the room at the window, surprising everyone. "Ooh," she screamed. "All these years I questioned why Luiz would come to Gardo and the answer was right in front of us the *whole bloody time.* Because *his mother is Sheila.* Oooh." Turning on her heel, she grabbed her bag from the side table and stormed out the door.

Spiros retrieved the paper and smoothed it out. *"Retired Detective Giancarlo Gardo and his wife, Sheila'."*

"Sheila?" Pedro went to his father's side. "As in?"

Spiros examined the woman. She was older, twenty or twenty-five years or so, but he recognised the face of the woman whose apartment he had woken up in back in '78. The woman he'd believed he'd slept with which had driven a wedge between him and Jenny for nearly four months.

"Papa?" Pedro held the paper. "Is it *the* Sheila?"

"I don't know. I never saw her. But I need to catch up with your mother." He hurried after Jenny while Carlos and Tomas moved to their brother's side.

"Does he mean Sheila, as in Sheila Manning?" Carlos looked at the photo.

"None of us know what she looks like except mama," Tomas said, curious to what Luiz's, and now James's, mother looked like.

The three of them traded glances while the other adults got up for a look at the article.

*****

Cabot touched Antonio on the hand, waking him.

Antonio sprang awake, his head moving back and forth to see what was going on. "What? What's wrong?"

"Tonee," Cabot said softly and pulled his arm back. He was lying on his side, curled up into a ball, feeling worse for wear and sorry for himself.

"Cabot." Antonio pulled his chair closer. He'd fallen asleep with his head on the bed and could feel the cramp in his neck that it left behind. "What's wrong?"

"I feel sick, Tonee. My stomach is awful, and my head aches. Ugh." Cabot groaned. "What happened?"

"Don't you remember?" Antonio brushed the hair aside from his brother's forehead. "Don't you remember what happened?"

"No. Did I get into a fight?" Cabot looked at his wrists. "What happened?"

Antonio sighed. "You got really drunk last night, Cabot, ended up on Brooklyn Bridge. Do you remember that?"

A faraway look came over Cabot. "No..." he said dreamily. "But I'm really tired. What did I do?"

"You took a bunch of pills with your alcohol, Cabot. You tried to overdose." He watched his brother's face for recognition. But there was none.

"I don't remember, Tonee. Are you sure?"

"Why else would you be in the hospital, Cabot?"

Cabot swallowed. "Ugh, my throat feels like it had something down it."

"It did. A tube for the charcoal they put in your stomach. It made you vomit, but the pills had already been diluted, so they gave you something to counteract the pills.”

“What about my wrists?” Cabot picked at the bandage on his left arm.

“You smashed the vodka bottle and slashed your wrists.”

“What?” Cabot looked up in surprise. “Why would I do that, Tone? I’ve just gotten over my face being beaten up, so why would I slash my wrists?”

“In an attempted suicide,” Dan said from the doorway. “Good to see you awake and talking.” Checking the chart and vitals, Dan made the decision to move Cabot upstairs. “You’re better, but we’ll give you another day before we release you. You just don’t need to be in intensive care anymore.”

“I just want to go home,” Cabot said. “My own bed, my own room, food.”

“You can in another day,” Dan said. “In the meantime, we’ve got you started on HAART and will get a counsellor in to talk to you. I’ll get the paperwork signed to move you up to a room.”

“HAART? What’s HAART?” Cabot yawned. He may have been out all night, but he was still so tired.

“It’s the drugs you need to stave off AIDS,” Dan replied, before leaving the room.

“You need it,” Antonio said. “You can be on it and be okay, and it won’t let your HIV turn to AIDS.”

Cabot burst into tears. “I have HIV, Tonee,” he sobbed and smothered his face in his pillow. “I have HIV.”

“Yes, Cabot.” Antonio climbed onto the bed beside his brother and took him into his arms. “You have HIV.”

“Tonee,” Cabot cried. “I don’t want HIV. My life is over.”

“No, it isn’t, Cabot.” Antonio kissed his temple. “I don’t want you to have it either, but you do, and there’s nothing we can do to change it. All we can do now is get you onto your meds and make sure you stay as healthy as possible.”

“Will you help me, Tonee?” Cabot’s muffled plea came from Antonio’s chest.

“Of course I’ll help you, Cabot. But you need to let Mama and Papa help, and Grandma and Dan and Derek. Can you do that?”

"No, Tonee. I just want you to help me."

*****

Spiros caught up with Jenny in the underground car park getting into the town car. "Jenny, wait, you need to know something."

"Get in and tell me. I need to get to the hospital." She ducked into the back seat and moved over for him.

The driver shut the door behind him and hurried around to the driver's side. "Where to ma'am?"

"Mount Sinai hospital," Jenny told him then turned her attention to Spiros. "What did you have to tell me?"

"Was the woman in that photo Sheila Manning?" he asked.

She sighed. "Yes. But what do you have to tell me?"

"Remember the woman whose apartment I woke up in, back in 1978?"

"How could I forget? I…" The cogs clicked into place, and the memories came flooding back. Her head slowly turned to her husband. "You're not saying that Sheila…"

"Was the woman from the apartment." Spiros stared at his wife. "She looks like her, just older. Although I didn't stick around for long."

Jenny's brows moved slowly down into a deep v. Giancarlo had told her he'd been investigating when he'd found Spiros's photo on the wall in some bar. He'd gotten the story from the barman, tracked down the cab driver, tracked down the woman, and found out she was newly widowed, just six months ago, and all of her friends had told her to get back out there and date. She'd gotten drunk with Spiros and taken him home, only to realise she wasn't over her husband. Nothing had happened, but she didn't have a chance to tell him come morning because he'd dashed out of there too fast. *So, does that mean…does that mean he lied to me? If the woman was Sheila, and he knew who she was, that he lied to protect me? Or to help me? But he ended up with her, which meant it was her he was married to in 1980 when we saw him in the department store. James was born on Valentine's Day '79, Spiros and I split in '78. She must have been pregnant then.* She calculated back. *Sheila would have been pregnant in May, and Giancarlo told me in June…he lied to me!*

They arrived at the hospital and asked for James Gardo. Getting directions to ICU, they took off at a quick pace.

*****

Dan came into Cabot's room. "We can move you now. You'll get your own room on the fifth floor for the night; tomorrow, I tell your grandmother."

"Aw, Dan," Cabot whined from his brother's arms. "I don't want her knowing."

"Stop it, Cabot, you need help, and Grandma and Dan are the best ones to give it," Antonio told him. "It's time to get your life together."

"But I'm scared, Tonee." Cabot snuggled into his chest. "I'm scared."

"There's no need to be. And we're all here for you." Antonio saw the orderlies come into move the bed. "Do I need to get off?"

"No, you can stay there," Dan said. "You didn't come in with anything, did you?"

"Just his personal effects," Antonio said and was handed two large brown paper bags with Cabot's clothes, shoes and personal items.

"Okay, we'll get you upstairs now." They rolled the bed out the door and to the lift, where they waited until it opened and then pushed the bed in. The lift opposite opened, and Jenny and Spiros stepped out to see Antonio on the bed and Dan saying, "I'll be upstairs soon, Cabot, Antonio." The door shut, he turned around and startled. "Ah, ah, oh, Jenny!"

Jenny blinked in surprise. "Dan…my grandsons are in this hospital?"

"Ah…" Dan flushed. "Long story…very long story…very, very, *very* long story and I was going to call you tomorrow."

"Why tomorrow?" She knew something was going on.

"Because we're keeping him in overnight."

"Cabot?"

Damn, how did she do that? "Yes."

"What's he done?"

"Were you on your way somewhere?" Dan slowly backed away.

"What floor?" Jenny demanded.

"Fifth." He backed further under her scrutinising glare.

"I'll talk to you later. Where's James Gardo?"

"Who? Oh, the cop on Alena's tour. He's here? Antonio told me last night…oh…" His face fell at having given that away.

"So, he's been in all night? I'll deal with all of you later. Right now, I need to see the Gardos."

"Probably through the door and down the hall," Dan said, backing on down the hall.

"Mmm," Jenny grumbled and took off with Spiros on her tail. They saw the couple talking to the doctor and slowed down to listen, trying not to look too conspicuous.

"The bullet hit an aneurysm. Has he been acting strangely lately?" the doctor asked. "It would have been causing pressure on the brain."

Giancarlo glanced at his wife. "The last few weeks, yes."

"Yes, well, he should get better now. The bullet landed in the aneurysm and blew it up, essentially. We cleaned it out and can bring him out of his coma in a few days. We want the swelling to go down first."

"But he'll live? He'll be okay?" Sheila asked fearfully.

"Fingers crossed," the doctor said. "But you never know. We'll keep him in a coma and keep him monitored. For the next few days, there's not a whole lot that will be going on."

"Okay, thank you, doctor." Giancarlo shook his hand.

Jenny waited for the doctor to be out of earshot. "Oh, the delicious sweet irony." She saw both of them turn around. "That *both* of *your* sons would get shot in the head," she told Sheila. "You know, until today, I haven't seen you in nearly thirty years." Jenny took a step closer. "Why is it, that the shit hit the fan yesterday? And I wouldn't have even known you were James Gardo's mother if my grandkids hadn't gone looking. Obviously, you know James was on Alena's tour." She glanced from Sheila to Giancarlo. "He would have told you. And because he turns up claiming to be Luiz, and then you, Giancarlo, show up with a bunch of paperwork, all of a sudden they come up with the bright idea to go to the library archives like James did and dig up a whole lot of information on our family and yours. And after I confiscated it, what did I see?" She glared at Sheila. "James Gardo's graduation from the academy photo with his proud parents, retired NYPD detective Giancarlo Gardo, *and his wife Sheila.*"

Jenny's head was moving as though she was watching a tennis match, back and forth between the two. "And who did I notice? Not Sheila Gardo, oh, no." Jenny waved a hand. "Sheila *Manning. Luiz's* mother. Still living on my money?" she spat. "The money I gave you for your son's death? Not expecting another lot are you? Because this one I really will fight in court."

"Jenny, not now." Giancarlo put his arm around his frightened wife.

"Not *now*, Giancarlo?" Jenny stepped forward, incredulous. "*Your* son comes to *my* home, telling everyone *he's* Luiz Manning, and scaring the shit out of my son Tomas, carrying on the way he did, and *you tell me, not now!* Oh, by the way," she stopped him before he could interrupt, "Spiros saw the photo as well, and wouldn't you know it, memories came flooding back for him, too. Memories of waking up naked in some strange woman's apartment and assuming he'd slept with her." She stared into his pale blue eyes. "And then I remembered the story you'd told me, about how you just *happened* to track down the woman and find out she's a lonely widow who was told by her friends to get out on the town."

"Nothing happened," Sheila cried out. "Nothing happened."

"*Nothing* happened," Jenny spat. "You got my husband drunk and took him back to your place. *That's* what happened. And James was born Valentine's Day '79." She turned to Giancarlo. "So, that means she was pregnant when you told me, which…" She waved a finger in his face, but then replaced it with her right hand as she swung it with all her might across his face. He stumbled back, his own hand flying to his cheek. "You *lied* to me on purpose. To what? Protect her?" Her voice was nearly a scream.

"Yes," Gardo bellowed. "Yes, Jenny, I did. I lied to protect the mother of my child from you. From what you would have done to her. She told me the story, and I believed her."

"Did you?" Jenny asked, her voice coming down a few decibels after noticing doctors and nurses frowning their way. "Or was it purely to protect the baby who, by the way, has turned out to be a *psycho like his brother*? Guess he found out about that, huh? What?" She looked back and forth. "Never told him? Surprised you didn't," she said to Sheila. "He looks like Luiz's twin for God's sake."

"I wouldn't know, I didn't see Luiz after he was seventeen. I don't know what he looked like." Sheila sobbed under her husband's arm.

"Exactly like James," Jenny said and leaned forward. "All the way down to those aqua blue eyes that seemed to have fascinated my family."

Sheila stared at Jenny, fearful of what could happen. She hadn't seen her since Christmas '77 when she'd gotten the money, and while she had followed the family, she hadn't seen her in person until now, and she was still frightening. "A lot has happened, and I don't want to lose another son."

"And I hope you don't," Jenny told them. "One child is enough to lose, and thanks to Luiz, I nearly lost Tomas, but he pulled through. Regardless of what James did, something is seriously wrong in his head and yes," she waved a hand to stop Gardo, "I heard the doctor, an aneurysm putting pressure on his brain making him act strangely. But that doesn't explain how he knew so much about my family. *That* he could not have read anywhere. Only Luiz would have known it thirty years ago, and James knows it now. So, how the hell are you going to explain that?"

"We can't," Gardo said. "We have no idea what's been going on in his head. Before he left, he was fine. On tour, we got the occasional call. When he got home, he disappeared and didn't go to work. We were all looking for him."

"And yet he rings up Alena yesterday morning and gets invited to brunch. How is that?" Jenny asked. "No one can find him, but he turns up at *my* home?"

"I don't know. Until he wakes up and we can talk to him, we won't know what he was thinking," Giancarlo said.

"What if he doesn't remember at all?" Sheila fretted. "What if he remembers none of it? None of *us*? What if he doesn't know who we are?" She clung to her husband, and Jenny finally got a good look at her.

Short brown hair in a stylish do, slimline clothes, well-tailored, a plump figure. Same height as her, same blue eyes as her. *Oh, my God, she looks like me!* Jenny thought.

"Take it easy, Sheila. We don't know what he'll remember until he wakes up, and that won't be for a few days. We'll just have to wait and see," Giancarlo comforted his grieving wife.

Jenny's eyes went back and forth between them as her brain ticked over.

Thirty years had come down to this.

Thirty years had come down to nothing.

She knew it was time to go.

Thirty years was thirty too long.

And thirty years were finally done.

"I hope he gets better. I really do," Jenny said softly, and she and Spiros walked away.

"Thank you, Jenny," Giancarlo called out behind her.

They made their way to the fifth floor and got directions to Cabot's room, where Antonio was surprised to see them.

Jenny held her finger to her lip to silence him. Cabot was asleep in his brother's arms and looking at peace. She noted the bandages on his wrists and frowned, and a worried look from Antonio sent her looking for Dan. She found him at the nurse's station.

"Let's go into the doctors' lounge and talk." He led them in and closed the door. "I was going to give him some time before calling you."

"From start to finish and leave nothing out," Jenny said.

Sighing, Dan sat and started with the assault in Mykonos and all the details he knew, and then moved on to the flu Cabot had recently, and how it wasn't the flu, but the onset of HIV in his system.

"He what?" Jenny asked, not hearing correctly.

"He's contracted HIV from the assault," Dan repeated.

"What? No…he…we…" The air flew out of her, and she imploded. Dan and Spiros caught her as she fell and sat her down. "Of all the… we taught them…"

"I know." Dan sat beside her. "But there's only so many times you can tell them. Only so many times you can give them updated brochures and booklets."

"And he got it from the rape in July?" Jenny asked, dumbfounded.

"As well as another STD I'm treating him for."

"And now…he what…?" She turned her head to stare at Dan. "Tried to kill himself? I saw the bandages on his wrists."

Dan's shoulders fell. "From what Antonio told me, he was out all night for two nights. He'd disappeared, then called Antonio. He was drunk, said he was on Brooklyn Bridge. Antonio found him, found the paracetamol packets, and called an ambulance. Before it got there, Cabot smashed a bottle and slashed his wrists. He told Antonio he was going to kill himself because his life was over."

Jenny sighed deeply from her gut. For all they had done, for all they had taught them, it still had not been enough. Finally, she said, "Can you get the meds ready? We'll be taking him home and helping him there."

"Of course. He's already on them, and I've got them ready to go. Derek's already packed our bags."

"Good. I'll need you to get me a top of the field psychologist, not only dealing with HIV, but all other issues as well, because Cabot's got a few of them and it's time someone got to the bottom of them. Tell them they'll be on a 24/7 retainer with a hotel room in Mykonos."

"Okay." Dan nodded.

"We don't want to alert the family, so I'll deal with it quietly. I'll say I, we," she glanced at Spiros, "need to get home for work, or something, um, I'll let Carlos and Viv know, we'll take Cabot home, and the rest can stay and come home when they're ready."

"Good plan. When do you want to do it?" Dan asked.

Jenny looked at her watch. "First thing tomorrow. I need to see the twins now." Back at their room, she found Cabot still asleep. Moving around to the other side, she gazed down at him, stroked his head, and dredged up memories of Tomas. Her eyes burned with tears. Her heart burned with fears. Fears that it was happening all over again. And it was.

Antonio watched silently, knowing Dan had told her.

"Mmm." Cabot moved. "Tonee?"

"Cabot," Jenny said softly.

Cabot opened his eyes to see his grandfather beside the bed, Dan at the end of it, and his grandmother behind him. He sat up, scared of what was coming. "Grandma."

"I know, Cabot," she said, her heart breaking. "And I am so, so sorry."

He blinked, realising she knew, knowing that the whole family would know, and buried himself on his brother's chest, sobbing.

"I'll be taking you home tomorrow," Jenny went on. "Your grandfather and I will take you and Antonio home. Dan and Derek will be with us, and I will get your parents on the plane as well. We won't tell anyone else just yet. They don't need to know."

"I'm not going home, Grandma," came out muffled from Antonio's chest.

"The time for talking is over, Cabot." Jenny's voice hardened. "We have let you get away with disgusting behaviour, and now we're pulling in the reins. You will do as you're told, and we will help you. It's time to grow up and be a mature adult, because the time for being a stubborn, snot-nosed little brat is over."

Cabot rolled towards her, eyes blazing.

"*Don't you even think* of opening your mouth to me." Jenny pointed a finger in his face, blue eyes blazed back, blue matching blue with anger. "You've said enough, and now it's time to listen. *You* will do as you are told, and *we* will get you through this. *We* are taking you home, *you* will take your meds, and *you* will speak to the psychiatrist that Dan will hire. *You* are going to get to the root of your problems, and I don't care if you like it or not. There will be no more modelling for you. You are on permanent holiday until you can get your life together, so Antonio," she looked over Cabot's shoulder, "you get to take a break too. But you," she stared at Cabot's scowling face, "will do *as you're told, when you're told,* and if you don't, Cabot Conroy Stephanopoulos, I will do one of two things. I will either release a story to the world that you are a homophobic fag fucker who pushed a conquest too far and got what he deserved, HIV, and ruin what career you have." Cabot's eyes widened in fear. "Or I can lock you up in the cove and leave you there until you break. If you don't do as you're told and finally get help and your medication, one of those two things will happen. And if you even *think* of running away, I'll have the security team track you down and lock you in the cove anyway. You won't get a choice then. *Do you understand me, Cabot?*"

He blinked in fury, not believing his grandmother could be so vicious.

"*Do you understand me, Cabot?*" She leaned in close, so one set of blue eyes was in front of the other. "You don't fool me. You don't screw me over. You will do as I say until you can prove you are a man, a mature adult that can deal with his life efficiently, effectively, and properly. *Do you understand me?*"

He gulped at the fury burning from her. "Yes, Grandma." Rolling over, he buried himself in Antonio.

Jenny got on the phone to Tilly. "Matilda? Jenny Stephanopoulos. You're fired. I'll have your severance pay forwarded."

"But I—"

Snapping her phone shut, Jenny saw Spiros and Dan's wide eyes and raised brows. "Let's get to work."

An hour later, they were back at home. Going upstairs, they found Dom hovering in the penthouse foyer. "Dominic. You smashed Danté's camera?"

He shrugged, having been too scared to enter the suite, but at least he had the decency to look ashamed.

"A shrug is not an answer. Yes or no?" Jenny demanded.

"It was an accident," he whined, hands in pockets, head down.

"Bullshit!" Jenny told him. "You're suspended from *SB3* until next year as punishment. Your trust fund is frozen, and if you can't live on the money you've saved, you can get another job outside of the family business. *That* is your punishment for your bad attitude toward Danté and smashing his birthday present. Do you understand?" When Jenny got efficient, she got downright efficient.

"Something's going on in the foyer." Angie looked towards the door, hearing loud voices arguing.

"Sounds like Mama and Dom," Pedro replied, not quite catching what was being said, but knowing it wouldn't be good.

Dom was stunned. "It's just a camera."

"If that's what you think, then clearly we have spoiled all of you into not having a healthy relationship with money." She opened the door and saw her family gathered in the sitting area. "I've dealt out Dominic's punishment, you," she pointed to Pedro who had stood at the sight of his son hovering in the foyer, "need to have a strong talk to him. I have some things to do upstairs before dinner."

"Did you see James?" Alena called out, but she got a shake of the head from her grandfather.

"Well, what did she tell you?" Pedro asked Dom, crossing his arms and standing in front of his son. "What you did wasn't cool, Dominic. That was an expensive camera we gave Danté as a family."

Shame still flittered across Dom's face. "I can't believe she did that. I can't believe she did it." His voice rose. "She just suspended me from *SB3* until next year and froze my trust fund," he yelled at his father. "And she told me if I didn't have enough money to find another job at a business that's not part of the family's. *She can't do that.*"

"Wow." Pedro raised his brows and glanced at Angie. "That's more than what I would have given you. But then you have been pretty snarky to Danté lately. Any reason why?"

"Why do I have to get suspended from *SB3?* That's my job, that's my life, that's my career." Dominic's hands gestured wildly with every syllable.

"And it won't be any of it if you don't get over yourself." Jenny came down the stairs. "Right now you are being more selfish than Cabot, so if you want a slap like he got, keep pushing it, Dominic." She stood before him. "I am *so* sick and tired of my grandchildren's childish, bratty, selfish behaviour. Between you, Alena and Cabot, why are you all a pack of spoilt, selfish brats? At least Alena finally had enough sense to grow up, but that took nineteen years and Alexis getting assaulted. So, what's *your* excuse? Huh?" She stepped closer to a shocked Dom. "Do I have to slap some sense into you, because you're acting very much like Cabot at the moment and giving a bad attitude."

Dom gulped. "No," quietly came out of his mouth. He was scared of his grandmother and the blazing blue eyes that raged at him.

"If you want to lose your job entirely, *and* your trust fund, open your mouth one more time and whine," she warned him. "We've dealt with your jealous bullshit for fourteen years, we dealt with Alena's for nineteen, we're still dealing with Cabot's, but it ends tonight. *Do you understand me*, Dominic Spiros Stephanopoulos?" He may have been over six feet to Jenny's five eight, but she was tall when berating her grandchildren. "Open your mouth one more time and whine, and your job at *SB3* is gone. Open your mouth and make a snide remark about your brother, and your job at *SB3* is gone, and you can get a job somewhere else, and you can get out of home and get your own place. I *will not* have whingers and whiners in my family. *Not anymore.*" She turned her head to look at her stunned grandkids. "That goes for all of you. No more bullshit from tonight." Staring up at Dom, she stepped toe to toe and stared hard into his eyes. Pointing her finger in his face, blue eyes flashed blue eyes. "No more, Dominic. I'm warning you, and this is your last warning. Whatever garbage you have against Danté, you let it go tonight. Do you understand me?"

Unlike Cabot, Dom didn't have a career outside of the family business, and unlike Cabot, he didn't have the balls to walk out on his family, or grandmother. "Yes, Grandma." He felt it. The shame, the embarrassment, the flames burning his face. He knew how Cabot must have felt, and it was horrible and embarrassing.

"Good. I hope you've learned your lesson, because I will not tolerate any more bullshit from my grandchildren. Hell, your fathers weren't even like this. I never had to slap them or fire *them* from their jobs." She turned to her family. "Who's making dinner? Spiros and I will be flying home tomorrow for some business thing, but the rest of you feel free to stay another week or two as scheduled. I have to finish off my packing." Walking back upstairs, she left her family astounded.

"Um, I guess we can get dinner," Tomas said slowly to Roger, who nodded. They made their way into the kitchen, even more stunned than the kids. "Bloody hell," he whispered, rubbing his forehead. "I've never seen Mama go off like that except at Cabot. Not even her reaming of Alena was that bad."

"It *was* shocking," Roger replied, getting a wok from the cupboard. "Especially since it's Dom."

Mike and Maggie excused themselves from the situation by taking their kids and leaving. Viv and Carlos got up to set the table, and that left Pedro and Angie to sort out Dom. Alena, Alexis and Danté shuffled over to them in shock.

"Do I need to say any more to you, Dominic?" Pedro asked, stunned by his son's attitude and his mother's outburst. In all of his fifty years, he'd never seen her go off like that until the last few months when Alena, Cabot, and now Dom had gotten a right royal reaming.

Dom's eyes stung, and his gut wrenched. His grandmother had never spoken to him that way before, and he hated it. It was horrible, and he knew tears were forthcoming. He also felt like running away to his room and hiding.

"I hope they are tears of embarrassment because you *should* be embarrassed." Angie stood by Pedro's side, ashamed that her children had acted the way they did. "We didn't raise you to be like that, Dom, and that behaviour, *today's* behaviour, has been absolutely appalling and won't be accepted by either of us."

Dom nodded, his lip quivered. He'd never been reamed out, and never wanted it to happen again.

"I suggest you take your punishment and use it as a learning tool," Pedro told him. "This is what you *don't do* in this family. Do you understand?" He got a nod. "This family does not do what Alena, and Cabot, and you do. We, your mother and I, will not accept this behaviour from you, and if it *does* continue," he stepped closer to his son, "Look at me, Dominic."

Dom looked up through glossy red eyes.

"Then I will side with Mama. If this behaviour continues, you will be fired from *SB3*, you will have your trust fund cut off, and you can move out of home and find your own place and your own job. Do you understand?"

Dom opened his mouth the protest, but the dead set serious look on his parents' faces made him shut his mouth and swallow. Thinking, panicking, he nodded. He didn't want to be kicked out of *SB3*. He loved it and wanted to follow in his father's footsteps. And he didn't want to be kicked out of home, as he got his meals and laundry done.

"Now, if you're still too embarrassed and need some time out to think, you may be excused for dinner," Angie said. "But stay in the apartment; we don't need you wandering the streets at night too."

With a tearful nod, he fled upstairs to the spare room, locked the door behind him, threw himself on the bed and buried his tears in the pillow.

Jenny and Spiros finished packing their things and went down for dinner.

"What business do you need to take care of, Mama?" Carlos asked as he placed bowls of stir-fry on the table.

"Don't worry about it now, we'll talk about it later. Let's eat." She sat down and noticed a few faces missing. "Mike, Maggie and the kids eating out?"

"They had plans for some new restaurant," Angie said. "They wanted to get in before we go home."

"You can all stay another couple of weeks and can share the penthouse. Obviously, Dom and Danté have the spare rooms, and I see he's not eating."

"He was too embarrassed, so I excused him," Angie told her.

"Good! He should be embarrassed," Jenny said. "His behaviour was atrocious. You don't treat other people's belongings like rubbish. Alena, make sure to get your money from him."

"Yes, Grandma. I plan on it," Alena said.

After dinner, Jenny helped Tomas and Roger put the dishes in the washer. "I want a word with you two. Are you planning on staying another two weeks?"

"If you're going home, Mama, there's no need for us to stay. Not after yesterday," Tomas said.

"I don't want you to worry about that anymore. I need to know how long you'll be."

"Why, Mrs S?" Roger asked, wiping down the cupboards.

"Let's just say, in a week or two, you will be needed at home."

Tomas narrowed his eyes. "What do you mean?"

"No more until then. So, when will you be home?"

"I, ah…" Tomas frowned. "I wanted to spend a few more days in Miami at the centre, make sure everything's running smoothly."

"Okay." Jenny tenderly brushed his hair out of his eyes before stroking his face. "You two go and do that, and then come home by next week. It will be important."

"Okay, Mrs S," Roger said. "If you're leaving tomorrow, then we might too."

"We'll be taking the jet, so you'll have to fly commercial."

"That's okay, done that before." Roger grinned.

"Did you leave food for Dom?" Jenny asked, straightening the tea towel she hung up. "He'll probably be hungry later."

"In a microwaveable container ready for heating. It even has a sticky note on it with his name and instructions," Tomas said.

"Good, good. The kids have been all over the place, having slumber parties and changing rooms. I can't keep up." Jenny wiped a hand across her forehead before running it through her hair.

"Grandma." Alena came up to them. "Did you see James before?"

Jenny sighed. "I went to the hospital, yes."

"Did you see James?" Alena stood expectantly, but also with trepidation.

"No, I didn't, because he's in ICU in an induced coma."

"Oh, my God." Alena's hand flew to her cover her mouth.

Jenny put her arm around her shoulder and led her to the lounge room where everyone else was. "Apparently, the bullet hit an aneurysm, and that is what was causing his strange behaviour. Other than that, I have no idea what's going on, or if he'll remember any of what happened."

"What about his parents? *Is* his mother Sheila Manning?" Pedro asked.

Taking a deep breath, Jenny let it out in a whoosh. "Yes, yes she is."

Murmurers went around the adults.

"Jesus," Tomas muttered. "No wonder he looks the same."

"Well," Jenny butted in, "no two children will look identical unless they're twins like Cabot and Antonio, or Summer and Melody. But for Sheila to have two children, to two different fathers, twenty-seven years apart, and for James to look exactly like Luiz, born a year and a half after Luiz's death, is just mind-blowingly crazy." She swiped a stray hair away. "It's just unbelievably crazy."

"So…what now? Will he be okay?" Viv asked.

"I don't know." Jenny sat down and sighed. "It would be horrible for Giancarlo to lose his son because of an aneurysm, or a bullet. James is his only child. He never had children with his first wife."

"He was married before?" Carlos looked on in surprise.

"Many decades ago when he was in his twenties. Joined the force, his wife couldn't handle being married to a cop and left him." She glanced at Alena and Tomas who were beside her. "I know what it's like to lose a child. It's incredibly painful."

Tomas smiled and sat on the couch next to his mother, sliding both arms around her waist and hugging her tight.

"What happens now?" Alena asked, sliding under her grandmother's arm and hugging her too. "How long will he be in ICU?"

"I don't know, sweetie," Jenny replied, leaning her cheek on her granddaughter's head. "But I think it's going to be quite a while." Getting a look from Spiros, she added, "Why don't you guys go downstairs and have some time as a family? Go for a walk, or watch TV. See what Diana's up to. She didn't come up for dinner."

"Okay, come on Alexis, Danté." Alena led them out the door.

"You two go as well," Jenny told Pedro and Angie. "Spend some time on your own, or with your kids. Go on, we'll see you tomorrow before we go home."

"You sure, Mama?" Pedro asked. "It's been a long couple of days."

"And that's why you need to spend it with your kids. Keep Alena away from James and the hospital."

"Okay, Mama. We'll see you for breakfast." Pedro got up and kissed his mother, followed by Angie. "We'll see you tomorrow."

"Night, sweetie." Jenny waited until they had left and then whispered to Roger, "Can you check if Dom is listening, or still in his room."

Roger frowned at the unusual request, but sneaked over to the stairs and walked up. Seeing no one, he came back down. "What's going on?" he asked quietly.

Jenny sat next to Carlos and Viv. "There's something I need to say to you." She held Viv's hand.

"Mama; is everything all right?" Carlos asked as a curious dread snaked through his gut.

"No, it's not." Taking a deep breath, Jenny started. "When we go home tomorrow, the two of you need to come with us. Don't make a fuss, don't give any details. I will tell you on the plane."

"No, Jenny, tell us now," Viv demanded, gripping her mother-in-law's hand. "Is it Cabot? I knew it." She looked at Carlos. "I knew it in the cemetery at Cabot's grave. I knew it, tell me." Turning back to Jenny, her grip got tighter.

"He tried to…" Jenny was skirting the subject. "He took a couple of packets of pills with a bottle of vodka."

"What?" Viv's head shook. "What?"

"He overdosed?" Carlos frowned in confusion. "You mean he tried to overdose on pills and alcohol?"

"Yes," Jenny said. "He's not well, Carlos. He needs psychiatric care to help him with whatever his issues are."

"Wait!" Viv sprung up and paced. "He overdosed? Was it drugs? Did he try to OD on purpose? On drugs? Which drugs?"

"Paracetamol," Jenny replied dryly.

"Wait, what?" Carlos guffawed. "He swallowed paracetamol with alcohol? Was that…can you even OD on that?"

"You can when you try and kill yourself," Tomas said softly from his spot on the couch arm.

"What?" Viv spun around to face him. "Cabot wouldn't…he…"

"Look, I didn't tell you to freak you out," Jenny said firmly. "I want you two to come home so we can get Cabot out of the lifestyle he's in and get him better. And yes, he tried to kill himself. He slashed his wrists with the bottle after he broke it. He needs help, Viv, and it's time we gave it to him. It's time we took him home and took charge, and I've already told him that. He agreed."

"You…saw…him… When?" Viv was puzzled.

"Bizarrely, he's at the same hospital as James Gardo. Antonio is with him."

"Is Antonio all right?" Carlos asked.

"He's fine. He went looking for him and found him on Brooklyn

Bridge. He called the ambulance, and they got him to hospital. He'll be okay."

"Is he?" Viv asked, incredulous. "My son tried to kill himself." She rushed over to the window and stared out into the night.

"Mama, how bad is he?" Carlos asked, shifting over a seat to sit beside his mother.

"Well, he got that fire in his eyes and was ready to argue with me, so I'd say he's doing okay, as long as Antonio's with him. But still, he needs to see a therapist to deal with whatever *is* going on inside of him, because clearly, we can't. And with Dom acting the way he did today, and Alena the way she was, it's time we took charge of these kids. Cabot needs help, that's all there is to it." She moved to Viv's side. "We need to get tough, Viv, and get Cabot out of the lifestyle he's been in. It's done him wrong, and we need to sort it out. When I learned of what had happened, I rang Matilda and fired her. She clearly doesn't do anything to help and hasn't stopped his behaviour. So, *we* need to. It's time to get tough, Viv."

Viv wiped her face. "All these years, I didn't know what I did wrong."

"We did nothing wrong. *You* did nothing wrong. Diana and Antonio turned out perfectly, but Cabot..." Jenny shook her head. "I just don't know. But I do know it's time to take charge now, so..." She directed Viv back to the couch. "You and Carlos need to pack tonight and come with us tomorrow. No mess, no excuses, no need to tell anyone anything. Just say you have some style business to deal with. The others can be told at a later date if you want to. But you need to get a grip right now. Take a breath," she breathed with Viv, "take it easy, he's okay, he's alive and whiny and pouty and Antonio's with him. It's okay, Viv."

Viv nodded, still breathing. "Okay. He's okay."

"Now, do we know what's going on with Diana? Is she still sick?"

They spoke for another half hour before Viv and Carlos retired to their apartment to pack.

"Mama. Did he try to kill himself because he's gay?" Tomas asked.

"No, baby." Jenny kissed his head and hugged him. "No. He didn't try to kill himself because he's gay. He has problems, and we're going to help him sort them out."

"So, we need to be in Mykonos in a week or two?" he continued.

"It would help, I think. He may need a…*mature* gay man to talk to, and you two are family and have been through it all before."

Tomas nodded. "Okay, Mama. We'll call when we're done in Miami."

"Okay. You two go and get some sleep now," Jenny said. She kissed them goodnight, and once they left, she rang Antonio.

"Hello," he whispered.

"How is he?"

"Sleeping."

"I told your parents he tried to kill himself by overdosing on paracetamol and alcohol. And that he slashed his wrists."

"Didn't mention the disease?"

"Not yet. We'll do it on the plane."

"Who's coming?"

"You and Cabot, Dan and Derek, your parents, and your grandfather and me. I've told Dan to be at the airport by nine. He'll have the two of you with him. I'll try and get your parents there by ten."

"Okay. See you then; night Grandma."

"Night sweetie."

*****

The next morning, they had breakfast in the penthouse, with Viv remaining calm, but apologetic about leaving.

"We'll be leaving too." Tomas tried to make it easier for her. "We're heading back to Miami to work at the centre for a few days. Maybe a week or two."

"Don't worry, you can have the penthouse all to yourselves," Jenny told the kids.

Dom had come down for breakfast and was quietly eating his food next to Alena at the opposite end of the table to his grandmother.

"That means we can have fun, now," Alena said cheekily. "We can run riot up here."

"Don't forget, *we're* still here," Pedro warned her. "We might take the master ourselves."

"I don't have a problem with that," Jenny said. "Everyone else has probably had a go after all these years." She looked at the clock. "We gotta go. The plane leaves at ten. Diana, what will you be doing?"

Diana looked up tiredly. She'd been slowly nibbling a piece of toast, but she hadn't got much down. "I leave in a couple of days for six or seven weeks of modelling shoots, so I'll stay here until then."

"Okay. We'll see the rest of you at home." Jenny kissed and hugged her way through the family, including Dom, who awkwardly hugged her back, and they helped carry the luggage down and out to the car. "Who's doing the dishes?" Jenny called.

"We will since we're taking the penthouse," Angie said.

"Have fun for your last couple of weeks," Jenny said from the limo window. "We'll see you when you get home."

"Bye, Mama."

"Bye, Grandma."

They got to the private hanger and boarded the plane. "I want to leave on time," Jenny told the pilot, who nodded.

"Where's Cabot?" Viv asked.

"Probably in the bedroom. Wait until you're in the air and then you can talk," Jenny said. "Sit down, Viv, and we'll get in the air."

Fifteen minutes later, they were winging their way home.

Jenny unbuckled and went into the bedroom to see Dan, Derek and the boys. "Did you tell him?" she asked Antonio.

He nodded in return.

"Your parents are on board. I told them you overdosed and tried to kill yourself, but nothing more. That's up to you," she told Cabot.

His face crumpled, and he ran from the room and into Viv's arms. "Mama."

"Oh, my baby, my poor, poor baby." She gripped him tightly. "Oh, my baby."

"Mama." He buried his head in her shoulder, breathing in her hair, burying himself in it while he sobbed. "I'm so sorry."

"It's okay, baby. It's okay. Now we have to get you better."

Carlos saw Dan and Derek emerge with Antonio from the back

hall and frowned. "What's going on? What are they here for?"

"To help Cabot," Jenny said. "They're coming home to help him and will stay as long as Cabot needs them."

The frown deepened. "No. This is something else." A cold, foul feeling swept through his gut, and he knew it was much more than just Cabot trying to kill himself. "What's *really* going on?"

Jenny glanced at Dan and Derek before turning back to Carlos. "Do you remember why we came home for your brother?"

The cold, foul feeling washed over him as he remembered 1981. "No," he murmured. "That was…Tomas had the gay plague. We thought he was…" He saw his mother's expression, and his entire body turned to ice. "No." His head moved mechanically from side to side. "No." He buried his head in his hands.

"Oh, Carlos." Jenny moved to his side and held him.

"What are you talking about?" Viv asked. "We thought Tomas had AIDS."

Cabot froze for a moment before leaving her arms and flying into Antonio's. "Tonee."

"It's okay, Cabot. They have to know. It's okay." Antonio held him.

"I don't want to tell them, Tonee." He buried himself in Antonio's neck.

"Tell us what?" Viv was confused. Between the solemn faces and Jenny hugging Carlos, she had no idea. "Why are we talking about Tomas and AIDS?"

Jenny left a crying Carlos and moved to her side. Holding her hands, she squeezed. "Do you remember when Cabot was assaulted in Mykonos?"

Viv stared dazedly at her. "Yes."

"It started off as sex, but the man wanted payment and pulled out a knife."

"Yes."

"Well," Jenny glanced at Dan and Derek, "From what we could put together, the man assaulted Cabot and then told him he'd gotten the disease."

"Disease? What disease?" Viv's confusion grew as her eyes darted back and forth from person to person.

"HIV, Viv," Carlos muttered. "Our son has HIV." He looked at Dan through tear-filled eyes. "Are you sure?"

Dan nodded. "Cabot came to see me for that flu he had a week ago. I gave him a full exam, asked a bunch of questions. And after he told me what the man said, I tested for it."

"And you're absolutely sure?" Carlos repeated feeling like an old man of a hundred, with a thousand years' worth of weight on his shoulders.

Another nod. "We tested three times to make sure."

Viv looked from Carlos to Jenny, to Dan to Cabot. "No…"

"The flu-like symptoms are from the body being infiltrated by the disease. It tries to fight it off, but it can't. Cabot has HIV," Dan told her.

"No," Viv cried, and collapsed onto the couch against the plane's wall.

"Oh, Jesus." Carlos collapsed beside her. "Oh, Jesus."

"That's why we're taking you home." Jenny sat opposite them. "To get him help and get him away from the lifestyle he's been living. We've got him started on HAART already. We *have* to do this." She took one each of Viv and Carlos's hands. "We *have* to do this for Cabot."

"No, I don't want AIDS," Cabot wailed in Antonio's neck. "I don't want it, Tonee."

"Well, Cabot, unfortunately, your lifestyle and stubbornness gave it to you." Antonio held him tight. "Your idiotic need to do what you wanted has now gotten you in this position, and we need to do what we can now."

"Tonee," Cabot sobbed. "Will you help me, Tonee?"

"Of course I will. It's what we're all here for." Antonio pulled away and indicated for Cabot to sit.

Looking around, Cabot sat beside Viv and shamefacedly stared at his hands in his lap. "I'm sorry."

"Oh, my baby," Viv murmured, and grasped both of his hands. "Oh, my poor baby." Wrapping her arms around him, she held him tight while he sobbed. "Is that why you tried killing yourself? Because you have HIV?"

"I don't want it, Mama. I don't want it," he cried.

"Well, we *did* tell you," Carlos told him. "We *warned* you, but *you* know better, oh, no, *Steele Stefan knew better*, and figured if his old man could fuck a lot, then he could too. Well, *I* never got HIV. *Neither* did your uncles, but *you* had to go and do who and what you bloody well wanted and try to prove us all wrong, and *now* look."

"Carlos, no." Viv shook her head. "The time for blame is over. He has it now and needs to deal with it."

"Mmm," Carlos angrily mumbled and stalked off to the back of the plane, leaving everyone uneasy.

"I'll go." Jenny stood and followed Carlos to the kitchen, closing the door for some privacy.

"Mama." Carlos gazed into her eyes. "He's got…"

"I know." Jenny teared up and slid an arm around his shoulders. "I know. And we can be angry all we like, but it won't change anything. It won't get rid of it."

Carlos couldn't hold it in any longer. "Mama."

"I know, I know." Jenny wrapped her arms around him, letting him cry on her shoulder. "We always tried to educate them, always pumped it into their heads. Safe sex, HIV/AIDS, we did all we could, and it still wasn't good enough."

"Oh, Mama. I know things have improved, but he's still got it for life. There's no cure for it. He can't just take a pill and make it go away." His heart was breaking for his son. When the twins were born, he knew they'd be a handful, and they were. But for all the bad things they did, they were generally good kids, until they became adults and Cabot went off the rails. Especially the last few years.

"I know." Jenny felt his pain and doubled it. She knew what it was like back in '81 when Dan had told her Tomas and Roger had the gay plague, and she refused to believe it. Refused to accept it all the while caring for her two dying sons. It had been heartbreaking, to say the least. The wasting disease he'd experienced, getting so painfully thin, dealing with diarrhea and contamination. It wasn't fun, but she'd done it because she loved Tomas. He was her son. So was Roger. Now they had to do it all over again. But this time, the medications to stave off AIDS were available. It didn't mean it might never progress, just that the pills would keep it at bay, so Cabot could have a fairly healthy life.

"How did it all go so wrong, Mama?" Carlos pulled back. "How did it go so wrong?"

"I don't know, sweetie." Jenny shook her head. "I just don't know. And I would love to know, but when it comes to the older kids, some of them just became selfish as the others came along and never grew out of it."

"And now they're paying the price," Carlos murmured. "Alena, Dom, Cabot. They're getting the one thing no one wants."

"What's that?" Jenny frowned.

"Being reamed out by Grandma." Carlos finally cracked a smile.

So did Jenny. "I wouldn't have to if they weren't selfish brats. But look at Diana and Antonio; perfect kids. How did we get it right with two and not three?"

"I don't know, but hopefully Alena and Dom are sorted now, and all we have to do is sort out Cabot."

*****

"Can we have the master?" Alena asked her parents as they lingered in the penthouse.

"Oh, we might have it." Pedro casually flicked through the newspaper.

"Do you *really* want to sleep in a bed where your mother and father have slept and had sex in?" Alena asked. "Ew, Daddy."

"Ew, Alena." Angie frowned. "No, actually, I don't."

"Do *you* want to sleep in a bed where your grandparents have slept and had sex in?" Alexis asked Alena with a cocked brow. "And God knows what Cabot's done in there."

"Ew, Alexis," Alena cried and covered her ears. "Don't want to hear it."

"Well, *I'd* rather stay in my own bed, thanks very much," Angie said. "It's the one we've had since before you were born." She smiled at Alena.

"Ew, Mama, I hope you've changed it in thirty years." Alena delicately screwed up her nose.

"Then *where* do you want to stay?" Pedro asked his girls.

Alena glanced at Alexis and shrugged. "Where we are!"

Alexis nodded her consent.

"So that means, Dom will keep his room, as well as Danté and Nick," Pedro said. The boys had been staying in the spare rooms of the penthouse as there was no space for them at Mike and Maggie's, or Pedro and Angie's. Diana or the twins had the second bedroom in apartment 3, so the only spare room among the family was Tomas and Roger's second bedroom. When all the kids were in town, there was just no room for all of them.

"No one gets the master," Alexis said with a shrug. "It would feel weird to sleep in Grandma and Grandpa's bed anyway."

"Yes, it would," Angie agreed and flipped through her diary. "We don't have plans for today; want to go out to lunch?"

"There's something I want to do first," Alena said. "It's only 11:30, so we have time." Turning to Alexis who was beside her on the couch in the sitting area, she added, "We need to go and have a chat with our brother." Grabbing her hand, she led her upstairs.

Dom was hiding in his room. Danté had gone out with Nick and his family to keep the boys separated for a while, and they would all meet up later.

Not bothering to knock, Alena barged into Dom's room. "Why are you such a shithead to our little brother?" She flopped down on the bed and waited for the surprised look to leave his face.

"What? What are you doing in here? Get out," he grumbled, sitting up on the bed. Glaring at his two sisters, he pulled the earbuds from his ears. He'd been listening to his iPod and the tracks he'd put together back in Mykonos in the studio.

"No." Alena sat up and faced him, Alexis by her side. "What you did was disgusting, Dominic, and Alexis and I are going to get to the bottom of why you did it, and why you've been an ass all these years."

"Like you can talk." He stuck his buds back in.

Alena leaned over and pulled them out. "Yes, *I can* actually. It took Grandma reaming me out, and *our* little sister getting raped to make me wake up to myself. All the years I allowed my anger and jealousy to ruin my life. She's *our* sister, and yet I treated her badly because I was jealous that another girl was in the family. Diana was all I had.

We were the only two girls in the family until Alexis came along. And instead of being the big sister and helping do her hair and make-up and talk about boys," she flung her arm around her sister's neck, "and go clothes shopping together, and do all the stuff we should have done, I blew it big time by being a snotty, jealous little girl. And you're being exactly the same when it comes to Danté."

Dom arched a brow. "What? A snotty, jealous little girl." His comment elicited a giggle out of Alexis.

Alena grinned and slapped his leg lightly. "No, silly. You know what I mean, Dom." She got serious. "You've treated Danté like I treated Alexis, as an enemy instead of a kid sister or brother. You had the twins to look up to and play with, Danté had no one except Nick. I had Diana, Alexis had Summer and Melody. That wasn't fair. They deserved their older siblings, not people who hate them. Why do you hate Danté?"

Dom scowled. "I don't hate him; he's just annoying. Always asking questions and getting in my way."

"Did you ever think he was idolising you and wanted to hang out with you, or *be* you?" Alexis asked. "As someone who knows, all we want is our older sibling to take us under their wing and teach us. Help us. Show us how to do things."

"And we missed out on that because I was stupid," Alena told her. "It took a horrible situation to make me realise what an idiot I'd been. Selfish and self-centred, and I missed out on my little sister growing up. *I* missed out on doing her hair and make-up. *She* missed out on having me do it. What is *your* problem with Danté?"

Shrugging a shoulder, Dom repeated himself. "He's annoying. I don't want him hanging around me. I want to be on my own to do my own thing. And why couldn't he pick something else to do? Why did he have to be a DJ like me? Why couldn't he do something of his own?"

"Why did *you* have to be a DJ like Daddy?" Alena asked. "You can't do what Daddy does and then expect Danté to do something else. It's in the family. *Music* is in the family. Besides, Danté raps too, *you* don't. He *does* do his own thing."

Another scowl. "Is that what you call it? Rapping," Dom said.

"Jealous that you can't?" Alexis asked. "I don't hear *you* rapping. You just said you want him to do something else, well, he raps. That *is* something else. What are you still bitching for?"

"He's your only brother, Dominic. What if something happened to him like it happened to Alexis? What if he was beaten up like Cabot? Beaten up by some group of thugs who wanted his camera or computer? What if he was taken, kidnapped for money, because, you know, the family *is* rich? What if a shark took him while he was out swimming, or he hit his head and drowned? How would you feel if all of that happened?"

Dom thought about it. He didn't hate Danté, just got highly annoyed at him. But if something did happen to him, he'd hate it. Just like he hated the fact Alexis had been assaulted, and he couldn't do anything about it. He couldn't take it back, make it stop, or make it hurt any less. He saw the bond the girls had now and remembered how Grandma had set her scathing attack on Alena at Diana's birthday, and then slapped Cabot, and now berated him. Maybe he'd better pull his head out. And if it made Alena re-evaluate things, then maybe he should too.

"Finding Danté annoying isn't good enough for the treatment he's received," Alexis told him. "Squirt's never done anything bad to you, or treated you badly. He's never smashed *your* camera on purpose."

"It wasn't on purpose." A frown slid onto Dom's face.

"Well, you had no care for it, *or* Danté," Alena said. "You threw a five-hundred-dollar camera like a piece of rubbish. And I expect you to pay for it too. All five hundred and twelve dollars. I booked it up, so you can pay the bill when it comes in."

"Yeah, yeah," Dom muttered. "You'll get your money, but considering I'm suspended and had my trust fund frozen, I'll have to go through my papers to find out how much I got in the bank. I still can't believe she did that to me."

"Personally…" Alena cocked a lip. "I would have fired you *and* kicked you out of home. But if that's all the punishment you get Dom, count yourself lucky."

"Lucky! I don't call no job and no income lucky," he spat.

"Then find another job," Alexis said. "There are other clubs in Mykonos, or try Santorini where Daddy used to work. You're not hard done by, Dom. You know what you want to do; I'm still trying to figure it out. And what you do, you can do anywhere. But you've got to let go of whatever you're resenting him for. Danté didn't come along to make your life a misery. He came along because Mama and Daddy wanted another baby and he happened to be a boy."

"Just like Alexis happened to be a girl," Alena added. "Not my fault, not her fault; Mama and Daddy wanted a baby. It just happened to be a girl. And it took something pretty damn bad to make me realise that none of what *I had* imagined happened actually happened, and *none* of it was her fault. So, whatever you've got going on with Danté, cut it out. Listen to what Grandma said, and boy, did she lay into you, even threatened to slap you like she did Cabot. You really pissed her off. More so than me."

"That was scary," Dom said, winding his earbud cord around his finger. "I hate it when Grandma goes off. She went off on you, then Cabot. I never wanted to be on the end of that."

"Neither did I!" Alena exclaimed. "And it was horrible. But it makes you wake up to yourself and realise what a jerk you've been."

"Yeah," Dom murmured. "I've never been reamed out by Grandma before. And never want to be again."

"Neither do I," Alena told him. "So, get over yourself and grow up. Take Danté under your wing, be a supportive big brother instead of a hateful one, hang out with him, regardless of the fact you're ten years older. He's your only brother, Dom. He's all you've got. Just like Alexis is all I've got."

He sighed thoughtfully. All he'd ever done was push Danté away. Reject him. He was the baby boy of the family and Dom was not. The role had been taken over by someone else, and he was no longer special. But instead of being happy that he had a brother, he'd revolted against the family and wanted nothing to do with him. And that wasn't fair to Danté. The more he thought, the more he became frustrated. Because he had no idea how he was going to make it up to him. But he didn't want to wait for something bad to happen either.

"We're all going to lunch, but I gotta make a call first. Think about what I said," Alena told him. "Don't wait until it's too late to be the big brother you should have always been." She got up from the bed and left the room with Alexis. "I'm gonna pop into Grandma's room to make a call."

"All right; see you downstairs."

Walking into the bedroom, Alena pulled her phone from her pocket. Dialling the number, she waited.

"Mount Sinai, how may I direct your call?'

"Um, yes, I'm ringing to find out the condition of one of your patients."

"Name?"

"James Gardo."

Tap, tap, tap. "He's still in ICU."

"Any idea if he can have visitors?"

"Mmm." Tap, tap. "Unless you're family, no."

"Uh, no. Just a friend ringing up to find out how he is. Any idea when non-family visitors can see him?"

"Probably not until he's moved to a room."

"Oh, okay. Thanks anyway. Bye." Sitting on the bed, she went back over all that had happened with James. The night they met at the Garden, the ten weeks on tour, him trying to kill Roger, claiming to be Luiz Manning. But from what they had read, and what they had heard their parents talk about, James was Luiz's half-brother by their mother, and Angie's half-brother by their father, the kid's grandfather. Andros Poulos was Angelina's and Luiz's father, and Sheila was Luiz's and James's mother. She let out a whoosh of air. How confusing! But one thing she *did* know was, she wanted to get to the hospital to see James, or to talk to his parents. She finally wandered downstairs to find Tomas and Roger. "Are you guys leaving?"

"Our flight's at four," Roger said. "We have time for lunch together."

"I think it's so cool what you did," Alexis told them. "Opening a centre in that old lady's house."

Tomas smiled brightly at his niece. "I think it's cool too. It's what Bette wanted, and she left the money for it, so I made it happen."

"*We* made it happen," Roger corrected, and got a cool look from his husband in return.

"Yeah, whatever." Tomas still wasn't quite back to talking to Roger just yet. Roger's carrying on over James/Luiz had caused a rift between them.

"Are you two *still* fighting?" Pedro asked, worried because his brother and Roger had never fought in their whole life together. "You *never* fight."

"Tell Roger that I have every right to be affected by some guy who looks *exactly* like my dead first lover who tried to poison me, kidnap me, and frame him for murder. Apparently, after thirty years, I'm not supposed to be affected anymore," Tomas huffed.

"Thirty years is a long time, bro." Pedro stared up at his brother who sat on the couch arm.

"Thank you," Roger murmured, glad someone agreed with him.

"But," Pedro went on with a glance at his brother-in-law, "it freaked *all of us* out. Some guy claiming to be Luiz just happened to be his half-brother. This whole situation is sick beyond belief. It's just too crazy to try and figure out. But as I've said before," he laid his hand on his brother's leg, "we can't possibly begin to know what it was like for you all those years ago. To be poisoned and kidnapped, stalked, framed for murder," he glanced at Roger, "it's a lot to deal with, and to suddenly have it all drenched up by the half-brother who is the exact identical twin to him." He shook his head. "That must have been so beyond freaky for you."

"Yeah." Tomas sighed, trying to corral his feelings. "You can't even begin to know what was going on in my head. I thought he'd come back from the dead to kidnap me again." His eyes welled. "I couldn't believe he was standing there. Looking the same. He hadn't aged. He looked *the same*, and he called out to me like he did back then. Ah…" He wiped away the tears. "It was freaky and creepy, and scared the fucking shit out of me, excuse the language," he told his nieces.

Alena shrugged. "We swear, we don't care."

"I do because I don't. Or at least, I rarely do," Tomas said.

"But I think the occasion called for it," Pedro said. "You wanna go get some lunch?"

*****

Jenny and her family arrived in Mykonos and headed for Carlos and Viv's place where they unpacked the twins.

"I don't want to be alone," Cabot said, refusing to set foot in his old room. "Do we have to be here? Can't we be on our own, Tonee?"

"No, we can't, Cabot." Antonio dropped his bags inside the door of his own room.

"Can I stay with you, Tonee?" Cabot made his way to his brother and wrapped his arms around him. "I don't want to be alone." The child in him was alive and well and rearing its childish head.

"You're not alone, Cabot. We're all here for you." Antonio gently patted his back.

"You have a choice, Cabot." Jenny came up behind them. "Your old room here, or your father's old room at my place. And then Dan can watch over you."

"But I want to be with Tonee in our own place," Cabot whined in a soft voice.

"You won't be alone. You can move in with Tomas and Roger when they get back. That's your third choice. Pick one."

Frowning, Cabot tried to act tough, but on the inside, he was panicking and angry. He didn't want to stay with his parents *or* grandparents. He wanted to stay with Tony. "Tonee, where do you want to stay?"

"In my room," Antonio replied. "I haven't stayed here for so long it will be good to be home again."

"Can I stay with you, Tonee?" Cabot tweaked his brother's golden-brown hair.

"Cabot." Antonio pushed his brother back, so they were facing one another. "I am here for you, but you need to be a grown-up now. You always wanted your own room. Well, now you get that again. We get peace and quiet and home. Sleep in your own room, Cabot. It will be okay. We're all here if you need us, but the time for acting like a child is over. We don't need to sleep in the same bed, or the same room. You'll be fine."

Cabot's bottom lip quivered. "Tonee—"

"Cabot," Antonio cut him off. "You're twenty-five, act like it."

The lip stopped, and the attitude came back. "Fine! I'll sleep in my room then." He stormed off down the hall.

"Do we need to lock you in?" Jenny called and followed to see him face down on his king-size bed. "Do we need to bar the windows and lock your door? Or do you need me to remind you of the plan? You do as you're told, and don't go off partying, or getting drunk."

"Yes, Grandma, you told me. Now leave me alone," Cabot mumbled from the pillow his face was buried in.

"Does Dan need to stay here the night? Maybe you should come home with me after all," Jenny continued. "We need to get your regime going."

Cabot rolled up into a sitting position to face off with his grandmother. "I'm perfectly capable of taking pills every day."

"Are you?" Jenny asked. "When you haven't been capable of acting like an adult who gives a crap about anyone but himself? When you haven't been capable of maturity and care *to* yourself? You got yourself into this mess, Cabot, and now we're trying to clean it up. I can call Tomas and Roger to come home early if you want to stay with them. It might be easier since they're neutral in all of this. Your mother will want to coddle you, your father will be angry and blame himself *and* you. Me, I just won't take crap from you, and your poor brother needs a break." She walked in and sat beside him on the bed. "It's time that Cabot Conroy Stephanopoulos found out who he really is on his own. And he has nothing to do with Steele Stefan."

Cabot frowned. "What do you mean?"

"Find out who *you* are deep inside, Cabot. Find out what sort of man you truly want to be and *be* it. Be the man you would be proud to call Cabot. Figure out what *your* problems have been and put them to rest. Find the real Cabot and let him out. He's not Steele Stefan any more than Antonio is Phoenix. Search your mind, your heart, your soul, Cabot, and find out who you truly are. From tomorrow, you'll be seeing a counsellor. We don't expect much, but if you want someone to talk to who has a vague idea of what you're going through, then I'll get Tomas and Roger home. Maybe there's something they can help with." She sighed. "And I know Tomas has some issues to deal with. You could deal with them together."

The words bounced around in Cabot's head, resonating on some level.

Jenny squeezed his hand and got up, but he didn't release her hand. Looking down, she saw conflicted thoughts pass over his face and through his eyes. Taking his face in her hand, she kissed his cheek. "I love you, Cabot. You're my grandson, but it's time to stop acting like a hurt little child and be a grown-up. You have grown-up issues to deal with now." She saw tears spring to his eyes and smiled softly. "Be a good boy, Cabot. I'll see you in the morning."

She left him and saw Antonio in the hallway, listening.

He silently mouthed *thank you* and walked into his room.

Back in the lounge, she hugged Viv and Carlos goodnight and left Dan to talk over Cabot's new regime. When she got home, she found Spiros and Derek drinking coffee in the dining room. "Where's mine?"

"In the pot," Spiros said. "You look as if you need it; take a seat, and I'll get you some." He went over to the counter, poured another coffee and gave it to her with a kiss on the cheek.

"What was that for?" She inhaled the aromas of fresh Greek coffee beans.

"For being you and taking control." Spiros seated himself and picked up his mug.

She sighed. "I just wish I'd done it sooner. Cabot might not have HIV. You both settled in?"

"Bags are in our room for you to sort out," Spiros said.

"And I've settled Dan and me into the guest room," Derek added. "I feel as if we were just here."

Jenny laughed lightly. "You were."

"Dan still next door?" Derek asked.

"Yes." Jenny sipped her coffee. Nice and strong. "He could be a while."

Derek nodded. "He went over everything on the plane, but now they're home, it needs to be gone over again. He could be a while."

"I told Cabot he'll be seeing the counsellor tomorrow, but I doubt he liked that idea much."

"Cabot's very Gen Y," Derek told her. "Very, *why me, why can't I have this, why can't I have that, me, me, me*. Arrogance level is high, so is denial that he's done wrong. And as long as it's been consensual, his sexual behaviour hasn't been wrong, until that fateful night. And he has that to deal with on top of whatever has been bugging him. So, it could take some time for him to open up."

"We'll give him a chance on his own," Jenny said. "I get that he may not feel that comfortable seeing someone, or talking to someone on his own, that's why I suggested calling Tomas home if he needed someone to talk to. And maybe they could see the counsellor together."

"Tomas needs to see a counsellor?" Spiros asked. "He hasn't seen one since '81 or '82 when he was in recovery. Oh…" he caught on.

"I'm not sure you quite got what I meant." Jenny smiled. "Yes, Tomas knows what Cabot is going through. In '81 he was told, by Dan, that he had the gay plague. But I was talking about this Luiz thing." She shook her head lightly. "I know it's thirty years, but Jesus, you saw his reaction to James Gardo. We were all shocked. Now that's dredged up a whole load of stuff that he clearly hasn't dealt with, or simply pushed down and ignored for thirty years." She glanced at Derek. "When does the counsellor get in?"

"Dan called up Xanthe Metlos from twenty-six years ago. She's still in business and is happy to stay indefinitely again. She already knows the family."

"Oh, that's excellent," Jenny said. "I remember her. She was so helpful with Tomas and knew his problems. Maybe she'll be able to help again." Glancing at the clock, she yawned. "But right now, I need to unpack and have a shower. What time is she coming?"

"On the first ferry, I think she said."

"Great. I'll meet her there and have a chat. But for now, I'll say goodnight to you, Derek. You waiting up for Dan?" Standing, she gathered the cups and placed them in the sink.

"I will. It's still relatively early, and he shouldn't be too much longer. Goodnight."

Jenny and Spiros retired to their room, closed the door behind them to lock out the world, and while Spiros got the bed ready, Jenny showered. Tomorrow was going to be a long day.

*****

Antonio sat staring at the wall in his room. He was back in his old room, with its old movie and music posters, awards, ribbons and school stuff. It had been a long time since he'd been there. Whenever he and Cabot came home, they stayed in the spare house, claiming it for themselves although it was usually reserved for visitors. But here, here he could be free. He could be himself.

"You okay, Antonio?" Carlos asked as he and Viv stood in the doorway. They'd just let Dan go and were looking in on the kids.

Sighing, Antonio gazed tiredly at his parents. "I'm home. I'm finally back in my old room again. I get to be Antonio again. No more Phoenix Stefan. I'm just plain old Antonio Stephanopoulos again. I get to be Tony again." He flopped backward onto the bed, staring at the ceiling covered in more posters.

"Yes, you do, my darling." Viv went to his side. "You get to be our little boy, Antonio, again."

"Viv, remember what Dan said. No more little boy stuff. They're men now, and must be treated as such," Carlos warned.

Her eyes connected with his. "I know. But my children will always be my babies. Look at how your mother called you her babies in your twenties. She even does it now."

"I know. But we never liked it." Carlos grinned.

"Liar!" Viv laughed. "You all loved it."

"True," Carlos admitted. "But times have changed, and now Antonio can have a break from life while Cabot gets help. You go and do whatever you want to relax and enjoy what's left of summer. And don't worry about your brother. We'll take care of him."

"Okay, Papa. I'll *try* and enjoy myself." Antonio's grin matched his father's.

"Good. We'll see you tomorrow. Come on, Viv."

She kissed Antonio goodnight and gave him a hug. "You have a good sleep, and don't worry about anything. It isn't up to you anymore. We'll carry the burden, okay? It's off your shoulders now."

"Okay, Mama. See you tomorrow."

They walked into Cabot's room, but he was busy staring out the window.

"Cabot, we've come to say goodnight," Viv said. "Are you all settled in, sweetie?" She glanced around and saw nothing unpacked.

"Mmm?" He turned from the window. "I'll unpack tomorrow."

"You were far away." Viv smiled at her son. "You looked serious."

He shrugged and gazed around the room. "Thinking about something Grandma said. My brain hasn't stopped spinning with things. It hasn't changed." His room was identical to Antonio's. The same pictures and posters, the same colours, the same layout.

"We had no need to change this room. But if you want to, it's your room. You might feel comfortable being in a place that's familiar," Viv added.

"Yeah." Cabot avoided their eyes. "Maybe. You were going to bed?"

Carlos observed the nervous twitch in Cabot's right leg. It always moved when he got antsy, and with crossed arms, Cabot looked as though he was up to something. "We are. So's Antonio. It's been a long few days for all of us. We've dead bolted everything, so you can't get out. But if you do, you know the security team will hunt you down, right?"

Cabot's leg stopped twitching. "Was she serious about that?"

"Cabot." Carlos stepped over to his son and held him by the arms. "She slapped you; she's serious. She *never* slapped any of us, didn't need to. But you, Alena, and Dom got reamed out because of your attitudes."

Cabot's eyes widened. "Dom got it too?"

"Yes, he did. He smashed Danté's camera that he got from the family for his birthday. They were out at the time, so Alena went and got Danté another one. Mama suspended him from *SB3* until the new year, froze his trust fund, and told him if he couldn't live off the money he'd saved, then he could get another job at a non-family owned business."

That shocked Cabot to the core. "Jesus, she *is* serious." The panic rose in his gut. He wanted to flee, to breathe, to be himself. But he felt captured, caught, a prisoner.

"The three of you needed pulling into line. And now it's your turn again. So, if you do escape, she'll hunt you down." Hugging his son, he moved back for Viv to have her turn.

"We're just around the corner if you need us, and Antonio's next door." Kissing his cheek, she stroked it. "I love you, Cabot. I want you to get through this."

His smile was grim. "I can't get through it, Mama. I have it for life."

Viv saddened. "I know, my baby. But we can help you deal with it and get your life back on track. So, try and get a good sleep, okay."

"Okay, Mama." He hugged her and closed the door after them. But sleep didn't come as easily for Cabot as it did Antonio. No, sleep didn't come at all. His brain worked overtime. Tears, fears, trepidation. He didn't want to talk to a counsellor, he didn't want to reveal his deepest thoughts and fears, hell, he didn't even know what they were himself. He wasn't even sure why he did what he did. He didn't want to go through this alone, and knew Tony deserved a life away from him, so he could get himself a girlfriend. They had been together forever, ever since the womb, and done everything together, but now he had something Tony didn't. HIV. And he couldn't pass that on to his brother. As much as he wanted them to do everything together, and live together for the rest of their lives, things were changing. And the idea of giving it to Tony so they could have it together excited but repulsed him. He couldn't give it to Tony. He didn't deserve that. He hadn't done anything wrong to deserve that. No. HIV was something he was going to have to live with himself for as long as he lived.

*****

In New York, Diana emerged into the penthouse.

"What have you been doing, cuz?" Alena asked from the couch in the sitting area.

"*Haus of Stefan* business." Diana yawned. "God, I'm so tired all the time. I think taking time off has made me tired." She sat wearily on the couch.

471

"What sort of *HOS* stuff?" Alena probed, having done none herself in months.

"Designs, ideas, legals, future ad campaigns, checking into sales, what's going on in London, Milan, Europe in general."

"We're getting ready to go out to lunch," Angie said. "Want to join us? Tomas and Roger are leaving after that."

"Where are you going?" Diana asked, the fog in her brain thick.

"Miami for a few days to check on the centre," Tomas said.

"That's cool. I love that you did that," Diana told him. "I'm hungry; what are we eating?"

A half hour later, they caught up with Mike, Maggie and the kids, and sat in *Rodriguez*, the Mexican restaurant they had first been to back in the early '80s.

"I can't believe this place is still here." Tomas looked around at the decor. "And it looks exactly the same."

"Yeah, it does," Pedro said as the waitress handed over menus. "It's funny how some stuff can't wait to change, and other things stay the same always."

"Miss 69?" Roger asked.

"Oh, God yes!" Pedro exclaimed. "When it's such a big part of your life, you always miss it. We partially modelled *SB3* on it, but I still miss it, *and* the people." He saw his family around the table. The girls, Angie, the boys, Dom had crawled out of his room, Mike, Maggie and the kids, Tomas and Roger. "Makes you even more grateful for what you have." Tomas sat next to him and he squeezed his hand.

Tomas squeezed back. "Yeah, it does."

"You two getting sappy again?" Alena rolled her eyes.

"Have you *not* learned anything from being in this family?" Angie asked her.

"Of course, Mama." Alena laid her head on Alexis's shoulder. "It only took me nineteen years to learn it."

"And a reaming out from Grandma." Tomas grinned.

"Ugh," another eye roll, "I never want to go through that again. I've had my turn."

"Yes, you have," Pedro told her. "And hopefully Dom will not repeat *his* behaviour either." He glanced at his son who blushed. "And now it's just Cabot to go."

"Anyone know where he and Antonio are?" Diana asked. "I haven't heard anything since Antonio came over on Sunday."

"No, nothing." Pedro glanced down at his menu. "But then that's not unusual."

After lunch, while Mike and Maggie took the twins, Nick and Danté, Pedro, Angie and the girls took Tomas and Roger to the airport and waited until the plane was in the air before returning home. Alena, Alexis and Diana went to her apartment to discuss *HOS* business, while Pedro and Angie enjoyed drinks on the rooftop terrace, and Dom retreated to his bedroom to continue sulking.

"So, how's *HOS* doing?" Alena flopped down on the couch in apartment 3.

"Good." Diana dropped the paperwork in her lap. "But more importantly, what are you going to do about James?"

Alena blushed. "What do you mean?"

"Are you going to see him in the hospital?" Diana asked.

"They aren't letting anyone in besides his parents. I called today. He's in ICU in an induced coma."

"Any idea when he'll be brought out of it?" Diana glanced over more papers.

"No. But I did consider going to the hospital anyway and talking to his parents."

"What!" Diana and Alexis glared at her.

"Are you stupid?" Diana asked. "With everything Grandma said."

"I know, I know. But I really liked him when he was on tour, but he didn't like me—"

"He liked Uncle Tomas," Alexis cheekily said.

"I *know*," Alena went on. "But now we know he had an aneurysm and wasn't himself. We need to find out what he remembers, and if he knows who Luiz is. You know he and Mama shared a brother."

"What!" Diana exclaimed. "How?"

"Well, on the papers we got from the library, and from what James said when he was here believing he was Luiz, he said as Luiz he was the bastard child of Andros Poulos and Sheila Manning. Andros Poulos was Mama's father. That makes Mama and Luiz half-siblings. And because Sheila had Luiz and James, *they're* half-siblings. So Mama and James share a brother."

"Jesus, does that make James and us related?" Alexis asked, chewing on her lip in thought.

"Um, no, I don't think so," Diana said. "Different mothers, different fathers. No, not genetically."

"But ew, how close is that," Alexis continued. "Way too close."

"What will you say to his parents?" Diana asked.

"I don't know." Alena sighed. "Maybe ask them to explain it to me. Grandma took the papers before we could read them properly."

"What will you say to James?" Alexis inquired. "What if he doesn't even remember you?"

Alena shrugged a shoulder. "I don't know. Thank him for his service and walk away."

"But you like him," Alexis prompted.

"But he looks like Uncle Tomas's first lover. I can't date a guy that freaks Uncle Tomas out. He doesn't deserve that." Alena frowned. "I'm not *in love* with him or anything. I just *really* like him."

"Like Uncle Tomas *really* liked Luiz?" Alexis asked.

"Hey, if he had been interested and wanted to sleep with me, I wouldn't have turned him down." Alena waved a hand. "He's hot and sexy and has incredible eyes. Did you see them?"

"Did you see Uncle Tomas's reaction to him? Poor thing thought it was his lover back from the dead," Diana said. "Did you hear what Luiz did to Uncle Tomas? Poison, kidnap, murder."

"What's the story, exactly, do you know?" Alexis asked.

"Luiz was engaged to a Bertha St John when he met and fell in love with Uncle Tomas," Diana said. "But when Uncle Tomas found out, he and Bertha dumped Luiz and flew to Miami. Luiz followed, stalked Uncle Tomas, killed four *Seralift* porn stars who worked with Tomas and Roger, and tried to frame Roger for their deaths to get him away from Uncle Tomas *while* he was poisoning Uncle Tomas to get him away from Roger. Uncle Tomas ended up in the hospital and Luiz kidnapped him from there. They found a seedy hotel, but another man killed Luiz and kidnapped Uncle Tomas. We don't know who he was or why he kidnapped Uncle Tomas yet."

Alexis and Alena looked at her in disbelief.

"You got *all of that?*" Alena asked, incredulously.

"I read the papers as they printed off and listened closely on Sunday, and every time our parents whisper in huddles," Diana said.

"Jesus." Alena raised a brow. "So, this Luiz Manning, James's half-brother, did all that to Uncle Tomas, and James freaks him out by looking like and talking like Luiz, and Uncle Roger wonders why he's freaked out?"

"It *has* been thirty years," Alexis pointed out. "Time to move on and all that."

"But they say James looks *exactly* like Luiz. They could be twins. So, do you want to get involved with a guy like that?" Diana asked Alena.

A sigh left Alena. "I don't know. I doubt anything will come of it, but I'd like to see him. We did travel together for over ten weeks. And I'd like to talk with his parents."

*****

The next day, Jenny met Xanthe at the wharf. She came with two large, two medium, and two small suitcases, plus two bags.

"I hope you won't be staying that long," Jenny joked. "That's a lot of luggage."

Xanthe laughed. "I brought summer *and* winter clothes, but the two small cases are my offices. Laptop, books, paperwork. I need something to do when I'm not counselling."

"Oh, what a good idea for travelling," Jenny said, wheeling a large and medium case with bags attached over to the car. "I'll have to remember that." Twenty minutes later, she was settling Xanthe into the spare house next to Tomas. "Here we are. Bedroom upstairs, office downstairs. All free of charge. I didn't get any food, but the grocery store we buy from will deliver. Just ring up with what you want, and they'll get it out today. We'll pick up the tab for everything, of course.

Did Dan tell you much?"

"He spoke briefly of Cabot's behaviour and that he recently contracted HIV from an assault." Xanthe removed her blazer and looked around. "Very nice. Part of your empire?"

"I had these last time when you came to counsel Tomas and Roger in '81 through '83 or '84." Jenny tidied up as she went.

Xanthe nodded at the memories. "That's right. And how are they?"

Jenny's brows rose at the question. "Long story, but I did want to talk to you about the family. A lot has happened, my granddaughter, Alexis, was assaulted in May, then something recently happened with Tomas, and he and Roger aren't on good terms. Then there's Cabot. Dom's at Danté's throat, but we hope that's ended. So, if anyone in the family wants to talk, you're on 24/7."

"Absolutely anyone, anytime, anything. Even you." She watched for a reaction.

Jenny's eyes narrowed. "I'm not sure I have…issues…with myself, although I do have them with the grandkids and would like to know where we went wrong with them."

"Who said you did?" Xanthe asked.

"Well…Alena, Cabot, Dom were all egotistical, selfish people. Alena has seen the light, and we hope Dom has. But Cabot's behaviour was not taught by us. Diana and Antonio turned out fine. So did Alexis and Danté."

"Jenny, they're adults. Adult behaviour is *their* responsibility. You can give them the tools and teach them until they're blue in the face, and you too, but once they leave home and live on their own, their behaviour is their own."

"Which explains Cabot, but Alena lives two doors down with Diana when they're in town, and Dom still lives at home."

"Well, if he'd like to talk, I'm willing to listen, the door is open."

"You know one of us could walk in anytime," Jenny said.

"Then I'll make sure I'm dressed," Xanthe joked.

*****

Tomas and Roger emerged from Bertha's house and drove to the centre. Even after a month, the place was still running smoothly.

"Did you expect it to fall apart?" Dr William Fender joked. "No. It's a very well-run centre, and we're taking care of all the patients."

"Has anyone…passed yet?" Roger asked softly.

"Not yet," William said. "But a few *are* close." He showed the boys through, and they sat and spoke with the patients, offering sympathetic words. They held the hands of the sick, and helped change beds, telling William their own story when he questioned why.

"Wow, even back then to be told you had the gay plague, it was the end of your life. That must have been terrifying."

"It was," Tomas said softly. "We owe everything to Mama and Dan. All of our friends died except for one, and they're all buried here in Miami."

"Do you attend their graves?" William asked, pulling a case onto a pillow.

"No. In '81 we couldn't take it anymore, so we stopped coming back, and then we got sick. It took years for Tomas to get better, and by then, we chose to be activists. We hadn't been back until August," Roger said.

"And you haven't attended their gravestones?" William repeated.

"No," Roger answered, wondering why he was pushing that aspect.

"But we should," Tomas murmured. "We attended the graves of my brothers and sisters-in-law's friends who died when we were in New York. And we realised we hadn't attended any in all these years."

"Do you know where they're buried?" William asked.

"Most are in Miami Gables Cemetery," Roger replied. "There's a few elsewhere, but most are there."

"How many?" William asked.

"Hundred, hundred fifty, more? We stopped counting." Roger fluffed the pillows on the next bed.

"Jesus. It was a bad time in the early '80s." William threw the dirty sheets into a laundry trolley.

"It certainly was," Tomas muttered as he smoothed out the blue blanket on the bed.

"Will you go to their gravestones?" William asked.

With a deep depressing sigh, Tomas said, "Yes."

"I'd like to come."

Tomas and Roger looked up in surprise. "What? Why?"

"Because I probably treated most of them."

Staring in shock, Tomas couldn't say anything; he just slumped onto the bed he'd smoothed down. Talk about coincidence.

"You're kidding?" Roger managed.

William sadly shook his head. "It was a rough time, '80 to '81 through to 2000 at least. So many died and *continue* to die from it. That's why this centre is so important. You can't get many in, but you know they won't have long, and another will have a chance to die at peace here."

"And where do they go?" Tomas asked. "Do we…"

"We pay for the burial, or cremation, as stipulated by you, and if their family doesn't want them, then we abide by their wishes and bury them, or scatter their ashes," William told them.

"And where do we bury them?" Roger wasn't sure he wanted the answer to that.

William's eyes traded back and forth between them, gauging their reactions. "Miami Gables Cemetery."

Worn out by the emotional baggage of it all, they spent the rest of the day helping then retired to Bertha's house.

"I think it's fabulous what you boys are doing, and I've changed my will, so you will be left the house. I want you to do the same as you did with Bette's," Bertha told them over dinner. "I think all the girls have done the same."

"What?" Shock settled over Tomas once more. It had been a day for shocks, as so many were lately.

"We're leaving you two our houses and money to turn into AIDS centres for the dying. In fact," she became animated, "I thought of starting the process now. I have an apartment I could move into, so the house could be renovated and turned into a centre. And then you two can be the owners when I die. Oh, that's a marvellous idea. I'm going to get started on it right away. I want to help while I still can, and I'm alive to see it happen."

"Oh, my God, Bertha. That's an incredible thing to do," Roger told her.

"I know all the right people to call because we just did it with Bette's house. I'll have no problems there, and I don't need all of this artwork and statues anyway. Someone else can enjoy it." She put a finger to her lip. "I might get all of the girls to do it, so we can share our wealth while we still can."

*****

The next day, Tomas and Roger stopped at five florists to get enough flowers for the graves. They met William at the car park and hauled the crates from the back of the van they had rented. After strapping the crates onto dollies, they set off for the section that held their friends. Reaching the top of the incline, they saw row after row of small white headstones indicating where their friends lay dead.

"Oh, God." Tomas closed his eyes, ready to implode.

"Take a deep breath and breathe slowly," William said, gazing over the grounds. "It's a powerful sight."

Tomas felt a hand on his elbow and opened his eyes to see Roger by his side.

"Together," Roger said.

A soft smile lit up Tomas's face. "Together."

They rolled the dollies along the path and stopped at each headstone to check for a name. Judd, Ethan, Johnno, Evan, Freddy, Braeden. Friend after friend after friend received a rose, a small prayer, and a crossing of the chest.

They had bought two hundred roses. They left with none.

Stopping at another florist they bought more, and found Zack and Adam's graves in another cemetery. Laying a bunch for each, they crossed their chests, bowed their heads, and left. It took all day and left them drained, so they sat on the back terrace at Bette's sipping iced tea.

"That was tough," William said. "I recognised a lot of names."

"So did we," Roger murmured. "I haven't been back there since 1981. It became too much to keep losing them, and then we got sick ourselves."

"Two hundred and two," Tomas murmured, dazed that they had lost so many people they knew personally all to one goddamned disease.

A while later, they left, and Tomas was quiet on the way home, but the moment they closed their bedroom door, he fell into Roger's arms. "I don't want to fight," he sobbed. "I love you, and we've lost too many."

"Oh, my love." Roger stroked his hair. "I don't want to fight either, and obviously I'll never know the full extent of Luiz's effect on you, and I shouldn't be so horrible about getting you to forget. But I think it's time you sorted out your feelings and finally let it go."

"I know," Tomas sobbed. "I know."

*****

Cabot sat for the third day in a row in Xanthe's office. Antonio or his grandma had escorted him there at ten every morning, and every morning he sat, or paced, or stared out the window.

Xanthe didn't care. She knew he would be a tough one, and that he needed to open up in his own time, so she worked on her papers while he paced, sat, or stared out the window. But finally, she asked, "Why did you and your brother come up with monikers?"

He frowned slightly at the sudden intrusion, but continued staring out the window. "What?"

Xanthe wrote a few notes. "Why did you and your brother choose stage names?"

Cabot shrugged. "Because they sounded cool."

"They do," Xanthe said. "I like them a lot and have seen your pictures in magazines. You and your brother are incredibly good looking. The modelling world must love you." Her eyes stayed on her papers.

Breathing in calmly, Cabot said, "Yeah, they do."

"Did you pick the names, did Antonio, or did you both?"

Finally, he turned from the window. "When we started modelling, I told Tone that our names sounded stupid, especially mine, so we should come up with cool names. Our sister goes by her middle name, which is Mama's name, and no one in the family goes by Stephanopoulos except our fathers."

"It is their name." Xanthe searched through a small pile of books for the one she was after.

"Yeah, but they didn't go by it when they were young. They all went by Stefan too. Did you know our father and his brothers were huge porn stars back in their day? Carlo, Pedro and Tomas Stefan. The *Porn Star Brothers* of the late '70s." Cabot stood smirking, thinking he'd shocked Xanthe.

But all she did was casually blink at him and smile. "Oh, I know all about it. Even saw some of their movies. But what does their career before you were born have to do with you now, thirty years later?"

"What?" Cabot blinked, confused momentarily by the lack of surprise.

"What do *their* careers have to do with *you* now?"

Frowning, Cabot stared at her. He comprehended the questions, just didn't have an answer.

"Something? Nothing?" Xanthe asked, knowing she'd stumped him. She knew all about the boys' careers, having counselled Tomas, and he'd spilled everything about his life, finding love with men, the deaths of his friends, his career, and how his illness and his mother's love had changed him.

"Um…" Cabot murmured.

"Your grandmother informed me that you had found your father's vault and found out the big, dark family secret," she joked. "Not that it was a secret, they just never told their children because it's none of their business. So…what does your father's past have to do with you now?"

"Um…well…" Cabot struggled for an answer, so he came up with the only one he knew. "Because it makes him a fucking hypocrite. *Literally*, it makes him a *fucking* hypocrite." Cabot stalked around the small office, skirting the two cosy chairs as he went.

"So your father's sex life, before and after his stint in porn, is the reason *you* have sex now? Explain that to me."

"Explain it to you?" he asked in surprise. "*You're* the shrink, *you* tell me."

"Okay." Xanthe sat back in her chair at the small desk. "You are attached to your brother your whole life. You want to live the same life, but it seems what, boring, dull? You're becoming a man, so sex has become important, and you start off with women because that's the norm. But as you get older, men interest you too, more than women. So, you experiment, which there's nothing wrong with, and life is going along okay until you find your father's movies and think what, how dare he? If he could do it, why can't I? So you become rampant like he was, thinking, who's he to tell me otherwise. And then your grandmother slaps you because you call your uncles fag fuckers and revealed to your cousins that your parents and uncles were in porn. They're telling you to stop or cut back on sex, and you call them hypocrites. Knowing and telling someone else's business made you feel big and strong, until your grandmother slapped you, and then you were weak and pathetic. So, at twenty-five, instead of manning up and taking responsibility for the choices *you* made, *you* blame your parents and grandparents." She studied him as his frown deepened. "Do you *not* *know* how to take responsibility, Cabot? Did your parents not teach you how to?"

He stared at her, wondering how she knew so much without having spoken to him. "You've talked to my family? That's where you got all of this from."

"Dan told me you have HIV, your grandmother told me how arrogant you'd become, and I haven't spoken to your parents or brother. I've only been here three days. I know the family, I've read up on all of you and your careers, I can read body language, and you're very shut off. You're shutting yourself off on purpose." Taking in his frown, crossed arms, and very straight pose, she knew he was in denial, full of anger and fear, but it was a matter of getting to the bottom of it.

"I don't want to talk to you anymore." Cabot stormed out the door only to be met by Antonio. "Tonee." He threw himself into his brother's arms. "I love you, Tonee."

"I love you too, Cabot," he replied, spying Xanthe over his shoulder watching the reunion with interest. "Are you finished for the day?"

"I'm finished forever. Let's go, Tonee." Cabot tugged his brother away from the house, throwing a scowl over his shoulder at Xanthe.

"I seriously doubt you're finished forever," Antonio said as they walked arm in arm down to the beach and sat on a stone wall watching the waves come in.

"I don't care. I don't want to go back," Cabot stubbornly said, running a hand through his hair.

"You know the rules, Cabot. You see Xanthe every day like clockwork."

"But Tonee—"

"*No buts,* Cabot. You don't get to make the rules until you can show you can follow them like an adult."

Scowling, Cabot noticed beachgoers staring, and realised it was because they were famous. Waving, he called out, "Hello, yes, it's us. The Stefans."

"Don't go there, Cabot, unless you want me to tell them you have HIV."

Cabot's eyes widened in shock. "Tonee, you wouldn't?"

"We're here to stay out of the limelight, Cabot. Get out of the public eye, and here you are waving to fans."

"But they're *fans,* Tonee." Cabot jumped off the wall to sign autographs and take photos with them.

Knowing he needed to stick by his brother, Antonio jumped down and joined in before pulling Cabot away. "Come on, let's go."

"But Tonee…" Cabot waved at the fans as they left. "You're being rude."

"And you're getting sucked back into the lifestyle we're trying to get out of. Let's get you home. We can sit on the balcony and have a drink." Antonio dragged him home and onto the balcony.

"Tonee, I want to go out and have fun." The scowl was etched into Cabot's face.

"And spread your HIV around?" Antonio handed him a light beer.

Cabot sighed. "Tonee, I don't like talking about it."

"Still in denial?"

"Still don't want to talk about it. Have *you* seen Xanthe yet?" He changed tack.

"Nope. But I've been wondering if I should. Sort some of my own issues out."

"Like what, Tone?"

"Like, what will I do now I'm not modelling. Like, what do I do now I'm not looking after my brother. Like, how do I go about getting a real girlfriend. Like, do I even want to model anymore or move into other areas like Diana wants to? Mama and Papa did." He shrugged. "We're twenty-five now, we have control of our trust funds if we want to set up a business. Maybe I'll do that, or just work for *HOS*. Maybe I'll bartend at *SB3*, or go work in *The Windmill*, or the meat shop. Maybe I'll volunteer my time and services, so I broaden my horizons." He finished his beer and sat back, staring over the ocean and stretching out his long legs. The warm breeze swept over his sun-kissed skin and made him warm and placid.

Cabot was impressed. And intrigued. "You'd really do all of that, Tone?"

Antonio shrugged a shoulder. "Why not? I want to stop being a model for a while and do other things. *Learn* new things. Explore Mykonos again, which we haven't done since we were kids because we haven't been here. And I know we're only in early September, but I can't wait for the cooler months. Thanksgiving, Christmas, New Year's. To sit in front of Grandma's roaring fire on a Sunday afternoon, all warm and toasty after a scrumptious roast chicken meal that she makes…God, I can't wait for that."

Cabot's mind went back to the times before they left the island to pursue their careers. They were teens, and Sundays were the best days because of Grandma's roast chicken. "Yeah, it was pretty cool. We haven't done that in years," he said wistfully.

"Yeah, and I can't wait to do it again," Antonio said. "I can just smell it now…"

"Do you think she'll make one this Sunday?"

"God, I hope so."

*****

After spending the night in each other's arms, Tomas and Roger woke. They'd never given one another the cold shoulder in the whole thirty years of their marriage, and they had never stopped talking to one another either. But that past week had taken its toll, and once more they decided to stop talking about Luiz. Tomas agreed to see a counsellor to try and resolve whatever issues he had where Luiz was concerned.

They spent the day at Bette's old home, and with help from the ladies, and William who went over all of the details again as a refresher, laid out plans for their houses to be turned into centres. The ladies promised to start next week and were more concerned about throwing Tomas and Roger a going away party than anything else.

"We don't need anything, really," Tomas told them. "Just a nice meal tonight and then we head off tomorrow."

"Nonsense!" Bertha exclaimed. "We'll have to make it a gala affair. After what you've done with this place, you've inspired all of us to do the same, and we want to do something nice for you."

"Which is nice, but not needed," Tomas said. "We just want a nice meal."

"Then that's what we'll plan," Bertha replied. "Come on girls, let's get back to my place and get it all ready."

Watching the girls leave, Tomas shook his head in wonder. "They never cease to amaze me."

"If they can turn their homes into care centres, it will be a massive help," William said. "And they get to see the impact it makes while they're still alive."

"True, true," Tomas agreed. Another two hours and they were ready for home. "We're not sure when we'll get back, but you have our number and Skype address, so call if you need help, and we'll be on a plane out here."

"Sure thing. It's been a pleasure hooking up with you boys." William shook their hands.

"Same here," Roger said, and they left, waving goodbye as they went.

They arrived at Bertha's to see the full setup in the luxurious dining room. "What's all this?" Roger asked.

"Dinner!" Bertha exclaimed. "And you have twenty minutes to change. The girls will be here at half-past."

With smiles as broad as can be, the boys hustled upstairs to shower and change, and made it down as the girls arrived. They escorted each one to their seat before seating themselves.

Tapping her knife on her glass, Bertha called for attention. "I'd like to propose a toast to Tomas and Roger; raise your glasses, everyone."

There were twenty-two people at the table; the twenty women who were left in Miami from their original group of friends thirty years ago, and the boys.

"I would like to propose a toast to Tomas and Roger. You have brought so much to our lives, and once again you have given it new meaning. Thirty years ago it was about getting a man that wasn't already mine." Tomas blanched and went red. "Now, it's about doing good for the community and following in our good friend Bette Olander's footsteps. What you have done with her home is commendable, and it has inspired all of us to do the same. We are opening our hearts, our lives, our homes to the needy HIV/AIDS patient who are no longer wanted by their families. We will take care of them until we need to be taken care of ourselves, and it's all down to Tomas and Roger." She raised her glass to them. "Tomas and Roger."

*****

On Saturday morning, Cabot was back in Xanthe's office. Silent, staring out the window, arms crossed.

Xanthe was at her desk, silent, poring over her papers, waiting for him to talk. When he didn't, she started. "Do you like being famous?"

Cabot cocked a brow. "*Are* models famous?"

"Do you have fame from your job?"

"I guess."

"Do you get recognised in the street?"

"Yes."

"Then you're famous."

"Yes." Cabot pondered. "I guess I am."

"Do you like being famous?"

Another ponder. "Yes."

"How so?"

"It gets me more jobs, more money, more attention. I get into clubs for free, get sent a lot of nice things for free, get lots of invitations to things."

"It must be nice to know that you're wanted?"

He thought about it. "Yes, yes it is."

"What sort of free stuff do you get?"

"Clothes, watches, jewellery, shoes, alcohol, bags. One company offered us a car for six months a few years back. That was nice."

"What sort of car?"

"Aston Martin."

"Nice!"

"I thought so. They gave us matching ones."

"Antonio gets the same stuff you do?"

"Of course. They always send two of everything."

"Do you usually get your own, or do you share?"

"We generally get our own, but sometimes we've shared. We've shared our whole lives."

"Do you share sexual partners?"

A frown slid across Cabot's face as he thought back to that time in the penthouse. "No."

"Never?"

Silence.

"Male or female," Xanthe went on.

"Mmm," Cabot grumbled.

"Do you want Antonio to get HIV too?"

"What!" Cabot spun around. "Of course not."

"Then, have you shared sexual partners?" Xanthe looked him straight in the eye.

But Cabot was too ashamed; embarrassed to even answer that.

"I'll take that as a yes. Were you both safe?"

He gulped before answering. "Yes."

"With each other?"

The frown deepened. "We don't do that together."

"I meant, if you shared a sexual partner at the same time, or have had threesomes, were you safe with each other?"

"Oh…um…yes…"

"So have you shared men or women?"

"Both," came out softly.

"At the same time?"

Shame flared on his face. "Yes."

"Condoms?"

"Always."

"Have you ever wanted to have sex with your brother?"

"What!" His eyes went wide. "Oh, my God, you're disgusting. What sort of quack are you? That's gross." He raced out the door and into the arms of his father. "What sort of crackpot is she?"

"One that clearly got on your nerves," Carlos answered. "And one that's clearly doing her job."

*****

New York was bright and sunny on Saturday morning, and the family were spending their last day in town.

"I have something to do today before we go; can we meet up for lunch instead?" Alena asked her parents when they suggested spending the day together. "I can meet you somewhere."

"I was going to suggest spending the day at the zoo or Coney Island," Angie told her. "But if you have things to finish off…"

"Or I can stay another week before coming home," Alena suggested. "Diana's here another week or two. I can stay with her to keep her company."

"I'll be off mid-week," Diana said. "I've got a full schedule if I'm going to make it home for Mama and Daddy's anniversary."

"Then I can stay with you until you go," Alena said. "Keep you company, so you're not all by yourself in this big old apartment building."

"That would be a good idea," Angie told Pedro. "And then we wouldn't need to worry about leaving Diana alone."

"Okay." Pedro nodded. "Then what do *we* do today?"

"Personally," Summer piped up. "I'd rather go shopping since we're leaving tomorrow."

Maggie shook her head in amusement. "Haven't you girls had enough shopping? You've been out every day. The plane will be full and won't be able to fly your stuff home, you've bought so much."

"Mother, it's hardly *that* much, oh, how you do exaggerate," Melody told her in a hoity-toity tone.

"Ah-huh. And does it all fit in your suitcases?" Maggie knew her daughters well.

The twins traded glances. "Of course it does," Summer finally said.

"Yeah, right!" Maggie quipped.

Angie laughed. "Sounds like us when we were that age. Whatever we're going to do, I suggest we make a decision and go and do it." She started clearing plates from the breakfast table.

Dom cleared his throat. "Um…there's an exhibition on today that… ah…I'd like to see and ah…I thought…um…Squirt might like to go…" He rubbed his sweaty palms on his jeans and stared down at the table nervously.

Everyone stopped what they were doing and traded glances with everyone else. Pedro at Angie, Alena at Alexis and Diana, Nick at Danté, Danté at Dom.

"Ah," Pedro started, surprised by his son. "What sort of exhibition?"

"Um…photographs of old New York. Apparently, it's got an old camera display there too. It's some sort of photography exhibition." Dom licked his lips and swallowed. "But if you all want to come…"

"Ah…" Pedro glanced from his son to Angie's wide-eyed expression.

She shrugged, unsure of what to say or do at the sudden change of events. "Where is the exhibition?"

"At the School of Visual Arts," Dom said, picking at his placemat.

"Oh, I know where that is," Mike said. "We went to a restaurant near there last week." He looked at Pedro, raised a brow, and gave a slight nod at his son.

Pedro caught on. "Um, okay. I have no problem with that if you have no problem taking Nick along."

Dom's eyes flew up to stare into his father's. "Ah, what?"

Pedro coolly stared back. "You can take Danté to the exhibition if you take Nick as well."

"Oh." Dom nervously looked around. "Um, okay."

"Good." Pedro watched his son. "What time is it."

"Um…" Dom looked at his watch. "It's open from ten."

"Then we can still have lunch together and do something this afternoon," Angie told everyone. "What do you girls want to do?" She turned to Alena and Alexis.

"Well, *Haus of Stefan* has dropped its fall line, so we'll check out that. Maybe do a bit of selling and get some customers in," Alena said. "Who's up for free clothes?"

"Oooh, me." Summer and Melody's hands flew up.

"Then it's settled. Alena will take the girls, Dom, the boys, and we adults get to spend some time together. Diana, what will you do?" Angie asked.

"Ah, I'll go to *HOS* with the girls, Aunt Angie." Diana's stomach was still unstable, regardless of the vitamins Dan had her on, and the energy she once had was gone.

"Where do we want to meet for lunch?" Pedro asked.

"How about *Club 54* on 69th Street?" Mike asked. "We haven't gone there yet."

"What do they serve?" Angie asked.

"Club sandwiches, mainly," Mike said. "Upper crust, nice, don't need to dress up though. They do other food as well."

"Sounds great. 1 p.m. okay?" Angie asked.

"Can we call?" Alena asked in return. "If we get caught up at the store, we may not be able to get away."

"Okay, *I* will call everyone when *I* think we should eat," Angie said. "It will be somewhere between one and two."

The girls left for the store and the boys for the exhibition.

"Well, what did you think of that?" Angie asked Pedro as the four adults took the car to the beach.

"I thought it was downright weird, but then who knows, maybe Mama's words got through. Maybe whatever the girls said to him got through. We'll see soon enough."

*****

The girls arrived at *HOS* and immediately checked out the stock. Alena did some re-arranging as the manager came flying out, and Diana moved the jewellery displays. Summer and Melody picked out new fall fashion, and Alexis tried on the shoes.

Word on the street got out, and visitors came through the door wanting autographs and photos. Diana and Alena said hello to fans, and many wanted Alexis's autograph, which stunned her. She posed with fans who admired her hair and funky style, and stock flew off the shelves. They quickly put in an order for more, and these were delivered from the warehouse out the back within half an hour.

The girls played stylist for their customers and helped pick out fall outfits for them, even giving a 30% discount if they purchased three or more items. They were having fun and considered opening a store in Mykonos or Athens.

*****

Dom, Danté and Nick took a cab to E 23rd street, making it there as the doors opened. They had been quiet on the ride over, Danté not knowing what to say to his brother to whom he hadn't spoken in ages.

Dom paid their way in, and they spent the next three hours looking at pictures of old New York and the kinds of cameras used.

"Cool, that one's a hundred years old," Nick said. "It must be the first camera ever made."

They continued on, not needing to say much. Dom left the boys to themselves, but stayed close by until he found a photo that piqued his interest. "Hey, Danté, get a look at our building."

Danté and Nick looked at each other in surprise before moving. The photo was of their NY home, all seven storeys, and the story of who built it and owned it.

"Built in 1816 by Gustoff Nikolai, wealthy oil baron from Russia. Sources say Gustoff built the home to house his wife, four mistresses, and their children," Dom read.

"Whoa! A wife *and* four mistresses," Nick said. "Dude must have been exhausted."

"I wonder if we could get a copy of this," Dom said. "I don't think Grandma ever dug into the history of our building. Maybe we should."

Danté got his camera out and took a photo. "We might be able to get a copy from the archive for historic homes."

Dom thought about it. "We've got Christmas coming up. We could do a photo book or something of all the buildings the family owns and their history."

"Won't that be a lot of work?" Nick looked from the photo to Dom to Danté.

"Not really," Danté said. "If we can get old photos and info, I can put together a document on the computer and print it out. Or we can get Yossi at *Prologue* to do it. We're already September, we've got school, but I could get the document done if you get the research done and info ready," he told his brother.

Dom nodded enthusiastically. "I wonder if we could get something done today?" He glanced at the bottom of the photo to see where it had come from, but it just stated who it was and where.

"The historical society?" Nick suggested. "We could try there."

"And if it needs longer, just email everyone when we get home," Danté added. "Surely they'll be able to send us stuff over email?"

Dom's phone rang, and he quickly answered it.

"It's 1 p.m., can you get to *Club 54* now?" Angie asked.

"Um," Dom looked around, "Yeah, we're just about done."

"Good. Your father's rung the girls, and they're on their way. It's on 69th."

"Okay, we're on our way, bye." He shoved his phone into his pocket. "Mama. Time for lunch, come on, Squirt." He put an arm around Danté's shoulder, which totally surprised Danté, and led the boys through the rest of the exhibition and out to the street.

*****

Early on Sunday morning, Cabot sat thinking. He'd been thinking since seeing Xanthe the day before. Did he share sexual partners with Tony? Of course he had. They'd fucked the same women, and some of the guys he'd fucked had sucked off Tony. Did he want to have sex with his brother? What sort of quack was she? Did she get off on those kinds of thing? They were twins, for God's sake. What sort of disgusting cow was she?

"Cabot, breakfast," Viv called.

Scowling, he climbed out of bed and made his way to the kitchen.

"And here are your pills," Viv handed him a small container and a glass of orange juice.

He threw them back and gulped down his juice. "What's for breakfast?"

"Bacon and eggs. You can have it on a roll, Antonio's making it," Viv said.

"Tonee!" Cabot happily went to his brother at the stove and wrapped his arms around his waist. Snuggling his head into his shoulder, he added, "Can I have lots of bacon, Tonee?"

"You can have whatever you want," Antonio told him. "It's grilled, so it's healthier, and the roll is multigrain."

"I want one egg and lots of bacon, Tonee."

Antonio quickly whipped together the roll and handed it over. "Here. Sit and eat."

Cabot let go long enough to grab the roll and shove half into his mouth. He carried the plate to the table, where he sat and inhaled the rest of it. "Can I have another one, Tonee? I'm hungry." He gazed expectantly at his brother who was sitting beside him trying to eat his own roll.

Antonio paused as his roll reached his mouth.

Viv saw that pause and got up. "You sit, sweetie," she told Antonio. "I'll make Cabot another one."

"But I like the way Tonee makes it," Cabot whined.

"Then you can wait until Antonio eats his own breakfast, and then he'll make you another one," Viv said. "Or, I can make you one now."

Cabot pouted and watched Antonio eating his bacon and egg roll. "How long will you be, Tonee?"

Antonio coolly glanced at him, deliberately chewing his food slowly. "Awhile."

"Aw! I can't wait that long." Cabot screwed up his face like a pouty child. "Okay, Mama. You can make it."

Viv smiled and laid four pieces of bacon on the grill and closed the lid. She cracked an egg in the pan, heated the roll, buttered it, turned the egg, and made up the roll. "Here you go, sweetie. One egg, four bacon."

Cabot shoved half into his mouth. "Mmm, mmm, mmm."

"You can wait until you've swallowed to repeat that." Carlos sipped his coffee. He was sitting at the opposite end of the table, so had a clear view of his son and his attitude.

Cabot swallowed, drank some juice and tried again. "This is good, Mama."

"I've taken lessons from Uncle Tomas and Roger too. Who do you think taught Antonio? Next time, you can make your own and try it out. It's simple."

"Mmm, maybe." Cabot finished off his roll and poured a cup of coffee while waiting for Antonio to finish his breakfast. "What are we doing today, Tone?"

"You've got therapy at ten," Antonio replied, casually drinking his coffee and not giving his brother his attention.

Cabot scowled. "That woman is a sicko. The things she said yesterday."

Carlos traded a glance with Viv. "Hit a nerve, did she?"

"Mmm? No." Cabot kept his tongue in check. He didn't want to give away too much. After all, the sessions *were* private.

Antonio drank the last of his coffee and checked the clock. "Go get ready. I'll take you in half an hour."

"Okay, Tonee." Cabot bounced out of his seat and went to shower and dress.

"Does he do everything you tell him to?" Carlos frowned thoughtfully.

"Pretty much," Antonio told him.

"And how do you like it?" Carlos asked.

"I feel smothered." Antonio eyed his father. "And I'm over it."

"Yes, I guess you would be," Carlos murmured. "Does he know you feel that way?"

Antonio shrugged a shoulder. "Who knows? Will the rest of the family be home today?"

"Yes. Pedro, Angie and the kids."

"Diana?"

"Not until November," Viv reminded him. "She has a busy schedule."

"She'll be the last to know then?" Antonio asked.

"Yes," Carlos said. "Unless we tell her over the phone."

"Although," Viv murmured, "I think she has something going on with her. Did you notice that she was quiet a lot and didn't really do much?"

"She said she was busy or tired," Antonio replied. "Maybe the food poisoning is going on longer than expected."

"Mmm, well I've never heard of that," Viv said. "Maybe I should ask Dan if she's okay."

"You can't do that; doctor-patient confidentiality," Carlos reminded her.

"You never know." Viv got up to clear the table.

"I'm ready, Tonee." Cabot came bouncing out of his bedroom, and Antonio got up to take him downstairs.

"Ugh, I really don't want to be here," Cabot grumbled as they stood at Xanthe's door. "You should have heard some of the things she said yesterday."

"That's for the two of you to sort out," Antonio said. "I'll see you later."

"Ugh, Tonee," Cabot whined and watched his brother walk away. With a sigh, he entered the home and found Xanthe working on her computer.

*****

Tomas and Roger were unpacking their cases in the bedroom, after a long flight from Miami, when they heard the twins walk past and stop next door.

Peering out the window, Tomas said, "Cabot's gone in, and Antonio's walking away. I wonder what going on."

"There's one person who can tell you that, and that's your mother." Roger closed his empty case and stored it in the walk-in closet.

"Then I suggest we go now," Tomas said, and they hurried upstairs.

*****

"Do you do that a lot?" Xanthe asked, not looking up from her computer.

"What?" The lip cocked up.

"Whine. Do it a lot?"

"No." The scowl was back, and he moved over to the window to stare out at the view.

"Scowl a lot?"

"No." Then he realised he did.

"Lie a lot?"

"What?" He turned to face her. "I don't lie!"

"Don't you?"

"No."

"Not even to yourself?"

"What?" The scowl was replaced with an unsure frown.

"You clearly lie to your family, except for your twin who knows everything. But do you lie to yourself?"

"I don't…" He stepped forward, but stopped. "I…" Racking his brain, he tried to figure the question out. Finally, he said, "I don't lie to myself."

"Not even about your sexuality?"

"What! No."

"Are you gay, Cabot?"

"What! No."

"You have sex with men."

"So!"

"That makes you gay."

"I also have sex with women."

"When was the last time?"

"Last time for what?" Cabot confused himself again.

"When was the last time you had sex with a woman?"

"Um…" He thought back.

"Do you even remember?"

"June…I think."

"You had sex with a woman?"

"Well…" He remembered back further. "I got my cock sucked."

"So, you *don't* have sex with women?"

Blink. "Not anymore."

"You prefer men?"

Blink. "Yes."

"So… You're gay?"

Blink. "No."

"So, you're lying to yourself?"

A sigh. "No."

"You're gay, but you can't say so. That's lying to yourself," Xanthe said. "If you're gay, there's nothing wrong with that. Ever called yourself gay? Accepted it? Do you call yourself a free spirit like your sister described you? Do you have sex with 75% men, 25% women? 50/40?"

*****

Tomas and Roger found Carlos and Viv when they arrived at Jenny's. "Who's next door to us? I saw Cabot go in, but Antonio walked away," Tomas said, as he walked into the dining room.

"Xanthe Metlos," Jenny informed him. "We brought a counsellor in for Cabot. Dan called her."

"The counsellor I had?" Tomas asked. "Back in the '80s?"

"That's the one," Jenny replied, doing a quick tidy of the dining room. "I told her there's a few in the family that might want to see her." She glanced at him. "Including you."

"Me? Why would I…?" Tomas's eyebrows slid down. "Oh."

"Yes, oh." Jenny almost laughed. "It's time to rid yourself of Luiz once and for all."

Tomas sighed and pulled out a chair from the table and sat. "Yeah…I know."

"Maybe Dom would like to see her too, although Pedro called, and said that Dom suggested taking Danté to an exhibition. He took Nick along too, so, who knew? That was a surprise," Jenny told everyone.

"Yeah, but how long will that last?" Carlos asked.

"Forever, I hope," Jenny replied.

"What's going on with Cabot?" Tomas went on. "The assault get to him?"

Everyone stopped and stared at him.

"What?" He suddenly felt as if he were under a microscope. "Is there something in my teeth?"

"You'll find out when the boys get here," Jenny said. "Cabot's the one who has to tell you." She patted his shoulder as she passed him on the way into the kitchen.

"Something serious, I take it, which is why you asked me home." Tomas watched her face for answers.

Jenny smiled brightly. "Just wait until the twins get here."

*****

"Your uncle is gay. He has been since he was twenty-two. He didn't know it until a man made him feel these things. We talked about it when I counselled him."

Cabot looked on in interest. "Did *he* know he was gay before that?"

"Oh, hell no." Xanthe laughed. "Most don't until they try out women *and* men. Tomas wasn't interested in either, he just worked and had a life and figured when the right person came along, he'd know."

"But then he met a guy, Luiz something." Cabot watched her intently.

"Yes." Xanthe smiled. "His face lit up when he first talked about him and how he made him feel. But as he talked about the bad stuff, his face fell. And it clearly caused him a lot of grief. But being sick caused him more. I suggested he take up a hobby to help. Your grandmother told me all of these paintings are his." She waved a hand around the room. "He's very good. Maybe you should take up a hobby."

A snort escaped Cabot. "Like what? Needlecraft?"

"What are you interested in? Besides men and sex."

He shrugged a shoulder. "I dunno."

"Are you gay, Cabot?" she asked softly.

Another shrug. "I guess."

"And what's wrong with that?"

"Nothing, I guess," he murmured, glancing everywhere but at her. "Unless it gets you HIV."

*****

The boys arrived at Jenny's for her famous roast chicken lunch and found Tomas and Roger ready to greet them.

"Hey, boys." Tomas hugged Antonio and then took Cabot into his arms. "How are you, Cabot?"

Unsure at first, Cabot reluctantly put his hands on Tomas's back.

Tomas sensed it. Knew it. "Cabot, what's wrong?" He stared into his nephew's shame-filled eyes. "Cabot?"

Cabot fled into Antonio's arms.

"You have to tell them, Cabot. You'll need to tell the others when they get home." Antonio rubbed his brother's back.

"Ugh, I don't want to. I don't want people knowing." Cabot burrowed deeper into Antonio's neck.

"They're not just people, they're your family, and they need to know, so they don't contract it." Antonio pushed him away. "You tell them, or I will."

Panic hit Cabot in the face. "Tonee, no," he pleaded.

"Cabot," Antonio snapped. "Be an adult and tell them. They *have* to know."

With a quivering lip, Cabot slowly turned to face his uncles. Without looking them in the eye, he said, "Remember when I got beat up, well the cock sucker told me he gave me the disease..."

Tomas frowned, and his head slowly shook. "The disease...oh..." Tomas's world fell apart as memories came flooding back of an AIDS-ravaged era he barely lived through. "Cabot...no..." He took his nephew into his embrace. "Oh, my boy, what have you done?"

"Me! I didn't do anything, Uncle Tomas." Cabot pushed him away. "The fag fucker did it *to* me. *He* gave *me* AIDS."

"Technically HIV," Dan said. "It's not AIDS yet."

"And don't use that language in this house," Jenny reminded him. "That's what I slapped you for."

"Is this what it's going to be like?" Cabot scoffed at his family. "You're always going to *blame me* for this because *I* got HIV. Because I'm gay?"

Tomas smiled broadly. "Thank you."

"What!" Cabot frowned. "For what?"

"For finally having the maturity to admit it," Tomas said.

"Wait, what!?" Cabot's brainpower was slowing down, and he was confused. Again.

"You finally admitted it, Cabot. To yourself *and* us," Tomas told him. "That you're gay and you have HIV. Not a lot of men want to admit to either…it takes a real man to admit it."

"But…no…" Cabot shook the cobwebs out of his head. "You were ashamed of me. I saw your faces."

"I'm disappointed that you contracted HIV. But a lot of people get it from rapes and assaults," Tomas told him. "Alexis is lucky she didn't. Unfortunately, you're not so lucky. And I'm sorry."

Cabot saw the shame whether they admitted it or not. He saw it and felt it.

"You know we'll be here for you if you want to talk about anything." Tomas touched his hand to his nephew's cheek. "Roger and I are both here for you. If you want to talk about being gay, or HIV, we're here."

"Um…yeah…" Cabot's frown deepened, as did his confusion. Thoughts ran wild in his head, and he couldn't catch on to one.

"The rest of the family will be here tomorrow. They'll have to be told," Dan said.

Cabot sighed and rubbed his eyes. "I really don't want anyone knowing."

"For their own safety, they have to, Cabot," Dan replied. "So they know not to touch you if you have cuts, or touch any of your bodily fluids, especially if it has blood in it. It will be infected, and so infect them. You don't want to infect your cousins, or sister, do you?"

Cabot shook his head. "No, of course not."

"Then they need to be told, and we'll get to educating everyone again," Dan added. "A refresher course is needed."

*****

On Sunday after breakfast, Alena and Diana waved their family goodbye from outside the apartment building.

"Bye, love you, see you in a couple of days," Alena called as she waved madly. When the car was out of sight, she dropped her arms. "Thank God for that. Now I can get to the hospital."

"Today?" Diana asked. "It's Sunday. They may want to spend the day with their son."

"I know, but I need to see him and find out what's going on," Alena said as they walked into apartment 3. She had moved her things in that morning.

"And what if the Gardos can't tell you anything else that we don't already know?" Diana sat on the couch and put her feet up. "It's Sunday, Alena, I fly out on Wednesday. Can't we spend some time together?"

"You can come to the hospital with me, that's spending time together." Alena pulled out her phone and dialled the hospital. "ICU, please." She waited to be connected and then asked about James. "Yes, I'm calling about James Gardo, he's a friend of mine. How's he doing?"

"He's out of the induced coma and is doing well."

"Oh, that's good." The butterflies settled down in her stomach. "Is he having visitors yet?"

"Just his family. But he is being moved to a room tomorrow and will be allowed visitors then."

"Oh, that's wonderful, thank you so much." Alena ended the call and flopped next to Diana on the couch.

"Good news, I take it," Diana said.

"He's awake and doing okay, and will he be moved into a room tomorrow."

"So, you can see him then."

"Yes, I can, and you're coming with me."

*****

"I hear Tomas and Roger are back," Xanthe said Monday morning. "It will be good to see them again. Did you tell them you're HIV positive?"

Silence…

"Yes."

"How did they react?"

His head bowed.

"Badly?"

"Not good," he murmured.

"What happened?"

"They were back, and I told them."

"And?"

"And they frowned, they teared up, and they looked ashamed."

"Of you or your behaviour?"

He finally looked at Xanthe. "Same thing, isn't it?"

"No. You are their nephew; your behaviour is changeable."

He thought about it. "I don't know. Both, maybe."

"Did they say?"

"What? That they're ashamed of me? No."

"Then how do you know?"

"Because of the expressions on their faces."

"Or, because that's what *you're* feeling inside, so you see it on everyone else's face when you look at them?"

"What?" Cabot shook his head. She had a hell of a way of getting shit out.

"Do you see shame on other people's faces because you feel it inside of you?"

"Why would I feel ashamed?"

"Because your behaviour made you contract HIV. Because after all the years they taught you, all the *things* they taught you, you arrogantly disregarded it and did what you wanted, and now you've acquired HIV because of your behaviour. Are you ashamed because of that?"

He didn't look her in the eye, just wrapped his arms around himself, bowed his head and bent over a little.

"You're withdrawing. Hiding, retreating. The answer is yes. All you have to do is tell the truth, and you will finally start healing, and finally be free."

Cabot's whole face fell, and his body sagged. He had never been ashamed of himself, but then his behaviour had never resulted in anything to feel shame for. Now things were different. "I can't...I can't..." His breathing came rapidly, and he ran for the door and out into Antonio's arms. "Tonee," he sobbed.

"Hey." Antonio held him tightly. "It's okay. It's okay. Therapy is a good thing. Just keep remembering that. Come on, let's go for a walk."

Xanthe watched the two walk away, studying the body language.

"He's too reliant on Antonio." Jenny stopped at the door, watching her grandsons. "Always has been. Very needy, wanting."

"Yes, and I need to show him he can be an individual," Xanthe said.

"How's he going?" Jenny asked.

"He's confused. I think he's got so much stuff going on in his head that it's confused him, and so his behaviour is a result of it."

"So, you clear the confusion and the real Cabot will finally be able to stand up?" Jenny asked.

Xanthe smiled. "I think so."

*****

At Monday lunchtime, everyone gathered in Jenny's home. She even called in the Gatoses. They sat around munching on sandwiches and drinking soda until it was time to drop the news. Jenny had packed a bag for Antonio to taken Cabot on a picnic to prepare him, and Xanthe was chatting with Tomas and Roger.

Finally, Antonio and Cabot arrived.

"Oh, no, no, no." Cabot did a u-turn straight into Antonio's arms. "I can't do this, Tonee. I can't. There are so many people here."

Xanthe came to his side. "It's okay to be scared, but the truth will prevail. Have strength; they are your family. They need to know so they can help you."

Jenny joined the trio while the family hovered around. "Do you want me to slap you again? Get that fire in your belly?"

Cabot's eyes blazed, and he spun around to face her. *"No, Jennifer, I do not."*

Jenny arched a brow and lowered her voice. "Jennifer?"

"Oh, I see where the attitude comes from. It's definitely inherited." Xanthe looked back and forth at the two sets of blazing blue eyes.

"*That attitude will get you slapped, Cabot Conroy Stephanopoulos,*" Jenny spat back.

Carlos and Viv saw the heat radiating from the two of them across the room. "Oh, I hope they're not getting into a fight right now," Carlos said.

"Mama's stirring him up," Tomas told him. "Or have you forgotten she does that when we're all being pathetic?"

"You're such a little boy, *Cabot,*" Jenny stirred. "You have *no idea* how to be a mature man. At this rate, you'll *never* be like your father."

"Oh," he growled and turned to everyone else. "Can I have your attention, family. Back in July, I was assaulted as you all know," he addressed his family who all looked on with piqued interest. "But I wasn't just beaten up or robbed. I was sexually assaulted. It seems a conquest of mine wanted payment, and when he found I had nothing, he pulled a knife and shoved his..." He spied Danté and Nick and stopped a moment. "*Himself,* up my behind while he held the knife to my throat. I fought him off, but he told me that he had given me the disease. Tony came along to save me. After a trip to Dan for my flu a few weeks ago, I found out I have contracted HIV because of the assault, and now all of you need to know."

He saw the shocked faces and concerned frowns on his uncle and cousins. "And because I wasn't ready to accept that I have it, I tried to kill myself by getting drunk and knocking back a packet or two of pills. When that didn't work, I broke the bottle and slashed my wrists." He pulled off the wide leather studded cuffs he'd been wearing to cover the scars and showed everyone. "Yep, I tried to kill myself, and now Grandma's in charge and has brought me home, and Dan has me on the meds to stop the HIV from turning into AIDS, and Xanthe here, who Uncle Tomas and Roger saw years ago, is back to be my counsellor. So, there you have it. Dan needs to tell you all how not to get AIDS from me, but I can't stick around because this is too..." he sobbed, "much..." He fell into Antonio's arms and stood sobbing.

Xanthe patted his back. "You did good, kid. The first step is admitting you have it. The second is getting medicated, the third is telling those who need to know."

Pedro sat in shock in an easy chair by the fireplace and stared from Cabot to his mother who was near the boys, to Carlos and Viv who were in the kitchen. Tomas and Roger stood by them, clearly already knowing.

"Oh," Angie murmured, remembering what it was like for Alexis to be assaulted.

Dom and Danté stood frozen, but Alexis was the first to move. She pulled Cabot from Antonio's arms and hugged him. "I know what it's like to be raped," she whispered. "It sucks. I'm sorry you got HIV from it."

That made Jenny tear up, and she looked at Xanthe who had a tear or two of her own. They watched Alexis and Cabot cry in each other's arms. "I think it's time for both of you to talk about your assaults," Jenny said to them softly.

Alexis looked at her and nodded.

Angie was the second to move and hug Cabot. "I'm so sorry. As a parent, I didn't deal with Alexis's assault very well, but it must be just as hard for you as it was for her. I'm so sorry it's been made worse with HIV."

"Thanks, Aunt Angie." Cabot sniffled. "I'm trying hard to deal with it."

"I know you are. You'll have a lot to change now," Angie added.

Pedro finally stood, slowly, as if he had old man's knees. He didn't know what to do or say, or who to go to first, so his mouth moved up and down.

"Pedro." Jenny motioned at her son.

"Ah," came out of his mouth. "I..." His head moved side to side. "I'm...conflicted."

"Why?" Jenny was curious as to how her youngest was feeling inside.

"Because I don't know who to go to first. My brother, or my nephew." He looked from one to the other.

"Understandable," Jenny said. "I raised you three to be close and to protect and defend. Of course, you'd want to go to Carlos first and console him."

Pedro stared at Carlos. His face was crestfallen, and he could tell his brother wasn't handling it well.

Angie pulled back from Cabot. "Pedro," she murmured.

Pedro's head turned to her and saw Cabot's tear-stained red face. He turned back to Carlos and saw his shame-filled embarrassed one.

"How about both of us," Carlos told him and walked toward Cabot while holding out an arm to his little brother.

Pedro moved over to them and enveloped both. "Jesus fucking hell," he whispered fiercely. "Jesus, Cabot."

"I know," Cabot moaned on his uncle's shoulder. "I know."

Pedro kissed his nephew's cheek, then his brother's, and saw Tomas come up in front of him.

"Room for one more?" Tomas wrapped himself around Cabot and Carlos.

"Room for two more?" Antonio asked and wrapped himself around Cabot, Pedro and Tomas.

"And that is what we tried explaining to the kids," Jenny said to the room. "The unity of siblings. No matter what, always love, protect, defend." With a sigh, she looked over at Dom and Danté who still stood in shock at it all.

"My turn," Xanthe told her and walked over to the boys, ushering them down the hallway to the bedrooms. "Are you two okay?" She got two blank stares. "In shock?"

Two nods.

"Not sure what to say?"

Two nods.

"Or to do?"

Two nods.

"Scared for him?"

Two nods.

"Not sure if you want to touch him?"

They looked at each other.

"You won't catch it from hugging him."

Danté sagged against the wall, and Dom opened his mouth. "It's just…"

"He's your cousin."

"Yeah."

"And you don't want him to have HIV."

"Nah."

"And you don't know what to do to help him."

"Yeah."

"Or if you want the burden of helping him." She got two cold stares from that. "Then what is it?"

Dom finally shrugged. "What do we say? What do we do?"

"*How* do we do it?" Danté asked.

"Oh, Little Danté," Xanthe said. "It is hard. Finding out that someone has HIV is a very hard thing. It's made harder by the fact he's your cousin. It will take some time for all of you to come to terms with it. Which is why my door is open to the whole family. Anything you want to talk about will remain confidential. Regardless of whether it's about Cabot or not. Okay?" She looked from face to face for confirmation and got two slow nods. "Okay. Let's go back in. Don't feel the need to hug him because you don't have to. You need to feel comfortable too. Now Dan's going to go over the basics of not getting infected, and we all need to see it."

"What about Alena and Diana?" Dom asked. "They're not here."

"I'll have to tell them when they come home." Cabot came up to them. "I get it. You don't want to touch me."

"Don't make assumptions," Xanthe told him. "They're in shock and don't know how to react. *You* were in denial, so don't criticise them. Just give them time to get used to it." She left them to it.

Dom sighed, leaned against the wall and looked up at the ceiling. "Why does so much shit happen in this family?"

"Because we're Stephanopouloses," Cabot quipped. "It's in the blood. Look at everything that happened to our fathers and uncles. Now it's happening to us."

Dom's head moved side to side. "Geez, dude, why did you have to go and get fucking HIV?"

Cabot pulled a face. "I just said, it's in the blood." A sigh left him. "But seriously…I didn't plan on ever getting it. Being assaulted's not fun."

"No." Dom remembered the helpless feelings he had when Alexis told him she'd been attacked. "It's not." Looking at his cousin, he added, "Geez dude, I'm sorry."

"So am I," Cabot replied. "So am I."

"What do we do now?" Angie asked the group. They were huddled around in shock, waiting for Dan's refresher course.

"You'll do what Dan tells you to." Jenny rubbed her back.

Angie rested her head on Jenny's shoulder. "Alena and Diana will need to be told."

"It's up to Cabot to do that," Viv told her. "Today was bad enough, now he has to tell his sister."

"Okay, everyone, we're doing the refresher course now," Dan called out.

Mike clapped Pedro on the shoulder. "Bringing back memories?"

"Oh, hell yeah." Pedro wiped a hand over his face. "Too many. Leon, Stan, Thomas, Eddie, Jamal, Stephano. Way too many."

"Times have changed. The meds help people with HIV live longer," Mike added. "He's got a good chance if he helps himself."

"We've lost too many, I can't lose another family member," Pedro whispered.

"Tomas and Roger are alive," Mike murmured. "Your family's just fine."

The boys came back into the room, and all sat through Dan's refresher on how to treat an HIV positive person.

"Cabot, you're going to have to be careful of any cuts you get, and any blood you shed. Sex should be out of the question while all of this is happening."

"Yes, captain, my captain." Cabot saluted him, standing near the adults in the open dining room.

"Always with an attitude." Xanthe stood near Cabot, fascinated by him.

"Don't you know." Cabot cheekily grinned. "It runs in the family. Just like the blue eyes side. You can blame Grandma."

"Geez, thanks," Jenny cracked dryly. "Blame me for everything."

"All right then," Cabot started.

"Don't you dare blame your grandmother for anything," Carlos warned him, standing close to his mother and wife and waving his finger around. "If it weren't for her we wouldn't live the way we do, or have the things we have. And Tomas and Roger certainly wouldn't be here. You have a very privileged life because of your grandmother. We *all* do."

"Oh, it definitely got handed down." Xanthe looked from Carlos to Cabot to Jenny and back. Blue eyes defying blue eyes.

"Can we get back on track?" Dan called from the lounge room. "Cabot, keep an eye on cuts and wounds, and don't go near anyone who has cuts or wounds. You got that?"

"Yes, Dan." Cabot rolled his eyes.

"Any questions?" Dan asked.

"Yes, I have one?" Cabot waved his hand in the air. "How long is my life going to be ruined for?"

"As long as you keep ruining it," Xanthe replied swiftly, waiting for his reaction. She had been prepared for his comments.

Cabot's head swivelled to look at her. "Doing your *psycho*therapy on me?"

"Not at all. You got yourself into this, you're the one who stuffs up, you're the one who needs to fix it. You have absolutely no problem getting angry when you feel slighted or wronged. You blaze like fireworks, but when it comes to being serious, you fizzle out and have nothing. You need to learn to keep a steady line and maintain it. Use that passion and anger you have for good instead of trying to ruin your life. Or anyone else's. Use the force for good, Cabot."

"Ba-ha-ha," Tomas laughed and quickly covered his mouth with both hands. When everyone looked at him, he said, "That was from Star Wars. It came out in 1977 when we all moved to America. Don't you remember?"

"I was too busy doing other things," Carlos said.

"Yeah, like how many women?" Cabot asked, getting a blazing glare in return.

"And I was too busy being the biggest DJ in the world," Pedro added.

"And I was too busy worrying about my three boys who had disappeared off the face of the planet," Jenny said.

"And I was too busy getting through Juilliard," Angie told him.

"And we were all busy getting married," Viv finished off. "'77 was a big year. We were all too busy to notice a movie."

"Not us." Roger grinned. "Even with everything going on, we saw it five times and have watched all of them in order since."

"Don't tell us you're a Trekkie," Pedro said.

"Ugh, Dad," Dom and Danté groaned. "*Star Wars* fans aren't Trekkies. That's *Star Trek.* Geez!"

"There's a difference?" Pedro feigned naïveté.

"Duh, Dad, of course, there is," Danté said. "If you're into *Star Wars,* you're just a fan. Ugh, old people, they think they know everything, but really know nothing." A cushion was thrown at him for that. "Help!" He ducked behind Dom who got the next one in the face.

"Hey!" Dom frowned fiercely at his father, then reluctantly cracked a smile.

With the family in a lighter mood, they spent the rest of the day together.

*****

In New York on Monday morning, Alena called the hospital. "Is James Gardo having visitors yet?"

"He's being transferred to a room as we speak. If you can wait until after lunchtime, he should be settled by then."

"Okay, thank you." She checked the time on her phone. Ugh, nine o'clock, what was she going to do until then? "Diana," she yelled out and went looking for her cousin, finding her in the bathroom. "I can't see him until after lunch, so I'm going back to the library to have another look at the files we found. Want to come?"

"I guess. I haven't got much else to do anyway." Diana set the last pin in her hair and gave it a spray of hairspray.

They gathered their things and took a cab to the library, where they went searching through the archives. They found all of the articles they had found before and printed them out. By the time they were finished, it was lunchtime, and they stopped for a bite to eat before Alena bought a bunch of flowers and they went to the hospital. After asking what room James was in, they went up to the fourth floor and made their way to his room.

James was talking softly to his parents, but saw the girls in the doorway. "Alena!" His face brightened upon seeing her, and his parents turned.

"Um, hi, I, ah." Alena gulped. "Heard you were out of ICU and thought I'd ah, stop by to see you. Ah, this is my cousin, Diana." She waved a hand. "And I brought flowers coz I didn't know what else to bring, and ah, we ah, need to talk to your father for a few minutes." She gulped a second time as Giancarlo stood and towered over them both.

The light in James's eyes dulled. "Oh, ah, of course. I'll see you in a few minutes."

Sheila noticed the light appear and disappear and studied Alena with interest. *She definitely looks like her parents,* she thought.

Giancarlo took the flowers and handed them to his wife. "We'll be back soon." He followed the girls down the hall to the waiting area. "So, what's this about? Does your grandmother know you're here?" He saw two sets of her eyes. "You both have her eyes."

"You knew our grandmother?" Diana asked.

"Yes, yes I did." He smiled at the memories. "Not for long though. I hadn't seen her since 1980."

"When you had James and Uncle Tomas was with Grandma?" Alena said.

He studied both girls. "How much do you actually know? Because if Jenny hasn't told you, I don't want to."

Alena traded a glance with Diana. "They never told us anything except for Uncle Tomas and Roger getting sick. But now we're finding out about kidnappings and Luiz Manning. Who is he, Mr Gardo?"

"How much of him do you know?" Giancarlo marvelled at how beautiful the girls were.

"What James said in the penthouse, and what's in these articles from years ago." Alena pulled the paperwork from her bag.

Gardo nodded. "The same articles James found. I found them in his apartment along with my files on the case from '77. He'd stolen them from the police archives."

"Why did he think he was Luiz?" Diana asked softly.

Gardo shook his head. "We don't know, and he doesn't remember anything. So, say nothing to him. The doctor said he's not going to remember a lot of what's happened, so don't mention it."

"Did you ever tell him he had a brother?" Alena asked.

Gardo sighed and indicated for them to sit. "My wife, Sheila, had Luiz in 1952. She was an unwed mother. She met Luiz's father, Andros Poulos, the year before when she was on holiday in Santorini. He denied the baby was his and left her without help or support. When Luiz was seventeen, she kicked him out of home and never saw him again. I didn't know any of it when I knew Sheila. We had been seeing each other off and on for a couple of years. I became involved in your father's case when a drug kingpin was known to have helped Andros plant drugs in your father's car and cut his brake lines. Your father crashed and ended up in hospital," he told Alena and then looked around. "Bizarrely, *this* hospital. And it's also where your mother ended up after being shot by a hired hand of your grandfather."

"What!" Alena exclaimed. "She never told me that."

"From the sound of it, there's a lot they've kept from all of you, and for good reason."

"To protect us," Diana said.

"And because it's nothing to do with you."

"But then what?" Alena interrupted.

"Well, your father had a stalker who crashed your father's car into your grandfather, and then he was kidnapped by your grandfather's associate. I chased him to Chicago, but your father was smart and was able to get out of the trunk. The FBI took over at the airport where I met your uncles, and I didn't see any of them again until late November, early December, I think. And that's when I met your grandmother. The boys had gotten married and had the two of you on the way." He gazed at both of them. "You both look like your parents, and you both have Jenny's blue eyes."

They smiled. "So we're told," Diana said.

"So, James came along?" Alena pushed the conversation along.

Gardo sighed. "Yes. He was born Valentine's Day 1979."

"Same day as our fathers," Diana murmured.

"Yes," Gardo replied. "Coincidence? I saw Jenny on the odd occasion from '77 through to '78, and then not until July 1980 in the department store."

"Did you ever tell James about his brother?" Alena pushed.

Gardo shook his head. "Sheila was heartbroken at losing her only son. When she ended up pregnant with James, she didn't want him turning out like Luiz. She packed up the things she had left and put the box in the attic. It hasn't been touched since."

"Could James have found it?" Diana asked.

"I doubt it," Gardo replied. "But he did have a strange pull to Tomas. He always dreamt of him and called out his name. And when his obit hit the front page of the paper, he stood up from the floor, came over to me, pointed to the picture and said, *Tomas, Dada, Tomas.* It left my blood cold. I'd never seen Luiz; never saw a photo. Sheila doesn't have one past the age of seventeen, so neither of us knows what he looked like."

"According to the family, he looks exactly like James," Diana told him. "All the way down to his aqua blue eyes. Uncle Tomas swears it's Luiz back from the grave to kill him."

"Yes," Gardo frowned. "He poisoned and then kidnapped him from the hospital."

"James knew those details, but how could anyone?" Alena asked. "Only Luiz and Uncle Tomas would know, and he doesn't."

"And neither do I," Gardo added. "We've been asking him questions all day; what do you remember, what have you been doing? He remembers going on tour, but said it became fuzzy, as if he was always underwater, or in the background. He didn't know why. We told him it was the aneurysm. He believes us so far."

"Will you tell him what he did?" Diana asked, knowing her energy was flagging.

"About Luiz?" Gardo asked in return and sat back tiredly in his seat. "He doesn't need to know about a half-brother who died before he was born."

"Doesn't he have a right to know?" Alena asked. "Especially if he starts remembering what happened. What if one day he says, who's Luiz Manning?"

Rubbing his tired eyes, Giancarlo yawned. "I don't know. We'll deal with it if or when we come to it."

"So, what am I supposed to say to him?" Alena asked.

"Anything other than Luiz Manning."

*****

"So, you remember Alena and being on tour with her?" Sheila asked James.

His face lit up. "Yeah, I do. But it's fuzzy. I don't know why. The brain thing, I guess. She's awesome, gorgeous, pretty, beautiful, so talented, gorgeous."

"You said that." Sheila smiled. "You like her, huh?"

"Yeah." The grin was ear to ear. "I'd like to spend some time with her if we're not on tour anymore."

"Not possible, I'm afraid." She and Diana entered with Gardo behind them, and they stood by the side of the bed.

Worried, Sheila stood to be by her husband's side, but she got a small nod and knew he'd speak to her later.

"The tour's over, so we have time." James frowned. "I don't really remember."

"It finished about three weeks ago," Alena said. "You, ah," she looked at his parents, "had a holiday because of the hard work you put in, and that's when this happened. And I've been with my family, but they left yesterday, and it's just us left for a few more days." She indicated to Diana. "I wanted to see you before I left." They gazed down at aqua blue eyes. His head was shaven, so most of his hair was gone, cheeks sunken, but his skin was a normal colour. "You look okay."

"The doctor says I'll recover. It's just a matter of time." *Oh God, she's beautiful*, he thought. *Why didn't I kiss her on tour? We had ten weeks.*

"That's good. I, ah, told my family about you, and we thank you for helping at the Garden that first night, and I thank you for protecting me and saving my life."

"Even though we didn't find a shooter?" James smiled up at her.

She was still dazzled by that smile and felt the butterflies flutter around her insides. "Um, so…we should go and let you rest."

"Will you come back before you go?" James managed to grasp her arm.

"Oh, ah…" She startled, and Diana looked on in surprise. "Um," Alena looked from James to his parents to Diana. "Um…I guess so…"

"Great. Can you stay now?"

"Ah, um, I don't want to wear you out. You need your rest and to get better. So um, I'll see you tomorrow." She pulled back. "Okay?"

James's smile waned. "Okay."

"Okay." Alena backed away, pulling Diana with her. "Okay, um, bye."

"Bye." James watched her leave, but kept smiling to himself. "Isn't she incredible?" he said to his parents.

Sheila looked at Gardo, worried for what it meant. James had fallen for the niece of his brother's lover. What a mess that could lead to.

"Yes, son, she is." Giancarlo held out Sheila's seat then sat himself. For all women to get involved with, it had to be a Stephanopoulos. What the hell was Jenny going to say when she found out?

"I really like her," James went on. "I don't remember much of the tour. I was always on duty, but she's awesome, don't you think?" He looked to his parents for confirmation.

"Yes, darling, she's lovely." Sheila held his hand.

"What the hell! You're coming back tomorrow?" Diana said as they went down in the lift. "We fly out the day after."

"I know, I know," Alena wailed. "But did you see those eyes?"

"The same eyes Uncle Tomas fell for," Diana told her as they hailed a cab. "You can't fall for him, Alena. Grandma won't allow it."

"I already did fall for him on tour," Alena told her cousin. "And that was all before we found this out. But I didn't think he was interested, so I stopped it…but now…"

"Oh, you cannot be seriously thinking of getting involved with him?"

"I don't know," Alena cried. "I have no idea what to think. What to feel. What to do. But yes, we fly out the day after tomorrow, and I suggest we read all of this paperwork before we leave so we know what we're dealing with."

Three hours later, they sat back in their apartment and sighed.

"This is way too much to deal with. Mama was shot and assaulted, Daddy was stalked and kidnapped, and the FBI got involved. How serious could all this be?" Alena asked

"I don't know," Diana replied, "But it's made me feel sick, except it's also made me hungry. You want pizza?"

*****

Sheila was thoughtful all the way home. She and Giancarlo had only been home twice in the last week, staying in the hospital with James. But now he was out of his coma, and out of ICU, they were told it was okay to go home.

Giancarlo noticed how quiet his wife was and asked what was wrong as they pulled up to their house.

"Mmm?" Sheila came out of her reverie.

"What's wrong?" he repeated, gently grasping her hand. "Is it Alena?"

Sheila sighed. "He can't get involved with her. It's just too…"

"Awkward?" Giancarlo said before he alighted. Retrieving their bags from the trunk, he opened his wife's door. "We're home. Let's not worry for a while. We'll have a nice hot shower, a strong cup of coffee, and relax. James is going to be okay." He escorted her inside, relieved to be home. A half hour later, they rested on the lounge drinking their coffee.

"I've been thinking," Sheila murmured. "We should discourage James from liking Alena. It won't come of anything, and it wouldn't be good after what you told me he did. Thinking he was Luiz. How could he? He knows nothing of Luiz."

"He found out from my old files," Gardo said. "He circled Luiz's name and yours."

"But I also wonder what would be the good in telling him about Luiz," Sheila went on. "I haven't thought about Luiz in years. When

James was born, I noticed he had the same eye colour. I figured that was a genetic thing from me because Andros had brown eyes like Angelina. But I noticed similarities as James grew. Subtle ones, nothing major, but then he seemed to grow out of them, and I stopped worrying. But now…" She gazed up at the ceiling. "I think…" a sigh, "I think you need to get Luiz's box down from the attic. I think it's time I went through it."

"Are you sure?" Giancarlo and Sheila had had a good life. While their rocky start across '75 to '77 wasn't smooth, once she became pregnant with James they had seen each other differently. And the five million dollars from Jenny for Luiz's death had afforded Sheila a makeover. She had become the woman she'd always wanted to be. And the kind of woman he had always wanted. That was why he'd had such an infatuation with Jenny when they met. Those blue eyes sucked him right in. And then once Sheila had her makeover, he'd noticed how blue her eyes were, and how they radiated. He realized what he'd wanted was right under his nose all along. They married in October '78, had James in February '79, and had been happy ever since. Living off his retirement pay and her part-time work, he'd been a stay-at-home dad and loved it. They lived wisely off the rest of the five million, and still had a healthy amount left, although some of it would be going to James's medical bills. They'd still managed to holiday somewhere nice every year, and afforded nice presents for birthdays and Christmas, and paid for James's education. They had a great life, though he was eighty-three, and Sheila seventy-seven, they were still spry and full of life, and hoped to see grandchildren before they died. "Do you really want to dig up those memories?"

Sheila tearfully looked at her husband. "With Luiz's name being brought up, I'd say it's time. It's nearly thirty years." Flashbacks of thirty years ago came to her mind. The letter from the morgue asking if she wanted his body, her refusing because she had no money to bury him, and she had been ashamed of him being gay, so she wanted nothing to do with him. The morgue buried him cheaply, but years later, after receiving the money from Jenny and having James, Giancarlo helped track him down, and they exhumed the body. They had stood there while the coffin was raised and a representative for the city needed to look inside to confirm the body was there. But she couldn't look. Giancarlo forbade her to look, making her turn away. "I'll do it," he'd said. "You don't want to remember him this way." She'd turned away while he confirmed it was a six-foot male with a gunshot wound to the skull. Once it was done, they had the body taken to the funeral home for cremation, and his ashes still resided in the small urn on her bedside table. "Can you get the box down, please?"

"Are you sure?" He was concerned for the memories it would dredge up.

She smiled sadly. "No, but it needs to be done."

Nodding, he got up, walked up the stairs all the way to the attic, and searched for the box in the farthest corner where he knew she'd put it. Blowing off the dust, he carried it downstairs and sat it on the kitchen table as Sheila came to his side. "You don't have to do this, you know."

"Yes," she whispered, looking at the box. "I do."

He found a Stanley knife in the utility drawer and sliced open the tape. "There are no holes, so probably no rats, roaches or mice."

"Let's hope not." She stood staring at it, and finally, reaching out, pushed back the flaps. The box contained a few of Luiz's toys, a couple of knick-knacks, and two photo albums. She didn't have a lot of money, but she did afford to get a roll of film developed every now and then. Photos were all she would have. Pulling a teddy bear from the box, she smiled. One eye was missing, and his arm was falling off, but it was her son's favourite teddy. There was a small train, a block set, and a few books, all still in good condition. She pulled out the photo albums and wiped them over. Her smile turned to sadness, and she sat down at the table.

Giancarlo sat beside her, ready with a box of tissues for the tears to fall.

Opening the first album, she came across his birth certificate and death certificate. The photos were of him as a baby, and her finger gently touched the words she had written underneath. Luiz Andros Poulos, after his father, but since Andros didn't want him, she'd changed it on his paperwork to Manning. "Eight pounds, four ounces," she murmured.

"Same as James," Giancarlo replied.

"Yes." She studied each photo, moving slowly through the album. Each birthday was represented, each special occasion, starting school, plays, graduation from middle school. High school, although he'd quit to bum around the neighbourhood at seventeen, not even finishing. Coming to the end of the second album, she stared at the last page she'd filled, two pages shy of the end. There were four pictures of his seventeenth birthday, the last time she'd taken photos. The last photos she had. The aqua blue eyes were bright, the scowl in place. She could only afford supermarket cake and some cheap clothes. They had lived on her wage for eighteen years. Since Andros never paid for his son, she had to get a job while pregnant and support them both, so presents were only twice a year, birthday and Christmas, and even then she couldn't afford a lot. He got clothes for the new year, and a special present that she saved up for on his birthday. That year it was a transistor radio and they didn't come cheap. James popped into her head as she stared at those pictures. "Can you get me James's photo album? I want to compare them, see if…"

Giancarlo complied and retrieved the albums from the cupboard where they were kept. He laid them on the table next to Luiz's albums.

Sheila flicked through James's, comparing him as a baby to Luiz. His birthdays, his looks, his height, all the way to seventeen years of age. "Oh, my God, look."

Giancarlo looked over her shoulder and saw the four pictures of Luiz on his seventeenth next to four pictures of James on his.

Sheila looked at him in shock. "They're identical."

He blinked, first at the album then at her. "No…they…" He stared at both sets of photos. His detective's brain kicked in, and his eyes moved between face shapes, build, stature, stance, eyes, nose, shape of the head and body. Finally, he pulled back. "Jesus. They *are* identical?"

"It's no wonder the family freaked out. I read about what Luiz had done; it made the papers here. He killed four men and poisoned Tomas before kidnapping him. No wonder the family went nuts thirty years ago. But Jenny always seemed so…" She thought back. "Caring.

She wasn't angry with me, or vicious. Just angry at what Luiz had done. But now that James—"

"James is different," Gardo cut her off. "He's *not* Luiz."

"He's identical to him!" Sheila exclaimed. "You can't deny it. And as they looked the same at seventeen, they must look the same now. Oh…" she thought, "You know what I mean. He would still look the same as Luiz. But why does he *think* he's Luiz? It can't just be the aneurysm?" Pushing away from the table, she moved to stand by the open back door for some air. This was now freaking *her* out.

"I don't know." Giancarlo stared at the photos. "I have been racking my brain as to how, and I came up with a very vague answer."

"What? Tell me so I can understand," Sheila said.

"Well, remember he was at the department store with me when we ran into Jenny, and then Tomas came up, and James reached out to Tomas and said his name. Now, he could have just been repeating what Jenny had said. I don't know. After that, he would say Tomas's name when he played, as though he was an imaginary friend, and he would call out to him at night when he woke. *And* when they made front page news with their deaths, well, James got up from where he had been playing on the floor, came over to me and pointed to the paper and said, *Tomas, Dada, Tomas.*" He shook his head. "That kid remembered Tomas's face, but I think it was no more than an overactive imagination of a little boy. He grew out of it and never said his name again. But, this tour business and remembering things he did, I reckon he started doing research on the family and dug up way more than he bargained for. I think the aneurysm jumbled it all up in his head, and when he found out you had another son who was related to Alena's mother, hence related to him, it probably became too much for his brain to cope with and became one big jumbled mess." He got up and stood beside her. "Maybe that bullet was a blessing. It stopped the clot in its tracks and showed the doctors what was wrong. Basically, it was the arrow that pointed the way to James's strange behaviour; it saved him."

"But now my baby is scarred, and his brain has been removed." She fretted and clung to him.

"It has not," Giancarlo chided. "They removed small fragments that were damaged, but it won't affect him overall. The doctor said he'd recovered well and will continue to do so. He's going to be okay, Sheila. *Better* than okay. The aneurysm is gone, and he should get back to his old self."

"And what if he remembers Luiz, or Tomas, or the paperwork he saw?"

Gardo sighed. "Then we tell him the truth."

Sheila closed her eyes for a moment. "Maybe we should tell him anyway." Her eyes opened. "If he wants to get involved with Alena, he will need to know that he and her mother shared a brother. That maybe it's not a good idea *to* get involved with each other."

"And are you going to stop him?" Giancarlo asked. "Our son is bull-headed and headstrong."

"Just like his father." She smiled softly and stroked his cheek. "And I love you for it. But all of this has shaken me up, and I'm terrified."

"Of what? Your son knowing he had a brother?"

"Of him being Luiz." The tears rolled over her cheeks. "If he looks exactly like Luiz, then what if he *is* Luiz and that's why he remembered."

"Sheila, Luiz died in 1977, James was born 1979; he is not Luiz."

"If he's reincarnated he could be," Sheila sobbed, having never believed in any of that until reading a story on Jenny Stephanopoulos and her beliefs. It was after Tomas and Roger recovered and become AIDS activists. Jenny had done a story in a magazine talking about the disease, death, and afterlife. And the more Sheila had thought about it, the more she'd questioned whether Luiz had come back as James.

"I don't believe in reincarnation, so get that fool thought out of your head," Giancarlo told her. "He is *our* son, James Giancarlo Gardo, *not* Luiz Manning. *He* is gone, *he* is cremated, his ashes are sitting on your bedside table. He is not James. James is not him."

"No," Sheila whispered. "But I think it's time he knew."

*****

Tuesday morning, Cabot stalked around Xanthe's office for his daily visit.

521

"So…how do you think yesterday went?"

"Oh, like clockwork," Cabot snarked. "Did you see their faces? Shame, disgust, horror, it was all over the place." He waved his hands at every word before running them through his hair.

"Then clearly we saw two very different things," Xanthe told him. "Yes, there was shock, but you let rip with your woeful tale of assault then HIV then suicide. How did you expect them to react?"

He shrugged and crossed his arms. "I dunno. I just don't want anyone to know."

"And if you cut yourself and someone tries to help you?"

Another shrug. "*I don't know!* I'll deal with it when it happens."

"Except you can't. Just as they can't be near you if you do. Unless they know what to do. Use gloves and a face mask."

"Yeah, because I'm going to carry all of that stuff around with me to protect everybody from me." The frown was deep, so was the cocked lip.

"Didn't ask you to, but you need to be prepared if the need arises. You, your father, and grandmother are very much alike."

Cabot snorted. "Yeah, right. The only thing my father and I have in common is our ability to fuck a lot." He ran his fingers along the books on the wall shelf.

"You also have the blue eyes, the temper, the same golden-brown hair. And your left brow does that cocky thing where it rises when you're annoyed at something."

"What?" Cabot turned to face her. "I don't think so."

"I think that's why you're always at war; too much like one another. Jenny and Carlos were at war when he was a kid and teenager, and you're very much like him back then, but they got along like a house on fire after Tomas rose from the ashes and they started the company. Carlos is very dedicated to his mother. Just as Tomas looks like Spiros, Jenny and Carlos are two peas in a pod, and you're the third. But you want your independence and don't feel at home with the two of them. It's as if the shell isn't big enough for all three of you and they've pushed you out, almost. There's no room for you anymore, so you fight to save what you can."

His frown turned upside down, and his brows rose. "Have you been drinking, or snorting, coz you are *clearly* on something?"

Xanthe laughed. "No, I'm not. Are you?"

"Hardly," he scoffed. "I haven't been allowed to drink, not that I care to after drowning my sorrows in countless bottles of alcohol, and I haven't snorted in months."

"So, you had no problem doing drugs? Which ones?"

"Pot and coke mainly." He walked around the easy chair to the window. "It wasn't habitual. Just here and there if we were partying. I'd do a line before we went out. If we were home, I smoked a joint."

"Do you know how many lovers you've had?"

"What?" He spun around. "Why would I know that?"

"Your father does. And I doubt it's anywhere close to the number you've had."

"My father knows how many women he's slept with?" Cabot's brows hit his hairline. "How many, do you know?"

"No. I never asked. But he did volunteer that he'd kept a list out of curiosity when he was your age. I doubt it's as many as you. I'd say you've probably tripled, if not quadrupled the list."

That made him laugh. "Yeah, that's a good one. I've quadrupled it."

"How many?"

"How would I know?"

"Do you not keep a list? Photos, memories? Would Antonio know?"

"I doubt it."

"Maybe we should ask him."

"Why would you do that? He won't know."

"You sure?"

He stared hard at her face. "Why would my brother know how many lovers I've had, or how many people I've fucked?"

She stared back, not blinking. "Because he's your twin; you've been together since birth. He lives with you 24/7, so he *would* know."

"I doubt it, but go ahead." He dismissed her.

Xanthe set the phone to speaker and dialled Antonio's number.

"Antonio Stephanopoulos, who's calling please?"

"Antonio, Xanthe. I'm here with Cabot debating how many lovers he's had, and I asked if you'd know. He doesn't believe you would. Would you happen to know?"

"Hang on." Antonio checked the notes on his phone. "Over all the years you've been having sex, at last count, 4242. And that includes the ones you've been sucked by, or fucked, and the guy here on Mykonos who turned around and attacked you. At least they're the ones *I know of,* anyway. You've clearly had many I don't know about, so it could well be over 5000 for all we know."

"No," Cabot growled. "No, it's not possible."

"Of course it is, Cabot. You're rampant. Can't keep your eleven-inch cock in your pants, that's how you're in the mess you're in. See you at lunch."

Xanthe disconnected the phone and sat back in disbelief. Of all things she'd ever heard of, or been told, that took the cake. "Well… there you go. 4242 at last count, and possibly more. What do you say about that?"

Frowning, Cabot's nostrils flared, and he breathed heavily. "No. It's not possible. It's not possible that I've fucked that many. No. I don't believe it."

*****

Tuesday morning, Alena and Diana had a late breakfast out. It was Diana's last day and Alena's if she left on time, but she was having second thoughts.

"You can't be serious!" Diana exclaimed. "You're thinking of staying longer?"

"At least until the end of the week," Alena told her. "I really should stop by and see him."

"You did! Yesterday," Diana reminded her, sipping her juice. "Isn't that enough? But no, you're going back today. And now you're telling me you're staying until the end of the week. Will you see him every day?"

"I don't know." Alena blushed behind her hair as she looked down at her food. "I suppose."

"Suppose my foot! Of course you will." Diana delicately picked at her food. "You told him yesterday you'd be in today. And now you're telling me you'll stay longer. What will you tell your parents when they call because you didn't come home on time?"

Alena shrugged. "I don't know. That I have some *HOS* stuff to do."

"Why lie, Alena?" Diana chided. "Why not just tell them you stayed to see James?" She placed a forkful of scrambled eggs in her mouth and felt like vomiting. But she forced it down with juice. The pills Dan had given her helped, and she had kept taking the anti-nausea ones, but sometimes, with some food, they just didn't work.

"Why are you lying about your illness?" Alena countered, watching her cousin go green around the gills. "You've barely eaten since August. Food poisoning *my* foot."

"I think I've gone off eggs since the poisoning," Diana told her. "It seems to have turned me off a lot of food. But then I guess vomiting it back up will do that." She glared at Alena, defying her to say something.

"Ew, Diana. You'll put me off *my* food. Ew." Looking down at the rest of her eggs turned her off, and she pushed her plate away. "Look, I don't know if I'll see James every day. His parents may turn me away. But I did say I'd be back today."

"Then why not leave it at that?" Diana finished her coffee. "Leave him your phone number or email address, and he can get in contact with you when *he's* better. None of this is up to you, Alena. His parents need to take care of him, and he'll probably be on sick leave until next year. They won't let him back until he's able to return to duty. Let him live his life and don't lead him on. Let him recover with his parents."

Alena pulled a face at her cousin's sage advice. "Yeah, I guess you're right. And he does already have my phone number. We could Skype if he has a computer."

"And if he doesn't?"

Alena shrugged. "I'll get him one."

"Do you know when he's going home?"

"No."

"He'll be staying with his parents for a while no doubt."

"I don't know."

"You can't intrude, Alena." Diana finished up and placed her napkin on the table. "I'm done. I have some shopping to do before I pack. I leave at 1 p.m. tomorrow, and we need to clear out the fridges. Will you be leaving tomorrow too?"

Glancing away, Alena sighed. "I don't know, D. It will depend on today."

"Oh, for God's sake, Alena." Diana paid the bill the waiter brought. "Seriously think about what you're doing, who it involves, and what the ramifications could be for our family. Now." She stood up. "I have to go. What time will you be home by?"

Alena checked her watch. It was after ten-thirty. "I'll be home by three definitely."

"You'll be staying at the hospital that long?" Diana asked as they walked out into the sunny fall day.

"I don't know. If not, I'll do some shopping. If I do, then you'll know not to wait."

Diana sighed. "I hope you know what you're doing because I certainly don't, and I know Grandma and Uncle Tomas won't. I'll see you later." With a flick of her shimmering rose-coloured calf-length silk dress, she walked off down the street.

Oh God, Alena thought. *I wish I knew what I was doing, because I don't.* After catching a cab, she got to James's room just on eleven to see the doctor walk out. "Is everything okay? I can come back later." She glanced at the Gardo family.

"No, no, come in." James lit up. "It's good news. The doctor says I'm doing well and should be out of here next week sometime." He watched her walk around the bed slowly, her eyes flicking from him to his parents.

"That's wonderful," she said. "If I'm intruding, I don't mean to. I *can* come back." She expected Mr Gardo to kick her out while Mrs Gardo had a protective hand on her son's arm.

"No, it's okay." James looked to his parents who smiled.

"We could leave you two alone for a while if you like," Giancarlo said.

James struggled to sit up. "Can you? Please."

"I don't mean to rush your parents out of here," Alena said quickly. "If it's inconvenient…" She watched Mrs Gardo help her son by fluffing the pillows behind him.

"It's all right, Alena." Giancarlo put a hand on Sheila's elbow. "I'm sure you two have a lot to talk about. Reminiscing about the tour and all. Come on, Sheila, we'll leave them alone for a while. We'll be back shortly."

"Okay." James waited for his parents to leave before speaking. "Hi," he gushed. "There was so much I wanted to say to you yesterday, but you had to leave, and my parents were here. But they've gone now. I wish they wouldn't worry and flit around. Mom especially."

"You're their only child, so it's natural to worry. What happened to you was horrible." Alena sat on one of the chairs vacated by his parents.

"Yeah. Dad told me I was in Central Park and got caught up in a chase. Officers were after a perp, and I yelled out 'stop police', but instead of stopping, the perp shot me." He carefully shook his head. "I don't even remember being there."

"What *do* you remember? Any of it?" Alena was curious to see how much he did remember, if any at all.

"I remember being told we were on duty for your concert. I remember running in the underground car park and getting you out of the way when the shots rang out. I remember your mom said she knew my dad. I remember my captain putting me on bodyguard duty, and I went home, packed a bag, and came back to meet your cousins. Twin boys; can't remember their names, though."

"Cabot and Antonio."

"Right. Six-foot brunets, one blue-eyed, one green."

"That's them."

"And your mom and sister were there."

"That's right."

"And they stayed for two weeks and flew home from Miami, then we continued on for weeks."

"Ten weeks in total," Alena said. "Do you remember all of it?"

His head moved up and down. "Yes…yes, I do…but it's as though I was underwater. It's fuzzy on sound, dull, I'm not quite catching it." He thought back, a faraway look on his face. "I saw everything from afar. As if I wasn't the one doing everything. I was just the watcher, looking on." He sighed. "It really is very bizarre, and I can't explain it. The doctor said any strange behaviour would have been caused by the aneurysm. Did I exhibit any strange behaviour on tour?" He gazed into Alena's electric blue eyes and saw her smile. Her giggle was music to his ears.

"No, you didn't. Although you didn't appear interested in me, which I found strange since all good-looking young men fall for my charms."

"Oh." His face fell. "Oh...I...don't know how to explain that. I..." He blushed and looked away.

"It's okay. It's not a requirement of working with me that you have to fall for me."

"No...it..." He didn't know how to put it into words.

"What?"

A sigh left him. For all the thinking he'd done since being out of a coma, words failed him now. He vowed to be honest and grab the bull by the horns. "I *do* like you, Alena. *A lot.* But I have no idea why I didn't kiss you, or hold your hand, or something except to say either I was keeping it professional, or this brain thing made me a whack job. But I don't know why I didn't do anything, and I apologise if I offended you by not doing anything."

Alena burst out laughing. "Oh, my God," she gasped. "Do you mean to tell me that you really wanted to kiss me, but didn't out of responsibility?"

"Or my brain thing." James grinned. "I have no idea why I didn't."

"That's okay." Alena's smile was broad. "You had your brain thing. You're forgiven."

His grin grew. "Really? Am I? That's great, coz I'd really like to get to know you when I get out of hospital and maybe kiss you for real."

Alena's smile disappeared. "What?"

James panicked; he'd said too much too soon. "I'm sorry. I shouldn't've pushed it. It's just with everything that's happened, I've thought a lot about life and chances, and risks, and I decided to take the bull by the horns and just do things, and one of those things is kiss you..." He really, really hoped he hadn't made a fool of himself.

"Oh." Alena had no idea what to say to that, or what to think.

"I'm moving too fast?"

"Yes," she murmured, unable to look at him with everything that had happened. She didn't want to upset her Prince Tomas by falling for James, the man who looked just like his first lover, who did so much damage to him, and just happened to be the half-brother of his lookalike.

"Oh, my God, I'm sorry. Sticking my foot in it again." James groaned and looked away, desperate for his parents to walk back in.

"Look, let's talk about the rest of it, and get your mind on other things," Alena said. "Do you remember what happened after the tour?"

"Ah…" His mind wandered back. "Not really. I think I was in my apartment a lot. I think I was drinking a lot. I think I was going to the library."

"What about before that? The last night of the tour. Back at the Garden. You disappeared, and no one knew where you were."

"Really?" He pursed his lips. "I think I was there, but I can't really remember."

"Oh, what about Sunday? When all this happened?" Alena pushed.

He shook his head. "I've tried remembering before, and I can't."

"You rang me that morning to ask me out to lunch or dinner."

"I did?" His eyes widened. "I don't remember."

"I didn't know you had my number; you said you got it from my phone."

"Did we got out to lunch or dinner?"

"No. I ended up inviting you to brunch in the penthouse, so you could meet my family."

"What time?"

"I said come at eleven."

"Did I make it?"

"Well…" She saw the Gardos hovering in the hallway. "You made it across the street."

"And then I was shot," James said. "Dad's told me all about that. So has Denny, my partner; do you remember him?"

"From the Garden that night; he saved Alexis."

"Yeah, well, he stopped by last night after work. Brought a huge card that the guys from work all signed." He pointed to the side cupboard where a two by one foot get well card sat. "He told me his side of things. He saw me run across the street to the park and yell out, but the perp shot me and down I went. He's the one who called for help."

"Yes, that's what we were told." Alena saw the Gardos listening closely. "My whole family went out for a look and saw you taken away. My grandma helped your father look after you."

"Oh, that was nice of her. I should thank her. Did my dad? I don't remember any of it, and Dad hasn't told me all the details."

"Probably thinks it would be too much to deal with so soon. Or maybe he wants you to remember on your own."

"Yeah, maybe. I definitely remember the tour, but it's fuzzy. And I don't remember that day."

"Did the doctor say you'd never remember, or it might come back?"

"He said it might never come back, so don't expect too much." Shifting on the bed, he finally saw his parents in the hall. "You don't have to spy, we're not making out or anything."

"Oh, hey, what!" Alena became alarmed.

"My son has a sense of humour, Miss Stephanopoulos." Sheila walked into the room. "It seems with everything that happened, he managed to retain it."

James grinned at Alena. "Sorry if I freaked you out. I crack jokes like that to diffuse moments."

"Oh." Alena blushed. "Okay. I wasn't expecting it."

"Most people never do." Sheila patted her son's arm and smiled affectionately.

"Well, I should go. Let you rest and have lunch. Spend some time with your parents." Alena stood and gathered her things.

"Are you really going home tomorrow?" James asked, not wanting her to go.

"Mmm," she paused. "I was…"

"Can you stay? A few more days at least," James went on.

Alena glanced at Giancarlo and Sheila. "If your parents don't mind. I don't want to step on their toes."

"I think if you want to visit again, that will be fine," Giancarlo said.

Alena glanced from him to Sheila. "Mrs Gardo?"

"Mom, I want her to visit," James told his mother.

Sheila finally smiled. A fake smile, anyway. "If that's what you want, and what will make you better, then it's okay with me." Gently touching his face, she let her smile grow, genuine this time.

"Okay. I'll be back about the same time tomorrow. My cousin's leaving, so it will be after that." She backed out the door. "So, um, bye…"

"Until tomorrow." James leaned forward to see her off.

"Yeah, um…bye." She fled out the door, but she stopped halfway down the hall to catch her breath.

"Alena."

"Ah." She jumped and spun around. "Ah, Mr Gardo, you scared me."

"I'm sorry, I wanted to ask you something. You asked James if he remembered the last night of the tour, and you told him he'd disappeared, and no one knew where. Can you elaborate?"

Frowning, Alena wasn't sure she should say.

"Did something happen?" Giancarlo noticed her unease and instantly knew something was wrong. "Did James do something?"

"I'm not sure I should even say." She shifted from one foot to the other.

"Please. If it had to do with his behaviour, I need to know."

With a confused sigh, she recounted Roger's assault and Cabot's word that it was James who had attacked.

"And what day was that?"

"August 20, Saturday, the last concert of the tour at Madison Square Garden."

"And Cabot swears it was James?"

"He said he'd recognise those blue eyes anywhere." The whole conversation made her uncomfortable. "So did my Uncle Tomas. That's the way he felt about Luiz. The eyes seem to attract everyone. It's what they remember about him, about Luiz. Are they really both the same?"

Giancarlo moved her further down the hall. "I'm not sure. Yesterday, Sheila made me dig out the box of Luiz's things. She hasn't seen them in nearly forty years. There were two albums of photos; the last lot of Luiz was his seventeenth birthday. She asked me to get James's album, so she could compare them, and the way James looked on *his* seventeenth birthday made him identical to Luiz on his. I couldn't tell them apart, and I was a cop for over thirty years." A sigh rumbled through his body and finally left him. "Sheila thinks it's time to tell James about Luiz. But I don't know."

"Will he remember what he said or did as Luiz?"

"I don't know." Giancarlo studied her. "What I *do know* is you have your father's and grandmother's blue eyes, and James has fallen for you the way I fell for your grandmother. So, maybe it runs in the family."

Alena blinked in surprise. "You fell for Grandma?"

Giancarlo glanced over his shoulder to make sure Sheila wasn't there. "When I first met her in '77, I thought she was everything." His face softened with the memory. "But she was with your grandfather, and I had been seeing Sheila. So, obviously, it was never going to work out. By '78, the crush was over, but now I see James has fallen for those blue eyes too, and I don't want him to be hurt, Alena. If your life is not here, but with your family, then please don't lead my son on."

"Oh, I have no intention—" she started.

"I know you may not." Giancarlo stopped her by putting his hand up. "But he likes you very much and might want to pursue some kind of relationship. I'd like you to not do that. Just tell him you can be friends, but he's got his career, and you've got yours."

"He said he wants to make detective by thirty," Alena said. "He told me on tour."

Gardo nodded. "That's his plan. I'd like that to happen."

"You'd also like him to fall in love and settle down with a girl who's not a Stephanopoulos in any way, shape, or form." Alena wasn't sure if she should be offended.

"Yes, we would."

Alena exhaled slowly. "So, don't get interested in your son. Don't lead him on, go home, and leave him alone."

"Please," Giancarlo said softly.

The pain rocketed into her chest, and she was annoyed and understanding at the same time. Annoyed because she liked him, but she understood. "What will you tell him when I don't turn up tomorrow?"

"I will tell him you rung earlier to say you had to go home for a family emergency. He'll understand."

She shifted from one foot to another. "Not sure I do."

"James shared a half-brother with your mother. That half-brother could have been his identical twin and was the lover of your uncle. *That* is a mess."

A low laugh came from her. "Yeah, one hell of a mess this family is in, huh?"

"We'll make him understand, Alena. Your life is in Greece with your family. His life is here with us and his future career and wife."

"I never said I wanted to be his wife." Tears burned her eyes.

Giancarlo's heart went out to her. Not only because she was Jenny's granddaughter, but because his only son thought the world of her, and he was destroying that world before it had a chance to really get going. "I know. But this way, it stops him from falling for you too hard, and he can move on from it."

"From me, you mean." Moving backward she could barely talk. "Tell him whatever you want." She turned and ran for the lift, catching it as it was ready to close. Managing to hold herself together until she got home, she flung herself onto the twin bed in Diana's room and cried.

"Hey, what's wrong?" Diana came in from the bathroom.

"His parents hunted me out. They told me to go home and not get involved with him."

"Well, considering who he is and who he looks like, that's a good thing." Diana rubbed her back. "Tell me everything."

For the next few minutes, Alena recounted her visit, and how she'd told Gardo that they thought James tried to kill Roger at her last concert.

"How did he take that?"

"Well." Alena wiped her face. "But then he told me it was better for James if he didn't fall for me, and to just leave and never see him again."

"I'm surprised you left. Will you go back?"

"What's the point?" Alena flung herself back into her pillow.

"I guess it's just as well. There's no point getting involved with a man who lives so far away. You know it won't work out."

"That doesn't mean we shouldn't get to know each other and spend time together."

"Didn't you do that on tour?"

Alena lifted her head and sniffled. "Yeah."

"So, why do you need to spend *more* time together? You had ten weeks."

"Yeah, I guess. And he does have my number." Alena sat up and wiped her face free from tears.

"And he's a cop. If he wants to find you, then he can come looking for you. Prove that *he's* interested in you. Although, considering the family…"

"Yeah, that's what Mr Gardo said."

"Well then. Leave the family to it, and if James is serious, *he* can find *you.*"

"Yeah, yeah, he can," Alena agreed. "Let him find me."

The next morning, both girls boarded the family jet for Europe, leaving James wondering why Alena didn't show up, and if his parents had something to do with it when he heard his father's excuse for Alena's no-show. His cop instinct kicked in. He'd spent ten weeks with her, there was no way she'd just leave without telling him. No way at all. He vowed to track her down and find out why his father had lied to him.

Alena made it home, after a stopover in London to drop off Diana, and into the arms of her family. "I missed you all so much."

"We've only been gone a few days." Angie hugged her back. "Are you okay, sweetie?" Pulling back, she gazed into her daughter's face.

"I'm okay, Mama, probably just tired from the flight. I need to go downstairs and unpack. Alexis, you wanna come help?"

"Um, okay." Alexis allowed herself to be dragged down to the house Alena shared with Diana. "What's going on?"

Alena locked the door, and they dragged her bags upstairs where she threw herself onto the bed and bawled her eyes out.

"Whoa, okay…stop that!" Alexis had never seen her sister cry like that and had no idea what to do.

Alena sat up and wiped her face. "It's horrible, Alexis. What am I going to do?"

"Tell me what's going on first of all." Alexis sat on the bed and listened to the whole story of James Gardo, what his father had said, and how much she liked him.

"You know that won't go down well with Grandma and Uncle Tomas."

"But he's *not Luiz*," Alena wailed. "He's *James*, and I printed out all of that stuff we found on the family." She pulled the pile from her tote and showed them to Alexis. "Here, read them. What Luiz did was horrible, and what Mama went through was horrible at the hands of *her* father."

Alexis quickly read the papers and sighed. "But none of this is *our* business. It all happened before we were born. It's about James, Luiz, and Uncle Tomas. You can't get involved with someone who's related to the family in such a way. Besides the fact he lives seven hours away in New York and is a cop. Do you expect him to give up his career for you?"

"Oh, God, of course not." Alena walked over to the window. "But I like him, and he said he liked me and wanted to kiss me, but he didn't, and now that I know that, what am I supposed to do?"

"He told you all of that?" Alexis moved to her sister's side. "How would you have a relationship?"

"Who said anything about a relationship?" Alena said.

"If you like each other and kiss, then you might end up in a relationship. What then? You're here, will you move to New York and marry a cop?"

"What! Alexis, I'm not talking marriage." Alena slapped her on the arm.

"But you're talking relationship," Alexis argued. "That means living together, sex, marriage, children."

"Oh, my God. I'm not thinking that far ahead." Alena ran her hand through her hair. "I don't know. I don't know. I like him. I know he likes me."

"You need to see a counsellor," Alexis advised her. "There's one two doors down that Grandma brought in for Cabot. She's up to see the whole family."

"Brought in for Cabot?" Alena frowned. "Why would Grandma bring in a counsellor for Cabot?"

"Oops," Alexis glanced at her watch, "he should be with her now; probably a good time to go see them and he can tell you while she's there."

The frown deepened. "Alexis?"

Alexis backed away. "Go see them. He needs to tell you and having a therapist present will help. I'll see you later. You might want to talk to her while you're there," she called as she walked down the stairs and out the door.

Puzzled, Alena walked two doors down and raised her hand to knock, but Cabot opened the door, ready to barge out.

Scowling, he snarled, "What are you doing here?"

Used to Cabot's outbursts, she was unfazed by his tone. "Alexis told me Grandma brought a counsellor in for you and that I might want to see her for my issues. Apparently, you have something to tell me, cuz."

Xanthe came to the door. "You must be Alena. Come in, come in." She ushered them both in. "Cabot refused to talk today. But now you're here, he may as well tell you. Go on, Cabot." She waited.

"Tell me what?" Alena looked from one to the other. "Tell me what?"

The scowl had stayed in place, but Cabot almost hissed. Crossing his arms, he became defiant. "Grandma dragged me home and got me a *psycho*therapist." He rolled his eyes. "All because they claim I tried to kill myself." He'd been arrogant for a couple of days, arguing with himself about the things Xanthe had gotten out of him, and what questions they stirred up inside. Questions he did not like because he either didn't have the answers, or he didn't want to think about the feelings he was having.

"You what!" Alena stared in shock. "You what!" Her head swivelled between Cabot's cocky face and stature, to Xanthe's amused grin and back again. "Cabot!" She whacked him hard on the arm. "What the fucking hell did you do that for, you fucking dickhead?"

"Hey!" He backed away from the attack, arms up in defence. "No need to assault me. I've already been through one of those."

"What?" She was confused. "*What* are you talking about, Cabot? *From the beginning,* and don't leave anything out." She saw his reluctance. *"Now!"*

Xanthe wandered into her office to give them some space, but she could still see them in the hallway. "You have to tell her," she called.

Cabot sighed. "Okay, *Xanthe.*" He rolled his eyes as hard as he could, but stopped when he saw Alena's furious expression. Gulping, he began. "Do you know about me being beaten up in July? Here in Mykonos?"

"It's been mentioned. You were robbed and beaten."

"Well…" His voice went higher. "Not quite."

"Cabot," Alena warned, tired of the dragging out.

His energy flagged, and it came out in a rush. "It was the night after my birthday, I got angry at the family and Grandma slapping me, so I stormed off, got drunk at a club, and had sex with a guy, but the guy wanted payment, and when I didn't have anything, he pulled a knife and demanded it. He groped my pockets and then shoved me against the wall and shoved his cock up my ass. I fought him, managed to knock the knife away, and get him off me, but he started hitting me in the face, and we rolled around on the ground hitting each other, and then a couple came along and helped me, and then Tony came along and got me to the hospital."

"Oh, my God, Cabot. Why did you cover it up?" Alena's shock grew.

He sighed. "I didn't want anyone to know."

"So…why would you try and kill yourself over that?" Alena asked.

"Um…" Biting his lip, he glanced at Xanthe and saw her small nod. "Well…you know how I had the flu in New York?" He couldn't look his cousin in the eye.

"Yes."

"It wasn't the flu."

"What was it?"

He scuffed a toe and looked down at it. "My body getting AIDS."

Alena's brows rose. "What?"

His eyes moved to the ceiling. "The bastard who attacked me gave me HIV and some itchy red spot STD that Dan's been treating me for."

"Oh…my God…Cabot…" Alena didn't know what to say or do, so she looked at Xanthe who nodded again. "Oh, my God." Her energy zapped out from her feet and into the ground. "You've got that for life, Cabot."

"Yeah, cuz. I know."

"So, that's why you tried to kill yourself?"

"Yeah," he said softly. "At first I was in denial. Dan told me. Tony found the packet of info he'd sent and tried to get me to admit it. But I got drunk instead. I was actually in the park when that cop got shot. I'd gotten drunk the night before in the park and saw the whole thing. But I ran back to the hotel and showered, and finally read the info. Then I ran again, got drunk again, and downed some pills and tried to throw myself off a bridge. I rang Tony to tell him I loved him, but he found me. I smashed the bottle and tried to slash my wrists, but I didn't do a very good job of it. Tony called the paramedics and got me to Dan at the hospital. Grandma found out and told me she was taking charge, and I had to lump it. So, here I am getting *psycho*therapy every day on the dot of ten. Why are you here?"

"Alexis told me about Xanthe, and that you had something to tell me and I should come here because you'd be here." The last four weeks had been complicated, and now the tears flowed forth. Again. "I'm so sorry, Cabot." She went into his arms and hugged him. He was four inches taller than her, and he laid his chin on her head as she rested it on his shoulder. "I'm so sorry."

"So am I," he murmured. "I really cocked up, didn't I?"

"Yes, you did," she replied. "And so have I."

"You?" he asked curiously. "What have you got to do with this?"

"Not with you." She stared up into his steel blue eyes. "I meant with *my* life." Glancing at Xanthe, she added, "Can any of us see you?"

"24/7," she said. "You're welcome to stay now."

Nodding, Alena let go of Cabot. "If you're done, I guess it's my turn."

"Okay. I'll see you later. Grandma has me cooped up with the olds, and she's on guard duty, so I don't get to go far unless someone's with me."

"And that would be me, right now," Antonio said from the doorway.

"Tonee!" Cabot bounced over to his brother and flung his arms around him. "I missed you."

"You saw me at breakfast." Antonio pushed him away and hugged Alena. "How are you, cuz? Dickface told you how he's fucked up?"

"Tonee!" Cabot was shocked that his brother called him such a thing. But then, only Tony could *and* would get away with it.

Alena giggled at the name. "Yes, he has. That sucks."

"Yes, it does. But he did it to himself, so he has to deal with it. Xanthe." He nodded at her amused expression. "I'll take him off your hands now. Come on, Dickface. Let's go for a walk." He walked out the door without a backward glance.

"Tonee," Cabot whined as he ran after him. "Don't call me that?"

"Why not…you are…"

"Oh, my God." Alena choked back a laugh as Xanthe shut the door. "Dickface! Antonio has never called him that." Laughter got the better of her and came out.

"Yes, that is a new one." Xanthe led her into the office. "It surprised me too."

"Have you seen anyone besides Cabot?" Alena asked. "Like Antonio?"

"Not yet. But I think he will come when he's ready. Like you." She sat on one of the easy chairs. "I hear the tour went well. Apparently, there's a hot cop that's related to someone the family knew. That must have been crazy?"

Alena looked up in alarm. "How the hell did you know what I wanted to talk about?"

"I didn't, but your reaction just told me. I was merely making conversation."

Freaked out by her astuteness, Alena didn't know where to start.

"From the beginning." Xanthe saw her discomfort and some reluctance.

Wide-eyed, Alena told Xanthe all about the tour from start to finish. Then she launched into what happened that fateful Sunday and how she felt about James. "His father all but told me to get out and not come back."

"Interesting," Xanthe murmured, making notes in a large black notebook. "Does your family know you've discovered all of this?"

"Grandma confiscated the first lot of papers, so Diana and I printed another lot."

"And how do you feel about what you read in them?"

"Shocked!" Alena exclaimed. "Mama was assaulted by her father, shot by some man, Daddy had a stalker who killed our grandfather, then Daddy was kidnapped. Jesus. What sort of life did they have before us?"

"What does it matter?"

"What?" Alena looked at Xanthe like she was crazy. "*Of course it matters,* they're our parents."

"And it all happened before *any of you* came along. It's none of your business, doesn't include you, didn't happen to you. So, why does it matter?"

"Because it's come back to haunt Uncle Tomas."

"And what does that have to do with you?"

"It has to do with me because James looks *exactly* like Luiz, Uncle Tomas's first lover, who did so much to him and Roger."

"What Luiz did, is over. *Was* over in 1977. Tomas told me all about it when I counselled him after he was sick. That has nothing to do with any of you *now* in 2007."

"It does because James is Luiz's half-brother, he looks *identical* to Luiz, and it freaked Uncle Tomas, and everyone else, out that day in the penthouse."

"Do you know for a fact they're identical?"

"Besides everyone telling us that?"

"Who's everyone?"

"Uncle Tomas, Grandma, Mr Gardo."

"Three people is not everyone."

"You know what I mean!" Alena was exasperated. "James and Mama share a half-brother, who happened to be Uncle Tomas's lover. That's kinda gross, kinda creepy."

"Doesn't make you related to James, though, so if you wanted to pursue a relationship with him—"

"I couldn't," Alena cried in alarm. "Mr Gardo warned me off, and Grandma would kill me. Not to mention what it would do to Uncle Tomas."

"What would it do?"

"It would…" Alena looked around for answers. "It would…kill him…"

"How?"

"Well…what?"

"How would it kill him?"

"Well," Alena blinked, "I guess it wouldn't physically, but emotionally…"

"How?"

"Well…um…it would hurt him to know his niece had gotten involved with someone who not only looks like his former lover, but just happens to be the half-brother of him."

"Yes." Xanthe nodded. "It would hurt him. And maybe that's why it's time for Uncle Tomas to deal with Luiz once and for all. But apart from all of that, remove who James is from the equation. Remove his ties to Tomas. How do you feel about him as a woman and man?"

The smile lit up Alena's face. "I like him…a lot. On tour, I wished he'd kissed me, and if we'd fallen into bed, I would've had no problem with that whatsoever. In the hospital, he told me he wanted to kiss me, but wasn't sure why he didn't. Responsibility as my bodyguard, or because of the brain thing. So, if he hadn't been sick…"

"Forget that you live in two different continents," Xanthe said. "Would you pursue a relationship with him?"

"Not necessarily." She blushed. "I like him, I'd like to spend more time with him without our work getting in the way. If we kissed, we'd see where it went. If we ended up in bed, we'd see where it went. I can't say it's going to turn into a relationship. I just know I really like him and want to spend time with him."

"Would you tell your grandma that?"

"Oh, God no." Alena's eyes widened in alarm.

"Your Uncle Tomas?"

"Nope, definitely not."

"Why not?"

"The same reasons as before."

"And I can repeat my answers from before. You and James have nothing to do with Tomas and Luiz."

Alena's sigh was deflating. "Yes it does; you know it does."

"Then clearly it's time to sort this out once and for all," Xanthe said. "For everyone's sake."

*****

Alexis, Summer and Melody caught up with Cabot and Antonio on the beach, and Alexis pulled Cabot aside while the girls kept Antonio amused. "Cab, have you talked about your assault with Xanthe?"

"Not in minute detail." He casually laid his arm around her shoulders, and she wrapped hers around his waist as they walked along.

"I was thinking I should talk to her about *my* assault. The counsellor I saw back in May wasn't very good." Alexis watched her cousin frolic with her friends.

"I will say *this* about the *psycho*therapist. She has a way of getting shit out of you and asking questions you never thought to ask yourself." Cabot jammed his free hand into his jeans pocket.

"She's *that* good? What's she gotten out of you?" Alexis grinned.

He grinned back. "Never you mind, cuz. Those sessions are private, and no one's getting any info out of me."

"I should talk to her then?" She saw the girls try and drag Antonio towards the water, but he was resisting.

"If you feel the need, yes. If you need help dealing with something, absolutely." Cabot saw Antonio pull Melody back and wanted in on the fun. "Hey, Tone, you need to get wet." He ran after his brother, who ran away, but he caught up, flung him over his shoulder, and ran into the surf, dumping them both.

The girls cheered and clapped the boys as they surfaced and spluttered water everywhere.

"Oh, think it's funny, do you?" Cabot grinned and climbed to his feet. He flung his hair back and wiped the water off his face.

"*Of course* it is," Alexis said. "Most things you two do *are* hilarious."

"Is that so?" He shook his head to spray water over the girls and grabbed his cousin.

"No, Cabot, no," Alexis cried as she was flung over his shoulder and dumped in the surf. She came up spluttering, "No fair," and splashed him as he trod water nearby, rolling along with the surf.

"Whoo," Summer and Melody cried. "Alexis got dumped."

"And so will you two." Antonio came up behind them, an arm around each waist, and ran them into the water, screaming.

"No, Tony, no," Summer cried before she was swamped by a wave. "Ah!" She stood up, wiping her face. "My hair."

"*Your* hair? What about mine?" Melody cried. "And my clothes." She wrung out her wet *Haus of Stefan* top. "It's ruined."

"So what!" Alexis told her. "You'll get another one." She dunked Cabot who grabbed her waist and lifted her into the air. "Ah!" She was dunked again.

They played for an hour or so before heading back home, somewhat dry by the time they stopped at Viv and Carlos's for Cabot and Antonio to shower and change.

Jenny opened the door, as she'd been visiting Viv, and saw the dishevelled appearance of the kids. "What have you lot been up to?"

"Just gone for a swim, Grandma, no biggie." Cabot dripped all the way to his bedroom with Viv wiping up the mess behind him.

"Have fun?" Jenny asked, glad her grandchildren were finally cutting loose in the last days of the summer warmth. "Looks like it."

"Yeah." Antonio grinned. "Destressed after God knows how long. We did have a lot of fun."

"Good." She smiled. "Lunch is waiting next door. Have you seen Alena?"

"Left her at Xanthe's," Antonio said. "Gotta get changed, Grandma, see you at lunch." He kissed her cheek and ran off, leaving her to close the door behind him. "And what about you three?" she asked the girls.

"So much fun, Grandma," Alexis said, ruffling the last remaining drops from her hair. "Haven't had fun like that in ages."

"I'm glad you did. And you got to spend time with your cousins, which is rare." She walked them to Pedro and Angie's door.

"Yeah, I did, and it *is* rare, but now that we're all back home, except for Diana, we can have fun like a family again." Alexis opened her door. "And even Dom and Danté are getting along, albeit, stiffly."

"At least *they are* getting along," Jenny replied. "I'll see you for lunch." Turning to the twins, she added, "Would you like me to walk you?"

"No thanks, Mrs S, we can make it. It's only five houses down the street."

"Okay. If you want to come for lunch, there's more than enough."

"Thanks, Mrs S." They waved and set off.

The smile was still on Jenny's face when she walked through her own door.

"Something good happen?" Spiros asked from the kitchen where he was making iced tea.

"Alexis and the girls just spent time with Cabot and Antonio. All had fun getting drenched in the surf."

"Things are looking up then?" He handed her a glass of chilled mint tea.

She sipped it. "Mmm, nice and cold. It would seem so. And Alena's talking to Xanthe, so I wonder what that's all about."

"You did tell the family all were welcome to see her." Spiros added another sprig of mint to his glass.

"Yes, but what could Alena have to talk about?"

*****

"Here we are, darling." Sheila opened the door and led James into their home. "Home, sweet, home." She quickly fluffed the pillows on the couch and helped him sit.

"I'm okay, Mom. I don't need help sitting." Shooing her away, he glanced around. "Still the same as always. I still don't know why I couldn't just go home to my place. Oh, my God, the rent and bills!" He struggled to get up. "I have to pay them, or I'll lose my apartment."

"Already taken care of James, just relax." Giancarlo set his son's bags down and closed the door. "We've told your agent we'll be paying for the rent for the next three months while you recover."

"Dad." James settled back. "You didn't have to do that. I should be back home in a few weeks. I *should* be home *now*."

"You heard what the doctor said." Sheila placed a crocheted blanket over his legs. "Take it easy and don't be on your own for at least a month. You have to ease back into doing things."

"Mom, I don't need a blanket, I'm not cold. I just…" He stopped when he saw her crestfallen face. "Mom, stop. I don't want to feel like an invalid. I can walk and talk and brush my own teeth. The doctor said I can do everything on my own, I just need someone around." He took her hand, squeezed it and pulled her down beside him. "I want to go for walks and get some air and do the stuff I used to do."

"You won't be back on the force until next year, at least." Giancarlo sat in his easy chair across from the couch.

James sighed. "Yeah, I know. And that sucks as far as I'm concerned. It's my job, it's what I love doing, and I'm not doing it."

"But you need your rest," Sheila told him. "And your brain will take a few months to fully recover, and you'll have to have more tests to see if you're okay to go back to work. Until then, I want you here with me, with us, so we can take care of you."

"Well, I guess it's just as well you grabbed my stuff during the week. I wouldn't want to be robbed while I'm away," James said.

"I told the agent I'm an ex-detective, and if anything happened to your apartment, or you were robbed, he'd be paying," Giancarlo told them.

"Good old Dad," James joked. "Still think you're a detective thirty years on."

"Hey." Giancarlo pointed a finger at him. "Just because you came along, didn't mean I gave it up completely. Just wait until you get to my age."

James frowned at that. "I didn't even think I'd get to thirty with what happened. And when I get to eighty-three, you'll be gone." Tears welled in his eyes. "I don't want you to be gone."

"Oh, sweetie." Sheila teared up.

"Son." Giancarlo moved to the sofa and sat next to him. "We started late with you and that's why you're still young and we're old.

That's life. As a cop, you know that. Life and death happens. Now, would we love more time with you? Absolutely. Do we want to die yet? Of course not. Would we like to see grandkids? Obviously. But that may or may not happen in our lifetime. I've got at least ten years in me, your mother a good fifteen," he told his son, pulling him into his arms. "I wish we had found each other sooner and had you sooner. So much could and would have changed." He and Sheila had been talking a lot since opening Luiz's box. By '77, the two of them had been seeing each other for two years; maybe he could have saved Luiz, had James sooner. But at the end of the day, they knew that it had all happened the way it was meant to, and that meant having only had twenty-eight years with James, and maybe having only ten to fifteen more. That made every day that much more precious.

"Aw, Dad," James murmured into his father's chest. "I love you."

"I love you too, James." Giancarlo kissed his head. "I wish I could do more for you. I wish we had more time together."

"You could live to a hundred, you know. That's another seventeen years," James said, feeling the heavy weight of losing his parents in so short a time; especially after what had happened to him.

Giancarlo laughed. "Yeah, yeah I could."

"Look, ah, I'd like to go and unpack my stuff, see my old room again." James sat up and looked from one to the other. "If you don't mind."

"Of course not, it's just how you left it," Sheila said.

"Messy and dirty?" James laughed.

"Silly, I *have* cleaned it up. Come on, we'll help you."

With Giancarlo carrying James's bag, they went up and let the early fall air into the room.

"You have clean sheets and new pillows; everything's in its place." Sheila puffed up the pillows on the bed.

"Yeah, it is. I guess I didn't take too much when I moved out." James gazed at the posters and pictures still on the walls before looking out the window. "Still the same old house on the same old street."

"This house is a hundred years old and still standing." Giancarlo settled the bag on the bed. "And it will be yours one day soon for you to bring a wife home to."

"What if my future wife wants to live in the city in a nice apartment?" James turned from the window. "Or another state? Or another country?"

Panic flitted through Sheila. Was he going after Alena? "Why would she want to live in another country?" she asked, trying not to let her panic show.

James shrugged. "What if she has to move for work? Or her family?"

"That doesn't mean you can't keep the house," Giancarlo said. "I had it for many years before I met your mother, and it fell into disrepair. When we knew you were coming, we had it renovated and have kept it up since. It's all we have to give you except for a small inheritance."

"Dad," James said softly, going over to his father and hugging him. "I don't know what the future holds for me. Whether I'll make detective, whether I'll get married or not, whether I'll even become a father." He pulled back. "But I will treasure this house always and do my best to look after it."

Giancarlo sucked back a sob. "That's my boy. Do your papa proud."

"Would you like help unpacking?" Sheila walked over to them, so proud of her son. "We left your other case and bag for you to unpack."

"No, I've got it, Mom." James kissed her cheek. "I'll have a rest after I finish, and you can come and get me for dinner."

"Okay, sweetie, you rest." Sheila kissed him back and followed her husband downstairs.

Quickly unzipping his case, he hung or folded his clothes, then got into his bag to find toiletries, some books he'd planned on reading, his brand-new laptop, and some other personal effects. Jumping on the bed, he cringed as pain shot through his neck to his skull. "Shit! Better not do that again." He opened his laptop, connected to his parents' internet and went searching for any news on Alena. She had a website with photos of the tour, plus there were websites for *Haus of Stefan*, her cousins Diana, Steele and Phoenix, who were currently holidaying at home due to health issues, websites for each of the family businesses and members of the family. He found her parents, aunt, and uncles; even her grandparents turned up on a website where Jenny sold her books.

Unable to find a phone number for her, he searched his phone to see if he had it and luckily, he did. He quickly texted her to get her Skype number. *'Alena, James Gardo, out of hospital, would like to Skype, what's email?'* He hit send then pulled up Skype on the screen. While waiting for a reply, he read more on her website.

Beep beep. Alena pulled her phone from her pocket and read the text. *Oh, my God, he's out of the hospital,* she almost shouted, but kept her cool as they were at Jenny's house. Casting a sly glance around the room, she texted back, *'give me five'* and casually stood up. "I gotta go do some stuff online. I'll see you all tomorrow, yeah. Night everyone." She quickly kissed her grandparents and parents goodbye and made her way out the door. Once it was closed, she raced down the stairs, let herself into her home, locked the door, raced upstairs, and booted up her laptop. Five minutes later, she texted back her email address, and thirty seconds later, James popped up, and she clicked on the call. "Oh, my God, hi!" She eagerly stared at the screen, and he grinned back.

"Hi. You never came back to the hospital. My father said you had a family emergency."

"Ah…" Her face fell. "Yeah, um, sorry about that." Her brain grabbed at something to tell him. "My, ah, cousin is going through some pretty tough things right now, and Grandma wanted us all together."

"Your cousin? Diana, or one of the twins?"

"Cabot. The one you threatened to turn into a woman on my tour bus that night. He's dealing with some pretty heavy stuff right now."

"Anything you can tell me? I saw on their website they're taking time out to spend with family."

"Ah, no. Cabot's business, not mine to tell. What about you? You look good. You got home today?"

"Yeah, well…my parents' home, not mine. Mom insisted I come home so she can look after me till I can look after myself again. The doctor suggested not being on my own for another month or so."

"How are you healing?" She studied him as best she could on screen.

"Scarred," he said. "But my hair will grow back, or so I was told."

"And how do you feel?"

"Um." He thought about it before answering. "A bit of everything. Bored, ready to go back to work, like I should be out doing something, not lying around doing nothing. I wanna get back to work, you know."

"Yeah," she acknowledged. "Like now. I'm not working, just hanging out with my family, but I want to be doing something. Daddy says we'll film a music clip next week, and nothing's stopping me from writing music or recording it. So, I might get back to that."

"When are you coming back to New York?" James so desperately wanted to see her in person, and a small picture on a screen wasn't cutting it.

"Ah, I'm not. At least not this year. We holiday there every summer, and that was my first tour, but I won't be doing another one. I might stop in on the odd occasion for *Haus of Stefan*, or to see Diana or the twins, but they're not there."

His face fell. "So, I won't see you again?"

"Mmm, probably not this year unless you come here. Maybe I can convince the family to have Christmas and New Year there. We're there every couple of years or so for that. We've also been to Australia for Christmas New Year's, or had it in London or Paris, or in Athens. Who knows what will happen between now and next year?"

"Alena…" He decided to get serious. "Do you like me?"

"What!" Her head pulled back, and her eyes widened.

"It's just that I've been thinking. I really like you, and I wanted to spend more time with you, getting to know you, because I don't have a clear memory of the tour, so I wanted to get to know you all over again. But now that you've said you probably won't be coming back, I have to wonder if it's worth my time, our time, pursuing this. That's why I asked. I really like you, Alena, but if we're on two different continents, it's going to be hard."

"Yeah." She saddened. "I've been thinking about it too. I do like you, a lot. And if you'd kissed me, I would have kissed you back, and if it had gone further, I wouldn't've stopped you. But now…and I've thought about it…we're just not going to be able to get to know each other in person, and that kinda ruins it."

He nodded. "Yeah, totally agree. With you there and me here, unless you can come here, we're not going to get a chance to be together. Explore where this could go."

"Do you think it could go somewhere?" The butterflies started up in her stomach.

"I'd like to see where it could go. Maybe it wouldn't go any further than a kiss. Maybe we would end up in bed. I don't know, but I wanted a chance to find out."

"Yeah, so did I."

"So, what do we do?" James asked, perplexed, distressed, and freaking out over not spending time with Alena.

"I guess we could continue to Skype and get to know each other that way. And then if we ever do meet up, we can see where it goes."

"Alena…" He got even more serious. "If I had kissed you, would you have kissed me back?"

"Yes."

"And if it had gone past a kiss?"

"Yes."

"Yes to what?"

"Yes to all of it."

*****

"Why don't you kids take the boat out before the beautiful weather disappears into autumn?" Jenny said on Friday. "There's only a week or two left in September, so why don't you all go and have fun." The kids were all lazing around her lounge room trying to come up with something to do.

"Could we, Grandma? You wouldn't mind?" Alena asked. After her Skype session with James during the week, she'd been quite emotional and needed time out.

"Of course not, it *is* the family yacht, and besides, your fathers are busy at the studio with your mothers." Summer, Melody and Nick were also in attendance. "Carlos and Viv have their things to do, and Tomas and Roger are busy with Dan and Derek on some AIDS thing."

Cabot glanced up sharply. "Was that a hint, Jennifer?"

"Call me Jennifer again, and I'll *slap you* again," she warned him. "They've been working on AIDS campaigns and education since you were born; it's not all about you, Cabot." She wearily turned to the girls. "If you want the boat, I'll call up the staff to get it ready."

"Yes, Grandma, thank you." Alena jumped up and kissed her. "Come on, let's get our swimsuits on. New *HOS* for everyone."

"Whoo," Summer and Melody followed her out the door, and Alexis kissed her grandmother before following. Antonio dragged Cabot up, and Dom, Danté and Nick followed.

Jenny called down to the dock to get the boat ready for the day and thought nothing else of it.

The kids piled onto the boat forty-five minutes later. They would have been there sooner, but the girls couldn't choose which swimsuits to wear.

"Let's get this show on the road," Cabot yelled, fist pumping the air. "When was the last time we were on the boat, Tone?"

"A couple of years, I think." Antonio sat next to his brother on the lounge deck, both wearing tiny swim shorts to show off their packages. They were already golden tanned Adonises and didn't need the extra tan.

"Oh, God, I look positively pasty next to you two," Alena complained, glancing at her fair skin. "Better soap up the sunscreen. Who's got it?"

"I do." Alexis had it and helped her sister rub it in, and then Alena helped her. Summer and Melody did one another, and offered to do the boys.

Alexis helped Danté and Dom, then all settled down to soak up the rays as the captain went out of the harbour to anchor off the coast of home.

"God it's beautiful," Melody murmured as they all sipped juice, water or soft drinks and relaxed in the sun.

"It certainly is," Alena replied. "It's always good to be home."

"As much as I love home, I love visiting other countries," Alexis said.

"Travelling's great, but it can get boring," Antonio told her. "Coming home is always a treat for us."

"Yeah, but you guys are *always* away, so, of course, it would be,"

Alexis countered. "Whereas I'm always here and *barely* getting away."

"Still don't know what you want to do?" Summer asked. "We never did figure it out, and then we ended up in New York."

"Yeah, I know." Alexis sighed. "And now we're here again, and I still don't know what I want to do."

"Are you designing for *HOS*?" Alena asked. "Those dresses you made Diana and me were awesome."

"Yeah, I did all that when you were on tour, but I want to do something else. I feel like I should be *doing* something else."

"Yeah." Alena sighed and put her face up to the sun. "I know the feeling."

"Well *I* want to know the feeling of water on my body, so let's go swimming." Cabot grabbed Antonio's hand and raced downstairs and off the back of the boat that had been put down.

The others followed, and they spent a few glorious hours swimming, jet skiing and diving before lunching on local seafood and icy cold beverages. Afterwards, the girls sunbathed on the top deck, while Cabot and Antonio lounged on the middle deck. Danté and Nick were still jumping off the back of the boat or snorkelling, and Dom kept a close eye on them both as his grandmother and parents would want him to. He sat watching TV in the cabin that opened up to the back of the boat, and occasionally watched the boys fish. They caught a few, and he helped release them back from knotted lines. He left his diving knife on the kitchen island bench and grabbed a drink from the spacious kitchen's double door fridge. Cracking the can open, he saw the boys on the back deck.

He thought about what Alena said to him that day in the penthouse. What if something happened to Danté? What if he was beaten up like Cabot, assaulted like Alexis, taken by a shark? He didn't know then how he'd feel. Sick with guilt as he thought about it. But now that he was watching his brother with his best friend, he thought about it again. And he'd feel sick about it. Danté was *his* brother. Not the twins'. They had one another. He had Danté, and Danté was it. Yet for all those years Danté and Nick had been the brothers while he hung around with Cabot and Antonio because they were only a year apart; like Danté and

Nick. And it had been the same for Alexis, Summer and Melody. They were her best friends and sisters because Alena wasn't. But now they were getting along like a house on fire and were all up on the top deck sunbathing. Cabot and Antonio would always have one another, not him. He was their cousin, not their brother, so he'd never be as close to them as they were to each other. Danté was all he had as a brother, and he'd come to stop feeling hard done by. It wasn't Squirt's fault, he was just the kid brother. It was *his* fault for feeling hard done by for no reason, and now he needed to step up and be the brother Danté wanted *and* needed.

"When do you think we have to go in?" Nick asked, dangling his legs in the water as they sat on the back of the boat. He looked at his diving watch. "It's already five."

"Already? Geez, we've been out that long?" Danté said. "It's like we just got here." He dangled his legs in the water next to Nick. "Should we go for another swim, or snorkel for a while?"

"We should drink!" Nick said and got up. "Want one?"

"Sure, get me a Pepsi," Danté told him and waited while Nick went into the cabin and grabbed two cans. "Hurry up, I'm thirsty, and hot, and I'm gonna get wet." He slid off the back of the boat to wet himself and then hauled himself up, so his lower half was still in the water. "Where's that drink?" He watched Nick crack it open and hand it to him, but something sharp clamped down on his right his leg and dragged him away underwater. He barely had time to scream.

Nick dropped the cans in shock as his best friend suddenly disappeared under the water. "Oh, my God, Danté. Shark, shark's got Danté," Nick screamed, looking around for someone to help. Watching as blood floated to the surface about fifty feet from the back of the boat, he saw Danté's hands flail up through the water.

Dom snatched up his knife from the bench, raced from the cabin, and dived off the back of the boat into the water towards his brother, swimming like a dolphin, with all the power and strength he had. But he couldn't see them. Surfacing, he took in great gulps of air and saw Danté's head barely above the water just metres from him, screaming and thrashing his arms.

The girls had heard Nick's initial screams and came pounding down the stairs. "Oh, my God, what's happened?" Alena cried.

"Danté, shark," Nick stuttered.

The girls, with Antonio and Cabot, watched in horror before Cabot grabbed the jet ski hooked to the side of the boat.

Dom dived, and kicked off toward the great hulking animal that had his brother in its jaws. He saw Danté hitting its head, but *he* needed to get the shark to release Danté's leg.

Danté's leg stung. He struggled for air, but he kept thinking, knowing he had to hit it in the face, especially the eyes to make it let go. But it wasn't letting go, and he was ready to pass out from lack of air and loss of blood. The water was murky with it, and he was losing steam. Fast.

No strength…no energy…feel sick…feel weak…feel…

It was lights out for Danté.

With as much force as he could, Dom swung his right arm through the water and jammed that knife into the shark's head, cutting its gills and yanking out its eye. It let go of Danté's leg as he stopped fighting.

While the shark swam off, trailing blood behind, Dom grabbed Danté around the middle with his left arm and surfaced to find Cabot on the jet ski.

"Take the life ring," Cabot yelled and threw the lifesaving ring at him. Dom caught it, and Cabot gunned it back to the boat, hauling them behind.

Antonio and the crew pulled Danté, then Dom, up onto the back of the boat.

"Get strips of material, or bandages, to wrap the wounds," Dom yelled. He saw Danté wasn't breathing and gave him CPR until Danté spat the water out, then went to work on his leg. He held the towels to Danté's leg that had great geysers of blood spurting from the wounds. "Get the back up, get back to the dock, call the ambulance," he yelled to the crew, and the captain started the engine. The boat roared to life, and they were on their way, the jet skis left behind, but no one noticed as they hurried around finding things to wrap Danté with.

Alexis covered his torso with a towel and held him to keep him warm.

"Here's more towels." Cabot came running up. "I'll hold them down."

"Get away from him," Dom yelled. "You can't be near him." He was wrapping ripped up pieces of towelling around Danté's leg.

Everyone glanced at Cabot, and Antonio spoke from his spot holding towels on Danté's leg. "Cabot, you know you can't. Just don't touch anything."

"But I only want to help," Cabot murmured, feeling like a leper with the looks he was receiving.

"I know, Cabot," Antonio told him. "But you can't be around open wounds. So stay back." He moved his hand out of the way while Dom wrapped another wound. He watched him wrap from the top, around, underneath, and then tie the ends on top to keep the wound together. "I take it you did first aid."

"Never thought I'd need it for shark bites on my brother." Dom glanced at Danté's face. His eyes were closed and his teeth chattering. "Hang on, Little D, we're almost at the dock. Has someone called Dan?"

"I will." Cabot pouted. "Since it's the only thing I *can* do without being near my cousin." He walked into the cabin and dialled Dan.

"Cabot, you okay?" Dan and Derek were soaking up the last rays of the day on the beach sipping cocktails.

"Danté's been eaten by a shark; can you get to the dock?" He saw they were approaching the dock and there was an ambulance waiting. "Oh, no, wait, we're here, and there's an ambulance. Can you get to the hospital?"

"We're on our way." Snapping his phone shut, he told Derek, "Danté's been bitten by a shark, we gotta get to the hospital."

The boat pulled into the dock, and everyone saw the ambulance waiting. The paramedics came on board and quickly hooked Danté up to an IV. Dom lifted his brother and carried him carefully off the boat and onto the stretcher. "I'm going with him. The rest of you get there, and call Mama and Papa." The doors shut and they were gone.

"We gotta call," Alena screamed hysterically, gripping her face in shock. "We gotta call Mama, we gotta call Daddy."

"Get a grip." Alexis slapped her arm until she stopped. "Let's get to the hospital." They hightailed it to the hospital in several cabs and piled into emergency as Danté was being rolled in and Dan and Derek came in with him.

"What happened?" Dan saw them and knew what Cabot had said was true. "We'll get him into surgery, you call your family."

"I guess *I'll* call." Alexis called her mother.

Angie was in *Sync's* office at the studio when her cell went off. Seeing it was Alexis, she said, "Hey sweetie, enjoying your day?"

"We were. Mama, you and Daddy need to get to the hospital, Danté's been hurt." She glanced at her family who were still in shock.

"What do you mean, Danté's been hurt?" The fear froze in place.

"He was bitten by a shark. We were swimming off the boat, and he got bitten. Dom got him out and wrapped him up, and now we're at the hospital. Just come, Mama. I'll call everyone else." She ended the call.

"Danté? My baby," Angie whispered.

"Angie? What's wrong?" Maggie was with her as they had been working on music sheets. "What is it? Has something happened to the kids?" The panic she saw on Angie's face rose in her chest.

"Danté," the whisper came out again. "In hospital. Shark." She grabbed her bag and ran for the studio. "Pedro, Danté's been bitten by a shark, and he's in the hospital." Her voice rose hysterically.

"What?" he spun around in his seat, Carlos next to him.

"Danté's been bitten by a shark," she screamed, not comprehending reality as fear made her crazy. "Hospital." She dashed away.

Pedro glanced at Carlos, and they both ran after her with Maggie on their tail. He grabbed the keys from her hand and drove them to the hospital.

*****

"Grandma? Alexis. Danté's been bitten by a shark. He's in the hospital. I've called Mama and Daddy, they're on their way."

"What! Oh, my God. So are we." Jenny hung up. "Danté's been bitten by a shark; he's in the hospital," she told Spiros, Tomas and Roger. They dropped everything and drove to the hospital, making it just behind the others. They all rushed into emergency and found the kids standing around.

"What happened? What happened?" Angie cried hysterically, and Pedro held her.

"Mama!" Alexis and Alena threw themselves at Angie in a hug.

Summer and Melody went to their mother, and she grabbed Nick.

"What happened?" Jenny demanded. "How the hell is there a shark in Mykonos, and who the hell does he think he is biting my grandson and trying to get away with it? Dom, Antonio, Cabot?"

"Don't look at me." Cabot put his hands up in defence. "They didn't let me touch him. Wouldn't even let me near him."

That brought a frown to Jenny's face as she watched Dom and Antonio finally turn around. They were covered in blood. "Oh, my God."

"Oh, my God, Dom," Angie cried. "Is that…?"

Dom looked down. He was caked in it. "Danté's blood."

Antonio was not so bloodstained. "Nick and Danté were still swimming when the shark grabbed him. Nick screamed out; we were all on different levels of the boat. Cab and I raced downstairs to see Dom swimming for the bloody mess in the water. He got Danté up, and Cabot got out on the jet ski to pull them in. We pulled them onto the boat and Dom performed CPR, then we wrapped his leg. Alexis kept him warm in a towel. Alena and I ripped up towels and bandages. We got back as soon as we could and got him in the ambulance." It all sounded mechanical as he'd said it, but then he *was* on autopilot.

"Oh, my God," Carlos murmured, and Tomas clung to Roger.

"Who's in with him?" Jenny asked.

"Dan, Derek and Lorenzo," Antonio told her.

"Why don't you boys go and get cleaned up at least? I'm sure the staff will let you use their staff room, and give you some scrubs," Jenny said. "It could be a while."

"Yes." Angie moved mechanically. "Yes, Dom, come, we'll get you cleaned up." She led him and Antonio away, grateful for something to do to keep her sane.

Jenny turned to see Nick sobbing in his mother's arms. "Nick, sweetie." She went over and sat with them. "Can you tell me what happened?"

"It's just as Tony said. We were swimming off the boat, and I went in for drinks when Danté dropped in the water to cool off and get wet. He was half in the water when it grabbed him and dragged him away. There was blood everywhere." He choked and sobbed on Maggie's shoulder.

Mike came barrelling through the door. "What happened?"

"Dad!" Nick flew into his arms, and the others quietly told him.

"It's okay, little man, you're okay, and Danté will be okay too." He hugged him tightly, knowing it could have easily been him.

"Why don't you take the kids home?" Jenny told them. "There's no need for you to stay, and the kids *are* in shock."

They agreed and said goodbye to everyone.

Hours later, Pedro almost yelled when he saw Dan and Derek walking towards them. "Dan; how is he?"

Dan joined them. "Lucky. Bloody lucky. Missed all major veins and arteries, but he did bleed a lot. We've cleaned the wounds and stitched up the worst ones. Lorenzo's finishing off now. You might want to get a plastic surgeon to fix them up at a later date," he said to Jenny.

"Oh, if I know Danté, he'll want them the way they are. A badge of honour so to speak," Jenny said.

Dan went on. "He's sedated and will be in ICU for the night to make sure he's okay, and he'll need to stay a few days to prevent infections, and you know, just in case."

"But he'll be okay?" Angie came up to them. "My baby will be okay?"

"At this stage, yes, Angie. He'll be fine. We just have to look out for infection. You can see him in another hour or so, so you all don't have to stay." He spied Dom and Antonio. "You two look as if you could do with showers. Go home, have one, get some food, come back in an hour."

"I want to stay with my baby." Angie's brain was not computing.

"Go home, come back in an hour. You can't see him now," Dan told her. "All of you, go home, have showers, get that mess off you. You can come back and see him later. Go home, eat, drink, come back later." He ushered them toward the door.

Jenny caught up with Cabot who had moved ahead and slid her arm through his. "You said something before, about not touching him.

What was that?"

He shrugged, tears coming to his eyes. "I wanted to help, but they didn't want me touching him."

"Do you understand why?"

He sniffled. "Yes. But it doesn't stop me feeling useless, like I don't matter anymore."

"Maybe you should go see Xanthe. Get this out with her. Obviously, there's something troubling you. Go and see Xanthe, and then you can come back with us in an hour."

"Okay." Wiping his face he stepped forward, but then thought better and stepped back to kiss his grandmother's cheek. "Thanks, Grandma." He ran pell-mell for Xanthe's, leaving Jenny in surprise.

Running all the way, he burst into Xanthe's and collapsed on the lounge floor in a blubbering mess. She came out of the office and made him tell her what had happened. "I feel like a failure. Like I'm no longer welcome in my family. I don't belong anymore. I can't even help my cousin. I don't want to be me anymore. No one wants me. I can't touch anyone. I can't help my cousin for fear of infecting him. I don't want to be me anymore."

Xanthe left him crying and rummaged around in her bag in the office. Coming back, she placed three items on the coffee table in front of him. A bottle of black hair dye, a pair of brown contact lenses, and a pair of clear glass thick black framed glasses.

Cabot noticed and stopped sobbing. "What are they for?"

"You just said you didn't want to be *you* anymore. Well, this is your chance to be someone else."

"What are you talking about?" Cabot looked up at her, not understanding.

"If you don't want to be you, then become someone else. Change the way you look, and it might change the way you feel. About yourself, and everyone and thing else, and come up with a name you'd like to use. If you don't want to be Cabot, just don't use Steele, or anything ridiculous. Ordinary, so you blend in. Now run along, I have the rest of the family to see. Come." She walked him out the door, and he held the three items to his chest. They hurried upstairs to see everyone had arrived home. "You go, I'm needed elsewhere." She walked to Pedro and Angie's door, but Jenny opened it before she could knock.

"Perfect timing; come in."

Xanthe walked in and saw Angie standing in the middle of the lounge room in a state of shock. "Let's start with Mama." Gently holding her by the arms, she started talking to Angie.

In the girls' bathroom, Alexis was in the shower while Alena was waiting. They were talking about what had happened and how scared they were. Even though Alena had her place downstairs, she didn't want to be away from her family right now.

"I can't believe it happened. A shark here in Mykonos. Not the whole time I've been alive." Alexis finished off. "Pass me a towel."

Alena handed a towel to her sister. "I've been thinking of cutting my hair. It takes so long to wash." She held out a strand to look at it. "It takes ages."

"How short will you go?" Alexis wrapped the towel around her and stepped out of the cubicle. Grabbing another towel, she dried her hair off.

"Shorter. I like Mama's hair, but maybe a bit longer. Like a longer bob, or Cleopatra cut." She shrugged. "If I don't like it, it will grow out."

"He'll be okay, Alena." Alexis knew her sister changed the subject when it came to hard issues.

Alena looked up dazedly. "Will he?"

"Of course he will. He's a Stephanopoulos. We survive anything."

Out of the four kids, there were two bathrooms. The girls shared one, the boys the other. Dom stood in his, in his shorts, having dumped the scrubs on the floor, not doing anything but crying. He sobbed for his brother. Sobbed for the shock of seeing Danté dragged away. Sobbed for the shock of what he did; dive in and kill a shark to save his brother. Shock at the extent of Danté's wounds, shock at tying them up and carrying him off the boat. "Argh." He crumpled against the wall, his face screwed up, his ears deaf to the door opening.

"Oh, Dom." Pedro removed his watch and laid it on the sink, then pulled off his shirt and pants. "Dom." Stepping into the shower, he held his son. "It's okay. Danté's okay. He's going to be *okay*. You did good, Dom. You did good."

Dom sobbed on his father's shoulder, feeling his world fall apart.

"It's okay. Danté will be okay, and if we're getting back to the hospital, we need to get you washed." He grabbed the body pouffe and soap and started scrubbing the dried blood from Dom's arms.

Dom came to a rattling halt and saw what his father was doing.

"Come on, let's get you cleaned up," Pedro said, and Dom finally came to. They cleaned him down then Pedro got out for his son to finish off. After wrapping a towel around himself, he held one out for Dom as he turned the tap off and opened the door.

A few minutes later, Dom was getting dressed, and Pedro was changing.

*****

"Angelina, you need to snap out of it," Xanthe said.

"My baby, my baby," Angie murmured, glassy-eyed and out of it.

"Snap out of it and get tough." Xanthe shook her gently.

"No…my baby." Angie's brain wandered off.

"You may need to slap her," Jenny offered.

"We don't slap people these days," Xanthe said.

"Could be the only way to get her out if it," Jenny countered. "I'll do it."

"Jenny." Xanthe looked disappointedly at her. "It's 2007, not 1807."

Jenny shrugged. "If she wants to get back to the hospital she'd better snap out of it."

"Hospital?" Angie was in dreamland. "We have to go to the hospital?"

"See what I mean?" Jenny told Xanthe and took Angie by the arms. "Angelina, Danté is in the hospital, we need to go."

"Danté? In hospital?" Angie looked straight through Jenny.

"Okay, here goes." Jenny slapped Angie firmly across the face.

"Mama, what the hell? What are you doing?" Pedro had seen the whole thing.

"Snapping your wife out of her hypnosis." Jenny looked into Angie's eyes.

"Mama, what'd you do that for?" Angie's hand was on her cheek. "You've never slapped me."

"You've never gone into a catatonic state before," Jenny said. "You can't get weak or fade out now, Angie. *You're a Stephanopoulos*, you *need* to get tough and deal with this."

"Yes," Angie murmured. "Get tough and deal with this." Her head moved up and down, and her eyes cleared. "Yes. Get tough and deal with it."

"You're a Stephanopoulos, get tough and deal with it," Jenny cheered her on.

"Yes." Angie fist pumped. "I *am* a Stephanopoulos. I *will* deal with this."

"I told you so." Jenny glanced at Xanthe. "Good, now do you all want something to eat?"

In the bathroom, Alena stepped out of the shower. "Will you cut my hair for me?" she called into Alexis's room.

"What?" Alexis was pulling on her shoes. "You want me to what?" Walking into the bathroom, she said, "What did you say?"

Alena had combed her hair straight back. "Will you cut it for me? Four or five inches off. Just past my shoulders."

Alexis blinked. "Are you nuts?"

"Grandma did *your* hair, and I can't be bothered paying hundreds for a few inches off, so will you cut it for me?" She held up the scissors from the cabinet.

Shaking her head, Alexis moved over to her and grabbed the implement. "You're nuts."

"It's just hair. I do like Mama's cut, but that's a bit short for me."

"Okay, you sure?" Alexis held up the scissors to her sister's hair.

"Yes. It's too long to deal with anymore."

"You absolutely sure before I cut?" Alexis warned.

"Just cut it!" Alena demanded.

With quick snips, Alexis cut five inches from Alena's hair, leaving it about two inches below her shoulders. It fell to the floor in long wet strands. "There, all done at the back. Brush it, and I'll trim up the sides." She watched Alena brush it into its normal style and then trimmed off the long bits. "It will shrink an inch or so when it dries."

"That's fine." Alena shook her head. "Feels lighter already." Digging in the cabinet, she found a tube of conditioner gel and smoothed some through.

"Hey, don't use all of that," Alexis called as she cleared up the hair. "I'm nearly out." She dumped the hair into the bin under the sink.

"I'll get you some more tomorrow," Alena promised and combed her hair out. "I hope my old clothes fit. I can't run downstairs in my towel." She ran into her old room and quickly found something to put on.

Alexis walked into the lounge room to see Xanthe waiting. "Hey."

"Hello, Alexis. I came to see if you all needed help dealing with Danté's attack."

"No. I'm okay for now. The shock has worn off, and I just want to get back to Squirt." She saw her parents and grandparents in the kitchen getting food.

"My door is open if you need me. Ah, Alena, how are you?" She watched the older sister adjusting her clothes as she walked out.

"Fine." Alena was busy adjusting the old jeans and sequined top. "But these clothes really don't fit anymore."

"Had a haircut I see," Xanthe said.

"Yeah, I just got Alexis to cut it."

"You what!" Angie looked up from the kitchen. "You what?"

"Got Alexis to cut a few inches off." Alena swung her head for her hair to move side to side. "So much lighter. Who knows, I might end up going shorter like Alexis, or you, Mama."

"Now who's copying who?" Alexis grinned. Alena had accused her for years of always copying her; now she was doing it.

Alena grinned back. "Yeah, I know."

Dom finally walked out and saw everyone standing around. "We getting back to the hospital? The hour's nearly up."

"Have a sandwich, so you have something in your stomach." Angie put the platter on the table in the dining room while Pedro set down cans of soft drink. "A bite to eat, and we'll go."

"Not really hungry," Dom said, but cracked open a can and sculled it back.

"Have something, even if it's half." Pedro laid a hand on Dom's back. "You need to keep your strength up after being out all day."

*****

Carlos was catching Viv up on everything that had happened. She'd been busy with interviews and style items and had no idea until he and twins came home.

"Oh, my God. You sure he's going to be fine?" she asked, shocked that after all the years they had been swimming in the waters off Mykonos a shark had suddenly appeared.

"Dan said nothing major was bitten, so he should be fine, apart from a possible infection." They were in their kitchen getting salad sandwiches together.

"Poor Danté. Poor Angie. How's she dealing with it?" Viv cut a sandwich in half.

"Mama went home with them, so probably not well."

Cabot sat staring at the items Xanthe had given him while Antonio was in the shower. Become someone else, pick a name, become someone else. It wasn't a new idea; they'd already done that when they took on Steele and Phoenix as names, but he'd always hated Cabot, though Tony had told him that him hating his name was his fault and he should stop. So it was not as though it would be all that new. But to be someone else to hide in society? To hide out from everyone and not have everyone know who he was, was kind of exciting. To disappear into the crowd, and not have fame or celebrity. That might be nice for a while. He heard Antonio emerge from the bathroom and took his place, thinking more about becoming someone else. Dressing, he took one last look at the items and decided they weren't for him right now. Not with Danté going through what had happened.

*****

A half hour later, everyone poured back into the hospital and stood outside of ICU where Danté would be staying.

He groggily looked over and waved. High on drugs, he felt no pain. Certainly not like he had earlier when he'd been swallowed by the shark. That had freaked him out. The pain searing through his leg. The blood, the diving under the water. He'd managed to hold his breath and fight, punching the animal in the face, eyes and nose, trying to get it to let go. But it hadn't, until Dom had sliced into it and it swam away. He didn't remember much after that, just being held by Alexis while Dom wrapped his leg. His thigh was forever scarred, unless Jenny got a plastic surgeon to fix them. But he might keep them. He had to see how cool they looked first.

Lorenzo saw the family and came out. "Two at a time, three minutes each, and I suggest you go last," he told Angie. "Because you might not want to leave him, but it's ICU, and you can't stay unless we set you up next door."

"I just want to see him," Angie said. "But I'll wait." She motioned for Alena and Alexis to go in and watched while they visited.

"Um, Grandma." Cabot sidled up to Jenny. "You know the jet skis got left behind out there today."

"I know. The captain called. He went back out and found them not far from where you were. They also found a shark floating on the water, its gills and eye ripped out, apparently. About three metres long, so not full grown according to the captain."

Dom quietly glanced around to see everyone staring at him and shrugged. "I sliced it open to make it let go. Is it the same one?"

"The captain towed it in. You can go down tomorrow and have a look." Jenny watched his expression, hopeful that Dom had finally come around to loving Danté.

The girls left, and Spiros and Jenny entered. "Hey, sweetie, how are you?" She kissed his forehead. "Can't wait to look at those scars, I'm sure."

He grinned weakly. "Yeah. I hope they're cool."

"Well, if you don't like them, I'll get a plastic surgeon in to fix them."

"I know you will, Grandma." He held his arms out for a hug and got a tight one.

"You get some rest, Danté." Spiros gave him a hug and kiss, and they left.

Tomas and Roger went next, hugging and kissing him. "Oh, my God, are you okay?" Tomas asked. "You had us so scared."

"I'm okay, Uncle T." He yawned sleepily. "Just tired."

"We'd better let you go then. We'll see you in a couple of days." Another kiss and they left for Carlos and Viv to go in.

Antonio and Cabot were next with Cabot keeping his hands tucked under his armpits.

Danté hugged them both, and another yawn escaped him.

The twins came out, and Dom looked at Nick. With a nod, he indicated for him to go in and followed him into the room.

"Danté, you okay?" Nick fretted. "Not cool man! Getting taken by a shark and making me drop a can of soda."

Danté grinned. "It's only a can, dude. At least my leg's intact."

"And you'll have some cool scars to pick up all the chicks with. I'm jealous." Nick scowled.

"Jealous of being taken by a shark? Dude, you're a dick," Danté said. "Nothing cool about being eaten and devoured to death."

"Yeah, I suppose. I meant I'm jealous that all the girls will be hanging around you now. Checking out your scars, telling you what a hero you are. Cool stuff like that."

"I'm not the hero." Danté's eyes were half cast. "Dom's the hero. He saved me from the shark and gave me CPR when I wasn't breathing." He watched his brother sleepily, seeing him standing at the end of the bed behind Nick with his hands on his hips, looking all concerned and brotherly.

Dom shrugged nonchalantly. "You're my brother."

Danté weakly held out his arms and Dom didn't hesitate. He flew into them, wrapping his arms around his brother tightly and sobbing.

"Aw, look." Jenny teared up. "What we finally wanted to see."

"He broke down while he was having a shower," Pedro told everyone. "I had to get in there to help him wash the blood off and hold him while he fell apart in shock. I've never seen Dom like that before. It shocked *me*."

"He'd just saved his brother's life," Jenny said, wiping her tears away. "It's bound to shock everyone."

"Just a pity Alena's words came true for it to happen," Alexis said.

"What?" The others looked at her, and she blushed, explaining how in the penthouse she and Alena had torn strips off Dom for being hateful to Danté.

"And I said, what if he was taken by a shark." Alena shuddered.

"Didn't expect it to actually happen." Her phone beeped, and she stepped away to read the text. It was from James, asking if she could Skype. She texted back, *'not now, busy'*, and turned off her phone.

Dom and Nick exited the room, and Angie and Pedro went in, staying with him until he fell asleep.

*****

On Saturday morning, Dom went down to the boat deck to check out the shark the captain had brought in the night before. Three metres, small mouth, a slash through its gills and out one eye. He took photos from every angle to show everyone and asked the captain what he planned on doing with it.

"Fish food for the fishermen," he said and prepared to haul it up to the bait shop.

Dom took a few more photos and turned to leave, running into Cabot and Antonio who were a few feet behind him.

"Is that it?" Antonio asked, staring at it.

"Yep," Dom said quietly, eyeing off Cabot who stood by, silent and brooding.

"You really did a number on it," Antonio walked around it and nudged it with his foot.

Dom shrugged. "It had my brother. It deserved it."

"You going to the hospital this morning?" Antonio asked as they made their way back to the path.

"Lorenzo said to come after lunch, so we'll go after lunch," Dom said, not caring much for his cousins' company anymore.

Antonio nodded. "We'll come too. See you then." He veered off with Cabot and headed for Xanthe's while Dom headed for home. "You were quiet," he said to Cabot. "Shark got your tongue?"

"Har-har!" Cabot rolled his eyes. "Just didn't have anything to say. It was pretty heavy, man."

"Yeah." Antonio stretched his arms above his head and yawned. "It was."

"You didn't sleep?" Cabot asked, tickling his brother's side.

"Not once you came in," he replied, casting a sideways glance at his brother. "*You* slept fine."

"I always sleep when I'm with you, Tone." He had been so upset by the turn of events that he'd sneaked into Antonio's room and snuggled into his side. It hadn't mattered to Antonio, who allowed him to stay, needing his brother close after what had happened. They arrived at Xanthe's door. "Ugh, we're here."

"I'll leave you to it and be back in an hour. Then we'll go to Grandma's."

"Why Grandma's?"

"Because you know everyone congregates there. See you then." Antonio walked off.

Going in, Cabot found Xanthe looking through her books. "What'chya doin'?"

"Looking up animal attacks and how to deal with them." She managed to glance up briefly, but did a second take. "You haven't done anything yet?"

"Nah." He shook his head and paced the room. "Figured with everything happening with Danté, it might seem selfish of me if I did it. Like I was vying for attention and taking it away from Little D. So, I figured I'd wait a week, or two, and let him have his moment in the sun for a while."

Xanthe was impressed. "That's very mature of you, Cabot. You're definitely improving. Have you thought about it, though?"

"Yeah, yeah I have. It's intriguing, and kind of exciting. Being someone else, out of the limelight, not recognised at all. But how would it work?"

"Well." Xanthe sat back in her seat. "You dye your hair, put in the contacts, wear the glasses, become someone else. Have you picked a name?"

"I was thinking of Darren. Kinda an Aussie name, maybe get back to the other side of the family's roots and stay away from the Greek side."

"Okay, that's an idea." Xanthe nodded, seeing he'd been seriously thinking about it. "Anything else?"

Cabot shrugged. "Not really. I haven't thought past that since I have to be here every day and stay with the family. You'll need to tell me what else I *can* do."

"Okay. You'll need to move out of home and into somewhere your family, parents and Antonio, won't be. I'm thinking your uncles'."

Cabot's brows lowered. "Uncle Tomas and Roger. But *they* are family."

"I meant your immediate family. You can't stay here with me, and you can't be on your own. You still need supervision until your problems are sorted, and you can be a mature adult."

"Can't I stay with Alena? She's two doors down."

"But with her family all the time. You need to be with people who don't have a problem taking you on. And that's Tomas and Roger."

"So, what will I have to do if I move in with them?"

"Continue your therapy. I can give you some exercises to do. Lists of questions to find answers to. Get you to write down stuff."

"What, like a diary." He sneered.

"Like a paper copy of the crap going on in your head," Xanthe told him. "That's part of your problem, Cabot. You've got so much stuff going on in your head that you can't think straight and get a proper thought out."

"I can too," he argued.

"How long has it taken to admit you're gay?"

"What?" A scowl replaced the sneer.

"How long have you been having sex with men?"

He glared at her. "My early 20s."

"So, four or so years, and you've just recently admitted you're gay. How long does it take to admit to other things? Or sort things out in your head?"

A shrug. "Awhile."

"And that's because one, you've never been taught how to fend for yourself, so two, Antonio's done it all for you, and three, there's a lot of stuff going on in your head. So, when we, or should I say you, start clearing it out, you'll be able to think clearly."

"That's all well and good, Xanthe, but I don't have any more problems. The only problem I had was the HIV and trying to kill myself, and that's over now." The stubborn, defiant streak was back.

"Is it?" she questioned, watching the expressions fly over his face.

"You told me you felt like a leper yesterday because you couldn't help your cousin. That Antonio and Dom yelled at you to get away, so you didn't infect Danté. That hurt, didn't it?"

His leg twitched. "Yeah," came out softly.

"Then you need to learn to live life not just as a gay man, but as a gay man with HIV. And one who needs to learn to fend for himself."

"But I'm rich, I can afford a maid," he scoffed. "Why do I need to learn how to do anything?"

"Because you've had your parents and then Antonio look after you for twenty-five years. You've never had a maid. Your family don't have maids now; they all do their own housework. It's time you manned up and learned to do your own jocks."

Looking at her in horror, he distastefully said, "I wear boxer briefs, *not* jocks. And besides which, Mother and Aunt Angie both use a cleaning service and have done for years."

"Whatever." She dismissed him with a wave of her hand. "It's time for you to be a man, Cabot, and do everything for yourself. I'll see if your uncles will teach you."

"And if they don't want an AIDS-riddled supermodel living with them?" he asked curiously.

"You're not AIDS-riddled." Xanthe rolled her eyes. "And you won't be a supermodel. You'll be Darren, their house guest."

*****

James finally caught up with Alena on Skype after the family visited Danté in hospital. "Hey, you couldn't talk yesterday."

"No." Her lip quivered, and she burst into tears.

"Oh, my God, Alena, what is it? What's wrong? Has someone died?" He'd been annoyed that she'd fobbed him off. Of course he knew of the time difference, and she'd have other things going on, but still.

"My brother got bitten by a shark and ended up in the hospital. That's why I couldn't talk." She was on her bed, sobbing into her pillow.

"Jesus. Which one?" Now he felt guilty. They weren't dating, or even a couple, and he was getting annoyed that she couldn't talk on Skype, without even thinking she might have her own issues to deal with. Talk about selfish.

"Danté. He's only fourteen years old." She grabbed the box of tissues from the bedside cupboard and wiped her nose.

"Oh, Jesus, Alena. I'm so sorry." He was such an idiot. "What happened?"

"All of us kids were on the boat in the harbour, and we'd been swimming and jet skiing, then we had lunch, and us girls sunbathed, and Nick and Danté were still swimming. The shark grabbed his leg and pulled him from the back of the boat. My brother Dom swam over and stabbed the shark to make it let go, and he got Danté back to the boat with Cabot's help. He'd gone out on a jet ski and pulled them in. We wrapped Danté up and got back to the dock where an ambulance took him to hospital. He spent the night in ICU, and we've just come back from seeing him." It had all come out in a stuttering, botched up mess of a story.

"How is he?" He felt like a right dick. Yesterday he'd gotten angry that she couldn't Skype, and clearly, he'd overreacted. What a moron!

"The doctors stitched him up and said the shark didn't bite anything major, so he should be okay. He'll be in hospital for a few days."

He shook his head. "I'm so sorry. I'm sorry for your bother, for your family, and most of all for my behaviour."

"Your behaviour?" Alena wiped her face. "What did *you* do?"

"I got bratty and shitty when you texted me back. I thought I was being fobbed off and I'm sorry." He gently slapped his forehead with his palm. "Clearly I need to stop thinking that it's all about me. You have a big family, anything can happen. Yet I thought about no one but myself. I'm sorry."

She didn't know what to say to that. "Well…if all of this is going to be an issue for you, maybe we shouldn't even Skype."

"No, I," he cried in alarm, but quietened down with a glance at the door. "It's just that I want to spend time with you, but you can't come here, and I can't go there, and I get the feeling my parents are keeping something from me. They generally don't let me out of their sight when I'm downstairs. They've been very overprotective."

"They're your parents. They love you. You're their only child, so, of course, they're going to be like that."

"Yeah." He rested back on his pillows. "I guess. I just want to get back to my life. I'm cooped up and bored. I can't date you, I can't go for a walk, so I'm stuck here reading or watching TV, or getting on the internet. It's boring after a while."

"Yeah, I guess it would be. Danté's going through that now, being cooped up in hospital, and then he'll be home for some time. And he has to see a physio to make sure his leg works properly. How's your head?"

"Good. Still a bit achy if I'm not careful. That's the thing. I forget. When I feel good I forget I've been shot and sliced open, and then I go and do something, and I get pain shooting up my neck into my skull."

"Ouch. Guess you'd better take it easy then," Alena said.

They talked for another couple of hours before being interrupted by his parents.

"James, are you coming back down?" Sheila knocked on his door.

"Gotta go," he whispered and shut down Skype. "Do I need to?" he called.

Sheila entered the room to see him lying on the bed with the computer. "You're on that a lot. Should you be looking at such a small screen all the time?"

He shrugged. "What else am I gonna do except check out stuff online, or shop on eBay and buy useless stuff I don't need?" he joked.

She smiled. "Your father suggested going to the beach tomorrow and getting some sea air. We can have lunch or dinner down there. Or both."

"Oh, finally." He shut off the computer and jumped off the bed. "I get out of the house. I'll get my stuff ready now."

Not being too tech-savvy, Sheila wondered if he'd been talking to Alena on the computer, and watching him pull clothes from the closet, she wondered what he did for hours on his own.

*****

After dinner, Alena called Diana as no one in the family had told her about Danté yet, and she'd put her hand up to do so.

"Hey, Alena. Is it a nice Saturday where you are? It's raining here."

"Yep. It's been nice and sunny. Have you got time? I need to talk and tell you a bunch of stuff."

Diana stood by the window looking out at the Parisian landscape. "I'm in my hotel room watching the rain pour down. Nowhere to go, so shoot."

Alena told her all about her conversations with James, and how he'd told her he wanted to kiss her and more. But because they weren't even in the same place, they both figured it wouldn't be going anywhere. Then she told him about Danté.

"Oh, my God, you're kidding?" Diana's hand went to her mouth, and she fell into the closest chair. "Is he okay?"

"Dan and Lorenzo said he'd be okay. Remember Lorenzo? I dated him a few years back."

"The hot doctor Grandma helped? Why didn't you continue dating him?"

Alena rolled over on her bed. "The chemistry fizzled out. He's hot and all, and a great kisser, but that was it."

"Didn't you sleep with him?"

"Who said anything about sleep?" Alena cheekily replied.

"Oh, my God, Alena!" Diana exclaimed. "You naughty girl. You're as bad as Cabot."

Alena laughed. "Hardly. Do you know how many lovers he's had? I can count mine on one hand. Have you spoken to him?"

"No. None of the family has rung. But then, neither have I. Been too busy."

"Well, if you've got the time, I suggest you do. He's got something to tell you, so make sure you're charged up and have the time."

"Why? What's going on?"

"Up to him to tell you, not me. I'm sure Danté wouldn't mind a call from you, and Dom could probably do with a chat."

"After saving Danté the way he did, he must be in need of some help."

"Daddy did say Dom fell apart in the shower, but Xanthe is here for the whole family to talk to. Grandma brought her in for Cabot."

"Who's Xanthe and why did Grandma bring her in for Cabot?" A frown darkened Diana's beautiful face.

"Remember when we were little, and Uncle Tomas and Roger were sick? She got brought in to counsel them for a few years."

"Oh," The memories flooded back for Diana. "You mean the large lady with the bun and sharp attitude? She always made people laugh and spent time talking to us about Uncle Tomas."

"That's the one. Dan and Grandma brought her back."

"But why does Cabot need a therapist?"

"You'd better call him. Or better yet, text to see if they can Skype you. Got your laptop?"

"Yes. What time is it there?"

Alena looked at her clock. "Just after eight."

"Then we have time. Do you know if he's out?"

"Nope. Not allowed out. It's one of the rules Grandma has set up."

"Rules! Now you *really* have me intrigued."

"Then give him a call, and maybe you'll get Antonio as well."

"Okay. I'll talk to you in a few days if I'm not busy."

"Okay, bye."

Diana ended the call and texted Cabot to see if he and Antonio wanted to Skype.

He checked his phone. "Hey, D wants to Skype, Tone, let's go." They said goodbye to the family and went home to see their sister. "Hey D." They were on Cabot's bed staring into the laptop.

"Hey boys. What have you been up to? Alena just told me about Danté."

The boys took turns telling her all about it, and she became horrified once more.

"It sounded bad when Alena told me, but now it sounds even worse. How is he?"

"He'll live," Antonio said. "He'll have a leg full of scars, but Grandma's told him she'll bring in a plastic surgeon for him."

"And he wants the scars to look cool, right?" Diana laughed.

"That's Danté, always making the best out of a bad situation," Antonio said.

"And what about you two? Enjoying your time home?"

"Oh, I am," Antonio told her as he reclined on some pillows. "Walks on the beach, hanging out with our cousins, meal times. It's all awesome. When are you home?"

"Not until November. I think I fly in the day of our parents' anniversary."

"That's cutting it close," Cabot said. "Will you be spending time here?"

"Absolutely. I'll be home till after the new year. Then I have some serious thinking to do."

"About what?" Cabot was intrigued, and lay nibbling on his fingernail.

"Remember in, what was it, July, when I popped in to New York? I mentioned it was time to re-evaluate my life. Well, it is. I'm thirty next year, I'll have my trust fund, and will need to sort out what I want to do. So, I will be."

"What are you planning?" Antonio asked.

"Not sure yet. Not even sure where I'll live, or who I'll live with. I can't live with Alena forever, and if I want a child, or partner, or husband, I *definitely* can't live with Alena. So, I've got a lot to sort out."

"Still want a family?" Cabot asked. "They're overrated."

"*Hey, I'm* your family, and so's Antonio, so don't knock us," she chided. "What have you done for you to get in a shit with the family again?"

"I'm not in a shit." He shrugged a shoulder. "I haven't been slapped lately."

"But he keeps calling Grandma Jennifer, so he's looking for one." Antonio poked his brother in the side.

"Cabot, you don't call Grandma by her first name. Are you looking for trouble?" Diana asked.

"Yes, he is," Antonio answered and nudged Cabot with his foot. "Go on, tell her what you've done."

"I haven't done anything," Cabot countered.

"Tell her, Cabot. She's the last in the family to know."

"Know what?" Diana asked.

"I don't want to," Cabot stubbornly said and clicked off the call.

"What did you do that for?" Antonio shoved him aside and called her back. "There you are."

"Did we get disconnected?" she asked, looking at her computer to see if it had happened on her end.

"Cabot ended the call." Antonio rolled his eyes and sat on his brother's back. "Tell her or I will. She's our sister, our *only* sibling. Tell her."

"Tell me what?" She frowned. "Is it bad?"

"Very bad," Antonio told her.

"What? Tell me."

"Argh, Tonee, get off me," Cabot growled, stuck under his brother.

"Tell her, Cabot." Antonio pulled on Cabot's ears.

"Hey, let go. Don't do that, Tonee," he whined and grabbed his brother's hands.

"Tell her, Cabot." Antonio pulled harder.

"What *are* you two doing?" Diana had seen them play around, but not like this.

"Tell her." Antonio was straddling Cabot's back and was prepared to do other things besides pull his ears.

"Tonee," Cabot whined. "Stop it."

"Tell her."

"Tonee… I got raped and got HIV, and then I tried to kill myself. There, you happy, Tonee? You couldn't just let me tell her when I saw her." He managed to shove Antonio off and stumble off the bed, landing near the window, dismayed by his brother's actions. "Tonee, you're mean."

"He what!" Diana exclaimed. "Oh, my God, did I just hear that right?"

At Antonio's urging, Cabot told her the whole story, but off-screen. He sat on the floor at the end of the bed, unable to look at her. His sister. His one and *only* sister. The shame was just as hard as it had been admitting it to Tony. And he felt like shit. The last member of his family finally knew.

"Oh, Cabot, my God." She sat back in shock, hands on mouth, unable to say anything else. She saw Antonio looking at his brother off screen and could only imagine how hard this was for him. "Are *you* okay, Antonio?" she finally managed.

He glanced at the laptop. "Yeah, sis, I'm okay. Xanthe's here to help him, so I don't have to. And he seems to be growing up a bit, which is good."

"And Cabot, is Dan looking after you? Are you taking the medications for it?"

Reluctantly, he nodded. "Yeah, Dan's got me on it, and I'm getting lots of healthy food and exercise."

"Oh, Cabot. I'm so sorry. What *is it* in this family? Alexis is raped, you're raped, but you're the one who gets HIV, Danté's bitten by a shark, and all of this comes thirty years after our fathers went through all of their own mess. Have you been told anything more about it?"

"Nope, no one's talking," Antonio said, resting his head on his hands as he lay face down on the bed in front of the computer. "Just the odd argument Cabot brings up, but it gets shut down pretty quick."

"And how's the *whole* family dealing with this?"

Antonio's head moved as he spoke. "Okay. Finding out in small groups at a time. Grandma and Grandpa, Mama and Papa, Uncle Tomas and Roger, Uncle Pedro and the cuzzes, as well as the Gatoses and Xanthe."

A deep sigh left Diana, making her empty. "Well, I'm the last. Does the rest of the island know? Or the world?"

"The website just says we're on holiday at home due to ongoing health issues," Antonio replied.

"And that's the way it will stay," Cabot piped up, still on the floor. "Grandma sacked Tilly and cancelled our work until next year."

"Would you want to work while you're sorting this out?" Diana asked.

Cabot thought about it and finally shook his head. "No. I don't want anyone knowing. That's why I'm no longer going to be Cabot Conroy Stephanopoulos. Or even Steele Stefan. Not after next week."

*****

They brought Danté home from the hospital a week later, and settled him onto the sofa in the lounge room of Pedro and Angelina's.

"You okay, Squirt? You want a drink?" Alexis asked.

"You want food?" Alena added.

"You need a blanket?" Angie laid one over his lap.

"I don't need a blanket, Mama, it's not cold." He settled himself back with Nick on his left. "Just wanna watch TV or play games."

"Okay," Angie fretted. "I guess I can't expect you to do too much for a few weeks. It's not as though you can go out running or DJing."

"But I want to get back to that," Danté said. "I want to get back to DJing and hitting the decks."

"All in good time, kid." Pedro ruffled his hair. "I only just went back last night. We've all been worried about you."

Danté smiled up at his father, always knowing he'd get love and support from him. "I'm okay. You heard the specialists, nothing major hurt, and the scars will heal with physio and that cream they gave me. And I'm still taking antibiotics and easing off the painkillers."

"Geez, he's got it down better than us," Alexis murmured. "Clearly the kid knows what he's doing, but if you need something to do, Little D, I got a project I need help on."

"What sort?" he asked, as the others wandered into the kitchen for food.

"A website. I've made some sketches, but I need some other help with it. And I'll have to talk to a few people first."

"I can set you up one in an afternoon, but it will take time to tweak. Got pictures and a bio ready? You'll need stuff to fill it up with."

"Yeah, I've been working on that." Alexis sat on the couch arm. "I made some graphics, and have some stuff written up ready to go. I'm not sure how I'm going to run it."

"As what? A blog or website?" Danté asked.

"Yeah, exactly. I want it to be a place for women to go, but don't necessarily want to blog a lot."

"So, a website with a blog?" Nick asked.

She shrugged again. "Yeah. I guess. I haven't figured out what I'm going to do. That's why I need to talk to a few people first."

"All right, just let me know. Have you got a domain name?"

"No, not yet." A sigh. "I don't even know what I want to call it. It's all going to depend on what I make it. Guess I'd better have those chats with people." She ruffled his hair and wandered off.

"We *are* the computer specialists in this family," Nick told Danté.

"How many websites would that make it?"

Danté counted on his fingers. "The nineteenth for my family. How about yours?"

"The girls have theirs together, there's mine, and one each for Mom and Dad. But they're really just info pages and not full websites like the girls and me. What's business, what's blogs in your family?"

"All of the businesses are business websites, Alexis is a web and blog, along with mine and Dom's because we wanted to blog more. The twins, Alena and Diana are more websites with information, portfolios and news updates." He distractedly scratched his chin while thinking, his gaze wandering off into the distance. "We need to start our own business."

"Not another one." Jenny brought him a tray of food, while Maggie brought Nick one. "Don't we have enough to run?"

Danté grinned. "We were just talking about how we're the IT specialists in the family. Running all of our family's websites. We should start our own business."

"Well," Jenny said as she considered it. "That's not a bad idea. You do get paid for the hours you clock on with all of our websites, and I know you do more than the requested two hours."

Danté nonchalantly shrugged a shoulder. "Once they're up and running, they basically run themselves, and the managers and publicists have a hand in it to keep adding information all the time. I just come in and run the back ends and keep it all smooth like clockwork."

"Mmm," Jenny murmured, a small smile on her face. Her left brow rose. "Well, you know you can't use your trust fund for it, but…I will consider funding your venture if you get a business plan in place and show me how you'll manage it around your school work, which you already have a lot of since you're taking time off at the moment."

"It won't take much, Grandma, just a website and a list of the things we do."

"Maybe so, but you may need to apply for a business name and tax number, especially if you trade as a business and make money, and you're underage, so I may need to look into that."

"Then you'll have to let *us* know because I have no idea what to do with websites and running a business. Nick runs our things," Maggie said.

"Of course. We'll sit down and discuss it together," Jenny told her. "*And* make a plan for business hours, so it doesn't mess up your schooling. *That* is important." She and Maggie left them to it. The whole family was there, normally at Jenny's, but since it was Danté's home, that's where they were congregating.

"Cool." Danté and Nick high-fived and dug into their roast beef and coleslaw sandwiches. "Mmm, good," Danté mumbled around a mouthful.

Cabot had been hovering nearby and wanted to talk to Danté without the family listening in. "Little D, how you doin'?" he asked quietly and sat beside him.

"Good." Danté nodded at his cousin.

"I…ah…" Cabot cast a glance over his shoulder to see if anyone was watching or listening. "I ah, have something to ask you."

"What?" Normally Cabot had nothing to ask him, so he was surprised and intrigued. "Want me to overhaul your website?"

"What? Ah, no, ah…" Cabot wiped his sweaty palms on his jeans leg. "Ah, Xanthe has suggested an experiment for me to do, to try and get to the root of my problems, and it requires me not looking like me."

"You going to put a mask on or something?" Nick asked.

"Ah, no, Little Nick. Xanthe gave me hair dye and contacts. She thinks I need to stop looking like myself for a while and basically become someone else to sort out my issues. So, my question is, would you mind if I wasn't me anymore and didn't see you for a while. I don't want to take any attention away from you by doing it. That's why I've waited, and Xanthe told me I've been very mature in thinking about someone else instead of myself. So, I thought I'd ask you if you minded me getting some attention for a bit before I disappear." He casually crossed his legs.

"Where are you going?" Danté asked.

"Well, if Xanthe's spoken to Uncle Tomas and Roger, then their place. I need to be away from the fam, but with a "supervisor"," he made quote marks with his fingers, "and she thinks with me being gay that I need to stay with gay men to sort some shit out." He swung his leg gently and hoped no one had heard.

Danté glanced at Nick before turning back to Cabot. "Will we still see you?"

"On the odd occasion. Xanthe says this is the time for me to become independent and man up. Learn how to do stuff for myself instead of having Mama or Antonio do it."

Danté shrugged. In the grand scheme of what he'd been through, Cabot's thing was nothing to worry about. "Okay. I don't mind."

Dom was sitting at the dining table, mouth full of food, not chewing or swallowing, watching the exchange. Now that Danté had been hurt, he didn't like Cabot being near him, and was wondering what they were talking about. He saw Cabot grab Danté's face and kiss his cheek. His blood boiled.

"Thanks, Little D," Cabot said. "I might do it tomorrow or Monday. The first of the month. It might make it easier doing it on the first. I better grab some food and leave you to it." He patted Danté on his good leg and got up, only to see Antonio standing nearby. "Tone?"

"Cab. What's Xanthe got planned for you?" he asked quietly and leaned against the wall with his arms crossed.

"Nah…just something to try and help me grow up, but today's Danté's day. You eaten?" He headed for the kitchen.

"Not yet." Antonio followed him, and they got big fat roast beef sandwiches and cold sodas. They took a seat next to Dom who threw a black look at Cabot. Antonio noticed and frowned at the daggers Dom was letting loose on his twin. Dom saw him watching and looked away.

Well, that was strange, he thought, *why would Dom look at Cabot like that…he's never looked at one of us like that, only Danté, but now…* He noticed Dom gazing adoringly at his brother, and it piqued his interest. *Well, that's a change from just a few months ago. But what's with the black look at Cabot?* He ate his food in silence, but continued to watch.

"When will the physio come?" Angie asked as they stood making sandwiches in the kitchen.

"Every day for an hour during the week, for two weeks, and then three times a week for two weeks, then once a week for two weeks. I just want to make sure he's okay, and his leg is back to working order," Jenny said and handed two more plates of food over. "How many more?"

"Four," Spiros said. "Everyone's got one except for us." He grabbed a plate from Tomas as he handed it over.

"Nearly there," Tomas said and finished off his mother's plate. "Mama."

"Thank you, my baby." She took it and sat down, waiting for the boys. Carlos, Viv, Pedro and Angie had waited, as had Mike and Maggie, for the rest of them. The kids finished off and sat in the lounge room.

"And we're done." Tomas and Roger carried their plates to the table. "Let's eat, I'm starving."

They ate for a few minutes without speaking and watched the kids debate what to watch on TV. They watched Dom sit protectively beside his brother and cast dark glances at Cabot.

That brought a frown to Jenny's face. *Now what,* she thought. *Is he really going to have a problem with Cabot? Oh, for God's sake.*

Afterwards, Xanthe dropped by to see how everyone was going, along with Dan and Derek, making Cabot scowl at the intrusion.

Alexis saw that scowl and pulled him aside, dragging him to her room. "I want to talk to you about something."

"What? Not going to ream me out for something are you?" He flopped on her bed and lay staring at the ceiling.

"No. I want to talk to you about your assault, or more importantly, what we can do to help others."

"What?" He rolled over, putting his head on his hand. "What *are* you talking about?"

"Well…" she began, fidgeting with the bedspread. "I've been thinking about my assault, and while I haven't spoken to Xanthe about it yet, or not in great detail, I was wondering what I could do on a bigger scale. And…I want to start a support group and website. And," she looked at him for an expression, "I want to set it up in conjunction with one for men who have been assaulted, gay or straight, HIV or not, or maybe a couple of groups to cover the bases." She waited expectantly. "Well? What do you think?"

"If you want to set up a support group for women, fine, just don't expect me to take part in a men's group."

"Why not?" she demanded. "Is Xanthe doing enough for you? Do you know how many other gay men there are with HIV on this island?"

"Do you?" Cabot countered. "Xanthe's already got an experiment planned for me. I doubt setting up a support group would be a part of it. Besides, I don't want to sit around telling complete strangers my problems. I could barely tell my family." He rolled into a sitting position and dangled his legs over the side of the bed. "I don't know, Lexi." He saw her frown and corrected himself. "Alexis, I'll support you to do it, but I just don't know if *I* can."

"What about helping to set it up then? And volunteering to make coffee and tea? You'll be there hearing other men's stories, but won't be participating, keep it low key. At *least* help me set it up," she pleaded, jumping on her bed and grabbing his hands. "And I need to talk to Dan and Xanthe about it because I'm going to get them to volunteer their time while they're here and provide medical advice for the website."

"So, you have this planned out already?" Cabot asked, seeing her enthusiasm. "It sounds like something you've been thinking about a lot."

"I have. The therapist I saw before was useless, and I'm hoping this will be what I've been looking for to fill that hole I've wanted to fill."

"It can't hurt to ask." Cabot jumped off the bed. "May as well do it while they're all here."

They walked back into the lounge and Alexis cornered Xanthe, Dan, Derek and her grandmother. Cabot hung around to eavesdrop.

"I wanted to talk to you all about something," she said. "Um…I wondered about um…setting up a support group for women who have been assaulted like me. But I'm not sure where, and not sure how to go about it, and wondered if I could get advice from you guys." She looked at Xanthe and the boys. "You're all doctors, and I also wondered if we should set up a group for men who have been assaulted. And anyone who has HIV or AIDS from assault." She waited for them to stop staring at her.

"That's a wonderful thing you want to do, sweetie, and I'll back you all the way." Jenny rubbed Alexis's arm. "I'm behind you one hundred percent."

"So am I." Dan cast a glance at Cabot in the background. "I'll help with materials to give out. Brochures, booklets, folders, that kind of stuff."

"And we will need to set up some guidelines." Xanthe smiled, proud of the girl. "And you know, Cabot," she said as she turned to see him lurking, "this would be beneficial to you too. To hear of other men's experiences and how they're coping. It could be a part of your experiment."

"Experiment?" Jenny perked up, all ears for information.

"Yes," Xanthe told her. "I want Cabot to become someone else, so he has the freedom to talk without fear of retribution."

"Why would there be retribution?" Jenny asked. "And he's already become someone else. Steele Stefan."

"But this person will not only look different, he will not be famous, or a celebrity. And he will *not* be a Stephanopoulos."

Jenny didn't like where this was going. "And this was *your* idea?"

"Yes. I believe it will remove the constraints he's put upon himself and allow him to be free to finally relieve himself of these constraints."

"And you're sure it will work?" Jenny persisted.

"Yes." Xanthe nodded enthusiastically. "I believe it will."

"Well!" Jenny looked at Cabot. "Okay then. But back to the support group. I think it will be beneficial for Cabot to go. Even if he starts as a volunteer helping with tea and coffee and putting out chairs."

"That's what I told him," Alexis said. "So, will you guys help?"

"I don't see why not," Dan told her. "We'll be here a few more weeks anyway."

"Why don't you stay until the boys' anniversaries, or Thanksgiving?" Jenny asked. "You're more than welcome."

"Of course we are." Dan grinned. "We may as well move here since we're here so much."

"Then, it's settled. You'll all help me set up a support group and help with the website? I want to set up one that supports rape victims, and gives out info and advice from specialists. I'm not sure if I want to add a blog or forum, or something to it for people to chat to each other, but I want to set something up for people."

"Why don't we have a brainstorming session?" Xanthe suggested. "We can give you ideas on what to have on it, as well as in the support group, and that should help you come up with something."

"Awesome. Can we do it tomorrow?" Alexis asked.

"Come by after Cabot's session, and we'll start talking," Xanthe said.

"Awesome!" Alexis repeated and wandered off into the lounge room.

"Well, Little A is growing up," Dan said, using the nickname she had. Dom and Danté were Big and Little D, and Alena and Alexis Big and Little A.

"Yes," Jenny murmured, smiling as she watched her grandchildren talking in the lounge room. "Yes, she is. Now it's time for Cabot to grow up." Her eyes moved over to him, and he blushed.

"I'm getting there," he mumbled, self-conscious now their eyes were on him.

"Ugh, I can't believe I let you cut my hair." Alena groaned and ran her fingers through it. "It's so short."

"It is not," Alexis scolded. "It's exactly where you told me to cut it. You wanted it off."

"I know, but I didn't think it would look so short. It's ruined and makes me look like I've got a helmet on."

Alexis laughed. "You do not. Stop whining. My hair was longer than yours, and I just cut it off."

"Yeah, but look at you." Alena grabbed Alexis by her arms. "You're gorgeous, tall and skinny like Daddy. It suits you. I'm short and dumpy like Mama."

"Hey, I heard that!" Angie turned around. "I am *not dumpy*, and besides, you're three inches taller than me." She looked down at her body.

"Alena, that wasn't nice," Pedro chastised his daughter. "Your mother is as beautiful as the day I met her. Telling her she's dumpy is mean. That body carried you and your brothers and sister for nine months each, then brought you all into the world, so don't insult your mother. She's still in great shape."

"Yes, Daddy." Alena blushed at the telling off. "Sorry, Mama. But I feel so short next to Alexis, and she's so skinny." Her lip pouted.

"So were you at nineteen," Jenny reminded her. "But you now have the body of a twenty-nine-year-old. You've spread, sweetie." She bit her cheek to stop from laughing.

"Ah…" The breath left Alena, and her eyes went wide. "Grandma! How could you say that! I haven't spread, have I?" She compared her thighs to Alexis's and realised they were wider. "Oh, my God, I've spread," she wailed.

"Okay, cool it," Jenny called out. "Enough with the rubbish. We are all fit healthy people thanks to Tomas and Roger. You have what you have, and you just happen to be in the middle of your parents. Whereas Alexis is like Pedro as is Dom. Danté's still growing, so we're yet to see how tall he'll get." They glanced over as he fist pumped something on the game he and Nick and Dom were playing on their Wii. Dom didn't notice what his sister was wailing about. He was just having a good time with his brother.

"Yes, Alena, cool it. No more comparing yourself, and don't ever call your mother dumpy again," Pedro warned her.

Her face fell. "Yes, Daddy. Sorry, Mama." She dragged Alexis off to their bedrooms with Summer and Melody following.

Angie was still looking at her body, turning this way and that.

"What are you doing?" Pedro pulled her into his arms.

"I'm not dumpy, am I?" she asked.

"Oh, for God's sake," Pedro chastised her. "You are *definitely not* dumpy."

"Well, it's just that I've had four kids."

"And you're in great shape for doing so," Pedro murmured in her ear. "You're still hot and sexy to me."

She giggled. "Pedro, not here."

"Why not?" His eyes looked up to see who was watching, and no one was. "It's our home; we could sneak away for an hour or two."

"Oh, an hour or two," she murmured. "Do you *really* think you last that long anymore? You haven't gone for an hour or two since we met."

"Angie!" He recoiled in shock. "I was a porn star, I can go for an hour or two." He kept his voice down, so the kids didn't hear.

"Yeah, thirty years ago." She grinned. "Times have changed, buddy boy."

"Oh," he gasped and let her go. "Well, I *am* shocked. No more for you."

Angie burst out laughing as he walked pouting into the kitchen. "Party pooper. You're just getting old, face it. It doesn't work as well as it used to."

His jaw dropped. "Angie, how could you say such a thing about Pedro Junior?"

"Ew, no." Tomas shook his head. "I don't want to hear about it."

Pedro looked at his brother. "What? It's my house, if I want to talk about Pedro Junior, I'll talk about Pedro Junior." Pedro's grin was ear to ear.

"Then we're leaving." Tomas rose. "The leftovers are in the fridge, say goodbye to the rest of the kids for us." He kissed his mother goodbye, and he and Roger left.

"And we'll take that as our cue to leave," Carlos said. "I don't want to hear about Junior either." He and Viv left, followed by Mike and Maggie.

"Tell Alexis I'll see her tomorrow," Xanthe told Jenny. "And Cabot." She grasped his arm as she passed. "You might want to stay after your session to see if you can be helpful in setting up the support groups."

"Mmm," he grumbled from his chair, where he sat with one leg over the arm. "Maybe."

Dan and Derek followed Xanthe, and the twins decided to say goodbye as well.

"That's one way of getting rid of the family." Pedro's grin was still on his face.

"If you wanted us gone, you just needed to say." Jenny playfully slapped his arm. "No need to talk about your penis size. We all know you outdo Carlos by an inch."

"Mama!" he gasped, his eyes wide. "How could you know such a thing."

"I remember all of those posters from your movies and the photo releases that were put out. Besides which, I gave birth to you all, and I could *clearly* see you all took after your father."

"Oh, no, ew, I'm with Tomas." Pedro covered his ears. "Don't want to hear it."

"And yet you had no trouble showing it off all those years ago," Jenny reminded him and kissed him on the cheek.

"Yeah, but I was young and a stud then," he added.

"What?" Angie asked in all seriousness. "And you're not now?"

*****

On Sunday, after Cabot's therapy, Alexis, Dan and Derek joined them for a brainstorming session. Xanthe gave her a bunch of information to put on her website, as did Dan and Derek, but for some reason, a name just didn't come to her. "What will we call the group therapy?" she asked. "I have no idea what to call assault therapy. Do you call it assault therapy?"

"No, you call it Cognitive Behavioural Therapy," Xanthe said. "And I don't think it matters too much what you do call it as long as people know what it's for. You can't be the only one here on Mykonos who's been assaulted."

"There can't be too many men who have been assaulted here on Mykonos, either," Cabot murmured. "I don't want to be the only one who turns up. And I sure as hell don't want to be the only one there with HIV."

"You shouldn't be surprised at how many gay men there are on Mykonos and the surrounding islands," Dan said. "But you might be surprised at how many have HIV or AIDS."

Cabot raised a brow and leaned forward in his seat. "Really? How many?"

"There are quite a few gay men besides yourself, and I know there are a few HIV people around. They may not want a support group, so I agree with doing several groups, one for assault, one for living with HIV, and maybe one for people who know people with HIV and don't know how to act. We can also do one for young men who are in the process of coming out and counsel them."

"Could we do the same for women, then?" Alexis asked. "Those who have been assaulted, those with HIV, those coming out?"

"That's at least four support groups each," Cabot said.

"Unless you make the one for people who know HIV people and make that inclusive for men and women, then that's three each and a joint," Xanthe said. "You might want to make a couple unisex just to keep the classes minimal."

"And where do we hold these classes?" Alexis asked. "I've looked around. There's the town hall, and the health clinic off the hospital. Or we could rent a space in the middle of town. Or the edge of town. Would people be ashamed to come to a support group? Everyone knows everyone on Mykonos."

"A lot of assault victims are ashamed, so possibly not. The health clinic could be a good idea, as people could claim to be seeing a doctor," Dan said. "I'd veto the town hall; too public."

"And I suppose the church would be too sanctimonious." Alexis grinned.

"Yes, wouldn't want the added pressure on them," Xanthe said.

"The health clinic it is then. If I can get the hospital to agree," Dan said. "I know Jenny's donated a lot to get it up to scratch the last twenty-six years, so it shouldn't be too hard. They have a meeting room that joins the clinic to the hospital."

"And we'll be able to use it a couple of nights a week?" Alexis asked.

"That will depend on the schedule they already have," Dan told her. "I think it's empty most days, so if we supply the tea and coffee, plus the doctors, then we should get it for nothing. If not, I'm sure Jenny will have a word in the administrator's ears. In fact, I think it was her money that built the clinic in the first place. If you're sick with flu or cuts, you go to the clinic instead of the ER. That keeps it free for emergencies and the hospital free for patients. We should be able to get it. I'll call up tomorrow for a schedule to see what days would be available."

"Cool," Alexis said. "Then I will get started on fliers to put out around town. And hopefully, Grandma will let us advertise in all of the companies. We have billboards at the club and meat shop. I'll have to check with *The Windmill* and see what they have to put fliers on. Now, all I need is proper titles for the classes, times and dates, and a name for the whole thing."

"How about *The Mykonos Assault and HIV/AIDS Support Centre*," Cabot suggested casually. He'd been listening intently, taking it all in, and thinking about possible names for the centre and how they could work it. "It isn't aimed at one gender, it tells people it's for both, and why don't you just set up a proper centre for it? I'm sure Grandma owns a building somewhere you could use. She owns half the island."

Everyone stared at him, surprised at what had come out of his mouth.

"What?" he asked. "Didn't think I had a brain in my head?"

Alexis grabbed him and planted a kiss on his cheek. "Oh, you clever boy."

"Whoa." He pulled back in surprise. "What'd *I* say?"

"Exactly what you needed to," Xanthe told him. "You came up with a name that encapsulates exactly what it is, and where it is, and you had the idea for a centre. Do you think your grandmother will go for it?"

"She set up the clinic for Derek and me twenty-six years ago, and people to run it. Plus she put *The Bette Olander AIDS Centre* under the family business, so she probably will," Dan said.

Alexis was on her phone. "Grandma, can you come down to Xanthe's? We've got a proposition for a business."

"Oh, goodness, another one? I'll be down in a few minutes." Jenny hung up. "Now we have Alexis wanting to set up a business. It seems I've taught my children and grandchildren well," she told Spiros, Tomas and Roger. "Everyone wants to set up a business in this family."

"That's because it's easy to do it. You supply the money," Roger joked.

"Yes, but all of you know after three years it's up to you to keep it running without constant financial help from me. And all of the businesses are doing well. I'm surprised Cabot and Antonio haven't delved into their trust funds for a business venture."

"I don't think they've had the time to figure it out, let alone think about anything other than Cabot's HIV," Tomas said. "But I'm interested in what Alexis has to say, so I'm coming too."

"Me three." Roger got up and followed Tomas.

Spiros came up the rear. "Me four."

"Where are you all going? We were coming for lunch." Carlos was waiting outside his house for Viv and Antonio to be ready.

"Off to Xanthe's, Alexis has a business proposition," Jenny said.

"For what?" Pedro and the family were coming up from their side.

Jenny saw Dom piggybacking Danté and smiled. "Alexis has a business proposition, so we're going down to Xanthe's to see what it is." They hurried down the stairs beside the house and piled through the door.

Cabot saw Antonio and pulled him aside.

"So, what's going on?" Jenny asked. "Is this about the assault and HIV group?"

"Yes, it is, Grandma. And not only did Cabot come up with the perfect name, he suggested you might know of a place that you might own that we could use to set up a proper centre instead of working out of the hospital's health clinic," Alexis told her.

Jenny cast a glance at the whispering twins and racked her brain for a possible space. "I *might* have one handy," she said.

"Tone, have you any ideas on what you want to do with our trust fund? We can draw on it for business and stuff," Cabot whispered.

"Why? And why are we whispering?" Antonio leaned toward his brother.

"Because I want to help Alexis out and use my money to set up the clinic."

Antonio drew back in shock. "That's a very selfless thing for you to do, Cabot."

Cabot shrugged and glanced around awkwardly. "What about you, Tone? Do you want in, or is it just me?"

Antonio was tempted, but he had a very strong feeling that this was something Cabot had to do on his own. "I think you should do it to prove to yourself you can do something good. And I will support you emotionally, and physically."

Cabot beamed. "Thanks, Tone." They walked back to the group as financing was being discussed.

"If you have volunteers, that's one thing, but you'll need money to do the place up and run it like a business because that's what it will be," Jenny told her granddaughter. "I can hire a manager to run it, but will you be a part of it?"

"Absolutely! Dante's already said he'll do the website, and I can run off fliers. We just need to get volunteers." She looked hopefully at her family.

"I have no problem cleaning and painting." Pedro was a hundred percent behind his daughter, as was the whole family.

"Now we just need the funding, Grandma," Alexis pleaded, entwining her hands and shifting nervously.

Antonio nudged Cabot to say something.

"Um," Cabot struggled. "I might be able to help there." Everyone turned to stare at him. "Ah…" Embarrassment and shyness overcame him. Steele Stefan, shy and embarrassed. That was a new one.

"Go on," Antonio urged, but seeing Cabot's reluctance and flame red face, he continued for him. "Cabot's offering his trust fund for start-up money. We're twenty-five, we can use it for business, and Cabot's offering his help."

"Oh, my God, I love you." Alexis jumped on him, wrapping her arms and legs around him.

"Whoa, uh, hey." He stepped back in surprise, having never had a cousin, or any other family member, jump on him.

Jenny captured her two grandchildren in her arms. "I love you, too." She kissed Cabot on the cheek. "That's very mature and adult of you, Cabot. I'm very proud of you."

"Um…" The redness of his face deepened. "Yeah…well…um…"

Alexis let herself down. "Yay!" She jumped up and down excitedly. "We're doing this."

"If he's putting in, then Antonio should too," Alena said. "We can all put in and help out."

"Ah…" Alexis stopped and looked at her. "Ah…"

Jenny knew what was going on; she had that sixth sense when it came to her family.

"Ah…um…Alena…" Alexis glanced at Cabot.

"I think, that as wonderful as that offer is, Alena, this is something Alexis and Cabot have to do themselves, for obvious reasons," Jenny calmly said.

Alena's face fell. "Oh, ah, of course. I just wanted to help out too."

"And you can." Jenny moved to her side and put an arm around her shoulders. "You can help get the centre ready and be a volunteer. But this is something Cabot and Alexis have to do for themselves. It's not about you." Her brows rose.

Alena caught on and nodded. "Okay, Grandma. Not about me. About my little sister and my cuz helping themselves through horrible times, and I will be there to support it." She hugged her sister. "In any way I can."

"Aw, thanks, Princess Alena." Alexis joked.

Alena tucked her hair behind her ear. "Have you decided what colours yet? You'll need something light and bright to make people feel welcome."

Jenny watched the girls for a moment and turned back to the family. "Now that that's settled, it's time for lunch."

"Oh, my God, the ovens!" Tomas cried and ran out the door.

"Tomas, I wanted to talk to you," Xanthe called out.

"Why don't you come up for lunch? You can talk then," Jenny suggested as the family piled out the door.

"Oh, I don't want to intrude," Xanthe said. "What are you having?"

"Roast chicken," the kids said in unison.

"Well…it is a Sunday." Jenny smiled. "I always make it every Sunday, and there's more than enough to go around."

"Oh, well then, thank you for the invitation. I'll freshen up and be there shortly."

"Want me to carry you, Squirt?" Dom crouched down and grabbed Danté's calves.

"Ah!" Danté cried out and clutched his leg.

"Danté, sweetie, what's wrong?" Angie flew to his side.

"Stabbing pain, in calf," Danté managed through clenched teeth.

"Looks like we'll have to carry you," Pedro said. "Crouch and I'll pick you up."

"You can't pick me up, you're too old," Danté joked through the pain of the cramp.

"I'll show you old," Pedro told him in mock anger.

Danté crouched, and Pedro picked him up, his bad leg against his chest, so it wasn't being held. "God, Danté, how much do you weigh? Weren't you just a baby yesterday?"

Danté giggled. "Papa, I'm fourteen. I'm a big boy now."

"You certainly are." Pedro walked slowly up the stairs with Dom in front, ready to take his brother if there was a problem. But they made it to Jenny's and safely deposited him at the table set up for the kids.

Mike, Maggie, the girls and Nick met them there, and the kids sat around talking about the centre, with Alexis telling the girls of her plans. They readily volunteered and thought it was a great idea.

With plates at the ready, Tomas and Roger began serving, and Xanthe came through the door to enjoy one of Jenny's roast chicken meals, only served on a Sunday.

After dessert and drinks, Xanthe cornered Tomas and Roger on the balcony. "I have a favour to ask of you two."

"What is it?" Tomas sipped his light beer that he only drank on Sundays with his mama's roast chicken, as the flavours bounced off one another perfectly.

"Besides the fact *you* haven't come in to see me yet, I was wondering if you could take Cabot on. Have him move in with you." Xanthe eyed Tomas and watched his face for an expression.

"What!" Roger exclaimed, almost choking on his beer.

"I'm putting him on an experiment. He's going to become someone else. Looks, talks, walks, he's going to be someone else in the hope that when you take away all he is, he will finally find his true self and all of the garbage will be gone."

Tomas raised a brow in disbelief. "Yeah, right. Sounds interesting, but why move in with us?"

"I want him away from his parents and Antonio, so they can have a rest, and since he can't be on his own, and can't live with me, I figured who better than his two gay uncles who can help him cope and live as a gay man. He'll need to be taught how to be independent, washing, cooking, cleaning, that kind of stuff. Plus, who better to talk to about HIV than the two who lived through it?"

Tomas sighed and gazed out across the ocean.

"Xanthe, that's going to be a big task," Roger said. "It was Viv and Carlos's job to teach him everything. Are we going to have to wipe his bum too?"

She laughed. "Of course not. I've already got it laid out. I printed out instructions on how to do everything, and we'll walk him through them a few times, so he gets the hang of it. It should only take a couple of weeks to a month to teach him until he gets it. Cabot is quite smart when he puts his mind to it; he just refuses to do for himself. This is forcing him to do so, and hopefully, it won't take long for whatever is inside him to come out."

"Who's he going to be?" Tomas asked.

"Not sure yet. We find out tomorrow," Xanthe said. "The experiment starts on the first of October."

"For how long?" Roger asked.

Xanthe thought about it. "I'd say we should be good by Christmas if he works hard at it and makes a go of it. We need a breakthrough in his behaviour, and after that, it *should* be smooth sailing."

"*Should?*" Roger raised a brow.

Xanthe shrugged. "You never know with these things."

October 2007

On Monday, the first of October, Cabot attended his therapy session with Xanthe. He'd brought the hair dye, glasses and contacts with him, set them on her coffee table in the office, then started pacing back and forth. She had just gotten through telling him how selfless he had been yesterday in helping his cousin with a centre name and finances.

A shoulder shrugged. "Yeah, well. It will do a lot of people a lot of good. Alexis was raped; she and other women need a safe place to talk about it."

"Is that all *you're* doing it for?" She watched him pace.

"Mmm, well…" He didn't want to discuss it in front of people. Xanthe was bad enough, but to talk about it to a group of people… blech!

"I get it. Talking to other people will be hard, but you can still volunteer to get coffee and tea and put out chairs. There's a lot you can do if you're not ready to talk about it. That's what changing your identity is all about. Getting inside of you and finding the *real* you. And then you won't be so embarrassed for people to find out because they won't be staring at Cabot Stephanopoulos, they'll be staring at Darren…who? Have you picked a last name?"

"Holbrook," Cabot said. "Darren Holbrook. What happens if I meet someone while I'm Darren and he knows who I am?"

"Tell him you're incognito," Xanthe said.

"And if I meet someone I'd like to get to know…?" His voice trailed off.

"Sexually?"

Shrug. "Maybe."

"Then I suggest you stay away from that until you know what status he is, and even if he *is* positive, still stay away. Getting sexually involved with someone is *not* a good thing at this time."

"What if I fall in love?" he said with a defiant shake of his head.

"You? Fall in love? Don't make me laugh. How many of your 4242 plus lovers were you in love with?"

That stopped him. "Why can't I fall in love, Xanthe?"

"Do you know what love is, Cabot?"

"Yes."

"How?"

"I love Tony."

"Like a brother?"

"Of course."

"Or a lover?"

"What?" His faced screwed up. "Are you back to that sick shit again? You're disgusting, Xanthe. Really!"

"How reliant are you on him, Cabot?" She didn't let him stop her.

"What? Not very."

"Not for getting you food, doing your washing, making sure you've gotten to where you needed to be on time, getting you jobs, on planes. Are you reliant on him for love? Does he love you unconditionally, warts and all?"

"Yes, Tony loves me. I'm his brother, and I love him."

"Does Tony want to fall in love?"

"He told me he did."

"And how did that make you feel?"

Silence.

"Part of me wants him to find a nice girl and fall in love."

"And the other part?"

Silence.

"The other part doesn't want him with anyone but you, is that it?" Xanthe asked.

"Well he *is* my twin," Cabot argued. "We've been together since we were one egg in our mother's uterus. Just because we split in two, doesn't mean we'll ever separate. We've lived our whole lives together, playing, school, modelling, working, living."

"And that's the problem," Xanthe said. "You may have originally come from one egg and be twins, but that doesn't mean you're the one personality. The one brain. The one body. You are not conjoined, Cabot. You never have been. You are two separate individuals living a life together. You have both become smothered by it. The fame, the celebrity, the modelling. Always being together has smothered you both and snuffed out the two flames that were burning. You need to both find that flame again. That flame that makes you Cabot and Antonio. Two separate people with two separate personalities. Two separate flames burning bright that got snuffed out by a life that smothered you. And now it's time for you to get that flame back. By leaving Cabot behind, you will find that flame and make it burn brightly once again. And this time, it will be for you, and no one else. Certainly not for Antonio. He needs to find his own flame again. And the only way you'll both do that, is by being alone. Being away from one another. Being separate. Are you ready to leave your brother, Cabot? Are you ready to leave your old life behind? The life that smothered you and took your flame away? Are you ready to find that *real you* deep down inside? The person that you truly are, and not some fake as shit supermodel called Steele Stefan? Which is a good name, but not the point. Are you ready to find your authentic self, Cabot?" She watched him pace the room, pace the lounge, and up and down the hall while he thought about everything she had just said. She saw the determined steps and stride as he moved, knew his brain was ticking overtime, and knew he was ready.

Standing in the hallway, he stared at the coffee table. Then snatching up the hair dye on the way, he ran to the bathroom and read the instructions. An hour later, he emerged, put in the brown contacts, and slid the thick black-rimmed square glasses on. As it was a cool October day, he pulled on a black knitted turtleneck sweater with long sleeves and adjusted the neck. Turning, he asked, "How do I look?"

Xanthe nodded her approval. "Like Darren Holbrook."

Knowing no one was home, he raced upstairs and got his bags that he had packed the night before and met Xanthe at Tomas and Roger's door.

Xanthe knocked and they answered. "This is Darren Holbrook, your visitor for the next couple of months."

Tomas and Roger stared. The change was dramatic. Cabot now had black hair, brown eyes and glasses. He wasn't Cabot anymore. In fact, he looked like Dom and Danté.

"Whoa," Tomas murmured, stunned at the effect. "That's a change."

Roger played along. "And where are you from, Darren?"

"Australia." Cabot carefully tried out the Aussie accent he'd heard his grandmother use her whole life, whereas Roger's was a hybrid like the rest of the family.

"Okay." Roger nodded. "We'll need to work on that accent, but we can do this; come in." He held the door open and let them in. "We have a small bedroom upstairs at the back. You will have your own bathroom too."

"Cool," Cabot said and looked around. He hadn't been in their home much; none of them had. It was full of paintings they'd done, and pictures from their travels, wedding, and anniversaries, all hanging on the walls.

"Would you like to get settled?" Roger asked, feeling very strange just asking that.

"Um, yeah, okay," Cabot muttered.

They led him upstairs and watched him unpack and set his toiletries in the bathroom.

"Well, we know you can do that for yourself," Xanthe said. "Let's go through the rest of the house."

Tomas and Roger led them room to room explaining the instructions for using the washer and dryer, plus the dishwasher in the kitchen. They told him about the food system they had, and cleaning up. They did the housework every Friday morning so they had the weekend free.

"There's also dusting, vacuuming, sweeping, mopping," Tomas said. "A whole bunch of stuff to do."

"Why do you do it when you can afford a maid?" Cabot asked, perplexed by his uncles need to do their own stuff.

"Because our parents raised us to do our chores, so when we

moved out of home we could do it ourselves," Tomas said. "Mama taught all three of us to clean up and tidy. Do the dishes, the cooking, the housekeeping. Carlos and Pedro are lazy, they let Viv and Angie do it, and *they* get a maid service in once a week."

"I'm surprised your mother doesn't own that business too," Roger joked.

"Don't laugh, she just might," Tomas told him before continuing. "We do our own housework, always have."

"So…now I have to learn it all?" Cabot asked, overwhelmed at it all.

"All of it just to say you've conquered it and can do it," Xanthe said. "Think of it as goals. Steps on a ladder. Each step you learn gets you closer to the top and closer to the reward."

"And what's the reward?" Cabot asked, intrigued as to what he might get at the end of all of this.

"Finding your true self," Xanthe replied.

"Ugh," Cabot threw his head back, "I'm sick of hearing that."

"But just think, if you achieve that, then happiness is yours. You'll be a more fulfilled human being who doesn't just think of himself all the time, and you've already showed that by waiting to do this while Danté was in the hospital, and by helping Alexis yesterday. You're growing and maturing as a person, Cabot. Now go and be Darren and really find out what you're like. If you cry, cry, if you wail and scream, wail and scream, if you need to punch someone, punch a pillow instead. Whatever it takes to get the *real you out* of you Cabot, we will do. And you need to do it without drugs and sex."

"Two of my favourite things," Cabot murmured wistfully, gazing around the lounge room laden with mementoes of travels gone by.

"What are the others?" Roger asked, wanting to learn more about his secretive nephew.

"Money, partying, freedom, and Tony."

"Well, you can't see Tony for a while," Xanthe told him.

"What about meal times?" Cabot asked. "Am I not allowed upstairs for food anymore?"

"I suggest you go once a week." Xanthe read the thoughts flitting through his mind.

"But Tomas and Roger are up there every dinnertime making dinner. What do I do then?" The whine crept in to Cabot's tone.

"What did you do when you were in New York?" Xanthe asked.

"Ate out," Cabot said. "Ordered in."

"Then that's what you do." Xanthe shrugged.

"And if I get fat?" Cabot cocked a brow. "I'll blame you."

"Work out at the gym," Roger suggested. "You're family, you get in for free. We'll train you up and get you in shape."

Xanthe was nodding. "Good idea. Between working out and helping Alexis set up the centre, you'll be busy. You need a hobby as I suggested before. Tomas and Roger took up painting; you can volunteer. Maybe there are some patients in the hospital who'd like flowers or chocolates delivered."

"What if I prick my finger on a thorn?" Cabot asked.

"Carry them in a vase," Roger said.

"What if I drop the vase and forget I have HIV and grab the glass?" Cabot countered. "You all told me to stay away from open wounds, I can't go near people in hospital."

Xanthe sighed. "At least you've been listening. Okay, maybe the hospital's not a good idea, but you can definitely volunteer at the centre."

"We'll leave it at that then," Cabot said. "And come up with some other stuff later."

"Okay." Xanthe nodded her consent. "That's what we'll do. In the meantime, I'll leave you all to it." She left and the others stood around staring at one another.

"God, you look so different." Tomas stared at his nephew.

"Yeah," Cabot huffed. "I didn't even recognise myself."

"You definitely look as if you could be one of Pedro's offspring." Tomas stepped closer for a look. "Height, build, eyes, hair. So…what are you going to do as Darren Holbrook?"

Cabot shrugged and pulled a face. "Find my true inner self."

*****

Diana sat in her hotel room in Switzerland. It was the third of October and she was thirteen weeks pregnant. Every month, on that day, she had measured herself, and for the first two months she was the same. But now, in the last month alone, she had spread three centimetres.

"Shit! What am I going to do?" She had another four weeks of modelling shoots to do and knew she wouldn't fit into the sample sizes. She could ring ahead and warn them she'd gained weight, but then they might fire her instead. *Well, looks like I'll have to do what I've been doing, and that's feigning ignorance and making the seamstresses take out the clothes.* But she knew it was futile. In another month she'd be swollen enough for people to notice. Maybe if she could get all of the shoots done in the next two weeks, that might help. But they had already noticed on the last two shoots, and it would be obvious in a matter of days.

Sighing, she lay on her bed thinking about Charles. *Where is he? No one's heard from him, or about him, in months. He can't still be on that photo assignment he was sent on. Surely someone must know where he is, or what he's doing? He deserves to know I'm having his baby. That he's going to be a father. But...he clearly doesn't care about me. I'm just another conquest of the great Charles Kensington. Clearly, he didn't care about getting conquests pregnant; probably thought I'd be on the pill, so it didn't matter.*

She thought back to their first time, and every time after, and blushed. Her fingers went to her stomach, feeling the small bump of a baby in there. A smile came softly to her lips and she remembered being taken by Charles. And taken ever so thoroughly. The way he made her move underneath him, the way his fingers applied just the right amount of pressure to her nipples or clitoris. The way his lips and mouth moved over hers. Her mouth, her breasts, her body. Oh, God how they moved…

She found herself aroused and longed for his touch, his lips, his mouth, his body, his penis. Oh, my! She rolled over and sat up. "Oh, God, I ache for you, Charles," she whispered fiercely while squeezing her eyes shut. "Where are you? Where are you?" She didn't know how she was going to get through the next six months, let alone raise a baby on her own. And she didn't want to; she wanted to raise it with him, as a couple. The birth was going to be scary enough, but to never see him, her lover, again. That wasn't fair to either of them. The baby shouldn't have to grow up without a father. She hadn't, neither had her siblings or cousins. It wasn't fair for her baby to grow up without a daddy. "Charles, where are, you damn it! Where are you?"

*****

Most of the Stephanopoulos clan were standing in Jenny's house debating which property would be perfect for a centre. The pictures and plans were all laid out on the dining table, and they were poring over them.

Alexis knew it had to be perfect, and had called Dan, Derek and Xanthe in for consultations.

"We should call Cabot in since he's footing the bill," Jenny told everyone.

"Oh, no, it's not *Cabot* anymore," Tomas told her. "It's *Darren* now."

"What?" The family looked up and stared at him.

"The experiment," Xanthe explained. "He's become someone else in the hope of finding his true self."

"So…we can still talk to him?" Alexis asked hesitantly. "To us, he's Cabot."

"You can still talk," Xanthe told her. "Just call him Darren. Once he's out in public, he's Darren. So get used to calling him Darren."

"Um…okay." Alexis texted him to come up and work on the centre.

He walked in five minutes later, to astonished faces. "Ugh…hello… my name's Darren…" He saw Xanthe nod enthusiastically, but he wasn't feeling it.

"Oh, my God…" Alexis went over to him and poked him in the face, pulling down his cheek to look at his brown eyes. "You look like us now."

Antonio came through the door. "I'm here. Anyone seen Cabot?"

"Tonee!" Cabot bounced into his brother's arms.

"Ah, oh, who are you? And why are you hugging me?" Antonio

pulled his head back in horror.

"It's me, Tonee." Cabot kissed his cheek. "I missed you."

Antonio stared into Cabot's eyes. "You *sound* like Cabot, but you *don't* look like him."

"Nope." Alexis threw her arms around Cabot in a hug. "He looks like *us* now, he's one of us, not yours anymore." Clenching her hands in Cabot's turtleneck jumper, she pulled him over to the table to look at the plans. "Here's one of four buildings we can use." She waved a hand at the paperwork

"God, you do look like us." Danté grinned and leaned on the table, favouring his right leg. "Not a golden boy anymore."

"Just wait till Mama and Papa get a look at you." Antonio shook his head at his brother's appearance. "Mama'll go nuts."

"So will Carlos since Cabot now looks like Pedro." Tomas grinned.

"Hey, what, no!" Pedro shook his head. "You've got the brown eyes, bro, he could pass as yours and Roger's."

Tomas glanced at Roger. "We *could* adopt him."

"Oh, hell no." Roger shook his head. *"Hell no!"*

"Geez, thanks, people. I *am* in the room," Cabot drawled and got back to the plans. "We need an office for health checks, a room for staff, a room for group meetings, and a patient waiting area, plus room for a counter, and we need to keep everything separate, but accessible for disabled people on walkers, in chairs, etc, plus people with pushers, prams and children, so no sharp bits floating around." He studied the four buildings. "Central, but not too far, need to be close for people to get there, but far enough away for privacy and space. Maybe not far from the hospital either…this one." He picked up the stack of photos of a building not far from the hospital, but still centrally located in a back street with privacy. "It accommodates all your needs and gives privacy to potential clients."

"Oh, my God, he's right." Alexis kissed his cheek. "You're a genius."

"I know," he said softly without a trace of arrogance. "Anything else?"

"Here are the financials on that building. You pay monthly rent and to fix it up." Jenny handed over the portfolio to the building. "After three years you should be able to make money from it, somehow."

"Grandma, it's a health centre; how are we supposed to make money?" Alexis asked. "We can't charge people to come to therapy." The thought of not having the money to run it the way she thought they would, was starting to make her want to cancel the whole thing.

"Charge a dollar for a cup of tea or coffee, fifty cents for two biscuits. If they get health checks there has to be some payment via the health department; there's paperwork for that. Write off as much on tax as you can, do other things to supplement your income, and we'll have this conversation again in three years. You'll be getting your allowance from your trust fund on your twenty-first. But that's two years away, so don't rely on it. You won't be able to fund everything on a weekly wage."

"My wage can go toward it," Cabot said. "We haven't taken a cent from it, so you cancelled it. The last four years of my money can go toward it. That should keep it running for a few years."

"So can mine." Antonio stepped up as a man to support his brother. "The last four years of my trust fund wages can be used as I haven't touched it."

"I haven't either," Alena added with a shrug. "Never needed to so you can have eight years' worth of mine." She looked at Dom who put his hands up in defence.

"Sorry, mine's frozen, not up to me."

"If you have enough in savings to get you through until next year, then we can take the money from your account," Pedro told him.

"I have enough in savings, barely," Dom said softly. "I guess I can give you three years' worth."

"I haven't got my trust fund, but I'm doing the websites and all the press and publicity; that's my contribution," Danté said.

"And we love you for it, Squirt." Alexis smiled brightly at her little brother and got a toothy grin in return.

"It's settled then. I'll go to the bank and have the money transferred from your accounts into one I'll set up for the centre. Are you sure about the name?" Jenny asked.

"Yes, Grandma, *The Mykonos Assault and HIV/AIDS Support Centre*," Alexis said.

"Okay. Since it's a business account, I'll put my name, your fathers' names, and your names on it. You and Cabot will be the only ones able to make withdrawals and pay the bills," Jenny told her. "It cuts down on thefts from staff and other people. Plus, with my name on it, they'll know it's a part of *Stephanopoulos Inc.*"

"Good old *S.Inc.*, getting bigger all the time," Tomas joked.

"Yes, it is, which is a good thing." Jenny smiled in return.

Don't put my name on it, Grandma," Cabot told her. "This is all Alexis. I won't be running it, or anything. Just giving my money and support."

Jenny stared thoughtfully at her grandson. "You sure?"

He nodded. "I'm sure."

"Oooh, I bet Diana will want to put in her wages." Alena pulled out her phone and called her cousin. "Hey, cuz, got a minute?"

Diana wiped her face. "Sure, I'm just sitting here in my Swiss hotel in Switzerland."

"Aw, Switzerland, nice," Alena said and went on to explain what Alexis and Cabot were doing with the centre, and how they were all donating their unused trust fund wages for the last few years. "How about you? Wanna give up your eight years' worth of money?"

"Absolutely," Diana said. "I think it's a wonderful idea, and I'm very surprised at Cabot for stepping up and being a man with this."

"Oh, his name's Darren now." Alena told her about Xanthe's experiment and that Cabot was now called Darren.

"Oh, good grief. What the bloody..." Diana sighed. "Well...if it helps my brother get this act together, then I will congratulate Xanthe and buy her a drink."

"I think we all will." Alena wandered down the hall towards her father's old room. "How are you? Coming home soon?"

"Early November. Probably on the day of the fourth."

"Got something good for your parents?"

"Have you?"

"All four of us are getting something special," Alena whispered. "What about you guys? Everyone's been focussed on Cabot, ah, I mean Darren."

"I told the boys months ago what I was getting them, and they left it all up to me. So, I'll have it when I come home."

"What is it?"

"Not saying."

"Aw, okay, I'll see you when I get home. I'll let Grandma know you're giving your trust fund as well."

"Okay, I'll see you in a month."

"Okay, bye." Alena went back to her family. "Diana's giving up eight years' worth of trust fund as well."

"Then that's five trust funds to transfer money from, and as per usual, I will also donate to the centre as I do for all of the businesses. Whatever the amount the trust fund money comes to, I will add the same amount."

"And I will donate to it as well," Pedro said.

"Me too," Angie jumped in. "It's about time I used the Poulos money. I haven't touched it. But you know what, considering how much my father seemed to have a love/hate relationship with women, my mother, in particular, I'll transfer a weekly wage over to the account for as long as the centre lives, so you'll always have money to pay for what you need."

"Oh, Mama." Alexis grabbed her mother in a bear hug. "Thank you so much."

"That's okay, sweetie. I should have thought of it sooner. The money's always been sitting in the account doing nothing but accruing interest. I have all of you to hand it down to, so it may as well get used now."

"So, then…what about this being something Alexis and I were doing?" Cabot asked. "What Grandma told Alena the other day."

"That is true." Alexis pulled out of her mother's arms. "It's just…" She looked guiltily at everyone. "I thought if everyone put money in they'd want to dictate what went on, and I didn't want anyone treading on my toes. *I* wanted to do this. *I* wanted something to do to make a difference. I didn't want it to be about everyone else. But after Grandma mentioned money…" She gently punched Cabot on the arm. "We can't really afford to run it for three years without help."

"If that's the way you feel, you should have said something sooner," Alena said. "I have no problem with giving my money as a donation if it will make you feel better, and I'll stay out of it every other way. You're in charge."

"If you give it as a donation, you could probably get tax on it," Jenny murmured.

"How about we all make a donation to *The Mykonos Assault and HIV/AIDS Support Centre* just to get it up and running," Tomas said. "Because I want to donate too. To help out my niece and nephew who have gone through hell."

"Same here," Roger agreed.

"And then once the three years are up, my money will fund it alone," Angie added. "I think it's a brilliant idea, Alexis, and I don't know why I didn't think of using the money earlier. I've let Mama spend all of hers all these years; it's time I followed in her footsteps and did the same thing for my children. Between you and Danté, it's been a horrible year, and now with Cabot, ah, Darren," she glanced his way and shook her head, "it's time for me to step up and help my children with everything they want to do. So, that will be my contribution. A weekly wage while the centre is running."

"Aw, thanks, Mama." Alexis hugged her again. "I can't believe how awesome this family is."

"Of course we are, we're Stephanopouloses," Carlos said from the doorway as he and Viv arrived. "And we wouldn't have it any other way."

"Is Cabot here?" Viv looked around, but saw only Antonio.

"He's Darren now." Antonio flicked a thumb over his shoulder in his brother's direction.

"What?" They both looked at their black-haired son. "No…"

"Hey. It's ah, Xanthe's experiment," Cabot said nervously. "I get to be someone else for a while, while I sort my shit out."

Viv stared up at his face, looking curiously at his hair and eyes. "You look like one of Pedro and Angie's kids."

"Ha! That's what I said," Tomas told her.

"And I said with his brown eyes he was one of Tomas and Roger's kids," Pedro retorted. "Not mine."

"And I asked Roger if we should adopt him and he said *hell no.*" Tomas grinned at Carlos's expression.

"Didn't I ask you not long ago if you wanted to adopt the twins," Carlos said, turning to the paperwork on the table.

"And we said *hell no* then, too," Roger said, his hands placed firmly on hips.

"So, what's this for? We setting up another business?" Carlos picked up the papers for office spaces on the beach.

Viv was still staring at Cabot, furtively glancing from him to Pedro's side of the family and back, hearing everyone's words floating through the air, and fretting that she was losing her child. And then Cabot hugged her, kissing her on the cheek to reassure her he was still hers. She smiled and hugged him back fiercely and Antonio hugged them both.

"Alexis and Cab, ah, Darren's centre. They've decided on which building to use, and the kids have donated their wages from their trust funds to run it. Plus, Angie's digging into the Poulos fortune for it," Jenny told him. "*They're* starting to do what your father and I did for you boys thirty years ago. Setting up for their children's and grandchildren's futures. They're roughly the same age as your father and I were too." She smiled warmly at her two youngest children and received smiles back.

"It's about time, Angie. That thing must be massive by now. What is it, thirty years?" Carlos said.

Angie brushed her fringe aside. "Yes, and I've only just recently remembered it. Alexis has figured out what she wants to do, so I'm putting the money in. Everyone's donated to it, but once the three years are up, I'll fund it myself. I'll get my accountant to divide the money into trust funds when we get the paperwork done at the bank."

"Oh, that's so sweet of everyone," Viv said. "Carlos, we'll donate to the centre too."

"Coming under the *S.Inc.* banner?" Carlos asked.

"Of course," Jenny replied. "But it's Alexis and Cabot's business. It's time for the kids to find their way and step up into being business owners. They will carry on the family name and business after all."

*****

For the next week, the family cleaned out, renovated and decorated the new centre. Jenny worked on the legals with Pedro and Angie, and Danté worked on the website fliers and press kits that would go out. They painted, laid new floors, hung new curtains, set up new counters and walls, and the local shops thanked them for their business. Once the centre was done, it was time for furniture to come and areas to be set up. By tools down Friday afternoon, the centre was complete, renovated, decorated, and the family celebrated with drinks.

"I want to congratulate my daughter, Alexis, and my nephew Cabot for coming up with such a great idea. The two of you have been through a lot, and if this helps you both recover from your own incidents, then all the better for it. To Alexis, Cabot, and *The Mykonos Assault and HIV/AIDS Support Centre.*" Pedro held up his glass and everyone cheered.

The centre had already gained support and popularity through word of mouth. Mykonos was an island, the Greek grapevine was punctual with its gossip and news, and many had come to support it. Staff from the hospital had volunteered to clean up, including Lorenzo, and all had offered to counsel group sessions, or people in need during their free time. Dan, Derek and Xanthe had participated, and even some tourists had stopped for a look.

"The sign for above the door will be ready on Monday along with the rest of the signage, plus all of the brochures and press kits that Danté has done will be ready next week. We can open after Wednesday," Jenny told everyone.

"I can't believe we've done this in a week." Alexis wiped the back of her hand over her forehead. "Is the air-conditioner on? It's warm in here."

"It's been replaced," Jenny said, giving her a hug. "We haven't turned it on yet since it's fairly cool outside."

"Well, I just want to thank you all for your help this last week," Alexis told everyone. "It means a lot to me to have such a big family that's ready and willing to help each other out...finally." She cast a glance at Dom and Alena who blushed with embarrassment. Alena had clung to her, and Dom to Danté, during the week.

"We're Stephanopouloses," Carlos reminded them all. "That's what we do. Mama taught us that, and we've tried to teach all of you the same values and morals." He glanced at Cabot. "Didn't always work though, but it seems that even my son is growing up…finally. I'm proud of you, Cabot—"

"It's Da—" Xanthe started.

"Don't ruin the moment, Xanthe," Carlos snapped and Xanthe nodded and backed away, realising her mistake to intrude upon such a moment. Carlos turned back to Cabot. "For all you have done, for all you are doing, trying hard to figure yourself out, and finally coming through with what you're doing with Alexis, and dealing with your HIV status, I *am* proud of you."

Cabot blinked rapidly, trying to get rid of the tears. "My contacts are going to come out if I start crying, and you're making me cry."

Carlos took his son into his arms. "Then take them out and cry. It would probably be a good thing if you did."

Viv and Antonio joined the hug, kissing Cabot and telling him how proud they were.

"And while the family's in a hugging mood," Pedro said, "Let's get my daughter in on it." He grabbed her in a bear hug, lifting her off the ground. "I am so proud of you, my baby."

"Thanks, Daddy." She hugged him as her own family crowded around.

"Well…I'd say we've done good," Spiros told Jenny as they stood watching the family.

"Yes." She smiled brightly. "We certainly have."

"I feel kind of left out," Tomas said quietly to Roger. "We don't have kids to be proud of, or to hug, or to help out with different things." A tear sprang to his eyes. "We didn't get any of this." He moved past Roger and out the door with Roger hot on his tail.

Jenny watched them go, saw the anguished look on Tomas's face and knew it was about not being a parent. Her heart broke. It always did when he got this way. Thirty years ago she'd set up a wedding ceremony even though it wasn't legal. She had fought hard for his rights as a gay man since. But the one thing she hadn't been able to do was give him a child; adopted, blood or otherwise. Gay men weren't allowed to adopt, and even if he could have used a surrogate, he didn't have the sperm count for it. The illnesses he'd experienced back in 1981 had killed his sperm off. Not even a surrogate would help, and they certainly couldn't foster children. Mykonos might be full of gay men, but like the rest of the world, they didn't have a lot of rights yet. And so, her heart broke for him. Again.

Alexis pulled away from her family. "Let's get this place tidied up and then we can go and eat. I'm starving."

Everyone ran around closing windows, straightening chairs and cushions, and giving the floor a quick vacuum as they all left.

Jenny tapped in the alarm code and shut and locked the door. "There. Now we just need to wait until Monday when the sign goes up, and then the centre will be open. Thank you, everyone, for coming. Lorenzo, I thank the staff at the hospital for volunteering their time this week, and after we open." He nodded his acknowledgement. "Thanks to the rest of you who helped. Go home, eat, rest, and we'll see you all next week."

They caught up with Tomas and Roger making dinner for everyone at Jenny's.

"Are you okay?" Jenny rubbed his back as he stood turning mince into burgers.

"I'm fine, Mama," he said. "Why wouldn't I be?"

"Because I saw you tear up and run out of there the way you always do when talking about children. You still miss not having any of your own."

His hands stopped mid-air, a ball of mince in them. Unable to say anything, he just breathed. The heavy weight in his chest and throat made everything constrict.

"Oh, my baby," she murmured in his ear. "I'm so sorry it never happened for the two of you. You, in particular. As my son, I would have loved for you to become a father. Unfortunately, and sadly, it just wasn't meant to be. And I know the pain of not having a child. I never got to have a daughter, but Angie and Alena made up for it. As did Diana and Alexis."

"Not Viv?" Tomas swallowed and went back to making burgers.

"Viv's too close to my age for me to see her as a daughter. But she is."

"First batch of burgers are nearly ready," Roger called through the balcony door where he was using the barbecue to grill them.

Angie and Viv quickly got the buns and condiments out and set up on the kitchen island. They had ten rolls ready for the burgers when Roger brought them in.

"Kids, come and get it," Angie called, and handed plate after plate over since Mike and Maggie were there with the kids. Nick, Summer and Melody got in on the burger action. Mustard, sauce, relish, mayo all got squirted onto a burger before they grabbed a can of soda from Jenny who pulled them out of the fridge.

"One left and I'm eating it because I'm starving." Angie grabbed the last burger and shoved it in her mouth. "Mmm, mmm, mmm." Her eyes closed. "Mmm, good."

Tomas finished with the mince and washed his hands, watching while Viv got the rest of the buns ready.

"Next lot's ready," Roger yelled and handed the platter to Tomas who handed it to Viv to make up burgers.

Jenny and Spiros held back while guests and family took theirs. "There's one left from this batch if anyone wants a second, or even share a half," Jenny called.

Danté swallowed his last mouthful. "I'll have a half."

"I'll get it." Dom pushed back his chair. "Nick, you want the other half?"

"Yes, thanks," Nick said from the other side of Danté.

"Where are you putting it all, Squirt?" Alexis asked her skinny brother.

"In my leg." He grinned. "There's less of it, so I gotta fill it back up."

A few looked at him in horror at the joke, but the adults knew, especially Xanthe, that it was his way of coping.

Dom quickly put together a burger and cut it in half before putting the plate in front of Danté. "Divide and conquer," he told them before sitting back down.

Jenny had been looking on in amazement that Dom was finally the young man he should have been instead of the grumpy little sod he was. Pedro caught her eye and she raised her brows in surprise.

"The last one's ready; here you go, Mrs S." Roger handed the platter over and Jenny set about making her and Spiros's burgers.

"There's three more if anyone wants to share a half, or even eat another one."

Cabot and Antonio traded glances. "We'll have half."

"Come and get it then," Jenny said.

Cabot went and got it, sharing it with Antonio.

Everyone else was so full, that the rest of the burgers were put in the fridge for a snack later on.

"Ah." Pedro sat back. "That's a big meal for me and," he checked his watch, "I have to go for my shift at *SB3*." Standing, he kissed Angie on the cheek. "Thanks for the food, Mama, Tomas. I'll see you all tomorrow."

"That means I better go too." Mike stood up. "Thanks for the food everyone, great as always. I'll see you at home, sweetie." He kissed Maggie and he and Pedro left.

"And I think that's it for me too," Angie said. "I'm pooped. You kids coming?"

"I want to talk a bit more with Cab, ah, Darren, about the centre," Alexis said. "Unless you want to come over for a while and Danté can show you the website?"

"One of my best." Danté preened in his magnificence.

"You lot go, we'll finish up here. There's not much cleaning anyway," Jenny told them. "Night all."

"Night, Grandma." They kissed her and Spiros before filing out the door one by one. Nick, Summer and Melody were staying with Alexis and Danté before going home, so they left too.

"Share a drink before you go?" Angie asked her bestie as they walked out the door.

Maggie rubbed her bloated stomach. "Sure, haven't had one for a while."

"Great. We can talk about how awesome our kids are." Angie giggled.

"Looks like it's our turn, Mama." Carlos got up and gave her a kiss. "With Cabot out of the house, we get a bit of extra peace and quiet to ourselves."

"Okay, I'll see you in a few days. Will you still be helping with the centre?"

"Not for a few days, I've got film to go through, so I'll try and make it for the opening instead."

"And I've got new videos to outlay," Viv said. "As well as new pictures for the website. But I'll definitely make the grand opening."

"Okay, I'll see you later." Jenny kissed them goodbye and saw Xanthe out next. "Dan, Derek, what have you got planned for the evening?"

"A nap and a night out at *SB3*," Derek said. "We love a good '70s '80s disco pop night. It takes us back."

"Yes," Jenny murmured as she cleared up the table. "Pedro was awesome at 69. And he continued it here at *SB3*, and every now and then I'll put the records on and blast out the music from that era."

"Definitely a riot to listen back to it." Derek grinned. "Ah, it takes me back."

"To when you were just a youngster?" Dan joked.

"Yes." Derek frowned in amusement. "I *was* young then, and so smooth and wrinkle-free."

"Sorry about that," Jenny told him, continuing the joke. "All those wrinkles were caused by my family."

"Yes, they were," Derek said. "And full of experience thanks to you."

"Well, thank *you* for taking care of my family. Both of you." Jenny gave them a hug each. "Without Dan, I would've lost Tomas and Roger, and now potentially Cabot. You're definitely generational." A smile lit up her face.

"Well, what can one say." Dan was chuffed at the compliment. "I try to help people of all ages."

"And in this family, you're covering all ages," Jenny said. "What time will you be leaving and coming home?"

They checked their watches. It was barely seven. "We'll leave just before eight-thirty and stay until we can't dance anymore." Dan fluttered around the room, dancing.

Jenny laughed. "Okay, don't forget your keys; you'll have to let yourself in."

"Yes, Mom." Dan and Derek grinned and headed for the guest room.

"What about you two?" she asked Tomas and Roger. "Got plans?"

"Nope." Roger plonked down on the lounge. "At least, not that I know of."

Tomas shrugged. "We didn't plan anything. Being a Friday night, it's TV, movie, or a book." He sat next to Roger and crossed his legs.

"That's a bit boring," Jenny told him. "Although, after the week we've had, we don't have plans either." Sitting in her recliner, she put her feet up and relaxed. "I could go over some paperwork."

"Leave that until next week," Spiros told her. "Just relax and enjoy the weekend."

"But you know the weekends are usually filled with family." Jenny flicked through the channels with the remote. "Most times, the nights are boring unless we're out to dinner, or at *SB3*."

"We could go out and enjoy a cocktail?" Roger suggested. "It has gotten cool, but there are some lounge bars open."

"Why don't you two go and do that if you want to. I'm actually quite tired," Jenny said. "I know it's still early, but goodness, I'm worn out."

"It's okay, Mama." Tomas eyed her carefully. "We'll stay. We'll watch you until it's time for bed."

"Sweetie…" She smiled at him. "You don't have to watch us." She patted his hand and he squeezed in return. "You're still young, get out and live your life while you still can. Especially after what you went through. Love every day to its fullest." At seventy-nine, Jenny knew she didn't have many years left. A good ten to twenty if lucky. Her parents had passed away ten years earlier, her father dying of a heart attack, her mother dying of a broken heart one day later. It had been tough on Jenny. She'd packed up the whole family and flown to Australia for the funeral service and stayed a month, helping to clear out her parents' house for sale. Everyone pitched in, and everyone was glad to see Tomas and Roger still alive and healthy. Since then, Jenny had lost two brothers and a sister, and it had taken a toll. Of course, they had stayed in touch after '81, when half of the family came over to see Tomas and

Roger to say goodbye. Every couple of years, Matthew and Sarah had flown over, or Jenny had shipped the family back to Aus. So, at least she had gotten to see them not long before they had passed. But it was still hard. Hard then and hard now. And now she didn't know how long *she* had, or Spiros, or any of her children and grandchildren. Three of them had been assaulted in the last year, and Cabot had come out of it with a life-changing disease. God, how had she dealt with it all? With the Stephanopoulos determination. That was how. And fortunately, she'd passed it down to her children and grandchildren.

"Mama?" Tomas wondered where she went in her daydreaming. "Are you all right?" He loved his mother dearly and didn't want to lose her. After dying back in '81, and the emotional rollercoaster that was, he knew, just like Carlos, that his mother was one hell of a woman. Special in every way, she would fight tooth and nail for her children and not give up the fight. If it weren't for her and Dan, he and Roger wouldn't be there now. If it weren't for the incredibly amazing mother she was, he and Roger would not have had a ceremony in '77, or exchanged rings, or travelled the world. If it wasn't for his mother, none of this would have been possible. "I love you, Mama." He leaned over and kissed her.

"I love you too, my baby." Her eyes welled up and she quickly wiped away the stray tears. "Why don't you make us a cocktail and we'll watch some TV, or a movie?"

"Can we watch my wedding video?" he asked hopefully.

The smile lit up Jenny's face. "Of course, my darling. Whatever you want."

By the time Dan and Derek left, they had gone through two cocktails and the first round of wedding video. While Roger made another drink, Tomas hit the play button to watch it again.

*****

At the Athens airport, people bustled around from all corners of the globe.

From two separate planes, two men disembarked; one from Los Angeles and one from London.

Neither had been to Greece before; neither had any reason to.

One was heading for Mykonos. One for Santorini.

But both decided to wait until morning.

Both men booked into the airport hotel and stayed the night.

Both men would be taking passenger planes to Mykonos and Santorini at twelve the next day.

Neither man knew the other. They had never crossed paths, had never seen one another, or worked together. But they had one family in common; one family that was going to give them answers, whether they liked it or not.

*****

On Saturday morning, Cabot paced Xanthe's office.

"So, how do you think the last week has gone?" Xanthe asked, ignoring his behaviour as usual.

"Well. Although, considering you told me to stay away from my family, I spent all week with them."

"But look at what you got out of it. Your father and mother being proud of you—"

"And he snapped your head off." Cabot grinned at the memory.

"Yes, well, I should have known better than to interrupt *that* moment." She blushed. "You'd think I'd know better after all these years."

"Yes," Cabot murmured. "You should."

"All right, all right." With a wave of her hand she changed the subject. "How do you like it at your uncles' place?"

"It's okay. They're teaching me to do my own laundry. Showed me how to dust without breaking anything. Mop, vacuum. It's all pretty easy, I guess."

"You only guess?"

He shrugged before lounging in an easy chair and laying across an arm. "Housework seems like a lot, but it's actually quite easy."

"So, you can do it then?"

"Of course."

"What about cooking for yourself?"

"They haven't let me near the stove yet. I can make cereal for breakfast, get drinks, etc, but I haven't cooked yet."

"Don't want to?"

"Don't think they want me cutting myself."

Xanthe smiled sadly. "Guess that's a fact of life you'll have to deal with. You've been very mature this week, Darren."

"Why, thank you, Xanthe," he mocked, "I *can* be when I want to be."

"So, why haven't you been before?"

Another shrug. "As you said, too lazy; everyone did it for me."

"And now you're doing it for yourself. What do you think of it?"

"It's okay, no big deal. I feel okay about it. The schedule you set out for me has given me structure, which was the point. I get up at the same time every day, shower, eat, make my bed, go and do something like housework or work, go home, have dinner on my own, watch TV, be bored, go to bed, do it all again the next day."

"Do you want something to do?"

"I want some*one* to do." He stared at the ceiling.

"Is sex that important to you?"

"Nah, not really. It was the intimacy. The feeling of naked flesh against naked flesh."

"The power?"

"The power of what?"

"The power you had over the men you fucked."

He thought about it. "I…guess."

"Did you enjoy the power?"

"Yeah. Bash them against a wall, hold their head on my cock, make 'em do whatever I wanted to do."

"Did you love any of them?"

He tried to remember back across so many. "No. But there was one who I had a thing for."

"What kind of thing?"

"A crush kind of thing."

"What did he do?"

"He's the guitarist in a band."

"Ah, the rocker type."

"Yeah." He smiled softly. "Long dark hair, lean mean body, my height. He's gorgeous."

"Is he gay?"

"Not at the time."

"What happened?"

"He finished the set and came back to the penthouse. I called up a couple of call girls for him, gave him pot and alcohol, added a bit of coke for the fun of it, sucked him off in the shower, he had sex with the girls, and I had sex with him."

"Consensual?"

"He didn't say no."

"How many times?"

"Three."

"Which way?"

"I was on top of him, then I back-ended him, then I sat on him. He disappeared before I woke."

"Is he gay?"

"If he wasn't then, he is now."

"Do you know that?"

His fingers laced together then parted, on repeat. "No."

"Then what makes you think that a straight man, who's forced by a gay man, would suddenly be gay?"

A shrug. "Ego, I guess. Fuck Steele Stefan and he'll make you gay."

"It was a conquest?"

"Yes."

"Do you love having sex with men?"

"Yes."

"More than sex with women?"

"Yes."

"Do you want to be with just men?"

"Yeah…I guess."

"Any man in particular you'd like to be with?"

Shrug. "Dunno."

"Do you want to fall in love, Darren?"

His brain computed the idea. "Yeah…I guess."

"Do you want to have sex with your brother?"

His brows furrowed deeply, and he scowled. "For fuck's sake, Xanthe, you're a sick bitch!"

*****

"That sounds really cool," James told Alena over Skype. "You must be so proud of your sister and cousin. From what I remember on tour, you hadn't been close, but you had just made up or something." It was 3 a.m. New York time and he couldn't sleep.

"Yeah. I had been a jealous hateful bitch for nineteen years, and when she was assaulted, I snapped out of it. I missed out on so much with her that I have a lot to make up for. Now I can by volunteering at the centre which will also be good for me. We're all privileged with the lives we have; it will be good to give back to the community and help out the family." She lay on her bed watching the weather blow the waves against the rocks.

"I wish I could have been there," James said. "I would have loved to help. I feel so cooped up here."

"Aren't you getting out at all?" Alena just wasn't feeling it any more with him. It was as if the fizzle had died out. Possibly it was because she'd been so busy and not thought of him.

"I am now. The last couple of weeks, Dad and I have gone for walks, we've gone for drives to the beach, up to Long Island, and they took me to the mountains for a few days. That's why we haven't Skyped all week."

"It must be nice spending time with the family," Alena said. "After everything you've gone through."

"Yeah. I worked hard to get on the force at twenty-one, and I want to make detective by thirty, but now…" He unconsciously touched his head. "I don't even know if I'll be able to get *back* on the force."

"You need to think positively," Alena told him and twirled a strand of hair around her finger. "If you want it badly enough, you'll get it done. You'll find a way to make it happen. Whatever doctors, whatever tests, whatever exercises you need to do, do them. But the problem's going to be your brain. Will it be okay by next year?"

"They'll probably stick me on desk, or light, duties and not let me out to play."

"And what's wrong with that?" Alena asked. "You should do anything you can to get back to work. So what if you have to wait awhile, at least you'll be back at work. That's better than nothing."

"Yeah," he murmured distractedly. "I guess. Hey…have you cut your hair?"

"Yeah." She frowned. "I got Alexis to hack off four or five inches, but I think it's too short." She sat up and moved her head from side to side so her hair swung. "What do you think?"

He shrugged. "What would *I* know about hair?" The grin slowly crept into place.

"Ooooh, you. No, seriously," Alena said.

"I like it long. But I'm just a guy."

"Yeah." Alena stared at a strand. "I do too."

"I suppose that's the good thing about hair, it *will* grow back."

"Yes, yes it will." She plonked down in front of her laptop. "How's yours?"

"Growing, albeit, slowly." He pulled his beanie off. "You're not the only one who got a haircut."

"Oh, my God, it's shaved," Alena cried, peering at the screen. "Turn around, let me look."

James turned his head left then right. "Mom thought I should get it all evened out, so Dad took me to his barber who carefully cut it. It's called a buzz cut. It's kinda military style, even though I'm not in the military."

"Wow. You definitely don't look the way you did."

"Yeah." He sighed. "But it also means I can't cover the scar. My hair was short back and sides before, but this is much shorter. At least it will grow."

"Yeah, that's the good thing about hair, it does grow back." She saw the clock on her laptop. "What time is it there?"

"3:30 a.m."

"Jesus, you should get some sleep."

"Can't, not the last few days. I've got too much going round in my head."

"Like what?"

"Like, what was I doing in the park if I was coming to see you? Like, what did I do for nearly three weeks between the tour ending and that day at your place? Like, why do I get the feeling I've done some bad things?"

"Jesus." Alena felt the bile rise in her throat. but swallowed it down. "How do you know you've done something wrong?"

"I don't *know* if I've actually done it, but I get the sense, the *feeling* that I've done *something*," he said. "I have no idea what it actually is, and my parents haven't said anything. I keep watching the news, I search the internet for any mention of me, but all I find is a bunch of articles on me getting shot."

"Have they tracked down the perp?" Alena nibbled on a strand of hair, worried that James would remember being Luiz.

"They actually got him that day. Shot him in another park about five miles away."

"At least that's something," Alena said.

"Yeah..." James murmured, looking far away. "Something..."

"You said your parents haven't said anything."

"Nah. No mention of that day."

"What about from the end of the tour? Did you go home, or call?"

"Apparently not. No one knew where I was, but Dad said from the look of all the beer bottles, I'd been getting drunk at home."

"And what do you think of that?"

"Must have been the brain thing because I remember none of it," he said, with a shake of his head. "Absolutely nothing."

"Wow." Alena frowned, but was secretly glad that he didn't remember. "That sucks."

"Yeah, it does. I have vague dreams or memories of doing things, but I just can't put them all together."

"Like what?" she pushed.

"Like going to the station and looking through files and going to the library. How did I even know where you lived?"

She shrugged. "Don't know. Maybe I mentioned it on tour."

"Yeah, maybe. I have no idea." A yawn came out of him.

"Guess you'd better go." She glanced at her clock. "It must be nearly four there?"

"Yeah." His eyes were hooded against the light from the screen. "I'll let'chya go, night."

"Night, James." Alena ended the call and walked over to the floor-to-ceiling windows and looked out over the ocean. *What was he remembering? He's asking questions; that can't be a good thing. What if he remembers what he's done? That he tried to kill Uncle Roger, that he claimed to be his dead half-brother, that he came storming into our home and freaked everyone out? And what about what I feel for him?*

She'd pondered her feelings these last few months and definitely knew the sizzle just wasn't what it used to be. Clearly, time and space had killed it off. Did she still like him? Not to the extent of before. So what did that mean? *That I like him as a guy who could be a friend, but don't like him as a guy who could be my boyfriend. Yeah, that's it, I don't really have those kinds of feelings for him anymore. No, not the kind of lovey-dovey, butterfly churning, heart-rattling girly crush I had in New York and on tour. Now it's just, he's a what? A friend? No, no romantic feelings at all. Maybe that's a good thing. His parents warned me off; my family warned me off. Oh, wait, they don't know I talk to him. Oh well, looks like it's fizzled out on its own.*

James pulled up Alena's website and checked for the latest news. All it had was a picture of her with her new hairstyle, and dates for the next single release. That was October 1st. *Wait, that's over a week ago. I haven't been on here in over a week? Wow, must be the mountain air that's cleared my brain of her. Do I still feel the same…? Not really. She's still gorgeous, beautiful, awesome, crazy, but I don't have that sizzle anymore. So, what does that mean?*

His brain thought some more, but it was tired and sore. *Was I ever in love with her? Was it a crush? Why can't I remember? What happened on tour? It's like there was a fuzziness come over me, like my eyes were blurry, and I couldn't see clearly, or hear clearly. I was underwater.*

Not once on tour had he broken protocol. He had been a cop the whole time, never holding her hand, never kissing her, never leading her on. Always being professional, on duty and *doing* his duty as her bodyguard. Though they had ten weeks to get to know each other, he couldn't recall knowing that much. Her mother and sister were there for two weeks, and then went home, but after that… His feelings only came after, when he woke up in the hospital. *Why was that? Why in hospital? Why after getting shot and having an aneurysm did I have feelings for Alena? And why don't I have them anymore?*

*****

The man from Los Angeles took the ferry from Santorini to Mykonos on Monday morning, booked into his room at *The Windmill Hotel*, asked for directions to Carlos Stephanopoulos's film studio, and made his way there. He hadn't seen Carlos in ten years, and hoped he'd be able to see him now. Standing at the front door of *S'Reel*, he pressed the buzzer.

"*S'Reel*, how may I help you?"

"Yes, hello. My name is Alfonso DeVille. I don't have an appointment with Carlos, but he knows me and knew my parents, Harry and Harriet DeVille. I need to speak to him."

"One moment please."

While waiting, he looked out over the paradise that was Mykonos. A little on the grey side today and chilly, but still beautiful nonetheless.

"Mr Stephanopoulos?" Margaret, the studio manager popped through the door. "There's an Alfonso DeVille here to see you. He doesn't have an appointment."

Carlos swung around in his chair. "Alfonso! My God. Let him in, let him in." He threw himself out of his chair, but stopped at the door. "Oh, Marty, can you finish that off for me? I don't know how long I'll be."

"Sure, boss." Marty turned back to the screens in front of him.

They were editing a movie, but he knew Carlos could disappear at any moment for family or personal reasons. That's why Marty was second in command and shadowed everything Carlos did. If the need be, he could finish his boss's work without a hitch.

"Alfonso!" Carlos saw him standing in the entrance hall. "My God, look at you. It's been what, ten years?" He gave him a slap on the back. "How have you been?"

"Good, good. How about you, big movie director, producer? Harry always knew you'd be a success." Alfonso had been adopted by the DeVilles when he was nine, after a promise to his mother to raise him. At thirty-five, and five foot eleven, he had a head of healthy swept-back dark brown/black hair, brown eyes, and an all-year-round tan thanks to his Mediterranean heritage.

"Good old Harry." Carlos was saddened at their passing. "I still miss them when I think of them. So, what are *you* doing here in Mykonos?"

"I came to talk to you about something that includes someone on the island."

"Oooh, sounds intriguing, come on in." Carlos escorted him into his office and offered him a drink.

"No, thanks. But you might want one when I'm finished." Alfonso watched his face for any sort of connection as he set his briefcase-style bag on a chair and laid his three-quarter length light grey wool coat and matching scarf over it. He was wearing dark blue skinny jeans, a snug dark blue, black and white small check print shirt that hung over his jeans with a grey wool vest over it, and a skinny black tie. The latest trend in black sneakers completed his outfit.

Carlos turned from the drinks cabinet. "Now you *really* have me intrigued, sit; take a load off."

Alfonso shook his head. "Too wired, too nervous. Mind if I pace while I talk?"

"Go ahead. Harry did it all the time." That took Carlos back to '77.

"Okay, here goes." Alfonso swallowed the lump in his throat and wiped his sweaty palms on his jeans. "When Harry and Harriet died, I went into shock. I had lost my mother years before, and never knew my father. I did wonder if one of the men on set was my father, but

Mom never said anything, and neither did Harry or Harriet."

"It was good of them to adopt you; to look after you for Suzy. She was a great lady, by the way, always making sure everyone had what they needed. And you were the cutest kid."

Alfonso grinned. "That's what Harriet always told me. Anyway, Harry had raised me to take over the business when he wasn't around, and so after they passed, I got stuck into resurrecting *DeVille* for the future. The noughties were coming, and I was in charge. So, I left everything the way it was, Harry's office in particular. I never sorted anything out; I left all of their stuff where it was, but I never found my legal documents. My birth certificate, my adoption papers... The lawyer said he had it all, and I didn't need to worry. Anyway, this year I finally took a holiday and planned on going through their things. Personal papers, etc, and you will never guess what I found when I checked the blueprints of the house when I was about to renovate."

"What?" Carlos's interest had hit its peak. "Tell me."

"A secret room in Harry's office," Alfonso told him.

Carlos's brows moved down. "You mean the one on the wall to the right side of the door as you walk in?"

"You knew!" Alfonso was shocked. "How did you know?"

"I saw Harry put screenplays and paperwork in there a few times. But I just figured it was like a storage-room-come-safe. What was in it?"

"A lot." Alfonso kept pacing. "Lots of old scripts, legal documents, a medium sized tin with a drug kit, bloodied rags, and pictures of some woman dead and naked. Harry left a note saying it was about you, evidence in a murder."

"What?" Carlos's brows did a one-eighty and hit his hairline. "From when?"

"1977," Alfonso said. "The girl's name was Rosalee Brentworth."

Carlos's brain flew back thirty years to that day he watched Rosalee, his then-girlfriend, be raped and murdered by a drug overdose. "Jesus fucking Christ! Harry kept that stuff?"

"All these years," Alfonso told him. "The note said he kept it as evidence in case it was ever needed. I left it alone and figured I'd ask you when we met. I can destroy it if you want me too. I could hardly bring it with sniffer dogs at every airport."

"No, no." Carlos wandered off to the past. "Jesus. I remember when Tony found it. He took it back to Harry."

"Tony's still around, still works for *DeVille* as a security consultant."

"Jesus! You're kidding." Carlos chuckled. "Tony and I had good times. He tracked me down when I'd been kidnapped. Do you know about that?"

"All in Harry's files." Alfonso chuckled along with him. "He never got rid of anything."

"Wow, um, yeah, destroy it," Carlos told him. "It's irrelevant and not needed. Destroy it."

"Okay. When I get back I will." Taking a deep breath, he continued. "I also found videos of all the movies, and ones of Harriet in her younger days. Did you know she was in porn too? That's how Harry met her."

"I did hear rumours back then." Carlos grinned. "And when they argued, they flung a lot of stuff at each other. Verbally I mean."

"Well, guess what else I found," Alfonso went on. "A small blue locked chest. The key was dangling from the handle. So, I opened it, and guess what was inside?"

"A video of Harry's first porn movie?" Carlos joked.

"No, but that would have been hilarious." Alfonso laughed. "No, I found my legal documents. My birth certificate, Mama's birth and death certificates, the adoption papers, and some bits and pieces she left for me."

"Why didn't Harry give those to you before he died?" Carlos may have known Harry well back in the '70s, but he'd always questioned some of the decisions he'd made.

Alfonso shrugged. "Have no idea, man. No idea whatsoever as to why he'd keep them locked away from me. He should have given them to me when I turned twenty-one. I have no idea why he didn't."

"Not even a clue in his will?" Carlos was astounded. Harry DeVille was one of the most organised men he knew. If he'd kept that box from Alfonso, he had a good reason.

"Nothing in his will. Not a note, a letter, nothing. Probably figured since I was inheriting everything, I'd find it anyway. But you'll never guess what else was in there."

"What?"

"A letter from my mother. She wrote it before she died."

"Whoa, oh, Alfonso," Carlos shook his head in regret. "I am so sorry your mother died and left you behind."

"Yeah." The sadness reached Alfonso's eyes. "But at least she left me with two people who cared about me. Harriet doted on me. They never had kids, you know."

"Yeah, I know." Taking a deep breath, Carlos cleared his thoughts. "So, what did your mother say?"

Alfonso looked down at his hands, unsure where to start. "Well… she said a lot of things." He turned to stare out the floor-to-ceiling windows at the view. "She told me she was sorry she was sick and dying, and couldn't look after me anymore. She told me Harry and Harriet would be looking after me from now on. And that they were adopting me so I would have someone to look after me and raise me like a son. She told me the DeVilles were great people and had been wonderful to her, and now they were repaying her by taking care of me." A sob caught in his throat. "Harry told me before he died that Mom had AIDS. They didn't know it at the time, just that a lot of people were sick at *DeVille* and Mom was one of them."

"Yeah, I heard. I'm so sorry, Alfonso." Carlos murmured his sympathies.

"Yeah, so am I. But I wonder why Harry kept that letter from me because it felt like she wanted me to have it *after* she died." He turned his head to the side. "But Harry kept it from me." Casting a glance over his shoulder at Carlos, he went on, "I don't know why. I can only imagine he thought it would hurt me."

"Why? Why would a letter from your mother hurt you?" Carlos was perplexed. "If she meant it for you to have after her death—"

"Probably because of what she told me in the letter."

"There was more?" Carlos stood behind him, arms crossed, wondering why Harry would keep something so precious from a child who had lost his mother.

Alfonso turned around. "In the letter, she told me about my father.

His name, where he was from, what he was like. She had met him one night in Hollywood and been instantly attracted to him. He took her for what she called the most romantic getaway of her life, and that's where I was conceived. When she told him about me, he denied I was his and threatened her with a lawsuit for slander. She was embarrassed and ashamed, and broke down in Harry's kitchen one night. He found her and got it out of her. He promised to keep her on and that she was welcome to have the baby and raise it there. When I came along, the DeVilles doted on me, and she knew that if anything happened to her, I was to go to them."

"Okay, so he's not the first man to deny a child." This was sounding very familiar to Carlos.

"Yes, well, I did some research on him. He died in 1977 when I was five, and lived on Santorini, she told me in her letter. His name is on my birth certificate, and there was a photo of the two of them, plus a bunch of newspaper clippings she'd kept about him, including his death in New York."

The cold crept down Carlos's spine. "He died in New York?"

"Yeah." Alfonso glanced down, not sure if he should continue.

"It must be hard finding out you're an orphan?" Carlos laid a hand on his arm. "I'm so sorry."

"Ah." Alfonso swiped his hands over his face and looked up at the ceiling. "I've spent the last weekend on Santorini, looking into him, and a few weeks in New York before that. Trying to track down anything on him."

"And what did you find?"

"That he had another son, an illegitimate one, who also died in 1977 in Alabama, the same night. And that he had a daughter, *who was* legitimate, and was with him in New York the night he died."

Carlos's blood ran cold. "How did he and his son die on the same night?"

Alfonso looked Carlos square in the eye. "His son was shot in the head in a seedy motel. *He* was killed by some woman speeding a car into him and crushing him to death."

It all flashed back for Carlos, hearing about it, seeing the reports, listening to Pedro tell it over and over. "Alfonso," he said, and his voice cracked, "Who is your father?"

Grimly, Alfonso said, "My father was Andros Poulos."

*****

The man from London had spent the morning searching bars and clubs, asking if anyone knew the man in the photo he showed them. There were a few who recognised the face, but no one knew the name, and no one could tell him where the man lived. As he was strolling the streets deciding where to go next, he saw a group of people in a side street. Stopping to watch, he saw a sign go up above the door and be fixed in place. Walking toward it, he saw what the sign said. *The Mykonos Assault and HIV/AIDS Support Centre.* The sign ran across the whole front of the building, and he watched the men disappear with their tools down the street when they were finished. Wondering if he should go in, he saw the grand opening sign on the front door for Wednesday. A black-haired man with thick black glasses stumbled out to give the windows a quick wipe down, and stuff a bunch of brochures in a metal stand. "Ah, excuse me?"

Cabot spun around to see the tall dark exotic beauty before him. "Hello, um, yes. Can I help you?" Oh, how he'd love to help this one in so many ways. *"Down, Cabot,"* Xanthe's voice came into his head. *"Keep it in your pants."* He kept the tingling to a minimum.

"Ah, I don't know." The man glanced over the inexperienced boy before him. "Are you open?"

"We officially open on Wednesday, but if you need help I can get you a doctor." Cabot flicked a thumb over his shoulder. "We also have a nurse."

"Um, no," the man said. "I'm trying to find someone, he ah…" He glanced up at the sign. "Wouldn't have been here if it's not open yet."

"Is he gay? Was he assaulted?" Cabot stepped closer and breathed in the spicy cologne wafting over him. Oh, heaven!

"Um…" The man stared at Cabot, feeling tingles in the pit of his stomach. *Cool it, just calm down, he's way too young, and considering what you've got, he's not for you.* "He's…gay…not assaulted…but…" He glanced away in shame.

Cabot knew the signs. He'd displayed them himself. "*You* were?"

The man's head turned up sharply. "I didn't say that."

"You didn't need to," Cabot said quietly. "I had that exact shame months ago. I…was…" He glanced down. "Assaulted."

"Oh." The man softened. "I'm sorry."

"So am I. For you, I mean." Cabot peeked over his glasses. "If you want to talk to a doctor, Dan's getting stuff sorted. Here, here's a brochure with all of our group sessions, and if you want one on one, we do that too." He handed over one of the brochures he'd been stuffing into the metal holder.

"Thanks," the man said, taking the brochure. "I…ah…might come along. How much is it?"

"They're free, with free tea and coffee and biscuits."

The man smiled. "You're not American; you said biscuits."

"Australian," Cabot said. "Well, part. You?"

"English, with some Colombian and Spanish mixed in."

"Oh, I knew you were an exotic blend," Cabot murmured. "Look at you. Tall, chestnut hair, quite an exotic eye colour you got there."

"My mother had green eyes, my father brown," he replied. "So they're a greeny hazely colour."

"All-year-round tan?" Cabot asked, casually checking out the man meat before him.

The man's smile grew wider. "That's the Mediterranean blend. What's your name?"

"Ah, Cab, ah, Darren, Darren Holbrook," Cabot stumbled. Suddenly shy, he backed off a step.

"Hello, Darren. I'm Tony. Tony Luca. Definitely nice to meet you." He held out his hand, and upon grasping Cabot's, held it firmly.

Cabot got the tingles in his arm and stomach. *And* his groin.

So did Tony.

*****

"Oh…ah…" Carlos breathed, unable to comprehend what Alfonso had just said.

"I don't mean your sister-in-law any harm." Alfonso put his hands up in defence. "I just want to meet her and find out about our father."

"Oh…this is *not* going to be good." Carlos stumbled over to the desk and leant on it. "All these years…"

"Yeah, I know. I've had no siblings. Neither has Angelina."

"Oh…" Carlos looked at him and collapsed on his desk. "You had a sibling. Luiz Manning. Neither of you knew about him." He breathed deeply. "What is it you want? Her money?"

"Oh, God no!" Alfonso exclaimed. "No, I just wanted to see where he lived, what he did, learn about my genetic history. And to meet Angelina. Hear what stories she has to tell me."

"Not good ones, I'm afraid. Andros was a pig by all accounts."

"I read the newspaper clippings about the assault charges being brought by her in '77. That's rough. Look, I don't want the money, I have the DeVille's, I'm well off. I just want to meet her, talk, find out stuff." He stood in front of Carlos. "Can you arrange for us to meet? In private, in public, whatever would be best. I don't want to freak her out."

"Oh, *you will*. You'll probably freak the whole family out. Do you know for sure you're Poulos's kid?"

Alfonso shrugged. "Not for sure. I'm willing to have a DNA test with Angelina to prove one way or another. I have no problem doing that."

"Ah." Carlos ran a hand over his face. *Okay, okay, calm down, Carlos, calm down.* He started pacing. "I ah…I ah, can maybe get the family together today. My parents will want to be there. Pedro, my brother, probably my other brothers, definitely not the kids."

"Whatever you think is best," Alfonso told him, watching him pace the room.

Carlos checked his watch. "Nearly lunchtime. I could get us all together if that will work." He got a nod from Alfonso, and quickly called his mother. "Mama, is everyone at your place for lunch?"

"Pedro and Angie are at the clinic," Jenny said.

"Can you get them home for lunch? Tomas and Roger too. I think

Viv's busy, but even she needs to eat."

"Okay. Why?" She knew her son, so knew something was going on.

"Something very strange has just come up, and ah, you all need to know about it. Can you get everyone there by twelve-thirty, but not the kids, definitely not the kids, and I'll see you then. Oh, by the way, I'm bringing someone to lunch."

"Oh, okay, see you then." She hung up knowing full well something was coming. Her Spidey senses told her so.

Carlos stood toe to toe with Alfonso. "It's happening today."

*****

Everyone was there by twelve-thirty, except for the kids, so the family were having pre-lunch drinks when Carlos walked in. "Hey, everyone, I want to introduce you to Alfonso DeVille. Harry and Harriet's adopted son from their maid, Suzy."

"Alfonso, so nice to see you again." Viv hugged him. "I haven't seen you since the funeral."

"Good to see you too, Vivian," Alfonso replied warmly.

Pedro got up to shake his hand. "Carlos has told us all about you."

"Not everything I'm afraid," Alfonso said and shook hands with everyone. "I've only just recently found out something about my parents and who I am."

"Would you like a drink, Alfonso?" Tomas asked. "Beer, mineral water?"

"Not right now, thank you, but I'll definitely need one later." Alfonso eyed all of the family, and his eyes rested on Angelina who was unaware.

"Oh, okay," Tomas said, surprised and intrigued by the comment.

Jenny watched Carlos and Alfonso, knowing there was something going on and it had to do with their guest. She saw Carlos look at her and turn away.

"Everyone, sit, please. There's something I need to tell you all," Alfonso said and followed them into the dining room.

The family traded curious glances, but sat at the table anyway.

"Okay, what's going on?" Jenny asked.

"Alfonso has a story to tell you." Carlos cracked open the beer Tomas gave him and drank half in two gulps. He only did that when something was wrong and he was stressed. "Quite a story."

Alfonso smiled shyly and stood near the island bench, so he had their full attention. "Um...I was five years old in 1977 when I met Carlos. My mother, Suzy, was the DeVilles' maid. She became ill in 1981 and died from what we now know as AIDS." Murmurs went around the table and he watched them carefully before continuing. "She asked Harry and Harriet to adopt me and they did. But when *they* died, I didn't bother dealing with their belongings; I just kept running the business. A couple of months ago I decided it was time to clear their stuff out, and I wanted to do some remodelling. I discovered a secret room off Harry's office and found a whole bunch of stuff inside. Including a small chest with all of my paperwork in it. My birth certificate, my mother's papers, the adoption papers, and some personal items she wanted to leave me. One of those items was a letter. In it, she apologized for getting sick and leaving me alone at nine years of age. She told me about my family. Her parents, siblings, etc. She also told me about my father."

Knowing he had all eyes on him, he pulled a photo from his pocket and stared sadly at it. "She told me who he was, what he did, and how it had been a week-long romance in 1972. He was on holiday, business, from Greece. He wooed her and then left. When she found out she was pregnant with me, she told him and he denied my existence. Denied her."

"Sounds like my father," Angie said critically, her left brow arched as she sipped her wine, ignorant of a panicking Carlos who finished his beer in another gulp, and not noticing Alfonso's facial expression.

Alfonso had looked at her sharply. "When Harry found out my mother was pregnant, he looked after her, and she asked him to look after me upon her death. They adopted me, and I didn't know about my father until two months ago. I searched the internet for news of him and found a lot." He slowly walked to his left, step by slow step. "I found his name in my mother's letter, and on my birth certificate. I found his name online in old newspaper clippings at the library. He was not just from Greece, he was from Santorini. He was a businessman. He died in October 1977 in New York, the exact same night that his son died in Alabama."

Jenny's heart went cold and she looked from Alfonso to Carlos and saw his panicked expression. She knew where this was going and couldn't believe it was happening again.

Tomas glanced at Roger, remembering Alabama, October 1977. He saw Carlos's expression and knew where this was going. Saw Carlos staring guiltily at their mother; and turned his head to see her staring back at Carlos, lips firm, expression grim.

Alfonso stopped next to Angie, ignorant of the others in the room, watching her face. "This is a photo of him and my mother." Handing it to her, he awaited her response.

Her eyes grew wide, the panic hit her heart, and eighteen years of memories flooded over her like a thousand-foot-high tsunami. "No! No!" Looking at Alfonso, she repeated herself. "No… No."

"Angie, what is it?" Pedro snatched the photo from his distressed wife's hand while she and Alfonso continued staring at each other. He studied the people in it. "Oh, my God. Angie, it's your father."

*****

"So, that's the centre." Darren walked Tony out the door. "We'll have four groups per day, Tuesday through Friday. Then volunteers run it on the weekend and it's admin time on Monday."

"It all looks great," Tony said, smiling at Darren. "And what's your part in it? You seem to know everything about it." And *he* wanted to know everything about Darren Holbrook.

"Um, I'm a volunteer," Darren said. "Here from the beginning. I've helped out a lot. And will be here a lot."

"So…I'll see you if I come to a session?" Tony desperately wanted him to say yes.

"Um…" A shy smile came to Darren's lips. "Probably. We do have sessions for women, so, probably not those ones."

Tony grinned. "Probably not. It was nice meeting you, Darren." He held out his hand to shake and Darren accepted. "Are you doing anything for lunch?"

"Um…" Darren stared into the exotic mixed eyes and fell. "No."

"Would you…ah…have lunch with me? You can tell me more about the centre."

"Um…" Darren dug a toe into the pavement, his leg twitching. "I guess."

"Great. Can you get away now?"

"Oh, absolutely," Darren murmured, still clinging to the hand in his.

*****

"Yes." Alfonso studied Angie's face. "The name of the man on my birth certificate is Andros Poulos. Mom told me about him in her letter. From searching online, I found you, Angelina. His daughter, my sister." He stared into her horrified face and rushed on. "I don't want money, or the estate, or anything like that; that's not what I want. I just want to know who he was, our heritage, what sort of man he was."

"A grade-A son-of-a-bitch bastard," Angie spat. "You *do know* what he did? You said you read the clippings from '77. You'd know he assaulted me and I brought charges against him. You'd also know he tried to have Pedro killed quite a few times. He was an asshole and not worth fighting over or talking about." She grabbed her wine and knocked it back. "I need another."

Tomas nudged Roger to get her a refill while the family sat waiting in suspense.

"I'm willing to take a DNA test to prove if I am or not, your brother, I mean," Alfonso rushed on.

"I can't deal with this right now." Angie rubbed her eyes and sculled her wine that Roger placed in front of her. "Yes. A DNA test and then we'll talk. Not before. You need to prove who you are to me. Do you understand?" She didn't bother looking at him even though he was still by her side.

Jenny looked from Alfonso to Angie to Spiros. "And the family keeps on getting bigger," she murmured, resting her chin in her hand. "Oi!"

*****

"So…um…I was um…assaulted…in July." Darren awkwardly moved in his chair at the restaurant bar and grill he and Tony were eating at. "And um…in August I found out…um…I had…"

"Contracted HIV," Tony finished.

Darren glanced up sharply then turned away in shame and embarrassment.

"So was I."

"What!" Darren's head shot up. "What?"

A half smile appeared on Tony's face. "In July last year I was here on holiday. Met a couple of guys, had sex, safe sex, of course. But one of them demanded payment afterwards. When I refused, he flicked a knife open and assaulted me. I found out I had HIV two months later."

"Jesus," Darren breathed. "That's what happened to me. Must be a bunch of arseholes on the island come summer."

"Just ripe for the picking," Tony joked and became serious. "So, you're still dealing with it?"

"Yeah. I'm seeing a therapist for it. To try and get through the denial."

"So, you're gay," Tony said softly.

"Um…yeah…" Darren said just as softly.

"But you seem new to it?"

"More like new to admitting it to myself and everyone else," Darren said.

"Ah." Tony knew. "Screw men, but don't believe you're gay."

"Screwed men *and* women, but it became more men in the last year."

"Ah," Tony repeated. "Bi."

"Well…" Darren sniffed and screwed up his nose. "Not so much anymore. *Straight out gay* my therapist said I was."

639

"A strange choice of words." Tony grinned.

"Yeah." Darren laughed softly. "Hadn't thought about that."

"So *all* of this is still new to you?" Tony asked.

"I've um…" Darren shifted in his chair. "Been with men about four or five years, but obviously, I've had to stop."

"Until you get the virus under control?"

"Ah…yeah…" Darren thought about it. "I suppose. My therapist told me to stop, so I stopped. She said I needed to sort my shit out, and this was just a small part of my problem."

"What's the rest of it?" Tony sipped his beer, liking Darren Holbrook more and more by the second.

"A lot of shit. I'm still sorting through it," Darren said. "It could be a while before I'm *straight*ened out. Get it."

Tony laughed. "I got it."

*****

Jenny called Dan at the centre. "Dan, we need a DNA test done. Can you take bloods and get them to the hospital?"

"Ah, sure. I guess. I'll dash home now." He told Derek and they rushed home to find a man in the living room.

"Alfonso DeVille, Dan Ardent and Derek Blaine. Dan, Derek, Alfonso DeVille. He needs a DNA test," Carlos said.

"To match to who?" Dan asked, looking at each member of the family.

"Angie," Carlos replied.

The boys' brows rose. "Angie!"

"Yes," Alfonso told them. "It's possible that I'm her brother via her father. We need to confirm it. Will the four glasses of wine she's had affect it?"

"Ah, whaddaya expect. I don't get drunk often, but when I do it's for a reason." She sneered, waved her glass around, and started on her fifth drink.

"Although this isn't really the time to get drunk," Jenny said.

Angie finished off the glass. "I'll be the judge of *that*, Jennifer!"

Everyone leaned backwards in shock, especially Jenny who raised her brows.

"Angie," Pedro gasped. "That's the first time you've called Mama, Jennifer."

"So! Thirty years apart I find out I have a half-brother. Clearly, my family is not my family." She wavered in her seat, feeling ill. "May as well take the blood now, Dan, because I think I'm gonna spew." And she did, all over Jenny's dining room floor, making everyone rush out of their seats, or take several steps back.

"Oh, Angie, oh, Mama. I'm so sorry." Pedro lifted his legs so he didn't get any on him, and watched his wife sit up. "Angie, how could you?"

"How could I what?" she mumbled, glassy-eyed, and hurled again.

"Oh, my God, Dan, do something," Pedro cried in alarm.

"Throw her in the shower," Jenny told them. "That will wake her up."

"I'm so sorry," Pedro kept repeating and managed to get out of his seat without stepping in any of it and led Angie away. "Get the cleaning stuff, I'll clean it up," he called out.

"I'm not leaving that crap there," Jenny said and collected the supplies from the laundry.

Tomas threw open the terrace door and dining room windows and stood by them breathing in the sea air.

"Ah, oh, my God, Pedro, that's cold," Angie screamed from the boys' old bathroom.

"Good. You just got drunk and barfed all over Mama's floor." He left her to Dan and Derek and went back to clean up. "No, Mama, let me do it." He hurried over and got down on his hands and knees, almost retching himself before putting on the mask his mother handed him. He looked up apologetically. "I'm sorry."

"Not your fault," Jenny told him and walked over to the front windows to open them. The door was next.

"I should apologise too," Alfonso said. "I didn't realise this would be such a shock."

"What *did* you expect," Pedro grumbled from the floor. "She'd welcome you with open arms?"

"Um…no…but I didn't expect her to get drunk."

"Neither did we," Jenny said dryly from the front door. "Oh, God, spray some of that air deodorant. Someone."

Tomas ran around spraying while holding his nose.

Dan and Derek got Angie out of the shower and into a towel and robe. "Let's get you lying down." Dan gave her a shot to ease the nausea, and took a blood and saliva sample while he was doing it. "We'll do two tests just to make sure," he said to Derek.

"Jenny will demand it anyway." Derek put both samples in bags.

"You rest, Angie." They left the room to take Alfonso's blood and saliva. "Have it to you in twenty-four hours," Dan told Jenny.

"Do I need to tell you?" she asked.

"Utmost discretion as always," Dan said and he stopped at the door beside her. "I gave her something to ease the drunken nausea."

"Thanks." Jenny closed the door and sat on the couch watching Pedro.

"I cannot believe she did that," he mumbled behind the mask.

"I can't believe she called Mama, Jennifer," Tomas said, watching Pedro as he passed through to the lounge room. "She's never called you that." He sat down next to her.

"No, but Cabot has." Jenny shrugged. "It is my name, and we did tell the three of them thirty years ago to call us Jenny and Spiros. Viv does."

"Yes, but that's because I'm older than Angie, and it felt more natural than Mama and Papa, or Mr and Mrs S," Viv said, still shocked by the events that had just unfolded.

"And all three of you call us something different. That's the way you are, and because of your ages at the time. Angie was eighteen," Jenny reminded them.

Pedro finally finished and dumped the bucket in the laundry, giving everything a quick wash out and leaving it to air dry before going back into the lounge room. "All done. I'd better check on her." He found her sleeping it off on his old bed and sat beside her and stroked her face. "You're gonna have a cracker of a hangover," he whispered. Leaving her alone, he went back to his family.

"Look, Alfonso, I think you'd better go," Jenny said. "Where are you staying? We'll contact you tomorrow."

"At *The Windmill Hotel,*" he told them. "It's very nice there."

"It should be." Jenny grinned. "We own it."

"Ah, well, I like it *very* much. I'll see you all tomorrow." He let himself out.

"So, what the hell do we do now?" Pedro asked, slumping wearily in an easy chair.

"Wait until tomorrow," Jenny told him.

*****

"Will you be back for the grand opening?" Darren asked Tony as they walked slowly back to the centre.

"Absolutely," he said. "And if I can volunteer, or help out in any way, let me know."

"I'll talk to Dan about it," Darren said. "He's the doctor on call and knows about my…uh…status…because he's my doctor as well. He's a specialist in HIV/AIDS with his husband, Doctor Derek Blaine."

"Ah, specialist," Tony said. "That must come in handy?"

"Oh, in more ways than one," Darren said. "You would *not* believe it."

"Try me." Tony smiled, wishing he could hold hands with the man beside him.

"Ah." Darren returned the smile. "For another day, maybe. Because I have to get back to work." They arrived at the centre and stood out the front.

"Will you be here on Wednesday?" Tony asked, not wanting to leave yet.

"I will be here every day this week," Darren said. "And probably every day next week. And the week after, and the week after."

"So, anytime?" Tony asked, delighted that he could see Darren every day.

"During the week anyway." Darren was secretly thrilled that he'd be getting to see the exotic hunk more often.

"And the weekends?" Tony took a step closer.

Darren shrugged. "I'm free."

"Cabot, can you come and help me with something, I need your height," Alena called from the doorway.

Tony looked on in surprise.

Darren momentarily froze before answering. With a roll of his eyes, he said, "My name's *Darren*."

"Oh." Alena's eyes moved back and forth between Cabot and Tony. "Sorry, ah, Darren. Can you come and help please?"

"Yeah, I'll be there in a minute." Darren turned his attention back to Tony. "That's not the first time they've done that."

"Can't get your name straight. Yeah, I get that." Tony grinned, wondering what the confusion was about.

"Yeah." Darren matched the grin. "Can't get my name straight. I gotta go." He backed towards the door. "I'll see you on Wednesday?"

"Absolutely." Tony's grin grew bigger.

"Okay." Darren nodded. "I'll see you Wednesday."

Tony's whole face was smiling. "It's a date."

*****

Angie woke an hour later, dazed and confused. "Ooh, what happened?" She was lying on Pedro's bed and her head pounded. "Ooh, what the hell?" She remembered and her face fell. "Oh, no." Five glasses of wine on an empty stomach and barfing on her mother-in-law's floor because some kid had told her he was her brother. "Ooh." She rolled over, the pounding continued and she sighed. "What the hell am I going to do?"

Pedro came through the door to check on her. "Hey, babe. You okay?" He sat beside her and gently stroked her hair.

"No," she mumbled. "I've made a fool of myself by getting drunk, calling mama by her name, which makes me as bad as Cabot, and then I barfed all over her floor. Oh, my God." She buried her head in the pillow. "How could I? I feel so stupid."

"No, you're not. You were in shock." He shifted as she sat up and moved to the side of the bed.

"I *am* stupid," she told him. "I disrespected your mother, I made a fool of myself. Oh, my God. I can't believe I vomited. Who cleaned it up? I'd better do it."

"It's okay, take it easy." He reassured his wife. "I cleaned it up, it's all done."

"Oh." She gazed up into his eyes and her lip quivered. "I'm sorry. I've never done anything like this before."

"Well!" He choked on a laugh. "You've never had a guy come to you and tell you he's your brother before."

"Argh." Angie let her head fall into her hands. "Another Poulos brother. Jesus, how many did Daddy have?"

"Maybe it's time to find out," Pedro said. "Get a private investigator onto it. Find out how many birth certificates your father's name is on."

"Ugh, how could we do that?"

He shrugged. "Put out a full-page ad asking for people with his name on their birth certificate."

"But then they'll want the fortune and I'm not handing it over after thirty years. After what he did to me, I bloody well deserve it."

"Well then." Pedro slipped his arm around her. "Thank God Alfonso doesn't want it."

*****

With everyone gathered around at dinner, Jenny brought up the centre's accounts. "Now that you have your grand opening in two days, and are basically up and running, we need to talk about the cost of running it. As your landlord, I'm offering the building for free for the first year, then rent will go up to fifty percent in the second year, and in the third year it will be full price," Jenny told Alexis. "After that, you'll have to fund that yourselves. You also need to pay for electricity and any other bill you acquire. Those, I can't help you with. After transferring everyone's trust fund into it, plus your parents' money, my money, and the donations from your uncles and aunt, you have a fairly healthy bank account." She retrieved the paperwork and set it down in front of Alexis.

Alexis's eyes grew as wide as saucers. "Oh, my God, you're kidding!"

"How much is it?" Danté strained to see from his seat.

"Two million, five hundred and fourteen thousand dollars," Alexis said.

"Bloody hell!" Alena exclaimed. "How much? How come it's that much?"

"Because I said I would put in the same amount as all of your trust fund monies came to, and that was seven hundred and two thousand," Jenny said. "Your grandfather and I added the same, as did your parents."

"And Viv and I matched Cabot and Antonio's contributions," Carlos said.

"And Roger and I gave a huge donation," Tomas added.

"So, it all added up," Jenny said. "Divide that by three, work out your sums, and you should know what you can and can't afford for the next three years. From what Ron and I figured out, you should be able to hire some staff, either full-time, or part-time. The rest can be volunteers."

"Oh, my God, this is awesome!" Alexis exclaimed. "Maybe I can make it last four, or five, years, or spend a little more and hold fundraisers or benefits to help out. Bring the community together."

"A part of running a business is doing the budget, and you'll need to do it well. Just because you've got the money doesn't mean you can blow it on stuff you don't need. You know Ron will help with accounts like the way he does with *HOS*, *SB3* and all the others," Jenny told her. "You need to get a plan in motion. Figure out who you can hire and who will have to volunteer. You know what money you have to budget with. It has to last for three years, and you have monthly bills to pay on top of staff."

"Yes, Grandma, I can do that tonight. What's the annual rate for a doctor and nurse?" Alexis asked. "Or a counsellor?"

"It varies, so you'll have to look it up." Dan peered over his shoulder. "But you should be able to afford full-time or part-time staff. Plus yourself, and a manager if you want one."

"Me? Why do I need a wage?" Alexis asked in surprise.

"You will be working there," Dan told her. "You're the one running it, you have to be there, so you'll need a wage."

"Me?" A faraway look came to her face. "I never thought about it."

"So, you expected what?" Jenny asked. "You and Cabot would get it up and it would run itself?"

Alexis stared at her grandmother. "I…guess. I mean, I can help out, and volunteers will help out, but I didn't think I'd be working there as a job."

"Then you'd better reassess that business plan of yours and figure out who's got what job. This business is yours and Cabot's, and while I don't expect him to run it, I do expect *him* to at least spend time there volunteering and helping out." She glanced from her granddaughter to Tomas. "How's he doing?"

"He seems okay," Tomas said as he cut up food for the next day's meals for his parents. "Maturing, becoming an adult. Learning to do housework. Growing."

"Maybe Xanthe's experiment is working after all," Jenny murmured, wondering what sort of grandson she'd have on the other side.

"Well, if he's maturing, I'm astounded," Carlos said from the lounge room where he reclined with Viv. "It's about time."

"Mmm, I wonder what she's getting out of him?" Jenny questioned. "He's only twenty-five; he can't really have that many issues."

"He's Cabot, he can have a shit load." Antonio lazed back on an easy chair and swung his legs over the arm.

"Yes." Jenny watched her grandson. "I guess he can."

*****

At Xanthe's the next morning, Cabot was excitedly telling her about meeting Tony. "I got the tingles," he said, moving frenetically around. "I got the tingles when he shook my hand and it raced up my arm and into my chest." He stopped. "I wasn't having a heart attack was I?"

Xanthe laughed. "No, no, that's what you call attraction. Have you ever been attracted to anyone before? Man or woman?"

Cabot pondered over his past conquests. "Yes. I've been attracted."

"Sexually or physically?"

"Um…sexually." He glanced up at the ceiling. "And some physically."

"Did they give you the tingles?"

"Some did."

"From what?"

"What do you mean?"

"What gave you the tingles? A handshake, dancing, looking in each other's eyes. What was it about them that gave you the tingles?"

"Ah…" Cabot pulled faces and bit on his lips as he walked around. "I've been physically attracted to men. It can be their eyes, their body. I've been sexually attracted to men because of a touch of their hand, a look in their eye."

"The spark?"

"Yeah." Cabot nodded in agreement. "The spark."

"And you had that with Tony?"

The goofy Stephanopoulos grin came over him. "Yeah."

"So…what does he look like?"

"Tall, dark, browny red hair, an exotic mix of eyes. They're greeny brown with a fire in them. He's a Colombian-Spanish-English mix. His mother is English. She has red hair and green eyes. His father was dark. He's muscular and well-built, manly. Older than me, I think."

"Is he a mature man?"

Cabot thought through all the times they'd seen each other. "Yeah, yeah, he is. In looks and speech. He sounds mature too."

"Have you ever been with an older man?"

He shrugged. "Wouldn't know, never stopped to ask. Although there was one that was older for sure. That guitarist I told you about. He's about five years older, but as for the others, I have no idea."

"So, maybe you need someone older to ground you?"

His head swivelled so he could look her in the eye. "Are you saying I'm immature?"

She looked him squarely back. "Yes."

He thought about it and relented. "Mmm, so I need an older man?"

"Maybe what you need is an older, *mature* man who has been through the same experiences, come out the other side, and become more adult, more mature, more educated, more *grounded*."

"So, I'm flighty, is that it?" He didn't know whether to be insulted or not.

"Are you going to come up with every word in the book?" Hauling herself up, Xanthe stood in front of him. "Darren, you are currently maturing due to one hell of a life experience, so maybe you need to hang around older, more mature people to give you some perspective about life. Someone you can ask questions of and get answers from. Share experiences, which is why the group therapy will be good. You get to hear that others have been through the same thing as you. You get to hear about how they handled it, or didn't handle their situation, you get to hear how they're coping on the other side. It is time in your experiment to make friends, Darren. You and Antonio have been superglued to each other for so long you don't lead separate lives. It's time to make new friends, and if this Tony person can be one of them, then great."

"What if I…" He glanced away. "Want to be *more* than friends."

"Don't even consider it," Xanthe told him. "Regardless of the fact he's HIV positive like you, you both need to step back from sex and just be still. Find *yourselves*, find *your* spot in this life. Don't jump into anything. Just make friends, hang out, and enjoy being twenty-five. Stop with the sex, because that's part of your problem."

Cabot was astounded. "But sex is good."

"Yes, sex can be mind-blowingly good with the right person. How do you think your grandparents, parents and uncles and aunt have stayed married for so long? Because their sex lives are mind-blowingly good."

"Or it could just be the men in the family have big cocks," Cabot muttered.

"Or it could be that." Xanthe smirked. "My point is, don't look at every man and see him as a sexual conquest. See him as another human being, a potential friend, a potential client, a potential informant. Not every man has to be a man you have sex with."

"Yeah, I guess." Cabot absentmindedly poked at a cushion on the easy chair.

"Do you *really* want to have sex with him?"

"It's…" Cabot bit his lip. "It's not as…not as much as I used to. It's like all of that has stopped. All of the frenzied rutting isn't necessary anymore. I don't need to get my cock sucked or shove it up an ass."

"That's good, Darren, you're maturing."

He sighed and deflated on the exhale, slumping on the arm of the chair, thinking about Tony Luca. "Yeah, I guess."

"But?"

"But...this is different. It's not just about sex and getting drunk and dancing and fucking in an alley or hallway. I *want* to get to know him. Spend time and hang out. I *want* to feel those tingles again."

"Good for you, Darren." Xanthe smiled brightly. "Now, if we could just break through that final hurdle, you would be home free."

"And what final hurdle would that be, Xanthe?"

"That hurdle called Antonio."

*****

Later that day, Dan took the test results to Jenny's house. The adults gathered, including Alfonso, to hear what they had to say. "We did a saliva DNA and a blood DNA, and did them both three times each," Dan said. "All are conclusive, you are siblings."

Angie burst into tears, sobbing as she hadn't since she was eighteen.

"Yesterday she drinks, today she cries." Alfonso had no idea what to do as he looked around at the family gathered there.

"Babe, hey, it's okay." Pedro rubbed her back. "You have a brother."

That just made her cry harder and Pedro looked at his mother with a 'I don't know what to do; you help her' expression.

"You need to remember back to Christmas 1977," Jenny told him. "She had lost her father, the *only* parent she had, *after* he did horrific things to her *and* you. She'd lost her mother eight years before, gone without a family, Christmases, birthdays. She was eighteen, pregnant, married, and her world had turned upside down." She went to her and Angie flew into her arms, holding on tightly. "I told you then we were your family now." Gently smoothing her hair, she waited a moment. "That you had Pedro, that Tomas, Carlos and Roger were now your brothers, Viv your sister, Spiros and I your parents. We are all you've had for thirty years. And the half-brother you *did* have, did horrific things, just like his father. They went to meet their maker at the same time." Soothing her daughter, Jenny laid her cheek on Angie's head. "And now after thirty years of having just us, you find out that your father had another child. And who knows, he could have more. But that doesn't mean you have to take them into your life. It doesn't mean you have to give yourself as a sister. It's okay, Angie. You're an adult now, you're a Stephanopoulos, *you can deal with this.*" She pulled back for Angie to adjust herself.

Steely determination flittered into Angie's eyes as she wiped her hands over her face and back through her hair. Letting out a deep breath, she nodded. "You're right, I've gone without a blood family for so long that you all became my family." She finally turned to Alfonso. "I can tell you about our father; the life we had, but don't expect anything out of me. I don't know if I have it to give."

Alfonso nodded eagerly. "That's all I wanted. To know about him and to find out my medical history."

The air whooshed out of Angie. "Okay, let's ah…get a drink and some food and go out on the balcony. I need air."

"Make the drink non-alcoholic," Pedro murmured and squeezed her hand as she passed him.

She looked up sheepishly and led Alfonso outside while Tomas got them a platter of food and mineral water.

"Thanks, Mama." Pedro kissed her cheek.

"For what?" she asked, offering Dan and Derek a drink.

"For helping her and understanding when none of us did," he said.

"Don't I always?" Jenny smiled. "And why haven't *you* learned to read your wife after thirty years?"

"What!" Pedro stopped pulling out his chair at the dining table and thought about it. "I…thought I could."

"Clearly not." Jenny laughed and seated herself. "Ah, this has been a hell of a year and we're only October. Anyone dressing up for Halloween?"

"We're a bit old for that, Mrs S." Roger grinned. "I think we stopped doing that years ago."

"Liar." Jenny's grin matched his. "We do it every year at *SB3* and you love it."

His grin turned to a laugh. "Yeah, I do."

Tomas came in from the balcony after delivering the food and drinks to Angie and Alfonso. "So, what *do* we do now?"

"We let them talk. As long as they need to. How long's Alfonso staying?" Jenny asked Carlos.

"Don't know. He flew in last Friday, went to Santorini for the weekend…maybe a week."

"Until he gets what he wants." Pedro looked out the window at the two of them. "You sure about him not wanting the estate?"

Carlos shrugged. "He's got the DeVille money, he doesn't need it. And Angie cashed it all in for money didn't she? There's no property left."

"Yeah, she sold it all off in '77 before we got married and flew out to New York," Pedro said.

"And if she'd forgotten about it until recently, then it's accrued a lot," Carlos went on.

"It *was* a sizable estate," Pedro reminded him. "Once it was sold off there was a lot of money, and she didn't touch it except to help you buy our old movies back."

"And with thirty years' worth of interest on top of what was left," Carlos prompted.

"Several hundred million," Jenny muttered.

"Jesus," Carlos murmured and everyone looked at Jenny. "How do you know?"

"I saw the paperwork because I helped her with it back in '77. She was eighteen and needed a legal adult to sign off on things. Add the same interest to hers as mine, and she's accrued millions. Time to put it to work for the family," Jenny said.

*****

After therapy, Darren walked up to the centre and found Tony lurking outside.

"Hey!" Tony brightened when he saw Darren. "I wasn't sure if you'd be in. I didn't see you."

"Had therapy." Darren's smile was ear to ear.

"Do you think we could...ah...maybe grab lunch?" Tony said, getting the tingles in his groin. *Hold back Tony, you don't want to rush him. He's going through therapy the way you did. And besides, you came here to look for the guy who assaulted you, not to hook up.*

Darren checked his watch. "It's only eleven-fifteen, a bit early for lunch."

"Well...how about morning tea?" Tony suggested, not wanting to spend the day without him.

"Um..." Darren peered inside the centre. "Hang on a minute." Dashing in, he asked, "Am I needed here today?"

Alena glanced up. "Not today. Hot date?"

The grin said it all. "Bye." He dashed out to jump in front of Tony. "They don't need me, let's go."

They walked down to the beach and along the sand, talking about everything. What they liked, didn't like, hated, loved, watched, listened to, did day to day.

"Ah, I'm taking time out from my day job to get counselling," Darren told him as they walked. The mist from the waves wafted around them. "I have no idea if I'll be fired or not, so I guess I'd better find a way of living now I have HIV to deal with."

"Yeah, I got fired from my job," Tony said. "After spending six months falling apart, I got into therapy."

"How did you fall apart?" Darren played with his turtleneck sleeve cuffs.

"Got drunk, turned on my friends, turned on my family, but then once they found out I had HIV, they turned on me, so I guess it was easy to part ways. Not that I had a family. I have half siblings. They don't care. Although they certainly cared before that when I inherited my father's estate when I turned twenty-five."

"How old are you?"

"Twenty-nine."

"Oh, same age as my sister and cousin," slipped out of Darren's mouth before he could stop it.

"And you?" Tony asked.

"Twenty-five."

"We're not too far apart in age, then." Tony smiled, liking Darren more and more. *At least he's old enough, getting therapy, dealing with it.*

"What happened after you turned on everyone?" Darren asked. "You look like you've gotten your shit together."

"Yeah, well, getting arrested for drunk and disorderly will do that to you. When the judge found out I was HIV positive, he ordered six months' worth of therapy. It was the best thing he could do. It took me a couple of months to get over being angry and get out of denial. And once I broke down and let it all out, I got better. The therapist told me what was going on in my head was normal and now I'd have to deal with something over thirty million other people deal with."

"That many! Jesus?" Darren went wide-eyed. "I thought it was something like ten million."

"Nope. The latest records from the World Health Organisation says over thirty million *worldwide*. Most of it seems to be in Africa."

"Jesus," Darren repeated. "That sucks. So, you're okay with it now? Mentally?"

"Yeah." Tony stopped to stare out at the ocean and breathed deeply. "I have HIV from an assault. The assault was not my fault, getting HIV was not my fault, but it is a life-changing thing I have to deal with. So do you." He laid a hand on Darren's shoulder. "It's a hard road, but you'll get there."

Tingles were racing through Darren's body and he looked from Tony's hand to his eyes. "Yeah, that's what my therapist says. It's just going to take a while. But I've made inroads. She got me to admit I'm gay, and to tell my family that I'm gay and have HIV from an assault. So, if I can admit it to myself and my family, that's a start." The headiness of Tony's hand and the tingles it was causing made him lightheaded, and it felt good resting where it was. Tony was a good few inches taller than him, but he didn't mind. In fact, he liked it, and liked Tony. *One step at a time Darren,* he told himself. *One step at a time.*

"Absolutely," Tony agreed. "How'd they take it?"

Darren gently shrugged his shoulders, not wanting to dislodge

Tony's hand. "Disappointed, upset, horrified, scared."

"Did they disown you? Kick you out of the house?"

Darren turned his head. "Did yours?"

Tony shrugged. "My stepfather called me a fag fucker, wanted to kick me out. His kids, my halfs, called me the same thing. It's not very nice."

"What did you do?" Darren asked softly, remembering calling Tomas and Roger that name and wincing.

"Well, I was bigger than my stepfather, which he hated. Small man syndrome, I'd say he suffered from. When I inherited my father's estate, he demanded payment for all the years he'd paid for me. My mother reminded him he hadn't as she'd received a weekly allowance to look after me until I was twenty-five when I inherited."

"What did you inherit? Something cool?"

Tony grinned. "A Spanish style hacienda castle kinda thing in Spain and a multimillion dollar trust fund. There was a lot of money in the family, and Mum told me my dad's parents had died, leaving it all to him. Then he died and left it all to me. It was quite a fortune in 1981. A small amount was taken out each year for the upkeep of the house and land, but there's a lot left over."

"It sounds cool. Got any pics?"

"On my laptop. I travelled there when I inherited and had a look. It's impressive, to say the least. Beautiful, but haunted, classic, yet old-fashioned. I love it and plan on keeping it, but I did organise to rent it out, so it could pay its own upkeep."

"It sounds awesome." Darren smiled. "I'd love to see it one day."

Tony matched his smile. "I'd love to show it to you one day."

*****

"Thank you, everyone, for coming to the grand opening of *The Mykonos Assault and HIV/AIDS Support Centre*," Alexis said over the loudspeaker the next day. "It means so much to me to be able to bring this centre to the community, for the men, women and children of Mykonos."

Applause from the crowd grew. It was a good five hundred strong and most were being nosy at what Jenny Stephanopoulos had done now.

"Sexual and physical assault is no laughing matter, neither is getting HIV/AIDS from it. We have opened this centre to serve the people of Mykonos. To support the people of Mykonos. And to help the people of Mykonos. My cousin, Cabot Stephanopoulos and I are proud to bring this centre to you. Thank you." With a huge grin, Alexis cut the ribbon across the door.

As people piled in to see what it was like, Dan, Derek, and Lorenzo, plus doctors and nurses, spoke to people in the crowd about the centre.

"It's fantastic," Tony told Darren as they mingled. "I wish I had something like this back in England when I needed it."

"Yes," Darren agreed. "It is wonderful. Just what the place needed." He'd freaked out a little when Alexis mentioned his name, but considering no one looked his way, all was well. Unless someone called him Cabot.

"How'd you manage to get away from your therapist?" Tony asked. "Aren't you normally in therapy right now?"

"Yeah, but my therapist thought it would be a good idea to be here, since I'm volunteering, and we'll do our session after we're done here."

"Oh, what a great therapist," Tony said. "Very amenable."

"Um, yeah," Darren replied, looking around for his family. "Flexible 24/7 if I need to talk. She's available for the family too if they want to talk to her."

"About your status and how they feel?" Tony inquired, wondering why his family would need a counsellor.

"Or about their own problems." Darren nonchalantly shrugged. "That's Xanthe over there. The portly woman in the garish floral top and pants." He pointed and she noticed.

Walking over, she shook hands with Tony. "You must be the young man Darren's mentioned. You were assaulted by a man here last year."

"Ah, yes." Tony was surprised that Darren had been talking about him. "Tony. Tony Luca." He shook her hand.

"Oh, I'm sorry, should I not have mentioned you?" Darren asked him, worried he'd offended him somehow.

"Um." Tony shook his head. "I don't have a problem with it."

"Good. Then say goodbye to Darren because we have a session," Xanthe said.

"Ugh, Xanthe," Darren groaned, twitching his leg like a kid about to throw a tantrum.

"A deal is a deal, come along." Xanthe set off for her office.

"Ah," came out in a sigh. "Sorry, gotta go." Darren walked backwards so he could still see Tony's face.

"Okay, will I see you later?" Tony asked.

"Maybe. I'll be back here this afternoon," Darren called and finally turned around to follow Xanthe.

Once back at her home, the session started.

"He's very good looking," she said. "Do you want to have sex with him?"

"What! Jesus, Xanthe, you know how to jump into it." He ran to the window, hopeful that Tony might walk past.

"Well, do you?"

Not seeing anyone, he flopped into an easy chair. "I'd like to, if it works out."

"Explain that."

He lifted a shoulder. "I really like him. I'd like to get to know him, I'd like to kiss him, see where it goes. Will it lead to sex? I don't know. I'd like it to, but I'm also scared of it."

"Why?"

"We both have HIV. Should we even be having sex?"

"You can with condoms. It's not as if you can catch it from each other."

"Yeah, I suppose." He scratched his head and pushed his hair back. His undercut had grown out, and all over it was a little longer than how he normally wore it. "I just…don't feel like rushing it."

"Good for you, Darren," Xanthe cheered him on. "Do you feel that way about all men, or just Tony?"

"Just Tony. Guess I want to see what he's like on the inside first. Whether he meets all my needs or not."

"And what needs are they?"

Both shoulders shrugged. "I dunno. To be loved unconditionally.

Accept me for me and all my flaws, and all my issues and mental problems."

"Sounds like the kind of love we all want." Xanthe watched his face. "Do you think Tony can give you that?"

"I dunno." He picked at a cushion cover that poked out under his arm. "I guess. He might. He seems interested in me. He knows I was assaulted. He was too. We both acquired HIV out of it. We're both on meds. We're both still dealing with it. We both know what the other is going through."

"Yes, I guess that is a good thing. Many gay men with HIV/AIDS hook up with other men with HIV/AIDS. One, they're not going to infect the other, and two, they both know what the other's dealing with."

"I don't know if we'll hook up. I'd really like something to happen down the track. But he's from England, I'm from here, so it might be a bit hard to make something happen."

"And in the meantime?"

He finally looked at her. "I deal with whatever issues are going on in my head."

When the hour was up and Cabot was gone, Xanthe started a game plan in motion. *He likes this new guy Tony, which is what he calls his brother. Coincidence? I don't think so. He clearly has issues with his brother, and that's what we're going to get to the root of. Something's holding him back and it has to do with his brother. But what could it be? He's clearly desperate for his brother's love, desperately needy that is. The way he clings to him, especially in the beginning. But since being apart, albeit only for ten days, he seems to be dealing with it. When they're together, he hugs and kisses his brother, clearly wanting his brother's love in return. So, it looks like we'll have to get the two together for a long session on Friday, so he has the weekend to recover. It's going to be long, and exhausting, but, I hope, we'll finally get to the bottom of it.*

*****

Diana had a fitting for her photo shoot. She was in Milan, fashion capital of the world, and was on set of the new campaign for *Maison Blanche's* brand-new Mercedes Benz. Her outfit was to be skin-tight denim jeans and a tight top, but clearly, that wasn't happening.

"God, girl, have you gained weight?" Mystery, the stylist for the shoot, asked. She was the number one stylist in Milan and worked with Diana often.

"A couple of centimetres," Diana mumbled. "I think I'm getting old and can't keep the weight off anymore." She had been fretting for the last month about her size.

"I don't think Viscount Blaison will be too happy with you changing clothes," Mystery told her. "But I can't do anything with these jeans. You'll have to wear something else." Thumbing through the clothing racks, she pulled out a dress. "What about this?" It was a dainty floral number.

"No. What about sequins; an evening gown?" Diana suggested. Anything to take the focus off her expanding waistline.

Mystery flung her long colourful braids over her shoulder and cocked a pierced critical eye over the rack of evening wear. "We've got a couple of sizes in each one."

"I'll take the next size up from my normal," Diana said, desperate to keep her bump covered. "The gold. It will go with my hair." Mystery handed it to her and she went behind the screen to change. "Ugh, I can't get it on. Can you try and zip it up for me?" She held her hair out of the way while Mystery yanked the zip. It broke off halfway. "Jesus Christ. I couldn't have gained that much." She frowned. "Next size." The third dress fitted and looked perfect, even if it did show a small belly bulge.

"You *have* gained weight." Mystery cast her critical eye over Diana's small, frame. "You went up three sizes."

"It must have been the burger I had for lunch," Diana joked. "We'll have to use this one." After removing the dress, she went to the hair and make-up room and sat for an hour while they styled her mane and coloured up her face.

"On set in half an hour," the floor assistant called. "Half an hour people."

Diana finished up in the chair and quickly donned her gold sequin dress. Walking out to the stage, she saw the car sitting in pride of place.

"Ah, Diana, my beautiful Diana." Viscount Blaison swanned over to her and kissed both cheeks. "How are you my darling?" He gave her the once-over. "No jeans and top?"

"It will be classier in a sequin dress," Diana sugar-coated her voice. "Don't you want your car to be glamorous, to show glamour and style? And what better outfit to do it in than gold sequins?"

"Mmm, you've gained weight darling. I don't like that." The Viscount stood with his hand on his chin, critically eyeing her up and down.

"Well, sorry that I'm growing up, Viscount, but I refuse to starve myself for a job anymore. You gotta problem with that?" Her hands landed on her hips in defiance. A lot had changed within her lately, and her take-no-shit attitude had grown.

"Well, yes, I do." The Viscount noticed the attitude.

"Then if you don't want me, you know where you can stuff your car," Diana told him with a finger point. Everyone gasped and waited. "I'm getting really sick and tired of starving myself for photo shoots. I'm a grown woman, I won't be thin forever. And if you want anorexic, get Kate Moss. So…am I doing this shoot or not?"

The Viscount's eyes narrowed, and his lips pursed. He didn't take attitude from any two-bit model, but Diana was not a two-bit model and he knew she would sell his car.

"Haven't got all day Viscount, chop, chop." Diana clapped her hands twice.

"All right." He clicked his fingers and everyone got to work.

Diana dazzled as she always did, flicking her mane in the wind created by the fan, pouting her lips, giving it her all, and by the end of the shoot, Viscount Blaison was happy. The sequin dress had looked great, just as Diana said it would.

As she stepped off the stage the Viscount warned her, "That will be your last shoot for us, unless you can get your weight down."

"Then you know where you can shove that car then." Diana snapped her fingers in his face and walked past him. Half an hour later, she was back in her hotel room sobbing. She was alone; no family, no Charles, and she couldn't wait to get home. A few more weeks and it was all over. The fittings, the letting out of clothes, the loneliness. She'd be back home with her family. Four months pregnant and yet still alone. Her desperation for Charles grew each day, and the nights were the worst. Lying alone in bed, a different one every few days, had taken its toll. She wanted to be in *his* bed, with *him*. Or her bed; she wasn't fussy. And clearly, hormones had made her extra emotional. But without word from him, she felt the fear. The fear that she'd be a single mother without the father of her child in her life. She had called Edie, editor of *Flair* magazine. No one had seen or heard from Charles since he left for the overseas assignment, and everyone was worried. There was no word from him, or anyone else, about where he might be. No numbers to call, no address to write to. There was nothing, as though he had fallen off the face of the Earth. Completely disappeared. Completely out of communication with the world. He could be dead.

"Oh no," she cried, ice-cold fear searing through her. "No, he can't be dead. Please don't be dead. Don't be dead, don't be dead," she whispered before bursting into tears. If Charles was dead, she had no father to raise the baby. The baby would never know him. Could she live without him? She had so far, but did that mean she wanted to spend the rest of her life alone? No. She didn't. She wanted to spend her life with Charles.

*****

Darren met up with Tony for lunch. "Hey."

"Hey." Tony lit up. "How was therapy?"

"Ah, you know, same old, same old." Darren shrugged, not wanting to talk about it.

"Yeah, it can get that way," Tony said. "But it's good for you, remember that." He pointed a finger at him. "It's good for *you*."

A grin slid across Darren's lips. "Yeah, I know. It just seems to be taking a while."

"Mine went for six months," Tony reminded him, "And I came through it."

"And you look good," Darren said. "Really good."

"Healthy mind, healthy body, healthy life. Or as good as I can get it." Tony reached over the table to squeeze Darren's arm and smiled. "And you can too."

The butterflies bounced around Darren's stomach and he smiled. "Yeah. I guess I'll get there. What do you want for lunch?" *Please say me, please say me,* he silently pleaded, and then blushed at his thoughts.

"Thinking something good?" Tony caught the blush and wondered if Darren was thinking about him.

"Thinking…grilled chicken sandwiches," Darren covered for himself.

"And two beers?" Tony asked.

"Sworn off alcohol at the moment." Darren pulled a face. "Which isn't a bad thing. I used to get drunk and have sex a lot."

"It's always good to cut down," Tony agreed. "In every aspect. In friends, and family if they don't support you. Shit in your life. Stuff you collect, drugs, alcohol. It's always good to cleanse your soul."

"Yeah, I haven't really wanted a drink or the drugs." Darren rested his chin in his hands and stared across the table.

"What sort?"

"Pot and coke." Darren pulled his sleeves past his palms. He lived in the same black turtleneck, black jeans, and chunky black boots. It just made life easier.

"Wow. I didn't expect that. Did you do them after finding out your status?" Tony was shocked.

"Before. A few years before." Darren nervously picked at the hem of his sleeves. "I'd do a line of coke before going out partying, drink to get drunk, do a joint or two at home."

"I'm surprised it hasn't aged you." Tony smiled at the waiter as he placed his plate in front of him. "You still look young."

"Thank God." Darren picked up half of his sandwich and bit into the juicy flame-grilled chicken with tomato, cheese, lettuce and bacon with ranch sauce on a grilled bun. "Oh, my Got, this is goot," he managed around the mouthful. "Mmm."

Biting into his burger, Tony took in Darren's appearance. Black hair with some regrowth at the roots, brown eyes, golden tanned skin which still looked pretty good. But the dark circles under his eyes gave it away. There was something there, something he was still keeping inside, and it was making his health and sleep a problem. "You don't sleep well, do you?"

Darren swallowed the first half and wiped his mouth with his napkin, debating whether to reveal all. He took a swig of water. "Most nights, no."

"When *do you* sleep well?"

"Um…" Darren stared down at his burger. Not sure about answering.

"When you're with a man?"

Brown eyes looked up and stared into the exotic eyes of Tony Luca. "I generally don't sleep with men. Although there have been one or two that have stayed the night."

"Were you comfortable with them staying the night?" Tony's eyes bored into Darren's.

Darren thought back to Adam Slayer and falling asleep in his arms and a tiny smile lifted up his lips. "Some."

"But it hasn't happened often?" Tony wanted to know how many Darren had been with, and whether any of them had been serious.

"It was very rare." Darren picked up the other half of his sandwich and devoured it, not wanting to talk about his 4242 plus conquests. *Oh God, what will Tony think if he finds out? Oh, my God, how bloody embarrassing.*

"Do you need to go back to the centre?" Tony asked, eating his burger, but wanting to eat Darren.

Darren glanced at his watch. "Yeah, I'd better. I am a volunteer, so I should be volunteering."

A grin spread across Tony's face. "Yeah, I guess so. Can I walk you?"

Darren finished the last of his water. "Yes, yes you can."

They talked more on the way back, and Darren agreed to have dinner with him.

"So, I'll see you at seven-thirty, or is that too late?" Tony said. "I'm used to eating late.

"Make it six-thirty and it will be the perfect time," Darren replied.

"Okay, how about that restaurant, what's it called…" Tony racked his brain. "The one at the marina."

"*The Bay Marina?*" Darren offered. "It's mainly seafood."

"Do you like seafood?" Tony asked, taking a step closer.

Tingles raced through Darren and he wanted Tony to step closer. "I love seafood. They do a great fried prawn salad."

"Okay." Another step. "So…I'll see you there at six-thirty."

"Okay." The Stephanopoulos grin spread across Darren's face, and his fingers laced together in front of him.

"Okay." Tony reached out and laced his fingers with Darren's, their hands only letting go when Tony walked away.

Waiting until Tony had gone, and he couldn't see him anymore, Darren finally made it into the centre.

"Nice of you to join us," Alexis said. "Who's the hunk?"

"His name's Tony," Darren said shyly, watching his cousin do paperwork behind the counter with the new receptionist.

"And are you in lurve?" Alexis grinned, filing brochures and documents into racks for people to take home.

"Mmm, I might be falling." Darren spun around into a pirouette.

"You're kidding! *You, in love?*" Her eyes were as wide as saucers. *"Get out!"*

"Alexis," Darren chided lightly. "No fair on the teasing." He bounced lightly into the meeting room and saw several people there talking to Dan, so he pottered around straightening up.

Alexis appeared by his side. "You're not kidding," she whispered in his ear. "Are you *really* falling in love?"

He shrugged lightly. "Maybe."

"Whoa! I really didn't think Cabot Conroy Stephanopoulos was capable of loving anyone but himself."

"Har-har funnee." Rolling his eyes, he reminded her his name was Darren.

"For how long?" Alexis asked.

"Don't know. Until I have the breakthrough Xanthe wants me to have, I guess."

"So, when we wrap the Christmas presents we bought for Cabot, do we have to put Darren on them instead?" she joked.

"Argh," he growled under his breath. "I'm just the butt of the family's jokes, aren't I?"

"Not at all. We just think looking like us is pretty funny."

"You might think so, but Dom certainly doesn't."

"Yeah, what *is up* with that?" Alexis crossed her arms and leaned against the refreshment table where Cabot was tidying up. "It's been since Danté was attacked by the shark. All of a sudden Dom turned on you and started crawling up Danté's bum. Finally, he's being the big brother he should have always been."

"I dunno." Darren gave another shrug. "He's been rude to me. Okay, yeah, I get it. I shouldn't have been near Danté when it happened. And I get why he yelled at me to get away from him. But what have I done since to piss him off? Me, him and Tony were always close growing up. You know, it was *that time he hated Danté's guts.*"

"Yeah, I know." Alexis sighed. "Maybe he feels guilty for not being there for him all those years. Maybe he's trying to make it up to him now, and is scared you'll pass on the virus. Who knows what's going through Dom's head? I don't even think *he* knows."

Darren giggled. "You're funny."

"I try," Alexis drawled dryly. "So, you sticking around? Our first session starts tomorrow. Are you coming in?"

"Isn't that one for women? In which case, probably not good that a man's here."

"Doesn't mean you can't set out tea and biscuits. I'll be a part of it."

"You? Why?" His brown eyes locked onto hers.

"To show people that I know what they're going through. And that I want to help."

"Aw, Alexis, how sweet of you." He kissed his cousin's cheek. "I suppose you expect me to talk about mine?"

"At some stage," she told him. "If it's okay with Xanthe."

*****

Xanthe pulled Antonio into the office. "I have a plan for Cabot, but I don't think it will work unless you're here."

"What can I do?" he asked, anxious to help his brother, but also wary of anything to do with a shrink.

"Have a session with us."

"What?" He frowned. "Does my brother *need* me here?"

She peered at him curiously. "Are you ashamed of him, Antonio?"

"What?" His scowl matched the one his brother always had. "Are you shrinking *me* now?"

She raised a brow at the similarity. "Well, I should see you just to have a chat. Surely Cabot's behaviour has upset you over the years?"

"Well..." His arms crossed over his chest and his lip twitched. "Yeah."

"Then I need you to tell him that on Friday. That's when the session will be." She watched him fall into an easy chair and sat opposite him.

"You want me to tell my brother his behaviour has upset me?"

"Disgusted you, shamed you, embarrassed you, whatever you, it all needs to come out for him, and you, to deal with."

"What do I have to deal with?" he asked, wondering what she had planned.

"Besides his behaviour? Not having a life of your own, no friends, no apartment, no career, no girlfriend." She watched his face fall. "When did you last have a girlfriend? A *real* girlfriend?"

"High school."

"What age?"

"Seventeen, eighteen."

"Do you want one?"

His eyes were red and glossy when he looked up. "Yes."

"Do you love your brother?"

"Yes."

"Do you want a life away from him?"

"Yes."

"For that to happen, we need to separate you. As I've told Cabot, you need your own friends, your own apartment, your own life outside of each other. You need to cut the cord from each other."

The thought scared, but also excited him. "And how do we do that?"

"By telling one another what you really think of the other."

*****

The next morning, the group therapy for women dealing with assault was on, and Alexis was a part of it. Xanthe had volunteered her time along with Regina, the therapist who'd be taking the sessions on a daily basis through the week.

"The important thing to understand is, it's not your fault. You do not make a man assault you, regardless of what you say, what you do, how you act or behave, what you wear or how you wear it. The *man* is responsible for *his* behaviour. You are responsible for yours," Regina told the small group of eight women who had turned up. "It doesn't matter what he says, 'you made me do it', 'you wanted it', 'you led me on', 'you flirted with me', 'you said yes then no', 'you said no but your eyes said yes'. It absolutely *does not* matter what he says, or what you do, *no* man is entitled to assault, attack or rape you."

Alexis nodded in agreement and glanced around the group. They looked to be mainly her age and slightly older. Late teens, early twenties, some even thirties.

"Now, as an adult, you need to step up and protect yourselves, be prepared to fight. Be prepared to punch them, dig your nails in, kick, scream, bite, because he won't be expecting that. They expect you to stand there, or lie there, and say and do nothing. And *your* fear makes that happen. I don't care if he says he's going to kill you, you fight to the goddamn death for your life. *To protect your life.* If you get cut or stabbed, consider it a war wound. You fought for your life and got away with a cut. He'll be so busy trying to get away from *you*, from the scratching and biting and kicking, that he'll forget about hurting you and run away. Fight with everything you have and then some. Because at the end of the day, it's all up to you to protect and save yourself. *No one else will.* There will be *no one else* around to stop him except you. There is no knight in shining armour come to save you. No passer-by to pull him off you. It's all about you and fighting for your life. Fighting for *your* safety. *You* have to protect yourself from the start and then be prepared to fight for your life. Now, I know that this is all too late for you ladies, but that doesn't mean you have to hide under a rock and do nothing. You take your experience and you learn from it. You learn how to better protect yourselves from the get-go and to follow through. If you feel guilt, stop. There is no guilt here. There is no room for guilt in your lives anymore. From now on, you will be empowered women, self-reliant women." Regina turned to her right. "Now, Alexis, you said you wanted to speak today."

"Yes, yes I did." Alexis wiped her hands on her jeans leg. "I am Alexis Stephanopoulos, and coming from a well-known family didn't prevent me from being assaulted. I was on the beach with my two best friends when it all started. A guy came up to us and hit on me. I turned him down. He called me a frigid bitch and a whore and a tease. I went after him and asked him if he knew who I was and proceeded to tell him all about my family, all the while hanging on to his penis and wrenching it." There were a few giggles around the room. "Well, a few days later, we were down the beach again and I went for a swim, and he swam up behind me, grabbed me, threatened me, groped me and I screamed rape."

Taking a deep breath, she brushed away a few strands of hair. "That time, fortunately, my mother and father showed up and Daddy came barrelling in to save me. But he couldn't save me when the rape happened." She glanced up to see Cabot standing in the doorway giving her the thumbs up. She smiled softly and continued. "My friends and I were at our club, and the jerk came in. We told the manager, my friends' father, who he was, and he threw him out. A few hours later when we left, my friends, unfortunately, walked off instead of waiting, and as I was racing to catch up, that's when he grabbed me."

Lorenzo came to a stop beside Cabot. "What's going on?" he whispered, looking into the room.

"Alexis is telling everyone her assault story," Cabot whispered back.

"Assault?" Lorenzo's eyes grew wide. "I didn't know she'd been assaulted."

"Shh, listen," Cabot told him.

"He put his left hand over my mouth and carried me into an alley. He pushed me against the wall, pushed my knickers down, pushed himself inside me and groped me rather painfully. I screamed, scratched at his face and head, and kicked his shins. But because he was behind me, it was quite hard to defend myself and do real damage."

She sipped some water and sighed. "I did what I could, but it didn't stop him. When he'd finished, he grabbed me by my hair, which was long then, and smashed my head onto the wall. I was dazed and fell to the ground. My friends called out my name and he went running. They found me and took me to Grandma's who got our doctor in to check on me. It was…" Her head shook as she looked down in embarrassment. "The exam was embarrassing and humiliating. I didn't want another man touching me, but my grandma helped out and it was over quickly. I didn't want to think about the rape. I tried to block it out. I stayed with my grandparents. My family found out one by one, even though I didn't want them to know. But…"

Another deep breath. "It made my sister and me closer. We'd never gotten along, but this brought her to her senses and we get along like a house on fire now. But none of that changed the fact I'd been raped. I ignored it the best I could, but would then burst into tears. A week or two after it happened, I was watching TV and flicking through the channels when I came across a talk show with women talking about their assaults. I bawled my eyes out." Her eyes were full of tears. "I ran into the bathroom, grabbed a pair of scissors, and hacked my hair off. My grandma found me and stopped me. I screamed at her that I didn't want it anymore because he'd grabbed me by it and smashed my face into the wall. She sat me down and fixed up the mess I'd made, and this is what I have." She ran a hand through her hair. "I haven't had short hair since I was little; it's always been long like Mama's and my sister's. But after I did this, Mama got hers cut into a short bob, and it looks good. Don't they say a change is as good as a holiday?" she said to Xanthe and Regina.

"Absolutely." Xanthe nodded. "And once this has happened to you, you might want to change your appearance too. A haircut is a natural thing. So is gaining weight, or hiding behind baggy clothes. Many women want to make themselves unattractive to men, thinking that they won't be noticed. And all of this is perfectly natural. It's a coping mechanism, but by using it, you do yourself a disservice. You stop being the woman you were; the person you want to be, all because some asshole made you feel unworthy."

"Well, I didn't," Alexis said. "But I credit that to a strong grandma and mama. Our family is strong and united, and I had awesome role models. I still get a little freaked out if I'm by myself, but with the number of people in my family, I'm rarely by myself. I'm with my grandparents, my parents, aunt or uncles. We have dinner every night when we can, lunch on Sundays, we hang out with friends, and I've been okay. I had therapy early on, but for some reason that didn't help. My grandma tried helping, but she told me she didn't know what to tell me because it had never happened to her, so she didn't know how to help me with it. All she could suggest was to see it as a very horrible sexual experience, and to try and think about the future and what I wanted to do and then to go out and do it. To get on with my life and not let him make me stop. I told the therapist that and she poo-poohed Grandma's idea, saying it denied that rape had happened. Quite frankly, I think the therapist was wrong. Because a lot of people say, even my grandma, that whatever you have to say to yourself to get through the day, say it. Tell yourself whatever you need to, to survive another day in life."

Regina agreed. "There *is* a difference between denial, and simply pushing it to the side to get through the day. As long as you accept what has happened, understand it, deal with it, you *don't* need to think about it 24/7. Deal with it during your therapy and then the rest of the time, forget about it and get on with your life."

"And that's what I've done," Alexis told the group. "I've gotten on with my life. I've holidayed in New York with the family, I've designed for my sister's and cousin's clothing label, and now I've set up this centre with my cousin for all of you, with the help from our family. So I am *definitely* getting on with my life. That doesn't mean I don't think about it on the odd occasion, though. I do. I just breathe, tell myself I'm alive and okay, and get through the day. It helps, it really does."

They spent the rest of the time hearing from the other women, who said they now felt more empowered to take back control of their life just from hearing Alexis speak. Finishing up, Alexis gave the women a hug and walked them to the door, telling them it would be okay now, they had support. When they left, she hurried back into the room to tidy up, and was putting they used paper cups in the bin when he spoke.

"I'm sorry, I didn't know."

Alexis turned to see Lorenzo standing at the refreshment table. "Didn't know what?"

"That you had been assaulted." He stepped closer. "I'm sorry. I know your family. I dated Alena a few years back, I've worked with your grandmother, it's not fair what's happened to you and Cabot, and I'm sorry. Neither of you deserves it."

A soft smile came to her lips. "I'm sorry too. That I didn't do more… to stop it, and Cabot…"

Lorenzo moved closer. "I heard you say you fought, so at least you did something."

"But I didn't stop it." Trying to hold herself together, she put the lid on the biscuit container.

"No," he said softly. "And you're still dealing with it. I'm sorry, Alexis. I didn't know. I did wonder why you and Cabot were setting up this centre; I thought it was because of what he went through. But to hear your story, I'm sorry."

"Thank you, Lorenzo," she murmured. "That means a lot." A tear escaped and rolled down her cheek. It was quickly followed by more as she clung to the container in her hands, her knuckles white from gripping it.

"Oh, Alexis." He moved to her side and gently put an arm around her. "It's okay, it's okay now."

She went into his arms and sobbed. And she hadn't sobbed over it in months, pushing it aside to work and keep her mind busy. Clinging to him, she let it out and he held her until she was done.

"Are you okay?" He cupped her face and wiped the tears away. Oh, how pretty she was. Her eyes, her face, she was beautiful and dynamic.

"I'm okay." She felt the tingle in her face and gazed into his chocolate brown eyes, his creamy smooth skin, his black hair swept back off his forehead. At six foot two, he was Greek, young, and hot.

"Ah..." She pulled back and wiped her face. "I must be a mess, I'd better clean up."

"You're beautiful," came softly to her ears as she dashed past.

"Oh," she spun around, "What?"

"You're beautiful," he repeated, staying where he was, just smiling at her. "You're an incredible woman, Alexis, and you've done so much for yourself, your cousin, and the men and women of Mykonos."

"Oh." She stared at the beautiful Greek man before her, seeing him differently from how she *had* seen him. She knew who he was, had seen him date Alena for a few months, but had never got to know who he was, on the inside. "Oh...I'd...ah...better... Oh." She spun on her heel, and raced for the small bathroom they had in the building.

Cabot saw her fly by and walked into the room "Smooth. You got my cuz in tears."

"She was crying over her assault," Lorenzo told him.

"Yes, I'm sure. You know, dude, she's only nineteen." Cabot stood, arms crossed, at his full protective height of six feet, regardless of the fact Lorenzo had two inches on him.

"Yes, Cabot." Lorenzo sighed and inwardly burned. "I know she's only nineteen."

"And you're how old?" Cabot countered.

Lorenzo paused before answering, eyeing off Cabot and wondering what he was intending. "Thirty."

"Yowch!" Cabot exclaimed. "Better not let her parents see you near her in any way other than professionally. The whole family's overprotective."

"Then how did you get HIV?" Lorenzo sneered. "Or was it because you just didn't want protecting?" He stormed past Cabot, into the foyer, and into the staff office behind the front counter. He was on duty for the men's group that afternoon.

Cabot stood speechless, not sure what to do. Did he move? Laugh? Cry? Run away? How the hell do you answer that kind of question?

"Is he right?" Xanthe asked from behind him. "Didn't you want to be protected by your family?"

He spun around, still in shock which was clear on his face. "I, ah, never thought about it."

"But you said it about Alexis, and Lorenzo countered back by putting it on you. It's a very good question." She studied his face intently, seeing he had no idea how to react to such a comment.

"And I have no idea what to say to it," Cabot told her. "I have absolutely no idea what to say, or what to do. Laugh at it, cry at it, fall apart, run away…"

"It stunned you?" she asked.

"Yeah." He nodded sporadically.

"Why?"

His eyes flitted around the room. "Because I have no answer. I don't know *how* to answer it, or what the answer would be."

"Well, let's break it down. If your parents had've protected you, then you wouldn't have been out having wild sex and getting HIV."

"I guess," Cabot mumbled, having no idea what he was actually feeling in that moment.

"But you were talking about Alexis being nineteen and Lorenzo thirty; that her parents would be overprotective because of the age difference. She's still a teen, he's an adult who knows better, and he shouldn't be interested in a nineteen-year-old."

"Yeah." He nodded enthusiastically. "That's what *I* meant. But what did *he* mean?"

"I personally think he meant it to attack you. He put you on the spot. You were telling him to back off because of overprotective parents, and yet, he was pointing out that your parents couldn't stop you from doing what you wanted, so Alexis is old enough to do what she wants," Xanthe said.

"You're overthinking it," Lorenzo said from the doorway, having retraced his steps and hearing them talk. "I just said it to get back at him for his comment and for butting in. That was all."

"Hey, everyone okay?" Alexis stopped beside Lorenzo in the doorway. "It's lunchtime and I'm hungry. Do you wanna order in, or go grab something?" She looked from a scowling, cross-armed Cabot, to an intrigued Xanthe, to a gorgeous defiant Lorenzo and back. "Everything okay?" The vibes from the whole conversation hung in the air.

"Fine." Lorenzo broke the stand-off. "Lunch sounds great. Why don't I get everyone's order and grab something from the bar and grill down the road?"

"Not for us, thank you," Xanthe said. "Darren and I will be running along."

"Ah, yes, your little experiment, how's that going?" Lorenzo mocked.

"Quite well, actually." Xanthe eyeballed him as she passed. "Maybe you should take a class in psychology, Lorenzo, you might actually *learn* something."

Cabot couldn't contain the grin on his face and did a brow lift as he passed Lorenzo. "She told you."

Lorenzo reddened and pursed his lips.

"What was that about?" Alexis watched them go then shifted her eyes to Lorenzo's darkened face.

"Your cousin and I don't see eye to eye on something and he overreacted to it," he told her, gently touching her arm. "Looks like he has to talk to his therapist about everything."

"If it makes him better, I don't have a problem with it." The tingles from his hand raced up her arm.

"No, I guess not," Lorenzo quickly said, not wanting to overstep his mark. "I think they both overthought my comment, that's all."

"And what comment would that be?" She gazed at him questioningly.

Smiling, he said, "Never mind. How about that lunch?"

*****

"Is he kinda slimy, or is it just me?" Cabot asked Xanthe as they walked back to her place.

"*That* was kind of slimy," she replied.

Cabot nodded. "He knows she's nineteen, yet he hit on her anyway. After she told a group of women she'd been raped. He was standing beside me, so he heard the whole thing from the doorway."

"Was he hitting on her, or is that *your* interpretation?" They arrived back at the house and went inside.

"He hit on her all right, but I think she saw it as caring, kindness, a friend of the family showing her kindness. He dated Alena, you know.

About five years ago. Didn't last long, but they had sex."

Xanthe raised a brow and looked at him. "You know that for a fact?"

"She bragged about it to Diana, and we know they were dating, so we found out from gossip sessions."

"And now he's after Alexis?" she mused.

"Who knows?" Cabot shrugged. "He could be, or it could be my wild imagination because he called me out. So…" He flopped into an easy chair. "Which is it?"

"Mmm." Xanthe sat behind her desk and thought about it. "It could be both. Now, tell me about Tony."

Cabot registered the change in topic and his face brightened. "We had dinner at *The Bay Marina* last night."

"Did you talk?"

"A lot."

"About your family?"

"Ah…" The air left him. "Yes…"

"Mention names?"

Horror replaced the smile. "God no."

She noticed. "Not ready to?"

"Not if my name's Darren Holbrook."

"Not introducing him to family yet?"

"Should I?"

"No."

"Then why did you ask?"

*****

Alena caught up with James on Skype that night. "Hi, how's it been?"

"Good, and you?" It was morning in New York, and he lounged on his bed.

She told him about the centre and the grand opening, how her sister and cousin had really stepped up, and now it made her want to do something else besides sing and design clothes. "We do support charities with *HOS*, as does most of the family's businesses, but I want to do more."

675

"Like what?" James munched on some crisps. "Work for the poor, homeless shelters, animal shelters, hand out food?"

She shrugged. "I dunno. Haven't put that much thought into it, just been feeling that I want to do more."

"Feeling outdone by your sister?" He grinned. "Not back to that, are we?"

A giggle escaped her. "No, it's not like that. I just think with everything that's happened this year, that we should, *I* should, give back because I'm grateful I'm alive. Alexis, Cabot, Danté are alive. They're the ones who were attacked, not me. But I want to repay the universe for keeping them alive."

"How *is* Danté? His leg okay?"

"He's got holes in it, or I should say, little craters from where bits were taken out. It's still pretty gross, stitch lines and lumps and bumps. He gets physio for it."

"It could take a while for it to settle down," James said. "At least the shark didn't bite his head."

"Yeah, I guess." Alena yawned. "Oh, God, I'm tired and it's only early evening."

"Too much worrying about your family. Have you been helping out at the centre?"

"Yep. And it's been busy, with the grand opening yesterday. We worked all day, every day, so no wonder I'm tired."

"So, the thing to do then, is to decide who or what you want to help next?"

"Yeah, I guess. I'm not touring, I have enough songs for next year, and film clips are all done. *HOS* is a day a week, and I'm not doing much else right now."

"What about helping shark attack victims?"

"So far it's only been Danté."

"What about gunshot victims?" he pushed.

"No one's been shot in my family except Mama thirty years ago." She glanced at the screen. "Oh, God, sorry."

He was grinning. "Don't be. But maybe you could help brain-injury people?"

"Maybe. I don't know. I'll have to look at what's on Mykonos and decide, depending on what's missing."

"You know what's missing in New York?"

"What?"

"You."

The blush rushed across her chest, up her neck, and onto her face.

"I would like to see you again, and not just on a computer screen," he said softly. "Maybe you can tell me more about you and your family. Your grandfather having your mother shot in 1977 must have been a horrible experience for her."

Alena frowned. "How did you know about that?" She pulled her legs up and knelt on the bed in front of her laptop.

"Know what?" he asked ever so innocently.

"Know that my mother was shot in 1977 by her father? I never told you the details. Hell, I didn't even know them at the time of the tour."

He shrugged. "I dunno. Maybe I read it somewhere online. You sure you didn't tell me?" Confusion rained down over him.

"Why would I? I only found out last month."

"Oh, well, I don't know. Like I said, I must've read it somewhere."

"I better go," Alena said. "Bye James."

"So soon," he cried. "We just got on."

"Yeah, I gotta go, bye." She logged off.

"Bye," he mumbled miserably.

Out in the hallway, Giancarlo had been listening and frowning, as his son had not only been talking to Alena, but had brought up information he couldn't possibly know. There was no way James could know that unless he'd seen the papers again, or he was remembering.

*****

"Are you ready for today's therapy session?" Xanthe asked Cabot as he sat in her office and threw a leg over the arm of the chair.

"What's so special about today's session?" His leg swung from side to side.

"Antonio's joining us." She waited.

Surprise flitted over his face. "What! Tony? Why?"

"So, the two of you can resolve whatever conflicts you have and move past them."

"So…" He thought about his issues. "How long will it take?"

"As long as it takes." She watched him get up and pace around the house while waiting for his brother. He was uneasy, nervous. The session would be a long one, possibly hours, but after everything she had seen and heard, she knew it was time for the two of them to talk it out. Or scream it out. The chat she'd had with Antonio two days previously let her know what he was feeling, and that he was all for helping his brother get through his shit. She'd also talked to Tomas and Roger in regards to Cabot's therapy, and they were willing to help as well.

Antonio came through the door and shut it behind him.

Cabot bounded into his arms. "Tonee."

"Cabot." Antonio stood there looking at Xanthe for a sign of what to do.

Xanthe simply moved from the office into the lounge room. "Come sit down, you two, and let's get started."

Clinging to his brother, Cabot led Antonio to the couch and sat beside him, clutching his hand as though his life depended on it.

Antonio saw Xanthe frown at it and removed his hand from Cabot's.

Cabot stared at his brother, wondering why he'd let go.

"Now, let's begin. I want each of you to tell the other how you feel about him. Not about the sex life, or after dark activities; just how you feel about each other as brothers."

"I love you, Tone." Cabot grasped his hand again. "You're my brother, my twin, my other half, my soul mate. You're there for me when I need you, you love me regardless of what I say or do, you pick me up when I'm down, you make me laugh and cry and scream and shout, but even when we fight you still love me. And I love you for that. You're my best friend, my brother, my partner in crime. You've been there every step of the way from Mama's womb to…" he pouted, "me getting HIV. You were there for me, Tone, even when I didn't want to admit it. You were there for me and I would be lost without you. Even though Uncle Tomas and Roger are teaching me how to do things, so I can become independent, I'd still be lost without you. Like having my leg cut off. I'd hate it. And I'd hate it if you went away."

"Even if you get a boyfriend, or Antonio gets a girlfriend?" Xanthe asked.

Cabot blinked in thought. "Just because we get partners doesn't mean he'll go away. We'll still be together. We're brothers, so we'll always be together."

"You don't know that, Cabot," Antonio said softly. "Yes, we've been together for twenty-five years, but that's not to say we will be for another twenty-five. What if I want to go and live in Australia with our family? Or I might move to London or Paris and get myself a Parisian wife."

"Then I'd come with you, Tone," Cabot told him. "Just coz we get partners doesn't mean we can't be in each other's lives."

"Antonio, tell Cabot how you feel." Xanthe nodded her encouragement.

Letting out a sigh from the pit of his stomach, Antonio stuck to the rules Xanthe had set. "I do love you, Cabot. You're my brother, my *only* brother, and if anything happened to you I'd feel empty and alone, and probably feel guilty for the rest of my life for not doing something, *anything*, to keep you alive. I…ah…" Shaking his head, he looked down at his lap. "As much as you've become a pain in the backside, I would hate it if anything happened to you. You're my brother. I love you. And while I do want a life and friends and a girlfriend, I would hate it if you were out of my life completely. I don't think I could bear it if you were gone from my life completely."

Cabot wiped his falling tears away and gripped Antonio's hand harder.

"Now, tell Cabot what you want for your future," Xanthe urged.

"I…" He stared at the ceiling, trying to gather his thoughts. "I want a girlfriend. I want to fall in love, be a dad one day, and maybe get married, though that's not so important. Travel the world without fanfare, celebrity, people wanting me, pulling me left and right, spend time with the family, maybe get into another career like Mama, Diana, Alexis, you." He looked at his brother who didn't look like his brother and squeezed his hand. "I'm proud of you for what you've done in the last month. I'm proud that you've stepped up. And with a lot of therapy, you've come a long way, Cabot. You've finally admitted you're gay, you finally admitted you have HIV, you're getting help for your assault and dealing with a lifelong disease. You're really maturing, Cabot, and I'm proud of you for that."

"Naw, thanks, Tone." Cabot smiled brightly through his tears. He loved getting praise from his brother because his brother meant the world to him.

"Okay, this next part is where you both be honest about the things you don't like about each other. Use any language you want, but be totally, absolutely, brutally honest. It's the *only* way things will be resolved," Xanthe said. "Cabot, why don't you go first."

"Okay, um…" He pulled faces while trying to think of things. "I don't really dislike anything Tone's done. He's always been awesome to me. He's friendly, gets along with people, never fights, mmm, nuh, nothing."

"Has he ever said anything or done anything that hurt you, or *to* hurt you?" Xanthe asked.

"Well…" Shame fled across his face. "The last few months before we came here, he started telling me how ashamed he was of my behaviour."

"Which behaviour?" Xanthe pushed.

The shame deepened. "My…sexual behaviour."

"What did he say?"

Cabot quickly glanced at his brother who was staring straight ahead and not looking at him. "That he was ashamed of me, disgusted with what I did." His head bowed.

"And what did you do?"

"I…ah…" Cabot bent forward, curling into himself. "Screwed a lot of men."

"Are you ashamed of that?" Xanthe asked.

"Now, I kinda am."

"But at the time?"

He shrugged. "I was just living life. Having fun doing what my father did."

"Your father never had sex with men, or got HIV," Xanthe reminded him. "You need to stop using him as an excuse for your own behaviour."

"Yeah," Cabot mumbled, "And I…I kinda have. It's not about Papa anymore."

"No, it isn't. It's about Cabot and *his* actions and what he, *you*, can do to change them. Only *you* are responsible for your actions, Cabot."

"Yes, Xanthe, so you've told me." He rolled his eyes.

"Did it hurt when Antonio told you he was ashamed?"

"Yes." His eyes lowered.

"Antonio, why don't you tell Cabot how you feel about his sexual behaviour and what it does to you."

"It disgusts me," Antonio said quietly, staring straight ahead so he didn't have to look at his brother. "When we were younger we dated girls, and that was fine. We double dated, we dated on our own, but once we flew to New York to live, it all changed. Once he hit the New York scene, it all changed. He went from being into women, to being into men too. At first, it was a shock to see him kiss a man. He's my twin, I'd never seen him like that, never seen him with a man. Next thing I know, he's having sex with them. After the shock died off, I realised, that if he *was* gay, that was okay. But he never actually spoke to me about it, never sat me down and told me he was gay, or into men, or men *and* women. And all of a sudden he was snorting coke and smoking pot and fucking men and women in public places, in alleyways, hallways, toilets, bathrooms, and half the time I was there. But this year, I was around just to keep him in line. Standing over him like a guard on the lookout. It was horrible, degrading, embarrassing, humiliating. We'd been so close for so long and all of a sudden I'm watching him having sex, or having his cock sucked. It was just…" He thrust up from his seat and paced around the room. "Revolting."

"Are you ashamed of me, Tonee?" Cabot asked in his child-like tone, feeling his cheeks burn with his brother's shame.

"Yes, Cabot, I am." Antonio knew he had to get it all out, so Cabot could deal with whatever the underlying issue was. "I am so bloody ashamed." Tears sprang to his eyes. "Do you have any idea how *I* felt standing there watching you fuck men?" The rage built slowly, like a volcano preparing itself. "How it made *me* feel? Did you even *care* how I felt? Did you even comprehend *how disgusting* your behaviour was, and that you'd made *me* a part of it?" The lava built, and his body shook. It was time for him to let it out. "I was *so sickened* by what I saw, by what I did, but I know that if I walked away you'd do something stupid like coke yourself to death, and I was supposed to be looking after you." His voice rose as the lava reached the top. "What would Mama and Papa say if you killed yourself on *my* watch? If you did it while *I* wasn't looking?"

The frenetic pacing grew. "How do you think *I* felt, Cabot?" he screamed. "How do you think *I felt* finding my brother, *my twin brother*, trying to kill himself because he couldn't tell me he had HIV? How do you think *I felt* knowing there was something wrong with you, but you couldn't even talk to me about it? How do you think *I felt* having to look after you and your irresponsible behaviour all these years? Do you *even know*, Cabot? *Do you even care?* Did you *ever once* stop to care about me and how I felt? *No,* because you're a selfish, self-centred, self-obsessed, self-absorbed, narcissistic little cunt who only gives a fuck about his-fucking-self." Antonio had the finger pointing happening while tears were pouring down his face.

Cabot was highly distraught, having never heard his brother speak to him this way. Tears poured down his face, his heart breaking at his brother's words. "Tonee…"

"Don't you dare," Antonio spat. "Don't you dare make this about you, you selfish cunt. I *hate* what you did, Cabot. *I hated* all of the fucking you did that *I* had to watch, or see, or stand over, while you did it. Like *I wanted* to see my brother, *my twin brother*, shoving his cock up some guy's fucking ass. Like *I wanted* to see my brother, *my twin brother*, shove his fucking cock in some guy's fucking mouth. I don't want to see you get sucked off, Cabot. I didn't want to watch over you, but I knew that if I didn't, Mama and Papa would be disappointed *in me.* They were already disappointed in *you.* I didn't want them to be disappointed in me too. I felt so fucking guilty. So much fucking guilt for hating you. Because I hated you, Cabot. For the last few years, I have come to hate your guts because of what you've done. *I hate* what you've done. *I hated* having to watch it, *I hated you* for doing it."

"Tonee, no," Cabot wailed. "Don't hate me, Tonee, please don't hate me. I love you, you're my brother, I love you, and I don't want you to hate me, Tonee. Please," he sobbed, and crawled over to his brother, clinging to his legs. "I don't want you to hate me. I love you, I can't live without you, Tonee."

"Well, you're going to have to, Cabot." Antonio saw Xanthe's nod. "Because I don't want to be around you anymore. I don't want to work with you, I don't want to be Phoenix Stefan anymore. I don't want to model. I don't know what I want to do, but *I* don't want to do it with *you.*"

Great gasping sobs went through Cabot. "Tonee, no. I love you, you can't leave me. I can't live without you."

"Well, you're gonna have to learn, Cabot. Because my name is Antonio DeLuca Stephanopoulos, and I *no longer* want to a model. I *no longer* want to share my life with my twin brother. I *no longer* want to be a part of your life." His heart was dead; broken into a billion pieces at what he was feeling, saying and doing.

"Tonee, no." Cabot pulled at Antonio's sweater. "You had no problem with my lifestyle when you participated in the penthouse that weekend. You loved it," he accused his brother. "You loved getting your cock sucked by a man."

"It disgusted me," Antonio screamed down at his brother who cowered on the floor from his wrath. "I was on pot and drunk, and most men like getting their cock sucked, and it just happened to be sucked by a man. A man whose ass you had your own cock up. You didn't mind fucking him while he sucked me off. Hell, you probably thought it was me you were fucking."

Cabot shrank back in horror, swiping at his face. He had come without the contacts or glasses as Xanthe had warned him. "Tonee, no…" he choked.

"Stop whining," Antonio screamed. "That's all you do, Cabot. Is whine. Whine my name, whine about this, whine about that. That's all you do outside of fucking. When are you going to stop? When are you going to grow up? Why is it that you and I are twins, but for some God only known reason, I matured, and you didn't? You stayed a bratty little shit who never grew up. I hate what you've become, Cabot. I hate what *I* have become. I hate the fact it's tearing us apart. That it's torn *you* apart because you throw a tantrum in Grandma's house and she slapped you, so you had to go and get drunk and get fucked, and now you have HIV for the rest of your fucking life because you threw a fucking tantrum. How fucking stupid can you be, Cabot? All the years we were told about HIV, all the years we had safe sex drummed into our heads, all the years you didn't care and did what you wanted and fucked up your life. How could you be so fucking stupid? You're a moron, a retard, a fuckwit."

The lava was well and truly flowing out of him as explosion after explosion came hurtling out. "I hate what you've done, Cabot. You're a dumb cunt who didn't do as he was told because he was so fucking arrogant he thought he knew better, and he went and got himself HIV. Congratu-fucking-lations, you dumb cunt, you got yourself HI fucking V because of your fucking arrogance. How *could* you, Cabot? How could you do that to yourself? To your family? To *me*?" He stared down at his cowering, broken-hearted, sobbing mess of a brother. "And *I* was the one who searched the city for you. *I* was the one you called to say goodbye to because *you* were trying to kill yourself. *I* was the one who raced to find you to save you."

He broke down in sobs on the floor. "How could you do that to me? How could you call me to tell me you loved me and that you were ending it all? How could you do that, Cabot? How could you think of no one except yourself? How could you not even think of your own twin brother? The person who had to find you and try and save you from killing yourself, you selfish, dumb cunt. *I hate you*, Cabot." His body jerked with the pain of hearing his brother trying to kill himself. "I hate you for trying to kill yourself, I hate you for making me watch over you. I hate myself for not walking away. I hate you for getting HIV. Why did you do that to me?" He stared forlornly at his whimpering brother. "How could you do that to me?" Squeezing his eyes tight, he gasped as he cried, bending until his forehead touched the carpet.

"Tonee." Cabot was torn apart. "I'm so sorry, Tonee." His brother, his one and only brother, hated him, and he couldn't live with that. Shifting over to him on his knees, he smoothed Antonio's hair. "Tonee, I'm sorry. That was the old me. I'm sorry. I can never make it up to you. Don't hate me, Tonee, Please don't hate me. I couldn't stand it if you hated me. It would kill me. Don't hate me, don't leave me."

"Still talking about yourself." Antonio rose from the floor. "*Still* thinking about yourself, you selfish cunt. I hate you, Cabot, and I never want to see you again." Getting to his feet, he headed for the door, slamming his way out and running next door to the open arms of his uncle Tomas who pulled him inside.

"Let it out, sweetie, let it out." He held his nephew tightly while Roger closed the door. They had been waiting as Xanthe had asked, ready to help their nephews.

"No, Tonee," Cabot screamed through his blinding tears. He stumbled for the door, falling to his knees at it while Xanthe locked it. It was time to unlock the door in his head. "Tonee, Tonee don't leave me, I love you, come back. I'll kill myself if you leave me. Come back, Tonee, I love you." He collapsed into a sobbing heap. "I love you."

Xanthe stood over him, watching him sob for a few moments. "Come, Cabot, come and sit."

"Tonee, no, Tonee." His sobs lessened, and he allowed Xanthe to help him back into the lounge room. He curled up in the corner of the sofa. "Tonee." His body shook with sobs and gasps, and he curled into himself, arms around legs, knees under chin. "Tonee, don't leave me, I love you."

Xanthe sat beside him. "Yes, you do love him, don't you, Cabot?"

"Yes."

She gently rubbed his back. "You love him so much you'd kill yourself if he ever left you."

"Yes."

"Yet you tried to kill yourself and leave him behind."

Gasping, he barely glanced at her. "I know."

"And telling someone you'd kill yourself if they left you, is something a lover would say."

"I love Tonee," he wailed softly.

"Yes, like a lover. But he's not your lover, Cabot," Xanthe said gently.

"I want him to be, I love him," Cabot whined in his delusional screwed up state.

"You want to share your life with him?"

"Yes."

"In work, in play, in bed?"

"Yes."

"Do you love him that much, Cabot? That you want him to be your lover?"

Confused sobs followed. "Yes. I love him."

"Because he loves you?"

"Yes."

"Unconditionally, all these years?"

"Yes."

"Regardless of what you did, what you said, he was there, by your side, loving you unconditionally, for all your faults and flaws?"

"Argh." Rocking back and forth, he buried his head, confusion flying thick and fast through his brain as he tried to comprehend what he was feeling, thinking and saying.

"You just want someone to love you unconditionally, don't you?"

"Yes."

"And because you were always together, it ended up being Antonio that those feelings went to. Oh, sweetie. No wonder you had sex with so many people, you confused it all in your head." Giving him a hug, she sat for a few moments. "Everything you ever wanted to find in a man was in Antonio. And everything you ever wanted in a man to love you, was what Antonio gave you. So, you go looking for it in a man and can't find it in anyone *except* Antonio, so that's where it stayed. Stagnant in brotherly love. And you confused it all. All of these men you fucked you were trying to find an Antonio alternative. Someone exactly like him because you couldn't have him, because he's your brother. It's called transference. The love you wanted from a man or woman you got from Antonio, but you wanted to find that unconditional love elsewhere and never could. That's why you've done what you've done. That's why you went through women and then men. You were trying to find an Antonio that wasn't your brother, but you couldn't, so you kept on looking. Meanwhile, you became dependent upon your brother for doing the shopping, buying food, getting you to jobs, for physical bonding, emotional bonding. You relied upon him for everything, and yet in the moment you needed him most, first, you turn him away, and then you want him. Have you been ashamed of your love for your brother, Cabot?"

After a moment of thought, he looked up through swollen hooded lids. "Yes."

"Because you thought you were in love with your brother?"

"Yes." He lowered his eyes in shame.

"Well, I'm here to tell you you're not. And you're okay. Everything will work itself out now. All you did was transfer your wants and needs in a partner onto your brother because he was always around and loved you the way you wanted a mate to love you. You transferred your feelings onto him and the pot and coke would have made it worse. But this is not you, Cabot." Pushing his hair aside, she smiled encouragingly. "There is no need to be ashamed for what a lot of people do; transfer feelings onto the most convenient person, instead of finding the person they need. It's like that with some women. They get what they need emotionally from best friends, they get what they want sexually from their husbands, or boyfriends. Just because you're emotionally attached to someone, doesn't mean you're in love with them. You and Antonio share a very special bond. You came from one egg and one sperm. You are twins all the way. And you will always have that special bond and love one another until the days you die. But it doesn't mean you're *in* love. You've gotten everything screwed up in your head, and so the shame made you fuck those men, trying to find someone just like Antonio to take his place. You've just been confused all this time and too ashamed to talk to anyone. Have you ever told Antonio how you feel?"

Cabot wiped his nose on his sleeve. "I always tell him I love him."

"That you're *in* love with him?"

"Oh, fuck no! He'd hate me and think I'm some deranged fuck and never want to see me again. But then," the tears flowed again, "he doesn't anyway."

"Don't worry about that. I will fix it. I promise you. What we need to do now is work on you. You've become too emotionally dependant on Antonio for love. We need to get you back on track, so you can get rid of all the crap in your head. Now, I have some papers for you to read." She collected them from the office and handed them over. "There's no need to be ashamed anymore, Cabot. We've broken through that barrier and you can let it all go. I want you to stay here for the rest of the day, so we can talk about it. In the meantime, I'll make some tea. We need sustenance."

Wiping his face and nose, Cabot read the title on the first page, *Transference of Partner Love onto Brotherly Love*. He began to read with interest.

*****

"I feel like crap," Antonio said as he lay curled up in Tomas's arms.

"Isn't that what Xanthe wanted?" Tomas hugged him. "For the two of you to get into a screaming match and for you to tell him you're done with him?"

"Yeah," Antonio sniffled. "Doesn't mean I liked it."

"But if it makes Cabot better, then it was worth it. Right?" Roger set down the tray of cups and teapot. "We stood listening; it was a hell of a match. You did most of the screaming."

"I can't believe I called him what I did." Antonio's eyes were blurry, red and sore from all the tears shed. "I was horrible, and I was screaming at *him* for being horrible. How could I?"

"If it makes him better, as Roger said, then he will come out on the other side, and hopefully, Xanthe can break through to whatever was holding him back," Tomas said.

"Yeah, I guess." Antonio sat up and rubbed his right eye. "I'd better go. I don't want to be here when he gets home."

"Xanthe said she'll keep him all day. He's going to need intensive therapy," Roger told him. "You're welcome to stay for lunch."

"I'm not hungry." Antonio sipped his tea, but his stomach grumbled, betraying his words. "Okay, I guess I am."

"We made a big pot of soup, so it will fill up that empty stomach of yours. It will be ready shortly." Tomas grinned and squeezed his nephew's hand. "He *will* be okay."

*****

Xanthe counselled Cabot all day, draining him emotionally, physically, mentally. He talked, she listened. She talked, he listened. She gave the advice he needed to get through the rest of his life. Ordering in pizza for dinner, he picked at it, hungry, but not having the energy to eat.

"Take it home," she said. "And keep it for later, you may need your strength."

"What for?" He yawned, worn out from the day.

"Because I want you to do something for me."

"What?"

"I want you to go to your uncles, go into their studio, and paint."

"What! I can't paint." Cabot stared glassily at her. His eyeballs were coated in desert sand and blurry.

"I know. But this is the therapy. They have laid out canvases for you on the floor, plus paint and brushes, and I want you to go and do whatever your mind tells you too. It doesn't matter if it's good or crap; the point is to see what your mind, heart and soul is telling you."

"And then what do I do?"

"You take all the time you need, and if you fall asleep, you fall asleep. While we're getting everything out of your head, you can use the paint to draw what's in your head. So, let's get you home." She helped him to his feet, unlocked the door and took him next door. "They won't be home until later, so you'll be alone to paint. Will you be okay?" She handed over the pizza box.

"I'll be okay, Xanthe, I promise." Taking the box with him, he shut the door and went upstairs, finding the studio empty except for the canvases, tarps, and painting supplies on the floor. He threw down the box and stood staring at it all. "What the fuck am I supposed to do with this?" Running both hands through his hair, he breathed and opened the windows, sucking back the cool ocean breeze. It cleared his head and made his stomach rumble. He grabbed a piece of pizza from the box, and walked around the room. Tomas and Roger had removed all of their paintings from the wall, thrown down the tarps, and left a bunch of supplies. Digging into another slice, he stared down at the canvases.

"*Paint what's in your head,*" Xanthe's words floated through his brain.

After finishing off a third piece of pizza, he grabbed the red and black paint and a medium sized canvas.

*****

"Antonio, sweetie, are you okay?" Vivian asked her son at dinner. They were at Jenny's where they always were.

"Tired." With half cast eyes he finished off his food.

She got up and felt his forehead. "Are you coming down with something?"

"No, Mama, just exhausted from Xanthe's session with Cabot." He gently pushed her hand away.

"How did it go?" Viv asked, worried for both of her sons. Antonio didn't look good, and if he didn't look good, things must have been bad.

"I hope it went well. But Xanthe said not to expect changes for a while. It has to sink in, and he has to digest it before changes can start taking place."

"I hope for Cabot's sake everything she's doing is working." Jenny studied Antonio's face. "It looks as if it half killed you."

Antonio glanced up through swollen eyes. "It did, and I hate it. I *hated it.* I hated what Xanthe made me do, and *I hated* the way it made me feel. *Like fucking shit!*" he sobbed, resting his head in his hands and making the rest of the family come to a halt. "She said she was going to fix it, but I don't know how. I feel like shit for what I had to say and do."

"But if it makes him better?" Jenny went to his side at the kids' table. "If all of this makes him better, makes him a man, a capable man, who can live life successfully despite having HIV, isn't it worth it?"

His head shook. "I don't know, Grandma. I just don't know."

Jenny hugged him fiercely. "I hope for the both of your sakes, she can fix this."

"Oh, my baby." Viv rubbed his back, tears in her eyes. "Let's get you home, you look exhausted. You must be exhausted. Let's get you into bed, come on."

He allowed his parents to take him home and tuck him into bed.

Finishing off their meals, Jenny turned to Tomas and Roger. "What *did* happen today?"

They traded glances before Tomas spoke. "Mount Vesuvius."

"Mount Krakatoa," Roger said.

"Mount St Helens," Tomas added.

"A volcano?" Jenny said dryly, drinking the last of her wine. "From who?"

Another glance. "Antonio," they both replied.

Jenny's brows rose. "Well, that's a surprise. Although it shouldn't be." Pushing her plate away, she stood and walked over to her recliner, falling into it in relief. "Obviously it's been building up for years in Antonio. We should have stepped in sooner."

"At least they're only twenty-five," Spiros told her as he sat in his matching recliner. "They still have time to grow up and be young men."

"True. Let's hope Xanthe's done her job," Jenny replied. "What's the plan for Cabot now?"

"Painting." Tomas grinned and sat on the couch between his parents' chairs.

"You're kidding?" Pedro asked, coming into the lounge room. "Please tell me you're kidding?"

"Nope. Xanthe asked us to lay out canvases and paint for him to come home to. She wants him to get everything out of him, his head, his soul, his body, so she can rebuild him from scratch. We'll see what's happened when we get home." Tomas finished off his water and got up for a refill.

"Do we know if painting will work?" Jenny asked. "I hope you didn't leave all of yours in the studio."

"We took them down and put them in the storeroom, so if he makes a mess, it won't damage anything," Roger told her as Tomas took his seat beside him on the couch.

"If it gets Cabot back on track, then we're right there beside him helping him," Tomas said. "I have no problems doing that."

After a night of enjoying themselves, Tomas and Roger walked into their home around two in the morning. They had spent some time at *SB3* enjoying Pedro's night, and reminiscing about where they were when they first heard a song or danced to it. All was quiet, the lights were out downstairs, and they wondered what awaited them. Flicking on the lights in each room to check the windows were locked, they didn't find anything out of order. Walking upstairs and into their bedroom and studio space, they found the studio lights on and Cabot asleep on the floor surrounded by painted canvases. They stared down at them, worried by what they meant. Lots of black, lots of red. And a peaceful Cabot on the floor.

"Can you go and get the spare mattress and blow it up?" Tomas softly asked Roger. "I don't want to leave him on the cold floor all night."

Within minutes, the mattress was ready next to their bed in the bedroom, and Tomas had thrown down a sheet over it, and gathered a quilt and pillows.

"Are you going to move him?" Roger whispered.

"Yes, carefully." Tomas gently rolled his nephew into a sitting position. Seeing paint all over his jumper, he pulled it over his head and left it on the floor. Cabot's hands were stained black and red but were dry. "Come on, Cabot, time for bed," Tomas murmured as he and Roger got under each arm and lifted him. Half walking, half carrying him, they laid him on the mattress and removed his boots and jeans.

Not waking, he curled up on his right side and Tomas tucked him in. "Sweet dreams, Cabot." He gently kissed his temple and stroked his hair while his breathing calmed.

Roger quickly tidied up and took the empty pizza box downstairs and threw it in the bin, returning to find Tomas had locked the windows and turned down their bed. After changing, they snuggled up together, both facing Cabot to keep a close eye on him with the light on low.

At some point, Cabot woke. It was still dark out, but the light was softly glowing in the room. Glancing around, he saw his uncles in bed and the studio was dark. Exhausted, he gathered the quilt around him and wiggled like a worm over to the bed, where he slowly rose to the bed edge to see if his uncle was awake. With wide eyes, he rose higher to check on Roger, then slid down and sideways along the bed to look at Tomas. His right arm extended out from the quilt and poked Tomas in the face, then quickly slid back and he retreated to the left.

Sensing someone was beside him, Tomas woke with a start and saw two blue eyes peering out of a cloud of quilt. "Cabot?"

He blinked slowly, looking like E.T. "I didn't want to wake you. I just…"

"Hey." Tomas cupped his face with his right hand. "It's okay, what?"

Another blink. "I didn't want to be alone."

"You're not alone." Tomas smiled at his nephew.

Cabot clung to the quilt. "But I need a hug."

Pulling back the covers, Tomas urged Cabot to get in and then flung the layers of bedding over both of them.

Cabot snuggled up to Tomas tightly, not wanting to let go.

"It's okay, you sleep some more," Tomas stroked his hair back from his forehead. "You're not alone, Cabot."

In the morning, Roger woke to find Cabot clinging to Tomas. He left them both alone to shower and dress, then went downstairs to start a breakfast of hot omelettes with lots of meat and vegetables, and a pot of hot coffee. *Strong and dark like my Tomas.* Roger grinned at the thought.

Before putting out the omelettes, he went upstairs and woke Tomas, who carefully disentangled himself from Cabot, exchanging himself for a pillow. He grabbed a quick shower and joined Roger for breakfast.

It was lunchtime when Cabot woke. Sighing and stretching his weary muscles, he looked around and realised where he was. *How'd I get here? I didn't come to bed, did I?*

Rolling over, he saw he was in his uncle's bed and there was a mattress and quilt on the floor beside him. "Oh, my God, how'd I end up here?" Grabbing his jeans and boots, he slipped them on, found his jumper in the studio, and glared down at the paintings.

"Fuck!" Not dealing with them, he went to his room, showered and changed, and found Tomas and Roger downstairs.

"Hey, you okay?" Tomas asked, closing the book he was reading by the window.

"Tired." Cabot scratched his head. "But…lighter."

"You dealt with your issue?" Roger asked. "And are you hungry?"

"Starving." Cabot grinned. "And yeah, I think I finally sorted out my issue."

"Good. Xanthe told us to call her when you woke so she can talk about those paintings of yours." Tomas watched him carefully.

Cabot blanched, and his arms crossed. "You saw them."

"Hard not to."

"Yeah, I guess."

"Lunch is ready," Roger called and ladled hot steaming soup into three bowls. "Hot bread's in the grill if you want it."

While Roger laid the bowls out, Tomas grabbed the bread, and they enjoyed the ham and pea soup they'd made the day before.

Cabot had seconds and thirds of soup *and* bread, and then they called Xanthe to come over.

"So…" She stared down at the canvases on the floor in the studio. "Care to tell me what these all mean?"

Cabot stood enclosed, arms wrapped around himself, head buried in his sweater. "I don't know, I just…painted."

Xanthe examined each one, six in all, all covered in black and red paint. Some had a person painted in red, hands over face, while the background was black. Some had a red background with a black paint person covering their face. Others were of broken hearts. "Well, from what I can guess, you feel alone and broken-hearted, most likely to do with your brother."

"Yeah, and other stuff," he mumbled.

"What other stuff?" Xanthe's ears pricked up.

"Having HIV and being alone. The only one in the family to have it. Being an outsider because of it. Not being loved, or wanted, or needed by my family. My brother. That's him there." He pointed to a tiny little figure in the background of a painting that had another figure in the foreground covering his face. "He's left me and I'm all alone."

"Except you're not, you're still here, surrounded by family, including him."

Cabot was miserable. "Not anymore."

"You might be surprised," Xanthe said. "Who broke your heart?"

"No one, everyone," Cabot murmured. "It's all part of feeling alone."

"Do you feel *that* isolated from your family?" she asked, seeing the forlorn expression on his face.

After a few moments, a reply came. "Yes."

"Why?"

He shrugged and looked down at the six paintings. "I've been away from them working, growing, changing, it's changed me and they don't like the person I became. So, I...they stopped loving me and isolated me."

"You were going to say something else," Xanthe prodded.

"Yeah..." He moved to the window and flung it open. "I isolated myself from them. Is that what you wanted to hear?" Resting his right foot on his left, he leaned against the window, staring at the ocean, trying to take comfort.

"Why did you isolate yourself?"

"Because I was free to become the person I wanted to be and they didn't like it, *like me*, so I stayed away from them."

"Isolated yourself from everyone but Antonio?"

"Yeah, and now my behaviour has isolated me from him and him from me. *My* behaviour has isolated everyone."

"Why?"

He frowned and turned his head to her. "Why? Why have I isolated everyone?"

"Yes."

"Didn't I just say why?" Another shrug, which he did a lot and had become a habit. His gaze flitted to the paintings. "I don't really know. It's a combination of the hypocrisy of my father being a porn star, and then not wanting me to have sex. It was me trying to find myself in a family of bigwig producers and musicians and models. It was me trying to find my way through puberty and life as a twin. As much as I love Antonio and love being with him, I also wanted to be me. That's why I changed it up. I wore my shirts undone, pranced around, wore bandannas and jewellery and painted my nails, did what I thought was cool to fit in while also finding myself." Rubbing his tear-filled eyes, he went on. "I just wanted to find myself and fit into a family of superstars. Make my mark and my name without help from anyone else. I just wanted to be myself."

"And have you found yourself yet?"

He shook his head. "No. I'm getting there, though, I think."

"Why go into modelling? Your mother and sister did it, why you?"

A sigh came from him. "Because *they* did it. We were tall, good-looking kids, were extras in our father's films, got modelling jobs, sprouted to six feet by sixteen, and had everyone lapping at our feet."

"So, you had people telling you how fabulous you were at a young age, you didn't have time to go through puberty, let alone find yourself?"

"And yet Uncle Pedro knew he wanted to be a DJ at eighteen and was one. He was playing at *Studio 69* at twenty years of age for God's sake. Diana wanted to be like Mama her whole life, and she is. Alena wanted to be in charge of everything and everyone and sang her whole life. Dom and Danté grew up around music and wanted to do what Pedro and Angie do. But now Danté's also into the internet and runs all of our websites. He and Nick are little IT ninjas, so he's got that and photography. *And* he raps. Alexis didn't know what she wanted to do until just recently. She sings, writes songs, designs for *HOS*, models for them, basically everything Alena did she had to do too. But it wasn't until the centre that she found something else away from the family business. Although it's *in* the family business. And Uncle Tomas was always a trainer, and he and Roger have the gym, and now that AIDS centre in Miami. But what do Tony and I have? Nothing except for looking pretty."

"You and Alexis share the centre," Xanthe reminded him. "Is that something you want to go into more? Or how about helping Roger and Tomas with their centre when they go to Miami?"

"I don't know." He wandered aimlessly around the room. "I don't know what I want to do. What *can I* do outside of modelling? I don't sing, I don't DJ, I don't dance, although I get out on the floor. I don't write books. I don't write songs or play instruments, I don't make music. All I know is how to model clothes, jewellery, cars, whatever. Put something in front of me and I can model it."

"Okay." Xanthe pointed to his paintings. "Model one of those."

"What?" He saw her serious face. "Oi! Okay." Picking up a canvas, he set to work modelling, pouting, throwing his head back, posing. "See, I told you."

She was amused, highly curious, and nodded. "I'm impressed. You definitely can model anything. That's a talent in itself. But what else do you want to do?"

"Oh, I don't know, take the rest of the year to figure it out. I've got a trust fund, so I don't know." His hands rested backwards on his hips and he slowly walked around the room. "Do I *need* to decide now? I'm tired."

"No, I guess you don't. But these paintings have said a lot about you, Cabot. You're not alone, you never were, life can get in the way sometimes, and between what your family wanted, what your parents expected, and what *you* wanted and needed, it just all got jumbled up in your head. But now that it's clear, hopefully, life will be too. Take the rest of the year off, be with your family. Spend Christmas, New Year, Thanksgiving, Halloween with them and just learn to appreciate them for who they are. They did their best, now *you* need to, and don't worry, I'll have a chat with your parents and grandparents about cutting the apron strings. You have to stand on your own two feet now you're an adult. And while you've made stupid choices, you need to deal with the consequences of those choices, and that is making you grow up very quickly. So, I suggest you rest for the remainder of today. Stay in, don't go out; you're too emotionally vulnerable right now. Read, watch TV or DVDS, paint more if you want. You're actually quite good. Maybe you can do that?"

"Like Uncle Tomas and Roger?" His arms wrapped themselves

around him like a safety blanket.

"Why not? Why don't you surf the internet and look for different jobs that you might like to do, or something that might interest you like working with animals or other HIV infected people."

"I can barely deal with myself right now, let alone help others with it," he told her as they walked downstairs.

"Then have a read of the papers I brought you." Digging them out of her bag, she handed them over. "Read thoroughly. It's a step program that you might like to partake in. Pick which steps you'd like to do, and then follow through. It might make you feel good to start making amends."

"Yeah," he murmured, scanning the paper. "There's one I want to do now."

"And what's that?" Xanthe asked as they reached the lounge room and found Tomas and Roger waiting.

"Apologise," Cabot told her.

"To whom and what for?" she asked.

"To Uncles Tomas and Roger." Too embarrassed to look at them, he kept his eyes on the papers in his hands as they all stood waiting.

"What for?" Xanthe repeated.

"Um…back in July I called them something pretty horrible. I even called the guy who attacked me the same thing, but um…Uncle Tomas and Roger didn't deserve it. I was angry at Grandma, and then angry at Papa, and it all came spewing out and Grandma slapped me for it. So, um, I am sorry that I called you that name. I shouldn't have. I was angry for a bunch of reasons, and you were just the two I took it out on, and I'm sorry."

"Oh, Cabot. That's probably the most mature thing I've heard you say," Tomas told him. "Followed by what you've done with Alexis at the centre." He took Cabot into his arms. "Considering that's the only time you've said anything bad to us, I forgive you. I know the whole porn star thing seems hypocritical, but it was before any of you were born. It wasn't your career, it was ours for a while, but it's over. Thirty years ago, over." Pulling back, he held Cabot's face. "You're my nephew, I love you, I will help you through whatever you need help with. Thank you for apologising. That's a big step for you."

"And one he will be repeating," Xanthe said. "Amends needs to be made on both sides, and this is the start. I'll see you tomorrow morning before lunch and we'll sort something out then." She touched Cabot's arms. "Including Antonio."

*****

Antonio woke late, much later than normal. But then, since they were taking time out from work, normal wasn't normal anymore. Rolling onto his back, he stretched the muscles either side of his spine. His eyes were gritty and sore, his body weary. Staring at the ceiling, he barely registered that it was Saturday. Since they had been back in Mykonos, every day blurred into the next, and time didn't really matter. He didn't have to get up for work, didn't have to stay fit, look after himself, or anything. He could do what he wanted, when he wanted, and no one told him otherwise. But he knew. He knew his routine was shot and he needed to sort something out. He needed to sort his problems with Cabot out.

God, I hope Xanthe can fix things between me and Cabot. I really don't want to leave them like we did yesterday. I don't want to lose him; I'd hate it if we never saw each other again. He's my brother, my twin, and I want him in my life, just in a healthy way.

Sighing, he stared at the window, seeing daylight around the curtain. He didn't know what the time was, and didn't care.

There was a knock at the door. "Antonio?" Viv said softly.

"I'm awake," he called and grabbed the clock on his bedside cupboard to see what the time was.

Viv opened the door and saw him checking the time. "It's one p.m. are you okay?" Quietly moving to the bed, she sat beside him. "You okay, my sweetie?" She stroked his hair off his forehead.

"I'm okay, Mama. Worn out from yesterday still." As much as he was a grown-up, he still loved the attention from his parents.

"Hungry? I can make you something."

"Kinda. I could do with a bacon and egg roll or two."

"Then how about you have a shower and come out, unless you want lunch in bed?"

He grinned. "Nah, I need a shower. Think you can manage two rolls?"

"I'll make as many as you want." She kissed his cheek and left him to it.

Ten minutes later, after a hot shower and a good scrub, he settled at the dining table to two hot rolls and a steaming cup of coffee.

Carlos came from his home office where he had been working on a movie. "Hey, you didn't tell me we were having bacon rolls for lunch." He kissed the top of Antonio's head. "Hey kid, you doin' okay?" He accepted a plate with two rolls from Viv and sat next to his son.

"Worn out." Antonio finished off his first roll and drank some coffee. There was a touch of chocolate to it, and he knew his mother had made his favourite one.

"Still?" Carlos asked. "It must have been some session."

"You mean you didn't hear us?" Antonio cocked a brow. "I'd be surprised if the whole of Mykonos didn't hear us."

"Was it that bad?" Viv sat down with her own roll. "I've been so worried about Cabot that you've been left behind. I'm sorry, sweetie." Laying a hand on his arm she squeezed lightly. "We've left you behind. Are you okay? Do you need more therapy?"

"Probably," Antonio replied. "My problems are with Cabot and the life we've lived the last four or five years. I hope Xanthe will be able to fix the mess she caused because, for all of his stupid faults, I love him, and don't want him out of my life completely."

"Neither do we," Viv murmured. "I'm just sorry he had to contract HIV."

"It's a consequence of his actions and he has to deal with it," Carlos said. "You know what we all went through with Tomas and Roger. Thank God Dan was wrong with that diagnosis. Back then, just about every man that contracted it, died from it. But times are different, and so is the medication. He should be able to live healthily enough to last well past fifty."

"If he doesn't catch another disease like hepatitis, or some other

STD that will flatten his immune system leading way for opportunistic infections to get in the way," Antonio added. "He has to stay healthy to live longer." He finished off his coffee and stared at the cup. "What if he doesn't—"

"Don't say that," Viv rushed in to interrupt.

"It's possible," Carlos told her.

Running his hand through his hair, Antonio asked what everyone was doing.

"Relaxing day for most," Carlos said. "I think Dom, Danté and Nick are working on something IT or web related. I'm working on a movie, and the girls are at the centre, I think. What do you want to do?"

"Today, or for the rest of my life?" Antonio returned.

*****

Danté was behind his computer putting together the book interior he and Dom were making for their grandparents for Christmas. They had got emails back from the historical society in New York containing photos and links to their apartment building. "If Grandma's going to keep adding to the business," he said to Nick and Dom who were in his room, "shouldn't we do a book that can be added to?"

Dom was sorting out printouts and news clippings of all of their family's buildings on Danté's bed. "Are we able to find a printer who can do that? Who knows where it will stop? Just in the last few months alone Uncle Tomas's centre and now Alexis's centre have been added to the list."

"She already had that one," Danté reminded him, absentmindedly rubbing his shark-bitten leg as he stared at the screen. "And she has more that the family's not using; but are being rented to other people."

Nick noticed his best friend rubbing his leg. "That okay, dude? You rub it a lot. And how was all the girls checkin' you out at school." He glared daggers at Danté. "So jealous!"

Danté grinned. "Yeah, I've become the flavour of the week. It won't last long."

"It still hurt?" Nick asked.

"Aches," Danté replied. "Especially when I've sat for too long, which I obviously have." He spun around in his gas lift office chair to speak to Dom. "Do we have photos of *every* building she owns in Mykonos?"

"Yep." Dom straightened and his back cracked, making Nick flinch and pull a face. "Grandma owns twenty buildings here on the island, and one in Athens."

"*Stefan Productions*," Danté murmured.

"Yep. The rest are homes, these six, plus office spaces, and the businesses."

"Geez, regular entrepreneur your grandma is," Nick said. "And you all get to inherit it one day."

"If it's still left by the time we get it, but that won't be for a good few decades," Dom told him. "Papa's only fifty, and Mama forty-eight. By the time he and Uncles Carlos and Tomas die, we'll be old and have kids of our own to train."

"That's if Grandma doesn't sell off half the buildings in the meantime, or our parents and uncles. They could downsize by the time we get it." Danté swung around in circles. "By the time we get the company, there could be nothing left."

"Maybe." Dom picked up a photo of *SB3* when it was built twenty-five years earlier. "I hope she appreciates what we're doing. Did you say we could add to the book or not?"

"I'm sure there's albums that can be added to, or we'll make one up," Danté said. "Have you scanned them all into the computer?"

"Just got a couple to go...here..." He grabbed a photo and its clipping and scanned them on the printer.

Danté pulled up the image and added it to the document he had open. "That's all of them. Twenty here, one in Athens, one in New York. How does it look?" He slowly scrolled through it for Dom and Nick to see. Page after page had titles, dates, photos, news clippings, articles on each building all in the order Jenny had bought them. "Is the layout all right?"

"If we're doing an A4 vertical book. What about a coffee table book?" Dom asked. "Do we even know what size, or shape, we're doing it in?"

"Ah…" Danté looked at his brother. "Nope."

Sighing, Dom shoved some papers aside and sat on the bed. "I think it should be a square album. Thirty by thirty maybe, something like a coffee table or photographic book."

Danté quickly googled both categories and checked what was selling on Amazon. After searching for photography and book printing stores, they came across the appropriate sizes for printing.

"Hey…" Nick had a thought. "You guys *own* a printing plant. Why don't you just get them to print it up?"

Dom and Danté looked at Nick then each other before smacking themselves on their foreheads with the palms of their hands.

Danté pulled up the website and checked sizing. But, since it was a small press, mainly for the family and the island, he decided to ring Yossi, the manager of the press, instead. "Hey, Yossi, Danté Stephanopoulos, how are you?"

"Oh, my Little Danté," Yossi said. "Good, how are you after your shark fight? Getting better?"

"Yeah, I am Yossi, thanks. I have a question. Dom and I want to get a book printed up for Grandma, a photographic timeline of all the buildings she owns, and we were wondering if you could do it?"

"Of course, of course, what size would you like?"

"We're not sure. I've just done the interior in A4, but we saw that thirty by thirty was popular for coffee table and photography books."

"It can be. Did you want a dust cover or printed hardcover?"

Danté exchanged a glance with Dom. "Printed hardcover, but we were wondering if it could be added to over time? If Grandma buys more buildings, can we add to the book?"

"Mmm," Yossi's deep timbre voice came through the line. "Then it would have to be some sort of folio book. One that could be undone and added to. I have seen them, but not done them."

"Are you able to?" Danté asked. "Otherwise we'll just have to do it up until this year."

"Let me look into it, Little Danté. When do you want it by?"

"It's a Christmas present for Grandma and Grandpa, so it has to be done by December first at the latest," Dom said.

"Ah, Big Dom, you are there too. I will call back next week and we can get it done by December. Okay?"

"Okay, Yossi, bye." Danté ended the call. "So, looks like I have to rejig the size then." He made a few clicks on the document and set to work moving everything around.

*****

Alexis had spent the morning at the centre with Melody and Summer, but she was now lunching with Lorenzo. They sat in a local restaurant gorging on roast lamb and vegetables. And, of course, all meat was supplied by *Stephanopoulos Meats*, as most of the town's restaurants bought from there.

"How are you after the other day?" He sipped his wine.

"Better," she said shyly, noticing how long and black his lashes were. *Were they always that long or that black?* she thought. *I certainly haven't noticed before. I wonder if Alena did.*

"It was very brave of you to discuss what happened. Will your cousin be doing the same?"

"Probably. It Xanthe thinks he's ready. It will probably be for the gay men's HIV group and that's starts on Monday."

"I think it's wonderful what you've done with the centre," Lorenzo went on, staring into her big doe eyes all chocolatey and warm. "You're amazing, Alexis. Pity your sister wasn't more like you five years ago. But I'm glad she grew up so the two of you could have a relationship."

She had deflated at him mentioning her sister, but still felt warm and gooey on the inside. Not just from knowing she had the relationship she always wanted with Alena, but from the way he was praising her. "I didn't do it on my own. My whole family helped. It certainly wasn't the idea I originally had. A website slash blog or forum. But after thinking about the centre, where Cabot and I could both come, it started rolling. Cab came up with the name, picked the building, and gave his money. Then the family gave their time and money. It's all been awesome, and so is having a relationship with my sister. You two…ah…" She shyly glanced down. "Didn't last long."

"No, we didn't. Three months I think it was. She was very self-absorbed with herself and her career, and both came first before anyone else. We dated, did things, moved on." He slid a hand across the table and onto hers. "I think it's wonderful how you're giving back to the island."

A soft smile lit up her lips as the tingle lazily drifted up her arm and across her whole body. "That's, that's so sweet." Oh, how she wanted to kiss his sensuous lips.

"So are you, Alexis. You're growing into quite a young woman." He felt the tingle too, in his groin, but knew that sex would not be on the cards until she was ready, and he would not be pushing her, knowing full well what the family was like, overprotective when it came to the kids. So, if anything *did* happen, it would not be happening at a great rate of knots. Not after what happened to her. He knew he had to take it slow, and that was okay. His father had raised him to woo and to court. It had happened fairly quickly with Alena, but Alena was different, not only in looks, but in age and maturity. And besides, he'd never felt that tingle with Alena. It had been pure attraction and sex, not much else. No deep meaningful conversations, no charity works, or setting up centres. It had been all about Alena, and three months of that was three too many. No, Alexis was different. Kind, sweet, caring. Thought about others, not herself. *And Cabot is right. She is only nineteen and I have to figure out if it's worth getting involved with a girl who's not yet a woman physically, but who is well beyond her years mentally. I have to do it the right way and make a decision, and if I decide to date her, then I need her father's permission to do so since she's under twenty-one.*

"Lorenzo?"

"Mmm?"

"Are you okay? You faded out." Alexis had noticed the faraway look in his eyes and wondered who he was thinking about.

"Of course." He smiled brightly. "Just thinking about how awesome you are."

"Aw, how sweet." She blushed and heard the beep of a text. "Oops, gotta get that." Pulling her phone from her bag, she read it. It was from her mother telling her to be at her grandmother's before dinner as she had something to tell the kids.

"Everything all right?" Lorenzo asked.

"Mama wants us at Grandma's before dinner to tell us something. I wonder what it is. Oh, well, I'll find out soon enough." She put her phone away and went back to basking in Lorenzo's praise.

"You're one hell of a girl, Alexis." He gave her what she wanted.

"I'm not a girl anymore, Lorenzo. My family, my life, my experience has made me a woman," she boldly claimed.

"Yes," he murmured, finishing off his wine. One hell of a woman.

*****

The four kids turned up before dinner to find a man they had never met.

"Kids, I want you to meet an old friend of mine, Alfonso DeVille." Carlos took charge and introduced them all, and they shook hands before he wandered away and left Pedro and Angie to it.

"I, uh, need to tell you kids something." Angie gathered them around. Pedro was to her right; Alfonso her left. "I…ah…" She clasped her hands in front of her. "It seems that after many a decade, ah…" Looking everywhere, but the kids, she struggled to finish. "It seems I have a half-brother. Alfonso is your uncle," she rushed on.

The four of them stood in shock, jaws hanging, eyes wide, looking from their mother and father to the stranger in front of them.

"You're kidding!" Alena exclaimed. "When…? How…?"

"I have only recently found my birth papers," Alfonso told them. "My mother left me a letter when she died. I was nine, it was 1981, and her boss, Harry DeVille and his wife adopted me. They died ten years ago, and I only just went through their things a few months back. I found belongings my mother had left me, and all of my paperwork. My mother told me in her letter who my father was. Is. Andros Poulos. I searched the internet for him and found your mother. I already knew Carlos, so I came here to find out about my heritage. Your mother and I have been talking all week." Smiling nervously, he glanced at Angie.

"Um…yeah…" Angie finally looked up into the eyes of her four children. "It's been hard for me, having been an orphan for thirty years, and now a sibling pops up. Dan did DNA tests, and it is true, he is my brother. So um…your uncle."

"We already have three," Danté said slowly, suspiciously eyeing the man who didn't look much older than Dom.

"That's okay." Alexis flashed a glance at Danté. "It's okay to have another uncle."

Danté frowned, and murmured, "I guess. How old are you?"

Alfonso smiled softly. "Thirty-five. I was born in 1972."

"Well, I'm unsure of the whole thing." Angie scratched the nape of her neck. "I don't know if I can offer Alfonso a sister because I've been an only child all of my life. It's very awkward for me, and I told him not to expect anything from me in that regards. But we thought you should know before he goes back home. I've told him all I can of my…ah…*our* father, and about the business he was in. I only have a few photos, so I've given him copies, other than that, he leaves tomorrow." She turned and fled for the kitchen and the wine cabinet.

"Look, kids," Pedro said, "Alfonso's not—"

"A part of the family," Alfonso finished for him. "I don't want to intrude, that was not my plan. I just wanted to know my history, and I have found that out. We also figure I'm not the only one left out there. It seems your grandfather had a wandering eye, so I have no plans to disrupt your mother's life any more than I have. My being here has upset her, and I completely understand it. I have my own life and career in Hollywood. I just wanted to know who my father was. So please, don't be upset with your mother, and don't be upset with me for not staying to get to know you. Just meeting you is enough, and knowing I'm related to some very special people is enough for me." He glanced at Pedro. "Your parents and grandparents have asked me to stay for dinner, so we can talk, but as of tomorrow, I'll be flying home."

"What do you do?" Dom asked, curious about this stranger who sort of looked like his mother.

"I'm a film producer," Alfonso said.

"Like Uncle Carlos?" Alena asked.

Alfonso's smile widened. "A lot like your Uncle Carlos. That's how

I met him many a year ago."

"And we haven't really told the kids about those days, Alfonso." Pedro flung his arm around Alfonso's neck. "We tend to keep *our* jobs a secret."

"Except we all found out." Alena rolled her eyes and went to her mother's side in the kitchen. "You okay about this, Mama?"

Angie knocked back her first glass of wine. "Well, besides the fact it's made me a drunk this week, sure."

"Aw, Mama." Alena hugged her tightly. "I guess Grandpa was like Cabot and couldn't keep it in his pants."

That made Angie snort wine from her nose and she cracked up laughing. "Oh, my God, thank you, my baby." She wiped her nose, but kept laughing. "That has made my day and put everything into perspective. No, he couldn't keep it in his pants. God knows how many other siblings I have, but at the end of the day, none of them is important to me, or my life here on Mykonos, or in this family. Because the Stephanopouloses *are* my family, and have been for thirty years. End of discussion. Now, let's eat. Your Uncles Tomas and Roger are staying with Cabot for the night, so it's the rest of us, and we made soup."

*****

Having spent the day reading Xanthe's printouts and pottering in the studio, writing down how he felt and what he wanted, Cabot was surprised when he found Tomas and Roger in the kitchen. They'd made a huge pot of pasta and heaped it into bowls. "You not going to Grandma's for dinner?"

"Not tonight," Tomas said. "I called and said we were staying with you." Smiling, he handed over a basket of freshly baked bread.

"Mmm, smells good." Cabot bit into a warm piece of dough and sat chatting about what he'd done all day.

"You feel better?" Roger asked. "All that talking with Xanthe, everything you've done and read has helped you?"

"Absolutely." Cabot nodded. "Now I just need to start making amends to all of the people I pissed off. Although I don't think I could find most of the men I had sex with." His face reddened with embarrassment and they let the conversation go.

After dinner, where Cabot scarfed down seconds, Tomas and Roger sat on the couch to watch a movie with a huge bowl of popcorn between them.

"What'chya watchin'?" Cabot wandered back in from freshening up and spied the bowl. He grabbed a handful and snuggled up to his uncle.

"Star Wars 1 to 3, or should I say, 4 to 6," Roger said. "Good old '70s classics."

"How many are there?" Cabot asked, reaching for more popcorn.

"Six so far," Roger told him, noticing the interest.

"Can we watch all of them?" Cabot munched. "I haven't seen them."

Tomas and Roger traded glances.

"You sure?" Roger asked. "It will take hours, all night even."

Cabot shrugged. "Not like I haven't stayed up all night before."

"Okay." Roger got up to change the disc in the DVD and sat back down.

Tomas lifted the bowl and nodded for Cabot to jump between them.

Like an eager puppy, Cabot hopped over his uncle and settled down in the middle, grabbing the bowl of popcorn as Tomas and Roger spread the faux fur blanket over them.

Tomas grinned at Roger behind Cabot's head. His nephew had finally come back from the dark side.

*****

On Sunday morning at ten, Antonio knocked on Xanthe's door.

She let him in and led him to the lounge room where Cabot was already waiting. "All right, you two, face one another."

They quietly stood facing, unsure of where this was going.

"The other day I told you both to be brutally honest, and you were." Xanthe watched them intently. "I want you both to understand, especially you, Cabot, that this was for you. To get things out in the open, so you could deal with whatever was inside you, so you can get better. And Antonio, I know it would have been hard for you, and feel free to come and talk to me about it anytime. But right now, the two of you need to make up, because we all know you're important to each other. What you said the other day stays in the other day. It doesn't come back into your vocabulary, and it doesn't come back into your life. It is over and done with. Now, is there anything else you want to say to Cabot, Antonio?"

Antonio was still emotionally drained from Friday, and as he thought, he didn't have any more bad words for his brother. "Not to add from the other day, but I do want to add something today."

"Okay, what is it?" Xanthe asked.

"That for all your faults and flaws, I don't want to lose my brother." He shyly stared Cabot in the eye. He had never been shy with his brother before, but this was weird and new and he felt different, and hoped Cabot did too. "I love you; you're my twin. I do think we need to back off a bit and do something separately. But if I ever lost you, I'd be devastated, and I don't want to lose you."

Xanthe smiled. "And Cabot, anything you want to say from the other day?"

"Um," he mumbled into his sleeve. He had his hand curled under his chin, his jumper sleeve pulled past his fingers. What his brother had just said warmed his heart. "All of those things you said the other day, Tone, did you mean them? Do you hate me that much?"

Antonio let out a deep sigh from the pit of his soul. "I meant them the other day when I said them. It's how I'd been feeling for some time. A lot of things had been building and it all came out. And now that it's out, I feel better. Tired, but better. Because I think it needed to be said. I needed to say it, and you needed to hear it. I hated your behaviour because it was bad, and I hated you because you refused to change your behaviour. But that's changing now, and I see that you are finally taking on board everything that's happened, and everything people are telling you. Clearly, Xanthe has helped."

"So, you still love me and won't leave me?" Cabot rushed on, feeling vulnerable and wide open in front of his brother. That was weird since he had no problem being naked in front of him, but physical nakedness was nothing compared to the emotional nakedness he was feeling now.

"I will always love you, Cabot. You're my brother. It just doesn't mean I have to love your behaviour. And I won't leave you. None of us will leave you. It's just time we did some things on our own. Like making friends and having partners and getting hobbies outside of each other."

Cabot nodded slowly. "Yeah, Xanthe's told me that. We need to find our own identity even though we're twins."

"And what do you have to say to Antonio today, remembering to leave all said on Friday in the past?" Xanthe said.

"Um…I love you, Tonee, I can't live without you, and I don't want to. But it would be nice to hang out with people and make new friends. I hope you don't think I'm leaving you, coz I'm not." Cabot smiled lightly at his brother.

"I know you're not, Cabot." A grin lit up Antonio's face. "We just need to spend half our time with other people, so we can breathe."

"I love you, Tonee." Cabot flung his arms around his brother and hugged him fiercely. "I don't want you to go away."

"I'm not, Cabot." Antonio hugged back. "I'm here as long as you need me as a brother. You just need to stop being a dickface."

"Tonee." Cabot laughed. "Not funnee."

"Yes, it is." Antonio kissed his brother's cheek and pulled back.

"Okay, I have a set of rules for the two of you to follow." Xanthe handed them a piece of paper each. "The first one's more for Cabot."

"Call my brother Antonio, not Tony, and stop whining his name," Cabot read. "But I've called him Tony for years."

"Yes, but his name is Antonio, the adults call him that, and if you want to act like an adult and be treated as one, you have to step up and treat your brother like an adult and not whine," Xanthe explained. "Besides, you have that new friend named Tony, and you don't want to get the two confused, do you?"

"You made a friend?" Antonio asked, intrigued because he didn't know, and a little jealous because there was another man in his brother's life called Tony. "When did you meet him?"

"A week or so ago." Shyness overcame Cabot. "He came to the clinic and asked about it. We hung out." He shrugged. "No big deal…yet."

"But you like him?" Antonio pushed. "Had sex with him yet?"

"Tonee, no." Cabot frowned. "It's not all about sex anymore."

That made Antonio's brows rise. "Since when?"

"Since I banned him from it," Xanthe told him. "He hasn't been with anyone since coming home."

"Fucking hell, you're kidding!" Antonio exclaimed and crossed his arms. "How the hell did you get Steele Stefan to stop having sex?"

"I didn't," Xanthe said. "The HIV did. With everything going on in him, he had a lot to deal with. And then I banned it, especially while he's getting his medications stable and seeing me. I'd say the next step for him is a proper relationship. No more rutting in back alleys. Streets or men's."

Antonio snorted. "Oh, I can't wait to see Cabot not screw some random guy and maybe find a relationship. Is this Tony person a potential mate?"

"Maybe." Cabot dug his toe into the carpet and hid in the turtleneck of his sweater. "He's nice, and makes me tingle, but he knows what I'm going through because he has it too and he went through therapy."

"He has HIV too?" Antonio was astounded. "Is that okay? Healthwise?" he asked Xanthe. "Two HIV people having sex."

"It's not as though one will give it to the other," Xanthe reminded him. "But if the relationship goes to that phase, we'll sit them down and talk to them."

"What?" Cabot's eyes widened and his head rose out of his sweater neck in alarm. Like E.T. raising his neck. "Ah, no, um, what?"

"Cabot, if you enter into a relationship with another HIV person, the two of you will need to be told what to do. You'll need to be completely honest about everything. Your sexual histories, medications, physicals. You'll need to know everything, so you can still be careful. Especially about contracting other STDs, which Dan tells me you got from the person who assaulted you."

"Yeah, but he treated me for that," Cabot muttered. "It's all gone now."

"Many STDs stay in your system, even after you've treated it. Like the herpes viruses of which you have one. They never leave the body,"

Xanthe explained. "So, either way, if you two get sexually involved, you will need to know."

"Well, I think that's a long way off," Cabot scoffed. "It's only been a week, and we're still getting to know each other."

"Good; but keep it in mind. Now, the two of you, when you walk out of here today, leave all of Friday behind, and you will both be adults. You will learn to open up more to each other, and the rest of your family. Okay, Cabot." She waited expectantly.

"Yes, Xanthe." He rolled his eyes.

"Good, and remember, Cabot, you are loved, no matter how alone you feel. You're not. And now I'm off to discuss it with your family."

"You're not going to tell them what I've said, are you," Cabot cried in alarm.

"Of course not. But I think your mother needs a stern talking to." Xanthe left them alone to go upstairs.

"What do you think she'll say to Mama?" Cabot panicked.

"That she needs to let you grow up and be an adult. To stop treating us like children," Antonio replied.

Cabot sighed and felt weary. "Yeah. Sometimes it's nice being treated that way, but mostly it's annoying." He shyly sidled up to his brother. "Tonee."

"Ah! What did Xanthe say," Antonio reminded him.

"Antonio," Cabot said softly. "I love you, and I'm glad you're my brother. I'd be so lonely without you."

"You're not alone, Dickface." Antonio grinned at Cabot's horrified face. "I'm here if you need me, Cabot."

Xanthe made her way to Jenny's and found the adults. "Ah good, you're all here. Let's chat about Cabot."

"How is my baby?" Vivian rushed over to her.

"For a start, he's not a baby, and you need to stop treating him like one, Vivian," Xanthe said sternly. "It's time you understand he's twenty-five and dealing with very grown-up issues, and he's struggled hard to deal with them while growing up. He's not your baby, he's your *adult son* and you need to treat him as such." She saw Vivian open her mouth to reply, but cut her off. "Don't even use Jenny as an excuse. Yes, she calls her sons her babies, but she had always treated them as adults and men who she's had no problem verbally slapping into shape. She may use the word, but she hasn't treated them like babies since *they were* babies. Take a leaf out of her book. It's *you* that needs to grow up Vivian, because Cabot needs strong parents who will give him guidance and leadership, not treat him like an incompetent baby. He's made great strides this last month, and you should be proud. He's come a long way in a short time."

"Have you got to the root of his problem?" Jenny was curious as to what Cabot's problem actually was.

"Yes, yes we did on Friday. He spent yesterday being by himself, and now he's with Antonio making amends with him. I want him to come to lunch and make amends with all of you, and to slowly come back into the family. He feels very distant from all of you, very alone in a world of superstars, and he's just Cabot with no particular talent except for modelling and being born gorgeous. His life has done nothing but jumble up in his head and confuse him. What his grandparents wanted for him," she waved a hand at Jenny, "what his parents wanted from him," she frowned sternly at Viv, "what life gave him, what it offered him, and he's tried to fit in since he was a teenager. And, of course, discovering his sexuality on top of it, and moving out of home and living in a big city with just his brother, he finally had the freedom to find himself. The problem was, that he felt you all hated the person he became, and that made him feel more isolated and lonely."

"Oh, my baby," Viv murmured. "Where did we go so wrong with him and not Antonio?" Wringing her hands, she clung to Carlos.

"You probably pushed him into *your* version of him instead of letting *him* be himself. Regardless of what that was," Xanthe told her. "Now, it's time to cut the apron strings and let him be the man he wants to be, gay or straight, model or slacker. Whatever he wants to be, you need to let him be it. And for the love of God, stop treating him like a child, Vivian." Xanthe rolled her eyes. "You've done them both a disservice."

"I didn't mean to," Viv cried, tears pouring down her face. "They're the only boys I have. Diana's the only girl, and they're *all* my babies."

"Except they're not." Xanthe stood in front of her. "They are *not* babies, Vivian. You need to see them as adults, and let them *be* adults. Do you treat Antonio and Diana the way you treat Cabot?"

Viv delicately dabbed at her eyes with a lace hanky. "No."

"Why not?"

"What?" She looked into Xanthe's eyes. "Because he acts the way he does and needs more help."

"Because he *acts* like a child," Carlos told his wife. "So you *treat him* like one."

"Oh, that's not why," Viv protested.

"Of course it is," Xanthe scolded. "Diana and Antonio don't act like children, so they don't get treated like children. Just Cabot, because he's always been a bit wild, a bit out there. The only difference is, that was all an act on his path to finding his spot for himself in life in general. Trying to find *his* personality, *his* way to being an adult. Throw in his sexuality and you've got one emotionally mixed up kid. Now, the thing you all need to do is be supportive. He fucked up by getting assaulted and contracting HIV, now he's dealing with it. Don't even bother using it against him all of his life because that's *you* trying to make him feel guilty," she told the adults. "Let it go and deal with Cabot *now*. The person he's finally becoming. He has choices to make about where his life's going, and he may take the rest of the year. So what, who cares? Let him do it. He's been through a lot, and he's coping quite well considering. He has no idea what his interests are outside of modelling, but helping Alexis with the centre is a very big start."

"How much longer does he have to be Darren?" Pedro asked, quite amazed by Xanthe's inside scoop on Cabot.

"Probably just another week, if that. He'll slowly become Cabot when he's ready. I think the name and who he was named after had a big impact on his life," she said to Carlos and Viv. "Knowing he was named after a gay photographer friend who died from AIDS is a big deal to dump on a kid. That hasn't helped, either. He thinks he's lived up to the moniker, and who the other Cabot was."

Viv sighed and slumped into an easy chair. "Yes. I guess naming our children after dead friends wasn't a good idea. But it seemed right at the time. Same with Antonio."

"Except, Cabot hates his name, but I think he'll come around to that too." Xanthe smiled. "That will be the next step in therapy, getting him to accept the person he is, or is becoming."

"So…we just accept his apology and move on?" Jenny asked.

"Exactly. And he already started on Saturday with Tomas and Roger by apologising for whatever he called them months ago."

"He did?" Jenny's brows rose in surprise and she looked at her sons.

"Yes, Mama, he did." Tomas nodded. "And we accepted it."

"Well, blow me down," Jenny quipped. "I *am* surprised."

"And that's just the start," Xanthe added. "He'll apologise to everyone else at lunch."

"I can't wait then," Jenny said. "Should we film it for prosperity? You know…*you remember that one and only time you apologised.*" Everyone grinned.

"No, no." Xanthe laughed. "No need to." She was interrupted by the kids coming through the door. "Well, hello there, let's have a word about Cabot." She explained to them what she'd just told the others and almost all agreed to give him a second chance.

Dom stood quietly by, frowning, arms crossed. He'd outwardly agreed, but inwardly disagreed vehemently and didn't like it. He wasn't sure what it was, but since Danté's attack, he just hadn't cared for Cabot.

"And this one has issues." Xanthe noticed Dom's stance. "Care to talk?"

"No." He left it at that and walked into the kitchen for a drink.

Surprised, the others traded glances and left it at that when they saw Xanthe heading in Dom's direction. They moved into the lounge to give them some space.

Xanthe walked up behind him and kept her voice low. "There's no reason to hate your cousin. I know finding out he had HIV freaked you out, but what is it now?"

Dom shrugged. "Nothing." Gazing out the window, he avoided her eyes.

"Bullshit! Tell me."

His blue eyes flitted to her and her no-nonsense approach. "I don't know. I just…"

"Yes…"

Another shrug. "Have had a problem since Danté's shark attack."

"Why?"

"Don't know."

"Bullshit!"

He sighed. "Is that all I'm gonna get from you? I *don't actually know why.*"

"Of course you do; think."

Closing his eyes, he thought about it. "I was scared he'd give Danté HIV and I didn't want him near my brother. And after I just…I dunno…didn't want him around at all. I feel angry, or something, when they talk, when Cabot shows him attention." Embarrassed, he knew his cheeks were flame red.

"Ah." Xanthe nodded knowingly. "Jealousy."

"What! I am not," Dom flared crossly.

"Of course you are," she told him. "You spent years not caring for your brother, and so the only boys in the family to show him attention were the twins. Now that Cabot has HIV, and you woke up to yourself where your brother's concerned, you're jealous because he still gets attention from Cabot. *You're* his brother, *you're* the one who should be showering him with attention, not Cabot. But why not Antonio? Because Antonio can't hurt him. Look, Dom," she said and rested her hand on his arm, "Cabot can't hurt him unless there are open wounds. He's not going to hurt him by hugging him."

"Yeah, I *know* that. Doesn't mean I want him around." Dom scowled.

"You look like Cabot when you do that." Xanthe grinned and it made him scowl harder. "Lighten up, Dom, the world isn't over because Cabot gets HIV, Danté gets bitten by a shark, and you finally get over yourself. When it comes to Danté, it took long enough, *and* being punished by being suspended from *SB3*, how did you feel about that?"

"Sick," he growled.

"Good! Smashing an expensive camera and being punished for it *should* make you feel sick. At the end of the day you need to get over yourself. Nothing has happened to you, but it's happened to your brother, sister, and cousin. At least Alena got over herself." Xanthe left it and walked away.

Antonio opened the door and pushed Cabot inside. "We're here."

"Oh, my—" Viv started, but was cut off by Xanthe. "Sons…" she ended. "How are you both?" She hugged them and held Cabot's face in her hands. "How are you? I love you both so much."

"I'm fine, Mama." Cabot rolled his eyes at Antonio and grinned. "She just can't help herself."

"Of course not, you're my babies. I'll always worry," Viv said, then corrected herself. "You are my *grown adult sons*, and I'll always worry."

"Yeah, talking of worrying." Cabot gently removed his mother's hands and cleared his throat. "Um…I…ah…Tone, ah, Antonio," he flashed his brother a glance, "has told me I've been a big fat dickface for the last four or five years." Giggles came from most of the kids and snorts from the adults, and he grew red with embarrassment. "And Xanthe told me that on my way to recovery I need to make amends, so I guess I'll start with the head of the family." Putting one foot in front of the other, he moved over to his grandmother and hugged her. "I'm sorry, Grandma. I've been a big fat dickface and deserved to be slapped, and for all the times I've called you by your first name. I'm sorry."

Jenny felt the difference in his body language and realised he had actually grown up and was sorry. She hugged him back. "Thank you for apologising, Cabot. Your apology is accepted."

Smiling shyly, he moved on to Spiros before his parents who hugged him as though the world was ending, then to Pedro and Angie, and then the kids.

Dom didn't hug back. He just stood there with his hands on his hips and a scowl on his face.

"You look like I did a few months ago," Cabot joked. "I get it, you don't believe me, and I know it will take time to show you I've changed. But *I will* show you, Dom. I will." He hugged Tomas and Roger, and finally Dan and Derek, thanking them for taking care of him and helping him through it.

"That's what we're here for, Cabot. To take care of the family." Dan gave him a man slap on the back. "Think you're ready to talk at the centre now?"

"Oh, I don't know. I know there's a session on Monday and I'll be volunteering, so maybe I'll just hang around in the background with the biscuit container."

"I thought you were getting off them," Antonio teased. "You *have* gained weight lately."

"Argh, don't tell me," Cabot groaned. "We both have to hit the gym." He turned to Tomas and Roger. "We talked it over and wondered, as a part of a healthy new lifestyle we both need to take on, if you'll train us in the gym a couple of times a week? Please?" He held his hands together, praying they'd say yes.

Tomas and Roger pondered the questions as they glanced at each other, dragging out the moment. "Well, I guess we could."

"Yay!" The twins hugged their uncles, leaving Carlos a tad jealous.

He watched his sons go over and hang out with their cousins and then moved to his brother's side. "You know when I told you, you could adopt the twins, I didn't actually mean it."

"Feeling jealous?" Roger chuckled. "We're getting more love than you."

Carlos eyeballed him with a cocked brow. "I am a bit. He wants to spend time with the two of you and not us, and we're his parents. But..." he conceded, "if it means being with the two of you is helping him be gay, or deal with his gayness, or whatever it's called these days, then more power to you. You're helping my son, and I love you both for that, and hope that it helps him grow up."

"Aw, Carlos." Tomas kissed his cheek and hugged him. "It hasn't been easy for him, but he will get there. He just needs time to find himself."

"Yeah, I know. I keep being told." Carlos hugged his brother back. "We nearly lost you, and I don't want to lose my son."

"You won't, at least we'll hope not. He has to stay healthy and on his meds, and he should live long enough to see you die." Tomas grinned.

Carlos snorted. "Because he'll be the death of me, you mean."

*****

On Monday morning, after Cabot left for his volunteer session at the centre, Tomas and Roger set about clearing up the studio. Paintings came back out onto walls, and they cleared up the paints and tarps on the floor, resting Cabot's paintings against the wall.

Tomas stood staring at them, wondering how long all of it had gone on inside his nephew, and why he hadn't sought therapy before. All those years. That's how he'd been feeling. Lost, alone, scared, full of loneliness. A kid just trying to find his way in the world, a kid just trying to find and figure out his sexuality, his path, his profession. It had left him empty of love, lost and alone. He remembered back to the age of twenty-five, 1980, when everyone they knew started dying from the gay plague, and it only got worse over the next year. Being reported in newspapers and on TV, dealing with the scare of their lives. Being told they had it, the gay plague, the disease they thought Luiz had given him. Because it couldn't have been Roger. He'd always worn condoms. So it *had* to be Luiz.

Luiz bloody Manning. The bane of my bloody existence, Tomas thought. *The man who started it all. Started me on the gay route to love, cheated on his fiancée with me, killed four men to frame Roger, poisoned me to get me away from Roger and then kidnapped me from the hospital. What did James say when he was Luiz? That we were in the throes of passion when that man shot him. How the hell would he know that? He wasn't there. But I was, and I've never remembered. I didn't want to remember what Luiz did to me. After '81 I didn't want to think of him at all. Even being here on Mykonos, I didn't think of him. But this year. Thirty years on. All I've done is think of him, and thanks to the kids digging it up and James coming into our lives, all it's done is awaken everything I thought I'd forgotten. So, what now? What or why did James have to come into our lives, my life, and pretend to be Luiz for? What other word would you call it? It wasn't a dream, it did actually happen, plain as day, plain as the nose on my face. Luiz Manning was standing in the penthouse right there in front of me as if thirty years hadn't even passed. Looking exactly the same as he always had. Beautiful, tanned, and tall. And those eyes...*

He saw them as clear as day as if Luiz was standing in front of him. Those eyes were the same, exactly the same. The same shape, the same size, the same colour. His hair was the same colour, his tan the same colour. He was identical. *How the hell can that be? How the hell could Luiz have been resurrected from the dead thirty years later to stand in front of me as if he'd never disappeared, as though thirty years had never passed? How could he?*

"Tomas?"

Tomas didn't hear. Didn't care. He just stood in front of Cabot's paintings choking back sobs that had been held in thirty years too long.

"Tomas." Roger touched his shoulder and he spun around. "Hey, you okay?" He saw the expression on his lover's face, saw the pain in his lover's eyes, and knew what was going on.

Tomas hastily wiped the tears away. "It's October."

"Yes…it is." Roger wondered what had upset the love of his life.

"It's thirty years…" Tomas's voice wandered off.

"Yes."

Tomas breathed in. "Since we were kidnapped, and I was poisoned, and you were framed, and Luiz kidnapped me…it's thirty years this month."

"I know." Roger saw where Tomas was going and let him go there.

"It's been thirty years since I left Mykonos. Since the three of us left Mykonos and made new lives in America. It's been thirty years since Stefano Papadopoulos tried to ruin our lives and kill us. It's been thirty years since Luiz tried to ruin my life. *Our* life."

"Does this mean you're finally ready to deal with him?" Roger asked, arms casually crossed as he stood two feet from his lover.

Brushing away more tears, Tomas said, "Yes, I finally think so. I'm going to see Xanthe next door. Don't wait for me."

"Okay." Roger kissed him as he passed and followed him downstairs. "You going to be a while?"

"Yes. But I need to see Mama first. I hope she's in. I'll see you later." He grabbed a light coat from the rack in the passage and left.

"Okay," Roger murmured, crossing his fingers that all would finally be healed.

Tomas walked through the door of his parents' house. "Mama, you home?"

"In here," Jenny yelled from his old room that she had converted into an office. It made her feel closer to him, knowing he had died and been reborn in that room. He'd taken his bed, clothes, and personal effects when he and Roger moved out, so she'd put in a desk, shelving and drawers for all of her work. She was making notes at her desk when Tomas came in.

"Mama, have you still got that picture of Luiz?"

"Why?" She looked up from her work.

"Because…" He took a deep breath. "I'm going to talk to Xanthe about it all…finally."

"Okay," was all she said and studied his face for a moment before walking into his old closet. She dug through boxes of personal items she'd brought back from New York. The photos happened to be in there. After twenty-seven years of them sitting in the penthouse safe, she'd actually brought them home. "Here."

"I just need this one." Tomas took the one of Luiz on his own. "Do you know if Alena has pictures of James?"

"Ah, I see where you're going. Probably. Let's check her website. She may have posted tour shots." Jenny quickly pulled up Alena's website on her computer and found photos from the tour. "Here we go, let's see if he's here." She scrolled through the photos, but she found none of him. "You know what, let's just ring her." She called Alena. "Sweetie, just wondering if you have a photo of James Gardo for Uncle Tomas."

"What does he want one for?" She was in the studio doing new music with her parents.

"He wants to have a chat with Xanthe and needs a photo of James. Do you have one?"

"Let me check." Alena quickly looked through her photos on her phone and found one. "Do you want me to send it to you?"

"Email it to me and then I can print it out."

"Okay, hang on." Alena emailed the photo to her grandmother. "Got it?"

Jenny refreshed her email a few times and up it came. Clicking on it, she enlarged the photo and gasped. The similarity still shocked her. "Thanks, sweetie. I'll see you tonight." Jenny clicked off and hit print on the photo.

"Mmm, that was strange," Alena murmured, putting her phone on the mixing desk.

"Who was it?" Pedro sat behind the board working on the music.

"Grandma wanted to know if I had a picture of James for Uncle Tomas."

"What does he want one for?" Angie asked as she scribbled music notes on sheets of paper. She was sitting at the desk against the wall.

"Grandma said he's going to see Xanthe." Alena leaned back in her chair and spun around, her hair hanging over the back as she slumped.

"Wow, finally." Pedro's brows rose. "We were wondering how long that would take him. Have *you* seen Xanthe?" he asked Alena.

She kept spinning in circles. "Why would I need to see Xanthe, Daddy?"

"Because you have issues with it too," he replied, staring at the computer screen in front of him.

"I don't think so, Daddy," she scoffed, a frown settling over her pretty face. "Not like Uncle Tomas."

*****

Cabot was setting out the hot water and tea and coffee for the session when Tony arrived.

"Hey, I haven't seen you all weekend. I've been coming by every day to see you, but everyone said they had no idea where you were." Tony had hated not seeing him, and not only felt snubbed, but a little lost without him.

"Ah, oh, hi." Cabot blushed and went gooey inside. "Sorry. I had an epic therapy session on Friday. It went all day and then Xanthe had me be by myself on Saturday, and then yesterday I had to make amends to my family. I've been exhausted for days. Milk, one sugar, right?" He handed over the cup and his fingers brushed Tony's. The tingle sped up his arm.

"Um, yeah, how'd you remember?" Tony asked, making Cabot's blush even redder. "It must have been a pretty powerful session. You *look* okay." Tony smiled slightly at the tingle, and mentally kicked himself for being pushy. *Of course* Darren's therapy came first, it had to, and at the moment he was just a spectator in Darren's life.

"Yeah, yeah, it was." Cabot made coffee for two more members. "My brother and I really got our issues out into the open, and then Xanthe finally got to the bottom of *my* issues. Then we talked all day and she had me paint my feelings. That was weird, but really helped. And then we talked some more. Yesterday, she got my brother and I back together and helped us make up. Hopefully, it will bring us closer together."

"You're twins, weren't you already close?" Tony asked, sipping his coffee.

"I thought we were, but my sexual behaviour repulsed him, and he got mad and kept it all inside. It's finally out, and we know where the other stands now, so it's good. We had lunch with the fam yesterday."

"Your sexual behaviour repulsed him? You couldn't have been that bad?" Tony had a hard time believing that a twenty-five-year-old could be that bad sexually, or that rampant.

"Oh." Cabot blushed again. "You'd be quite surprised at how bad I was. How do you think I got HIV?" He welcomed two more people and offered coffee and tea.

"How many partners have you had?" Tony was split in two. Part of him was jealous that Darren wasn't his partner, and the other was worried that he'd had too many.

"Oh, way too many to count." Cabot's blush spread down his neck.

Dan and Derek walked in to begin the session, but they lingered while stragglers came after them. Finally, they shut the door and started.

Cabot hung back, sitting, watching, and listening to fellow Mykonosians talk about their HIV status and how they got it. Through assault, drug use, or unprotected sex.

Tony stayed with him, fascinated by what Dan and Derek had to say, but not wanting to leave Darren's side. At the end of the session, he stood up and asked if he could talk.

"Of course," Dan encouraged.

Tony stepped forward. "Um, last year in summer, some friends and I came here for a holiday. I met some guys, we hooked up, and it was all consensual," he told them. "And then there was one guy who I thought was into it. We had sex, I…was *in* him," embarrassment overtook him, "And once I had finished I pulled out and thought that would be that. But he demanded payment, grabbed at my pockets for cash or my wallet, and when I didn't have any, he flicked a knife open. I should have run," he said wryly, shaking his head. "I grew up in London, I know how to defend myself, so instead of running, I thought I'd fight. But how the hell was I to know he was going to stab me with the knife? I became disorientated and stumbled. He used that moment to haul me over something, I think it was a low wall or something, and shove his cock in. Once he was done, he left me there, laughing and saying that he had given me the disease."

****

"Hey, can I come in?" Tomas asked Xanthe at her door. "I need to talk."

"Of course, come in." She waved him into the office and sat. "Coffee, tea?"

"No, no, thank you. Um…" He sat on the other easy chair. "I want to talk about Luiz. And everything that happened. And something that's happened this year that might surprise even you."

She lit up. "Ooh, this'll be good."

He recounted every single moment with Luiz and how he felt about it, speaking of the idea that Luiz had given him AIDS, and that he'd moved on from it after recovery. Then he brought up seeing Giancarlo Gardo and his son in the department store in 1980, told her how James had ended up on Alena's tour, his attack on Roger, and ended with James turning up at the penthouse claiming to be Luiz and how he was shot in the head. "It turns out," he said, "that James Gardo is Luiz Manning's half-brother. They share a mother. And obviously, that means James and Angie share a half-brother. So, it's made it all very complicated for this family."

"Jesus," Xanthe said, already knowing much of it from Alena. "I knew about Luiz from before, but to now have his half-brother pop up on your doorstep thirty years later claiming *to be* Luiz, that must have freaked you out." She peered closely at his expressions, and into his eyes for some acknowledgement. "But he can't look *that* much like him. They do have different fathers."

Tomas handed over a picture. "That's Luiz. It was taken here on Mykonos in July of 1977. He was engaged to Bertha St John and had met me and probably done it with me already."

"Oh, *he is* gorgeous," Xanthe breathed. "No wonder you fell in love with him. I would've too."

"Mmm, not love…more lust," Tomas corrected her softly, fading out with a small smile on his lips.

"Bullshit!" Xanthe exclaimed, jarring Tomas out of his memories. "I knew it twenty-six years ago when I counselled you that it was love, but considering you had other health issues to deal with, I left it. But now, after thirty years of meeting him…" She studied the surprised light in his eyes. "I still see it in your eyes. You lit up when you talked of meeting him and that first kiss, the first touch. He was your first lover. Period! He's bound to have an effect. But still, his brother can't look identical to him."

Tomas nearly scoffed and handed over the photo of James, watching Xanthe's eyes widen.

"Holy Jesus mother of God," she whispered. "No wonder it freaked you out. When did *he* die and when was *he* born?" Her eyes flitted back and forth comparing the two.

"Luiz died thirty years ago this month. James was born Valentine's day 1979. I was twenty-four the night James was born. You know it's thirty years for all of it."

She finally looked up. "Tell me."

"It's October." He shrugged. "We were in Miami, Carlos in Hollywood, Pedro in New York. We were all kidnapped this month thirty years ago. Carlos went through a girlfriend being killed, and Aneeka being kidnapped. Pedro went through a stalker and Andros trying to kill them, and I was poisoned by Luiz, while Roger was framed for the murder of four castmates. I ended up in the hospital *all because of Luiz.* James knew what happened in that hotel room after he kidnapped me. I don't know how he could. His aneurysm couldn't make him know details like that, and there's only one person alive who was in that room that night, and I was drugged off my face. So, how does James Gardo, who was nowhere near being born yet, know what happened?"

Xanthe looked from the photos to Tomas and back. "I don't know, you've definitely intrigued me, but first, let's get you admitting how you *really* felt about Luiz. You can say it's lust till you're blue in the face, but it doesn't make it so. Forget everything else, everything bad. When he looked at you, when he touched you, when he kissed you, what did you feel?"

A small smile came to Tomas's lips and the air left him in a soft sigh. "Heaven. He was *so* beautiful." His eyes closed at the memories. "I hadn't been with anyone, had no idea I could be gay, but it felt so right, so perfect, so beautiful."

"Did your heart sing?"

"Yes." He breathed out slowly and his heart raced.

"Did your pulse race?"

"Yes."

"If he was single, would you have been with him?"

"Oh, God yes." Bowing his head, he remembered. "I told Mama in July 1980. She suspected it. If he hadn't been engaged we would've been together. I don't know for how long, but he would've been my first relationship."

"Does he still make your heart sing?" She handed the photo of Luiz back and watched his face as he gazed at it.

The smile came back. "Yes. It's those eyes. Those lips. The body. Look at him, he's beautiful. God-like. But gone." He sighed. "He's gone. I couldn't live with the betrayal of cheating on my friend with her man, and I ended it with him. So did she. We moved to Miami and I met Roger that night. A week or so later we fell into bed together and have been a couple since."

"But Luiz still affects you?"

"Yes. In every way because of all he did. I loved him." He looked from the photo to Xanthe. "All right, I admit it. I loved him. And remembering the way he made me feel and my first time with anyone, I'll never forget it, but I'll also never forget what he did. He poisoned me and killed four men to frame Roger. Both to get us away from the other. *That is not love.* Killing four people to get your lover *is not love.* Poisoning the person you claim to love *is not love.* Kidnapping the person you claim to love *is not love.* And now James Gardo is claiming to be Luiz. That's scary shit."

"And yet you still love him, even now."

"What! No." Tomas got up and stalked around. "It's not love, Xanthe. It's first love memories, when he was good, before he'd done anything bad except cheat on his fiancée. My God." He swiped a hand through his hair. "Who does that kind of shit?"

"A stalker."

Tomas glanced sharply at her. "So, he went from being my lover to my stalker? Oh, my God. But what about James? Thirty years later he's standing in front of me telling me he wants me back. He tried to kill Roger at the last show of Alena's tour. Cabot stopped him. I can't believe *he did* all of that." He stared out the window at the overcast day and grey rolling seas, feeling every ounce of those crashing waves inside his chest, pounding away at his resolve.

With a sigh, Xanthe hauled herself out of her chair and over to him. "What is it you want?"

"I want him to stop affecting me." Tomas turned his head to look at her. "I don't want to fall apart every time I see, or hear, or think about him."

She took the photo of Luiz from his hand and held it up. "How do you feel?"

His eyes darted to it like a moth to a flame. "Love, lust, sexual attraction followed by horror."

She lowered the photo and held up the one of James. "Now how do you feel?"

His brow furrowed. "Horror."

"Interesting."

"Why?"

"Because the before," she held up Luiz's picture, "induces love and attraction. The other," she held up James's picture, "induces horror. So, you're stuck on the horror." Staring at the two pictures and the two men in them, all she could say was, "I can't really tell you how to deal with it. It's an incredibly strange and unusual situation. What I *can* say, is to let it go. Just simply let it go. Of course, you're going to remember beautiful moments of first love, first attraction, first intimate experiences, but all of the horror has overridden it. *Luiz is dead.* James *is not Luiz.* Just his half-brother who looks incredibly like him." She stared at both photos and shook her head. "James himself has done nothing to you. As James Gardo, has he hurt you? Assaulted you? Kidnapped you, poisoned you?"

He blushed at the ridiculousness of it. "No."

"Right. Now, how he thought he was Luiz, we don't know. Aneurysms can wreak havoc on the brain, so unless someone can explain *that* to us, I'm stumped. Maybe he read all of the stuff on the family and his brain jumbled it up. Who knows. What I *do* know, is that Luiz *is not* James, and James *is not* Luiz. Maybe if you talked to James you would see what sort of person he is and disconnect the two. Either way, Luiz is dead and has been for thirty years. Do you know if James remembers what he did?"

He shook his head. "No idea. We haven't seen or heard from that family since. Even his father knew what was going on. Detective Gardo came into our penthouse to talk James down. He and Mama ran outside after him and stayed with him until the paramedics came. Mama went to visit them in hospital after realising James was Sheila Manning's son. Mama's a big believer in reincarnation."

Jenny chose that moment to walk through the door and stand in the doorway of the office. "We need to talk."

"We're in the middle of a—" Xanthe started, annoyed at the interruption at that precise moment, but knowing full well she'd said her door was open 24/7.

"Yes, I know." Jenny waved a hand and turned for the lounge room. "I meant about Luiz." She all but collapsed on the sofa.

"Mama, what is it?" Tomas flew to her side and grasped her hand. "Are you ill?"

"No, no, just tired of all of this." She patted his hand. "It's been thirty years. After you left, I sat thinking about Luiz and James and staring at the photos of the two, and reliving all that's happened, and realised that thirty years is too long. I thought the same way in the hospital when I went to see them. Thirty years is too long. Thirty years had come down to that. James being in the hospital. Thirty years had come down to nothing." She gazed at Tomas and shook her head in time with her words. "Thirty years is done, Tomas. No more of this. It's time to let it go. Luiz was your first love, your first lover, *nothing* else. *James is nothing to you.* Let them both go, *they are not yours. Neither* is yours. All you have are memories. Remember the good ones, the beautiful ones, and forget the bad. Forget about James Gardo and Luiz Manning."

With tears in his eyes and pain in his heart, he nodded. Because Mama always knew what she was talking about, and Mama was always right.

*****

Dan glanced up sharply to see Cabot leaning forward with interest.

"The little fucker told me I had the disease. At the time I didn't connect what he was saying because I was bleeding out, but some friends found me and got me to the hospital. I recovered from the stab wound, and thank God it was only superficial, but then I found out that I had contracted HIV." He looked around the group and saw Cabot inching closer. "I just wondered, for those of you who'd been assaulted, if any of you had been through the same experience." A couple of men nodded. "I also wondered if it could possibly be the same person. He was an exotic mix, not quite black, black hair, brown eyes, average height."

Cabot moved closer still. It sounded like his attacker. Could the same person have attacked both of them?

Tony pulled a picture from his jacket pocket. "My friends went through their holiday snaps and we found this. This is him." He held out the photo for the group to see, and two of the men excitedly chatted. It was him.

Cabot finally got a look at the photo and thought hard. He was drunk that night, but he definitely remembered the exotic mixed man he'd danced with, and then fucked, and then had been assaulted by. "Oh." He stumbled back, pointing at the photo. Bad memories and even worse mistakes came flooding back. "Oh, that's him. He's the one who, oh, no, I—" He spun around, ran out of the room and out the front door.

"Darren," Tony yelled and flung the photo at a shocked Dan. "Here, you take it." He ran after Cabot down the street and to the beach.

Cabot collapsed on the sand crying like there was no tomorrow. He'd huffed all the way there, breath escaping as the shock fluttered over him. It was the same man. The same man assaulted them both. With blurry eyes, he dumped the glasses on the sand and removed the contacts. Why did he have to meet a guy who'd been assaulted by the same low down dirty butt fucker?

"Darren." Tony collapsed next to him. "What is it? Did you recognise the man?"

"It's," Cabot sobbed. "It's the man…who…assaulted me."

"Oh." The news hit Tony hard. "Oh, my God. I never imagined that we, oh, my God. I'm so sorry." He rubbed Cabot's back as he sobbed. "Oh, wow, what a damn coincidence."

"I'm so sick of this." Cabot rubbed his eyes. "I'm so sick of it. I fucked up badly that night, and if it wasn't for my fucking every man that walked, I wouldn't have HIV. And I wouldn't be here now pretending to be someone else, or having to deal with this shit. I'm so over feeling stupid for making such a stupid mistake."

"Hey, it's not your fault," Tony said, noticing the glasses and two small brown dots on the sand, but it didn't connect. "We all wish we could pretend to be someone else and wish our bad stuff away."

"Except I *have* been pretending to be someone else." Cabot looked at him and Tony registered the bright blue eyes. Even on an overcast day they stood out. "It was all Xanthe's idea. To stop being me for a while, so I could focus on my issues without the constraints of my family or my fame."

"Your family or your fame?" Tony scoffed and then it connected. "Wait…you're *not* Darren Holbrook? Who are you?"

"No, I'm not Darren Holbrook." Cabot stared him straight in the eyes. "Xanthe told me to pick a name for my new identity and that was it. My real name is Cabot Conroy Stephanopoulos. My grandmother owns half the island, my parents are a famous model and movie producer, my sister's a model, and runs a fashion label with our cousin Alena who's a world-famous singer, famous spawn of a world-famous DJ and musician. Her brothers are DJs at the family's club, and Alexis you've met. My uncles, who I've been staying with while dealing with my gayness, are Tomas Stephanopoulos and his husband Roger Dencott, both are famous AIDS activists and gay advocates. They run a gym here on the island and added an AIDS care centre in Miami to the family business. My twin brother and I are world-famous models who go by Steele and Phoenix Stefan. Although Antonio doesn't want to be Phoenix anymore. Can't say I blame him. Xanthe says the family's success and fame had a hold on me, and I needed to stop being me for a while, so I could remember what normal felt like." Smiling softly, he slid a finger down Tony's cheek. "It's been good." Looking away, he added, "But now I totally get it if you don't want to see me, either because I've lied to you, or you don't want to be involved with a famous family. Or, because the guy who assaulted you also assaulted me and gave both of us HIV."

Tony breathed deeply, his brain going a million miles a minute. *One, two, three, breathe, Tony.* He understood the therapist making Cabot become Darren. His own therapist had suggested role play to figure out what was going on in his own head, but to find out Darren was really Cabot a.k.a. Steele Stefan… He'd seen the boys in magazine ads and actually gotten a hard-on over them. They were good looking boys. "I saw, I've seen, some of your ads in magazines. One was for watches. You and your brother work well together."

"Yeah." Cabot brightened. "I love Tone, ah, Antonio. Another of Xanthe's rules is to be treated like a grown-up, and to treat others like a grown-up, so I have to call my brother Antonio from now on."

"That's funny, I'm Antonio too, but have been Tony all my life." Tony grinned at the gorgeous boy before him.

"Really?" Cabot returned the grin with a smile. "You'll have to meet. But that's another of Xanthe's rules. Start having separate lives, friends, relationships. Spend time apart. Um…" He picked at the sleeve of his sweater and decided to broach the subject, regardless of the fear clenching his stomach. "How long are you here in Mykonos for?"

"However long I want to stay," Tony replied. "I'm on my inheritance, I don't need to work, or rush back to anything, or anybody."

Cabot's shy smile said it all. "So, there's no one special back home?"

"Not back home." Tony matched the smile.

"I um…" Cabot gulped. "Guess I'd better tell you everything then." He recounted his whole life story, ending with his suicide attempt. Pulling back his sleeves, he showed off the fading scars. "I wanted to kill myself, but Tony, ah, Antonio, saved me. Grandma flew us home and Dan and Derek have been looking after me. I see Xanthe every day, and I do as I'm told. I'm staying with my uncles, and I've taken up painting. Other than that, I have no idea what I want to do with my life."

"How about just taking it easy for the rest of the year and dealing later?" Tony suggested. "I'd only just come out of therapy before I flew out here. My therapist said one way of dealing with it was to track the bastard down and have him for assault, or at least for spreading HIV, which is actually a crime now."

"It is? I didn't know that." Cabot shifted to face him, staring into exotic green-brown eyes.

"Yes. If you know you have HIV/AIDS and you willingly have sex with someone without them knowing you have it, or wearing a condom, it's a crime."

"So…" The news excited Cabot. "If we can track him down, we can have him for assault and jailed?"

"In America, you could. Would have to check the laws here."

"So, you don't mind…" Cabot tried changing the subject. "That um…I'm not Darren?"

"No. I understand. My therapist suggested something similar. I get it. And you have a famous family. But you also have a lot to deal with personally. Xanthe wanted you out of that to get to the root of your problems." He smiled. "I don't hate you if that's what you think."

"It's just that um…I…" The blush raced up Cabot's neck to his face. "Really like you and um…I just…"

"Want me to get to know the real you?" Tony finished for him and grinned. "Yeah, I get it. When do I get to meet the family?"

"Oh, God, not yet. I want you to myself for a bit longer, ah…" His face went the same red as a ripe tomato, and he hugged his knee and rested his chin on it.

Tony laughed. "Okay. And how long will that be?"

"Well," Cabot said shyly, sneaking a glance at the hot hunk beside him. "My parents and uncles all have their wedding anniversaries the first week of November, the fourth, fifth and sixth. It's their thirtieth. You could uh, maybe, hang around for that. And then there's Thanksgiving two weeks after."

"Are you asking me to be your date for your parents' anniversary?" Tony's grin was ear to ear.

"Um, well," Cabot tried stringing the sentence together, but the words were a jumble in his head. "I'd have to ask for the seating arrangements, but um…yeah."

"I'd love to."

Cabot heaved a sigh of relief. "Oh, thank God, coz this dating thing is damn hard."

*****

Jenny and Tomas sat talking, deciding on a new path to take. Xanthe nodded, intrigued by the whole thing, and they called Roger and Spiros who both declared it ridiculous.

With some push and shove, they came to a decision. Tomas would let it go and not let Luiz or James have a hold on him again, and they came up with a plan to make it all go away and to forgive and forget.

Scrolling through her phone, Jenny found the number she had

been after in New York and made a call.

"Hello, Gardo residence."

"Hello, Giancarlo, it's Jenny Stephanopoulos. Once a cop, always a cop, huh? I wasn't sure I'd catch you this early."

"Jenny?" The surprise hit him hard. He hadn't even recognised her voice.

"I've done some thinking, Giancarlo, and I'd like to know if you've told James about Luiz, or what he's done."

"Not yet. Although he has been remembering things. Sheila wants to tell him. I'm not sure what good it will do."

"Well, I'd like to propose a plan." She went on to tell him what she'd come up with, but it all banked on telling James, *and* being honest.

"That's one hell of an offer, Jenny. I'm not sure Sheila would jump at it, but then you never know."

"If you decide it's what you want to do, call me and let me know. I'll arrange everything. It could be the only way for this thirty-year battle to be over. For all of us."

"Yes. You could be right," Giancarlo murmured, hearing someone behind him. He turned and found Sheila standing in the doorway. "I'll talk to Sheila and get back to you."

"Okay. Goodbye, Giancarlo."

"Goodbye, Jenny." He replaced the phone in its cradle and told his stunned wife of the plan.

Jenny called Pedro and Angie, Carlos and Viv, and once they arrived at Xanthe's, she told them of her plan.

"Oh, no, now wait a minute," Carlo interrupted. "We kept it from them for a reason."

"And now they know so much we may as well finish the story," Jenny told him. "They're not children anymore, and since Alena, Dom and Cabot have all sorted themselves out this year, and Tomas has finally sought help with his Luiz problem, it's time the family story came out. They *know* things, Carlos." She looked at him as she spoke. "It's time to tell them the rest of it."

*****

"I guess we should get back to the centre," Cabot said. He stood and brushed the sand off his jeans and boots. "Ew, my jeans are all wet. We'll have to stop off for me to change."

"Then we'd better stop off for me to change too." Tony was looking at his soggy jeans. "Where are you?"

"Not far, one street in," Cabot said. "What about you?"

"I'm at *The Windmill Hotel.*"

"Ah, yeah, that's ours." Cabot grinned. "It's where the anniversary parties will be for three days straight. They had their receptions there thirty years ago when they got married."

"Really? So, you're family's like, rich, huh?" Tony asked as the left the beach.

"Yeah. Not sure how, just that we had money and the family has all these businesses. *Stephanopoulos Meats…* Grandpa inherited that from his father, and his father before that. Then came *SB3*, the nightclub slash function centre in '82 which Uncle Pedro still DJs at on Friday nights. All '70s and '80s stuff. Then Dom and Danté DJ as well. Then they bought *The Windmill* and the houses surrounding Grandma's. The family has its own publishing house for Grandma's and Mama's books. Mama's Vivian Villiers, famous supermodel and cosmetics queen. She's also a stylist and does videos."

"Yeah, yeah, my mum had some of those. Your mother's gorgeous." Tony shoved his hands deep into his jeans pockets to keep them warm.

Cabot grinned. "Yeah. And then Grandma paid for the health clinic attached to the hospital, plus she owns a bunch of other properties. Papa owns *S'Reel,* Uncle Pedro has *Sync,* and together they have *Stefan Productions* in Athens, with offices here. My sister is Diana Villiers—"

"Oh, my God, she's gorgeous," Tony butted in, which made Cabot stop and stare at him. "Hey, a gay man can still admire a woman."

Cabot laughed. "Yeah, I guess we can. And she *is* gorgeous. She'll be home for their anniversary. And Alexis and I have the centre, and Uncle Tomas and Roger have the gym where Antonio and I will start working out next week. We've both gained way too much weight being here. Grandma also financially supports Dan and Derek's AIDS clinic in New York. They're world-renowned specialists in it. Plus, she took Tomas and Roger's recent acquisition under the banner which we call *S.Inc.*"

"*S.Inc.*?"

"*Stephanopoulos Inc.* And now Danté wants to set up some IT web business with his best friend Nick. He runs all of the family's websites. And I mean *all* of them."

Tony kicked a loose stone as they walked across the centuries-old cobblestones. "God, what a family."

"Oh, and I forgot our apartment building in New York," Cabot said. "And here we are." He stopped at Tomas and Roger's front door. "My uncles' home." He let them in and called out. "Uncle Tomas? Roger?" Getting silence in return, he shut the door and led Tony up the stairs. "I'll show you their studio. They paint. You've probably seen their pictures at *The Windmill.*"

"Oh, wow, they're beautiful." Tony stood still, completely absorbed by the paintings on two and a half walls. "They *are* good."

"Yeah, well, they're mine." Cabot pointed to the six on the floor leaning against the wall opposite them. "Mine suck. But look around, I'm gonna change. My room's just back there." He raced off down the hall into the back bedroom and ripped off his jumper and t-shirt then kicked off his shoes and socks. After pushing off his jeans, he grabbed a dry pair from the closet and pulled them on.

"That's some package you've got, Cabot." Tony hungrily eyed him from the doorway.

Cabot froze, his jeans halfway up his legs. "Um…" His whole body went red. "Runs in the family. Got it from my father who got it from his." He quickly adjusted himself in his jeans and zipped them up before grabbing a black t-shirt and another black turtleneck sweater.

Tony continued his observations. "You always wear black?"

Cabot grinned, relaxed once more now he had clothes on. "It's just easier. If it gets dirty, you can't see it." After pulling on dry socks and stepping into another pair of chunky black biker boots, he grabbed his wet clothes. "I'll just drop these off in the laundry. Let's go." He ushered Tony downstairs and quickly dumped his clothes in the laundry room at the back of the house. "Okay, let's move." They hurried to *The*

Windmill where Tony quickly changed, and Cabot cautiously stayed downstairs, but decided, because it was lunchtime, to grab a bite to eat in the dining room. They munched on fried chicken and hot greasy chips before heading back to the centre.

"Oh, hey, Darren, there you are. We were wondering where you'd gotten to," Alexis said as they came through the door.

"It's okay, Alexis, he knows I'm Cabot. I've told him everything," Cabot told her.

Alexis stared at him and saw the contacts were gone. "Oh, okay… *Everything?*"

Ignoring that, Cabot introduced them. "This is my cousin, Alexis, and this is Tony, my…friend…"

"Friend?" she asked with a cocked brow. "As in *special* friend?" Holding out her hand she shook Tony's.

"I hope so." Tony grinned. "Nice to meet you."

"Ah…Cabot's got a *special friend.*" Alexis matched his grin. "About time, cuz, with all the dogging around you've done."

"Yes, yes." Cabot blushed. "I've sorta told Tony about it."

"Only sorta?" Tony inquired, watching Cabot's blush rapidly spread and liking how shy he went.

"Well, it's not like I put a number on it." Cabot wished the ground would open up and swallow him whole.

"Oh, hello there, I'm Lorenzo." Lorenzo came over to them and shook hands with Tony. "I'm one of the doctors volunteering here."

"Oh, right." Tony nodded. "I've seen you around."

"Are you Cabot's boyfriend?" Lorenzo hoped to catch him out, but he was too late to the party.

"Not yet, but I hope to be." Tony stared him down. He knew arrogant dicks when he saw them.

"Oh." Lorenzo saw he was being put in his place by Tony's hands on hips and steely-eyed stand. He went for one last dig. "So, you don't have a problem with Cabot being HIV positive?"

"Why would I, when I am myself?" Tony said, and chose to ignore Lorenzo and the strange look Alexis was giving the hot doctor. "Actually," he said to Alexis, "it turns out the same guy assaulted us both and gave us both HIV. We hope to track him down and do something about it."

"Oh, no. I hope you catch him," Alexis said.

"There you are." Dan and Derek came out of the session room. "Turns out, the other two assault victims in the group earlier were assaulted by your guy." He handed the photo back. "Looks like we've got a rampant gay attacker on the island. We may be able to track him down."

"I've tried that." Tony took the photo. "I've asked at bars and clubs and hotels. People either don't remember, or they recognise the face, but that's all they know."

"Well, Jenny's got a team of specialists on call, oh, that's Darren's—"

"He knows," Cabot told them. "All of it...sorta."

"Okay." Dan nodded and continued. "She has a team of specialists who can track down people. If he's doing it here, he's doing it elsewhere."

"Can they track him back to where he lives?" Tony asked, intrigued at the power the family seemed to have. An Onassis type of power.

"Grandma's team can track an ant in an anthill," Alexis said.

"And what will you do once you find him?" Lorenzo was fascinated by the conversation, but pissed off that he had been left out of it.

"Depending on where he's from, have him arrested," Tony said. "It's a crime to knowingly spread AIDS to people."

"You should know that, Lorenzo," Dan told his colleague. "Especially if you keep volunteering here. You'll need to know the current status of all laws pertaining to HIV/AIDS."

"Yes," Lorenzo murmured, annoyed at showing his ignorance and being pulled up by Dan, the boy wonder. "I'll have to brush up on that. Excuse me, I have some work to finish." He left them to it and went back to the office.

"Arrogant bastard isn't he?" Tony said to the group.

"He can be, but he's young," Dan said. "Wants to prove himself and tries hard. But when he doesn't get it, he gets snarky. He just needs to learn to calm down and learn it all one step at a time."

"I think he's great." Alexis blushed and the others stared at her squirming.

"*You* would," Cabot teased. "You do know he slept with Alena?"

"That was five years ago and they dated for three months," Alexis defended Lorenzo. "That's all it was."

"Ah-huh. *Or* he could have been trying to get an in with Grandma because he did." Cabot raised a brow at Dan. "Lorenzo got a scholarship from Grandma; she paid his way through medical school."

"Did she now?" Dan muttered. "And now he thinks he can wheedle his way into the family, does he? Better keep an eye on him."

"Guys, stop," Alexis demanded. "I don't care, either way, he's a nice guy and he's offered to help out here. And I'm grateful."

"Grateful for the attention he's heaping on you, you mean," Cabot snipped.

She threw him a black look and stormed off into the session room.

"Aw, fuck it!" Cabot exclaimed. "I better go apologise." He wandered off after her, leaving Tony to talk to Dan and Derek more about the attacker. He found her sorting brochures and flyers on the table for the next session. "I'm sorry. In my defence, though, I *am* a dickface."

She burst out laughing despite herself and hugged him. "That's hilarious. When did Antonio come up with that?"

"A couple of weeks ago." He grinned. "I'm sorry, I want you to be happy with everything you've gone through, but he's older *and* he dated Alena. Do you really think the family will approve?"

"We're not dating, Cabot." She went back to the brochures. "Yet."

"Do you want to?"

"Yes."

"Even though he's been inside Alena?"

"Ew, Cabot." She bashed him with a handful of fliers. "That's gross."

"But true," he returned. "*And* he's thirty. You're only nineteen, not even an adult. *And* are you ready for that? A relationship? Sex?"

"I don't know." She stopped him. "I just know I like him and he makes me tingle when he touches me. Not that *you'd* know about such things."

"Oh…you'd be surprised," Cabot told her.

"Ah…" She turned to face him. "Tony gives you the tingles, does he?"

Cabot's blush crept back. "Yes, yes he does."

"You've only known each other, what, a week?"

"About that," he murmured, glancing over his shoulder to see Tony still talking to Dan and Derek.

Tony saw him and flashed a smile back.

Alexis noticed and zoned in on Cabot. "And is he the *only* one to give you tingles?"

Cabot turned back to her. "So far. But then I am only twenty-five."

"So…then *I'm* not allowed to get the tingles for someone?"

He sighed. "Alexis. Uncle Pedro will not like the fact he's thirty and you're nineteen."

"It's not like I haven't thought of it." She looked down, embarrassed at discussing the whole thing.

"But he gives you the tingles anyway?" Cabot saw the rosy cheeks and soft smile.

A smile that said it all.

*****

"She's willing to do all of that?" Sheila asked her husband. "I can't believe it."

"She did lay it all out," Giancarlo said, sitting beside her at the kitchen table. "But a prerequisite is we tell James everything we know that concerns him. You're the one who said we should tell him about Luiz."

"Yes, I know, but I wanted to do it when the time was right, not because someone else told me to." Sheila finished her first cup of coffee and went back for more. "How are we supposed to cope with this?"

"Like two mature adults," he said. "It's been thirty years, Sheila, Jenny knows it was you whose apartment Spiros spent the night in, and she slapped me for lying to her. I took the brunt of that *again*."

She sighed. "Yes, I know, and I love you for it. But she didn't seem overly angry. She was angrier about James and Luiz being half-brothers, and how he could possibly know all of those things. And I can't believe he could do all of those things she said he did, like strangling Roger.

Why would he? Oh, I don't know what to do, Giancarlo," she fretted. "After all these years, do we really have to dredge it all up?"

"It wasn't us that dragged it up. It was the kids," he said. "James stole my files from the precinct, and found more on file at the library, just as the Stefan kids did. I was involved back in '77, and whether *you* like it or not, because you had a child with Andros Poulos, *our* two families are tied together."

"Yes, but that only made Luiz related to Angelina, not Alena."

"But Luiz found his way to Tomas and they became lovers, so Luiz tied himself to the Stephanopoulos family whether we like it or not. Now, Jenny's offering a way to end it all. I say we do it. We end it. And we do that by telling him."

"But you didn't think any good would come of it. Or are you just agreeing with your precious Jenny Stephanopoulos?" Sheila argued.

Giancarlo gave her his steely detective glare which made her wither. "I didn't. But that was until I heard James say something to Alena the other day. He remembered something and claimed he didn't know where he'd read it. It could have only *been* from my files, or old newspaper clippings. He's remembering, *that's* why I now agree with Jenny. Because if he remembers all of it *before* we tell him, God knows what he'd do again."

"Do you think he'd do something stupid?" Sheila asked, knowing he was right.

"I hope not, but then you never know. He might fly to Mykonos just to see Alena to get the whole story. Problem is, even she doesn't know it."

"When do we have to decide by?"

"November first at the latest for arrangements. But we should do it now, so James can get his head around it first."

"But what if he tells her before the family?"

"Well, we can take his computer away; that might stop him talking to her. But it won't take him out of commission completely."

"What if we wait until the last minute?"

"Then he could remember anything in the meantime."

"We could tell him on the way there."

"We could. But dumping all of that on him at the very last minute could do some damage."

"So, then, when do we tell him?"

Giancarlo leaned back in his seat. "He has a doctor's appointment today. Let's wait and see what he says, and if James is doing well, we'll tell him today."

"Oh," she fretted, "I don't know if I can." Clutching her coffee cup, her knuckles turned white.

"We have to. He has a right to know. So, if he wants counselling before going back to work, he can get it."

"I just hope it doesn't affect him too badly. I don't know if I can stand my baby being hurt again."

"He's not a baby, Sheila, he's a grown man who's done some things he needs to know about. And it's time to tell him."

"I hope you're right. What time's the appointment?"

Giancarlo glanced at the clock on the kitchen wall. "It's at twelve. But he has scans and x-rays at eleven."

"So, we'll tell him when we get home?"

"Yes. This afternoon after the appointment and lunch. He'll need sustenance."

"I think I will too," she said. "It's thirty years we're dredging up."

"I know. But hopefully, he'll take it well and not act too much like a child."

"I'd better get breakfast ready then."

"And I'll go and see if he's awake." Giancarlo scraped back his chair.

James scurried back up the stairs and did a quick u-turn. Coming down, he met his father, making it look as if he was just coming down.

"Ah, I was just coming to get you. Your mother's getting breakfast and you have an appointment at eleven and twelve."

"Yes, Dad, I know." James made his way into the kitchen and helped his mother with breakfast.

"Oh, no, sweetie, you don't have to help," Sheila said. "I'll do it."

"Nonsense. I can get my own toast and butter it, Mom." He kissed her cheek and watched the smile remain on her face all through breakfast. *Which is clearly a change from what they were talking about,* he thought. *So what would it be that they have to tell me and what plans are they hatching?*

At twelve, they entered his doctor's office at the hospital.

Doctor Robbins was just sitting behind his desk. "Hello, James, how are we?"

"Good, thanks." He sat between his parents. "So, how am I?"

"I've checked your scans, x-rays, MRI, cat scan, everything looks good. Obviously, we had to do repair work, and you do have some scarring from that, but that's of no importance. We examined your motor skills and had you do a walk and talk test, and your balance and speech are fine."

"Can I go back to work?" James asked eagerly, leaning forward to see what the doctor would say.

Robbins chuckled. "Eager pup, aren't you. No, you can't. I've recommended having the rest of the year off for a reason. And I will be contacting your superior with your latest test results."

Disappointed, James slumped in his seat. "So, can I go back to living on my own again?" As much as he loved being with his parents, he was eager to get back to single life.

"I suggested taking the rest of the year off for a reason," Robbins repeated. "You need to take it easy on every level. If you go back to living on your own, you'll just want to run around like before. You can't do that, but you can up your exercise. Do some gentle weights, fast walking, light jogging. If it *doesn't* make you feel good, don't do it. And for the love of God, don't get involved in shoot-outs." He closed the file in front of him. "You're free to go. I'll see you back here sometime next month. Make your appointment on the way out." He escorted them to the door.

"Thank you, doctor," Sheila said and went to the counter to make the appointment. They stopped for lunch on the way home and finally made it back at two.

"Oh, that was a good lunch." Sheila set her bag on the hallway table. "Anyone care for coffee?"

"I'll take a cup." Giancarlo settled into his easy chair in the lounge room.

"I'll take a cup of truth," James said, and got two confused looks in return.

"I heard what you were talking about this morning and I want to know what you've been keeping from me."

Giancarlo sighed and glanced at Sheila. "Looks like it's time to tell. But we're going to need that coffee."

Five minutes later, they were settled at the dining table, Giancarlo at the head, Sheila on one side, James on the other.

"Okay, what's going on?" James asked, and, pointing to the box in the middle of the table, added, "And what's in the box?"

Sheila traded a glance with her husband. "It's a very long story, James, one that goes back a long time, and has to be told from the beginning so you understand."

He was puzzled by the secrecy. "Okay, just start from the beginning."

With another glance at Giancarlo, Sheila began. "It started in the summer of 1951. I was twenty-two, fresh out of college, and spending June of my summer holidays in Santorini, Greece, with my friends. I met a man there and was wooed. We slept together and I ended up pregnant. I was disowned by my parents. I was kicked out of home. I had to get a job and support myself and the baby, which I did. He was born in 1952. I named him Luiz Andros Poulos after his father. But since his father wanted nothing to do with him, or me, I renamed him Manning."

"Andros Poulos," James murmured. "Isn't that…"

"Alena's grandfather," Giancarlo told him.

James's eyes grew wide. "Oh, my God, I'm related to Alena?"

"No, no," Giancarlo hushed him. "You share a half-brother with her mother. It does not make you related. Now listen."

Sheila opened the box and pulled out Luiz's toys, setting them beside each other on the table. "When Luiz was seventeen he quit school. I never married, and I let myself go. Could barely afford to buy him things, but I kept a few toys. He bummed around, and eventually, I kicked him out. He was just seventeen." She lovingly held his teddy bear. "What I had bought him, and he didn't take, I pawned for money. It wasn't much, but it helped with the bills. I kept a box of stuff. These toys and two photo albums." Retrieving the albums, she opened the first one. "I'm sorry to say, I never really loved him. I hated the world at the time. Myself for being stupid enough to have sex, my parents for kicking me out. Andros for denying him. Luiz for existing."

"You could have adopted him out," James said quietly. He had a brother; he already knew that.

"Yes, I could have. But, I thought, after he was born, Andros would come to his senses. I sent a letter and photo, and his lawyer sent back a letter of refusal. He refused to accept Luiz as his son, so I kept him because I didn't believe in abortion and I figured I had to suck it up and deal with it." Flipping through the album, she smiled. "He was a gorgeous baby, and maybe I did love him in my own way. When he died, I couldn't afford to claim the body and bury him, but after I married your father, he persuaded me to track down his grave and dig him up. We cremated him, and I have him in that urn on my bedside table."

"That blue jar thing?" James asked. He'd seen it every time he'd gone into his parents' room. One day he'd even opened it to see what was inside. He figured it was dust, but now he was finding out it was his dead brother.

"Yes, that urn holds the ashes of your brother, Luiz." Sheila slid the album over for him to look at before continuing her story. "I didn't see him after I kicked him out, and I have regretted it ever since."

"Why did you kick him out?" James scanned the photos, looking for something, anything.

Sheila swallowed the big fat lump in her throat before answering. "Because he was gay and having sex with the underage neighbourhood boys."

"What?!" James's head flew up. "Oh, my God, you're kidding?"

"No." Sheila flushed with embarrassment. "I kicked him out before there was a complaint. I couldn't afford to be kicked out of my apartment, so I kicked him out instead. I had to find out from newspaper clippings that not only was my son dead, but his father had died on the same night."

"You're kidding?" James had a vague recollection of something.

"I was the detective on the Poulos case here in New York," Giancarlo told him. "I dealt with the death."

"Whoa." James stared from one parent to the other. "And then what?"

They took turns telling him they'd already been in a relationship for two years at that stage, and how Sheila managed to acquire five million dollars from Jenny Stephanopoulos.

"Alena's grandmother?" James's aqua blue eyes were saucer wide.

"Yes," Sheila said. "She inherited the fortune of the man who killed my son. By law, I felt I was owed something and she agreed. I received five million dollars before Christmas that year."

"And what did you do with it? It would have been a lot in 1977," James said.

"It was," Sheila replied. "It came in $250,000 increments every week until it was paid off. The first lot, I spent. I gave myself a makeover, moved into a new apartment, bought new furniture, new clothes, quit my old job and got the job at the museum. And once your father and I got married, I spent some doing up this house, so it was worthy of raising children in."

James looked around and his head nodded slightly. "It's held up well."

"We've kept it in good shape," Giancarlo said, glancing at his old house.

"So, what happened then?" James turned his attention back to his mother. "I was born on Valentine's Day 1979, and all I remember is seeing Jenny and Tomas in the department store. That haunted me for years and yet you kept telling me Tomas was a figment of my imagination. Why?" he asked his father. "I don't get it."

Giancarlo glanced at Sheila who took a breath. "In 1977, Luiz met Tomas Stephanopoulos, and for a short time, they were lovers. From what we know, Tomas dumped him and fled to Miami where Luiz followed. He was obsessed with Tomas and ended up killing four men from a porn movie company called *Seralift*. Luiz used to work there years before. He framed Roger Dencott, Tomas's new lover, for the murders to get him away from Tomas. He poisoned Tomas to get him away from Roger, and Tomas ended up in the hospital. Luiz kidnapped Tomas from there, but was found dead in a hotel room the next day.

Tomas was gone. It came out in a newspaper article and the report, the police file I was sent from Miami, that Luiz had been shot by a man working for Stefano Papadopoulos."

"And who's he when he's out?" James asked.

"He was a huge underworld mob boss who got what he wanted," Giancarlo kept up the story. "I was with the FBI when we tracked all three of the Stephanopoulos boys to Chicago where Papadopoulos was flying out. He didn't succeed in getting any of them, but all of his men were killed in the process."

James's brain ticked over. "Okay, so I have a half-brother who shares a father with Angelina Stephanopoulos, Alena's mother. He also happened to be the lover of Alena's uncle, Tomas. Tried to poison him, and frame Roger for four murders. What does any of this have to do with me except in relation to Alena? Which does not make us related genetically, I know."

"Well, we thought it stopped in 1977," Giancarlo replied. "But it started up again with you this year."

"With me?" James pulled back in surprise and saw his mother push the second album at him.

"Take a look, especially the last ones. Tell me what you see."

James quickly flicked through and stopped at the last pages of photos. "I have the same colour eyes. So what."

"James." Sheila handed a separate single photo of him over. "*That's* you at seventeen."

James studied his photo then looked at Luiz's. "Shit, we looked the same."

"And we have it on good authority that you look like Luiz when he was twenty-five," Giancarlo added. "The two of you are identical. Even to my detective's eye."

"Okay." James put the photo down. "We look identical, so?"

"You ended up on Alena's tour. Her mother knew me back in '77; she would have told you." Giancarlo watched his son for lies and betrayal.

James screwed his face up in thought. "Um…yeah…I vaguely remember. It's fuzzy, so?"

"Angelina never knew her brother, so she wouldn't have recognised you, but the doctor blames your aneurysm for your strange behaviour."

"What behaviour?" James asked. "You two are confusing me."

Giancarlo sighed and glanced at Sheila. He told James all about the assault on Roger and what he'd said. How he'd disappeared for two weeks, somehow managed to obtain his old files from the precinct, drunk a lot, and ended up at the Stephanopoulos penthouse that Sunday morning. "I went to your apartment to check on you. I found my old files, printouts, and the note about brunch. You had gone looking for the family and you found almost everything."

James blinked. "I remember some things, but they're fuzzy. Bits and pieces mainly, not details. I remember digging through boxes of papers. I remember the headaches. I remember the tour, but not what I did to Roger. And why would I go to the penthouse?"

"You rang Alena at nine that morning asking her out to lunch. She invited you to brunch instead. You turned up at eleven. When I found the paperwork at your place, I threw on the siren and hightailed it over there. I found you telling Jenny your name was Luiz Manning and you were back to claim Tomas as your lover. The whole family was there."

"What!" James exclaimed. "Why…why would…I don't understand."

"Your father believes that your health affected everything. That you jumbled it all up in your head and you believed you were Luiz because you'd found out in the apartment that I was his mother," Sheila said.

James shook his head, unable to comprehend what was being said. "Would an aneurysm make me do that?"

"Possibly. Not even the doctors know what it makes people do exactly," his father said. "It made you sick, son. And it messed you up in the head."

James leaned back and ran his hands over his bare head. "So, are you telling me, I went there to claim I was someone I'm not, and somehow got myself shot in the head?"

"No, that part was always true. You ran from the building; your head was making you crazy. You ran across the road, yelled out, *stop, police*, and was shot right in front of me. Not something I ever wanted to see, or want to see again, believe me. Jenny and I helped you until the ambulance came. You went into surgery and you know the rest."

"So, if I looked identical to Luiz, clearly I must have freaked the family out. Do we know for certain? Do you have pictures of Luiz at my age?" James asked, finally learning the whole truth.

"No, I don't. Seventeen was the last age I had any," Sheila said. This wasn't something she wanted to tell him, ever, but after the last few months, it was clearly going to come out whether she liked it or not.

"Oh, my God." James pushed back from the table and prowled around the room, his adrenaline rushing all over. "Oh, my God. I just…" His hand rested over his mouth. "I just can't believe it. I can't believe I did all of those things. Are you sure?" He spun around to his parents. "Are you *absolutely sure* I did all of those things?"

"Yes, son." Giancarlo went to his side. "I was at the penthouse. I saw the pain you were in. You were grabbing at your head before you ran out."

"I have never…" James sputtered at his father. "I have never tried, or thought of killing someone, or trying to. I still don't understand why I would try and kill Roger. I've never met him."

"Not formally," Giancarlo said. "But you came face to face with him at the concert and the penthouse."

"But again, why would I? I'm not my brother, and even if I did jumble all of that information in my head because of the aneurysm, why would I? I don't believe any of it."

"You clearly remember things about her mother that Alena said she hadn't told you," Giancarlo reminded him.

"Yes, I'm remembering things, but not trying to kill someone." James paced the room. "I don't get it, I just don't. Does Alena know all of this?"

Giancarlo looked over his shoulder at Sheila. "They, the family, never really discussed Luiz with the kids. They believed he was none of their business as it was before their time."

"Yeah, okay, I get that," James said. "Alena would only know what happened in the penthouse that day?"

"Yes."

"So, even if I talked to her about it, she wouldn't know any more than I do?"

"No."

"Oh, Jesus." James slumped onto the couch in the lounge room.

"Are you okay, James?" Sheila rushed to his side.

"Yes, Mom. It's just a lot to take in. Is Roger going to press charges against me? Is any of the family? I don't even know where to begin to make it up to him or them."

"No one's pressing charges; they know you were ill and not in your right mind." Giancarlo sat on his other side. "But Jenny Stephanopoulos does have a plan."

He and Sheila spent the next half hour telling James what she had in mind and explaining it all to him. It meant closure for all of them after thirty years. Even though James had only become part of it that year after his involvement with Alena, it would mean it was finally over for all of them. And after a lengthy discussion about not contacting Alena until it was over, he agreed to go along with it.

November 2007

Diana arrived at the Mykonos airport to no fanfare. No one recognised her. She wore dark blue jeans, a big baggy black turtleneck sweater, chunky black shoes, and a black newsboy cap. Her hair was braided and hung down her left side, and she wore no make-up or jewellery. The only accessories she wore were a watch and tinted sunglasses. She didn't want the fanfare; she didn't want to be seen, but she did want to get home without anyone knowing. Jumping into a taxi, she was home in fifteen minutes.

"Alena? You here?" She waited, but heard nothing. "Oh, thank God." Hefting her bags and cases up the stairs and into her room, she removed her glasses and flopped down on her bed. "Oh, it's good to be home." She sighed, staring up at the soft blue ceiling. The room was done in soft, pretty shades of blue, pink and peach, and it always made her calm and relaxed to be in it. But she didn't have long, and she knew that the family would start coming after lunch for her parents' anniversary, even though it was a Sunday.

"Everyone must be out if Alena's not here," she murmured and rubbed her bulging belly, hence the baggy jumper. "Well, baby, we're gonna have to reveal it all soon. Mama's going to be shocked; Daddy too. But I guess with a family as big as ours, it won't take long for them to love you too. And I have to have my first ultrasound. I hope you're okay in there." Grabbing her phone from her bag, she texted her grandma to see if anyone was home.

'Just me and your grandfather. No one's coming until lunchtime. All sleeping in, it is Sunday, are you back yet?'

'Nearly,' Diana texted back and dug in her bedside drawer for the key to her grandparents' house. Sneaking out of her place, she made her way up and through the door of her grandparents' home, but found no one there. "Must be in the bedroom or laundry." Noticing the tables laid out for lunch, she wandered down the hall to her father's bedroom. "Grandma, you home? I'm back."

"Diana?" Jenny looked up from the spare fridge in the laundry slash walk-in freezer. She and Spiros were getting the meat ready for the next three days. "Diana?" Stepping out of the room, she caught the tail end of her granddaughter as she turned the corner for her father's room. "I wonder why she's gone to Carlos's old room," she said to Spiros. "Have you got the meat?"

"Right here." He closed the door and followed her out, his arms laden with lamb, beef and chicken.

"And the store's supplying the hotel." Jenny continued marking off her list.

"Already there and being prepared, I hope." Spiros set the meat in the fridge, but left the chicken out to defrost. "I'll get the rest of lunch done; you go see if that was Diana."

Jenny hurried into her son's room and found her very plain-looking granddaughter sitting on the bed staring out the window. "What's with the clothes? You're dressing like Cabot."

"Grandma." Diana got up and hugged her, making sure not to push her belly against her.

But Jenny knew. "What's the matter?" she asked, staring into her grandchild's face. "Are you ill? Is something wrong?"

Diana sighed and moved to the window. "*Everything's* wrong."

Jenny sat on the bed and faced her. "Tell me."

Diana didn't hesitate. She burst into tears and collapsed at her grandmother's feet, crying into her lap, telling her everything she could. "I haven't seen him since, no one knows where he is, and I miss him. Oh, Grandma, I love him, but he's disappeared."

"Okay, let me get this straight. You're in love with a man who's disappeared since the last time you saw him, and no one knows where he is, is that right?"

Diana nodded through her tears.

"And yet no one knew you were in love with anyone, and you didn't say you were seeing anyone, so what's the real story?" She lifted Diana's chin gently. "You didn't say anything in New York. When did you see him last?"

"July four. We spent it together and then he left on assignment," she sobbed.

"Is he a journalist?"

"Photographer. He's done some of my shots." Diana burying her head back in Jenny's lap.

The cogs clicked into place in Jenny's brain. "Not that Charles Kensington you complained about months ago?"

"Yes." Diana's muffled reply barely came out.

Jenny's brain went into overdrive and the cogs connected the dots. "You're pregnant." Diana's tears came in hulking sobs, and Jenny pulled her up from the floor onto the bed. "Tell me again why he's missing."

Diana told her the story. None of the magazine editors knew where he was, his phone wasn't connecting, and he hadn't been seen or heard from since. "I don't know what to do. Either he left my life, or something happened to him."

"Do you know where he went?"

"No."

"What about the person who sent him on assignment?"

"I don't know who that was." Diana wiped away her tears before a fresh batch started. "I don't want to be a single mother. I don't want the baby growing up without its father."

"Do you have a photo of him? I can have Marco look into it," Jenny said.

Diana quickly flicked through her phone and pulled up the only photo she had of Charles. It was a black and white one from his website.

"He's very good looking," Jenny said. "Send it to my email and I'll get it to Marco, but I need all of the details you have. Who he worked for, where he lived, his number, his friends. Come, we'll send the email off now." They went into her office and sat at the desk, and ten minutes later she sent the email to Marco, labelling it urgent. "Poor boy, he's just got back from searching for Cabot's attacker."

"Did they find him?" Diana wiped her face and straightened her cap.

"Yes, they did. We made sure to make it front page news across America since that's where he's from. He's been arrested and charged with multiple counts of assault. Cabot and his new friend Tony filed charges, as well as ten other residents of Mykonos, but apparently, there have been more. They're all coming forward, claiming he robbed them at knifepoint. So far, he's up on fifty charges of assault and robbery."

"Oh, that's good. Cabot must be relieved." Diana paused. "You said his *new friend, Tony.*"

"He's met someone." Jenny smiled. "He's keeping him grounded."

"Wow! Sounds like my little brother has changed a lot."

"You're going to be very surprised. We are. Now, back to you. When did you find out?"

Diana blushed and sat down in an easy chair. "In New York when I saw Dan. I thought it was food poisoning, but, turns out I was with child."

"Do you love him?"

Diana lit up. "Oh, yes, Grandma, I do. I think I always did."

Curious, Jenny asked, "How long have you known him?"

"I met him on a shoot when I was nineteen. He was nice and polite, we worked together off and on for years, and then he left and came back the biggest ass in the world. We fought and bickered every time we worked together, and then after the party, the twins and I attended on the third, he came to the penthouse and we fought. And then we had sex." She blushed and looked down at her hands in her lap. "We spent the whole time in bed, and then on Thursday morning he left for his assignment."

"That's a long time to be gone," Jenny said. "Too long. Four months, one week."

"Yes," Diana slid her hand under her sweater. "I have to tell Mama and Daddy."

"They'll be okay, don't worry." Jenny got up and sat on the arm of the chair to hug her granddaughter tightly. "I've got the Charles thing under control, and they'll love the fact you're having their grandchild. *I* love the fact you're having my *great*-grandchild. Everyone will get a kick out of it."

"I don't think I can face everyone at once," Diana whispered. "We're a big family."

"You could wait in your father's room and I'll send your parents in. You can tell them, make it all good, then come out and announce it."

"Oh, I don't know if I want to do that. I haven't even had an ultrasound yet."

"We can get Dan to do one today." Jenny checked her watch. "No one's due until one, it's only eleven. We can get you up to the hospital, in the back door, and out before you know it."

"Oh, I don't know," Diana murmured, wringing her hands with the stress of it all.

"Don't you want to know if the baby's okay before you announce it?"

"I guess." Diana's mind wandered off.

"Come on then, we'll get Dan up and get to the clinic." Jenny led her to Dan's room and knocked just as Dan came out fully dressed.

"Oh, hey Diana, you're back." He kissed both cheeks. "Derek's just finishing up."

"We need an ultrasound at the health clinic," Jenny told him and Diana lifted up her sweater.

"Oh, my God, you have grown," Dan said. "You haven't had one yet?"

She shook her head. "No. I didn't want it getting out. Figured I'd just get it done here."

"The clinic's not open until later," Dan reminded them.

"And I have a key, and someone's already there setting up. Let's go," Jenny said.

"Hey, what's going on?" Derek came out of the bedroom.

"Off to give Diana an ultrasound," Dan said. "Baby's growing."

"Baby? What baby?" Spiros called down the hallway.

"Grandpa." Diana went and hugged him. "I'm having a baby, but please don't tell anyone if they turn up. We're off to get my first ultrasound."

"Of course, my darling. That's your business to tell." He kissed her cheek. "Congratulations."

"Thanks, Grandpa." She kissed him back. "We won't be long."

They peeked out the door and ran to the car out front, arriving at the clinic five minutes later. They rushed in through the back door, set up the machine for an ultrasound, and a half hour later they were back home with pictures of the baby and recordings of the heartbeat and movements.

"I can't believe it," Diana whispered. "Did you see it? He moved." The thought of having a child had hit home while watching the monitor. Hearing the heartbeat, seeing the tiny person inside of her, made her realise even more she didn't want to be a single mother. She wanted Charles to come home.

"I saw it." Jenny sat with her arms around her, gently rocking back and forth. "I saw him. He's going to be one gorgeous baby."

"Yes," Diana choked. "If only Charles was here to see him. To be at the birth. To hold his son."

"Oh, Diana," Jenny soothed her. "We'll find him. One way or another we'll find him."

"I hope so, Grandma, because I love him and want him to know he's going to be a father."

"Well, *I* need to go and get lunch ready," Jenny told her. "You stay here and rest. Is there anything you want?"

"I feel like a packet of crisps, but you probably wouldn't have any," she mumbled, suddenly craving salty food.

"Oh, you'd be surprised what I have in this house." Jenny grinned. "I'll bring you something and let your parents know when they arrive."

"Okay." She returned the grin. "Thanks, Grandma."

Jenny retrieved the chips and a bottle of drink for Diana, then set to work getting her famous chicken on. Regardless of it being Carlos and Viv's anniversary, it was still a Sunday, and she knew she had extra guests coming. Cabot had asked if he could invite his friend Tony, there was Dan, Derek and Xanthe, the Gatoses, and Alexis had invited Lorenzo. Lunch was going to be busy. Not to mention the dinners at *The Windmill*. Some of her family had managed to come, a lot of the boys' cousins, and some of her sisters and brothers.

Finally, the food went into the ovens at twelve on the dot. Thank God she'd had a second one installed once all of the kids had come along. It made life a lot easier to put the meat in one and the veggies in the other. And thank God for dishwashers, because there was no way she was doing all of the cleaning by hand.

Tomas and Roger came through the door armed with multiple desserts. Cabot was helping them out.

"Well, look at you." Jenny smiled at him. "Helping with lunch."

Cabot grinned, and set two dishes on the kitchen bench until Roger found room in the fridge for them. "It's just dessert, Grandma."

"Yes, but once upon a time you didn't want to help," she said.

He grinned shyly and nonchalantly shrugged a shoulder. "That's the old selfish Cabot, I'm the getting there and improving Cabot."

"So, you don't have a problem with your name anymore?" Jenny leant against the island bench watching her grandson.

"Well," he sighed, "I have a problem with being named after a dead friend of Mama's, especially one as rampant as him. But, Tony likes my name. He says it's unusual, and we googled the other Cabot. His photos were cool, and he took really good ones of Mama, so," he shrugged, "guess I'll live with it."

"And when's Tony coming?" she went on.

"I told him lunch was at one, so probably just before that."

"And what's he like?" Jenny noticed the smiles Roger and Tomas were trading behind his back.

Cabot went all giggly. "He's nice. We've been hanging out and getting to know one another, watching movies, going to *SB3*, having dinner."

"So…he's a…*boyfriend?*" Jenny smothered her giggles.

Cabot's shyness grew and he looked everywhere but at Jenny. "Not yet…maybe…I dunno."

"Ooohhh, look at you, all shy and giggly over a boy," Jenny teased. "Now I've seen everything." She playfully pulled at his sleeve.

"Grandma," he complained, secretly chuffed at being teased.

Carlos, Viv and Antonio came through the door. "Smells good already, Mama."

"Tonee!" Cabot cried then stopped and put his hands up. "Antonio." He bounced into his brother's arms and hugged him happily. "I love you."

"I love you too, Cabot," Antonio said. "Are we meeting this other Tony of yours today?"

"Yes." Cabot pulled back. "I've invited him to lunch and he'll be at the dinner tonight."

Antonio turned to Dan and Derek. "So, what's he *really* like?"

"He's actually quite nice," Dan told him. "Don't worry, we've got an eye on them both, watching their status, and Xanthe's still counselling Cabot."

"Oooh," Jenny remembered. "Diana's in your old room, Carlos, she wants to talk to you both before the rest of the family."

"Diana! Oh, why didn't she come home?" Viv cried and went racing off with Carlos hot on her trail.

"Because of a lot of issues," Jenny murmured and glanced at Dan and Derek.

Tomas and Roger overheard and gave her quizzical looks, but she raised a brow and turned away.

"Diana!" Viv burst into the room to see her daughter standing at the window. "Oh, my baby."

"Mama." Diana burst into tears and fled into her mother's arms.

"Oh, my sweetie, what is it?" Viv hugged her tight and felt the expanded waistline. "Diana?" She looked her in the eye. "Are you…?"

"Pregnant," Diana blurted and pulled up her sweater to reveal the bump. "Four months, one week."

"But…the…father…" Carlos stared at his daughter. "You're not in a relationship."

"He's missing." Diana gulped and swiped away her tears. "He left on assignment after we were together, and no one's seen or heard from him since. Grandma's got Marco onto it, but I might have to deal with never seeing him again."

"Jenny?" Viv frowned. "You came here first? You told her first?" Oh, the hell she didn't like that. Not being first to know her only daughter was pregnant.

"I wanted to talk to her first about Charles. That's his name. And Dan took me for an ultrasound at the clinic." She showed them the pictures. "It's a boy."

"Oh." Viv teared up. "We're having a grandson; look Carlos."

But Carlos was more interested in his daughter. "Diana." He took her by the arms. "Were you in a relationship?"

"Were you and Mama?" she countered. "It's 2007, Daddy, times have changed. I may have to be a single mother."

"Then we're all here for you." Hugging her tightly, he added, "My baby girl's having a baby. I'm gonna be a grandpa."

Diana giggled softly. "Yes, Daddy, you're gonna be a grandpa."

"Your brothers are outside. I'm sure they'll want to see you," he said.

"Who else is out there? I can't cope with all of the family at once."

"Your uncles Tomas and Roger, and Dan and Derek at the moment," he told her.

"Well…" She ran her hands over her face. "Guess we'd better go see the boys. Tell them they're going to be uncles."

"Oh, they'll love that," Viv said, and led the way. "Everyone, Diana's here."

"Hey. D's back." Antonio and Cabot hurried over and picked her up at the same time.

"Hey, you two." She hugged and kissed them both and stopped to take in Cabot's dark hair and glasses. "You *look* okay. Think the glasses make you look smart." She pinched his cheeks.

"Yes, yes I do," he said. "Have you gotten fat? Because you're heavy." Putting her down, he looked at her. "Hey, we're dressing the same. You hiding too?"

"Um, yeah," she murmured, and figuring she'd better dump the information quickly, she let it out. "Look, I have to tell you something, um, I'm having a baby."

"What!" Cabot squealed and bounced up and down on his tiptoes.

"You're having a baby?" Antonio repeated, shocked that his sister was knocked up. "Who's the father? You're not seeing anyone."

"Not at the moment," Diana said. "Because he's out of the country, but I hope he'll be back soon."

"Who'll be back soon?" Alena asked from the doorway as the rest of the family poured in. Spying her cousin, she screamed, "Diana," and flew across the room into her arms.

Alexis and Angie followed suit with the boys bringing up the rear.

"So, who's not here and when's he coming back?" Alena repeated, noticing her cousin's baggy clothes.

"Um…" Diana glanced at her parents.

"May as well tell them," Viv told her.

"Um…" Diana gulped and breathed in. "The father of my baby isn't currently here."

Silence.

"Baby," Alena screamed, "You're having a baby! Oh, my God." Bouncing up and down she hugged her. "Oh, my God you're having a baby."

"Okay, Alena, reduce the decibels," Pedro warned her. "It's Sunday, tone it down." He congratulated his niece, and brother and sister-in-law and headed for the kitchen for a drink. "Is it too early to drink?"

"I've already cracked the champagne," Tomas called, and Roger handed out glasses.

"Oh, just a juice for me," Diana said.

"Got one right here." Tomas handed her a glass of half lemonade and half orange juice.

They toasted Diana and the baby, and she told the rest of the family about Charles being the father and how he'd disappeared.

"I knew you had a thing for him!" Alena exclaimed. "All the way back in May."

"Well, if the truth be told, I had a thing for him all the way back when I met him. But I was young, and there were rumours that he'd come back from some traumatic experience. He was always nice and polite. Until a few years ago," Diana explained.

"So, you hooked up July Fourth," Antonio said, astounded at his sister's behaviour. "After that party where I bawled him out for the way he was treating you."

She shrugged, embarrassed by the turn of events. "He came over."

"Oh, he *came* all right." Cabot pointed to her stomach.

"Cabot!" everyone complained in unison.

"What!" he cried and shrugged a shoulder. "It's true, just sayin'."

Outside, two men were walking toward the same door from either end of the street. One had three bunches of flowers, the other had nothing. They reached the door at the same time and eyeballed one another.

"Lorenzo," Tony greeted him coolly. "You invited too?"

"Tony," Lorenzo said just as coolly, eyeing the flowers in Tony's arms. "For your boyfriend?"

"You really are an arrogant little dick, aren't you?" Tony asked. "Everyone but Alexis sees it."

"And you're a little fag with HIV dating the fag grandson of my benefactor," Lorenzo sneered. "I got her money for school, and *you're* giving her flowers."

"That's because it's the polite thing to do." Tony boiled inside. "*My* mother taught me manners."

"*My* mother taught me to use anyone I needed to get where *I* wanted to go, and I have no problems doing so." Lorenzo was proud of that fact.

"No problems screwing over Jenny Stephanopoulos and her family, you mean." Tony glanced up and down. "Look at you, you even dress arrogantly." He took in the charcoal grey suit pants and black turtleneck with matching black accessories. "You're also dressing like Cabot. Seems black turtlenecks are all the rage here in Mykonos. I'd better get me some."

"At least I bothered dressing up for lunch with the family." Lorenzo glared over Tony's black jeans, top, and leather jacket. "You look as if you're about to jump on a bike and ride off with your fag lover on the back."

"Have you ever jumped on a bike, Lorenzo?" Tony asked. "Or a man?"

"I'm not a fag like you and Cabot," Lorenzo flared. "I'm into women."

"*Girls*, like Alexis, you mean," Tony replied. "Just as you were into Alena five years back. How long did that last? Three months. Purely sex, I hear."

"*What would you know?* You've probably never been inside a woman before, and here you are bringing them flowers." Lorenzo flicked the bouquets in Tony's arms.

"I *have* been inside a woman, *my mother*, she gave birth to me. But at least I know how to be polite to my hostess and potential partner's mother. What did *you* bring? *Nothing!*"Tony knocked on the door.

"I'll get it." Cabot bounded over to the door and flung it open. "Tony!" He saw the flowers in his grinning friend's arms. "Naw! For me? How sweet."

"No, silly, for your mother, aunt and grandmother." Tony's grin got bigger.

"Naw, none for me." Cabot grabbed his hand, pulling him into the house. He shut the door, but it stopped and he saw Lorenzo. "Oh, didn't see you there, Lorenzo," he said coolly. "Here for lunch?"

"Yes, actually," Lorenzo replied just as coolly.

Cabot pulled Tony into the house. "Um…everyone…this is um… Tony." He smiled brightly and slid an arm through his.

"Oh, hello, it's nice to meet you, finally." Viv came forward.

"These are for you, Mrs Stephanopoulos." Tony handed over a small bunch of red roses. "I hope you like them."

"Oh, how beautiful." Viv took them and buried her nose in the rich red sea of petals, impressed by the young man before her. "Thank you, Tony."

"You're welcome." Tony smiled shyly. "And I have these for the other Mrs Stephanopoulos." He handed a small bunch of red roses to Angelina, catching her and everyone else, by surprise.

"Oh, thank you, Tony." She reached out and took them. "I wasn't expecting anything. Thank you, they're beautiful."

"That's all right, Mrs Stephanopoulos, my mother taught me to thank my hostesses, and you're one of my hostesses." He turned to Jenny. "And these are for *you,* Mrs Stephanopoulos."

"That would be me." Jenny walked from the kitchen, where she'd been watching Alexis bounce over to Lorenzo and he kiss her on the cheek. Alexis had blushed, thinking no one had noticed. "I'm Jenny, nice to meet you, Tony." She shook his hand and accepted the flowers. "Ah, Lorenzo, did you bring anything we need to take care of?"

"Oh." Surprised, he looked from Alexis to Jenny and back. "No, I'm afraid not, Mrs Stephanopoulos. Alexis said I didn't have to."

"That's okay, just asking, in case." Jenny smiled and winked at Tony and Cabot.

"And this is what I normally look like," Cabot said as Antonio came over. "Tony, this is wait…no…ah…Antonio, this is Tony." Cabot shook his head at the confusion. "Fuck, this is going to be hard to keep straight," he muttered.

"Nice to meet you, Tony." Antonio shook his hand and grinned. "Hope I don't get confused either."

Tony laughed. "Just as well I go by Tony; my real name's Antonio too."

"Really?" Antonio's brows rose and he cast a side glance at Cabot. "Cabot went and picked a guy with the same name as me. A coincidence, I ask?"

Cabot blushed and went all girly. "Tonee…argh…Antonio, I am *so* not gonna keep this straight."

"Cabot, why don't you introduce the rest of us?" Pedro said, standing near the fire to keep warm and watching his nephew get all giggly over a potential partner.

"Oh, right." Cabot giggled. "Our Uncle Pedro and Aunt Angie. Their kids, our cuzzes, Alena and Alexis who you know, and that's Dom and Danté." He pointed them out as he went as they were all huddled in the lounge room around the fire.

Tony nodded at the girls and shook hands with the others. "DJ and world-famous musician," he said to Pedro and Angie. "and DJs and

IT ninja I think Cabot said," he said to Dom and Danté. "And shark bite survivor as well."

Danté grinned, despite the ache in his leg. "Yeah, I have some pretty cool scars."

"And Uncle Tomas and Roger who you met yesterday," Cabot dragged Tony around and went on with the introductions.

Tony nodded at them in return and said hello.

Cabot stopped in front of his grandparents. "And my grandparents, the mega heads of the family, Jenny and Spiros."

Tony shook hands. "Thank you for inviting me, it was unexpected, but very nice."

Cabot pulled him on. "And big sis Diana who's having a baby, yay," Cabot squealed as he introduced his potential mate to his pregnant sister.

"Hello, Ms Villiers, nice to meet you; you're gorgeous." Tony smiled brightly at his potential sister-in-law, hoping to make an impression.

Diana blushed. "Oh, my, thank you, Tony, that's so sweet."

Cabot moved them on. "And, of course, Mama, Vivian Villiers, who's now a proud grandmama-to-be."

"Mrs Stephanopoulos, nice to meet you formerly." Tony kissed her hand, taking in her youthful appearance.

"Oh, Tony, lovely to finally meet you." Viv blushed at the hand kissing. Not even Carlos did that, and the last time it had happened was sometime in the '70s, or '80s at the latest.

Cabot waved a hand at his father. "And this is mega movie writer, director, producer, head of *our* family, Papa, Carlos Stephanopoulos."

Tony knew this impression was the most important, and hoped he made a lasting one. "Mr Stephanopoulos, pleasure to meet you, sir. Thank you for letting me come to your anniversary dinner tonight."

"You're welcome, Tony." Carlos noted the firm handshake and maturity in the tall lithe young man before him. He noted the dark features and exotic green eyes. "You got a last name?"

"Luca. Tony Luca," Tony replied. "My full name's Antonio DeLuca Junior, but I've always gone by Tony Luca."

Carlos froze, his hand clenching Tony's, staring at the young man before him, the resemblance bashing through his skull and surging forth the memories of decades past as his body went ice-cold at the mention of the name.

"Oh." Viv's hand flew to her mouth, and the rest of the adults gasped and fell silent, leaving the kids puzzled and wondering why.

"Is something wrong?" Tony stared at the silent shocked faces and fear raced through him. Had he made the wrong impression? Had he said or done something to insult the family? He noted the expression of dread on Carlos's face. "Mr Stephanopoulos?"

"Your name is Antonio DeLuca?" Antonio asked from the other side of Cabot.

Tony glanced his way, thoughts racing through his brain. "Yes."

"Wait, Tone, that's your full name," Cabot said to his brother, confused as to why two guys close in age would have the same name.

"What?" Tony looked from Antonio and Cabot to Carlos who still had his hand in a death grip. "Sir, Mr Stephanopoulos?"

"Argh?" Carlos pulled back and spun around, lumbering across the room to fall on the wall behind him. Jenny went to his side, as did Tomas, to support him.

"What is it? Have I said something wrong? I didn't mean to offend anyone." Tony was alarmed that the good impression he thought he was making just went up in smoke. Looking around at the family, he saw the strange, curious expressions on the adults, and confusion on the kids. Whereas Lorenzo was just smirking.

"Your father," Viv murmured. "Was he Antonio DeLuca?"

"Yes," Tony replied. "Did you know him? My mother told me they met here in 1977 when he worked as a bartender."

"Your mother?" Carlos gasped, having nearly no breath left as the memories pounded through his body.

"Yes, Cynthia York. A British redhead with green eyes." Tony watched his potential father-in-law's facial expressions and knew something was drastically wrong.

Carlos slowly straightened. "I…think I remember her. She spilt her drink and Antonio got her another one."

"Yes," Tony said eagerly, knowing he was going to get the information he had been seeking for years. "That's the story Mum told me. She said she'd been eyeing off the other hot bartender when she tripped and dropped her drink. Dad came to the rescue and helped her up and gave her another one on the house."

Carlos choked back a half laugh half sob and put his hand over his eyes. "I was the other hot bartender. Oh, my God, I was there the day your parents met. I knew your father, I worked with him for three years. He was at our…" Tearing up, he gasped. "He was at our wedding." Looking at Viv, he fled into the kitchen and out onto the balcony to cry like a baby, with Jenny, Spiros, Tomas and Pedro following.

"Wait." Antonio put a hand up. "Is that *the same* Antonio DeLuca *I'm* named after?"

Tony looked at him in confusion. "What?"

"Yes," Viv said solemnly, forlorn at the turn of events for her husband and the young man before her.

"Someone please explain what's going on to me because I'm lost," Tony told the room, glancing at face after face and getting nothing.

"Antonio, your father, worked with Carlos at a bar here on Mykonos for three years, 1974 through to 1977. I met Carlos around the same time, because of your grandmother, Connie DeLuca. She was a dear friend of mine, and I met Carlos because of her." Viv teared up at the loss. "We didn't talk much after the wedding. Antonio was there, Connie was unable to attend. She and I spoke on the odd occasion. She told me she had a grandson and was ecstatic. But we lost contact with your father and…" She breathed deeply. "We received a letter from a mutual friend that your grandfather, Stephano, had passed, followed by Connie, followed by Antonio. It hit us both hard because we hadn't known, and we didn't know Stephano and Connie were ill. Your father died shortly after, in early '81. We found out in January '81. We're so sorry, Tony. We are." Reaching out, she grasped his hand. "I'm so sorry. When the twins came along we named them after our dearest friends, Cabot Conroy, and Antonio DeLuca. And now look. Thirty years to the day that we last saw your father, you are standing before us. You're a fine-looking man, Tony, your father and grandparents would be proud." She touched his cheek and stepped away.

"Oh…" Tony deflated and leaned on Cabot who quickly slid his arms around his man.

Jenny came back in. "Everyone; let's give him some space to breathe." She waved her shocked children and grandchildren on. "We have food to prepare."

Cabot sat Tony down on the couch. "I am so sorry. I didn't know either."

"So am I. I've never heard that before. Mum just told me that my father and grandparents had died. She never went into detail." Tony's eyes glazed over, and he stared blindly into nothing.

"That's their estate you inherited," Cabot said. "They must have prepared that, they thought of you." He gently squeezed Tony's hand.

Antonio pulled a chair over and sat in front of his brother. "I never knew the story either. They just said it was after a friend of Papa's."

Tony looked at him through glassy eyes. "He's dead. And you all know him."

"Not all." Carlos set down a dining chair in front of him and sat. "I should tell you the rest."

"Please," Tony begged, reaching out to Carlos and desperately clutching at his hands. "I want to know the truth. How did they die?"

"It's shocking, and will hurt you," Carlos told him, squeezing tight. "Are you absolutely certain you want to know?"

"Yes, please. My mum didn't tell me much. I don't even think she knew. When I turned twenty-five I inherited the estate in Spain. I've been there. It's beautiful, but haunted, like something bad happened."

"It did." Viv sat beside him and patted his arm. "And we're *so, so* sorry."

"Please tell me," he pleaded, his exotic green-brown eyes fixed on her cat-like emerald ones.

Carlos reluctantly started. "In 1977 I had worked with your father for three years. I knew, we both knew," he cast a glance at Viv, "your grandmother, and knew that your grandparents had been separated for about five years. It was more of an open marriage, and Antonio used to tell me all the time how much he hated it. After our wedding, we left. We all moved to New York and I didn't see your father again. We got the odd note from Connie, about life, and her grandson. And then one day in January 1981 we received a letter from a mutual friend informing us of their deaths…ah…" The air left him and he stared down at their entwined hands, not even wanting to proceed. "It…we…know your grandfather had many lovers, as did your grandmother, but the difference was, your grandfather's lovers were men."

Tony's brows rose at the tidbit of information. "He was gay?"

Carlos nodded, unable to look the kid in the eye. "Turns out."

"Oh, my God," Tony breathed. "Oh, my God."

"During 1980, he became ill and passed away," Carlos continued. "When he died, there was an autopsy, but your grandmother didn't believe the results. She ordered more, but by the time she got those results she was very ill."

"From what?" Tony asked, wanting and not wanting the answer at the same time.

"Ah." Carlos breathed deeply. "The autopsy showed your grandfather had multiple STDs which he had passed on to Connie, which is what made her sick."

"Oh, my God." Tony's eyes bulged, fearing the worst. "Don't tell me?"

"Since it was 1980, no one can say for sure, but we believe he had what was known as the gay plague. The gay cancer."

"AIDS," Tony whispered, his face screwed up in anger. "My grandfather gave my grandmother AIDS?"

Carlos nodded. "It turns out, Connie couldn't believe that he would give her such diseases, and she became heartbroken. She thought he was sleeping with women, but, like her, he was sleeping with men. She died not long after."

"Of AIDS?" Tony asked. "It killed her that quickly?"

"Ah…no…" Carlos stared at Viv and saw her nod. A sigh deflated him. "Your grandmother was heartbroken at being given STDs by your grandfather, and with the thought of him sleeping with men, she…"

"What?" Tony asked eagerly. "What did she do?"

"Oh, Tony, I'm so sorry for what I'm about to tell you." Carlos let go of Tony's hand and buried his face in his. "Connie threw herself off the turret of her home. Your father found her dead on the driveway."

A squeak came from Tony as all the air left him, and his body slumped against the back of the couch in shock. His jaw hung open, his eyes as wide as saucers.

"Poor bastard; look at him," Pedro murmured to his family in the kitchen. "What a way to find out about your family's deaths."

"Yeah, it's going to affect him for a while," Tomas replied. "Maybe even for life." He went back to refilling glasses.

"It must be so sad," Alena whispered to Diana and Alexis. "To find out about your family that way. It must be horrible with all of us around." They were standing near the fire that crackled gently in the grate.

"Then stop staring," Diana chastised her cousin. "Give him space, don't stare."

Alena blushed. "Can't help it. Let's talk about something else like the teeny tiny baby in your tummy," she squealed quietly and tickled Diana's stomach. "I can't believe you're having a baby."

Diana grinned. "Neither can I."

"She…?" Tony started, unaware of the whisperings around the room.

"I'm sorry, Tony." Carlos looked up through red glassy eyes. "Your father couldn't deal with losing both of his parents so he…he joined them."

"What?" Antonio muttered, glancing between his father and mother. "You mean he—" He saw the small shake of the head his mother gave him and stopped talking.

"How?" Tony asked forlornly, knowing what was coming.

"Shot himself," Carlos replied simply. "But only after packing up all of the paperwork for the house and bank accounts. Looks like that all went to you."

"He shot himself?" Tony breathed in. "In the office…? I felt it, like something was there. It was cold and made me feel ill," he whispered. "I always said it was beautiful, but haunted. I'll never be able to look at it the same way again."

"At least you have something of your family," Viv said. "It's a beautiful home. I went there a couple of times in the '70s."

"But I want my father and my grandparents. I don't want their house. I want *them*." Tony couldn't breathe and looked around wildly for a way out. "I just…" The panic set in. "I can't breathe, I need air. I…" Jumping up, he stumbled over Carlos and Antonio and ran out the door.

"Tony," Cabot yelled and took off after him, finding him at the beach as they had done on reverse just two weeks earlier. They had spent the last two weeks hanging out and getting to know each other, but he certainly hadn't known all of that. He fell onto the sand beside Tony. "Oh, God, I'm so sorry. I didn't know."

"Neither did I," Tony sobbed. "My bloody father killed himself. My mum didn't know. She was just told they had died in an accident and that's all she told me. But now, oh, God." He broke down and cried in Cabot's arms.

*****

"Jesus fucking Christ," Carlos spat. "I never thought I'd ever have to live that again." He stood up so fast his chair toppled backward. "Fuck it!" He back kicked it across the room.

"Hey! What did that chair ever do to you?" Jenny walked over to the chair.

Carlos stopped, hands on hips, frown on face. "What?"

"I'm serious." She picked up the chair and looked at him. "You should know this family by now, Carlos, it's a very convoluted web of people and secrets."

"Yeah, but I never thought…I never thought I'd have to tell that story. *Ever!*"

"Neither did the rest of us, but a lot has happened to this family. *In* this family. Sometimes stories need to be told." Jenny set the chair back at the table. "Lunch is nearly ready. We'll eat. I doubt they'll be back in a hurry."

Quietly, they lunched on Jenny's roast chicken and chatted about the parties.

"Oh, my God, this is so good. I've missed it." Diana closed her eyes. She was in heaven devouring her grandmother's food.

"There's more if you want seconds," Jenny told her.

"Oh, God, yes, please. I'm starving." She was served seconds and devoured that too.

"Eating for two are we?" Alena joked.

"Just one that I know of, but it's a boy, so clearly he's a hungry little beast." Diana scraped up the last of her food and laid her utensils on the plate. "Bring on dessert."

After lunch, most left. Angie took the kids, Vivian went with Diana. Lorenzo, Dan, Derek, and Xanthe, who'd turned up after Tony had run out, left as well, to give them some space if they returned, which they did.

"They're back." Antonio saw them through the front window and jumped up to open the door as Cabot tapped on it. "Hey."

Cabot led Tony in and they went into the kitchen. "Sorry, we didn't make it back. Guess we're too late for lunch."

"It's warming in the oven," Jenny said, seeing Tony's forlorn expression. She wrapped her arm around him. "I'm so sorry you've gone through this. Today of all days. It must be very hard to comprehend. Unfortunately, this family is a very large one, and we've gone through thirty years of heartbreak. Like this. First in 1977 then '80 through '82 and now in 2007. We're very sorry for your loss, Tony. Your father was a nice young man. He didn't deserve the ending he got."

Tony stared at the floor, not registering her face. "I'm sorry I ruined lunch," he mumbled quietly.

"That's okay, you didn't," Jenny told him. "It's understandable. Now, if you're going to be a part of Cabot's life in that particular way—"

"Grandma, not now." Cabot frowned at her.

"Don't interrupt," she scolded lightly then continued. "If you are going to be in Cabot's life as his partner, then that makes you a member of this family. And for Carlos and Viv, you kind of already are. But it means we look out for each other, so if there's anything we can help you with, or do for you, let us know. And if you want to talk to Xanthe, feel free. She's here for the whole family."

"And she's good," Cabot butted in.

"Are the two of you hungry? You're definitely cold. Take your coats off and come sit by the fire. Carlos, stoke the fire, and get another log on. Tomas, get the lunch. Come." She led them to the two easy chairs by the fire and sat them down. "We'll get you some coffee to warm you up." After spreading lap blankets across them both, she went for the coffee while Tomas and Roger set their dinner trays on their legs.

While they ate, the family that was left cleared up in the kitchen to give them some peace.

"We're to blame," Carlos murmured. "I should have told her."

"Don't go back over that," Jenny told him. "It's twenty-seven years ago and there was nothing you could do."

"I could have told her." His face was black with anger. But he was more angry at himself rather than at anyone else.

"And if she didn't believe you?" Jenny fiercely whispered in his ear. "She would have slept with him anyway. He was her husband."

"You okay, Tony?" Cabot asked as he wiped up the remainder of his gravy with his buttered roll. Popping it into his mouth, he licked the remnants off his fingers.

"I'll live. Unlike my family," Tony sadly joked. "It was nice what your grandmother said."

"Yeah, I don't give her enough credit for holding us together," Cabot said, glancing at the kitchen to see her whispering furiously with his father and wondering what was being whispered about.

"Maybe I should talk to Xanthe like your grandmother offered."

"If you want," Cabot replied. "She doesn't take bullshit and is brutally honest in return."

"Maybe that's what I need." Tony stared into the fire. He was toasty warm and didn't want to move. It was the most familial home he'd been in in a long time. And it was nice. Even if he'd found out devastating news.

Carlos came and stood by the fire. "I'm sorry. I never dreamed I'd meet his son one day. I certainly didn't think I'd ever tell his son what happened."

"That's okay, Mr Stephanopoulos." Tony looked at him. "I didn't think it would happen either. I've been coming here for years trying to find out about my father, and then I was assaulted, and now I've met Cabot. Who knew his father knew my father thirty years ago!"

"The thing is, Tony, tonight we'll be playing my wedding video, and your father is in it." The words stuck in Carlos's throat.

Tony choked. "He's in it?"

"Yes, he is, for about a minute. He was a great guy, and I don't want to upset you tonight as well, so I thought I should let you know."

"Thanks for telling me, Mr Stephanopoulos. I only have the photos Mum took of us."

There was a small knock at the door and Danté entered. "Done it." He handed the package to Carlos and left.

"I had Danté copy and record the snippet onto a flash drive for you and make some photos of your dad." He handed over the business-sized envelope to Tony.

Tony opened it to find a small flash drive and two pictures. "Oh," he murmured and Cabot peered over his shoulder. "This was 1977?"

"Thirty years ago today," Carlos said quietly. "He'd already met your mother, but she wasn't there, and he didn't mention her."

Tony stared at the photo, a sad smile on his face. "When I found out about the estate and went to see it, the law firm took me through it. There were no photos, but they had been packed in the family vault off the office. We managed to open it and I found them. They looked so happy in them. There were albums and personal effects, all sorts of things belonging to my father and grandparents. I never knew all of that stuff, and all of a sudden I had my whole heritage in front of me. Spanish, Colombian, one whole half of me. Thank you, Mr Stephanopoulos." Standing, he shook Carlos's hand. "Thank you for telling me the truth. Not even the law firm handling the estate would.

You're the only person who has."

Carlos shook his hand in shame, regret and sadness. "I'm so sorry, Tony."

"There was nothing you could do to prevent it," Tony told him. "Not even me being alive could prevent it, apparently. Dad preferred to be with his parents than live for me." The sadness was deep within him, so deep it was embedded in his gut.

Carlos opened his mouth to say something, but his mother came to his side. "Why don't you boys go and rest in Carlos's old room for a while. I'll come and get you when it's time to get ready."

"Okay, Grandma." Cabot led Tony down the hall and into his father's old room, while Tomas and Roger cleared their trays.

"You can't tell them," Jenny murmured to Carlos. "You heard what he said. His father didn't even think about him. Antonio killed himself because he'd lost his parents and the shame of his father's homosexuality. Connie killed herself because of the same shame. You could not have stopped it. You don't even know if she would have listened to you."

"At least I could have tried," he sobbed. "Even if she had've ignored me, I still would have tried."

"Oh, Carlos." She took him into her arms and he cried. "I'm so sorry."

*****

"Hello and welcome back to *The Windmill Hotel* and our thirtieth wedding anniversary." Carlos gazed across his family. Thirty years ago there was a least a hundred people, now they were down to about fifty. "As we all know, in the last thirty years we have lost some people. Our great-grandfather, Papa's grandfather, went a week after the wedding. Mama's parents, Grandma and Grandpa Matthew and Sarah Marsh. We've lost some aunts and uncles, and some couldn't make it tonight. And that's okay. We also…" He choked up. "We lost a good friend of mine who was here that night. Antonio DeLuca. I think he sat with David and Beth and we all had fun. Well, bizarrely, his son is actually here tonight, thirty years later, as a friend of my son, Cabot." He turned to his right to see Cabot and then Tony sitting at the table next to him.

Cabot smiled softly at Tony and slid his arm through his, squeezing it to reassure him that it would be okay.

Carlos shook his head. "The memories and timing are mind-blowing, but I hope you all have fun. All remember thirty years ago… if any of you still have memories."

"Cut the crap, ya yobbo and get on with it," Chris yelled. He'd been at all three weddings and had been one of the cousins to come back when Tomas and Roger were dying.

"You know you caused trouble at my wedding too." Carlos wagged a finger at him. "I haven't forgotten that."

"All right, all right, enough of that," Pedro called from his spot at the side table. "As the resident DJ in this town I'll be spinning the discs for this shindig, so let's get on with the toasts so I can get playing."

"Yes, yes, all right," Carlos mumbled. "Thank you all for coming, we will be playing the wedding video later, so you can all see what dickheads you made of yourselves back then, but for now, here's Viv."

She stood up in her white ethereal *Haus of Stefan* chiffon creation to a round of applause and wolf whistles. The placement at the tables and chairs was the same as thirty years ago, except this time she and Carlos had their children at the table with them, and the rest of the family were at another. "Little did I know what sort of family, or life, I was getting into when I married Carlos thirty years ago." Guffaws were heard all round. "And little did I know that thirty years later I would be just as happy as I was then. Thirty years ago I was forty, and what most of you didn't realise at the time, was that I was almost two months pregnant with our beautiful Diana." She smiled down at her glowing daughter who sat with Antonio to her left. "My precious angel has given me permission to reveal to you all that tonight, thirty years after I sat here pregnant with her, that's she is also pregnant with our first grandchild."

Cheers, applause and whistles went through the crowd. Diana blushed delicately at the attention and smiled graciously at everyone.

"The father couldn't be here tonight due to work, unfortunately," Viv said diplomatically, "but we wish him a quick and safe return home to our Diana and their baby soon. Then along came Antonio and Cabot." Groans rolled around the room. "Yes, we know," Viv laughed, "but he *is* coming good with a lot of help from poor Xanthe who I'm sure is going to need to see a shrink herself very soon."

That had Xanthe laughing and nodding her head vigorously.

"So, please, remember our night thirty years ago, and enjoy our night tonight, thirty years on. Thank you." She sat down to more cheers and whistles and the food came out. It was the same menu as in '77, with meat supplied by *Stephanopoulos Meats.*

After dinner, Pedro got on the decks and spun the tunes from 1977, and the home movie of the wedding played on four screens set up around the room with the reception video playing after it.

Carlos kept an eye on the video, watching as he watched his sons. Cabot was dancing with Tony, Antonio with Diana, his parents were out on the floor as they had been thirty years ago, and he saw Alexis rocking down with Lorenzo, Dan with Derek, and Xanthe with half his family.

"I can't believe I got to sit at the head table," Tony told Cabot. "That's a bit embarrassing."

"Why? Because people thought you were a member of the family?" Cabot spun around and flung his arms in the air. "Or my boyfriend?"

Tony laughed and moved closer as they danced. "I didn't think I'd be on show."

"We're the Stefans, we're always on show." Cabot spun Tony around.

Carlos waited for the moment in the video to go up to his son and Tony. Laying a hand on his arm, he nodded to the closest screen when Tony looked at him.

Turning, Tony saw his father with Carlos thirty years previously, talking to the camera, arm around Carlos, beer in the other. Absentmindedly stepping closer to watch, his hand moved up to touch his father's face and a tear rolled down his cheek. The video moved on, and the moment was over.

Carlos led them just outside to the terrace. "That's what's copied onto the flash drive I gave you this afternoon. You'll be able to hear his voice, see him, know him. I also copied these for you." He pulled a bulky envelope from his jacket pocket and handed it over. "I don't recommend reading them now. They'll upset you. It's the letter from Harry telling us of their deaths, and six pages of obituaries, one for each of them in English and Spanish. I'm sorry, Tony, I really am truly sorry."

"Thank you, Mr Stephanopoulos," Tony tearfully said. "It means a lot to me. What you gave me today and now…thank you." He shook Carlos's hand, took the envelope, and stood looking at it.

"I'll leave you two alone. Come in when you're ready." Carlos went back inside into the arms of his teary wife and mother and teared up himself.

"Oh, wow," Tony breathed. "I've never seen their death notices before."

"Do you want to leave it till later? It might make you cry and more miserable than you were this afternoon," Cabot said, sliding his hand through the crook of Tony's arm.

"Yeah, it could." Tony frowned and slid the envelope into the inside pocket of his jacket. "I'll look at it later. Let's go back to the party." He squeezed Cabot's hand, and they went back in.

*****

On Monday at lunchtime, everyone rolled into Jenny's for sustenance.

"Ugh, I need food," Carlos groaned. "I'm starving."

"Same here." Pedro stared into the oven. "What's for lunch?"

"Beef lasagne," Jenny said. "So don't open it."

"Yum, my favourite." Yawning, Pedro grabbed a beer from the fridge.

"Did you not have enough of that last night?" Jenny asked, getting the plates ready.

"I don't drink when I play, Mama. So, I only had one with dinner. Do you want to talk to Dom now?"

"I guess we'd better," she replied.

"Talk to Dom about what?" Carlos asked, munching on potato chips.

"Dominic, can you and Danté come here, please?" Pedro called to his sons.

They managed to get up from the couch where they'd flopped down and walked into the kitchen.

"You only use my full name when I'm in trouble, so what have I done now?" Dom asked.

"You haven't done anything. We just want to talk to you both," Pedro said.

"Your father and I have talked at great length about your attitude the last fourteen years, especially towards Danté." Jenny's eyes flicked to his surprised face. "And we've talked at great length about your attitude the last two and half months. The way you finally got over yourself and stepped up. Especially when Danté was bitten and hospitalized." With a quick glance at Pedro, she went on. "That's why your father and I have decided to release you from your punishment and allow you to start back at *SB3* next week."

"Ah." Dom's eyes and mouth were huge o shapes. "You're kidding? Oh my God. I love you, Grandma." He hugged her, nearly knocking her off her feet.

"Whoa, hold on there, my, what a strong boy. Okay now." She patted his back.

He let go and hugged his father. "Oh, my God, thank you, Papa."

"Now take it easy." Pedro hugged back and then pushed him away to look into his face. "You're on probation for the rest of the year. Screw up again, you're done. Do you understand me?"

"Yes, yes I do." Dom bounced from one foot to the other.

"Tonight we want you both to do something. Since it's mine and your mother's anniversary, how would you two like to play DJ for the night?"

"Really?" Danté's eyes lit up. "Cool."

"But," Pedro calmed them with a finger point. "*I* have already decided on the music and what order, *you* just have to play it. *And,* Danté goes first so he doesn't fall asleep waiting for his turn. *They* are the rules." He glanced from son to son.

"Yes, we get to play, we get to play," Dom sang as he bounced.

"Yes, you get to play." Pedro grinned.

*****

That night, everyone danced up a storm as Danté hit the decks. Dom stayed by his side in case he needed anything and watched as his family enjoyed themselves. He'd get his turn later. At the end of the set, they stopped for dinner and speeches.

"To my beautiful wife, Angie, I love you more and more each day." Pedro drank in her classic beauty beside him as she sat shimmering in the black and silver *Haus of Stefan* creation Alena and Alexis had made for her. The girls were on her left, the boys on his right. "And the four beautiful children you gave me, including Alena with whom you were pregnant thirty years ago today." The crowd cheered and Alena did a little wave. "We have two beautiful daughters that look just like you, and both of them have grown into amazingly talented individuals. You all listen to Alena's music, right?" he asked the crowd who cheered back. "And Alexis has showed you all the centre?"

"Yes," echoed around the room.

"And then we have our two devastatingly good-looking sons who look just like their father," he joked. "Dominic, and Danté whom you've seen DJ. And you'll see Dom after dinner. They are incredibly talented, and Danté raps and does our IT as well. He's even setting up a company with his best friend, Nick Gatos." Pedro held a hand in the direction of Nick. "Because it's not enough that he runs all of *our* websites, but he has to run other people's as well."

Danté blushed and Nick yelled out, "Whoo, yeah, *IT Web Solutions.*"

"And there's Nick getting in a plug in for their business already," Pedro said. "I'm sure they'll be handing out business cards soon, if they haven't done it yet."

"I have," Nick yelled out, making everyone laugh.

Pedro continued. "And something we also discovered this year, just a couple of weeks ago, in fact, is that Angie has a half-brother, Alfonso DeVille, who's sitting at the table with my family."

Alfonso gave a small wave. He had been invited, but Angie still kept him at arm's length. She didn't want to get too close for the sake of her own comfort.

"And for all of you who remember thirty years ago," Pedro went on, "Carlos worked for the DeVilles and knew Alfonso when he was just five years old. So, let's finish with dessert and get back to dancing. I hope you haven't taken your boogie shoes off yet." He raised his glass. "Here's to thirty years."

"To thirty years," everyone cheered, and the party continued.

*****

On Tuesday at lunchtime, the family were back in Jenny's house enjoying a lamb lunch for Tomas and Roger's thirtieth.

"I'm a bit sad, actually," Roger was saying. "My parents and siblings weren't there thirty years ago, and they're not here now. I'm just glad you at least managed to get my mother over here in '81, Mrs S. We only got to see her a few more times before she and Dad died."

"She was ecstatic to see you alive, though. When did you go and visit her?" Jenny asked.

"In '88, for the bicentenary in Sydney. When we all went over."

"Oh, that's right. I vaguely remember you going off for the day. And you got to see her before she died?"

"A year before." Roger sipped his beer. "We kept in contact via letters that I sent to her sister, and she sent me the rest of my things, or pictures of my brother and sister and their kids."

"Have you seen them since the funeral?" Pedro asked, knowing Roger's family disowned him long before he'd hooked up with Tomas.

"I was at my brother's funeral, and only because a family member contacted me. I barely made it. But my sister still wanted nothing to do with me."

"What about your nieces and nephews?" Carlos finished off his lamb.

"We've had a couple of them visit and introduced them to you," Roger said. "I think they came purely out of curiosity because the Stefan family is famous, and they wanted in on it. Ironically, two of my brother's boys have come out as gay, and my sister's daughter is lesbian. So, how's that for a slap in the face for my brother and sister. However, they didn't come out until their grandfather had died because of his blanket homophobia. They didn't want him knowing."

"Wow," Angie murmured. "That's rough. To hang on to something that long and then wait until someone dies just to be yourself. Very rough and tough way to live your life."

"So is finding out you have a brother after thirty years," Tomas said quietly.

"Oh, you have *no* idea," she told him, placing her cutlery on her plate. "But you, Roger and Carlos are my brothers, and I've had you for thirty years, so three are more than enough. Imagine if I went in search of *all* of my siblings? Bloody hell. There could be hundreds or thousands. What would I do then?"

"Run." Roger grinned.

"Hide," Tomas added, making her laugh.

"Yeah, I feel like it," she said.

*****

That night, Tomas and Roger sat at the head table as they had thirty years previously, with his parents to his left, and Pedro and Carlos to Roger's right. They had the same meal, the same music, the same guests.

"Um, thirty years ago I didn't think it possible to have the kind of life I wanted," Tomas told the crowd. "I watched my brothers get married and cried like a baby because I wanted to get married to Roger, the love of my life." He stared down lovingly into his husband's chocolate brown eyes and set a hand on his shoulder.

Roger gently covered it with his hand and smiled up at his husband.

"Thirty years ago gay marriage wasn't legal, but that didn't stop Mama."

"Whoo, Aunt Jenny," Hayden yelled and the others followed, cheering her on. She blushed and waved at them to stop.

"No, Mama. You deserve it," Tomas told her. "You did what no one else thought of doing, getting me married off." Laughter rippled through the room. "You gave us the most beautiful wedding and reception, and a week in the hotel, which we now own, of course. And then you set Roger and I off on a lifelong holiday. And even when the shit hit the fan in 1981, you came through even more for us, *for me. Your gay son.* If it wasn't for you and Dan Ardent that year, we wouldn't be here now. And I will forever be grateful to both of you, for the rest of my life."

Derek wiped away a tear from his eye and applauded with the rest of the group. Hugging and kissing Dan, he made sure to embarrass him.

"And while Roger and I never got to have children of our own, and are unable to adopt or use a surrogate, unless we did it illegally, we do have seven amazing and incredibly talented nephews and nieces thanks to my amazing, incredible brothers and their amazing and incredibly beautiful wives. Carlos and Vivian, and Pedro and Angelina."

The family cheered and gave a standing ovation.

"I'm not finished yet," Tomas warned the crowd. "And our honorary members in Dan and Derek," more cheering, "and Pedro and Angie's bestest friends in the whole wide world," he joked, "Mike and Maggie Gatos, and their daughters Summer and Melody, who are Alexis's best friends, and Nick, who is Danté's best friend, business partner, and partner in crime.

"Don't forget *IT Web Solutions*," Nick yelled out.

"And quite a businessman too," Tomas told everyone. "I just want to end this by not only thanking Roger, my husband, my best friend, my partner in life, my lover of thirty years, but my parents for having me and accepting me and my lifestyle, and my brothers who were there when Roger and I needed you most. All of you did things a grown man shouldn't need his parents and siblings to do, but you were there all the way, and I will be eternally grateful and thankful and proud to know that you were all there for me when I needed you the most. I love you, I'm proud of you, including everyone in the room." He pointed out to everyone. "I love you all, and I thank you for being here for us thirty years later. I hope to see you all in another thirty. Let's enjoy the night." He set the microphone down and fell into his mother's arms. "Oh, Mama," he sobbed.

Viv and Angie spoke to the kids who sat opposite and beside them at the same time. "And that's how we raised *you* to be."

"So take note," Angie added.

Viv watched Antonio and Cabot, with Tony on the other side. The twins hugged it out before including Tony in on it.

Pedro got in on the hugging and held his brother tightly. "What I said thirty years ago still goes, big brother."

"I know," Tomas mumbled into his brother's shoulder. "It always will."

"Come on, I want some of that," Carlos said and grabbed them both.

Jenny got up to hold all three of her boys and Spiros and Roger joined in.

"Group hug," Pedro called, and the rest of the family joined it.

They partied the night away dancing and singing, just as they had back in 1977.

*****

On Wednesday afternoon, with a flaming hangover, Tony met Cabot at Xanthe's. He hadn't read the papers yet, or looked at the flash drive, but he took his computer along to watch it. Cabot had insisted he come for a session with Xanthe and talk to her about his feelings. And after the year he'd had, being assaulted, getting HIV, and doing the damage he'd done, he figured why not.

"So, you haven't read them yet?" Cabot asked from beside him on the couch in the living room.

"No. I wanted to talk it all out first before getting into it," Tony said.

"Start from the beginning then and don't leave anything out," Xanthe told him.

For the next hour, he told Xanthe all about his life. His father had died when he was two; his mother didn't tell him much after that, and

785

he didn't remember much either. He recounted years with his stepfather, and then discussed the estate, and finding out about it. He visited the house, but never imagined two deaths had happened there. "They're buried on the grounds. There are no gravestones, but they're buried there so no one could find them. The lawyer said he didn't know where. And my father wrote a long letter for me upon my twenty-first birthday, and made copies of everything, but the lawyer didn't give me one. Or my mother didn't. There were photos, portraits, paperwork, some jewellery. Diaries. He left his watch, a signet ring and ID bracelet from his parents, and a necklace. There were some rare coins and stamps. The lawyer said it looked like he'd prepared it all before his death, yet he never told me how he died. The vault was neatly organised and laid out. He even left catalogues of everything in there, what they cost, and what the value was at the time."

"He sounds as though he knew what he was doing," Xanthe said. "He was looking after you."

"But he killed himself to be with his parents," Tony yelled. "*He left me.* I was two years old and they both killed themselves." He broke down in Cabot's lap.

"Leaving you alone." Xanthe teared up and watched Cabot comfort him. "You need to read what's in that envelope."

"I don't know if I can," Tony sobbed.

"You have to. They're long dead. Now man up."

His head lifted, his brow was furrowed. "Do you talk to everyone like that?"

She grinned. "Damn straight. Now read them."

Reluctantly, he removed the papers and read the letter first, breaking down once more. Handing the letter to Cabot, he went through the obituaries and saw how loved his father and grandparents were. "Why didn't they love me like that?"

Cabot finished the letter and handed it to Xanthe before reading the obits.

"You can't know and will never know what depression truly does to a person," Xanthe said softly. "From what I can gather, Connie was devastated by her husband's scandal, and the diseases he gave to her. So, the only way out was death."

"Okay, I understand that, he gave her AIDS. She would have died like him, but my father," Tony wailed. "Why did *he leave me?* Why couldn't he decide to live life for me and raise me? I missed out on him. I missed out on my father."

"All I can say, is that Antonio must have been very close to his parents, especially his mother, so I'd say," she glanced at the letter, "it would have devastated him to the point that the only way out of his pain was death. That decision had nothing to do with you. He organised that trust fund for you. He did it all for you. Because at the end, all he had to give you was the family's belongings. He couldn't give you himself because his self wasn't good enough. He needed an out, and he made sure you were going to be okay before doing it. He thought about you, Tony, his son, his namesake, Antonio DeLuca Junior. He thought about you down to dotting every i and crossing every t. He just couldn't give you him."

"But I don't care about the house. Now that I know he and Grandma killed themselves in it, I don't want it. And all of the other stuff doesn't matter either."

"But they're buried there," Cabot said, placing a hand over Tony's. "You can't get rid of it. He's there in spirit."

"But I want *him*," Tony cried tearfully, feeling like a lost little boy. *"I want my father."*

"Of course you do." Cabot wrapped his arms around him to comfort him. "Why don't you play the video. Go on."

Tony loaded the flash drive into the laptop and clicked on the video. His father and Carlos came up, music playing in the background.

"My name is Antonio DeLuca, and I've known this guy here," he pointed to Carlos, "Carlos Stephanopoulos for three years. We've bartended together during the day, and now I'm at his wedding to the incredibly gorgeous Vivian Villiers." He grinned. "After three years of getting his rejects and sloppy seconds, he goes ahead and marries the woman I would have loved to have had."

"Hey," Carlos protested. "She's mine and you're lucky to be here."

"Yeah, yeah. Congratulations man, who'd have thought you'd get married at twenty-four and settle down before I did. And with a supermodel sixteen years older than you. You suck, and I'm jealous. But seriously, congratulations, man."

"Thanks, man," Carlos said and the camera turned away.

"That's what he sounds like." Tony replayed the recording to see his father. "I finally know what he sounded like. I finally get to see him walk and talk and…be…himself."

"And that's a good thing," Cabot said, squeezing his arm. "That's good."

"Yeah, I guess," Tony murmured. "I finally get to hear what he sounded like."

*****

In the early hours of Saturday morning, Jenny received a call from Marco. They had found Charles in a small backwater hospital in some godforsaken Middle Eastern country, sick and on his deathbed in a shell-shocked state.

"Get him out." Jenny slid her feet out of bed and sat up. "Whatever it takes, no matter how much, the money's in the account, do what you need to. And I mean *whatever* it takes."

"Yes, ma'am. We have a chance to grab a flight out in a few hours. We'll try and be on it."

"If not, buy a damn plane," Jenny told him. "You pay your way out, or shoot your way out, as long as you *get out*, do you understand me? Take him to Athens Memorial Hospital. I'll have people on standby. How far away are you?"

"About five hours, maybe less, add the time to wait for the flight."

"I'll see you later today," Jenny said and clicked off the phone.

Spiros had rolled over to listen in. "They found Charles?"

"Marco has him." Jenny checked her clock. "Two a.m. I need to call the hospital." She quietly called the specialist Dr Azmed Alfarti who she had spoken to during the week, and he told her he'd organised the unit that was set up and ready to go. She told him she'd see him later and hung up. "I'd better get ready."

"Do you need to go yet?" Spiros leaned up on his elbow and watched her get her clothes ready. "It's still dark; can't you get a few more hours' sleep."

"I can sleep at the hospital," she said. "Besides, I'll only be gone a day or two. Just enough to see how he is and give orders."

"Dan and Derek going?"

"Of course." She paused to give him a kiss. "Don't tell anyone, especially Diana. If anyone wants to know, I'm in Athens and will be back. Probably tomorrow."

"I was going to say, who'll make your famous roast chicken." He grinned. "I don't think anyone else can do it like you."

"That's because they don't know my secret ingredient." She laughed and ran into the bathroom for a quick shower. An hour later she knocked on Dan's door.

Dan answered with a yawn. "Ugh, Jenny, what is it?"

"Marco's found Charles. He says it will take about two hours to catch a flight and about five hours for that. I've told him to go to Athens Memorial. I could have let you sleep in a bit, but I'm not sure of the time zones and delays. I've rung Alfarti, he's getting the team together."

"Okay, we'll shower and pack. Any idea how long we'll be gone?" he asked as Derek came to the door.

"I want him here by Thanksgiving, so two weeks or so," Jenny said. "Unless something happens in the meantime. We'll leave in an hour. I'll get some coffee and toast on."

"We'll be ready."

She quickly called the airport to get her plane ready and set about making coffee and toast. They ate and were on their way to Athens on schedule. Arriving, they met Alfarti and the rest of the team at the hospital.

"I have no idea what condition he's in," Jenny told them. "But I want every test known to man. Every parasite, STD, HIV, inside, outside, blood, urine, saliva test known to man. I want to know what's wrong with him, so we can fix it. Test for cancers, diseases from insects, anything and everything he could possibly have that we need to know, so we can get him better. We have until Thanksgiving to get him healthy enough to travel to Mykonos, but I don't want him near Diana if he can pass something on. Don't worry about the cost, it's on my tab." She glanced at her watch and then at the team of doctors. Alfarti and Veroke were the specialists who had treated Tomas and Roger thirty years previously. There were specialists from around the world in every field.

"We have two to three hours left, depending on time zones. I haven't heard back since, so hopefully, they won't be too much longer." Breathing in, she added, "And let's hope they have the right man."

"He doesn't know?" Dan was surprised.

"They had a photo, and information on old broken bones, marks, scars, etc, but if he's been sick, or has wasted away, or been tortured, who knows," Jenny said.

"*Has* he been tortured?" Alfarti asked.

"I hope not," Jenny told him. "But, if he has, we'll get a specialist in to help with that too."

Three hours later, Marco and the team called from the airport. "We're here, but they won't let us through with him. I have the airport manager on the line."

"Put him on," Jenny said, hearing voices in the background.

"Ah, yes, hello," his broken English came down the line. "We cannot let this man through without passport."

"You listen to me. I am Jenny Stephanopoulos. My grandfather-in-law was Giorgio Stephanopoulos, I inherited Stefano Papadopoulos's fortune, and I run a very large part of Mykonos. That man has been tortured and detained by terrorists and needs help. I am here in Athens Memorial with a team of specialists waiting to help him. Let him through, or I will come down there and kick your arse. Do you understand me?"

"Ah, yes, Mrs Stephanopoulos. But he has no passport."

"Then get the American consulate to sort it out. He's coming to the hospital, or do I have to call the chief of police to escort him and my team?"

"Ah, the chief of police, oh, no, no, we will let him through." Clattering noises followed.

"Ma'am, he's letting us go, we're on our way."

"There's an ambulance and SUVs waiting outside for you; go with him in the ambulance. I'll see you when you get here." Hanging up, she added, "I should have just called the chief of police for an escort. What a waste of goddamn time. But they're on their way, so not long now."

Fifteen minutes later, a decrepit version of Charles Kensington was wheeled into emergency by Marco's team and moved into an isolation room.

Jenny held the photo from his website up to his face. He was an old, sick version of himself; thin, bony, and discoloured. "Are you Charles Kensington?" she asked him, noting the yellow glassy eyes. "Are you Charles Kensington?"

He nodded slightly, unable to speak.

"We found these in his pockets." Marco handed her two photos of Diana. "He still had his ID and wallet on him, along with SD cards. No camera or passport though. Looks as if he was robbed of his expensive stuff. He only has one small bag."

She held the two photos up to Charles. "Who is this? Who is this?"

His mouth moved and out came, "Diana."

"Your wife? Your girlfriend?" Jenny pushed.

A painful look came over him.

"Do you love her, Mr Kensington?" She leaned in close. "Do you love this Diana?"

"Yes," he managed through dry, cracked lips.

"Good. Because she's my granddaughter and she's pregnant with your child. So, I suggest you cling to that, Mr Kensington. She's pregnant with your son. Do you understand me?"

What looked to be joy and happiness washed over him, but it was hard to tell.

"Here's a sonogram of him, and a picture of Diana with her bulging belly." She showed him the two new photos. "Live for them, Charles. Live for them. Do you hear me? *You do not die on my watch.*"

Not today. Not ever. You don't get to make my granddaughter pregnant and then leave them alone in this world. Do you understand me? You don't get to leave them. Get better for them, cling to them."

Shoving the photos in his hand, she left the room for the doctors to do their jobs.

Watching, she paced as Marco told her the whole story. They had traced him to Baghdad which was his assignment. From there, he travelled across the border into Iran and on to Pakistan where he was taken hostage. From what they knew, the place was bombed and he'd been shifted from the refugee camp to hospital across the border into India.

"We're not sure what's happened to him. We found him in the hospital this morning. He had the photos and SD cards on him, and just his backpack with some clothes and stuff. We've checked it *and* him over for bugs, receivers, transmitters, etc. He's clean."

Jenny took a moment to breathe. "Amazing what you can do in one week with a bunch of money. Did it cost much?"

"About five million."

She winced and breathed in. "Jesus, bloody hell. Well, you did good, Marco. Between Alexis's and Cabot's attackers and this, you'll all deserve your bonuses this year. And they will be hefty ones, don't you worry. Go home, have a break, write up your reports, and I'll see you next week. And don't forget to have your medicals."

"Ma'am." Marco nodded and left Charles's bag with her. Walking outside, he indicated to his team to go, telling them of the big bonuses coming and to take a week off. He knew Jenny was generous, and the bonuses would be big. With the three things they'd had to do this year, he knew they would be paid well. Christmas was gonna be good this year.

Jenny paced for hours, called Spiros to see how everything and everyone was, and tried to get some work done. She'd brought her mobile office with her, but didn't get far.

Finally, everyone stopped and Charles was taken into a quarantined area and given a good scrub down. Jenny stood nearby, making sure he was taken care of while the specialists ran all of their tests.

Dan and Derek came up to her. "He doesn't have AIDS or any other STD that we can tell."

"Oh, thank God." She breathed a sigh of relief.

"But, as you can see, he's severely dehydrated and wasting disease has set in. We'll get him on a cocktail to boost up his system, but until we know the full extent, we can't properly treat him."

"Could it just be that he's malnourished?" Jenny asked.

"Could be," Derek said. "We'll know more with each result. And here comes some now." He nodded in the direction of Alfarti and Veroke who were walking towards them.

"He has parasites, so we're getting the medications ready," Alfarti said. "Considering what he's been through, it was to be expected."

They all watched the two specialists dressed in hazmat suits wash Charles down and dry him off before moving him into another room. They stayed behind to wash themselves off. In the next room, he was tested for radiation and dressed in a hospital gown. He was then wheeled into another room where they took him to ICU.

They followed into the room and Jenny handed back the photos of Diana and the sonogram. "Mr Kensington, do you feel better?"

He nodded, no longer glassy-eyed, but still unable to speak.

"We have a vague idea of what happened to you and we're sorry. Right now you need to get better for Diana and your child. Do you understand?"

Another nod as he stared at the photos. He was going to be a father? How the hell did that happen? They were only together on the fourth of July. He was going to be a father.

"Get him whatever he needs to make him feel better. Fill him with every medication you need to make him better," Jenny told the doctors and nurses before turning to Dan and Derek. "I've arranged for a couple of rooms to be filled with beds for you boys, at least until next week, so you're stuck with a hospital room for accommodation."

"Do we get to wear hospital gowns too?" Derek grinned.

"Better not," Dan joked, "they'll think we're the patients and not take us seriously."

"Sorry about the accommodations. Once he's out of the woods you can grab a nice hotel room nearby on me. And needless to say, you'll be getting big bonuses from me this year."

"Yay, Christmas in Hawaii," Derek said.

"Oh, that's where you're going. I was going to invite you to stay with us," Jenny said.

"We've already spent enough time taking up your house. We're not going to take up your Christmas too," Dan told her. "That wouldn't be fair."

"You know I don't mind," Jenny said. "With what you've done for Cabot, and now Charles, it all adds up, you know."

"We know, and you have no idea how much we appreciate everything you've ever done for us," Dan replied. "The clinic, putting us on the family payroll; it kept us in our home because there's not a whole lot of money in HIV specialists."

"After what you did in '81 we owe you, Dan," Jenny told him. "For the rest of our lives."

"Well…you don't have to go that far," he replied.

"Yes, she does," Derek joked. "Let her go on."

Across the rest of the day, test results came in for Charles. Overall he wasn't too bad, parasites had attacked his body wrecking his immune system and letting wasting disease set in. He was undernourished and dehydrated. His skin was dry and ashy. He was set up with high powered drugs to defeat the bugs, and high doses of protein to get muscle mass back. Vaseline was rubbed into his skin every few hours, and he was given a shave and haircut.

With him stabilized, Jenny flew home on Sunday in time for lunch. "It smells good," she said, closing the door behind her.

"Grandma!" Hugs and kisses abounded.

"I've only been gone a day." She laughed and untangled herself from her grandchildren. Spying Tony near the couch, she stopped to bend down and squeeze his hand in comfort. "How are you?"

"I'm okay, Mrs Stephanopoulos," he said shyly. "I took you up on your offer of seeing Xanthe. Cabot came with me."

"It must have been one hell of a shock, and I'm sorry," she said softly.

"Thank you. But I found out more information from your family than I ever did, and I'm glad about that." His eyes flitted to Cabot. "I'm glad I met you, too."

Cabot flushed. "Aw, Tony. I'm glad I met you too."

"Lunch is ready," Tomas called. "I hope we did it justice, Mama."

"I'm sure you did." She winked at Spiros with a huge smile on her face. Sitting down, they dug into the meal prepared by Spiros, Tomas and Roger. "Mmm, this is good," Jenny murmured. "I haven't eaten since yesterday and I'm starving."

"Jenny, you didn't have breakfast?" Spiros playfully scolded his wife from the other end of the adults' table.

"You know I don't eat much Sunday mornings. I keep my stomach empty for lunch. Did you do dessert?"

"Mixed berry pie, and apple cinnamon ice cream," Tomas said. "So, you like it?"

"I love it," Jenny told him. "I'm so used to the way I do it, I've never bothered doing it differently. But I love the citrus tones. I can taste lemon, a touch of lime and garlic…what else?"

"Ginger," Roger said. "We've been using the mix on other meats and they taste divine. Is it good enough for Sunday roast?"

"Of course." Jenny sipped her water. "In fact, come up with more marinades and we'll try them out."

"Ah, can we not?" Alena called from the other table. "It's nice Prince Tomas, but I come for Grandma's roast chicken every Sunday. So, I want *Grandma's* roast chicken."

"Yeah," everyone else agreed.

"Looks like we're outnumbered." Roger cocked a brow at a grinning Tomas.

"And what happens when the day comes that I'm not around to do my roast chicken?" Jenny asked. "Or Viv's not around to take over?"

After several horrified looks, Tomas said, "Then I'd better learn your recipe, Mama. I know what goes in the potatoes, but I'm not sure about the marinade. I want to continue the tradition."

"So do I," Diana added. "Guess I'd better learn to cook it for baby Stephanopoulos. If he's anything like Daddy and the boys, he'll eat me out of house and home."

"Hey," Cabot protested from beside her. "We don't eat that much, do we, Tone…argh, Antonio."

Antonio glanced at his brother over his beer bottle. "We did as kids, and then cut back for modelling. But we have been eating our fair share of the island's food these last months."

"That's why we're working out with Uncle Tomas and Roger," Cabot replied. "To try and burn off Grandma's food."

"It's easy enough," Jenny said to Tomas. "You've just never figured out the secret ingredient." Everyone at the tables stopped and looked at her.

"What secret ingredient?" Tomas asked. "I know what you put in the potato coating, and the other veggies are plain. And the gravy's just gravy."

"No, it's not." Jenny raised a brow. "Have you not figured it out after all these decades? It makes the skin nice and tasty."

"Soy sauce, garlic, cheese something or other," Tomas said, his brow furrowing as he concentrated on figuring out the ingredients.

"Nope. Well, nope to the soy sauce," Jenny teased.

"We give up, what is it?" Pedro asked.

"One heaped tablespoon of Vegemite melted in one litre of warm water. Half goes in the gravy, half in the marinade. But I do use garlic and parmesan as well as a few other things."

"Vegemite?" Pedro screwed his face up. "We haven't eaten that salty crap since we were kids in Australia."

"You've been eating it every week in my roast," Jenny told him. "That's where the salt comes from. No soy sauce."

"Well, blow me down," Carlos said. "I never knew that."

"What's Vegemite?" Danté asked over his shoulder.

Jenny and the boys turned to look at the kids who all had puzzled expressions.

"Is that like Marmite, Mrs Stephanopoulos?" Tony asked before explaining it to the others. "We have that in London. It's a salty black yeast spread for toast, bread, crackers, stuff like that."

"Yes, it is, Tony," Jenny replied warmly. "It's also for cooking. And call me Jenny, or Mrs S. Mrs Stephanopoulos is too long."

He blushed at the warm gesture. "Thanks, Mrs Steph, ah, Mrs S."

Cabot squeezed his leg and smiled brightly.

"Then I'm going to have to learn it, so I can continue making it for the family every Sunday," Tomas said.

Carlos changed the subject. "Dan and Derek not joining us today?"

"Still in Athens," Jenny said casually. "We had some medical business to take care of. They may not be back for a while, but should be here in time for Thanksgiving."

"Are we all here for Thanksgiving? Or do we have extras?" Carlos asked.

"Extras," Jenny told him. "Not sure how many, so we could be huge this year."

"Will we be putting up the Christmas tree and decorations?" Danté asked. He loved Christmas and couldn't wait. He also hoped to get cool presents that year, considering he'd survived a shark attack and all.

Dom nudged him and grinned. "*You'll* get lots of presents this year." He'd been working on a special presentation for his brother. Since most of their performances were filmed, he'd put together film clips of Danté rapping and DJing as a present.

Danté grinned back.

"Yes, we will, Little D." Jenny smiled at her youngest grandchild. "And I'm sure Dom's right, you'll get lots of presents this year, as will baby Stefan."

"Oh, God, he's got *that* name already." Diana laughed.

"Oh, my God, I just had the best idea," Alena shrieked. "A *Haus of Stefan* baby line. It will be fabulous."

"Dragging the next generation into the slavery of fashion already, are we?" Cabot said. "Look out, D, she'll want him modelling the clothes too."

"Oh, my God, that's an excellent idea," Alena's voice rose higher still.

"Tone it down a notch," Pedro called out. "We can hear you clearly without you shrieking."

"Sorry, Daddy." Alena moved around in her seat as if she had worms. "But I'm just so excited by all the ideas I'm having."

"Then write them down instead of shrieking." Pedro rolled his eyes and finished off his beer.

"Time for dessert?" Jenny asked, containing her laughter.

"Will you need to go back to Athens, Mrs S?" Mike asked. He, Maggie and the kids ate with them most Sundays. "It's Dom's first night back tomorrow; will the whole family be coming?"

"Yes, we will," Jenny said. "But if I have to fly back then I'll have to fly back. I definitely wouldn't miss tomorrow night."

*****

On Monday night after conference calling Dan and Azmed, Jenny joined the family at *SB3* to see Dom's comeback. The stand-in DJ had been performing for the last few months while the family was on holiday, and then for Dom's suspension, and Danté's time off. But now Dom was back in his element playing '90s and noughties music.

The family were on the floor with their boogie shoes on. Mike was prowling around, keeping an eye on things as manager. Carlos decided to take a spin behind the bar and resurrect his bartending skills, showing his sons and Tony what he could do in his younger days. Danté and Nick hit the floor, as did Summer and Melody with Alexis. Viv danced with Diana, while Alena was coming up with more ideas for the new baby line, and Spiros was sitting on the balcony above the bar enjoying the music by swinging his foot as he sat with his legs crossed.

And Jenny…

She stood at the balcony's balustrade and watched over it all. Her children, her grandchildren, the in-laws, and honorary members of the Stephanopoulos family that just kept growing. She watched over the club she started for Pedro, and now continued with Dom and Danté. This was the business she offered him after leaving *Studio 69* in 1981. While they had a life in Mykonos before, they had a life in New York for three and a half years, but just because Tomas and Roger were sick, didn't mean Pedro and Carlos had to go without their jobs, their lives, their loves. And she had catered to them. To all of them. It was thirty years since the boys had left Mykonos. It was twenty-six years since they had all moved back. Now, the next generation was coming. Diana and Charles were having a baby, and soon so would Alena, Antonio, and maybe even Dom, and eventually Alexis and Danté.

The next generation of Stephanopouloses is on its way, and we need to be prepared. Prepared for growth, maturity and expansion. Financially, business-wise, and family-wise. Because expansion of the Stephanopouloses is coming and it will not be stopped. The Stephanopouloses will never be stopped.

*****

Saturday was Danté's first day back as DJ. It had been two months since he'd been attacked, and the doctors had given his leg the all clear for healing. He was able to move and dance without much pain, and he did stretching exercises every day to keep his muscles limber. He was doing the 12 to 6 p.m. shift he had done since he'd turned fourteen back in March, but their holiday in New York, and then the attack, had set him back. But he was back in it and was going to start his Sunday gigs as well. He rocked out to Lenny Kravitz's *Are You Gonna Go My Way*, and rapped to Eminem's *My Name Is*.

Dom supplied the food and drink, being there as guardian since Danté was underage. But this time he didn't mind. Things were different after the shark attack; he actually admitted to himself that he loved his brother and it wasn't so bad being with him. Besides, he got a lot of work done backstage on his laptop, because that was all he was interested in.

Glancing at his watch, he saw it was nearly time for Danté to finish. He had to make sure they got home, and could then start getting ready for his own set that night. Finishing off his track, he saved it and removed his headphones. Watching through the curtains, he saw the crowd of school kids going crazy and remembered back to when he had done it. It was all Jenny's idea for the kids of Mykonos. When he'd started at fourteen, she set up Saturdays for under 18s. For a small door fee, they got free cheeseburgers, fries, and drinks for six hours. As he'd gotten older, so did they, and he stopped the under 18s when he turned twenty-four and Danté turned fourteen. He took over, and Jenny continued with the free food. The kids of Mykonos saved their pocket money every week and blew it all on *SB3* on Saturdays and every second Sunday.

Danté finished off his set. "Thanks for coming to my first set back, everyone. I'll be back tomorrow to do it all again. Don't forget your free drink on the way out, and I'll see you again tomorrow." He waved and left a twelve-inch playing, before limping off stage. Weary, he sat at Dom's table and rubbed his leg.

"Is it hurting?" Dom asked as Nick came backstage.

"That was awesome, bro. I can't wait to do it all again tomorrow," Nick excitedly gabbled.

"Yeah." Danté sighed and knocked back the drink Dom had pushed in front of him. "I just want to get to Grandma's for dinner and then into bed. *I'm exhausted.*"

"First night back took it all out of me too." Dom grinned. "I think Uncle Tomas has made pizzas and garlic bread. Get your stuff, Squirt, I'm taking you both home." They arrived at Jenny's as the food was being served and a commotion of seating arrangements occurred.

"I want lots, I'm starving," Danté declared and wearily slumped on his seat.

"How was your first day back, sweetie?" Angie asked and set a plate of hot pizza in front of him.

"Tiring. Can I go home to bed after this?" He shoved a slice into his mouth.

Surprised, Angie asked, "It wore you out that much?"

"Yeah," he mumbled. "And I gotta do it again tomorrow, so I may as well get to bed early."

"Oh, okay. I suppose we could." Angie smiled at him and went to attack her own slices of Tomas's chicken and prawn pizza.

"How was the show, Squirt?" Alexis asked Danté before shoving pizza into her mouth.

"Good," Danté replied. "Everyone came back coz I haven't been there in ages." He finished off his first piece and picked up his second.

"It was awesome," Nick enthused. "He got welcome back presents from all his groupies. I'm gonna have to become your manager, dude."

Jenny gazed across at the kids' table in amusement. "I'm going to have to get a manager for Danté now?" she said to Pedro who grinned. "Oh, that reminds me, boys," she called and saw all of the boys turn to look at her. "I mean Cabot and Antonio." The others went back to their food. "When you decide to go back to work, we'll need to get you a new manager slash agent slash publicist for you as your last one didn't fulfil her duties. So, we'll need someone who can."

"Tilly was fine, Grandma." Cabot munched on the crust of his pizza.

"No, she wasn't," Jenny replied. "Your manager's duties are to look out for you and keep you all out of trouble. She didn't, otherwise," she pointed a finger at Cabot, "*you* wouldn't have been in constant trouble."

Cabot grinned. "Yeah, I was a bit of a troublemaker. But that's *so* long ago now." Guffaws were heard all around, but he turned to Tony. "I used to get into *so* much trouble according to all of them."

"I don't believe it," Tony joked.

"Believe it," Antonio said dryly. "I witnessed most of it."

"Naw, sorry, Tone…Antonio," Cabot said. "I did apologise for all of that."

"Yes, you did, but that doesn't mean I've forgotten it, it's all burned into my retinas and memory," Antonio told him.

"I suggest since so much has happened this year, that you take the rest of it to decide what you want to do," Jenny said to everyone in the room. "So, that we can do any business overhauling come January when Danté freshens up your websites. Between Diana having a baby, the twins taking time off, and Danté's attack, it's time to reassess your careers."

"Already ahead of you, Grandma," Diana said. "I've been doing it for a few months now."

"So have I," Alexis added. "I didn't know what I wanted to do before my attack, and now I've set up an assault centre with Cabot. But bizarrely, I still don't know what I want to do. I feel there's something else I need to be doing."

"Like what?" Alena asked, finishing off her soda.

Alexis shrugged. "Dunno."

"Xanthe suggested to me that I should go through the internet to see what sort of stuff I *could* do. You never know what's out there until you look," Cabot told her.

"Have *you* looked?" Alexis asked.

"I have, a few times," he replied, and popped the last of his pizza into his mouth.

"And what did you come up with?" Alexis persisted.

Cabot swallowed. "Nothing yet. I'm still trying to figure it out."

"Maybe I can help you," Tony said. "I had no idea how my life was going to be after the assault, and not too many companies want a HIV person working for them. I've had to re-evaluate my life too. Right now I'm doing nothing."

"And what did you do before, Tony?" Jenny asked.

"Well, bizarrely, I was a bartender." Tony smiled. "Must run in the family. But I do love photography and books. I read like crazy."

"Cool, I love photography too." Danté finished off his food. "We should get together and compare photos some time." He yawned. "But now I need to get home to bed. Can I go now?"

Dom glanced at the clock. "I gotta go, so I can drop him off." Getting up, he pushed his chair under the table.

"We'll be along soon," Angie said. "But I don't want him on his own. Nick, do you want to stay the night?"

"Yes, please." Nick left his plate in the sink and followed Dom and Danté to the door.

"We'll go too." Alexis motioned to Summer and Melody to follow. "Then Squirt's not on his own."

"Okay, I'll be home later," Angie said. "I'll tuck you into bed."

"Mama," Danté wailed, rolling his eyes at everyone. "I'm fourteen, I don't need tucking into bed. I can do it myself." He followed Dom out the door with Nick hot on his heels. "God, how embarrassing."

Angie grinned. "Aw, my baby's growing up."

Jenny laughed. "Now you know how I felt."

*****

On Monday, Jenny was back in Athens at the hospital. "Mr Kensington, you look much better this week." Staring down at the frail man in the bed, she saw his colour was back, his eyes were white and bright, and his cheeks not so sunken.

"Mrs Stephanopoulos," he rasped slowly. "Thank you."

"You're welcome, Mr Kensington. Now, let's have a chat." Settled in a chair by the bed, she proceeded to tell him all about Diana.

He listened intently, his eyes widening when she brought the conversation back to him.

"I have no idea what you've been through, or whether you even have a wife or children, but you need to make up your mind about my granddaughter. Do you love her?"

Thoughts of Diana flooded his mind. "Yes."

"You want to have a child with her?"

Those thoughts moved to his heart. "Yes."

"Do you want to have a life with her?"

"Oh, yes."

"Has it all come about from your experiences?"

"Before," he mumbled, a frown creasing his brow.

"Okay." She stared at him, noting he looked a little fuller and not so bony. "It seems the doctors I hired have made a lot of progress. You need to do the rest. Do you think you'll be able to come to Mykonos on Thursday? It's Thanksgiving."

"Yes," he managed and licked his lips. "I want to see her. Diana." He slowly moved a hand over to Jenny's. "I love her. How is she?"

"Desperate to see, or hear, from you." Jenny sighed. "We didn't even know she was in any kind of relationship, but apparently, she wasn't. You and her were together on the fourth of July and that's when she fell pregnant. You were sent on assignment the day after."

"Yes, it was okay for the first month, or two, but then..." His eyes

803

closed briefly, a crease forming between them. "The shit hit the fan and I was in trouble. I can't believe all of that happened. I can't believe I've been saved."

"How did you survive, Mr Kensington?" She gently laid her hand over his.

"By believing I would somehow find my way back to Diana. I had no idea she would be pregnant, or that she would love me."

"If she didn't love you, Mr Kensington, she wouldn't have slept with you. Now…what about you? Did you love her then?"

"Yes." His lips moved upwards into a smile. "I've loved her since I met her, but she was too young, and I was too devastated." His eyes glossed over.

"By what?" Jenny's curiosity was piqued.

"By the death of my wife and child." Old painful memories covered his face. "I met Diana one year after, but she was too young. A few years back I went on assignment and the world changed me. I came back angry, and took it out on her and other models because of the vapidity of the whole industry." He breathed in and out and his eyes closed. "I'm sorry if I hurt her when I loved her. She's a beautiful young woman and I loved her, but the assignment changed me. Now, now I can't do this anymore." Tears slid down his face. "I can't do photo shoots anymore. I can't even be in that environment." He choked back a sob. "I thought about Diana to get me through; she's all I thought about."

"And now, Mr Kensington," Jenny urged. "What will you do now?"

"Be with her." His eyes opened and he looked directly at Jenny. "If she'll forgive me and have me. I've been so horrible to her the last few years. It's…I don't know why she doesn't hate me."

"She thought she did, until she found out she was pregnant, and then things changed. Not hearing from you, *no one* hearing from you, made it worse."

"I'm surprised the magazine didn't come looking for me. I work for a conglomerate, shooting for whatever magazine they want me to. Most times it's fashion magazines, but this time it was for *World*, the political magazine that talks about all things money and war."

"And you got caught up in what you were documenting," Jenny murmured. "Has your perspective changed then? From the man you were before to the man you are now?"

"Yes," he cleared his throat, "Yes. All I thought about was getting back to Diana. Being held captive in a war zone with bombs going off isn't fun. It isn't life. I feel sorry for the people who live like that, but I don't. My life flashed before me, my life before I met Diana with my wife and child, their deaths, coming back from what I thought was hell to work again. Meeting Diana and life after it. Those assignments have changed me. Life is too short. I would cry over her photos, cry because I may never get a chance to tell her how I really feel. Cry because I wasn't ready to die yet. Cry because I would never see her beautiful face again. No one could even imagine what sort of experience it is. It's the worst thing I've ever been through."

"I have a psychiatrist who is willing to talk to you about it. Willing and waiting on Mykonos. She's been helping my family with a lot lately."

"How is Diana? Is she and the baby well?" he asked weakly.

"Physically they are, but emotionally, she's a wreck over you."

He deflated. "Yes. I guess she would be. Unmarried mother-to-be."

"That's not why." Jenny laughed. "It's 2007; she was worried that she couldn't find you to tell you that you were going to be a father."

His lips moved into a soft smile. "I'm going to be a father again."

"I'm sorry about your wife and child, Mr Kensington," Jenny said softly. "If you want to be with Diana, that means you will be a part of this family. And as a part of this family, that means you get all the support you need."

"Thank you, Mrs Stephanopoulos. Thank you for everything."

"You're welcome, Mr Kensington. You get some rest. Have sweet dreams about Diana and your future son, and give your recovery everything you've got, because you'll be seeing them on Thursday." Watching his eyes close and his breathing regulate, she went outside to Dan and Derek. "How is he?"

"Doing better." Dan stared into the room. "The medication is killing off the parasites, the protein and all the vitamins we're giving him is making him gain weight. It will take some time, but he'll recover."

"Are you able to look after him at home? Will you be able to bring him home on Thursday?" Jenny asked.

"If he makes strides in his recovery until then, yes," Dan said. "He'll still be weak, but we'll do what we did with Tomas and Roger, and the hospital is nearby if he needs it."

"Okay. Can you order in whatever you'll need, co-ordinate with the hospital, and prepare for your departure on Thursday?" Jenny asked.

"We're leaving on Thursday itself? What time?" Dan asked.

"Nine or ten. I want him settled by lunchtime, so Diana can spend some time with him and slowly introduce him to the rest of the family. He'll be weak, and will only be able to stand so much. Can he eat food?"

"Not at this point. Besides the protein, his stomach needs to get used to food again, so even a little bit could make him sick."

"Okay. At least that's one less person to make food for," Jenny joked lightly. "But then it will be a buffet meal during the evening anyway."

"Not a sit down?" Derek asked, knowing she was up to something.

"For a quick lunch, but not for dinner. Not enough room at the tables," Jenny replied. "The kids can use trays, and the adults will sit on dining chairs. If that's the way it works out. Just get him ready by Thursday."

*****

On Thursday morning, Dan, Derek, Alfarti and Veroke prepared Charles for the plane trip to Mykonos. They travelled with him to the airport where they settled him in the bedroom of Jenny's private plane, and half an hour later, Dan, Derek and Charles were on their way to Mykonos. Within the hour, he was set up in Carlos's old room which Jenny had cleaned and dusted.

She fluffed the pillows behind him and smoothed the bedspread, then stepped aside for Dan and Derek to finish hooking him up.

"I will never be able to thank you enough for this, Mrs Stephanopoulos," Charles said. He was physically stronger, vocally stronger, and able to speak clearly.

"Repay me by loving my granddaughter and looking after her and your future children, Mr Kensington. I don't expect you to marry, but in this family, it would be appropriate. I'm sure that's something you'll discuss with Diana over the next year, or so. You need to regain your strength. Just concentrate on that. You look much better."

"I feel better." He smiled. "And I will try to live up to your expectations."

"If this experience has changed you the way you say it has, then I'd say you will. And call me Jenny, or Mrs S, it's easier."

"Thank you, Mrs Stephanopoulos, ah," he caught himself, "Jenny."

"I'll let Dan and Derek finish up then call Diana. She'll be shell-shocked to see you." Jenny was smiling as she left the room.

After confirmation that he was fine from Dan, she called Diana. "Sweetie, can you come over, please. There's something I need to tell you."

"Okay, Grandma, on my way." She turned up five minutes later to the aromatic scent of roast turkey. "Mmm," she mumbled, and heard her stomach grumble. "Food… Hungry… Can't wait."

"It will have to, because I have something to tell you." Jenny held Diana's hands. "Marco has found Charles."

Diana gasped and she clenched her grandmother's hands tightly. "Oh, my God, where, how, is he alive? Oh, my God."

"Calm down," Jenny said. "He was gravely ill. He'd been held captive and was found in a hospital. We've worked hard to make him better."

"What? We? Grandma? You're not making sense. Do you have Charles?" Diana was in panic mode, having not heard anything for two weeks since she'd told Jenny. "Oh, Grandma, is he okay?"

"Come." Jenny squeezed her hand and led her to Carlos's room.

"Charles!" Diana cried and leapt onto the bed next to him.

"Whoa, take it easy," Jenny called, her hand flying out. "He's weak, you're pregnant, take it easy."

"Oh, Charles, where have you been?" Diana planted kisses all over his face. "Where have you been?"

"It's a long story, my love." He stopped her. "I have a very long story to tell you."

"Okay." She slumped back, puzzled by his tone. "Is everything okay?"

"I've been ill, but thanks to your grandmother, I'm getting better, and there are some things I need to explain that you need to know."

"You know I'm pregnant?" She pulled her jumper up to show off her stomach. "Twenty weeks."

With his whole body radiating the love he felt, he gently placed a hand on her stomach. "It's a boy."

"How do you—?" She was even more puzzled.

"Your grandmother told me so I had something to fight for. I was so desolate and lonely. You were all I had to cling to, hope and pray for. I fought for the two of you once I was told."

"Oh." Snuggling beside him, she slid an arm through his. "I guess you'd better tell me that story now…"

*****

Lorenzo straightened his shirt and jacket before knocking on the Stephanopoulos's door. It was Thanksgiving day, mid-morning, and he held two bunches of roses in his arms. He was on a mission, and he needed to get it done now since he'd be spending lunch at the centre and wouldn't be with the family until later.

Pedro answered the door. "Lorenzo," he said, shocked because he wasn't expecting him. "Uh…what can I do for you?"

Lorenzo cleared his throat. "Uh, Mr Stephanopoulos, I am here to ask your permission to woo your daughter…" He held his breath.

Pedro frowned. "Alena? You already dated her."

The air came out of Lorenzo. "Ah, no sir, I meant Alexis."

Pedro's brows rose all the way to his hairline. "Alexis?"

"Yes, sir." Lorenzo licked his lips nervously. "Alexis and I have grown close working at the centre, and I would like your permission to woo her."

"Who is it?" Angie asked as she came into the room.

"Lorenzo," Pedro replied. "He wants permission to woo our daughter."

"Alena?" She was puzzled. "But you two—"

"Not Alena." Pedro glanced at her over his shoulder. *"Alexis."*

Angie's brows rose all the way to her hairline. "Alexis?"

"Yes. Mrs Stephanopoulos. Oh, these are for you by the way." He handed over a bunch of beautiful red roses, having taken a leaf out of Tony's book when it came to presenting himself. Not that he'd ever tell Tony.

"Oh, ah, thank you, Lorenzo," she said. "They're beautiful, but I'm not sure—"

"What's going on?" Alexis came out from her room where she'd been getting dressed for lunch. "Aw, Lorenzo."

"These are for you." He smiled brightly and gave her a kiss on the cheek as he handed over a large bunch of red roses.

"Aw, they're beautiful. Come in." She glowed as she shut the door. "Why didn't you let him in?" she accused her parents.

"Because he shocked us," Pedro said. "We couldn't do anything."

"And how'd he shock you?" she asked.

"I asked for your father's permission to woo you," Lorenzo told her.

She blushed as red as the roses. "Naw, Lorenzo, that's so sweet, but you don't need it. You just need to ask me."

"Oh, doesn't he?" Pedro crossed his arms and stared at his daughter.

"Daddy," Alexis chastised, "I'm nineteen, I can date boys."

"One, *you're nineteen*, not an adult, and two, Lorenzo's a man, *an adult*, not a boy," Pedro explained. "I don't like the age difference."

"Neither do I," Angie added. "Sweetie, after everything that's happened to you—"

"Mama, I'm okay. I'm not going to do anything foolish," Alexis calmed her.

"Mr Stephanopoulos, ah, Mrs Stephanopoulos, if I may," Lorenzo said under their intensive expressions. "I have no intention of rushing your daughter, or pushing her into anything serious. I just want permission to court her in the old-fashioned sense. Like my father courted my mother. He told me from childhood to always ask permission. So, that is what I'm doing. I was thinking movies, dinner, special occasions, breakfast and lunch, the club, swimming. Just hanging out and having fun."

"You dated Alena," Pedro stated. "Now you want to date Alexis.

What are we supposed to think about that?"

"I understand, Mr Stephanopoulos, but that was five years ago. Alena and I were not well matched, and I think I was just a bit of fun for her anyway."

"Is Alexis a bit of fun?" Angie stared hard into his eyes, hoping her message was conveyed.

"I would like to have fun with Alexis, yes." His insides were in knots and they weren't untying anytime soon. "We have grown close at the centre, and I would like to hang out with her *outside* of the centre. That's why I'm asking, why I'm here today."

"Oh, for God's sake." Alexis rolled her eyes. "I'm dating him whether you like it or not."

"We don't," Pedro told her point blank. "And don't take that attitude with me, young lady. You're *still a teenager, not an adult.* And considering what happened to you back in May, your mother and I have every right to be concerned about whatever man comes into your life. Even," he cut her angry expression and open mouth off with a pointed finger, "if it's someone we already know."

"He's right, Alexis," Lorenzo said. "They have every right to be concerned. Do not be angry with them, at least you have parents who care, unlike many young girls." He stared wistfully at her. "You are very lucky to have such an incredibly caring family who were there for you when you needed them." He knew how to suck up to older people; he'd been sucking up to Jenny for the last twelve years, her son and daughter-in-law were a breeze.

Alexis relented. "Yes, I am lucky, I know that. But I'm *nineteen,*" she stressed the word to her parents. "I'm old enough to date."

"A thirty-year-old man?" Angie arched a brow. "I don't think so."

"Mama, I'm gonna do it whether you like it or not," Alexis said. "I like Lorenzo; he's sweet and kind and caring. And he's interested in what we're doing at the centre. What I'm *not* interested in right now is sex, so that is way off the agenda. I just want to date a nice guy and have fun. Go out to the movies and dinner. Hell, you were having Alena at nineteen, so you can't really dictate, now can you?"

"But your father wasn't eleven years older than me, and I had your grandmother and Viv. *Big* difference." Angie didn't like the attitude she was getting from her daughter, but…she did have a point. "I had *no* parents to teach me, or look after me. I only had my in-laws. But you have us, and it devastated us when you were raped."

"I hate that word," Alexis spat. "At least assaulted is commonplace and can mean several things without the embarrassment."

"Oh, sweetie." Angie handed her flowers to Pedro and went to her side, resting her chin on Alexis's shoulder. "Times are different to when I had Alena. Times are different to May before you were assaulted. We just want you to be okay and careful. And not rush into anything with anyone." Her eyes flitted from her daughter's chocolate brown ones to Lorenzo's, making sure she got her point across.

"Having dinner and dancing and fun is rushing into something?" Alexis asked incredulously. "For God's sake."

"That is all I want to do, Mr and Mrs Stephanopoulos; to take Alexis out and have fun. My father taught me to ask for permission and I've done that," Lorenzo said. "But she *is* over eighteen and she will do it whether you want her to or not. At least you know me. I'm a doctor, I live here on the island, your mother paid my way through medical school, the family knows me. I'm not some stranger."

Pedro glanced at Angie and she shrugged at him. He relented, grudgingly. "It also means that if you hurt my baby girl, Lorenzo, I will do damage to you. Do you understand me?" He hoped his six foot, crossed-armed physique would put Lorenzo off. It didn't.

"Thank you, Mr Stephanopoulos. I will not hurt your daughter." There was only one Stephanopoulos Lorenzo knew could threaten his life, and that wasn't Pedro.

"Thank you, Daddy." Alexis threw her arms around him and kissed his cheek before doing the same to her mother.

*****

A couple of hours later, everyone started slowly rolling in to Jenny's.

"Is there enough food for all of us?" Carlos asked, bringing in a platter of food. "How many are coming?"

"A lot." Jenny put the tray of veggies back in the oven. "We're having lunch and then the rest will be for across the afternoon and into dinner. It will be a buffet dinner. Carlos, I want a word about the meat shop." Pulling out the turkey rolls, she checked the temperature.

"What about it, Mama?" He peered over her shoulder and breathed in deeply. "No turkeys again this year?"

"I want to know what you'll do with it after your father and I are gone. You know you boys never liked working there, so you're not exactly meat aficionados. Will you keep it or sell it?"

"Well," Carlos leaned against the counter and thought about it. "I hated working there. I hate the smell of raw meat."

"So did I." Pedro kissed his mother on the cheek. "Happy Thanksgiving, Mama. When's lunch?"

"Soon. I want to know what you'll all do with the meat shop when we're gone. Sell it or keep it?"

"Selling it off would be an atrocity," Tomas told them. "It was Papa's father's, and his father's; it belongs in the family."

"So, again, who's going to take it over?" Jenny persisted. "How do you think we've always had good meat all these decades? How do you think *The Windmill* and *SB3* are provided for? By *Stephanopoulos Meats.*"

"If you want it in the family, then I guess we'll keep it," Carlos said, shrugging at his brothers who were crowded around the island bench. "But I'm not taking it over. We'll just keep a manager on."

"And if *he* has no idea about meat?" Jenny washed and dried her hands.

"I don't know, Mama," he replied. "We'll get a guy who does."

"We'll take it, Mama," Tomas said as he looked at a nodding Roger. "We've become the cooks in the family after you, so we'll take it, and keep running it until it gets passed down to the next lot who takes over."

"And which one of the kids will that be?" Jenny raised a brow. "They all hate raw meat too. Or are you training Cabot to cook?"

"We are, actually," Tomas said.

"Speaking of kids, is Diana here yet?" Viv asked, hovering between the kitchen and lounge rooms looking out for her children.

"She is. You and Carlos go and see her in his old room. She has someone to introduce to you." Jenny saw the quizzical looks flit over their faces.

Intrigued, they went to see Diana and found her with a sickly-looking man in the bed. "Diana?" Viv said, looking from her to him.

"Mama, Daddy," she excitedly said. "Come and meet Charles Kensington. Grandma found him, and he's been through a terrible time, and she brought him here, so we can be together."

Viv glanced from them to Carlos. "Oh. The photographer." She moved around the bed and shook his hand. "It's a pleasure to finally meet you."

"Thank you, Mrs Stephanopoulos. You too. I've seen many of your photo shoots, and it's easy to see where Diana gets her beauty from," Charles said warmly.

"Oh, oh my." Viv blushed. "Thank you, that's very kind."

"And true." Charles smiled.

"And I'm Diana's father, Carlos Stephanopoulos." Carlos stepped forward and grasped Charles's hand in a death grip. "Where the hell have you been? You've upset my daughter terribly."

"I know, I know." Charles nodded. "Not my fault, truly." He launched into his war story.

In the kitchen, Jenny kept an eye on the clock, and when twenty minutes were up and they didn't return, she sent in Antonio and Cabot.

"Hello?" Cabot asked when they walked in. "Grandma sent us in. Ew, Charles!"

"Sit and listen," Viv told them, and the boys sat and listened to Charles's story and how it changed his life.

"So, why were you a shit to our sister? I bawled you out for that at the *Flair* party." Antonio scowled, still annoyed that his sister had slept with Charles *after* he'd defended her against him.

"Long story short," Charles replied. "I lost my wife and child one year before I met Diana. She was my first assignment back at work and I fell in love. But she was too young and it was inappropriate. A few years ago I went on an assignment which made the whole world of modelling seem so vapid and stupid. Teamed with my infatuation, I took it out on your sister. I have apologised to her and she's accepted my apology. I hope you will too." He squeezed Diana's hand. "I love your sister so very much, and what I've been through has shown me how short life is, and I want to make it up to her."

In the kitchen, Jenny was chatting with Tony. "So, Tony, do you cook?"

He leaned against the kitchen counter, unsure of what else to do. "I can cook a few things, Mrs S. Beans on toast, spaghetti on toast, toast." He grinned.

She laughed. "You sound like most of the boys in this family." Pulling out a bowl of cranberries and a few other things from the fridge, she set them on the island bench. "Tomas is teaching Cabot to cook; maybe you can join in?"

"Yeah, we don't mind." Roger snagged a handful of cranberries. "We teach him every meal time. He can make his own bacon and egg rolls now." He threw a cranberry at Tomas who caught it in his mouth.

"Aren't you the ones who taught everyone how to do those anyway?" Pedro asked from the dining table where he was enjoying a beer.

"Yeah, we were, and we don't mind teaching you too, Tony," Tomas said, glancing from his nephew's special friend to his mother. "Mama, how much longer?"

"About fifteen minutes." She saw Viv, Carlos and the boys come into the room. "Enough time for you two and Angelina and Pedro to go and say hello to Diana and her friend in Carlos's old room. Scoot now." Ushering them away, she watched Cabot move to Tony's arms, and Carlos and Viv hover near the fridge. "Well?" she asked quietly.

The adults entered the bedroom and found a man in Carlos's bed.

"Oh, everyone." Diana beamed. "This is Charles Kensington. Grandma found him, how wonderful is that? This is my Uncle Tomas and his husband Roger Dencott." Holding out her hand she made introductions.

"Nice to meet you, I've read a lot about your work." Charles shook their hands. "I'm very impressed with what you've done."

"Thank you," Tomas said, noting his condition. "And we have

been where you are, in bed wasting away."

"Yes." Charles nodded in remembrance. "You were told you had AIDS, but you didn't. You were brought home to die."

"This very house," Tomas told him. "Two rooms that way." He pointed to the wall behind Charles. "It's not fun."

"No, I guess it wouldn't be," Charles said quietly.

"And this is Uncle Pedro and Aunt Angie," Diana added.

"Hello, nice to meet you." Angie shook hands. "You look as if you've been through hell."

"I have." Charles gave them a quick rundown of the last few months.

In the kitchen, Carlos was talking to his mother and Viv. "Well, he's been through a hell of an experience. But will he be able to cope with a child, or a wife and child? I don't want him getting violent with Diana and the baby. I'll kill him."

"Oh, Carlos, don't be so dramatic. When Diana first mentioned him months ago I checked up on him," Viv said. "He seems like a perfectly reasonable man. He's just been through a very traumatic time."

"That's why I'm asking Xanthe to stay and counsel him," Jenny said. "Think he'll fit into the family?"

"Think Tony will?" Carlos looked across the kitchen into the dining room at his son and his partner.

Jenny glanced over her shoulder, seeing them leaning against the floor-to-ceiling built-in cabinet near the window, almost as if they were hiding in the corner for privacy, and smiled. "Yes. I think he will."

"Tony?" Cabot said softly as he sheltered in his friend's arms. "Would you think it okay if you stayed?" He popped a cranberry in his mouth. "I'd have to ask Uncle T and R."

"You mean stay here?" Tony teased as Cabot popped a cranberry into his mouth.

"No, silly." Cabot snuggled closer and played with another berry from the bowl next to him on the cabinet. "At our place…with me…" He rubbed the berry against his lips, and then pressed it into Tony's mouth.

"With you? How?" Tony feigned ignorance as he tightened his arm around Cabot.

Cabot rolled his eyes. "With *me*, silly. In *my* room?"

"Oh." Tony faked catching on. "You want me to sleep on the floor?"

"Tonee." Cabot stomped his foot childishly, making Antonio look up from his seat in the lounge room in confusion at hearing his name. But seeing he wasn't being spoken to, he frowned and glanced away.

Cabot went on. "Stop teasing. I mean with me in *my* bed."

"Whoa, I heard that!" Dan stopped in front of them as he came in for a drink. "You know Xanthe's banned you from sex."

"*I know, Dan.*" Cabot rolled his eyes again. "I wasn't talking about sex. I just thought," glancing at Tony, he blushed, "We could just snuggle and fall asleep in each other's arms. It *is* Thanksgiving, you know."

"Yes, Cabot, I know." Dan watched them both, trying to gauge how serious it was getting.

"And we *will* be wearing pyjamas," Cabot went on.

"I happen to know *for a fact* that a penis can find its way out of a pair of pyjamas and into things it shouldn't," Derek said as he grabbed some berries from the bowl.

"Oh, my God, Derek!" Cabot exclaimed and buried his head in a chuckling Tony's shoulder.

Dan covered his eyes in embarrassment. "I can't believe you just said that. *Why* would you say that?"

"Because it's true." Derek laughed. "Pyjamas don't stop it."

"Ew, no." Cabot blocked his ears. "No, no, no."

"Look." Dan pulled Cabot's right hand away. "As long as nothing happens, and it's purely the two of you finding your way together, then ask your uncles."

"Ask your uncles what?" Pedro asked as they all walked into the room.

"Um, Uncles Tomas and Roger," Cabot said shyly, watching them watch him.

"Okay then, I know when I'm not wanted." Pedro turned and saw his mother talking to the kids.

"Diana has someone to introduce. No screaming, no shrieking, no rubbish," she warned Alena. "*And I mean it.*" She watched them hurry off and went back to setting the tables.

"You wanted something, Cabot?" Tomas asked, walking over to him and grabbing some berries.

"Um, Uncle Tomas, Roger, um…" He was sure his face was going up in flames. "Is it okay if um…Tony stays over…um…with me…?"

"In your room?" Roger asked, hands on hips, looking from Cabot to Tony, to Dan and Derek.

"Um…yes…" Cabot couldn't look either of them in the eye.

"I thought Xanthe banned you from sex?" Roger continued while Tomas thoughtfully studied his nephew.

"Argh, it's not *all* about sex," Cabot growled, stomping his foot like a petulant child. "Why does everybody think that?"

"Because you're Cabot a.k.a. Steele Stefan," Antonio explained as he grabbed a beer from the fridge and everyone looked his way. "It's always about sex. Sex is all you think about."

"Well, not this time, Tonee…ah…Antonio." Shaking his head, Cabot added, "I'm really not going to get this name thing. But this is about just being together. It *is* Thanksgiving after all."

"And you want to *give* thanks, or *be* thanked?" Antonio asked, making those around them grin.

"Tonee." Cabot frowned at his scowling twin. "It's not like that anymore."

"Sure, we'll see," was all Antonio said before walking into the lounge room, a frown on his face and worry in his mind.

In the bedroom, Alena walked through the door. "Hello." She gasped. "Oh, my God, Charles Kensington. What are you doing here?" She hurried around the bed. "You know you're Diana's baby daddy?"

"Alena," Diana complained, then asked Charles, "Do you remember my cousin from the Monte Carlo fashion show?"

"Of course." He smiled. "And this must be the dark side of the family."

"My sister, Alexis." Alena pulled her close then pointed to Dom and Danté. "And our brothers."

"Yes, Dom and Danté. I remember from an article somewhere," Charles said. "I've been out of commission for a while."

Diana quickly brought them up to date on the last few months.

"I've been bitten by a shark." Danté shrugged. "Nowhere near as bad as you, dude."

"Wow, but bad enough. I'm impressed." Charles nodded. "How's *your* war wound?"

"It's my right thigh. Still scarred." Danté rubbed it. "Still sore sometimes."

"And Diana said you opened a centre, Alexis, with her brother Cabot." Charles turned his attention to her.

"Yeah, an assault and HIV/AIDS support centre," Alexis replied, taking in his thin gaunt appearance.

Jenny came through the door. "Lunchtime. You kids go and get your food, and Diana can eat in peace." She set the stable table on Diana's lap after she sat up. "Sorry, you can't have any, Charles."

"That's okay, Jenny, I'm salivating anyway." He stared down at the tray full of delicious turkey and vegetables smothered in gravy.

"This is just a quick lunch," Jenny added. "Everyone else will start arriving this afternoon. We'll be putting up the Christmas tree, so we can bring you out then if you're up to it." She saw Diana finish off her turkey.

"God I'm hungry!" Diana exclaimed. "I'm always hungry."

"It's the sea air." Jenny smiled. "Makes everyone want more." Hurrying back to the kitchen, she and Tomas finished serving and they gave their thanks. The afternoon was going to be busy, and so was the evening.

Around three in the afternoon, Alfonso knocked on the door. "Hello, Mrs Stephanopoulos, thank you for inviting me," he told Jenny as she let him in.

"You're welcome, Alfonso, you're part of the family now. You should be included in celebrations."

"Thank you, thank you." He removed his coat and handed it to Pedro who hung it in the coat closet. "Angie." He kissed her cheek.

"Alfonso," she replied coolly, still not sure how she felt about having another brother, but a few long talks with Jenny had brought her around to at least inviting him to celebrations as a way of getting to know him. Jenny had reminded her that besides her children, he was the only blood relative she had, that she knew of anyway, and she should at least make an effort.

"Hello, everyone, thank you for inviting me." Alfonso shook hands as he made his way through the group.

"Would you like something to eat, Alfonso? We've been keeping everything warm and are about to get more cooking," Jenny said.

"Oh, if it would be no trouble. It does smell good." He stopped beside the kitchen bench and inhaled deeply.

Jenny and Tomas quickly whipped up a plate of food and he devoured it.

"Oh, that was good. Sorry I couldn't make it here on time. The planes have been delayed."

"But you're here and that's what matters," Jenny said.

There was another knock on the door and Alexis peered through the front window. "Oh, that's for me." Jumping up, she opened the door. "Hi," she said brightly as Lorenzo kissed her cheek.

"Hello, Alexis." Lorenzo came into the house. "Hello everyone. Mr and Mrs Stephanopoulos, I come bearing gifts this time." He handed over the two six-pack cartons of wine. "From my father's shop."

"Thank you, Lorenzo." Jenny accepted the gift. "Please take a seat and make yourself comfortable."

"Thank you." He slid off his coat and Alexis put it in the closet. Grabbing his hand, she led him to the chaise lounge by the fire, sat him down and sat next to him.

"Just don't make yourself too comfortable," Pedro muttered over his shoulder as he watched them.

"And what's that about?" Jenny asked the adults hovering in the kitchen.

Pedro heaved a very heavy sigh. "He came by this morning to ask if he can woo Alexis."

Jenny raised her brows and a noise emanated from her throat. "Really? He's homing in on her now?"

"Yeah, that's what I thought," Pedro murmured. "He turned up with a bunch of flowers for Angie and one for Alexis, and then asked my permission to woo my daughter." He glanced over his shoulder and back. "I thought he meant Alena and asked him, but he said no, Alexis. I can tell you I was shocked." Crossing his arms, he frowned. "She's too young."

"She's nineteen, and he's not the first guy she's dated," Jenny said.

"I know, but he's thirty and has already dated Alena," Pedro replied. "And from the family gossip, they had sex," he pulled a face, "and now he's into Alexis. I don't like it."

"Well, you knocked up Angie when she was eighteen, so at least Alexis isn't pregnant," Jenny reminded him to stunned expressions. "Oh, please. Thirty years ago it was inappropriate, now it's not. I don't like him being that much older, but maybe she needs an older man to comfort her. A young one did her harm, an older one might make her at peace."

"Ooohhh," Pedro grumbled. "I don't like it."

"I'll have a word with him, don't worry," Jenny assured him. "He won't get away with hurting her. Dan said he's been an arrogant little twat lately, which is surprising since he's only ever been nice and polite to me. I'll need a word anyway." She gazed over the scene. Cabot snuggled in Tony's arms on the couch, Dom and Danté talking to Tony, Lorenzo and Alexis talking to Antonio, and Alena warily eyeing Lorenzo and Alexis.

"Are you two dating?" Alena asked Alexis and Lorenzo. "Because if you are, that's gross. You dated me, and now you're dating my sister who's ten years younger than me and eleven years younger than you. She's not even an adult yet."

"Alena." Alexis rolled her eyes. "We're just hanging out, nothing's happened yet."

The fear rumbled inside Alena. "You're only nineteen, Alexis, and he's thirty. That's too old."

Alexis frowned in return. "Don't ruin what *we've* gotten this year, Alena. Let it go. For the sake of *our* relationship."

Alena frowned and gave Lorenzo the evil eye. "You hurt her, I'll kill you."

Lorenzo smiled smugly. "I'm sure you will."

"And if I don't, *Grandma will*," Alena murmured and leaned closer. "The guy who attacked Alexis never got off the island. He was *never seen again*." With a warning look, she got up and walked into the kitchen, leaving him wide-eyed and alarmed.

He saw Jenny's face as the family looked their way and knew there was some truth to it.

"Ooh, that makes me sick." Alena crossed her arms.

"Join the club, sweetie." Pedro put an arm around her.

She wrapped her arms around his waist and rested her head on his chest as he rested his chin on her head.

"Dan, Derek, why don't we bring Charles out? We'll be setting up the Christmas tree soon," Jenny called and led the way to the room. "Hey, time to come out. You'll meet a couple more people, and we'll be putting the tree up soon."

Diana stirred from Charles's shoulder. "Mmm, Christmas tree."

"I take it you both napped." Jenny smiled and removed the tray. "Dan and Derek will help Charles. Diana, can you spread that blanket?" She nodded to a brightly checkered one across the end of the bed. "Put it over the wheelchair to keep the cold out. I'll just take this to the kitchen." She took the tray and came back to find Diana straightening the blanket. "Boys in the bathroom?"

"Yes. He wanted to freshen up and put some clothes on. He wants to look respectable." Diana finished spreading out the blanket.

Jenny smoothed the bed covers and pillows while waiting, and finally, Dan and Derek helped Charles walk back to the room.

"I'm not that strong yet," Charles said. "But I'm getting there." He'd changed into a t-shirt and sweater that Jenny had bought him. She'd quickly done some shopping so he had clothes and toiletries when he came to stay, but he left the PJ bottoms on. "If I have a blanket over me, no one will notice. But the top half will look decent." He was settled into the wheelchair and Dan rolled him out.

"Everyone, Charles and Diana are joining us and we'll start putting the tree up shortly." Jenny made room next to the fire in front of the upright piano. The Christmas tree would be going on the other side in the corner next to the front window. "Here we go. Diana, you use the piano bench if you like, or we'll grab you another chair."

"I'll use the bench, Grandma," she said. "It won't matter for now."

"Well, it will matter when our other guests arrive," Jenny replied. "We'll need to make room for everyone."

"How many more are coming?" Alena asked, sliding onto the bench seat beside Diana with a bowl of chocolate popcorn.

"Oh, yum." Diana dug in by grabbing a handful.

"Three." Jenny stood and looked around. "That I know of. On top of the Gatoses."

"What do you mean, that you know of?" Carlos asked. "Are we expecting drop-ins?"

"Unless Dom, Antonio, Danté or Alena have invited people and haven't told me, then Mike, Maggie and the kids should be here soon, and so should our other guests."

Right on cue, there was a knock at the door. Opening it, Jenny invited the Gatoses in and took their coats. Diana introduced them all to Charles. They shook hands and made a brief introduction of who they were. They said hello to Lorenzo and Alfonso, and accepted drinks from Pedro and Angie. Nick attached himself to Danté, and the girls sat near Alexis for a chat.

"Can you boys get the Christmas tree and containers of decorations from the basement, please?" Jenny asked.

"Basement? Since when do we have a basement?" the boys asked, looking at one another.

Jenny laughed. "Since always. We just didn't use it. But I've had it cleared out and I'm using it for storage. You know…there's a hidden room down there that's never been opened," she teased.

"A what?" Nick's head spun around. "A hidden room? Cool."

"Yes, we found it when we cleaned out the basement. It's not on the plans for the house, and no one knew about it, or mentioned it. So, imagine that, a hidden basement." Jenny's eyes widened in simulated surprise.

"Oh." Pedro made noises at the back of his throat. "You know we gotta check that out," he told his brothers.

"The door wasn't opened and I don't want to know if there are dead bodies in there," Jenny called as Carlos, Pedro, Tomas and Roger raced off with all the boys after them.

Carlos barged into the laundry room with the others right behind him but didn't see a staircase. "Wait, is it off the laundry?"

"Grandma," Cabot called from the hallway. "How do we get down?"

"There's a door at the back of the utility closet," she called back. "All very mysterious it is. Don't forget torches and lamps on the shelf."

Frowning at his brothers, Carlos opened the utility closet door and found another door as the back wall. Opening it, he felt for a switch and turned on the light. Bright white flooded the area. White stone steps and walls led down. "Cool."

"Come on, let's go," Cabot urged.

One by one they made their way down a short flight of stairs to a landing and turned right down a second flight into the brightly lit, white painted basement to find it covered in utility shelving for storage.

"There's the tree." Carlos pointed to the corner where it was wrapped in plastic and resting in a barrel.

"But where's the other door?" Danté asked excitedly, hobbling in.

Looking around, Carlos led them under the stairs to the other side of the room.

"There," Nick said and rushed over to the door with a black metal handle and old-fashioned padlock. He tried opening it. "It won't budge."

Carlos and Roger tried. "It's gotta have the padlock cut off. Is there a bolt cutter on the shelf?" Carlos asked.

"Wait." Roger looked closely at the padlock. "It's clean." He pushed and poked and it popped open.

"Ah," Pedro muttered. "Mama's already been here coz that should have been old and stuck."

"Okay. Who's ready for a look?" Carlos asked.

"Get on with it," Cabot muttered. "We haven't got all day."

"Bossy boots." Danté grinned over his shoulder at his cousin.

Cabot wrapped his arms around Danté's shoulders in return and rested his cheek on his head.

With Carlos pulling and Roger pushing, they managed to shove back the door. It slid on rusty old hinges to reveal a dark, dank room.

"Phwoar, that's gross. Who died in there?" Nick screwed up his face and held his nose.

"Ew." So did everyone else.

Shining flashlights and lamps into the dark underworld basement illuminated a sight before them that made them gasp.

"Do you boys have the tree and decorations yet?" Jenny called down. "It's nearly five." She went back to the lounge and giggled.

"Grandma," Diana said suspiciously. "What *are* you giggling about?"

Jenny smiled in amusement. "They think we didn't go into the room. We did, but locked it off. It stinks to high hell."

"Dead bodies down there?" Lorenzo asked casually, still alarmed after Alena's comment.

"I thought there might be considering the family business." Jenny eyeballed him. "Or a room with coffins."

"Grandma," Alexis frowned, "That's gross."

"Yes," Jenny murmured. "Lorenzo, can I have a word in private please?"

"Of course, Mrs Stephanopoulos." He followed her down the hallway to the bedrooms "What is it? What can I help you with?"

"Lorenzo, Pedro told me you stopped by to talk to him and asked permission to woo Alexis. I'm not thrilled about that."

"I have no intentions of forcing Alexis into anything," he quickly explained, not wanting to upset her, or put her offside. "We've gotten to know each other at the clinic and she's a sweet girl. I just wanted permission to hang out with her, woo her, nothing heavy, just date. My father told me to ask, to always ask."

"Grandma, you're not giving Lorenzo the third degree, are you?" Alexis asked from the hallway.

"Go and sit down, I'm not done talking," Jenny told her.

"Grandma!" Alexis crossed her arms and frowned.

"Sit down, Alexis," Jenny snapped, and waited for her shocked granddaughter to go back to her chair. She turned to Lorenzo. "You've become obnoxious lately; why?"

His lips pursed into a thin line. "I believed my manhood was threatened. Silly of me, really. Dan and Derek aren't normally here, and I'm the resident doctor at the hospital's clinic. I felt threatened and that was silly." Blushing, he lowered his eyes. "I haven't been very nice to Cabot or Tony, and that is wrong of me. I'm not sure why I've snapped at them, but I do not want to get on the wrong side of you, Mrs Stephanopoulos. You have helped me greatly. If it wasn't for you, I would not have been able to get through medical school, and I am very grateful for that."

"Do you like Alexis?"

He looked into her eyes. "Oh, yes, very much. She's so different from Alena."

"Not selfish?"

"Yes." A small smile lit up his lips. "She was very much about herself. Alexis is about others, and that's what has attracted me, which is why I'd like to woo her."

"You know she was assaulted?"

"Yes," he said sadly, "and that is horrible. That is why I have no intention of pursuing something serious until she is ready. I just want to take her out and do things."

"You know she's only nineteen." Jenny crossed her arms and raised a brow.

"Yes, I know." He nodded.

"And you're thirty."

"Yes, Mrs Stephanopoulos."

"And you've already dated and slept with Alena."

The red blush rose up his neck to his face. "She was twenty-four and I was twenty-five; we were consenting adults."

"Yes…I know…but Alexis is not an adult. Not legally. So, while I appreciate you asking permission to court her, I'm hoping there will be no sex involved with it."

"Um…I planned on letting her take the lead," he murmured and shifted his weight to his left foot.

"Mmm," Jenny mumbled. "I'm going to give you one warning, and one warning only, Lorenzo." She held up her forefinger. "Whatever snit you've been in lately, get out of it. No more being a jerk at the centre, or to my family, and two," stepping closer she lowered her voice as the boys hauled the tree and containers up, "if you so much as hurt Alexis the wrong way, I will hurt you in *every way* imaginable. Physically, financially, materialistically, I will have you removed from the clinic and centre. I *will ruin you*," she murmured. "*Do not* push the limits, Lorenzo, because I will push back a million times harder. So far, you've been nice and polite to me. Stay that way." Letting her eyes linger on his, she walked away. "Who wants to put the tinsel on?"

"Me!" Danté and Nick yelled out and quickly covered the tree in colour.

"Mama, why didn't you say you'd been in the basement." Pedro grinned. "You know there's nothing in there."

"*Now*," she said. "But who knows what your grandfather had in there. It stinks to high hell."

"So, why let us believe there was some big secret?" Carlos asked, disappointed that there wasn't a bigger mystery than some old locked room in the basement.

"Because at heart, you're all still kids. It was a bit of fun." Jenny touched his face gently. "It's Thanksgiving, so live a little. The little boy in you loved it." All four of her sons grinned in return.

Alexis pulled Lorenzo onto the chaise lounge. "What did she want? Did she give you the third degree?"

Smiling nervously, he said, "Of course she did. She's your grandmother. She cares for you and just wanted to make sure I was serious about this. She doesn't want you to be hurt again. Which is understandable after what you went through, and I did date your sister." He squeezed her hand reassuringly.

"You sure?" She gazed at him, worried that her grandma had overstepped the boundaries.

"I'm sure." His smile became strong. "She loves you; she's looking out for you."

Alexis's lips moved into a small smile. "Yeah, she does love me, and I'm thankful for that."

"Okay then, stop worrying about it," Lorenzo said.

There was a knock at the door and Dom got it.

"Hello. Have I made it on time?" Xanthe asked and slid out of her coat. "I worked all day and thought I was running late."

"No, you're not." Jenny pulled a pack of decorations from a container. "We're just starting the tree, and dinner will be a buffet that we'll put out soon."

"Oh, good." Xanthe accepted a wine from Roger and settled in on the couch to watch the decorating.

By five-thirty the tree was finished, lights were put up around the room and turned on, and stockings were being hung on the mantel.

"My, that's crowded," Xanthe said from beside Charles to whom she had been talking at Jenny's urging. "There will be even more added next year. Have you thought of a name yet?"

"Not yet," Diana said. "I haven't even decided where to live. New York, or my place downstairs."

"Here in Mykonos." Jenny hung the last stocking on the mantel. "Charles will take a while to recuperate. We could have his things packed up and shipped here," she said as she turned to them. "We could all pitch in and do up the house below Carlos and Viv. You can stay there."

"But I live there," Alena piped up from her spot on the couch.

"Not for long," Jenny told her. "Unless you want to live with them."

"Mmm, not really," Alena grumbled.

"Then you'll have to move home for now," Jenny said and felt her phone buzz in her pocket. Glancing at the text, she added, "But for now, I need you to do me a favour. Come with me." Waving at Alena to follow, she pulled her into her office. "I need you to go to the airport and fetch our guests. They're staying at *The Windmill,* so you'll need to escort them there and then bring them here."

"Why me?" Alena frowned. "Why do I have to leave the warmth and good food of home?"

"Because our guests are James Gardo and his parents."

Alena's eyes grew wide till they could widen more. "What?" she barely managed. "You're kidding? Why?"

"No." Jenny shook her head. "I'm not kidding. It's time to put an end to the last thirty years. It's a long story and it will take time to tell. Thirty years in fact. Say nothing, just get your coat and leave. There will be a car to get you to *The Windmill*, and you can use it to come, or you can walk home. It's up to them. Now go, they're only a few minutes out." Ushering her out of the office and to the front door for her coat, she closed it behind her and turned to see curious faces. "Our guests will be arriving soon." She noticed the kids had moved around and were spaced out. "We just need to re-arrange you a bit. Can you all move?" Organising the lounge room and its chairs, the kids and the guests, took ten minutes before she was happy. "Okay, you will all need to sit there later. Don't forget to keep your spot. You'll need it."

*****

Alena got to the airport just as the family plane landed, still not believing her grandmother had invited the Gardos. Shaking her head, she had no idea what to expect. Her and James hadn't spoken in weeks, and whatever they may have had fizzled out before that. Standing in the family's private hanger next to the car, she waited until the plane taxied in and stopped before stepping forward. The door opened and the stairs were rolled in. A stewardess smiled at the passengers, and James alighted through the door.

"Alena," he shouted excitedly and hurried down the stairs. Picking her up in a fierce bear hug, he swung her around.

"Oh," she cried out in surprise. "That's some welcome."

He set her down and planted a kiss on her lips, something he had been wanting to do for quite some months.

Sheila and Giancarlo stopped mid-stair and watched in surprise. James hadn't mentioned anything about kissing Alena, but then, it wasn't as though he really would have told them.

And Alena was right. The fizz wasn't there, and he realised it too.

"It's not gonna happen for us, is it? Time's run out." Letting his arms fall, he stood staring at her. "It's not gonna happen."

"No, I don't think so." She smiled sadly. "It just wasn't our time."

"Yeah, the timing sucked," he agreed, then brightened. "You look great."

"Thanks, James." She peered around his shoulder. "Mr and Mrs Gardo. Grandma asked me to escort you to *The Windmill Hotel* and then to her place. Do you have all of your bags?"

"Yes, Alena, we do," Sheila said, nervous now she was actually on solid ground. Not knowing what to expect, she got into the car after Alena and they set off for the hotel where they checked in.

"Mr and Mrs Gardo, your room key." Marcel, the desk clerk, handed over their key. "And Mr Gardo, your room key. We have turned down your beds, put on the electric blankets, and set the room temperature to a nice and toasty twenty-five degrees. We hope you enjoy your stay here at *The Windmill Hotel*." He nodded to each. "Miss Alena."

"Marcel." She smiled warmly. "I'll take them up."

"Of course." He nodded and watched them head up in the lift to the palatial grand rooms on the second floor. They overlooked the island, and had a view of the ocean.

"I'm to wait if you want to freshen up or unpack." Alena stood in the hallway. "Do you want to walk to Grandma's? It's about ten minutes, if that. Or we can take the car."

"Oh, I think a walk would be nice in this brisk air after being cooped up on a plane," Giancarlo said, and placed his case on the baggage rack at the end of the bed.

"We'll just be a few minutes," Sheila told her and closed the door.

"Okay." Alena paced the corridor.

"Nice room, nice hotel," James called from his room.

"Yeah. It's the family's." Alena stopped at his open door. "My parents and aunt and uncles had their thirtieth anniversaries here a couple of weeks ago. They had their wedding receptions here in 1977."

"Wow! Talk about history," James said. "I'm just gonna pop in the bathroom."

"What do we do?" Sheila whispered to her husband as she sprayed perfume on her neck and wrists. A fresh coat of lipstick followed.

"Why are you whispering?" Giancarlo teased. "She can't hear us.

And we're going to act like normal human beings, adults even. The family invited us to end this rubbish, and we're going to tonight. Did you see Alena's reaction to James kissing her? Looks like long distance made it over before it started." He brushed his short grey hair, having lost all of the blond years before, but he still had his precision cop haircut. "Ready?"

"No, I'm not. I feel sick." Sheila grabbed her stomach. "I feel sick."

"Calm down, Sheila. It's going to be okay. Now, let's grab our coats and go."

"Do I look all right?" She smoothed the royal blue pantsuit down and turned this way and that in front of the closet's mirror. She had good sturdy matching shoes on to compliment the outfit.

"You look lovely. Let's go." His eyes were twinkling as he helped her into her coat. It matched the pantsuit. "Ready?"

"No." She looked at his reflection in the mirror.

"Let's go," he said and moved her out the door. James was already waiting with Alena. "All set. The room is lovely, and so is the view."

"Thank you. Grandma's tried to do her best by keeping the charm of the old windmill and mixing it with modern conveniences," Alena told them as they went down in the lift.

"Your grandmother?" Sheila asked.

"Grandma bought the hotel in 1983. She's been able to keep it up to date, but still charming. The windmill out back are suites you can rent for months at a time." She paused as they stepped outside and pointed to the old windmill at the back and off to the side. "There. Four floors of private suits. Like little apartments."

"How charming," Giancarlo said. "The whole hotel is."

"Thank you. Shall we go?" Alena smiled and shoved her gloved hands into her coat pockets to keep them warm.

*****

While waiting for Alena, Jenny started filling one of the dining tables with food. Bowls of salads sat in bowls of ice to keep cold. There were novelty popcorn boxes and cones full of a variety of popcorn all set out on trays. Bowls of fruit and mixed lollies, nuts, chips, dips, a variety of crackers with a cheese platter, foil-wrapped chocolates, and small frosted cupcakes with turkey themes on them, plus heated buffet servers full of vegetables and slices of turkey roll that she had been cooking all afternoon. It was a fresh lot. Lunch's leftovers were in the fridge.

Carlos and Pedro helped Tomas and Roger set up the other table with buckets of ice for the beers, wine and soft drinks. And huge glass dispensers were full of fresh-fruit-laden concoctions Tomas had made.

"Now." Jenny surveyed the tables. "Do we have everything?"

"Yum, what can we eat?" Nick asked as he and Danté stood at the table with wide, greedy eyes.

"Nibble on some fruit, the main food's for dinner," Jenny told them and saw them grab lollies instead. "I saw that."

They giggled and went back to their seats.

*****

"So, your family owns the hotel?" James asked as he and Alena led the little group down to Jenny's.

"Yes, it was the third or fourth business Grandma had."

"Own most of the island, does she?" James joked.

Alena laughed. "Funny you should say that."

"You're kidding?" he said. "I was joking."

"I'm not." She grinned. "Grandpa inherited the family's meat shop. When the family came home in '81 for Uncle Tomas and Roger, she decided to set up businesses for Daddy and Uncle Carlos because they'd decided to move home to be with the family again. So, Grandma set up *SB3*. It's the nightclub come function centre for Daddy to DJ at and he did for years. Still does on a Friday night, and my brothers Dom and Danté are taking over from him. And I sing, which was a natural thing to do. Soon after *SB3*, she helped Daddy set up *Sync*, his music publishing company, and Uncle Carlos got *S'Reel*, his film company. They have studios here on Mykonos, and when it turned into something big, they set up *Stefan Productions* in Athens where Uncle Carlos makes his movies. Then came *The Windmill*, then Uncle Tomas and Roger got a gym where they train the rich and famous who fly in to work with Daddy and Uncle Carlos, then came the publishing company Grandma set up. She'd already taken on *Villiers Inc* for Aunt Viv. Dan and Derek, the doctors who helped Uncle Tomas get better, got help with their clinic in New York. Alexis and Cabot now have the support centre, and Uncle Tomas and Roger were left a house from a dear friend in Miami and turned it into a HIV/AIDS care centre. Grandma's got a bunch of other properties, including the five houses around hers. She bought them in '81 for the family to move into and then bought the ones besides ours and Uncle Carlos and Aunt Viv to join them together as we expanded, so we had the room. My brother Danté has just set up a business with his best friend Nick, and Diana and I have *Haus of Stefan* outside of our careers. But our office is in the *Stefan Productions* lot, so our fathers can keep an eye on us, and we used our trust funds to finance it as we all did with the centre Alexis and Cabot have."

"Trust funds?" Sheila asked as she clung to Giancarlo's arm. The streets of Mykonos were wearing her out.

"Grandma set up trust funds for all of us," Alena explained. "At twenty-one we can draw a wage, at twenty-five we can use the money to set up a business, but Grandma and our fathers sign off on it, and at thirty we get full control. Not that we need it. We've all got high paying jobs, so we earn our own money and pay our own way."

"Quite a charmed life you live, Alena Stephanopoulos," James told her.

Quite a rich life, Sheila thought. *Jenny could still afford trust funds for all of her grandchildren after giving me five million. It must have been one hell of a fortune.*

Giancarlo saw her frown and knew what she was thinking. He squeezed her hand and gave a slight shake of the head when she looked at him.

She blushed and looked away. He always had a way of knowing what she was thinking, and she knew deep down that the five million she did get had gone a long way. In fact, they still had just under four million left. Between a good budget, not blowing what they had, and doing simple repairs on the house, the interest had kept topping it up. So, at the end of the day, she was quite grateful to Jenny Stephanopoulos for the money, because, without it, she wouldn't have had the life she'd had. She wouldn't have been able to do herself up, buy new clothes, or impress Giancarlo. He'd only really become interested when she had her makeover and showed him the woman she wanted to be. That was the woman he'd proposed to, and he'd made her the happiest woman on the planet.

*****

"So, Alfonso…" Dom munched on some crisps. "What sort of movies do you make?" He was sitting with Antonio in front of the fire, while Alfonso was on a chair to the side.

"Ah, I cannot tell you." Alfonso smiled. "I have been sworn to secrecy."

"By who?" Antonio asked, his eyes flitting back and forth between Alfonso and Cabot who sat in Tony's arms on the couch.

"Oh…" Alfonso teased. "Your parents and grandparents."

"We googled you anyway," Dom said. "You make porn."

"Ah, the dreaded internet." Alfonso frowned. "It is all happening so fast. One minute there is no such thing, and the next you can't do anything unless you are all over it. But again, I cannot say anything."

"What do you have to do with Uncle Carlos? He worked for your father?" Dom pushed. "We sorta know already. They were porn stars."

Alfonso tried not to smile, but was unsuccessful and lightly laughed. "I cannot say anything. I have been told your grandmother will kill me."

Antonio tuned out of that conversation and into Cabot's and Tony's.

"So, *do you* wear pyjamas?" Cabot asked Tony, getting back to the conversation from before. He was snuggled in Tony's arms and liked the way it felt. "You might have to borrow some of mine."

Tony grinned. "I might have to. I normally sleep naked."

Cabot blushed. "Oh...um..." He desperately tried to change the subject. "It's Thanksgiving; what are you doing for Christmas and New Year's?"

"Oh...I might spend it here. What's Christmas and New Year's like on Mykonos?" Tony lazily ran his fingers along Cabot's arm.

Cabot shivered at his touch. "Boring, island wise. We go to the club at New Year's unless we're somewhere else like New York or Australia."

Tony was impressed. "Wow. It must be nice celebrating in Australia. Isn't your grandmother from there?"

"Yeah, she is. Grandpa emigrated in 1950, and they married in 1952, then had Papa in 1953, then came Uncle Tomas and Uncle Pedro. We had an aunt, but she died. Alena's named after her. She was a baby. Grandma had her early and she didn't survive. Grandma's kept her ashes. They're in that pink and blue urn on the mantel with the pictures." Cabot pointed to the mantel where it sat. "Grandma brings her out for celebrations so she doesn't feel lonely."

"Oh, how sad for your grandmother," Tony said, looking to the mantel to see the urn in the centre. He saw Antonio watching them closely and smiled.

So did Cabot. "Hey, Tone...Antonio, what'chya thinkin'? You don't look too happy. It's Thanksgiving, you should be happy." He could tell by the look on his brother's face that something was going on in his head.

Antonio gave a shake of his head. "Nothing's wrong. I just find it strange."

"What?" Cabot asked, munching on some popcorn.

"That the first guy you become serious about, not only has the same name as me, but we're named after the same person. That's a hell of a bizarre coincidence."

"I guess." Cabot nonchalantly shrugged his left shoulder.

"I agree with Antonio," Tony said. "I mean, what are the odds of you having a brother called Antonio DeLuca, and meeting a guy called Antonio DeLuca, and *we're both* named after my father. There are no odds," he added as he shrugged a shoulder, "you just couldn't bet on it because it's impossible *to* bet on."

Cabot shook his head in confusion. "I have no idea what you're all talking about, because I was asking you about Christmas and New Year." He popped a piece of cheese flavoured popcorn into Tony's mouth.

"Well, I know what I'm thankful for this Thanksgiving." Tony gently kissed Cabot on the lips.

Cabot's blush deepened in surprise and he quickly shoved popcorn into his mouth. Tony hadn't kissed him yet, and that was their first time. And he still looked like Darren, wearing the black framed glasses, with dyed black hair. He liked being different, looking different, because it was helping him become someone he actually liked.

Antonio watched all of it with a deep frown. He'd never imagined Cabot would get himself a boyfriend, someone else to spend time with, and he'd never imagined he'd feel jealous because of it. He'd always wanted freedom from looking after Cabot, and he had it. But he'd never counted on it making him feel lonely. He didn't have a partner to be thankful for that Thanksgiving, but Cabot did. How the fuck did that happen? With his jealousy boiling over, he glanced over his family. Dom and Alena were single, Dom was only a year younger than him, so he clearly had time. Alena had had a boyfriend; her ex was now with Alexis. He watched them. Alexis was smiling and happy in Lorenzo's arms. Danté was only fourteen and wasn't interested in girls yet. He was too busy following in Dom's footsteps of music to care about girls. Nick didn't stop thinking about girls and how Danté needed to get himself a girlfriend. Danté was talking to Charles about photography and was animated in describing how big the shark that bit him was. Charles was listening with interest and laughed when he was supposed to. Meanwhile, the adults were hovering in the kitchen, or around the food waiting for the new guests to arrive. *I wonder who they are?*

*****

"Does everyone know we're coming?" Giancarlo asked.

"Clearly not. I only found out when Grandma sent me to fetch you," Alena told him.

"So, we may not be welcome then?" James asked.

"You're obviously here for a reason, and Grandma always has her reasons. So, if she wanted you here…and we're here." They arrived at Jenny's door. "You all ready?"

"No," Sheila breathed. "I'm nervous."

"Grandma invited you. That's a big deal." Alena studied her face under the Christmas lights around the door and window. "If she hated you, you wouldn't be here."

"Really?" Sheila asked hopefully. All these years she'd never really hated Jenny either, she just needed somewhere to dump her grief, and Jenny had been it.

"Really," Alena insisted. "Grandma doesn't pull punches. She will tell you what she thinks and be brutally honest while doing it. It's the way she is."

"Well, from what you've said, this sounds like it's going to go well," Giancarlo said.

"Oh, I hope it does," Sheila murmured, hanging on to the leather-jacketed arm of her husband. "But I have a feeling it's going to be awkward."

"Either way, are you ready?" Alena turned from them and slid her key into the lock.

Jenny's ears pricked up at the sound and she turned around from the table. "They're here. Everyone behave, be respectful, well-mannered, and polite. *Do not* be rude. They are here for a reason," she told everyone just as Alena pushed open the door.

"We're here." Alena glanced at everyone and stepped inside to let James through.

He moved into the house and took everything in as his parents followed him.

Shocked murmurs went through the kids, but the adults, except for Jenny, frowned.

"Welcome to our home, happy Thanksgiving," she said from in front of the table. "Please come in. Carlos and Pedro will take your coats."

"Thank you, Jenny, for inviting us, it was quite unexpected," Giancarlo said as he slid his coat off and handed it to Carlos.

"Well, it has been thirty years, the time was right," she replied, stepping forward. She saw James hesitate at taking his beanie off. "You can leave that on if you feel more comfortable, James."

Smiling, he lowered his hand. "I don't want to freak anyone out with my scar. It's still pretty gross."

"That's okay." Jenny took another step. "This is a family full of scars, so you'll fit right in. Danté here," she put her hand on Danté's shoulder, "was bitten by a shark back in September. His right thigh is still full of teeth marks. And Charles here," she held out her hand towards him, "has just been found in a war-torn country, so he has physical *and* mental scars. Alexis and Cabot have survived assaults this year and opened up a support centre." She waved a hand at each person as she talked. "Tomas here still has scarring from what your brother Luiz did to him thirty years ago. Poisoned him with Nerium Oleander." Tomas was standing behind and to the right of her, almost too scared to even dare a look at James. "Angelina still has the gunshot wound from when her father ordered Pedro shot in 1977, and the emotional scars from her father's assault. And all three of my boys still have the emotional scars of what happened to them." She watched James's face move with different emotions. "There's a hell of a lot of scars in this room, James. You're just one in a room of many. So, don't believe you're alone in this, because you're not. Now, let me introduce you all." Making the introductions they came to Spiros, whom Sheila could barely shake hands with.

"I…ah…need to apologise, though it's thirty years too late," Sheila murmured, knowing she was flame red with embarrassment. "What I did in '78 was stupid, and I don't even know how, or why, I did it." Shaking her head sadly, she couldn't look them in the eye. "I am so, so sorry."

"Did anything happen?" Spiros asked her calmly, fully aware of every eye on them. His sons and in-laws knew the story; the grandkids did not.

"No, ah, no it didn't." Her head moved faster. "No, it did not. I was stupid and made a stupid mistake."

"Well, so did I." Spiros looked at Jenny. "And I paid for it."

"And it's all in the past," Jenny told them. "It's time we put all of this garbage to rest, and we will do that tonight." She looked at Sheila's shame-filled face. "I never hated you, Sheila. I had no need to. Even *now* I don't. I don't hate either of you if you ever thought that. It's time we all moved on." Glancing from one to the other she saw the shocked, but hopeful expressions. "In the meantime, it's dinnertime. Tomas and I will serve." She walked behind the table. "We have seats and tables along the walls for the adults; we have trays for the kids if you want to sit on the floor." They had moved one of the dining tables to be front and centre and facing the lounge room to serve as the buffet table. "We have turkey here, Tomas has vegetables, Roger has the hot rolls and gravy. Or there's nibbles and salads if you prefer." She handed each turkey-laden plate to Tomas who loaded them with vegetables and handed it on to Roger. The family hung back until the guests were served before getting theirs. There was enough to go around, and the guests sat at the café style tables that had been set up especially for dinner along each wall of the hallways. The rest pottered around eating at the table.

Alena sat with James at the table next to his parents.

"This is really cool of your grandmother," James said as he munched on a cheesy potato.

"Grandma does it this way every few years." Alena grinned, and saw her mother sitting with her father, Alfonso, and her grandfather. "The more the merrier. And we have more this year. Four more." She pointed to Charles. "He's Diana's partner and baby daddy. Alexis is dating my ex, Lorenzo," she nodded in their direction, "which is pretty gross. Cabot's got himself a *special friend* in Tony," she giggled as she made the quote marks, "then there's Alfonso, our long lost half-uncle. And Dan, Derek and Xanthe are here because they've been helping the family deal with all of the rubbish we've gone through."

"Would anyone like a drink?" Roger popped up beside them. "We have flavoured mineral waters, soft drink, beer and wine. Mr and Mrs Gardo?"

"A beer would go down nicely," Giancarlo said and turned to his wife. "Sheila?"

"A water will be fine," she said nervously.

"Berry or citrus?" Roger asked.

"Berry sounds lovely," she replied.

"James?"

James looked up. "Guess I'll have a soft drink, thank you."

"Okay, I'll be back in a moment." Roger went to collect the water, grabbed the beer, and cracked open the soft drink to pour it in a glass with ice, then carried the drinks over and went back to his own food, and Tomas, who had been cowering in the kitchen not wanting to serve James.

Jenny hovered around the table, serving seconds to the kids, and making sure everyone had what they needed, and once dinner was over, the leftover meats and vegetables went into the fridge along with the salads. The rest of the food on the table was re-arranged and restocked so it could be nibbled on all night.

"Dinner's over," Alena said after a lengthy conversation with James. "You need refills?"

"Not right now, thank you," Sheila told her. "But I do need to freshen up, if there's somewhere I can go."

"Of course." Alena pointed to the opposite hallway. "Down the hall, the last door on the left. I don't think anyone's using it." She collected the plates with James's help.

Giancarlo stood up for his wife and watched her walk off, and Alena walked off with the plates.

Viv and Angie came around and cleaned off all the tables while the boys re-arranged the chairs for more casual seating.

Alena pulled James over to the fire to chat with Diana and Charles, and Giancarlo wandered over to Jenny.

"Jenny, it was very surprising that you invited us here." Shoving his hands into his jeans pockets, he wasn't sure what else to say or do.

"It was a surprising invitation," Jenny said, looking into his blue eyes. "It wasn't something I ever thought I'd do, but after James, and being at the hospital, I realised that thirty years' worth of garbage had come to nothing, and it was, or needed to be, over."

"Yes." He nodded in understanding. "What James did, what happened, was so completely unexpected."

"Yes, it was. None of us could ever see that happening," Jenny said as Sheila came back and stood beside her husband. "No one could have predicted what happened to your son and what he did." She glanced over at James and Alena in front of the fireplace. He'd finally taken off his beanie and was showing Charles, Danté and Nick his war wound.

"No, none of us did," Giancarlo murmured, looking over his shoulder at his son. "Nor what happened thirty years ago."

Jenny felt Tomas appear beside her. "No. That's why we have something else." Urging Tomas to step forward, she let him take over.

"I…ah…" He cleared his throat nervously. "I think it's time for these to go to you." Handing over an envelope, he stood quietly.

"What are they?" Sheila accepted it and opened it to reveal several photos. "Oh," she gasped, her hand flying to her mouth. "Is it?"

"Yes, it's Luiz, in July 1977," Tomas told her. "He was twenty-five and engaged to Bertha St John. It's also around the time I met him…" He let the rest trail off.

"Oh." Sheila teared up and gazed at the one of Luiz on his own. "He was so good looking, just like James. Oh, they look the same, Giancarlo."

"Yes, they do," he murmured, sliding an arm around her.

"He was beautiful." Tomas gently clasped his hands in front of him. "He was so beautiful and I fell for him hard. We weren't together for long, but he had an impact on me then." He watched the range of emotions fly over her face and knew they matched the ones flying over his.

Flipping through the rest of the pictures, she saw him with Bertha on the beach, with the girls at a table with cocktails in their hands, with Bertha on a yacht. She came back to the one of him on his own, in small red swim briefs, hands on hips, a wide smile on his face, and a golden tan all over. "Oh, he was beautiful." Sighing, she deflated a bit. "But he caused so much trouble, even as a teenager."

James saw his mother looking at something, excused himself, and wandered over. "What's going on?" He saw the photos. "Oh, wow, is that him? He looks like me. Well, when I had hair anyway." Taking the photos, he peered closer. "Me with hair. No wonder you freaked out," he said to Tomas. "We look identical."

"You did." Tomas nodded, noticing James looked different with short cropped hair and a huge scar halfway around his head. He didn't look like Luiz anymore. "It's the eyes. You have the same eyes, same shape, same…colour…" Even now he felt it, because it was the eyes that still made him tingle in the pit of his stomach. But James wasn't Luiz. Luiz was dead, and James just happened to have blue eyes because both of his parents did.

"Yeah, um…look," James started nervously then looked back at the photo. "I'm sorry for what I did. I didn't mean to. I didn't know what I was doing."

"We know," Tomas told him. "We've been told of your condition. It freaked me out for a lot of reasons, all of which will be revealed tonight."

"And I think we should get started soon," Jenny said. "There's a long story to tell, and many people to tell it. We thought it was time for those photos to be where they belonged." She looked at Sheila. "As far as we know, they're the last ones taken."

"Oh, thank you," Sheila murmured. "Even after everything he did this means so much to me to know what he grew into, physically. He turned into a very beautiful boy indeed."

"Yes," Tomas murmured wistfully. "He did."

"Okay, kids." Jenny stepped away. "Time to freshen up. We have a very long story to tell, and you'll need to sit through all of it. There are four bathrooms to use, so use them."

The kids scurried off in four directions, and fifteen minutes later they were stocking up on snacks and drinks.

"Family on the couch, and around it. Tony, you and Alfonso are included, and you too James; you're all involved," Jenny called.

Tony and Cabot resumed their seats on the couch with Antonio and Danté. Dom and Alexis sat on the floor in front, and Diana and

Charles were off to the left near the door. Since Charles was in a wheelchair, it was hard to keep moving him around, so he stayed there. Alena, James and Alfonso sat to the right on dining chairs.

Lorenzo, Dan, Derek and Xanthe sat near the hallway leading to the guest room, while Giancarlo and Sheila sat at the other end near the piano.

The rest of the adults set up chairs between the two, and Mike and Maggie had their kids with them since they weren't a part of it, and they were sitting near the Gardos.

"Everyone got drinks and snacks?" Jenny asked.

"Yes, Grandma," came the reply.

"Okay." She nodded at Spiros, and while the children took their seats, they took their place, standing in front of the fire that crackled gently in the grate. Waiting until they settled, she nodded at her children and started the story. "This is going to be a long story. It wasn't one we ever thought of telling you, because it was before your time and none of your business, so we kept it to ourselves. But, it seems some of you decided to dig that story up this year and uncovered reports and old files of what happened back then. But you don't know the whole story. And that's what we'll be telling you all tonight." She gazed at the faces of everyone looking back. Fifty-five years of marriage with the man she loved dearly. Fifty-four years with three sons she would die for, and twenty-nine years with grandchildren she loved to pieces. And now a new generation was going to be born. "It's a thirty-year-old story that you, and we, think started in 1977. But that was just *my* family. *My* three sons and the adventures they were about to have. This family, the Stephanopoulos family, is a very convoluted, complicated one. It's like a family tree buried in the core of an onion and wrapped in a multi-layered spider's web. It's big, it's thick, and every time you pull some web away and peel off a layer, you find another person to be related to." She smiled at Alfonso who smiled back, and out of the corner of her eye, she saw Angie knock back her wine. "It is a family tree, a tale of intrigue, murder, marriage and children, all complicated by hatred, jealousy, *illegitimate* children, and a ravenous thirst for money and power."

"Grandma; are you writing a blockbuster novel?" Cabot joked. "Because that's what it sounds like."

Jenny laughed softly. "Well may you say that, Cabot, but I have been documenting it all and may turn it into a book. I swear though, you can't write stuff as good as our family history. And that history has now become yours because of what's happened this year. But now, it's time to end it." Her eyes flitted to her guests and her children. Sheila sat with the picture of Luiz in her hand. "Thirty years is thirty too long. The problem is, unbeknownst to us at the time, the issues had started long before even your fathers were born. Long before your grandfather and I were born. It all goes way back to Giorgio Stephanopoulos, your great-great-grandfather. And this is where your *grandfather* takes over the story." Jenny kissed Spiros on the cheek and went back to her seat beside Carlos.

"My grandfather, Giorgio, had two children with his one and only wife. My father, Giorgio junior, and my Aunt Marishka. Now, it's very complicated, as your grandmother said, so you might want to make a note of the names of people because they will come up later." He paused a moment to take in their curious expressions. "My aunt married a man by the name of Stefano Papadopoulos. They were both young, but my aunt was unable to bear him children. She died in her thirties, broken-hearted from being unable to have children, and because he did nothing but have affairs. My grandfather always blamed Stefano for his daughter's death, but never did anything about it. Stefano went on to marry a woman by the name of Caterina Vonwit. She had a son by her deceased husband. *Her* son was Andros Poulos who we know to be the father of at least three children. Two of them are in this room. Angelina, and Alfonso." He looked at them both. "And he had Luiz Manning by Sheila."

He glanced her way, as did the rest of the family, and saw her shame-filled blush before continuing. "Stefano had many affairs. We don't know how many children *he* sired, but we do know of Gustoff Dropopolous, whose mother is unknown, and Marta Effidopolous whose mother was Stefano's maid, Maria Effidopolous. Stefano became engaged to a young girl named Consuela Maria Da Vica; a poor girl sold off by her parents to a wealthy man. Her story came to a brutal end in 1977, as did Gustoff's, Maria's and Marta's. But, you'll hear about those later."

Gazing at his grandchildren, he realised what a full and happy life he'd led. He'd had Jenny by his side, they'd raised three sons, acquired three incredible in-laws, and been given seven beautiful, amazing grandchildren, and now there was a great-grandchild on the way. Yes, he and Jenny had been incredibly blessed.

"My grandfather, Giorgio, was a Greek tycoon. He made his money doing whatever he could, and he became a mafia-style boss. His fortune was massive, and it went to the first blood son as heir. Well, my father had died in 1967, and as you know, Jenny and I packed up your fathers and brought them home. As first blood heir, Giorgio's company would have gone to me and then to my sons. And that is where Stefano Papadopoulos had a problem. And *that* is where I let your parents take over." He took his place beside Jenny while Carlos and Viv took his by the fire.

"My story," Carlos glanced at Viv, "*our* story, starts in June 1977. I was twenty-four years old, a bartender by morning with Tony's father Antonio," he saw Cabot smile at Tony, "an oil sprayer by afternoon, and a masseuse by night. I was very much like Cabot, or should I say, Cabot's very much like me." He paused a moment to remember back thirty years. "I loved sex. I started screwing all the women I could at eighteen, and by twenty-four, I was charging for it."

"That makes you a prostitute." Antonio frowned at his father's behaviour. "A gigolo."

"Yes," Carlos admitted. "But, I saw myself as a businessman. I had sex with girls in my lunch hour, and sex with older women at night. I became known on the underground grapevine as the masseur who gave massages on the inside as well as the outside."

"Ew," the kids complained. "Gross."

"Yes, I guess it would be now." Carlos blushed. "But, in 1977, I was making ten thousand dollars for four hours, so it paid very well indeed."

"Jesus, maybe I should have charged," Cabot muttered, eliciting looks from Tony *and* Antonio.

"The problem, as I guess you could call it," Carlos continued, "was that one of the older ladies I massaged was Connie DeLuca. It's funny," he added as he watched that news sink in to Cabot and Tony, "that I felt no shame then, but I sure as hell feel it now."

"You had sex with Tony's grandma? Ew, Papa, how could you?" Cabot's face screwed up in horror and he buried his head in the neck of his black turtleneck sweater. "That's gross! Are we like, related?" he asked through the wool.

"Of course you aren't, Cabot, don't be silly," Viv chastised.

Carlos watched Tony's confused, horrified face. "I'm sorry you had to hear that. Your grandparents had an open marriage at the time. I think they'd been separated about five years, and your father hated it. Your grandmother had lovers, your grandfather had them as I told you. I just happened to be one of many of your grandmother's."

Tony blinked against the shock and swallowed the hard lump in his throat. "It seems there's still a lot I don't know about my family."

"Well, maybe Viv can help you with that. She has stories from her time with Connie in the '70s." Carlos looked at his wife. "That's how we met. Connie called her good friend Harriet DeVille, and she called Viv. She came over from Santorini and we met. Anyway, to get on with the story, I was continuing my work days and nights after meeting Viv, but they didn't last long. I was massaging a young lady when the previous customer came back with her boyfriend, and after calling the girl a whore, they fired a gun at me."

Shocked gasps went around the kids. "The young lady was, and I sure as hell didn't know at the time, Consuela Maria Da Vica, Stefano Papadopoulos's fiancée. The other woman and man were Marta Effidopolous and Gustoff Dropopolous. I knew none of their names, had no idea who they were, or who they were related to. I had just been going about my business. Connie found me running past her room and pulled me in. She came up with a way of getting me out of Mykonos. I raced home, grabbed my suitcase that I already had packed for emergencies, grabbed my money and papers, and took off down to the docks. Viv joined us, and told us it was all over the hotel.

Connie had brought along luggage trunks and told me to get in one." He smiled at the memories. "That's how I got to Hollywood. Smuggled out in a Louis Vuitton trunk. A few days later, they introduced me to Harry and Harriet DeVille." Gazing at Alfonso, he added, "Their maid was Suzy and she had a five-year-old son called Alfonso. No one knew who his father was except for Suzy. She was such a nice woman, Alfonso; she loved you so much. You used to run around the house pretending to be Harry, sucking on those chocolate cigars he gave you. He and Harriet *adored* you."

Alfonso smiled sadly at his own memories. "Yes, they did. It's always nice to hear good things about all three of them."

Carlos returned the smile. "Harry saved my bacon in more ways than one. And because of the size of my…" he blushed, "genetics, I became a porn star." He launched into the whole story from beginning to end, telling them about Barbara Weston and how Viv called her out, which was how they had met, the movies he'd made, written and starred in, the awards he won, and he showed them some old movie tapes and awards. They passed the awards around, the kids curiously holding them. Cabot tried to give one a blow job, much to the disdain of everyone else, so he handed it over and blushed in embarrassment, pulling his turtleneck sweater up over his head so just his eyes peeked out.

Viv admitted to her past in two porn movies for Harry, and Carlos talked about his girlfriend, Rosalee Brentworth, and her murder at the hands of Stefano's henchmen. He discussed meeting Aneeka, and how they were both kidnapped by those henchmen and ended up in the old quarry. "Aneeka got away, but I was taken, in the trunk, to Chicago. I managed to kick my way into the back seat and decided to fight my way out. I grabbed the steering wheel and we swerved all over the road, crashing through a bridge railing into the river. I helped my captor out of the car and swam for the surface. Tony, Aneeka, Star and Drew were there, and I told them he was heading for the airport. We got there as the Papadopoulos plane was taking off, and my captor was shot dead on the tarmac. We were all standing in the rain trying to figure out what to do next, when Star asked me if the people behind me were friends of mine. I turned and saw my brothers and a whole bunch of cops and feds."

Taking a deep breath, he let it out slowly. "And that's where my story," he turned to Viv and squeezed her hand, "*our* story, ends…for now, because now it's time for Pedro's story." He and Viv took their seats while Pedro and Angie took centre stage, leaving his family shell-shocked at the story. Cabot and Antonio had jaws hanging, Diana was white and being comforted by Charles. Carlos just hoped his children didn't hate him.

Pedro cleared his throat and gazed at his children and niece and nephews. "Our story begins, *also*, in June 1977. I was the DJ at a club called SantorPoulos, and it was owned by your grandfather, Andros Poulos. It's where I met your mother." Smiling down at Angie he slid an arm around her shoulders and she moved into him, resting her head on his chest. "Your uncle had already left, and the cops were all over the house. That's this house that we're in now. And then I started having trouble with Andros. I have no idea why, but he started drugging my drinks at the club. I got free food and drink, and I would come home high and wake up feeling like crap with the worst hangovers imaginable. It was Angie who told me she'd seen them do it, so I stopped drinking what they gave me and brought my own. After Angie and I met, we started seeing one another, and the night of her going away party, Andros found out and threatened to kill me. Angie hit him over the head with a trash can lid and we fled. Fled Santorini, fled Mykonos."

He went on to tell the story of Barbara Weston, what Andros did to Angie, getting a job at *Studio 69*, the people they met, and the things they did. Angie spoke of her assault at the hands of her father, the restraining order and charges, and getting shot in the shoulder. Pedro recounted his story of being in porn movies and told of crashing his car and having drugs found in it. Of hiring bodyguards Mark Monroe and Sara-Michelle Dubois, and of finding himself in the trunk of a car.

"I managed to get out on a back road when we'd stopped for a train, and that's when I was picked up by Mark and Detective Gardo. We made it to Chicago and ended up on the tarmac. My kidnapper was dead too." He turned to Giancarlo. "Would you like to add something, Detective?"

Giancarlo stood straight like a cop, and he noticed all eyes on him. "I was on the drug squad in '77. I had been tracking Nedro Scarvo for years, but I could never break him. I found out about Mr Stephanopoulos from his car crash and ended up on the case. We heard that Andros had been parked outside of 69 for a while and went to pick him up, and that's when we came across the scene of Mr Stephanopoulos's car smashed into Poulos and his limo with him dead, along with the young female driver of the Mustang. Monroe gave me a quick rundown of the situation, and that's when we realised Mr Stephanopoulos wasn't on the scene. We saw him being dumped into a car trunk, and that's when we took off in pursuit. We found him by the side of the road, picked him up, and took off for Chicago where we found a lot of people and a lot of bodies. It was a nightmare to clean up afterwards."

"Did you ever catch, Scarvo?" Jenny asked, recalling their conversation from thirty years earlier.

"Unfortunately, I didn't. I retired when James was born and my replacement didn't bother. The only good thing is Scarvo's long dead. Another kingpin apparently." He took his seat to rest his weary bones.

"Thank you, Detective," Pedro said and turned to the children. "That is where my story ends and Tomas's begins. And that's where all of this gets even more complicated and complex." He and Angie took their seats.

"I need more popcorn if this story's going to keep going," Danté said. "Can I get some more, please?"

Jenny and Tomas swiftly gathered the trays and passed the rest of the popcorn, lollies and chocolate around. The adults had the cheese and crackers, and any leftover chocolates. Drinks were passed around, and then Tomas and Roger took centre stage.

"Ah." Tomas breathed slowly and faced his nephews and nieces. "This is hard for me because I've...been so affected for so long. It affected me physically, emotionally, mentally, and my story goes longer than any others. My story goes for thirty years." He felt Roger squeeze his hand and stared up into his big brown eyes. Reassured, he went on. "I was never sure about much. I hadn't dated, I didn't feel the need to. I had no interest in bedding women like Carlos. I just wanted to work and save money and travel the world one day. And then Carlos disappeared and all of that controversy happened. And then Pedro disappeared and *all of that* controversy happened. And then I saw a…" his eyes closed, "beautiful-looking man on the beach, and all of a sudden I'm questioning my sexuality of which I had none. I hadn't had feelings for men or women. I just wasn't interested." Sighing, he looked at James sitting to his left with Alena and Alfonso and memories came flooding back as if they had just happened yesterday. "And then I saw him on the dock and sparks flew. And then he booked in for two hours of personal training one night and that's when things happened."

Tearing his gaze away from James in embarrassment, he looked down, his grip on Roger's hand tightening. "Luiz was my first. It was also the night I found out he was engaged to one of the ladies I trained in the gym. I felt as guilty as hell and vowed it wouldn't happen again. But it did, and the guilt grew. I told Bertha what had happened, and she told me he was bisexual." He glanced at Cabot. "But it didn't matter to her. Either way, we both dumped him, and I left to fly home with the ladies to Miami. I still remember the day I arrived. August the 1st 1977 was a beautiful day. Bette Olander set up a gym in her grand ballroom for me to start working on all of her friends. We dined at *Flair et Saveur,* and ended up at an over-forties club called *Sex et Faveurs* where Luiz turned up begging me to take him back. I didn't, and he was thrown out. We moved onto a club called *The Joy Stick* where I met Marie and Beatrice, and Violet Seralift." Smiling, he glanced at Roger and pulled him close. "It's also where I met this guy."

Roger kissed him lightly, making the smile grow bigger.

Tomas and Roger went on to tell their story, Tomas deciding to work at *Seralift,* Luiz vandalising Roger's car, killing four porn stars and framing Roger who was arrested, being poisoned by Luiz and rushed to hospital from the police station, and then being kidnapped by Luiz and then by one of Stefano's henchmen. And *then* finding his way out of the trunk of his car at O'Hare Airport and coming across his brothers.

"Looking back at that time, as I've done often, especially in the early days, I frequently wondered what would have happened if I'd stayed with Luiz, or taken him back." Tomas frowned slightly and thought about the long conversations he and Roger had recently had on Xanthe's couch where he finally declared his love for Luiz, and Roger declared his lies over sleeping with his fellow castmates. Both had got out the hurt and pain and had declared that day a fresh start for both of them. "I wouldn't have gone to Miami if Luiz had stayed here. We would have had a relationship. I don't know how long for, or if we would have lasted, but it would have happened. But, that also means I wouldn't have gone to Miami, I wouldn't have met Roger and had the life I've had with him." He rested his head on his husband's shoulder. "Then Luiz wouldn't have poisoned me, or killed four men to frame Roger. I had no idea what sort of mentality Luiz had, what kind of person he was deep down, because I'd only spent a few days with him. He broke into our home and poisoned my milk, killed four men and framed Roger and then kidnapped me. That is truly sick, and that is what has affected me for thirty years. That a man I gave myself to could so willingly treat me in such a way. Could tell me he loved me, and yet poison me and set my partner up for murder. The pure sickness of that makes me sick." His anger radiated around the room and his grip on Roger's hand turned deadly. "That the first person I gave myself to could turn around and do that to me, makes me *so* sick and *so* goddamn angry."

Sheila had been listening to the whole torrid story with sadness and fear; sadness that she didn't know about his life after kicking him out of home, and fear that there was going to be retribution for it. "I'm sorry," she whispered, looking down at the photo of her son. She didn't think anyone heard her, but Giancarlo had.

And Jenny heard it too. "It's not your fault," she told Sheila, making everyone turn their way. "What he did after he left home was *his* choice and had nothing to do with you."

"But it does." Sheila looked up with tear-filled eyes. "I know he knew I never really loved him. When I had him I was so damn angry with everyone including myself. My parents kicked me out of home and disowned me. Andros wanted nothing to do with either of us, and denied being his father. I was angry at myself for getting pregnant, and I was angry at Luiz for existing. I had to get a job and an apartment and not lose them. It was so damn hard trying to raise a child and work, and so I resented everyone involved. He felt it, he knew it. I know he did." Wiping her face, she stared at the photo.

"You did the best you could with what you had, which wasn't much," Jenny said. "But you got a second chance at it. You got Giancarlo and had James. The universe gave you a second chance, Sheila. That's more than some people get." Reaching across Giancarlo, she squeezed Sheila's arm. "You got a second chance."

Sheila stared at Jenny's hand before laying her own over it. Fresh tears flowed down her face. "I'm so sorry he did that to you," she told Tomas. "I didn't raise him that way. After finding out what he was doing at seventeen, I had to kick him out."

"And the choices he made after that are his and his alone," Jenny told her. "No one else's, not yours, not Tomas's, not Bertha's." Standing, she took Sheila into her arms and hugged her, much to her children's surprise, *and* Sheila's and Giancarlo's. "It's not your fault. He did all of that off his own bat. No one else's."

James watched his mother's anguish and his father's teary expression. Both had grief emanating from them and he felt it. No wonder he, James Gardo, had freaked everyone out. Luiz had done so much and harmed so many, and it was still affecting people thirty years later. He picked up his chair, carried it over, and placed it next to his mother's, and took her into his arms while she sobbed.

"I'm sorry, I'm so sorry."

"Hush, Mom, it's okay, it's okay." He gently soothed her hair. "It's over now. It's all over now."

Giving them a moment, Jenny saw Spiros collect a box of tissues and hand them over. Giving them to Sheila, she waited for her to be seated. "Tomas; are you finished?"

"Yes, Mama." He had stood where he was, watching the whole

thing in amazement.

"Then it's time to finish this part of the story. Spiros." She took her place as Spiros got up to stand beside his sons who gathered around him. Roger took his seat beside Viv.

Carlos began. "At the airport, we all moved into a conference room and met FBI Agent Payday. He's the one who'd been following Stefano Papadopoulos and traced him to Chicago. All of the cops and detectives on the cases filled in the details. I'd heard the name before, but I couldn't remember where. With the help of Aneeka, I remembered. I'd heard the name when I was seventeen years old, one day in the meat shop when I was working there. I didn't see him, and didn't know who he was. I told Payday and we flew here to Mykonos in the dead of night to find out from Papa. We then flew to Athens and visited his house, finally getting the story out of him. Stefano had orchestrated the whole thing. The henchmen, the kidnappings, Angie's shooting—"

"Which was meant for me," Pedro butted in from beside him.

"The reason was purely as Mama told you. Greed. He wanted the Stephanopoulos fortune and company when Giorgio died. But to do that, he had to get rid of any blood heirs of the firstborn. Us." Shaking his head, his laugh was mechanical. "It all came down to money. We found out later, once Giorgio had arrived, that Stefano had killed Gustoff and Marta, plus her mother. We also found out he was our great-uncle-in-law, and wanted to do all of that to us. What another goddamn nutjob." He sighed. "Giorgio shot him and we left. Giorgio came by our hotel room later and told us that he'd taken care of him, and how he'd sold off his estate and just the money was left. So, Stefano lost out regardless of what he did. Papa didn't want it, so Giorgio donated it all to charity."

"And in a melodramatic twist of irony," Pedro cut in, "Stefano's fortune had only close relatives to go to, and who do you think those close relatives were?" He spread his hands at his children and grinned.

"The Stephanopouloses," the kids yelled and the boys fist pumped the air.

"That's right." Pedro's grin grew bigger. "Mama took the money and made this family what it is today."

"Is that it?" Cabot asked. "The story ends there?"

"Not quite." Jenny and her in-laws joined the others by the fireplace. Carlos, Pedro and Tomas sat on the ottomans with their partners, and Jenny and Spiros stood behind them. "Once all of that was done, there were weddings to plan. We toasted for three days straight and enjoyed ourselves. You've seen the footage. You saw it at the anniversaries. At the last dinner here in this home before the kids flew out, Giorgio and my parents were with us. I had decided to fly to New York to be with Angie and Pedro to help with the baby that was on its way."

"The screaming hussy called Alena." Cabot smirked.

"Hey," Alena cried leaning over Tony to hit her cousin on the arm. "I wasn't like that."

"I liked New York so much I bought the building we were renting, and we still stay in it today," Jenny continued over her squabbling grandchildren. "I moved everyone else to New York, and then the girls were born, and we spent three and a half years there. Tomas and Roger travelled, Pedro DJd at 69, Angie and Maggie graduated from Juilliard. We celebrated birthdays, anniversaries, Halloweens, Thanksgivings, Christmases and New Years of 1979 and '80 in Australia…and then came back for our lives to move on. We celebrated birthdays at 69 on Valentine's Day 1980 and from then the shit hit the fan."

"People started dying," Pedro said sadly. "Leon, a co-worker and friend of Mike's and mine became sick and ended up in hospital. He died by the end of February, and from then they didn't stop. Officer Jamal Devron, 69 regular Stan Kosnov, Cabot Conroy," he saw Cabot's sombre face, "Thomas Derbon, friends of Tomas and Roger, and Carlos and Viv, friends of friends, people we knew, people we'd heard of, they all just…died." He closed his eyes and buried his face in his hands.

Tomas rubbed Pedro's back. "The year 1980 was the start of it. Pneumocystis pneumonia, Kaposi's sarcoma, opportunistic infections. We lost loved ones and attended funeral after funeral after funeral. It was horrible, and so emotionally depleting that we still get teary-eyed when we talk about it."

"And then came word in January 1981 of the deaths of Stephano DeLuca, Connie DeLuca and Antonio DeLuca." Carlos sadly looked at Tony who was looking as miserable as he was feeling. "With the deaths of each person, we connected them to another and another and another."

"*Seralift Productions* was absolutely devastated by AIDS. Marcus had to shut down in 1986, and he and Violet passed away, as did Bette. *DeVille* is still going because of Alfonso, but Greta Von Burro shut her doors too," Roger said. "And so many others we knew in Miami…the last funeral I went to was Freddy's. We'd already been to multiple funerals. Johnno, Ethan, Evan, Judd, Caden, Sam, Chris, Nathan. So many people we knew were dying in Miami." His face fell and his breathing laboured. "Tomas didn't come to Freddy's, I went alone, and that was the last funeral I attended. Unfortunately, unbeknownst to me, a passenger hitched a ride with me. A dirty little bug called a tick. We both got sick from it. So sick…" He laced his fingers through Tomas's. "Dan believed we had the gay plague."

"All signs pointed to it," Dan said and all heads turned to him. "And since we didn't know what it was, how it was spread, or even where to begin, it was all we could go by, so we dealt with it the best way we could."

"But I fought hard." Jenny took up the story and walked behind Spiros. "I fought for my sons and I fought until they died, which Tomas did." She slid her arms around Roger and Tomas and kissed Tomas on the cheek. "As we discovered, in time, the poison Luiz had given him had left damage to his insides and that's what the diseases latched onto. His immune system wasn't a hundred percent, and it took him a year to be able to walk without help as you all know. We opened *SB3* the night Cabot and Antonio were born, *Sync* and *S'Reel* after Dom was born. Tomas got better and they got *In Shape*. *Stefan Productions* was set up in Athens, we bought *The Windmill* for prosperity, and Alexis and Danté came along. I bought up other places around the island. The girls set up *Haus of Stefan*, Alexis and Cabot have the support centre, we have our homes, and who knows, now that Diana's having a baby, and Alena needs a new home, we might buy some more.”

She smiled affectionately at Diana and Charles who were sitting happily side by side, gazing wistfully at one another and holding hands. “We’ve acquired an AIDS care home in Miami, set up a publishing house of our own, have Vivian’s *Villiers Style,* Dan and Derek’s clinic, and now Danté and Nick have their IT business. We’ve always taught you kids to work hard at what you do and to be proud of it. It’s your future; all of this is for you and your children.” She gazed upon their faces. “We didn’t work hard for all of you to have it all come tumbling down, and this year it did. Thirty years ago terrible things happened to your parents and uncles. Thirty years later, it’s all happened to you. It seems history has repeated itself, and I don’t like it.”

Frowning, her eyes flitted back and forth to everyone. “Alexis is assaulted, Alena throws a hissy fit and makes it up to her then goes on tour where she meets, lo and behold, James Gardo. Who, lo and behold, has an aneurysm that’s screwing with his memory and brain, making the poor boy go nuts and think he’s someone else. Cabot’s assaulted at knifepoint and contracts HIV, and finally gets the therapy he needs. Thank you, Xanthe, you’ll have a massive bonus coming for Christmas.”

“Oh, goody, I need a cash injection,” Xanthe said.

“Dom gets himself into a huge amount of trouble and finally sorts himself out just in time to save Danté from a shark’s mouth,” Jenny went on, watching as Danté jokingly slung his feet over Dom’s shoulders, and Dom fling them off in annoyed disgust. “We’ve got Diana pregnant and alone because her baby daddy is off in a war-torn country getting himself held hostage and then hospitalised.”

Diana giggled. “Grandma, I didn’t know you knew that term.”

“I may be seventy-nine, but that doesn’t mean I don’t listen to or read what young kids are saying these days.” Jenny grinned at her granddaughter before moving on. “We have Tony Luca turn up to find his own attacker, and not only finds that he attacked other people, including Cabot, but finds out Cabot’s family knew *his* family. Unfortunately, in a most intimate way.” She lightly smacked Carlos over the head to giggles from the kids.

“Ow, Mama.” He ducked and grew sheepish.

"And you wonder why Cabot couldn't keep it in his pants," she said. "Like father like son."

Carlos flushed with embarrassment. So did Cabot.

"And then there's Alfonso; loses his mother at nine, and is adopted by the DeVilles and trained to take over the family business. Which we all need to do with you lot," Jenny told them. "And then there's James…" She turned to him. "He went through his own hell, not only having an aneurysm that made him believe he was his dead brother, but getting shot in the head. I'm sorry you had to go through both of those things. What some of us went through kind of fades in comparison, so I'm glad to see that you're back to normal and doing well."

"Thank you." He gave a small nod. "I am. A lot better than expected." He felt his mother squeeze his hand and happily looked at her and squeezed back. He saw his father's smiling face beside hers.

"And now *that* is the end of the story," Jenny said. "Except to say that there's been a lot of emotional help from Xanthe as several of you have processed things. Cabot and Alexis, Danté and Tomas. You've all had something to deal with, and hopefully, come the new year you will have all dealt with them. If you have any questions, ask them now, because after tonight that's the end of it. No more talk of the past. I'll get more munchies ready."

She urged Spiros into the kitchen while the kids all started talking at once. They listened half-heartedly while re-filling the table with help from Dan and Derek. Restocking the drinks, they saw it was only ten-thirty.

The kids finished with their questions and sat pondering as the parents got themselves alcohol. And lots of it.

"*That* was harrowing," Angie said and knocked back a glass of wine.

"Not as bad as I thought it would be, really," Jenny said, seeing Giancarlo and Sheila come for a drink.

"Quite a story." Giancarlo accepted a beer. "Even I learned some things I didn't know back then."

Jenny handed Sheila wine. "Oh, I think there was plenty people didn't know, particularly the kids." She glanced over to see them all huddled up while James and Alfonso sat chatting with Charles.

"So, what did you think of all that?" Antonio asked the others. "We already knew some of it, but the rest…bloody hell."

"Yeah, it is confusing, but Grandma's analogy of the family is a good one," Diana said. "A family tree buried in the core of an onion, smothered in a multi-layered spider web."

"Convoluted, congested and complicated," Cabot added. "Why didn't they just keep it in their pants and not force it on us?"

"Spoken like a true fucker who can't keep it in his own pants," Antonio said, giving his brother a scowl and getting a hurt frown in return before turning back to the others. "Either way, is it really any of our business? It was thirty years ago. If they can't talk about it, why should we? It has nothing to do with us. Long dead people made decisions that fucked up future generations. We can't change that, only learn from it, and move on with our own lives. It's none of *our* business."

The others agreed and dispersed.

"Oh," Sheila sighed, "I can't believe the grief I've felt. The *guilt* I've had all these years, even before '77 when I kicked him out."

"Why *did you* kick him out?" Jenny asked as they hovered around the tables in the kitchen.

Sheila blushed furiously. "His behaviour was less than stellar, and I believed it would get us kicked out of our apartment. All those years I hated everyone that let me down, including myself. There were times I loved him, and times I hated him. Sometimes, I'd look at him and think, I have a son, wow, a child. And other times, I'd be all, *oh, God*, I have a son. Life was hard back then. Unwed mothers in the '50s were sneered at and scorned. But I managed, and it was better when he left. I had less bills and less trouble. I could finally breathe. But all of those years I wondered, and reading about it in the paper only made it worse. I was ashamed and guilty and I still feel it now. Even all these years later, and now he's come back to haunt everyone again."

"But deep down you love him. He was your son," Jenny said to her.

A sigh from the pit of her stomach left Sheila. "Yes. A few years after we were married, Giancarlo asked about the papers he'd found. They were from the morgue asking about Luiz's body. I couldn't afford it, so they buried him, but he persuaded me to track him down and move his casket. We had him cremated and he sits on my bedside table in a small urn, except when we travel. Then he comes with me."

"I do that." Jenny smiled sadly. "My daughter, Alena, sits on the mantelpiece at the moment, so she can enjoy the festivities. I do that with every celebration."

"Your daughter?" Giancarlo was shocked. "I didn't know."

"Why would you?" Jenny asked. "She was born early. She would have been two years younger than Pedro, Angie's age. But she wasn't to be. When Pedro married Angie, she became my daughter. She was the same age and would have looked just like her. She was my substitute. And when their baby came along, I knew it was my Alena come back for another go. I'm a big believer in reincarnation, and believed it was my Alena. So, I suggested they use the name. She's more than lived up to it, and has the life I would have wanted for my baby girl."

"So…then…James…" Sheila couldn't finish the sentence.

"Could be Luiz reincarnated?" Jenny finished for her. "Well, considering they look identical right down to the tanned skin, hair colour and eyes, and those eyes give it away. Who knows? Different fathers, but the same mother. Maybe he did come back for another go." She shrugged a shoulder.

"Oh." Shock rained down over Sheila.

"Has he remembered anything?" Jenny casually glanced over at James.

"From the day of the shooting, bits and pieces," Giancarlo said. "But not enough to make me think he's Luiz come back from the dead."

"Well," Jenny raised a brow at him, "you never know."

"No, we don't," Sheila said. "But I do know it's time to go. I'm drained."

Giancarlo agreed and they collected James.

Jenny and Spiros gathered their coats, waiting while they got James and came to the door. "You have the room for as long as you want it. Take the time to look around Mykonos and have a holiday. We're here if you need anything else. Or just to talk," Jenny said, and opened the door for them. "And you have the plane to take you home when you're ready."

"Thank you, Jenny, for everything," Giancarlo said, and bidding everyone a good night, they left to walk back to the hotel.

Tomas and Roger wandered over to sit on the ottoman in front of the fire.

"How are you doing?" Roger kissed him lightly.

After letting go of a deep breath, Tomas smiled. "Better."

"Good. Ready to let Luiz go?"

The smile faded. "Can I ever? He did physical damage to me that I have to be careful of for the rest of my life. Can I ever let him go?"

"No." Roger sighed. "I suppose not. But at least you can try."

"So," Tony nibbled on Cabot's ear as they sat in their place on the couch. "You start off like your father, but you become just like your uncle."

Cabot made giggling noises and looked from Tony to Tomas and Roger, to his father standing in the kitchen talking to Pedro and Alfonso. "You think?"

"Oh, just look at you. Shy and retiring just like your uncle. You both get that silly grin on your face when we kiss you."

"That's known as the Stephanopoulos grin," Cabot told him. "We get it when we're in love." A sharp intake of breath and he realised what had just come out of his mouth. Blushing, he looked away, avoiding Tony's gaze like the plague.

"Are you in love, Cabot?" Tony asked softly. "Because I am."

Cabot's ears heard the words and his head swivelled back for his eyes to stare into Tony's. "You are?" he asked breathlessly.

"Yes," Tony murmured, just centimetres away from his soon-to-be lover.

"Oh," Cabot murmured back, and his heart pounded in his chest and made the blood rush through his ears.

"Well, that was quite a story," Lorenzo said to Alexis as they sat by the tree.

"Yes," she said, gazing up at the lights. "It was." Pulling his arms tighter around her, she snuggled into him. "We already knew a lot, but some of that other stuff, Jesus."

"Yes, it must have been disturbing for you to hear what your grandfather did to your mother." He gently rubbed his chin against her head, his eyes taking in everyone else in the room.

"Disturbing's not the word for it. The word is sick."

"Yes." Lorenzo nuzzled her hair. "I guess it would be." He saw Alena giving him the evil eye from across the room. "Will it make you all closer?"

"To each other, or to our parents?" Alexis asked.

"To one another?"

"Yeah, maybe."

Outside, a young man hovered nearby on the street, peering through the curtains at the family inside. He saw the person he was after and checked the photo in his hand. *Yes, that's him. That's the one I'm after.* Looking at the scene, he saw everyone happy and cheerful. Working up the courage, he moved to the front door and raised his hand. He inhaled and exhaled several times before his knuckles connected with the wood.

Jenny glanced at the clock. Eleven p.m. who could that be? Frowning, she hurried over to answer it and saw a young man of about thirty standing before her. "Yes? May I help you?" She didn't recognise him, but his features twigged at long forgotten memories.

"Oh…yes…sorry, I don't mean to disturb you, but I couldn't wait. My family and I only got in this evening and my wife told me to wait and come tomorrow. But I couldn't." He was rambling stupidly and his eyes moved to Roger who was staring curiously back.

"Yes?" Jenny asked. She stared at the six-foot brunet who looked vaguely familiar, and who clearly had an unusual interest in someone in particular.

The young man couldn't tear his gaze from Roger. "Um…my mother was an old friend of Roger Dencott's. I need to see him about something."

"Oh…" Jenny's suspicions alleviated somewhat. "Please, come in." Opening the door she stood aside. "Roger, it's for you."

"Me?" Roger stood up. "What's for me?" He saw the young man remove his coat. "Yes? Do I know you?" He didn't recognise him at all.

"Oh, no, not me, sorry," the young man said, moving into the room.

"You knew my mother. You worked with her in the '70s, in movies."

Roger's eyes narrowed. He knew which movies they were, and now, so did everyone else in the room. "And what was your mother's name?"

"Jan. Jan Metcalfe," the young man said, eagerly eyeing Roger for any sign of acknowledgement. "Brunette, young, pretty. I know I shouldn't be barging in, tonight of all nights, but I couldn't wait to see you. I left my wife and children at the hotel." He plaintively glanced around the family, making mental notes on everyone.

"Oh?" Tomas stood beside Roger. "Which hotel?"

"*The Windmill.* It's very pretty," the young man said.

"Yes." Tomas smiled. "That's our family hotel. We own it."

"Oh, I didn't know." The young man was a little bolder now as he glanced at all the curious faces.

"I remember your mother, but why did you need to see me?" Roger asked.

"Oh." The young man brought his attention back to Roger. "Well… she…um…" He licked his lips. "She passed away recently, and before she died she told me about her life before me and what she used to do. How she worked in movies with you a lot."

"Well, only a few." Roger crossed his arms. He had a weird feeling in the pit of his stomach.

"Um, my mother kept a scrapbook of everything you did, your activism and gay rights stuff. She was very proud of you and what you had achieved. I brought the scrapbooks with me, but they're back at the hotel in my case. She told me she didn't mind that you were gay, and that I shouldn't either. After all, I had a good upbringing and a stepfather who was wonderful. But she wanted me to know about you and everything you do." He swallowed the hard lump in his throat and was sweating bullets. *The family is huge,* he thought, *so many people here and all staring at us. At me. And who are those extras? I haven't seen them before.*

"I'm sorry." Roger shook his head. "I knew your mother many decades ago. A wonderful woman, so sorry she's passed away, but who are *you?*"

"Oh, I'm sorry." The young man became flustered and dropped

some of the papers he held. "I didn't introduce myself." Picking up the paperwork, he held out his hand to shake Roger's. "My name's Simon. I'm sorry I didn't introduce myself sooner, I'm nervous and it's all tumbling out."

Jenny sucked in air. She finally saw it. "Oh no," she muttered and those around her stared quizzically at her.

"What is it, Mama?" Carlos asked, amused at just one more thing adding to that night's story.

Jenny didn't stop staring at Simon. "The family just got bigger."

"What?" Carlos looked at Tomas, Roger and Simon.

"What do you mean it just got bigger?" Pedro asked, glancing back and forth at everyone.

Roger shook the young man's hand. "Simon, Simon what?"

"Oh." The young man flushed with embarrassment. "I expected you would at least realise. I'm Simon Dencott. Your son."

"What!?" Roger stared in shock.

Tomas's mouth opened into an O and grew as big as his eyes. The rest of the family and guests stared on.

"And the family just keeps on getting bigger," Jenny said.

"You're what?" Roger asked, his brows rising.

"Um," Simon faltered. "Your son."

Roger's head shook in spurts, guttural noises came from his throat. "No."

"She said she didn't tell you, but you must have figured it would happen?" Simon said. "Here." He shuffled through the papers. "My birth certificate, a letter from my mother, and my ID. She told me you were my father, a sperm donor basically. But she adored you. She said you were such a sweet man to work with."

Roger shakily took the papers and looked at them. "They don't really prove anything."

"Yes, I know," Simon said. "Mom said you might want a DNA test and I should comply."

"Oh, *hell yes*, you're having one," Roger said. "I'm not going to believe any of this until you prove you're my blood." Faltering, he was weak, and collapsed back onto the ottoman.

"Roger." Tomas sat beside him and rubbed his back. "Take a slow deep breath."

I don't believe it, Roger thought. *I can't...possibly...but...* He remembered back to the mid-'70s when he'd first met Marcus and done straight sex movies. It had only been a year, if that. *What was it, '75 or something. I did movies with a few girls, wore condoms. I remember Jan, she was a sweet girl, enjoyed the sex. She knew I was gay, so why would she...*

Jenny went over to them. "I'm Jenny Stephanopoulos, Roger's mother-in-law. I suggest you start from the beginning." She noted the panic in his eyes and resemblance to a young Roger. Tall, slim, brown hair and eyes.

"Oh, yes, Mrs Stephanopoulos. I've read about you, you go with Roger and Tomas to marches and such." He rapidly shook her hand.

"Yes, I do, but you need to talk now, about this, from the beginning." She held his hand to stop it.

He noted the grip and saw the determination in her eyes. She was not about to take this at face value and he would have to prove who he was. "Yes, yes, of course. My mother is Jan Metcalfe. In the '70s she worked in porn movies and that's how she met Roger. She said he was wonderful to her, and so sweet and kind that he was the sort of man she wanted to be the father of her child. She was single, he was gay, and wouldn't interfere with her in any way. She met my stepfather when I was ten, and he's been wonderful since. My mother died last month from cancer, and told me all about Roger and Tomas. She kept scrapbooks of everything he did, so I could see what he was like. She was proud of him, and told me not to hate him because he didn't know about me; she never told him and preferred it that way. But, she wanted me to get to know him. She lit up every time she remembered back to the '70s." He saddened and turned to Roger. "She was a wonderful mother, and Richard is a wonderful stepfather. And he agreed with her, that I should look for you. Since you're famous, it wasn't hard to find you." Glancing from him to Tomas and back, he added, "We arrived late and put the kids to bed, but I couldn't sleep. I had to come tonight. I couldn't wait. I'm sorry if I interrupted anything."

"Considering everything else that's gone on tonight," Cabot said, "you're not."

"Oh." Simon's face fell. "I did, I'm sorry. I should have waited and come tomorrow like Deidre said. I'm sorry."

"Stop apologising," Jenny told him. "Who's Deidre?"

"Oh, my wife," he said nervously. "She's asleep at the hotel with our kids, Stella and Liam."

"You have children. How old?" Jenny asked, hoping it might make him relax.

"Stella's five and Liam's two." Simon beamed. "They're adorable if I do say so myself."

"They sound adorable," Jenny said warmly, "and as you can see, there are plenty of children in this family, and more on the way—" She was interrupted by mumblings behind her and turned to see Carlos and Pedro. "What are you two doing?"

"Well, when he said he was Roger's son, we started seeing the resemblance and got one of the old photo albums out." Pedro held the album in his hands.

Carlos was beside him. "The resemblance is definitely there."

Pedro turned the album around to show two pages of Roger and Tomas from 1977. "Tall, brunet, brown eyes, your eyes are brown aren't they, Simon?"

"Um, yes, they are." Simon looked at the photos, interested in anything to do with his father as his mother had only a few photos of him from their time working together.

"Well, look, I..." Roger finally found his strength. "I don't want to do or say anything until we've done a DNA test and then we'll talk more. Dan, how long does it take?"

Dan wandered closer to the group. He and Derek had been with Xanthe, listening in shock as yet another member of the family came forth, and marvelling at Jenny's ease of acceptance. "An hour, if that. I can do one tomorrow at the health clinic."

"Great. We can meet at the hospital at ten, get the tests done, get the results," Roger said. "Until then, I'm in shock and need some air." He handed the papers back and ran outside.

"Roger," Tomas called out and followed.

"I seemed to have upset him. I guess I can't blame him. Mom did say it would be a shock." Simon looked from Jenny to Pedro and Carlos to the photo album. "I do look like him, don't I?"

"You certainly do." Jenny examined his features. "Same physique, same bone structure." She spoke her words carefully, but with warmth. "Look, Simon, this has been a shock for all of us, so why don't you go back to the hotel and get some sleep. Be at the hospital in the morning for the test, and then we'll all know for certain. If you *are* Roger's son, then you can bring the scrapbooks over, along with your family, and we'll sit down and talk. But until then, I think you should go back to the hotel and be with your family. We'll see you tomorrow." She went to the cupboard to retrieve his coat, and he followed her to the door. "This isn't the first time we've had to do this, this year, but we need to be certain before we move forward. I hope you understand."

"Of course, Mrs Stephanopoulos." Simon slid on his coat. "I understand. Mom said to expect it. Where is the hospital?"

"It's the big white building up on the hill. You can't miss it." Jenny smiled and opened the door. "The clinic is on the side. There are signs everywhere. Goodnight, Simon."

He nodded at everyone in the room. "Good night, everyone, Mrs Stephanopoulos."

*****

"Oh, my God, oh, my God, oh, my God." Roger finally came to a stop out the front of their home, leaned against the wall, and took great gulps of air. He bent over and rested his hands on his knees, squeezing his eyes shut against the tears that threatened.

"Roger." Tomas found him. "Roger, oh, God. Can you believe that? Are you okay?" Laying a hand on Roger's back, he rubbed it.

"No. Can you?" Roger gasped. "I'm gay for fuck's sake. The only time I had straight sex was in a couple of Marcus's movies before he went gay. I remember Jan; we had sex in several movies and I always wore a condom. She knew I was gay and not into it, but she did that to me anyway. How could she? How could she not tell me she'd taken my sperm and gotten pregnant? How could she not tell me I had a son? I always thought she was so sweet, and the bitch took my son from me." He rose and started pacing in time to his anger when he spat his words. "How could she take my son from me? He would have been born in what? '76, a year before I met you. Oh, Jesus fucking Christ, I've missed out on my son's life. *My child's* life, for fuck's sake." His pacing grew more frenetic. "She took my child from me and didn't let me raise him, or see him. I missed out on his first tooth, his first words, his first steps, his first day at school, high school, graduation. *Everything.*"

Roger stopped and ran both hands through his hair. "I missed out on his wedding and the birth of his kids, for fuck's sake. What the hell did she think she was doing taking all of that away from me?" The tears came with thirty years' worth of grief at not knowing his son. Folding in on himself, he fell to his knees on the pavement.

"Oh, Roger." A teary Tomas moved to his side. "Oh, Roger, I'm so sorry. I'm so, so sorry." He held his lover as he wept and saw Xanthe come around the corner.

"Come on, let's get him inside," she said, and took Tomas's keys from him. After unlocking the door, she flicked on the light and held the door open while Tomas helped Roger into the lounge room and onto the couch. Xanthe closed the door and followed. "Now, what's all this yammering about?"

"He's angry that he never knew. She never told him, and he missed out on everything," Tomas told her.

Xanthe sighed. "Yes, I guess he would be. But, unfortunately, there's nothing you can do about it. She's dead. She made the decision she made whether it was selfish or not. She got what she wanted, and clearly with you being gay, she never thought about you, just herself. At least in death, she wanted him to get to know you."

"Thirty-one years too fucking late," Roger spat, his eyes full of tears. "Too fucking late."

"For what?" Xanthe asked, sitting in an easy chair. "*He's* alive, *you're* alive, he's come to you to get to know you. What's it too late for?"

"For everything," Roger yelled. "His first step, first tooth, first word. I wonder if he ever said Dada." The forlorn expression on his face said it all. "I've missed his school years, his wedding, the births of his children."

"And all that sucks massive shit balls," Xanthe told him. "And unless he's got videos and pictures, you won't get to see it all. Look; be angry at her, it was *her* decision to exclude you, not his. He's just finding out about you in the last month or so, but at least she encouraged him and he came. *That's* something."

"But it means catching up on thirty-one years of his life that I've missed out on," Roger complained.

"So what!" Xanthe exclaimed. "What would you have done thirty-one years ago if she'd told you she'd gotten pregnant? Supported her or run away? And what about your job? Can't be a porn star and raise a kid, or even be on a permanent holiday like the two of you were."

He thought about it a moment. "I would have been angry at first, but then accepted it. I would have supported her and him financially and wanted to be in his life. I would have been his father. Things would have been different."

"And when you met Tomas?" she persisted.

His brain slowly defogged. "I would have told him the whole story. That I did straight porn for a while, which I told him anyway, and that it had resulted in a kid."

"Would it have mattered to you if Roger had a kid?" she asked Tomas.

"No." He shook his head. "After '81 I couldn't have children, so I got to miss out on it. Simon would have made up for it."

"So, why can't he now?" she asked them both.

"Because he's too old. We can't watch him grow up, or pick him up, and raise him. He already has been," Tomas said.

"So! Considering what this family has already been through, and the story it told tonight, isn't life too damn short to be whining about what *could have been?* People long ago made choices that fucked up everyone else's life. *You can't change that.* All you can do is move forward from this night on and make it all right. You may not be able to raise him, but you get a readymade family. Love him for the man she and her husband raised him to be. He seemed like a good sort." Heaving to her feet, she adjusted her coat and glared at Roger who sat like a limp rag on the couch. "You expect Tomas to stop living in the past with Luiz, well *you don't* get to live there either. What's done is done, get over it and move on from tonight. Tomorrow you'll find out he's your blood. Accept him and the family he has. And get to know *him,* be *his* dad, he'll be *your son,* you get a daughter-in-law and grandkids, for fuck's sake. Live life from now on as a father and stop whining." She left them with shocked expressions and open mouths.

*****

The next morning, Jenny and Tomas accompanied Roger, Dan and Derek to the health clinic where they met Simon and performed the DNA test. It was the longest wait of his life for Roger as he paced back and forth, running his hands through his hair and sighing. He'd had a restless night, barely sleeping at all, thinking about everything, going all the way back to 1975 when he'd met Jan, through to last night. He'd relived thirty-two years of his life in one night.

Finally, Dan announced the news. "Roger, congratulations, you're a father."

Roger felt like fainting. "Are you sure? Absolutely. Don't even kid with me, Dan?"

Dan grinned. "Just as with Alfonso, we performed saliva and blood tests, and ran them three times to make sure. Simon *is* your son."

"Oh, Jesus." All breath left Roger and he doubled over, leaning on his knees.

"Let's get some air and sugar into you," Dan said and helped him sit.

Derek scurried away for oxygen and jelly beans, and upon bringing them back, put the oxygen mask over Roger's face. "And breathe…"

Roger breathed, shoved a handful of jelly beans into his mouth and chewed, and breathed, and swallowed.

Simon stood silently by, noting the pale complexion of Roger's face. His heart fell, his stomach clenched, and he believed he knew the truth. Until he asked, "Does having a son make you this sick?" He wasn't sure what was happening, and *had* promised his mother to track him down and get to know him.

"No." Roger removed the mask and looked up at his son. "It makes me sick that I got to miss out on your life, your milestones, the big events, all because your mother absconded with my sperm and didn't tell me she was having my child. She knew I was gay, but that didn't mean I wouldn't have liked to have children. I could have supported you both and gotten to raise you and see you grow. I've missed out on everything, and that's your mother's fault. And I won't forgive her for that. For depriving me of my son." He took another breath and stood up. "She may have had good intentions for herself, but they were selfish ones that meant I missed out on you and that wasn't fair to me. It wasn't fair to you either." Placing his right hand gently on Simon's cheek he looked at his son. "Look at you. I got to miss out on you. You got to miss out on me, and that's so not fucking fair."

Simon was teary, his heart wrenching in pain. "I know. I bawled her out for keeping me from you and not telling me or letting me know. For keeping us apart, but it upset her and she was already dying. She asked me not to hate her, so how could I? She'd been an awesome mother."

"Who deprived you of your father and me of my son," Roger said, and after a moment's thought, took Simon into his arms and held him tight.

Tomas clasped his hands together, prayer style, and held them to his lips, smiling and crying at the same time.

Jenny stepped away and rang the hotel. "Marcel, Jenny Stephanopoulos. I need you to do something for me."

"Yes, Mrs Stephanopoulos, anything." He knew better than to say no to his boss.

"The Dencotts; Simon and Deidre, I want them upgraded to the family suite on the ground floor as they have two small children. I want them moved and their money refunded, or their credit card, however they paid. They will be staying free of charge for as long as they need to. The tab's on me."

"Ah, yes Mrs Stephanopoulos, family suite, ground floor, refund money. Anything else?"

"Make sure they get all meals and anything else for free." She glanced at Simon still wrapped in Roger's arms, both of them crying. "They're family now."

After everyone agreed to meet back at Jenny's, Simon rushed back to the hotel with Roger to find Deidre quickly packing their things.

"What's going on?" Simon frowned. "Are we being kicked out?

Our money was good."

"What's going on is, we've been upgraded to a family suite. The kids can have their own beds to sleep in, in their own room." She slammed her case shut. "And it's free."

"Free?" Simon's frown grew deeper. "I don't understand."

"Neither do I," Deidre said, gathering the kids' belongings.

"I do," Roger said softly, looking at the kids on the bed. "Mrs S did it."

"Mrs S?" Simon asked, seeing his father melting at the sight of his children.

"Jenny Stephanopoulos," Roger explained. "My mother-in-law. The family owns this hotel. She would have rung up and made it happen." He clasped his son's shoulder. "You're family now."

"Oh, that's so nice of her." Deidre saw the bond already growing. "I'm Deidre by the way, Simon's wife." She quickly kissed Roger's cheek and introduced the kids. "Liam, Stella, this is Grandpa Dencott. Remember we told you we were coming to look for Daddy's real daddy. This is him. Say hello."

"Huh-o, I Iam," the cheeky two-year-old said.

"He can't say his ls yet," Deidre explained.

A hiccupping laugh came from Roger. "Neither could my niece when she was little. Her name's Alena, but she always said A-ena."

"Oh, how cute." Deidre helped Stella stand. "Say hello, Stella."

"Hello, Stella." The bubbly five-year-old grinned.

"Ah, we have a comedian in the family," Roger said. "Well, hello Stella, Liam." He nodded at both. "My name is Roger, but I guess… you'll be calling…me Grandpa?" he questioned, looking from Deidre to Simon.

"Ah, yeah, I guess they will." Simon shrugged a shoulder. "You are their grandpa after all. My father."

"And what will *you* call me?" Roger asked him.

"Um…" Simon muttered. "Not sure. This is all new. I'm not sure what I *should* call you. Yes, you're my biological dad, but you weren't in my life, so," glancing around he thought about it, "I'll stick with Roger, until things settle in and we get comfortable."

Roger nodded. "Okay. Let me help you move." He carried their cases into the new room while they wrangled the kids.

The manager and a maid came to help, and they managed to find all of their things, especially the toys the kids had scattered all over the room. Once they were settled, the maid cleaned up the old room.

"All of your meals are free whenever you choose to eat here, and you have free access to whatever you need," Marcel said. "All courtesy of the owner."

"Yes, that's Mrs S." Roger grinned. "You're part of the family now."

"That's so nice of her," Deidre said. "We'll have to take her a thank you present."

"She's not expecting anything," Roger told them. "Just all of you for lunch. And on Sundays, she makes the most amazing roast chicken meal. And you will obviously be invited to that." He was starting to feel comfortable around his son and his family. "You'll be invited to a lot now."

"We don't want to overstay our welcome," Deidre said, noticing the body language her husband and father-in-law were exhibiting. It was of a relaxed nature and style compared to when they'd first walked in the room.

"You won't be. Mrs S will make sure you're all right before letting you go home, and speaking of that, we should head off. You'll meet the rest of the family in batches, so you're not too overwhelmed. So, when you're ready, we'll go."

Ten minutes later, they were back to Jenny's. "We're here," Roger called when he opened the door and saw Tomas in the kitchen.

"Hey, I'm in here, Mama's somewhere else." Tomas quickly washed and dried his hands, slid his black framed glasses back in place, and went to introduce himself as his parents came out of the laundry room. "Hello, I'm Tomas, Roger's husband." He shook hands with Deidre and said hello to the kids. "They're adorable."

Deidre blushed. "Oh, we think so."

"And I'm Tomas's mother, Roger's mother-in-law, Jenny Stephanopoulos, and this is my husband Spiros Stephanopoulos." She introduced them and shook hands. "Nice to meet you, welcome."

"Hello, nice to meet you," Deidre said. "You're the lady that gave us the upgrade in the hotel. That's was so sweet of you."

"Well, you are family now," Jenny said, "and welcome to ours. We have a large one, all of whom Simon saw last night. So, you'll probably meet most of them today."

"Neither of us comes from big families, so it could be challenging." Deidre's laugh was as cute as she was. "Although, when we found out about Roger and Tomas and the whole family, it did seem overwhelming. We never imagined we'd be related to people so famous. It's a bit nerve-racking." She slid a strand of dark brown hair behind her ear. At five-seven, she felt a bit short next to everyone. And she had some weight on her, so she wasn't as skinny as the girls in the family, and because of her weight, snub nose and round face, she was considered cute.

"We've worked hard to get where we are today," Jenny said. "It's been thirty years of hard work, and we've trained the kids to work hard too. Speaking of kids, here come two now." She saw Alena and Diana emerge from the hallway. "Simon, Deidre, this is Diana and Alena, Tomas and Roger's nieces."

"Hello." They both shook hands. "I guess this makes us…" Diana thought about it, "Step-cousins."

"Um, yeah, I guess," Simon said as he shook their hands.

"You're the two with the clothes," Deidre said. "I think I've seen your pictures in magazines, they're awesome."

"Thank you." Alena smiled. "That's *Haus of Stefan*, our fashion label."

"Oh, and your eyes, they're so blue in person." Deidre knew she was fangirling.

"We got them from our fathers who got them from Grandma." Diana smiled affectionately at Jenny. "And poor Uncle Tomas got Grandpa's side of the family," she joked.

"Nothing wrong with that." Spiros kissed her cheek.

"But you're both so different," Deidre went on. "Your colouring…I love your hair, Diana, it's so long and beautiful."

Diana blushed delicately. "Why, thank you, Deidre. It's a devil to maintain, though, and with the baby coming, I may have to shorten it."

"Oh, you're pregnant, how wonderful," Deidre gushed. "Your first?"

"Yes. Just over five months now." She patted her belly. "My partner Charles has been ill; he's in one of the bedrooms, but he may come out later."

"Oh, no, we won't catch anything will we?" Simon asked. "The kids seem to pick up every bug known to man." He glanced down at his children who were behaving themselves nicely, with not a peep out of them.

Everyone laughed. "That's kids for you, so did my boys," Jenny told them.

"No," Diana replied. "He's a photographer and went on a shoot in the Middle East. He was captured for months and hospitalised for the rest of the time. But he's on the mend now."

"Oh, how horrible!" Deidre exclaimed. "That must have been awful for you."

"Yes," Diana murmured. "I had no idea where he was, but Grandma put her team onto it and they tracked him down and brought him home."

The door opened. "Hey, Mama, you got some food?" Carlos stepped in. "Sorry, didn't know you had company." Viv and the boys piled in behind him.

"Sure you didn't." Roger smirked.

"Here's the rest of the golden side of the family," Alena muttered to Deidre. "Except for Cabot who's taken to dying his hair black this year."

"Yes, yes, just a little experiment I'm going through," Cabot said as they gathered around, and he pointed to his brother on his right. "I normally look like Antonio."

"*Finally*, he gets my name right." Antonio rolled his eyes.

"My sons, Antonio and Cabot," Carlos said to Simon and Deidre. "And Tony Luca, Cabot's partner, Viv my wife, and I'm Carlos, Tomas's older brother." He shook their hands and was introduced to Stella and Liam. "You've met my daughter, Diana," he nodded in her direction and asked, "How's Charles?"

"Tired after last night, but doing well," she replied.

"I just stopped by for food." Carlos looked at Tomas. "I gotta get to the studio to finish some work."

"And I have a book to finish, but I haven't done the food shopping," Viv added guiltily.

"We're just being nosy." Cabot shrugged. "Are we related and how?"

"Kinda step-cousins, I think we figured out," Simon said, looking at Diana, intrigued by all the people. Antonio and Cabot were clearly twins, but Tony was a good-looking boy who fitted right in.

"Legal or not?" Cabot went on. "Since Uncle Tomas and Roger aren't legally married."

"We've been together for thirty years, that doesn't matter anymore," Tomas told them. "Simon is Roger's son, that makes me the stepfather, so you're step-cousins."

"Okaayy." Cabot's brain ticked over. "After what Grandma told us about the family tree, it's just hard to keep it straight. So, technically, he's not *blood*-related to us, but just by a marriage that's not legal."

"Enough, Cabot." Carlos stood with his hands on his hips. "Cabot gets a bit carried away sometimes, but he *had* been coming good these last few months," he explained to Simon and Deidre and watched Cabot shrug again. "Is lunch ready? I need sustenance."

"I was just starting to put it on." Tomas quickly went back to the kitchen to put the turkey burgers on.

Carlos and Viv followed, leaving the kids to chat.

"How old are you, Simon?" Antonio asked point blank.

"Thirty-one," Simon replied, knowing he was more than likely going to be grilled by the entire family.

"Ah." Antonio eyeballed him. "Makes you the oldest of all of us. At least you've got the height."

Pedro, Angie and the kids came through the door. "Hey, visitors."

Roger introduced them to Simon, Deidre and their kids.

"Wow, it's a tall family." Simon shook everyone's hand.

"We get it from Papa," Pedro replied. "We'll leave you kids to it. We just stopped by for lunch." They headed for the kitchen. "Lunch ready?"

"About ten minutes." Tomas watched over the pans cooking the burgers. "Salads are leftovers from last night; we just need the buns."

"I'll get them ready, put the oven on." Jenny pulled burger buns from the cupboard and started cutting and buttering.

"So, what do you guys do?" Diana asked Simon and Deidre.

"Ugh." They glanced at each other. "Nothing at the moment, unfortunately. Deidre lost her job after New Year because the company downsized, and when Mom got sick I was fired for taking so much time off work."

"Oh, that's not good." Alena frowned. "Didn't they care that you were needed at home?"

"Unfortunately, no." Simon shook his head. "My stepfather told us to sell our house and move in with him, so we could help look after Mom, and she could get more time with us and the kids before she died. And that arrangement worked out great. But we can't stay there forever, and we didn't get much back from the sale of the house after the mortgage was paid off, so we'll have to get jobs once we get back home."

Antonio eyed them suspiciously, wondering if they were after money, or whatever they could get. Roger wasn't a multimillionaire like some of them, but he and Tomas had the gym and made good money. *I wonder if he's going to try and take Roger for all he's got?* He turned to head for the kitchen and saw Dom give him the eye. He arched a brow in return and knew Dom was thinking the same thing. Walking into the kitchen he asked if lunch was ready.

"About five minutes," Tomas told him.

"Diana; is Charles coming out?" Jenny called.

Diana turned and wandered into the kitchen. "If he wants, otherwise I'll stay with him. Not much point if he can't eat food yet."

"How much longer does he have to stay on the drip?" Carlos asked.

"I think Dan said this weekend," Diana replied. "They'll run some tests to check some things, and if they're good, they can take him off it. And then they'll start him on a special diet of high protein food and reduce his intake once he gets better."

"Ugh, I remember that drip," Tomas groaned. "It may have helped save my life, but it was horrible not being able to eat Mama's food. I salivated and dreamed about it all the time." He checked that the burgers had heated through to the centre.

"And now look." Jenny smiled. "You're the one doing all the cooking."

"Just dinner and sometimes lunch." He smiled back at his beloved mother. "Had to learn to do it myself once Roger and I moved out. He said he didn't want to be the only one doing all the cooking."

"And there's nothing wrong with that," Jenny said. "Just a pity my other two sons didn't think the same way…" She waited for their replies and got two groans instead. "You know what you should do, Tomas; document all of these recipes of yours and turn them into cookbooks. They'd be massive best sellers, especially among the gay community. Put your training and certified diet and nutritional education to use and do what Viv did. Food and exercise videos. They'd be huge, especially for the over-50s gay man." She took a breath and saw his half-shocked half-surprised expression. "What?"

"I don't think so, Mama," he said, turning off the pans and setting the burgers onto paper towel-covered plates.

"I'll start setting it up myself," she went on. "We have our own publishing house; it will be huge. Just you wait and see. Oh, my, God, you can even have your own cooking show. Film it here, or even at *S'Reel.*" She flicked a hand at Carlos who looked up in surprise.

"Mama; stop." Tomas blushed. "I prefer to be out of the spotlight."

"Then just stick to books," she urged. "At least think about it."

After lunch, everyone disappeared to do their thing, and Roger and Tomas sat with Simon and Deidre on the balcony talking. Jenny and Spiros watched over Liam and Stella in the lounge room with Diana and Charles, who had come out once everyone was gone.

"Do you have any other family?" Roger asked Simon. "Your mum's relatives? Your stepdad's?"

"Mom had two sisters. One's dead, one's unmarried and childless, so no more relatives on that side," Simon said. "Richard has siblings and I have step-cousins there, but I…" He frowned and looked down at his drink. "I don't think I was ever truly accepted by them."

"Because you weren't blood?" Tomas asked gently.

"Yeah." Simon gazed over the seascape. "I was ten when Mom married him. His family were accepting, I got along with the cousins, but this year, I don't know, it just seems that stupid jealousy and resentments came along. I have no idea why, but it's pulled us apart."

He screwed his face up and rubbed his eyes. "This year has been so stressful. Deidre lost her job, then Mom got sick, then I lost my job because I was helping to care for her. We had to sell our house and move in with Richard. Now, Mom's dead." Shaking his head, he finished the rest of his drink. "I think Richard's going to ask us to move out and that's going to make things worse."

"Why would he do that?" Roger asked, wondering where the conversation was going.

"I don't know, except Mom's medical bills got high and we both pitched in. But he might have to sell his house to get some money back."

Roger sighed and rubbed his leg. "That's not good. But we know about being sick, and the toll it can take on a family." He launched into his and Tomas's brush with death twenty-six years earlier. "It was horrible. I watched Tomas die right in front of me." He linked hands with his smiling husband. "He was dead for five minutes before the doctors brought him back. Turns out, we had a damn tick bite no one could figure out. Thank God for Dan and Mrs S; they fought like hell to make us better. And it took years. Charles is going through a similar thing, and now you tell me your mother did. It sucks to be dying."

"That's awful," Deidre said. "We read your story, but hearing it firsthand is different. It must have been so devastating."

"Saying goodbye was the worst. Although we tried not to. Just clung to every day that we had," Roger said. He remembered what Xanthe had said the night before. "Life *really is* too damn short."

Miami 1975

Twenty-three-year-old brunette beauty, Jan Metcalfe, groaned. Her lover, Roger Dencott, was longer than any man she'd had before, and it was driving her crazy. Her head tilted back, her eyes closed, and her breath came in gasps as she did.

"And cut!" Marcus Seralift, owner of *Seralift Productions* yelled. "Good job, Jan, Roger, let's get ready for the next scene, people."

Roger looked down at the woman beneath him. "You okay, Ms Metcalfe? I didn't hurt you, did I? I'm not used to sex with women."

Jan's laugh was delightful. "Honey, are you tellin' me you've *never* had sex with a woman?" She stared at the hunky piece of man meat that was still inside of her.

"Well," he said nervously as he moved, "when I was younger, but it was awkward and I began to consider that fact I was gay not long after."

"So, what made you get into porn movies with women then?" He was such a sweetie, calling her Ms Metcalfe, making sure she was okay, asking if he'd hurt her.

"I'm not really sure. I left Australia last year and came here looking to get into movies." Casting a look around the studio, his eyes fell upon Marcus Seralift, the porn king of Miami. "I wanted a place that was like back home, lots of sun and beaches, so it was Hollywood or here. I was actually en route to Hollywood when the plane detoured somehow and I got stuck on another plane. I had no idea where I needed to go and ended up here. I liked it, so I stayed. Marcus found me, asked if I wanted to audition for adult movies, and the money was good. So, here I am."

"Lying inside of me." Jan laughed. "But you're gay. How does a gay boy have sex with women in porn movies?"

"I have no idea." Roger grinned and leaned his head on his hand. His elbow was beside Jan's head. "The money was good, and I hadn't told anyone I was gay. I didn't even tell you. How did you figure it out?"

"It was obvious. Either you'd never had sex with a woman, so were a virgin, or you were gay," she told him. "Either way, you're very good, eager to please, eager to let the woman lead."

"Yeah, well, I've never done this before. Should I um…" He glanced around. "Still be inside…you?"

"You don't have to be; they're setting up for the next scene where we'll be doing it doggy style, so you'll have to prepare for that. I take it you've never done it that way?"

"No, no I haven't. Not yet." He nervously left her and settled by her side after dropping the condom in the bucket hidden behind the bed.

"It's all rather simple. I get on the bed on my hands and knees, you kneel between my legs and enter. Hands on my hips or boobs, whatever Marcus wants."

"I've only ever done it face to face." Roger was uncomfortable with straight sex, but he needed the money, and it was *good* money.

"How many movies have you made?" Jan shifted and tried to work a kink out of her leg by massaging it.

"Three."

"You're kidding." She laughed. "Don't tell me they've all been with me?"

He blushed. "Yeah. I only just started a few weeks ago."

"And does Marcus know you're gay?"

"I don't know. I haven't told him." Roger shrugged a shoulder. "He didn't ask. Just asked if I'd consider adult movies and it all happened."

"That quick huh?" Jan grinned. "I had to audition. Did you?"

"Um, just drop my pants and show him what I had," Roger murmured.

"Did you have to get an erection to show him how big you are?"

"Yeah, I did. That was bloody embarrassing, wanking off in front of him to show him how big I could get." Blushing at the memory, he moved on. "What did you have to do?"

"Have sex," she replied.

"Oh, you're kidding?" Roger groaned. "With how many?"

"Three men. It was a group thing. Pretty damn gross," she said. "But I dealt with it and here I am."

"And here *I* am," Roger said. "In bed with a woman."

"Okay, set up for doggy style," Marcus called.

"That's us." Jan jumped to her hands and knees.

"Roger, behind her," Marcus yelled. "Make it quick."

Roger reluctantly kneeled between her legs. "I need a condom," he called, embarrassed by it all. Someone came over and gave him one, and he wanked off to roll it on. "Ready."

"Okay, actors in places, cameras, lights," Marcus bellowed from his director's chair. "And…action."

Roger grabbed Jan by the hips and entered. Thrusting mechanically, he hated it. Hated doing it, but it was a job, and acting gigs in Miami were hard to come by unless you got a bit part in some action movie that filmed there. He'd had a couple of those, but hadn't got a big role, or even a mediocre one. Always bit parts. The guy in the background, the guy in the cab, the guy eating an ice cream. But here, he had the lead male roles, as awkward as they were. He got to be the good-looking lead who got the girl, and he got her good. They'd made three movies together now, but he still wasn't comfortable. He was gay; he didn't have sex with women. Period. And he'd been gay for a good eight years. At twenty-seven, he'd known for some time that he preferred men, but money was what he needed right now, and until his big break came along, he had to do what he had to do.

The day wore on, and they filmed scene after scene after scene, and by the end of it, both were sore and over it.

"Ugh." Roger groaned as he dressed in the unisex change rooms.

"Sore dick?" Jan asked, slipping her bohemian style dress over her head.

"Yeah." He carefully adjusted himself in his pants.

"Imagine how I feel," Jan said dryly, shoving her robe into her locker, and swinging her bag over her shoulder. "You hungry?"

"Starving," Roger said, shutting his locker door.

"Burgers?"

"Love some."

"Robbo's?"

"On Weston?"

"Yep."

"Sure, why not." Roger escorted Jan out to his car. "I can drop you home after."

"That'd be great." Jan gingerly sat in the car and swung her legs in. "I'm gonna need painkillers."

"I know what ya mean." He drove to Robbo's and stopped in the car park. It was a fifties-style burger joint that lingered from the past, but it still did the best burgers and fries in Miami. They went in, grabbed a booth, and ordered.

"So, how'd *you* get into the business?" Roger asked once the waitress had left.

"Because I like sex." Jan grinned. "But some days, not so much."

Roger frowned. "You became a porn star because you like sex?"

"Yep." Jan waited for the waitress to leave their drinks, and sipping her strawberry shake, she went on. "My sisters and I were raised fairly loosely. We grew up on a farm wild and free. Our parents were free-loving hippies who enjoyed orgies with their friends. Once we turned eighteen, we were allowed to join in. We were used to being naked as we ran around without our clothes, and so saw lots of others naked when they were at the house, so sex seemed kind of natural. I enjoyed it, but I needed a job, so what better job to have than having sex and getting paid for it?"

"Normally that would make us prostitutes," Roger managed before the burgers arrived and waited for the waitress to leave before continuing. "We get paid to have sex."

"True," Jan agreed. "And I guess in some cases it seems that way. But this is a production company that makes movies. We get paid to act in those movies. Whether it's sex we're acting or not."

"Yeah, I guess." Picking up his burger, he dug in. It was the extra-large Robbo Spectacular; a thick burger patty, egg, bacon, pineapple, lettuce, tomato and cheese. He'd asked them to hold the onion and gherkin, and it was as huge as a dinner plate.

They ate in silence for a few minutes and Jan watched Roger intently. He was sweet and kind and caring, and the perfect kind of man to be a father. Or the father of a child. She'd been considering her prospects for the last five years. Since becoming sexually active at eighteen she'd thought about her life, where it was going and where it would end. She knew she wanted a family; not necessarily a husband, as her parents weren't married, but a relationship with a man. Where, when, or how she was going to have one she didn't know. But being a pro in porn movies wasn't going to get her a man unless he was in the business. She definitely wanted a child, so if she couldn't find a man, a partner in life, a husband, then she had to find a way of getting a child, or pregnant with one.

She'd been considering the men that *were* in her life, and they were all associated with porn. So, what other choice did she have? Her parents had three girls, but didn't allow that to stop them living a free life. Her two sisters were working in jobs in the local area of Pennsylvania near where their parents still lived, but she had travelled to Miami for a better life. She could have gone to Hollywood, but she chose Miami instead. Roger was going to Hollywood, but he ended up in Miami. Was it a coincidence? He hooked up with Marcus not long after arriving, and now here they were, together, in the movies, having sex. But he wore condoms. Easy done, she could pierce a few with a needle and let it happen. He never performed without one, and she knew he didn't have diseases as Marcus made them get tested every month. He was clean, young, gay, wouldn't want a wife and child, and his genetics were pretty spectacular. Six foot plus, strong, broad, blessed with good looks, brown hair and eyes.

She studied him. *Our DNA would work perfectly together. We have similar looks, and it could really work. If our child got his height and looks, he'd be perfect.* It *would be perfect.* "So, I know you're gay and all, but do you still want to be a dad?" She sipped her shake casually. "This job doesn't really make it easy to have a family."

"No, it doesn't." Roger wiped his mouth. His burger was inhaled, his shake drunk. "I think so. Wanting children, I mean. But I'm twenty-seven. I've been out for about eight years, have no partner, can't adopt, can't use a surrogate, and so, unfortunately, I think it's out of the picture. I don't think I'll be a dad anytime soon. I'll give it some more thought once I turn thirty and see where my life is, who I'm with, what our life's like. How much money I have, where I am, what I'm doing, that sort of stuff. What about you?"

"Oh, I definitely want kids," she said. "But, you're right. It's a matter of seeing where I am now, and how do I get to where I want to be."

"And where do you want to be?" Roger noticed how beautiful she was.

"I want to be married with kids in a nice home, with a nice yard." She smiled at the thought.

"Not like your parents?" Roger grinned.

"Oh, God no. Twenty-one years of that was enough. That's when I left. I've been doing this for two years."

"Wow, a pro, literally." Roger's brow arched to join his grin.

"Yeah, yeah, I've been around awhile." Her grin matched his. "But, I don't know how much longer I'll do this. I've been saving hard and not spending when I don't need to. I don't commit crimes like tax fraud, I don't run red lights or stop signs. I've been a good little girl and abiding citizen."

Roger laughed. "Were you a girl scout too?"

"God, no," She rolled her eyes. "But, my parents raised me to do right, and I want a family, so I need to get a plan in motion for that. Maybe another year, if that, and then I'll move on."

"You sound as if you've got your head on straight, regardless of being in this workforce. I have no idea how long I'll last, but I can't go on in straight sex movies. I'm just not comfortable."

"At least finish out the year," Jan quickly said. "It's only a few months away and will give you a bit more in savings."

"Yeah, I guess. The pay is good, but if I'm gonna do it, porn I mean, then I'd rather do gay porn. Does Marcus even make gay porn?"

"Some," she said, setting her plan in motion. "But if you haven't told him yet, leave it a while and poke around. See whether they get the same pay, conditions, etc. But stay at least until New Years and then I'll make my decisions too." She crossed her fingers under the table. The plan was set.

Pennsylvania 2007

"And so I kept a brooch in my robe pocket and used it to poke holes in the condom packets to put holes in them," Jan told Simon and Deidre as they sat on her bed. "I wanted a child so much I didn't know how else to get one unless I had random sex with some guy I didn't know." She rasped through the ventilator mask. "But at least I knew Roger was clean, sexually speaking. No STDs to pass on. And he's a good-looking boy, tall and strong. I knew our genetics would work well together. I took a pregnancy test every week, and once I was pregnant, I planned it all out. I'd persuaded Roger to stay until the New Years and he did, which was just as well since it took a month or so to get pregnant. Come 1976, Marcus had decided to move into gay porn anyway. Straight porn sales were faltering in Miami, but gay was booming. So, he stopped that part of productions and I was out of a job. I moved back here and told my sisters of my plans, and we all agreed to get a house together. We all raised you until Richard came into my life. He loved you so much." Smiling sadly at her son, she weakly grasped his hand.

"Oh, Mom," he cried. "Why didn't you tell me? Why didn't you let me know about my father? I've gone without him for thirty-one years; how could you take that away from me?" He gazed imploringly at his weak and sick mother. Cancer had eaten her alive and she had mere days to live. Her hair was thin and grey, her eyes were sunken and cheeks hollow. He and Deidre had moved into Richard's house to help look after her.

"Don't be angry at me…please…" her voice came softly. "Please don't be angry." Blinking back tears, she knew it had been a mistake to take his father from him. "I made the choice to have a child, and Roger was perfect. I didn't want a male involved unless he was my partner, but Roger wasn't. He was just a sperm donor. I'm sorry if you feel you've missed out on a life with him, but he's still gay. He didn't change."

"So what!" Simon exploded out of his spot on the hospital bed they had set up in the lounge room so she could see the flowers in the front garden. "You kept my biological father from me. You told me you didn't know where he was. You lied to me, Mom." He felt disgust, anger, humiliation and misery. All of his life had been a lie.

"I'm sorry," she said. "I'm so sorry, Simon. Please don't be angry at me." At fifty-five, she hated the fact that the cancer had attacked her whole body; that it was killing her, and she would have no more time with her son, her daughter-in-law, or her two precious grandbabies. Cancer was about to rob her of the next thirty years of their lives, and so she had made some decisions. "I've talked it over with Richard. You're going to find your real father. He believes it's a good idea. He could never legally adopt you, so he's not your legal father. But he wants you to have contact with Roger. Now that I'm dying, and my parents and sister have gone, he's your blood. You should get to know him once I'm gone."

"Do you even know where he is, or what he's doing now?" Simon asked from the window where he stood looking out at Richard watering the lawn.

Richard saw him, smiled and waved.

Simon's hand half-heartedly waved back, then fell as he turned from the window. "Well? Do you?"

"Yes," Jan said and looked to Deidre. "Can you get me the scrapbooks out of the box in the cupboard there?" She weakly pointed to the buffet against the wall.

Deidre pulled out three boxes, found three large A3 sized albums, and placed them on the bed next to her mother-in-law.

Jan opened the first one. "Here, here's Roger and me on set in '75.

Wasn't he good looking?" Gazing wistfully at the pictures, she flipped through page after page, pointing out that he stayed in porn and made it big for another two years, and got married to Tomas Stephanopoulos. She'd kept news reports on the murders and kidnappings. She had the front-page obituary, and the front-page clippings from the marches and interviews, articles on the family's successes and businesses, the children and their fame, all the way through to articles about Alena's tour and albums. "I bought everything for you; all of their albums, cut all of the newspaper and magazine articles I could find. I have videos and DVDS of their marches and movies."

"Their porn movies?" Simon questioned. "Gross."

"No, no, their documentary films they made about gay rights and AIDS. Roger's mother-in-law is in it with them. They were made by his brother-in-law, Carlos, who was also in porn in '77. As well as their brother Pedro. He was a huge DJ at *Studio 69* in New York. I went to see him play. It was the night the whole family was there. I got to see how happy Roger was with Tomas and the life they'd made for themselves. I took pictures." Flipping back to the late '70s, she saw two pages of photos and sadness washed over her. "Those times were so good. Your aunts looked after you while I bussed it in and stayed overnight. I nearly went and spoke to him, but couldn't make myself move, so I just took photos. I couldn't ruin his life and what he had created."

"*You* ruined *our* lives when you lied to both of us." Simon painfully stared at the photo. He looked like him.

"Don't hate me, Simon, please. I don't have long, and I couldn't bear it if you hated me at my dying breath." Reaching up, she weakly grasped his arm. "I taped the movies, there in the box, along with CDS and booklets, pamphlets, catalogues, the kids have a fashion line, and your father's mother and sister-in-law write books. They're in there too. I wanted to get as much together as possible, so you could see what a big family you have waiting for you. Plus, there's the videos and photo album I have of you. All of your stuff that I have is in these boxes. Take them, they're your family; give them to Roger."

"But *they're* not my blood, *you* are. Aunt Jane is." Simon frowned and watched as Deidre set a box on the end of the bed and pulled out catalogues and books.

"*They* are your family now, Simon. I've had thirty-one amazing years with you. I got to be pregnant with you and give birth to you. Now, you get to spend thirty-one years with your father and his family."

"But *they're not my family*," he growled, and stalked around the room.

Deidre flicked through Jenny Stephanopoulos's book before picking up one of Vivian's. Even at seventy she still had style going on.

"Simon, please, don't hate me. What's done is done. I cannot go back and change it. I'm dying."

"Why didn't you think of me thirty-one years ago?" he asked, sadness making his whole body quake. "Why didn't you think of Roger, *my father?* Why didn't it occur to you that you were being utterly selfish and self-centred? Why didn't you think about the future and what *we* would have wanted? A father and son."

"You're right, of course, you are. I was selfish and self-centred and didn't think about anyone but myself and what *I* wanted. And I know him. He'll want a DNA test to prove you are his son."

"*I* want one too, to prove *he's my father*," Simon objected.

"And so have one," Jan went on weakly. "There's a letter to Roger in the box. I want you to promise me when I'm dead and gone, that you will pack up what you've got, and the kids, and go to see him. Spend time with him. I have a feeling the family will take you into their fold as one of their own. You won't be alone anymore, Simon. You'll have your father."

"And what am I supposed to do with a gay father at thirty-one?" he asked bitterly.

"Don't blame him, or hate him, for being gay for a start. That won't stop him from loving you all. It's a big family, and *they* will love you all, and will be able to give you what you need."

"And what's that?" he asked.

"A family," Jan replied. "Promise me, Simon. Once I'm gone, promise me you'll pack up the kids, and everything you have, and go and see him. He'll be able to help you because I can't. You've both lost your jobs, you're here caring for me, and it's not fair watching me die. You'll lose me, Simon, but you will gain a father and stepfather and a family. They'll love you and take care of you. They'll provide you with what you need. Family and help. I know all of this has taken its toll on you. Selling your house, losing your jobs, that's not fair. Neither is me dying at fifty-five, but you're not alone after I go. Far from alone. Promise me, Simon. Promise me you'll go and find him. They all have websites; you can find them online. They all live in Mykonos, Greece. I went there once, many a year ago, and it was beautiful." Her eyes glazed over as she reminisced.

Deidre stared wide-eyed and imploringly at her husband. "You *have* to do this, Simon. *We* have to do this, or you'll regret it."

"And why should we?" he asked. "*Our* life, *our* family, is here."

"Mine's in Florida, yours is in Mykonos. Your mother's dying wish is for us to go. You have to promise her, and we have to go," Deidre urged.

Sighing, he gently raised his mother's hand to his lips and kissed it. "Mom."

"Simon," she barely whispered, knowing her end was near.

"We'll go. We'll go to Mykonos to find my father and his family."

A small weak smile lit up her face. "Thank you, my baby. I love you all…"

She was gone.

Mykonos 2007

After spending the weekend getting to know one another, and having Jenny's famous Sunday roast chicken, it was all back to normal come Monday when Jenny had papers on Simon and Deidre in front of her. Their credit rating sucked, they had no money in the bank, and Richard had never adopted Simon, which meant nothing belonged to him. Both had lost their jobs, but both were highly qualified. Deidre was a dental technician, and Simon was an engineer. She was sure they'd be able to get jobs when they went back home, but she also knew Roger would be heartbroken if they did. He'd just found Simon and wanted to get to know him.

Sighing, she closed the file and wondered how much of Simon's story was true. Not about his mother dying; that was definitely true. But about what she'd told Simon. About what Simon had told Roger. His mother was dead, his stepfather wasn't his stepfather anymore, and they already knew about the family, having checked up on them after finding out Roger was his father. And why did Simon's mother wait until now? Because Roger was famous, and the family had money? She pondered this as she thought about helping them beyond their stay at the hotel. But did *she* have to help them? As Simon was Roger's son, *he* might want to, and that would be up to him and Tomas to consider. She knew Mykonos needed dental technicians and engineers, as did Athens. But whether Simon and Deidre would want to move here to be with Simon's family was a different matter. So, until it was sorted out, they'd stay at the hotel free of charge. *I just hope they don't start expecting Roger to make up for thirty-one years' of child support. If money's all they're after, that won't be good for Roger.*

*****

"This is the gym Tomas and I have." Roger led them into the gym atop the hill. "Tomas was a personal trainer when we met, and after we got better, I trained up and got my certifications. We eventually set up *In Shape*. What do you think?" He watched them look around.

"It's awesome," Simon replied. "*Everything* is awesome. You've all worked really hard to make something of yourselves."

"We have," Tomas told them. "Mama raised us to work hard and earn what we wanted, like Papa did. And *we* did. Carlos set up *S'Reel* and Pedro *Sync,* then together they set up *Stefan Productions.* We have family businesses that are sustainable incomes, and then our own companies all under the one umbrella."

"I think it's fantastic," Deidre said. "Your parents raised you to go after what you wanted and work hard. And now you're teaching your kids to do the same thing. I wish more people had that work ethic, but unfortunately, with the way things are headed in America, it seems a lot of people are losing their jobs. So, keeping a good work ethic is hard."

"It must have been awful losing your jobs," Roger said, gazing at the two of them. "Especially because you were looking after your mother."

"Yeah." Simon frowned. "You'd expect them to care, and my boss said he did, but he also needed an employee who was actually going to *be* at work. I understood where he was coming from, but it just ended up being an unworkable situation." Strolling over to the floor-to-ceiling wall-to-wall glass window, he looked across the island. "What an incredible view to work out to."

"It is." Tomas joined him. "We're in what we call the compound. *Sync* and *S'Reel* are nearby, as well as a home for the guests we have. Musicians, actors, all sorts come through to work with Carlos or

Pedro. They stay in the home, workout here, and go to work there. High flying celebrities love the views and privacy it affords them."

"It's quite a family you've got," Simon said, feeling wistful and melancholic. "And quite a family business. You all work together, but separately. Your names are side by side; your businesses are in a compound for goodness sake. Your family must own half the island."

Tomas smiled indulgently. "Far from it. Mama set up investments for the family and we've made them grow. She wanted us close by, so we have our businesses here, and our offices here, but *Stefan Productions* is a huge film lot in Athens, and it also houses head offices for *Haus of Stefan*, and *Villiers Inc.* The girls work from there when they can because that's its home base. We're all close to the European markets, and we spend a couple of months in New York every year working on the U.S. side of things. We'll also be travelling to Miami a lot. A dear old friend left us her plantation home and wanted us to turn it into a HIV/AIDS care home for the dying. We did that back in August and will be travelling there after New Year's. That's part of the Stephanopoulos business empire as well."

"I'm jealous," Deidre said. "My parents were raised the same way, to work hard and earn your way through life, and I was too. But now with the markets fluctuating and businesses downsizing, it's hard to keep a job for any length of time anymore."

"Have you thought of starting up your own business?" Roger asked Simon. "As an engineer, you could lend yourself to different businesses, and set your own fees for your talent."

Simon chuckled. "I had been thinking about it. But with everything I've dealt with this year, it just hasn't been top of my priority list. But I guess I could, and I have to start thinking about it for the new year."

"We could help you with a business plan if you wanted to set up your own business," Roger said. "Mrs S makes all of us set up a plan before she funds the start-ups, but after three years we have to take it over and make it work ourselves. The kids get to use their trust funds to set up businesses, but they have to submit a business plan. So, we all have plenty of experience at it."

"The kids have trust funds?" Deidre asked, trying not to sound envious. "But they're all so famous and have worked from teenagers."

"They did," Tomas told her. "Mama set up the trust funds at birth, but all of the kids ended up in their own businesses and making money, so they didn't need it. Except for the girls. They set up *Haus of Stefan* on it. Mama set it up so at twenty-one they draw a wage, and at twenty-five they can use it for a business. At thirty, they get full control, and just recently, they put all of their trust fund wages into Alexis and Cabot's support centre because none of them needed to draw a wage. They all work and earn good money. But that's not to say they had it easy. They all have talent, and they have worked hard at their careers and made huge successes of it all. They've been lucky. Alena writes music and sings because she was trained. Dom and Danté follow in Pedro's footsteps as DJs, and Alexis does a bit of everything. Diana followed in her mother's footsteps, as did the twins. They've all been extremely successful and extremely lucky."

"And we stand by and support them," Roger added. "If they need help we give it, but they are all headstrong and make their own way through life."

Simon shook his head. "Wow. This is all too much. The family is so big it's hard to keep track, not to mention everyone else who was around the other night. So many people."

Tomas grinned. "We are a big family, so there will be extras. Lorenzo is dating Alexis and used to date Alena. Tony's dating Cabot, Alfonso is Angie's half-brother, Charles is Diana's partner, Dan and Derek are honorary members after saving our lives in '81, and so are Mike and Maggie and their kids. Mike and Maggie have been Pedro and Angie's best friends since 1977. And Xanthe's the psychiatrist who helped us recover in '81, and she's back this year to help us with a lot of stuff." They made their way out of the gym and into the late fall sunshine.

"That's right. Danté mentioned being bitten by a shark, and Cabot and Alexis were both assaulted." Simon remembered the last four days and everything they had been told by his new relatives.

"That's right. We've had a lot to deal with this year." Roger watched the kids run around as they walked down the road and out the gate.

"Plus Diana's pregnant, Charles went through a kidnapping, Angie found out she had a long-lost brother, Tony found out that the same man that assaulted him assaulted Cabot, and he was hunted down and brought to justice. Then Tony found out Cabot's parents knew his dad and grandparents who died when he was little. The family keeps on growing." He smiled at his son.

"It's so much to remember," Deidre said. "I don't come from a big family. I have two sisters and we have two kids each. But we certainly don't have long lost relatives popping up all over the place."

Roger chuckled. "Be grateful, because it can make things very complicated indeed. Poor Angie, she didn't know the half-brother that died in '77. Her father died in '77, her mother ten years before that. She married Pedro in '77 then had Alena in '78, and now she's found Alfonso who only found out about his birth father a few months back."

"What happened there?" Simon asked, grabbing Liam and hauling him onto his shoulders.

"Carlos knew Alfonso when he was five, and his mother Suzy. Suzy became sick and died four years later, asking her boss and his wife to adopt him. They did, but died about ten years ago. He ran their company and didn't bother with much else. When he went to remodel the office in the house, he found a secret room containing lots of different things including a small trunk with all of his papers. Birth and death certificates for his mum, a letter from her, a copy of the adoption papers and a few other things. He found out who his birth father was, tracked him to Angie, and now they're having *discussions.*" Roger grinned.

"So many people discovering new family members," Deidre said. "It must be hard on everyone involved."

"Well, *this* has certainly been a shock to me," Roger said as they made their way back to their place for a late lunch. "It dredges up all kinds of things like, why did that person lie to me? Why did they not tell me? Why did I not know? And then comes, how do I make this work? What do we do now? How's it going to pan out?" He opened the door of their home and let everyone in. "Cabot, you home?" There was no reply. "He must be out, so we have lunch all to ourselves."

"Oooh, it's chilly." Tomas adjusted the heating. "I'll put lunch on."

The others settled in the lounge room, looking at paintings and photos. Simon saw the signatures on them. "You guys do these?"

"Yep." Roger stood beside him looking at a seascape. "Xanthe suggested it after we were ill. As a part of recovery we took up a hobby and this was it. Needless to say, our first attempts were horrible."

"Wow, they're really good." Deidre was looking at another painting.

"Thank you," Roger accepted the compliment. "We've done so many that we've distributed them across *The Windmill Hotel*, all of our homes, there's some in the gym, *Sync, S'Reel, SB3*, the centre, offices, everywhere. Our studio's upstairs off the bedroom so we have a better view of the ocean."

Deidre wandered over to the wall of anniversary photos. "Oh, look, Simon, their wedding and all the anniversaries." She gazed over thirty years' worth. "You make such a cute couple."

A little laugh came from Roger and he saw Tomas smiling in the kitchen and smiled back. "We think so."

Sitting down to hot turkey and vegetable pasta, Simon told Roger more stories of his life. He'd given Roger his mother's letter, and brought the albums and home movies over. They'd watched and looked over these on the weekend. Now, he recounted tales of his school years and growing up in Pennsylvania.

"Was your mum from there? I don't remember." Roger asked. "We worked together in Miami over thirty years ago, and I don't remember much of our conversations."

"That's where her sisters were, and she moved there by the time she had me," Simon replied. "Her sisters helped raise me, and then Richard came along ten years later."

"And now I've come along when you're thirty-one," Roger said, his heart breaking. "Thirty-one years too late for all of the milestones." It still depressed him, missing out on all the years he could have been a father.

Simon smiled briefly; his own heart broken. "I know. But I've missed out on you, too. The life you lived; I missed so much."

"But now you've found one another," Deidre said softly, glancing from her husband to her new father-in-law and noticing the matching emotions and expressions. "Now you can catch up and continue on from here. We can get duplicate photos made, and the videos dubbed."

"My nephew's good at that," Tomas said. "Danté can make copies at *S'Reel* for you, and he can whip up a design for the cover while he's at it."

"That would be wonderful." Deidre finished off her meal and cleaned up the kids, rubbing their sauce-covered faces with their napkins.

Roger's smile was sad as he watched the kids leave the table and go into the lounge room to play. "I missed out on their births."

"You didn't miss much, just a lot of screaming and pain," Deidre joked.

Roger's smile turned into a small laugh. "Yeah, I guess it would have been. But it hurts that I didn't get to hold my son when he was born, or my grandchildren when they were born." He stood up to clear the dishes as an excuse to not cry, knowing tears were welling, and he didn't want anyone to see. He'd read and re-read Jan's letter a hundred times in the last few days, especially during the night when he couldn't sleep, trying to understand why she had done it. To both of them.

Dear Roger,

I am writing to you now, and sending this letter with Simon, to let you know he is your son. I know you will hate me for tricking you, and not telling you he existed. I can only say I am sorry, as there is nothing I can say or do now that will make up for the years the two of you have missed out on. I have cancer and don't have long to live.

I have encouraged Simon to find you and get to know you as his father. I cannot make up thirty-one years' worth of time and memories, but I hope you can spend the next thirty-one years making memories of your own. You were so wonderful to me, and I considered you the best sperm donor to use. Clean, gorgeous, and gay. I'm sorry if all of this hurts you, I never meant to. And you're probably right if you think that you would never have known about Simon if I wasn't dying of cancer and encouraging him to find you. I'm sorry. For everything. Please forgive me and spend the rest of your life enjoying what I've just spent the past thirty-one years doing, enjoying our son.

He has Deidre, a wonderful girl I love and think highly of. She was raised well and comes from great stock. And I love Stella and Liam; both are so adorable and lovable. Please take care of them. Love them, look after them, raise them. Give them everything you have when it comes to love and family as I can no longer do so. Again, please forgive me, and don't blame Simon. Love him, nurture him, guide him. He is your son, and the most important thing in the world. I love him, and you, and I am so sorry.

Jan.

"And it hurts to have not been held by my father." Simon joined him, knowing Roger had been reliving his life with his mother and trying to figure out what he could have done differently. "Not to know who he was, or what he looked like, or to know if he loved me." He stared imploringly at Roger with tears overflowing. "There were so many times I wished for that. To have you to teach me how to play football and baseball and go to the park with." He broke down, gasping through his tears. "I hate that I've missed out on that, but I can't hate Mom for not telling me. She's gone. I don't have her anymore."

Roger took him into his arms and sobbed with him while Tomas and Deidre cleaned the table. "We have so much to make up for," he rasped. "Thirty-one years of playing and reading and teaching and learning. We have a lot to make up for, and it all starts now. This is who I am, Simon, this is *where* I am. And now it's your home too. Welcome home, Simon. Welcome home, son."

December 2007

Christmas was a festive affair with the whole family attending, a family that had grown by four.

Tomas not only became a stepfather to Simon, but a step-grandfather to Stella and Liam. Both he and Roger had beaten Carlos to being a grandfather, and Carlos wasn't happy. But Tomas was. He couldn't have children of his own, and now he had one; even if Simon was a step, he was better than none. He became an instant father and grandfather and loved them all to bits. And Deidre fitted right in with Alena, Diana and Alexis. Jenny and Spiros adored their new grandson and granddaughter-in-law, plus great-grandchildren, and being Jenny, she made them all family straight away once the blood test proved it, and lavished presents on all of them. Simon and Roger got on like a house on fire, and quickly got into their own father and son groove.

Christmas night got very merry for two couples in particular. Alexis and Lorenzo made love for the first time. It had started with simple kissing, but when Alexis got the tingles, she had no problem taking it further, all the way to naked city in Lorenzo's bed. It wasn't her first time at sex, but it was the first since the assault, and with Lorenzo, it was more beautiful than even she could have imagined.

And Tony and Cabot got it on. Xanthe, Dan and Derek had sat them down and had a thorough chat to them about sex and HIV. They both agreed to be careful and were, stocking up on condoms and using them proficiently. Tony took charge, as he was that kind of guy, and took the lead in bed, which infuriated Cabot as he always had. Learning to be the submissive one was a learning curve, but he loved being loved, and having Tony on top of and inside him, finally showed him what true love and making love was all about.

Charles was doing well, out of his wheelchair and walking with the use of a cane. And Diana was bulging at twenty-six weeks. But they had a small ceremony at the church and were married by the time festivities were over. Under orders from Jenny, Charles signed a prenup that meant he couldn't take one cent from Diana's trust fund, but Jenny had an idea, and made him the family photographer. He'd be covering the family, *S'Reel, Sync, In Shape, SB3*, and anything else the family was involved in. He'd earn a wage and be with his family in a beautiful place. She also suggested he might write a book about his ordeal which would be published by *Prologue Press*.

New Year's Eve was spent at *SB3* since some family members couldn't travel, and resolutions were made all round.

Alena was going to bring Alexis into the company more for her to design and to get her away from Lorenzo.

Alexis was going to put more time into the centre and her relationship with Lorenzo.

Lorenzo vowed to stay in the good side of Jenny Stephanopoulos, so he didn't end up dead like Alexis's attacker.

Dom and Danté promised to get along more, and Danté and Nick promised to get their business on the fast track to success, while Nick promised to get them both girlfriends.

After a lengthy chat with Tony and Antonio, Cabot made some decisions about his life. He still wanted to model, but only part-time, which suited Antonio fine. That way, they had time for other things and other people. He was also going to be an advocate for safe sex like his uncles, a move Tony agreed with wholeheartedly and made the decision to do himself. Tony also vowed to get Cabot and his family to holiday at the family home in Spain, so they could find his family's graves and give them headstones and a proper goodbye. Carlos and Viv promised they would.

Antonio made the resolution to meet a girl and take classes in everything, so he could learn more about life, and film classes were top of his list. Dom made a second resolution to not only meet a girl, but get a business of his own figured out by the time he reached twenty-five, so he could dip into his trust fund to do it. He just had to figure out what that business would be.

Pedro didn't need to make resolutions; he had all he wanted and was *all* he wanted to be.

Angie resolved to be nicer to Alfonso and to spend the Poulos fortune. And Alfonso resolved to torment his older sister and maybe track down more siblings; much to Angie's disgust.

Carlos resolved to love his family more. And Viv resolved to smother her first grandchild in lots of love and hugs and kisses. She was going to be seventy-one by the time the baby was born, so she was getting on in life.

Tomas and Roger resolved to be…well…fathers. Simon had been raised well, so they didn't need to do any parenting, but it was new to both of them, and they needed a bit of help.

Simon resolved to spend more time getting to know his two fathers. He saw the Stephanopoulos family as a family he could get used to living in. Deidre adored everyone in the family and wanted to stay in Mykonos longer. The kids weren't in school yet, and both had lost their jobs and spent their last cent flying over there. And considering what his mother had told him, he had no family outside of his aunt, and Deidre's was in Miami. With the fact his fathers had a reason to travel to Miami a lot for the AIDS support centre, it seemed that Mykonos might be a place they could start calling home. His father was there, a new family was there, Deidre's was in Miami. Maybe it could work out after all. And Deidre had been thinking about doing teeth for the dying. Why not die with dignity? Maybe she could help those at Alexis's centre, and Roger and Tomas's AIDS care centre in Miami.

Dan and Derek resolved to take a holiday and try and get back to New York at some stage. But they both needed to face the facts, they spent more and more time in Mykonos and considered moving there.

Xanthe had one resolution, to finally get back to her own home and spend the bonus money Jenny gave her on something frivolous.

Summer and Melody's resolutions were to get in on *Haus of Stefan* more and fill their closets with cool free clothes for the next year.

Mike and Maggie thanked God they got through another year with three teenagers.

In New York, the Gardos were celebrating in Times Square with the ball drop. They had done it every year with James and this was no different. They had much to be grateful for. Their son was alive and doing fine, and he'd met a nice girl when they'd returned from Mykonos. In fact, her and her family had joined them for Christmas and then in Times Square.

And last, but definitely not least, Jenny stood on the balcony of the office looking down at all of her family and extended family and resolved to make it even bigger. *Stephanopoulos Inc.* was an empire that would continue growing, and one day, take over the world in true Stephanopoulos style.

2008

The celebrations continued in February when Carlos, Pedro and Tomas celebrated their fifty-fifth, fifty-third and fifty-first birthdays on Valentine's Day with Pedro taking to the decks to play '70s and '80s tunes to remind them of how young they all used to be.

In March, Viv celebrated her seventy-first birthday, and Danté his fifteenth.

On April 1st, Roger celebrated his sixtieth birthday with his son and grandchildren for the first time, crying a lot at the overwhelming emotions of being a new father and grandfather. A few days later Diana's water broke, and after a three-day labour, she brought her first child into the world to much screaming and fanfare, plus a full-page celebratory notice in the *Mykonos Daily Times*.

'Spiros and Jennifer Stephanopoulos would like to announce to the world that their first great-grandchild, Adam Charles Stephanopoulos Kensington was born at 4:02 a.m. Sunday morning, April 2008. Proud grandparents, Carlos and Vivian Stephanopoulos were on hand, as were the baby's great aunt and uncles, and cousins. Proud parents, Diana Villiers Stephanopoulos and Charles Peter Kensington dealt bravely with the three-day labour, and now have a beautiful baby boy. Mother and child are both doing well.'

About the Author

L.J. has been writing since 2006, when her first of many novels, *The Road To Vegas,* was born. In 2016 she created the *Porn Star Brothers* series about three sizzlingly hot Australian born Greek Island raised brothers who became the hottest porn stars in '70s America.

L.J. lives in Australia, loves '80s music, disaster movies, and collecting Jackie Collins books as Jackie is her inspiration and mentor.

L.J. Diva is the adult pen name for author Tiara King. You can find more about Tiara on her website; follow her on social media, or visit her publishing house, Royal Star Publishing.

Socials

tiaraking.com.au/ljdiva

royalstarpublishing.com.au

Sign up for *Tiara's* Newsletter...

Make sure you're always in the know and never miss free exclusives, the latest news, book updates, and so much more with newsletters from...

tiaraking.com.au

Have you read these?

Or these?

NOVELS

Burning Desires
Anything for You
Falling for London
The Road To Vegas
Hollywood Dreams
The Billionaire's Dirty Little Secret

SHORT STORIES

The Body
The Perfect Plot
The Star of Your Own Crime Scene